OF SINS AND SACRIFICE

VERONICA LANCET

PREFACE

Of Sins and Sacrifice is the **second** book in the House of Cryos trilogy and cannot be read as a standalone.

Start the trilogy with 'of Ice and Villains'!

Hope you enjoy this new installment in Minnie and Marlowe's story.

ONE

HOUSE OF CRYOS, APERION, MANY YEARS AGO

IT'S BEEN two hundred and eighty-five days since I've last killed a demon.

Two hundred and eighty-five days since I've been on a battlefield.

And now I am forced to stand witness to the musical atrocity in front of me. All in the name of being seen in high society. All so I can be seen as ladylike and not a heathen who enjoys making demons bleed before sending them off back to the Source.

I tighten my fingers on the leaflet detailing tonight's performance, and a gust of chilly air blows through my hair, messing the updo my maid had painstakingly spent hours to style.

"Minerva," my mother hisses in my ear.

I glance at her from the corner of my eye.

The scowl on her face accompanies a deep frown that ought to permanently get etched into her features. It really should, considering how often she sports it. But alas, she's a powerful deity from a reputed clan. Despite her advanced age, she only looks slightly older than me, which she never fails to point out.

She's a beauty. A scowling beauty, but one nonetheless. And there's nothing worse than a female who is well aware of her attributes. Somehow, her sullen appearance makes her even more intriguing to the male population, which she greatly enjoys.

It's disconcerting how many admirers she has—males who openly profess their adoration to her even though she is married. To a king, nonetheless.

But my father is most often oblivious. Or if he notices, he turns a blind eye.

He is busy with *important* matters, not frivolous ones like monitoring what his wife is wearing or if she flirts with half of Aperion. In his eyes, she has done her duty. She provided him with three children: an heir, a spare, and a female—yes, that is exactly how both of my parents refer to their *precious* offspring.

It's laudable to have three children, considering an Aperite female has an average of one point five children. Not to say that they birth halves, though perhaps that happens sometimes? I've never personally witnessed a birth, so I cannot say how those little creatures come into the world, nor have I been allowed to investigate it, though I have been curious about it.

It's a matter for the worldly female, my mother would say, snatching a book on the topic from my hands. *"You will learn about it after you get mated."*

That means that no matter how many military treatises I read or how many classic works on the topic of demonology and spiritual energy I memorize by heart, I will never be allowed to investigate matters that are of a more...intimate nature.

Those are for the worldly female only. And why? Because not only my mother, but other females within our circles believe that worldly knowledge equals temptation. Once a young, unmated female becomes aware of those secrets, she is naturally bound to want to explore them.

Alas, it seems I am about to find out soon enough, seeing as how I am betrothed to be married.

I have been engaged for two hundred and eighty-five days. The connection between my new betrothal and my lack of demon killing is clear, though perhaps not as intuitive as one might think.

My fiancé is a refined male. A bit of a peacock if you ask me. Unfortunately, my parents chose him for me without even seeking my opinion.

But I gave it nonetheless at the engagement party they sprang up on me.

Quite loudly.

Quite...unladylikely.

Oops.

Who told them to spring up on me a surprise of such magnitude in public? I am not the type to silently acquiesce to everything, which my parents are well aware of. Perhaps they thought that by announcing the engagement in front of an audience, I would be less inclined to throw a fit.

Oh, well...

Theron of the House of Pyros is by all accounts a perfect match. He is a reputed warrior who has recently gained favor with Commander Azerius for his last mission. Rumors say he might make general soon.

Now that is quite the achievement, and I'm almost jealous about it—if it were actually deserved. It's no secret it is my ardent wish to excel in the army and become a general myself. The *first* female general in Commander Azerius' army. You would think that Theron, a warrior himself, would appreciate my aspirations.

No.

Not. At. All.

After my rather loud outburst in which I may or may not have said that he *is* a peacock—perhaps I should have chosen a different word for it, but I was too annoyed at the time to mind my vocabulary—he announced that he would magnanimously forgive me for my careless words. With a caveat, of course. I was to stop all unladylike activities and dedicate myself to becoming the model of decorum.

His prestige alone would be enough, so I do not need to concern myself with such business.

Psh! What an arsehole!

I would have said that to his face, too, if my parents had not promptly removed me from the ballroom.

As it stands, both families have signed the mating contract. The wedding is as good as done. But that doesn't mean I am pleased about it or that I bow down to what they dictate.

It's just a matter of...figuring out the best course of action.

So for now, I will smile and keep my mouth shut while silently planning my next move.

After all, it's not as if Theron likes me either. With his enormous ego, he probably thinks I am not fit to be within a few paces away from him. But egocentrism is not his only quality, you see. He's also a mamma's boy. And if his mother has decided on a bride for him, then he will of course do as she says.

Ugh!

"Minerva! Was that a snort I heard?" My mother gasps.

I bite my lip to stop a retort I know will *not* be welcomed. Instead, I put on my fake smile.

"Something was obstructing my breathing, Mother," I murmur in a low voice.

Her eyes narrow at me.

With a huff, she turns her attention back to the musical.

I release a sigh of relief.

I wonder how much longer I will have to withstand this cacophony.

My mother suddenly rises to her feet. Her eyes sparkle as she looks to the side. I follow her gaze, and my lips flatten in displeasure.

Theron and his mother, Olivia, are heading toward us.

He's proudly wearing his military uniform. On his jacket, he has displayed all his honors, including the ones that are more of a...participatory nature. But one would only know that if one happened to be in the military as well. To the rest of the world, so many medals on his jacket must be highly impressive.

Peacock.

It's on the tip of my tongue to tell him that I own most of

those medals too. But that would earn me a scolding—the last thing I need now.

"Olivia, dear," my mother calls out. "And dashing Theron." She studies his medals with interest. "I did not realize you were such an accomplished soldier. My congratulations."

Theron grunts. Tipping his chin up, a proud smile prods at his lips.

"Thank you." He inclines his head.

"Minerva," my mother whispers, giving me a look. "Isn't Theron so impressive?"

"Of course," I add with a fake smile.

He preens.

"I would never boast around with a participation prize. But if that gives him joy..." I trail off.

Theron and Olivia gasp at my words.

My mother is a little slower in understanding what I mean, but when she does, she elbows me in the ribs.

"She just meant that Theron must be quite involved in a lot of activities, no?" my mother says in an attempt to cover for my blunder.

Theron's eyes flash at me.

"Why don't we give them some time to talk during the recess," she continues. "They must be excited to get to know each other."

"It's not proper, Mother—"

"There are so many people around." She waves her hand to the rest of the audience mingling around for the break. "It is quite proper, I assure you."

Olivia agrees, and they all but shoo us to a more discreet corner so we can *get to know each other*.

We're still within their sight, but now there's no one to save me from having to make small talk with him.

Great.

Just what I needed on an already abysmal day.

Theron studies me, his lips curled with disdain.

"That mouth of yours will get you in trouble," he comments in a bored tone.

I shrug.

"At least I keep my mouth *out* of other people's arses. Who knows how many you had to kiss to get those *distinctions*," I grumble.

He reddens with anger. His hands are balled into fists by his sides, and he makes to grab me. But realizing how many people are around, he thinks better of it and stops himself before doing something *scandalous*.

"You will learn how to behave after our nuptials, Minerva. If I have to muzzle you, don't think for a moment that I will not."

"What?"

"I don't like you. In fact, I actively dislike you. But Mother has decided your family name is good for us, so we will marry. But do not for one moment think that I will let you behave thusly after we are mated."

"Really?" I ask drily. "And how will you have me behave?"

His lips press together in annoyance.

"As if you did not exist," he replies through gritted teeth.

Oh, my! That's quite the auspicious beginning to my marriage.

I smile sweetly and bat my lashes at him. While he's distracted—or better said disgusted—by my charms, I gather some of the moisture in the air and fashion it into a block of ice.

I should make a spear and stab him through the heart. Unfortunately, that will only get me in trouble, not only with my family but with the law as well. Alas, I must resign myself to something...smaller.

While he's scowling at me, I carefully manipulate the ice and send it flying toward his crotch, imbuing it with a little chant so it melts on impact.

The moisture splashes across the front of his uniform pants.

He stumbles back, his eyes alarmed, and as he takes in the big wet spot on his light uniform, I can barely hold onto my laughter. He stares at the wetness for a moment, almost as if he's too flabbergasted to react.

"I hope they give you a participation prize for that, too," I say with a wink.

His mouth opens and closes, his eyes now a stormy black as he slowly looks at me.

Energy swirls around him, threateningly so.

Oops. Or maybe make that double oops.

"Is that Theron of Pyros?" someone asks, pointing a finger at him—or rather, his crotch.

People stop to look at him. Well, at his crotch. Some even say he must have been overly excited. I suppose that's one way to empty one's bladder while in public. Safe to say, the whispers abound. Mayhap I did not plan for such a thorough humiliation before. But now that it's happened?

My, my. This is rather delicious. If Theron's humiliation had a taste, it would be a cloyingly sweet one. Of course, for someone who lives off sweets, there is nothing better.

"Minerva," he utters my name in a low, dangerous voice.

"Is that his betrothed? That's why he was too excited..." another voice comments.

So many people have stopped to comment that I see this as my chance to make a run for it. Before he can put his hands on me and strangle me—I will not put it past him at this point seeing how angry he is—I slip away and rejoin my mother.

"What happened?" she asks, her voice the epitome of motherly concern. She eyes the commotion suspiciously.

"I think Theron had an accident," I whisper. "Perhaps it's time to leave."

"Accident?" Olivia intones. "What accident?"

A crowd is gathered around Theron.

Mother frowns, but as she looks at me, it dawns on her that I must have had something to do with it. She releases a long sigh before she addresses Olivia.

"Perhaps we should cut this evening short. I see that my daughter is not looking too well."

Olivia barely minds her as she tries to find her son in the crowd.

"We will be in touch, of course."

"Of course," Olivia replies absentmindedly.

Taking advantage of everyone's distraction, my mother and I slip out of the music room. We increase our pace as we go down the palace doors until we find our carriage.

"I cannot believe you, Minerva!" she bursts out when we're in the back of the carriage and on the way home. "What did you do?"

"Me? Why do you think I did anything?" I pretend to be insulted by her accusations.

"I know you." She narrows her eyes. "You did something. Otherwise, we would not have left in such a hurry."

I shrug.

"As I said, Theron had an accident. I was just as surprised, you know. Someone of his age should be able to control his bodily functions better."

My mother gapes at me.

"W-what? Bodily functions?"

"Perhaps it's all that time in the military. It must have affected his..." I trail off. "Poor male." I shake my head.

"Do not try to deceive me, Minerva. I *know* you must have done something." She pauses before a concerned look crosses her face. "How will I face Olivia now? How will we face Theron?"

"Maybe we...don't?"

She gives me a harsh look.

"The marriage is on, whether you like it or not. But you have made a fool of your betrothed now, and if he treats you badly, then it is on *you*."

"So you will allow him to treat me badly?" I blink.

"I will not be able to do anything. You have brought this upon yourself."

"But, *Mamma*, you'll let a male treat your daughter badly?" I ask in an attempt to appeal to her emotional side.

She snorts.

"Perhaps it is high time someone did. Your father and I have been giving you too much freedom and it shows. By the Source, Minerva, you are a *princess*! I don't think there is anyone else with your status in Aperion who has such a disregard for manners and social protocol."

"I didn't exactly have time to cultivate manners in the army, Mother. I could hardly go to a demon and say *pretty please, can I kill you?*"

She glowers at me.

"And this is why you should have *never* been allowed to enroll. Goodness, Minerva. You're little more than a heathen *despite* your royal upbringing." She removes a handkerchief from her reticule and wipes away a fake tear. "I don't know where we went wrong with you. I really don't."

"Have you ever thought that maybe I don't want to get mated? That my purpose is not to be a paragon of decorum, but rather to keep the universe safe?"

She releases another snort.

"You?" she asks in disbelief.

"Yes, me. I did well in the army. You know that. I have the skills. I have—"

"You have only opened your fifth gate, Minerva. I would not call that *having the skills* as you put it. Look at your brother. By the time he was your age, he had already opened his ninth gate."

"Because I was hardly given the opportunity to!" I cry out.

She shrugs. "You would have if you were good enough."

"Good enough? What? I've had dozens of opportunities in the last few hundred years to take the next exams. Every time I registered, something happened and I *never* made it to the exam. As if I don't know you and Father had a hand in that."

"Males do not appreciate overly ambitious females," she mutters. "It is for your own good."

"What?"

"You already have your pedigree. The fact that you've opened your fifth gate is in your favor, of course, but your future mate will not care about that. Your job will be to deliver him strong children—stronger than both of you combined."

"Mother!" I exclaim.

"We have arrived. This conversation is over. You must go to your room and craft a letter of apology to Olivia and Theron."

"But—"

"No buts. You will apologize, Minerva." Another harsh look and she's gone from my side.

I hunch down my shoulders and stomp to my room, careful to avoid running into my father. The last thing I need is another lecture about how I am *not good enough* for the military, only for popping out children.

The moment I'm in my room, I release a loud groan and kick the first thing I see—which happens to be a wooden table.

"Ugh!" I yell out in frustration.

"Am I to understand your outing with Mother did not go as planned?" a voice calls from behind.

I swivel and come face-to-face with my brother.

"Kai!" I call out and run to him. "I didn't know you're back!"

"Well, not for long," he says with a chuckle, giving me a tight hug. "I was allowed one day at home before the next mission as it's going to be a long one."

"Next mission? What is it?" I ask excitedly.

He smiles indulgently at me as we take a seat at the table.

He's wearing his full military garb, which tells me he hasn't even stopped by his room before coming to see me. That warms my heart. At least one person in this wretched household believes I am *good enough*.

"It's in Anthropa. There is a violent conflict going on, affecting the entire world. Commander Azerius dispatched me and my regiment to prevent demons from consuming the souls of the mortals dying in the conflict."

"Oh," I murmur. I don't know where Anthropa is, but it's standard for an Aperite regiment to head to a world when there is a widespread conflict. Demons are always lurking around, waiting for such an event so they can swoop in and consume as many souls as they can.

"I am not sure how long we will be there, so I wanted to see you before I left."

"That's so sweet of you, Kai. I wish I could also be there." I sigh.

"You don't." He laughs. "It's not going to be pretty, Minerva. It will likely be bloody and dirty. That's not a place for you."

"I don't care about that. I only care about killing demons," I tell him. "And I can already imagine they're going to be swarming around."

He grunts.

"The casualties the House of Psyche reported so far for Anthropa are in the millions. And that is only the souls that have managed to cross over. We don't have an estimate for how many have already been consumed."

"Why didn't Commander Azerius send you there earlier, then?" I frown.

When a world becomes embroiled in such a conflict, Aperite forces are immediately dispatched to prevent the loss of souls.

Kai flattens his lips.

"He sent another regiment. But they are overwhelmed."

"There are *that* many demons?" I ask in awe.

He nods grimly.

"We don't know why, but lately there's been an increased demon activity. He sent a regiment based on the normal esti-mates in the case of such a conflict, but it seems this particular event is more violent than we thought."

"Violent how?"

He looks away for a moment.

"Genocide."

I blink.

"W-what?"

"It is not just the soldiers on either side that are dying or some unfortunate civilian casualties. There are people specifically targeted for extermination. Hundreds of thousands of them as far as we know. Maybe more."

"Genocide?" I repeat weakly. "On that scale?"

"Thousands die daily. The current regiment cannot keep up with it."

"And we can't do anything to help?" The words are out of my mouth before I can think it through.

"I wish we could do something about it. I wish we could do something about all the conflicts in the universe. But you know we cannot, Minerva." He sighs. "We cannot intervene in mortals' fates. If they wish to destroy themselves... They have the freedom of will to do so."

"But—"

"It saddens me just as much as it does you. Our only duty is to prevent demons from disturbing the natural cycle of a soul, nothing more."

"I don't like it," I grumble.

He gives me a sad smile.

"And that, my little sister, is why you would have never made a good soldier."

"Hey!" I suddenly stand up. "I am a damn good soldier and you know it," I declare emphatically.

"I am not talking about your abilities, Minerva. I am referring to your penchant for ignoring orders."

"Oh, well..."

"We both know you have a hard time following the chain of command."

"But I've been actively trying to be better. If only I could get a chance to prove it."

"Your betrothed does not want you in the field."

"Because he knows I might be better than him!" I exclaim.

Kai chuckles.

"That might be so. But Theron is a good soldier. He will make you a good mate."

"No. He will not," I retort with a huff. "He is an arrogant

peacock who only thinks of himself. The moment we're mated, he will lock me away and oppress me even more than I already am."

"Minerva..."

"Can I join you on the mission? Please? One last mission before the wedding. I know I cannot back out of it, but this way—"

"You know I cannot do that. You have already been discharged. And Mother and Father would have my hide if they knew I abetted you in any way."

"They don't have to know. We can just come up with something else. Besides, you need more soldiers, no? To keep up with the demons," I add excitedly.

"You think they would not notice your prolonged absence?" He laughs. "You are too naïve, Minerva."

"You could tell them you need me. You're the only one from Cryos in your regiment, aren't you? I'm sure you could use my skills and—"

"The answer is no, little sister."

He stands up to leave.

"But, Kai, please..."

"It is not the place for you. You have done your duty to Aperion, and you have proven yourself. Now it is time for you to marry and settle at your own home. That is safer."

"Safer for whom? Not for me. Not with Theron for a mate. He will make my life unhappy, Kai. You have to see it."

"This discussion is closed. It was good to see you, Minerva. Take care of yourself."

"But—"

He's gone.

Just like that, he's gone.

I scowl and kick the table again, though this time with intention.

Damn it.

Damn Theron and damn my family for thinking he would be a good match when I cannot stand the sight of him. Oh, and the feeling is mutual. Our mating would only be a disaster.

And of course, damn Kai for not letting me have this one thing.

Am I really to never kill a demon again?

I sigh and wipe the moisture from my lashes with the back of my hand.

I know he thinks this is what's best for me. But he doesn't *know* what's best for me.

Unless...

I bite my lip as a barrage of ideas inundates my mind.

He will never give his consent beforehand. But what if it's an accomplished fact?

Without regard for the consequences, I go to my closet and pull out my uniform.

TWO

THE TWO SUNS are slowly rising into the sky as I surreptitiously make my way outside the palace. Shielding my energy signature, I take the staff exit so no one can spot me.

With a little luck, my parents won't notice my absence until midday, at which point I should have already left Aperion.

If all works out, that is.

Kai may not have given me too many details about this mission of his, but it's standard practice for the regiment to meet with Commander Azerius before a mission to get direct orders.

Once I'm out of the palace, I leave the premises on foot until I'm sure I am outside the range of the protective runes of the place. Even if I hide my energy signature, if I teleport while on my family's land, they will know.

The staff who awoke with the dawn, ready to start the day's chores, pass by me without recognizing me.

A smile pulls at my lips. It seems like my disguise worked.

I styled my long hair in a bun and hid it under a black nondescript hat. I put on an old pair of dark gray pants and a loose woolen jacket to make it seem like I'm a street urchin. I also went through the pain of binding my breast to ensure no one can tell I'm a female.

Swinging my small bag containing my military uniform over

my shoulder, I double-check to make sure I'm off my family's land before I teleport to the Center for Military Advancement—the official building that houses all the send-off events for missions.

Getting inside the building is easy. For a military building, the security is quite lax. I go in search of a restroom to change into my uniform and then look for the event room.

I let my shield down and expel a burst of energy fly from me as I let my hearing roam through the building, listening to all the chatter.

The moment I hear the word *Anthropa*, I follow the source of the sound until I reach the designated room.

There are around fifty people inside. Eighty percent of them are male and only twenty percent are female. Despite the fact that the military is advertised as a free-for-all opportunity, there is still quite a disparity between the numbers of males and females.

It all comes down to ability and spiritual energy. Like me, a lot of high-ranking females are expected to marry well and are seldom given the opportunity to hone their abilities. The ones currently in the military are largely young females who have not yet been forced to abandon their vocation for a mate.

Unfortunately, most of them *will* be forced to quit at some point.

I've yet to meet an older female who's made her profession her priority, mostly because it's not always up to them. If they have a living family, best believe that they will be forced to give up their career dreams sooner or later.

Years ago, I did not think this would be me. In fact, I had resolved to be the exception.

The first female general.

Little did I realize that it would not be up to me any more than it is up to the other females.

Would I be able to refuse the marriage and run away? Yes, of course.

But then my family would disown me and I would be

branded a disgrace. No one in Aperion would look kindly on me, and the military would categorically *not* accept me anymore.

After all, family is the most valued thing for Aperites. And if you're willing to betray your family, who is to say you will not betray your realm, too?

As I get to the room, I sneak in among the people at the end of the line and keep my head down.

My brother is at the front of the room, giving a speech about the particularities of this realm. I'm only half listening, though, since I am more concerned with not getting caught.

Only moments later, silence descends in the room.

The crowd parts as a tall figure enters.

Commander Azerius.

He's dressed in a dark uniform with a purple belt wrapped around his waist that houses a white sword—the famed sword that has the power to kill a deity. Magical runes are etched on half of his face, swirling in different patterns as if they have a life of their own.

A shiver runs down my back. He is scary. But my apprehension is mixed with a sense of awe as he strides to the front of the room to join my brother.

Commander Azerius is a legend in itself.

I've only seen him in person a few times, but it never fails to leave me breathless. He exudes so much power, confidence, and discipline that it's hard not to admire him.

He is feared and hated—with good reason. But he is also a damn good soldier. The very best Aperion has to offer.

No one knows the full extent of his powers, but there are whispers that he is more powerful than all the Supremes combined.

My brother inclines his head at him.

"General Molokai has already briefed you on the particularities of Anthropa," he starts in an authoritative voice. "It is of utmost importance to ensure that those demons do *not* consume souls and ascend."

Everyone nods.

"But there is something else you need to be aware of." He pauses. "A few of our scouts have sent word that they have sighted Sons of Tenebreis outside of Tartareia."

Gasps erupt in the room.

Sons of Tenebreis? In Anthropa? But...

"I have not been able to confirm these accounts, but I would like you to be vigilant. I have already dispatched a small squad in charge of tracking the Sons of Tenebreis. But if that proves to be true, it is even more imperative that you do not allow any demon to ascend to a high level since they will likely feed that power back to the Sons of Tenebreis that control them."

"But... How can it be?" someone asks. "There has not been a sighting of a Son of Tenebreis in thousands of years."

Azerius regards the room with a bored expression on his face.

"The Chalice," Azerius states. "It appears they might be using the Chalice to move between realms."

My mouth parts in shock. Everyone has the same reaction.

The Sons of Tenebreis have been locked in Tartareia for more than seven thousand years. Although they couldn't leave their realm, they could remotely control demons. They used those lower-level demons to feed on the souls to increase their power. With every passing millennium, the Sons of Tenebreis became stronger and the barrier in Tartareia weaker. But so far no one has seen an actual Son of Tenebreis break free.

To hear that they might have found a way to get out of Tartareia? That is...

Terrifying.

We have a hard time keeping up with the myriad of lower demons preying on mortal souls as it is. The last thing we need is to have the Sons of Tenebreis out in the open.

If a high-level demon is powerful, then a Son of Tenebreis is infinitely more so. They are the elite warriors of Tartareia, the descendants of the Dark Seven themselves.

Aperion led multiple wars against Tartareia. But they were

all before my time. Still, if rumors are to be believed, a Son of Tenebreis is as strong as an Aperite Supreme. And that is...absolutely chilling.

"They have the Chalice?" Someone finally dares to ask.

Azerius nods.

"It appears that when Elias absconded with the Chalice, he joined the ranks of the Sons of Tenebreis."

It was a huge scandal a few years back when Elias, the King of the House of Bronte, and his high priestess disappeared together with the Chalice, the House of Bronte's most prized artifact.

Each one of the fifteen Houses of Aperion has one such artifact that was passed down by the fourteen Primordials. Initially, there were only fourteen Houses, a direct link to the fourteen Primordials that created Aperion. But the House of Psyche and the House of Moirai became separated soon after their creation. Their artifact, too, was split in two.

Given that the Chalice is imbued with the pure energy of a Primordial, it is exceedingly powerful. It doesn't surprise me that it would allow the Sons of Tenebreis to break free of Tartareia. But it does shock me that King Elias betrayed us and joined *them*.

Why?

Why would he have done that?

Why did his high priestess do it?

Just like every House has an artifact from the Primordials, they each also have a Temple and a high priestess in charge of guarding said artifact. Both the kings and their high priestesses take a vow to the Source to protect the artifact with their lives.

How could have King Elias and his high priestess gotten around that vow? It is physically impossible to do so.

"This is an alarming development, of course. But I am monitoring the situation closely," Azerius continues. His voice is... deadpan. There is no sign of alarm there, though I've never seen him exhibit any type of emotion before.

"I will now leave you to prepare for your journey. Make Aperion proud."

With that, the sea of people parts again for him as he departs the room. When he's gone, everyone is quiet, mulling over this new information.

Most of the people here were born *after* Tartareia was sealed off. But we've all heard the stories from before—of how scary and powerful the Sons of Tenebreis were.

Aperion and Tartareia were always at war. And because of that, the lifespan of a deity before was much shorter. We might be immortal, but we are not impervious. And the Sons of Tenebreis were one of the few things in the universe that could kill deities—just as deities could kill them.

In the seven thousand years since Tartareia was sealed, everything changed. No longer were the demons the most feared thing. Now it was... Azerius and his sword. The God Killer.

But where death at the hands of a Son of Tenebreis left the essence of a deity alive for the House of Psyche to cultivate it and prepare it for a future incarnation, Azerius' sword annihilates the very essence of a deity.

We exchanged bad for worse.

But despite the fear surrounding Azerius, he never does anything without a motive.

His executions are not random. They are the result of a fair trial. And to be sentenced to execution means you've *done* something.

Aperion is nothing but fair in that regard.

That hasn't stopped people from reviling Azerius. That also hasn't stopped me from admiring him.

The most loyal soldier of the realm—and the most powerful.

"You've heard Commander Azerius. It is imperative that you do not allow any demon to ascend. Ideally, we should be exterminating them while they are amorphous."

"But how do we do that without harming mortals?"

someone asks. "If they are amorphous, they will likely possess a mortal."

"Indeed." My brother nods. "But there is one exception. If enough time has passed since possession, the demon has already consumed its vessel's soul. In that case, the mortal is already dead. What's left behind is only a carcass."

"How will we know?" the same person asks.

I nod, curious about that, too.

In the past, we've usually avoided harming a mortal if it was the demon's first possession for fear its soul might still be present. As deities, we are prohibited from messing with mortals' lives. That means we cannot kill them, but we cannot save them either if their time has come to pass under normal circumstances. Of course demons present a rather *abnormal* circumstance. But still, we were taught to never take chances since the punishment would be...death. Killed by Azerius. Rather poetic if you ask me.

"You will each receive a small crystal. If a mortal touches it and it does not change color, then the soul is intact. If a mortal touches it and it becomes red, his soul has been consumed and now the only being inside that carcass is a demon. You may then act accordingly."

I blink. I'd never heard of such a crystal before or it being used.

The crystals are being passed around from front to back, and of course, by the time my turn comes, there are no more crystals because they were based on the exact number of the regiment.

Damn it.

Perhaps I can do it without a crystal?

But just as I think of ways I can still fight demons without the assurance of the crystal, my brother's eyes connect with my own.

Oh no!

His eyes narrow at me, and he shakes his head, his expression promising retribution.

I give him a feeble smile.

"You are dismissed. You may gather your belongings and prepare for departure. We will meet at the portal in one hour."

The crowd disperses.

I'm rooted to the spot, waiting for Kai to chastise me but also thinking of ways to appeal to his brotherly love so he will allow me to come with him.

"Minerva," he grits out.

Here it comes.

I take a deep breath.

He stomps his way toward me.

"Please, please, please, please, please," I burst out as I get to my knees and kowtow to him. "Please, please, please, please—"

"Get up."

"Please, Kai!" I continue to beseech him while bumping my forehead onto the hard floor in another kowtow.

"Get up, Minerva!"

"Please let me join you. One last time. Please, Kai..."

His hands cup my shoulders and he swiftly pulls me up to my feet.

He glares at me, his cheek twitching with displeasure.

"I already told you no. How did you even get in here?"

"Your security is not very tight," I say as I give him an awkward smile.

"I'm taking you home," he snaps.

"What? No, no. Please, Kai. This is my last chance."

"You were officially discharged from the army, Minerva. I can't just—"

"You can! You're in charge of the regiment. I'm sure you can squeeze me in."

His lips flatten.

"Please? One last time, I promise."

"Mother and Father will not like it," he grumbles.

"I will deal with them. I'll take the punishment. I'll even tell them I forced you. Just please..."

I'm close to tears as I realize he may very well send me home. Only a few seconds separate me from this place to my home should he decide to teleport there. And once my parents find out... They will lock me away for good until the wedding. I will not be able to go anywhere. They might even bind my powers to ensure my cooperation.

"One last mission," I whisper.

Kai stares at me, deep in thought.

"You will behave?" he asks eventually.

"I will *only* kill demons. I'm good at what I do. You know it. And as Commander Azerius said, you need everyone to be extra careful. I can be helpful, Kai."

He doesn't reply.

Taking his hands off me, he steps back and paces around.

I swallow hard in an attempt to ignore my rising anxiety. He can't send me home. Not yet.

"Please," I whisper again.

Once more, he doesn't say a word.

If anything, he looks pissed.

His entire body is tense. His features are tight and scary.

He stops his pacing.

Swiveling, he marches toward me, stopping suddenly.

I instinctively take a step back, ready to run if he's decided to return me home. I cannot go back yet. And if he won't let me join his regiment, I suppose I can try to sneak into Anthropa on my own.

Pulling something from his pocket, he thrusts it toward me.

I blink, not sure I'm seeing this right.

"This..."

"You will need it to assess the demons," he mentions in a low voice.

I take the crystal from him with both hands and carefully cradle it against my chest. I'm so scared of doing or saying the wrong thing and have him send me back that I simply stand still as a statue, my lips firmly shut.

"One last mission," he finally says. "Go get ready."

Not one to take my good luck for granted, I give him a wide smile and jump up to kiss his cheek.

His brows go up in surprise, and a small smile pulls at his lips as he watches me leave.

I did it.

I convinced him.

My heart beats wildly in my chest.

For a moment, I truly thought he was going to send me back.

But Kai isn't my favorite brother for nothing. He might not say it outright, but I know he's not exactly thrilled about my parents' plans for me or the fact that I had to quit the military when I was doing so well.

He knows how much I love to be on the field and how dedicated I am to my job.

Yes, I might have a *small* authority problem, but I make up for it in other ways—namely killing twice more demons than everyone else. That is my plan for this mission too.

If I can do something extraordinary, maybe kill a high-level demon, or even a Son of Tenebreis, Commander Azerius will praise me for my abilities. And when he'll hear I am going to quit, he's going to insist I don't, that I'm a valuable asset of the army and for the whole of Aperion.

My parents and Theron will not be able to say a thing against Commander Azerius. He *is* the ultimate authority, after all.

I smile to myself.

Yes! I just need to distinguish myself in this mission and I might escape my fate.

A few years back, a deity was given a medal and special treatment for killing the most demons in a mission. Even if I don't kill a Son of Tenebreis—though I would *love* to, just to say I did it and watch Theron's face mottle with jealousy—as long as I kill *the most* demons, I might get a distinction.

My plan is made, and an hour later, I'm standing in line with the other soldiers as we go one by one through the portal.

Anthropa, here I come!

Maybe I shouldn't be this happy about going to war, but how can I not when killing demons is so much fun?

THREE
LONDON, ANTHROPA, YEAR 1943

THE CITY of London is in disarray. Buildings are collapsed. Some are totaled to the ground while others sway with every little breeze, ready to tip over. The air is filled with the smell of powdered concrete, rubber, and death.

Yet despite the destruction all around, people continue on with their lives.

The night sky is clouded, the moon barely visible.

I've been in Anthropa for a few months now, and I don't think I've seen a clear sky in all that time. It's always foggy, dark...foreboding.

When I decided to join Kai's regiment, I suppose I hadn't thought of everything this mission would involve.

It is war, yes. I'm killing demons, yes.

But it's getting harder and harder to ignore the casualties all around me.

Daily, I see people die. Horrible, asinine deaths. And for what? What is the point of this war? Why do so many innocents have to die?

I take a bite out of my sugar-glazed donut as I walk down a dimly lit street. It's getting close to the blackout time, and people are frantically running up and down the street, trying to get to their homes in time before darkness sets in.

There are, of course, some unsavory figures who wait for the darkness to come to commit nefarious acts. Unfortunately, I have seen plenty of those, too.

Like any person capable of empathy, my first instinct is to help. But I am bound by my own laws, and I cannot intervene even in a small incident since it might ricochet and have unintended consequences on people's lives.

Fate. Such a tricky thing. Even something so little as a walk on a bustling street can be a pivotal moment in someone's life.

I take another bite of my donut.

Food, too, is scarce around here. People are living on rations, and the portions are not only small but also have a questionable taste.

I went through so much trouble to procure this one donut from the so-called Yanks. They have a base not too far from London and have brought with them some of their products—a fact that makes the British very jealous.

I would be, too, if those Yanks had sugary goodness while the British have...potatoes.

Not that potatoes are bad. In fact, they, like any other vegetable, have their purpose. But when everything becomes about potatoes... Well, then I can see why people would tire of them.

There are, of course, other available items, but they are in short supply. Meat, in particular, is scarce to come by, unless you have the money to purchase it from the black market.

I suppose things are better in the countryside where people grow their own produce, but how many people can boast about that?

London is the most populous city in the entire of Anthropa. I can't imagine how many people are suffering and going without because of the lack of resources.

For the first time since I can remember, I hate war.

From the corner of my eye, I note a small child of about eight or nine staring at me. His clothes are dirty and torn, and his face is smudged with dirt.

To be more precise, he's staring at my donut, not at me.

I swallow against the immediate discomfort.

His eyes glisten with longing in the shadowy light of a street lamp. Not a moment after, his stomach growls loudly in hunger.

I shouldn't do this, but I cannot help myself.

In a couple of steps, I am in front of the child and hand him my leftover donut, together with the little food I had left in my pouch.

His eyes widen in shock and I can tell he's ready to refuse. I open his palm and place the items in his hand before I leave without looking back.

Not a moment ago, I was giving myself a mental lecture about the importance of not intervening in mortals' lives. That small quantity of food could have very well made the difference between life and death. And though I know I might get told off if that is the case, I find that I cannot turn a blind eye to this type of suffering.

The image of the starving child remains with me as I continue walking aimlessly.

The streetlights go out one by one. The buildings still inhabited go dark too. Some people turn off their lights while others pull heavy, dark curtains over the windows to trap any light inside.

In a matter of moments, everything is pitch black.

Cars are still driving on the street, though there is almost no visibility. A few cries erupt in the air from people who barely avoid getting hit. It's the same situation every day, except sometimes they do get hit.

I take a deep breath and try to ignore the commotion around me. As I keep walking, I devote my attention to scanning the area for demons. Nighttime is the perfect opportunity for them to roam around in search of victims. As if the war casualties are not enough.

I walk for close to a mile before I stop, my senses on alert.

They're near.

I tilt my head to the side and close my eyes.

One. Two? Maybe three demons.

They're not far from me.

I focus on the tingling sensation I get when a demon is nearby and follow it as it intensifies.

Eventually, I end up in front of a three-story building.

On the outside, it's as quiet and dark as the rest of the buildings on the street. The windows are all firmly shut and there isn't any flicker of light coming out from the inside.

I sharpen my hearing, and that's when the sounds come through.

Music.

Loud chatter.

The clinking of glasses.

I narrow my eyes.

A party. And it's coming from the basement.

I circle around the building a few times, trying to find the entrance, until it dawns on me that the way into the basement is by going down the stairs at the front of the building—the servant's entrance as they call it.

I could, of course, teleport inside—or attempt to. But I can only teleport to a precise location if I've visited it before. Given that it's a new place, the basement of a building nonetheless, I could end up falling from the ceiling in the sea of people. Considering the fact that I'm trying to keep a low profile, that would not be appropriate.

I knock on the door, and as it semi-opens, someone demands a password.

I frown.

Placing my foot between the door and the frame, I push it open and move past the person at the door. I wink at him as I erase my presence from his mind.

A long, winded dark corridor leads to the main room. There are no windows here, and the few in the back have been barricaded with pieces of wood so no light can sneak out. The light inside is strong, but the thick cloud of smoke from the cigarettes makes it uncomfortably irritating.

Everyone is smoking. Left, right. Males, females.

They're puffing their cigarettes and blowing clouds of smoke into the air.

My nose twitches.

I inhale sharply. The tingle continues. My eyes water and I lose my way through the bustling crowd. Someone even blows smoke in my face—the last thing I needed.

The tingling intensifies until I can no longer contain my sneeze.

I release a loud wheeze, followed by a harsh cough. My throat itches.

I've seen people smoke before but not on this level. How can they breathe in this noxious air?

My lungs? They can heal. Their lungs?

T.S.

I smile to myself, proud of my new vocabulary that helps me assimilate with those humans.

Although good thing they like to use abbreviations because tough shit just sounds vile. T.S., on the other hand, is more palatable. Of course I have been taught not to swear in any language I might speak. Not only is it highly disrespectful but it is also a sign of bad breeding.

My parents may have been rather autocratic, but they did provide me with a perfect education from my cradle—despite the fact that they are now bent on seeing me stop all my educational endeavors and simply devote myself to my future mate.

Ew.

I wave around the smoke in front of me in hopes I can help the air circulate better.

The signal from the demons is getting stronger. They must be here.

But there are just too many people, and it's not as if I can visually determine whether someone is a demon. We have a hard enough time when these demons take on humanoid appearances without minding the fate of the soul within.

Now? Not only do I have to go around and bless drinks to

see who is harmed by them, but I also have to touch them with my color-changing crystal to ensure the vessel's soul has not been consumed yet. Add to that the fact that I may also encounter high-level demons that are already humanoid on their own and my chances of success in this crowd are looking...not good.

Of course I would never complain about finding a high-level demon. Defeating one of those pests is sure to get me some notice from the higher-ups. But they are also rather...strong. One would be fine. Two? Maybe stretching it. But more than three?

I bite my lip in concentration as I try to come up with a plan.

From the corner of my eye, though, I see that the fates have decided to smile upon me.

There is an entire bowl filled with a drinking substance on the table close to the exit.

My eyes follow the movements of the humans until I am sure that bowl is where they source their drinks from. I nod to myself after I note quite a few of them serve themselves from the bowl, and I decide to start there.

Elbowing my way through the crowd—which is quite hard, seeing as I am the smallest person in the room—I attempt to reach the exit. All the human females are wearing heels, while the males are significantly taller than me. They are not as tall as some Aperites I know, but they are still towering over most females.

Their sweaty bodies move to the music, swaying from side to side.

It's...disconcerting.

This is the first time I have been in such an environment and I do not think I like it.

So far, I have not seen the more...debauched side of Anthropa since I've kept to the streets mostly, away from the crowds of people.

But this? Touching and eating each other's mouths in public? With so many people around them?

And if the murmurs I hear are to be believed, they don't even know each other.

One soldier admits his wife is across the ocean, but he quickly tells his partner that he might die soon, so he's going to have as much fun as he can. Then he leans in and licks her neck.

My eyes widen in shock.

Humans! Such libertines!

I cannot believe it. Why did Molokai not warn me about the obscenities I would witness here? I might have been only half-listening to his speech on Anthropa, but I am sure he never mentioned anything about their lascivious behaviors.

This is preposterous.

My mouth drops open in shock when I see a soldier's hand go up a woman's thigh, sneaking in under her dress until he...

"By the Source, what is this?" I mutter in disbelief.

He's touching her. In her private place.

She throws her head back, releasing a low moan as she lets herself be fondled like that.

Madness. This is madness! I must get out of here as soon as possible. I cannot witness this debauchery for much longer or I will become ill.

I put more strength into my elbow kicks, targeting especially those couples that are far too indecent. After a lot of shoving and witnessing even more outrageous behavior, I finally make it to the bowl.

Making sure no one is watching, I dip my finger in the bowl and start chanting the blessing ritual. Once I'm done, I find a more quiet place and start observing.

Unfortunately for me, that also means observing more obscenities.

If I'd known what was happening in Anthropa, perhaps I wouldn't have insisted on this mission.

Ah, who am I fooling? I would have insisted on it anyway

since it might be my only break before I'm forced to mate that odious Theron.

I try not to look too closely at what's happening on the dance floor, at how the bodies are writhing together, touching places that shouldn't be touched except by a mate.

Yet I can't deny that I'm also a little curious.

This is what my mother didn't want me to know, isn't it? This type of touching that is both scandalous and...intriguing.

I know the mechanics of mating—or at least I think I do. A male and a female are joined somehow and they exchange energies, after which the female becomes heavy with child, whom she later bears. I am not entirely sure how these touches I'm seeing on the dance floor relate to that, though.

I force myself to focus on the matter at hand—identifying the demons. But against my will, my eyes roam around the room, following the sighs and moans and every little hitched breath that comes with those forbidden touches.

Why?

Why do they make those sounds?

Is it pain? Pleasure? What is it exactly?

Is this what happens in Aperion too when males visit bawdy houses? They go there to watch this...? Experience it? But why? What are they getting out of this? So far, it seems that only the females are the ones being touched.

Deep in thought as I contemplate this matter of touching, I almost miss the hiss of pain that erupts through the air after a male drinks from his glass. The sound, low and harsh, filters through the loud music and reaches my ears.

My eyes flash, and I tense.

My gaze lands on the culprit just in time to see him deposit his glass on a nearby table. His face is contorted in pain that he tries to mask, but is unsuccessful.

The blessing chant works like a poison for any demonic energy. Though it is momentarily painful, depending on the level of the demon, it doesn't take them too long to recover.

I watch his expression closely, counting down the moments

it takes for him to shake the pain from his features. While this is not a foolproof method, it gives me an idea of what I'm dealing with.

Five, six...

Seven.

His face is back to a neutral expression as he shrugs off the last of the pain and puts on an affable smile.

Low level.

And seeing the way he ignores what just happened and continues to mingle around people, I realize he must be a really young demon, unaware of the power of a blessing chant—or the fact that it means an Aperite is on his trail.

Straightening my back, I make my way through the crowd, going straight for him.

The demon has possessed a tall male—well, at this point who isn't taller than me? He has short-cropped black hair and brown eyes. He's dressed in a military uniform like so many others in this room are, and his body language is just as sleazy.

As a young demon, I have no doubt that he still has ties to the physical realm. He might be little more than a corrupted soul, but he still remembers what it was like to be made of flesh —to use said flesh and enjoy all the perks that come with it.

Seeing the way he's eyeing the dance floor and studying the females in a lascivious manner, I can tell his first intent is to get some of that touching action. Next is, of course, consuming the souls.

Not under my watch, demon!

I get in front of him, but he doesn't see me.

Damn it.

His eyes are fixated somewhere above the top of my head, and with my size, it's like I'm invisible in front of him.

He's about to move through the crowd when I quickly improvise and throw myself against him.

"Oh, my," I murmur, purposefully slurring my words.

He narrows his eyes at me.

"Hello, handsome," I say and bat my lashes at him.

Ew! I'm about to gag the moment the word is out of my mouth, but alas, I am ready to sacrifice a little sweet talk for a future promotion.

He looks at me pensively for a moment before he smiles.

"Want to get out of here?" I whisper.

Say yes, please. Say yes and let's go out where I can exorcize you or kill you—depending on whether the mortal soul inside you is still alive.

He raises a brow at me before his lips slowly curve into a smile. He nods to me to lead the way.

Giddiness suffuses me.

My first kill of the night. So what if it's a low-level demon? It's still something. I'll add it to my killing collection so far and if I don't win over Commander Azerius' praise by quality, then at least I will do it with quantity.

I make my way through the crowd, keeping an eye on the demon to make sure he's following behind me. We get to the hallway, and as we move past the male at the door, we're finally out of the building.

"You have a place in mind?" he asks, his brows wiggling.

I nod and smile, beckoning him to follow me.

There is a small alleyway between buildings a few paces away. The perfect place for this demon to meet his end.

He's dumb, too. He doesn't even question why I'm doing this or who I am. He simply follows along.

The streets are dark, but the alleyway is even darker—if that's possible.

Luckily, I have rather good night vision, so I am able to scan my surroundings and position myself in the best spot to attack the demon.

His shoes scrape the ground as he enters the alleyway.

Caught you!

Before he can open his mouth and say another disgusting thing, I'm on him. But whereas before I would have killed first and asked questions later, now I have to remember to take out the crystal and confirm whether the mortal soul is gone.

I roll my eyes.

Rummaging for the crystal, I push it into the man's hand just in time to see it turn red.

Thank the Source!

Sliding the crystal back into my pocket, I will my energy to the surface. Two long ice blades descend from my hands, and I waste no time in slashing the demon in a crisscrossing motion.

The poor demon barely has time to react. Poor not because I pity him, of course. How could I pity demons and kill them in the same breath? No, no. Poor because no one taught him how to be a proper demon, and as such, this will hardly be a challenge.

He tries in vain to block the attack with his arms, but my blades are far too sharp. They cut through flesh and bone until the hands of the vessel fall to the ground.

He releases a loud sound of pain, but before he can wail some more—not that I would not enjoy that—I slash across his neck all the while murmuring a low chant to exterminate the demonic essence.

As the blood splashes out of the host, the demon struggles to keep control of the body. Despite the darkness, it's hard to miss the shadowy smoke coming out of the dead vessel. It's slow and aimless.

Extending my arm to the side, I will my sword to turn into a larger version, all the while murmuring the same chant.

The disoriented demon heads straight for my enlarged sword, which by now is shrouded in the holy chant. Upon contact, a sizzling sound erupts in the air as the smoke promptly disintegrates.

And that, ladies and gentlemen, is how you kill a demon.

My swords disappear and I pat my clothes to shake off the demon dust.

A smile creeps up on my face.

One down, a few more to go.

But just as I'm about to turn, my ears pick up on another sound. It's close and getting closer.

I swivel.

My eyes widen as I note another demon coming straight at me. But this time, he's carrying a weapon in the form of a long knife.

I smirk.

This one seems to be a bit more knowledgeable. He's charging at me as if he actually means to do me harm.

So he knows I kill his kind, doesn't he?

Feeling for the crystal in my pocket, I throw it at him, waiting for the flash of light that will confirm whether I can go ahead with the kill.

But just as the crystal emits a low, red light, another set of steps echoes in the alleyway.

I barely get to react before two strong hands cup both sides of the demon's face, and in a swift movement, they twist the head of the vessel.

It drops to the ground, lifeless.

I blink. The demonic essence fizzles out and vanishes without my ritual.

What?

I stare in shock at the fallen carcass.

"It's not safe for a girl like you to be alone at night, darling." A deep drawl sends shivers down my spine.

My gaze snaps up to the person who did this—the hands that snapped the neck.

He slowly walks past the fallen body and heads toward me. He's dressed in a military uniform too, but the number of medals on his blazer are far more numerous than any of the ones I saw tonight.

He might be a higher-up? I'm not too familiar with the human military to say for certain, but I think they take their distinctions as seriously as we do.

One thing is for sure, though. He is the tallest human I've ever encountered. Quite easily among the tallest males I've ever seen, too.

Green eyes sparkle in the darkness. Full lips smile lazily at me.

But there is something else.

Half of his face is badly scarred. A harsh, jagged line starts from his temple and goes down his cheek and neck, hiding into his uniform.

There's something about his presence. Something... imposing.

My brows knit together in a frown.

Is he an Aperite? A deity? Who is he that he can so easily kill a demon—granted, a low level, but they're resilient bastards.

I swallow hard, a little taken aback by his presence. Especially as he continues to advance toward me.

"Who are you?" I whisper.

FOUR

WHOEVER HE IS, he killed a demon, and that immediately makes me suspicious.

I don't detect any Aperite energy from him, nor demonic. He screams human to me, but he's a human who doesn't mind taking another's life. If it's so easy for him to kill, then he's well on his way to becoming a corrupt soul and eventually a demon.

Doesn't matter. Whoever he is, he will *not* steal my kills.

They're mine.

All the ones in this area.

I've laid claim to them and he will *not* kill a demon under my watch!

He already did kill one, Minerva. And you know better than to claim otherwise in your report.

Damn it!

"Who are you?" I demand again, this time louder.

"Lucien de Vitry. At your service," he says with a bow.

There's a wicked glint in his eye that I do not trust.

"You killed a man," I note as I slowly inch away.

He shrugs, his green eyes still on me.

"I don't take kindly to gents trying to hurt a lady."

I glare at him.

"Well, I could have handled myself just fine," I say with a huff.

"The right thing to say is *thank you*." He pauses. His lips quirk up. "Miss...?"

I roll my eyes at him. I am not certain what he wants, but the more time I waste here, the fewer demons I will kill tonight—especially now that he took one of my kills.

"The right thing to do is to mind your own business," I tell him sternly and move to leave.

He doesn't move. His eyes are tracking my movements, shrewd and calculating.

I don't know who this Lucien de Vitry is, but my instincts tell me to be wary. There's something about him that I don't like.

Perhaps it's simply my pettiness for him stealing my kill. Or perhaps it's the way he's watching me with that dangerous glint in his eye as if I'd ever allow him to come within a few paces of me.

Dream on, soldier boy.

"Still waiting for my *thank you*," he says when I move past him.

I glare at him.

"You might have to wait forever."

"A feisty gal. I like it," he murmurs appreciatively as he turns toward me.

"Take one more step and I will gut you," I warn in a harsh tone.

His brows shoot up in surprise. Then he smiles and takes a step forward.

My eyes flare. For all my talk, I *cannot* kill a human. Could I get away with a little torture, though? Just enough to wipe that smile off his face.

He moves slowly, methodically, until he's right in front of me.

It's dark. As a human, I doubt he can see much. But I can see him well enough.

And I *hate* it.

I hate that I have to look up at him as if he were one of those buildings that scrape the skies. I hate that he dared to kill *my* demon. Most of all, I hate that he's daring to talk to me as if we are equals.

"You puny little hu—"

"Little?" He straightens his back, towering over me.

I glare mutinously at him—*up* at him. Okay, maybe little is the wrong word choice.

His sole response is to smile. He *only* knows how to smile. It's not a bad smile, if I were to assess it objectively. But as of right now, I am anything *but* objective when he just killed my demon! Now he's making me lose precious time when I could be out there finding another demon to fill my quota for the night.

"Step away or I *will* gut you," I grit out.

Those pesky little demons will not kill themselves—though how I wish they did, but when you're evil to your core and your only purpose is to prey on those weaker than you, I suppose there is no reason to get depressed about life. Alas, this is not the moment to contemplate the mental health of demons—though, really, perhaps that is a good topic for a dissertation, which might earn me another commendation if all goes well.

Stop this, Minerva! You will not *get any commendation for doing nothing*.

In fact, the only thing I will get is a reprimand if I tarry for much longer, which will only serve to stoke my ire about not meeting my nightly quota, which might make me *actually* gut him.

I may not be too well versed in human biology, but I am pretty sure if I were to gut him, he would die, and I cannot have that. Not that I feel any type of empathy toward him since he didn't feel any toward that demon either—though from his point of view, he was merely a man trying to harm me, a small girl (okay, when you look at it like that, perhaps it doesn't look as bad).

But he's a human. Finite lifespans. Small, insignificant dots in the large scheme of things.

Honestly, I don't see why we cannot kill them.

"Big words for a tiny darling like you," he murmurs in a low voice.

Does he not sense the danger he's in?

So what if I'm tiny? I'm deadly!

My nostrils flare as I stare at him.

"Step. Away."

"Now, darling, let's not get all riled up. Where is your home? I will do my gentlemanly duty and see you home safely."

Another smile.

What part of *step away* does he not understand? Is he hard of hearing?

"I do not require your assistance," I mutter in annoyance as I make to move past him.

Once more, he blocks my path.

Surely I should be allowed to get away with a tiny bit of torture, no?

"Move aside, human," I tell him harshly.

My entire body is trembling with anger. Just who does he think he is to speak to me like this? To encroach on my space and block my path.

I am visibly shaking, so much so it's a wonder my spiritual energy is still under control.

He sees it too, and I expect him to finally realize the danger he's in and leave me alone. Instead, he releases a loud sigh.

"You must be terrified, you poor little thing," he continues as if he didn't hear what I just said. "It's all right. I will not harm you."

"No. I *will* harm you."

"There are so many bad gents around I'm sure you don't know who to trust. But rest assured. I will see you home safely."

He smiles again. This time showing his teeth. Rather nice teeth, though that is beside the point.

"Human!" I growl.

"There, there, darling. I know you must be scared but—"

"*You* should be scared," I burst out, pushing my finger into his—rather hard—chest. "We're in a dark alley. Don't you have any sense of self-preservation?" I grit out.

He chuckles.

"I should ask you the same thing."

This infuriating male! My anger rises to the surface and I do my best to calm down, lest I accidentally kill him. That would do me no good.

Humans are foolish, Minerva. They are young and inexperienced.

"You poor tiny thing," he murmurs, grabbing my hand and holding it tightly in place. "It's all right. I will keep you safe."

I blink, momentarily shocked.

He? He will keep me safe?

I can't even laugh because I am too astonished by his words —though this is quite a laughable situation.

I pull my hand and push him away from me.

"I will excuse your blindness due to the darkness since you humans have rather feeble eyesight," I start in a haughty voice. "But I will have you know I am the scariest thing you will encounter here tonight. So move along before I am forced to hurt you."

There. That's it.

I'm quite proud of myself for getting the words out so coherently and without any outburst of energy that might send him flying. Although by the Source would I love to see him flying, preferably far, far away from me.

Except my words don't move him. If anything, they seem to amuse him further.

"Tiny and scary, ain't that right?"

"Stop commenting about my height," I snap.

"It's rather obvious." He chuckles.

I narrow my eyes at him.

"It's dark," I point out drily.

He shrugs.

"I can hear you speak from down below," he drawls, amusement dripping from his words.

"You..."

My anger gets the best of me and I fail to stop myself from punching him. Although I should pat myself on the back later on for *not* stabbing him with my ice dagger. Ah, the little things.

Even though I am more powerful than him—yes, even with my tiny body—he manages to parry my blow.

I frown.

How?

He can't see in this darkness. That much is certain. Even I lack full visibility. Yet as I attempt to throw another punch, I am surprised to see him dodge that too.

How can he know where I'm aiming? Can he see through the darkness? Was my initial assessment wrong and he is *not* human?

But that's impossible. I cannot detect any supernatural signature coming from him.

Going by his amused grin and laid-back attitude, he's not even making too much of an effort to parry my blows. He's simply swaying from side to side, using my strength against me.

Just as I try to hit him again, he catches my fist and pulls me close.

"Careful, darling. That's quite dangerous."

Yes! I *am* dangerous. He should fear me! He should. He's only unscathed because I cannot afford to use the full extent of my powers on him. But if he were a demon or another deity... I would have already had him on his back, groaning in pain. Preferably with his insides spilling out.

"Wouldn't want you to hurt yourself," he murmurs softly.

"I'm not hurting myself. I'm hurting *you*," I say through gritted teeth. He's holding me tightly against his chest, and his breath fans over my cheek. It reeks of cigarettes.

Disgusting!

I push against his hold, still debating whether I should just send him flying in the air and wash my hands of this unfortunate situation once and for all. My brother will have my hide, but perhaps he will be understanding once I tell him about this unseemly harassment.

I mean, he called me tiny!

Tiny!

So what if I am tiny? But who says that to someone else's face? Who even allowed him to speak to me? He should be punished for that alone. I should cut his tongue for daring to do that. He could survive fine without a tongue.

Never mind the fact that he is *touching* me. Mayhap I should add his hands to the list of bodily parts I must sever, too. Can humans survive without tongues *and* arms? I have heard of war amputees whose limbs were severed to prevent infection and they survived, but I suppose they still had their tongues intact.

If only I could have the freedom to experiment with how many parts I could remove from him before dying *without* worrying I might be punished for killing a human...

Alas, I have learned my lesson that humans are quite obnoxious, so I will keep my distance from now on. As long as I don't interact with them, I won't feel the urge to kill them, right?

"You must have been taught that all gents are evil, but that's not true, darling. It's fine. You can let it all out. I'm here to protect you." His voice is so damn soft and warm.

Is he...dumb?

I blink slowly as I focus on his features.

His green eyes sparkle as he smiles at me.

He's not joking. He actually believes I'm some mere girl in need of saving when, in fact, *he* is the one who will need saving.

In a moment or two. Once I decide if breaking the rules is worth the future punishment.

I might be annoyed, but I have to admit that the cigarette smell is not all that obnoxious, especially combined with leather and spice.

Minerva! Focus!

"Get your hands off—" A loud noise coming from above cuts my words off.

It's a buzzing, almost static type of noise.

He looks up, too, face scrunched in concern.

Everything happens so fast. One moment, we're searching for the source of the noise. The next, his arms are around me, shielding me from a deafening explosion.

A burst of light erupts in the darkness, illuminating the surroundings.

"What..." I mutter, my eyes growing wide with shock.

Tendrils of fire blaze in the air, accompanied by shrilling screams of pain.

Another loud explosion, and debris flies in the air, together with smoke and fumes.

The previously dark sky of the night is now a thousand shades of gray and small, almost translucent yellow stripes reflecting the fire below.

"You good, tiny darling?" His voice penetrates my mind.

I slowly turn to face him.

The power of the explosion had propelled both of us backward and onto the ground. His arms are still around me, holding tightly—too tight.

My mouth parts as I get ready for another set down, but I don't even have time to speak as cries for help erupt in the air, together with wails of sorrow and screams of pain.

The stillness of the night is no longer still. It's clogged with suffering...and death.

He pulls me to my feet, looking me over a couple of times before he nods to himself. His features are tense, the scar on the right side of his face more prominent than before.

Without a word, he leaves my side.

As in, he leaves me alone.

I blink.

Well...that was unexpected.

This is what it took for him to finally leave me alone? An explosion?

"Humans," I grumble to myself.

He probably fled in fear.

Weak lot, these humans.

I dust my clothes and walk out of the alleyway. I should probably scout other areas for demons. If I'm lucky, I might be able to get another one before dawn. That would bring my total to one hundred ninety-five. Just five short of two hundred. Of course, considering some are close to five hundred already, I am still nowhere near where I should be if I want to earn that commendation.

I'm about to head in the direction opposite the explosion, but my eyes are inexplicably drawn to the mayhem.

Two buildings have collapsed—totaled to the ground. A fire is raging in the second one, eating at the wooden foundation and growing stronger by the second.

A couple of people have gathered around the ruins of the first building, grabbing onto rubble and pieces of concrete and moving them out of the way in search of survivors. Though with the state of the building... I doubt there's anyone still alive in there.

Wait a moment...

I glance around and retrace my steps from the party, counting down the buildings. My eyes slowly widen at the realization that the explosion occurred in the building where the party was held.

Something else catches my eye.

A military uniform, but the person wearing it is not among the casualties. It's one of the people working to get them out.

That male...

I take a step forward.

The fire illuminates his face. Sweat and soot are gathered on his brow as he wipes his ash-ridden hands against his skin. He's pulling onto a large piece of concrete by himself, but I doubt he's going to move it.

A whoosh of air sweeps past me.

I look to the side to see a dozen or more messengers appear on the street, walking in a procession toward the building.

One by one, souls rise from the rubble. They are disoriented and confused, the perfect combination to allow the messengers to take them to the afterlife in a smooth process.

Each messenger latches onto one soul and opens a portal toward P'asala, the intermediary realm through which all souls must pass in order to be sorted into their afterlife by merit.

There are maybe thirty or forty souls in total that are taken.

I await silently by the side to ensure no demon shows up to attempt to consume the souls.

But something isn't right. There were more than forty people in that basement alone.

I close my eyes and recall the images from before, doing my best to approximate the number of people at the party.

I did not see everyone, but I am certain there were at least double that number. And if their souls have not left their bodies then...

They're either alive or they've been consumed.

I purse my lips as I try to detect any demonic signature, but there is none.

At the same time, the male from before, Lucien, stops what he's doing. His hands are full of deep lacerations, his fingernails half broken and bloody.

He's breathing hard as he calls for more help to lift the big concrete block. The only other person present, another male, is working on the other side, pulling on some metal bar.

But he's not calling for help from that male. He's calling for help from the people who are watching this tragedy from their windows, their faces barely visible as they peek outside. But they're there. Watching. Not moving. Not coming down to help.

I glance around and note that some cars have stopped at the end of the street, but those people, too, just stand there and stare.

Perhaps it's the shock.

If I were human, a feeble creature with a limited lifespan, perhaps I would be shocked too. Afraid that something could happen to me. That I could be next.

A bomb likely caused the explosion. That buzzing sound? A plane—an enemy plane. And with the way the fire is raging out of control in the second building, it's easy to see why people would be wary to help. More planes could come and drop another bomb in the area, the fire serving as a beacon of death.

They could be instantly killed.

Yet that male...that soldier... He doesn't seem concerned with that.

In fact, he's oddly unconcerned about his own safety, despite the fact that he was so insistent I care about mine not a few moments ago.

Odd. Very, very odd.

"There are people down here!" he yells, looking around and pleading with the bystanders. "Alive."

The fire crackles in the air, the only sound other than his ragged voice.

"We have to get them out," he shouts in frustration when the concrete slab doesn't move no matter how much he pulls at it.

With a loud curse, he steps back, his chest rising up and down as he labors to breathe. He wipes his sweat from his face, smearing more soot and blood on his skin.

Then his eyes meet mine.

He tilts his head to the side.

"You. Come help!"

M-me? I can't do that! I can't get involved in mortals' lives. And if their fate is to die today, then I cannot stop that from happening.

He stares at me in an unusual manner.

"Give me a hand here, darling."

I ignore him and turn to leave.

FIVE

INSTEAD OF WALKING AWAY, I find myself walking toward the ruins.

In the distance, a succession of flashes lights up the sky, followed by more buzzing sounds. It appears the enemy plane has been shot down. Hopefully, that means help is on the way.

As I near the fallen building, I barely hide a gasp at seeing a lone arm among the rubble. A distance away, there is a foot—a detached foot.

I may gut demons for a living, but this isn't what I signed up for.

This type of war is not what I signed up for.

And to think that what I've witnessed so far is barely a hundredth of what people are experiencing on the continent, where the war rages on their own land.

A shudder goes down my back.

I do my best to avoid looking at all the severed body parts, especially since not even an hour ago, I had seen the same people laughing, dancing, and enjoying life.

Now... They're gone.

Just like that.

I reach soldier boy and realize why he's trying so hard to move that piece of concrete. There's a faint sound coming from underneath it. It's almost like a wheezing sound, followed by a barely audible moan of pain.

He doesn't acknowledge my presence.

Grabbing onto the sides of the slab, he pulls it up at the same time as he's pulling it toward him. There are rusty metal bars protruding from the concrete that dig into his flesh, but he doesn't stop.

He gives it his all.

It's almost...admirable.

"Grab that side," he says with a labored breath, pointing to the end of the slab that is still not budging.

I'm frozen to my spot, unable to move—either to run away or to help him.

More smoke comes out from the burning wood, making it increasingly harder to breathe. If I, an immortal, find this uncomfortable, I cannot imagine how it must be for a human.

The entire landscape is one of horror, reminding me of the hellish dimension where evil souls go. I've never personally visited it, but I've seen illustrations of it. And it's just like this.

Pain. Death. More pain.

The severed body parts and the pooling blood gathering onto the asphalt are the centerpiece of this horror.

So much death...

"I'm talking to you, darling," soldier boy calls out, his voice harsher than before. "Grab that side."

I blink and meet his eyes.

They're a dark green, but the darkness comes from within, from the things he's witnessed and the things he has yet to witness.

There is no more amusement in his features now. No smile to be found. And for some reason, I envy the me from moments ago, who was only regaled with that side of him—annoying as it might be.

"I...can't," I whisper.

His features contort in anger, followed by what seems like disappointment.

But why? He doesn't know me. He has no reason to be disappointed by my actions.

"You can't?" he asks harshly, his upper lip twitching.

His hands are full of scrapes and scratches, some so deep, blood keeps oozing out. His nails are broken, a couple of them hanging on by a loose thread and on the verge of falling off.

His uniform is destroyed. Blood, smoke, and dirt. It's also ripped in places from being snagged by the metal bars.

"I..."

I should go. Teleport out of here and disappear. He might find that strange, but perhaps after some time, he'd think I was an illusion.

I truly should go.

But why am I not moving?

"Don't tell me you're too delicate to lift some rubble."

"No, of course not."

"Time's of the essence. If you're not gonna help, at least run along and fetch the authorities."

He gives me one last stern look before he turns back to his slab of concrete and resumes his efforts.

I could swear I saw a shadow of disgust in his features as he looked at me. But why?

Thinking that maybe calling the authorities might not constitute as meddling in human affairs, I turn to leave.

But I don't take a step before I stop. A small sound reaches my ears. It's the breathy, pain-filled voice of a child.

"Ma... Ma."

I freeze.

"It's all right, little one, I'll get you out of there," the soldier coos to the child before he resumes his efforts to lift the slab of concrete.

He'll never succeed. It's far too heavy for him to do it alone.

"I want my mamma," the child whispers, her voice carried by the wind until it reaches my ears. I doubt humans can hear that. But I do. And what's more concerning is the way I react to that hopeless sound.

I should be able to turn my back on this and leave. Human tragedy is everywhere. This is war, after all. I cannot help everyone.

But you could help that little child, my inner voice tells me.

Can I?

It's against the rules. I will surely be punished for it if I do.

Mortals die every day. Children die every day. It's nothing new.

I take a step forward.

A loud bang erupts in the air and I swivel.

The soldier lost his grip on the slab of concrete and it slammed against the rest of the rubble, emitting a loud thud.

He's breathing hard. The growing fire nearby illuminates his face, and I can see the wildness in his eyes as he tries to save what may not be salvageable.

It's...honorable. But also useless.

Why do humans exert so much energy to avoid something that's unavoidable? Why do they try time and time again when it is all in vain?

In my time here, I've heard about the Blitz and I've seen the destruction firsthand. This type of attack is not new, nor is the loss of life.

Thousands, if not more, lost their lives in that bombardment. Tens of buildings were destroyed.

It is all part of war.

If humans are so concerned about preserving life, then why wage war in the first place?

It is paradoxical.

The soldier slowly turns to me.

His green eyes are full of anguish and something else, an ineffable emotion that tugs at my heartstrings.

And that's when I realize my own shortcoming. I might pride myself on being a good warrior, a good Aperite, but at the end of the day, even I am moved by the same basic emotions.

I squeeze my eyes shut. I know I will regret this.

With a loud sigh, I swivel and in a few steps, I'm next to the soldier. I give him a nod and position my hands on the end of the slab of concrete. Understanding enters his gaze, and he grabs on the other end.

"One, two, three," he says, at which point we both lift.

The slab moves, and we slide it to the side, revealing a hole between the big pieces of concrete. The child is at the bottom, barely visible. She's buried under rubble and unable to move.

Soldier boy is the first to dive into the hole next to the child. He starts unloading the pieces of rubble to the side before grabbing the little girl and giving her to me.

Her clothes are dirty and torn. Her face and hair are covered in dust. There are small cuts all over her body, but otherwise, she will survive.

I grab her in my arms and take her to an empty area to the side.

"My mamma..." she whispers. "Where is my mamma?"

"We'll find her, all right?"

What am I saying? Why am I promising such a thing when I don't even know if her mother is alive? Yet the words are out of my mouth before I can think about the situation logically.

The girl gives me a tentative nod, her eyes shining with unshed tears. Yet there's something else in her gaze. She's putting her trust in me. Those words that I so carelessly threw around mean everything to her.

I force a smile as I slowly back away and head back to where the soldier is.

He's digging through the rubble, and when I get near him, I note a hand sticking out of the sea of concrete.

Getting to my knees next to him, I touch the hand to feel for the pulse.

Nothing.

I meet his gaze and shake my head.

It takes him a moment to stop his efforts. He releases a harsh breath, followed by a loud groan of frustration. But he's not done. He switches his focus to another area, all the while calling out for survivors.

It seems unlikely that there would be many, or that anyone would answer him.

But I am once more surprised when a succession of voices calls out for help. They're faint. Barely audible.

Soldier boy doesn't hear them. But I do.

I do and...

Another pivotal decision.

Do I point to him where the voices are coming from and help him save them, or do I ignore them and let fate play out as it should?

But as I see him rush around in an attempt to find any other survivors, my decision is made.

"Here," I say and point out to where the sound is coming from.

He gives me a tight nod and gets to work.

His hands are beyond damaged now. The entire surface of his palms is covered in blood from the deep lacerations he suffered from the rusty metal bars. The backs of his hands are not faring much better, covered in scratches and scrapes as they are.

It must be painful.

But he's not complaining.

Swallowing my discomfort at the situation, I set to help him as best as I can.

We lift tens if not hundreds of stones of all sizes until we find the people buried under the rubble.

Some are still alive. Others are dead.

Seeing that I have a knack for finding the areas with survivors, he asks me to look around more while he drags the corpses of the unlucky people to the side.

I divide my attention in half, listening for breathing sounds or existing heartbeats but also surreptitiously studying him.

The people might be dead, but he treats them with the same respect as if they were alive. He covers the females up to preserve their modesty and closes the eyes of the males who'd died with a terrified expression on their faces. But it's the children he's most gentle with. He carries the dead children to the side with such care, it makes me guilty to think that just moments ago I wanted to leave this area and ignore the cries for help.

More than guilt, though, I feel...shame.

For every ten dead bodies we pull out of the rubble, we maybe find one alive but gravely injured. Even with my intervention, I doubt some of them will make it through the night.

Still, the soldier gives his all.

"When will help come?" I ask as we carry a female to the side. She's missing an arm, cut badly at the elbow. Blood is pouring out at an alarming rate and I fear she will bleed out before she gets any medical attention.

His lips flatten.

"They should come...eventually. But by the time they do, it might be too late for a lot of these people," he says, echoing my own thoughts.

Taking off his military jacket, now dirty and torn, he places it atop the female to warm her up. He's left wearing a white shirt—though it's not that white anymore—and a thin undershirt that peeks through the unbuttoned bit of the shirt.

He pulls on the bottom of his shirt, tearing a huge chunk of material, and ties it around her elbow where her arm had been severed.

We're about to head back to search the debris when flashing lights appear from the end of the street. A procession of cars pulls up at the site of the accident. The first to get out of the vehicles are police officers, followed by nurses and medical staff. The last to arrive are the firefighters.

One of the police officers approaches us.

"The people on this side are still alive," the soldier tells him. "The ones on that side are deceased."

The officer nods, his eyes narrowing at us.

"A yank," he comments drily.

"Major Lucien de Vitry, sir."

"Well, Major, you did your duty. Now it is our turn. I would like you to step away from the site so you do not impede the efforts of the *actual* professionals."

I blink.

His tone is downright offensive.

Aren't those yanks supposed to be their allies in the war?

I expect soldier boy to have a fitting comeback, but instead, he bites his tongue and turns to leave.

What?

The officer turns his gaze to me, probably about to make a similar remark. But I don't give him the opportunity as I dash after Lucien.

"You're going to let him speak like that to you?" I ask as I reach his side. He's walking fast. "After you saved all those people?"

"They wouldn't want it known that a *yank* saved those people."

I frown.

"Why?"

He stops and turns to me. "You're not from around here, are you?"

"So what if I'm not?" I challenge.

His lips pull into a smile.

"Perhaps it's better if you're not," he finally says.

Then he turns and walks again.

I increase my pace to keep up.

"You need to tend to your injuries," I tell him.

Why am I still here? I've done my duty—though it wasn't really my duty, was it? I should be gone. Back to my cozy little place on the outskirts of London, where there aren't any buildings on fire and people to save.

He blinks, then looks down at his bloody hands as if it just dawns on him that he was injured.

He's quiet for a few moments before he nods.

"I suppose I should."

"Good. Then have a good night."

There, I did my second *duty* of the night. Maybe *too* many duties. Alas, now I can return home and sleep. I am quite sleepy. I should probably wash, too, though the water in this world doesn't suit my skin very well. But I have some leftover cookies from yesterday. And I'm quite hungry.

Yes, that sounds like a perfect plan. I can eat my sorrows away since I clearly did not meet my demon quota for the night, and I also did something I wasn't supposed to.

Now I can only hope that my involvement did not mess with those people's fates *too* much. Perhaps I can get away with it.

Deep in my thoughts—mostly about the cookies, to be honest—I barely realize when soldier boy grabs my arm and pulls me after him.

He's getting his blood all over me! Never mind that he's also *touching* me. Unacceptable.

I open my mouth to tell him exactly that but find myself stunned into silence when I realize he's pulling me toward the riverbank.

I'll blame my non-reaction on curiosity. Yes, I should have left already, but it's not as if this human male can harm me.

I am stronger, faster, and entirely superior to him and his kind.

Perhaps I can wait a little longer to see what he has in mind.

I must admit that after seeing how hard he worked to save those people, I have a renewed respect for him. He might be *just* a human, but he's an honorable one.

We walk down some stairs toward the river.

The moon is high up in the sky, and its reflection in the water affords some type of lighting.

Everything looks so peaceful now. One could almost forget that people are dying everywhere, that people just died a small distance away.

The water is so tranquil, innocently flowing from one side to the other, entirely ignorant of all the bloodshed around—bloodshed that sometimes makes its way into its depths.

The soldier finds a spot near the banks and plops himself on the floor.

I raise a brow at him, unsure of what he wants me to do.

The navy blue skirt and blazer set I'm wearing are new. I just bought them the other day. It's not seemly to sit down on the damp ground and get them dirty. So what if they're already stained with soot and dust? That's not too hard to clean—I've experienced it before. The wet, slimy earth, however, might stain the material for good.

I might have an allowance, as every warrior does when we are stranded fighting in another world, but it is not a big sum. It is just enough to pay for my accommodation, buy food, clothes, some trinkets here and there, and go three times a week to the moving pictures. I've already exhausted my clothes budget for this month and the one thing I will not do is dig into my movie theater budget. Or my sweets budget.

Unacceptable.

The soldier surprises me, however, when he takes off what's left of his shirt and places it on the ground next to him and motions for me to sit on it. He's left only in his undershirt, which exposes his muscular form. His arms are bare, strong, and well-defined. The light fabric molds to his chest, emphasizing his pectoral muscles too.

I look away.

This is not proper.

Taking a seat on his shirt, I make sure to keep my gaze forward so I don't see more than I need to.

I clear my throat.

"Why did you bring me here?" I ask.

He rummages through the pockets of his pants and removes a silver flask. After pulling the cap off, he takes a big swig before offering it to me.

My lashes flutter in confusion.

"What is this?" I wrinkle my nose as I take the flask and smell the contents. It's strong and pungent.

"Whiskey," he answers tersely.

I've heard of whiskey. It's a type of alcohol humans love to drink, although I've heard that this, too, is rationed.

"Why are you giving this to me?"

"To take the edge off," he answers.

I frown again. "What edge?"

He tilts his head to the side, not understanding my question. "Just take a swig."

I stare at the flask. I'm not one to turn down a challenge, and I might be a little curious about this so-called whiskey and why everyone is so enamored by it.

The moment the liquid goes down my throat, I feel a sudden burn and choke.

"No, thank you. I will pass," I say in disgust and hand him back the flask.

He shrugs and takes another swig.

"You should use that on your hands," I point out. Alcohol is good for injuries in this world.

"And waste good whiskey?" He chuckles, then takes another drink.

I stare at him in shock. Is the whiskey more important than an infection?

Without a word, I snatch the flask for him. Shaking it, I gauge that it's only half full.

I can tell he's about to protest, but when he reaches for the flask, I forcibly grab his hand, turn it palm up, and pour some of the alcohol on his wounds.

He hisses in pain.

"Give me your other hand," I order him, and he surprisingly complies.

I empty the rest of the flask on his left hand.

Then I still.

What now?

He's holding his palms up, the blood from the injuries diluted from the alcohol. I need something to clean the residual blood with—and the dirt that's probably snuck into the open flesh.

There's nothing around that I can use. His shirt is already dirty from the soil. And I'm not about to use my precious suit.

I eye him up and down.

I suppose there's only one thing that will work.

Grabbing the hem of his undershirt, I tear a wide strip of cloth from it.

His eyes widen, but he doesn't move. He lets me continue.

I don't look at his torso, instead focusing solely on his palm as I use one side of the cloth to clean his wound before turning it to the other side and wrapping it around his hand. I repeat the process for his other hand, and by the time I'm done, his undershirt is half torn, now barely reaching his belly button.

That means I can see his stomach.

His very, very hard stomach.

Uhm.

I gulp down and look away.

I shouldn't be noticing that.

"Done. You can be on your way now," I suddenly say.

"Why would I leave when you're treating me so well, tiny darling?" he murmurs in a low voice.

I release a scandalized gasp.

"Stop calling me that!"

"Why?"

"It's... Well, it's not proper." I straighten my back and look straight ahead. The last thing I need is to notice the green hue of his eyes or the way they sparkle in the moonlight.

Good grief.

I've made my fair share of mistakes, but I'm pretty sure I've never made so many in a single day as I did today. Not only did I help save mortals, but now I am engaging in conversation with one! A half-clothed one, too!

He chuckles at my serious expression.

"Then I suppose I should have your name. Miss..."

His eyes twinkle with amusement. He watches me closely, waiting for my reply.

"M-Minerva," I grumble.

What am I doing? Why am I giving this stranger my name? *By the Source, Minerva, you must have gone mad!*

"Minerva," he repeats. But no amount of mentally berating myself can make me ignore the way he says my name. His voice is rough, and I detect a slight lilt in the way he accentuates each letter.

"I am Lucien. Pleased to meet you, Minerva."

"Well, I am not," I shoot back, folding my arms over my chest with a huff.

He raises his brows.

"You're not...?"

"Pleased to meet you. In fact, I am the opposite of pleased. First, you killed a man for me when I did not ask you to, which I will have you know, messed with my quota. Then you practically forced me to help you with that building. And *then* you drag me to this place and you made me dress up your wounds as if I were your personal nurse. You, sir, are far too presumptuous and I am *not* pleased about meeting you."

I finally catch my breath when I'm done speaking, but I nod to myself, pleased about the eloquent flow of my words.

The corners of his lips are curled up and he's watching me as if he's barely holding back laughter.

I frown. What is his problem?

"So let me get this straight. I killed a man without your permission."

I nod. Finally, he's showing some trace of intellect.

"Then I forced you to help those people."

Damn right. I nod again.

"And then I *made* you tend to my wounds."

Another nod.

"All against your will."

"Precisely," I say with a huff.

He stares at me for a moment before he bursts into laughter.

"Yet you're still here." He points to where I'm sitting. "I am not holding you hostage, yet I don't see any sign of you leaving."

"That's only because *your* sight is faulty in the darkness. I am actually in the process of getting up and leaving," I quickly counter.

"It's taking you quite some time to do so," he drawls.

"Well, I am tired. You did force me to move all those stones. It's quite natural to be slower after such an exertion," I say, though he is right. I still make no effort to get up and leave.

But I will.

In a moment.

I did not lie to him. I find myself rather tired after all that physical effort. It's the only reason why I'm still sitting here. It has absolutely nothing to do with him.

"You're an odd duck, Minerva," he murmurs, amused.

I glare at him. How dare he call me a duck?

First tiny darling, now odd duck? Who does he take me for?

"You puny human! How dare you call me a duck?" I thunder at him.

"Now, Minerva, darling, you're misunderstanding—"

"Don't you darling, or duck me, mister," I threaten.

"Duck you?" he repeats.

"Yes, don't you duck me!" I take a deep breath to calm myself. "Humans. Nasty creatures."

Lucien is still sporting an amused expression.

"But what if I *would* like to duck you?"

"You, sir, are offensive."

"Yes, that was rather offensive, wasn't it? I should apologize."

"You should." I nod, pushing my chin in the air. "It is very rude to call someone an animal, or a bird, or whatnot. I don't know what type of company you keep, but this is unacceptable."

"You..." he trails off.

I give him another glare.

"I hope the next words that come out of your mouth are an apology."

He nods solemnly. "I do apologize for ducking you."

"Good," I huff aloud.

"As long as you allow me the possibility of doing that in the future," he continues. "Duck you, I mean." He smiles.

I frown. "I do not understand you."

He releases a deep sigh. "Never mind. It was a joke."

"I do not like these jokes of yours. I do not call you names, now do I?"

"I thought I heard you say *nasty creature*."

"That was a generalization. I did not say *you*, Lucien, are a nasty creature. Whereas you said that I, Minerva, am an odd duck. See the difference?"

He takes a moment to consider my words.

"Odd duck is an idiom, Minerva. It means you are an odd person. I did not call you a duck of the fowl variety."

"Oh," I mutter. "Couldn't you have said so from the beginning?"

"I could have." He nods.

I frown again. I do not think we're speaking the same language.

"Then you are an odd duck, too, Lucien."

"Now *you're* ducking me?"

"Why not? You did it first," I state in a haughty voice.

"So we're ducking each other now?"

"Precisely. Do not think for a moment that just because I am female, I cannot best you."

"Ah, Minerva." He lets out a laugh and shakes his head. "You're a gem, aren't you?"

"Good on you to notice. Perhaps you do have good sight, after all," I mutter.

He smiles and shrugs.

Leaning back onto his forearms, he tips his head back. He grabs something from his pocket and slips a white stick between his lips—a cigarette. I cannot understand why humans find this practice so appealing. The smell alone is obnoxious and foul.

He lights up his cigarette and puffs it a couple of times.

The smoke immediately reaches me, and I barely suppress a cough.

Damn it all, but that is too much for my sensitive nose. It's already making me tear up. The smell aside, the smoke itself is abrasive as it travels down my throat.

It happened before, at the party where everyone was smoking. But now, with the source of the smoke so close, it's almost worse.

Reaching forward, I snatch the cigarette from his lips and put it out on the grass.

The smell still clings to the air, almost as if it doesn't want to leave.

I wrinkle my nose in distaste. This is what I get for hanging out with humans and their disgusting pastimes.

"Good night, sir," I mumble before I turn to leave.

He calls out my name repeatedly, but I give it no mind. And when I'm far enough that I'm out of sight, I teleport back to my lodgings.

Humans. Nasty bunch.

Good thing I'm never going to see that Lucien again or hear about his ducking ways.

SIX

KISSING.

That's what they call the act of lip touching between two people.

Now I have a name for what was happening at that party. It was kissing. That is what people in love do—or at least according to the movie *Casablanca*.

The kisses on the screen are intriguing. Full of passion and yearning.

Ah!

The romantic in me can't help but sigh dreamily at those scenes.

I've never seen people kiss before. Certainly not in Aperion. I wonder if mated couples engage in this activity or if it is strictly a human thing to do.

"Minerva," my brother's voice penetrates my mind. In a few seconds, he's seated next to me in the empty movie theatre.

"Kai!" I squeak. "What are you doing here?"

He has a grave expression on his face that morphs into distaste as he glances at the kissing scene on the screen.

"By the Source, Minerva, what are you doing?" he asks in an outraged tone.

"They're called moving pictures. They're really nice," I quip.

I don't expect Kai to get it, though. He's far too uptight for any type of entertainment. Me, on the other hand... How I love these moving pictures! It's even better than reading a story because you can see it in motion. It's rather fascinating, too, because I get to find out about more human customs and what life is like for people in different parts of the world.

There are plays in Aperion, but they're nothing like this! They simply recount old and mythical events that no one cares about anymore—or at least, I don't.

Where is the romance? The excitement? The thrill of action?

How can Aperion *not* have something like this is beyond me. More people would be paying to see those plays, too. In fact, if there were more stories like this, ladies wouldn't be going to their mates with absolutely no knowledge of what mating involves.

See? These stories are educational, too!

Kai bristles.

"But they're..." he trails off, his lips pursed.

"Kissing," I say. "They're kissing."

"You shouldn't be watching something like this," he grumbles. With a snap of his fingers, he stops the movie.

My eyes widen in outrage.

"Why did you do that?"

It was just getting to the most interesting part, too!

Casablanca is one of the most explicit movies I've seen so far—and I've seen tens of them. I was looking forward to getting more information about what couples do in the intimacy of their home. Of course Kai had to come and ruin my fun.

"It's also inappropriate for an unmated lady such as yourself."

I narrow my eyes at him.

"Is it? Don't people in Aperion kiss too?" I ask him.

Heat travels up his neck.

"Kissing. That is what they call it here?" He clears his throat.

That confirms it. Aperites kiss, too. And I have to wonder how my brother knows about it.

"So it does exist in Aperion, too," I remark drily.

"It is something only mated couples engage in. These humans are far too free with their attentions," he mutters under his breath.

"Then how would you know about it?" I ask as I watch him intently.

He shrugs.

"I will remind you I am three thousand years older than you," he mentions.

"And you're still unmated. So how would you know? Who have you been kissing, Kai?" I ask accusingly.

"Just because *you* haven't seen it doesn't mean I haven't," he replies lazily as he leans back in his seat.

I study his features for any sign of deceit. Then again, my brother *is* a stickler for rules. I do not see him going around kissing anyone without the benefit of marriage. And who would he even kiss? Highborn ladies are just as sheltered as me in that regard. The only other option would be one of those bawdy houses that I've heard so many rumors about.

I shake my head at the thought.

Kai would never step foot inside a bawdy house.

"Well, now *I* want to see it, and you are disturbing me. Please see yourself out and let me finish the movie. It was already hard enough to get a showing without all those humans loudly yapping around."

"I'm afraid I can't do that." He takes a deep breath. "You need to come with me," he says and grabs my hand.

"What? Where?"

The words are barely out of my mouth when he teleports us to a vacant building. I don't recognize the location, but based on the architecture and the steel appliances abandoned in a corner, I am certain we have not left England yet.

"What's the meaning of this?" I demand sharply as I pull my hand from his grasp.

"General Molokai. And Lady Minerva," someone says. The owner of the voice steps out from the shadows and my eyes widen.

He's garbed in a long, pearlescent gown tied around the waist with a wide red belt. I recognize the uniform immediately and what this means.

Damn it!

"Minerva, this is Groyo from the House of Moirai."

I nibble on my lip.

"H-hello," I murmur guiltily.

"I suppose you know why you have been summoned here, do you not, Lady Minerva?" Groyo asks.

I bite my lip as I sneak a glance at Kai. He's wearing a somber expression, his hands behind his back as he distances himself from me.

Not wanting to show any favoritism. Got it.

"Uhm, not really?" I force a smile.

With a wave of his hand, Groyo unveils a golden silk veil with one flickering dot.

"This human was supposed to have died twenty-three hours, forty-five minutes, and thirty-four seconds ago." He pauses. "The human is still alive."

"Oh, is that so?" I murmur.

Another wave of his hand and the golden veil turns into a canvas featuring a moving picture. The lighting is much better here than it was at the actual site of the incident, and I can clearly see myself reach into the mass of rubble to pull out a little girl.

Oh damn. How did they get this footage? It's not as if there were cameras around. Then again, I've never had to deal with the House of Moirai before, and according to rumors, they are all-seeing.

This is what happens when I break the rules. I'm caught.

"All right. I helped her," I admit. It's not as if I can deny it when the evidence of my misdeeds is staring right in my face. After all, I knew about the potential consequences, did I not? And yet, I still chose to get involved.

"You did *not* help her," Groyo says, his voice booming in the empty building. "You thwarted her fate and made us work over-time at the House of Moirai to undo the damage you have caused."

"What do you mean?" I frown.

"The girl will die, as she was meant to. But we were unable to schedule her death until one hundred and five days from now."

"So you fixed it. She's still going to die."

Groyo glares at me.

"No, we did *not* fix it, as you say it. It means she is going to live one hundred and five days *more* than she should have."

"But she's still going to die," I add weakly.

He gives me another harsh glare.

"It means that someone else died in her place to maintain the balance, Minerva," my brother mentions.

"General Molokai is correct. So not only you did *not* help, since someone did end up dying, but you also made it more diffi-cult for the House of Moirai as we sought a way to ensure that human will die on the exact same day the human who died in her stead would. I cannot even begin to tell you how many threads we had to unravel to make that happen."

My lips flatten. I didn't think of it that way. Damn it all, I really messed up, didn't I?

"We cannot, of course, let this go. It is our duty to ensure that the threads of fate run their course accordingly. It is for that exact reason that deities are not allowed to interfere in mortals' fates."

"What?"

"You need to be punished for your misdeeds, Minerva," my brother says.

"But—"

"As General Molokai said. We cannot overlook this or it

would send the wrong message to other deities, which in turn would mess even more with the order of things. You must be punished in accordance with your sin."

"And what is my punishment going to be?"

Groyo waves the silk canvas away. It dissolves into a myriad of fine particles until there's nothing left of it.

"One hundred and five days," he states. "You will need to repay the House of Moirai for the one hundred and five days you stole from the human who wrongly died."

"But how?" I whisper.

"You will be stripped of your powers for one hundred and five days. General Molokai will ensure the punishment is meted out."

My eyes widen.

W-what?

Stripped of my powers.

I quickly glance at Kai. He's not even looking at me as he nods.

"But I'm on a mission. I can't—"

"You are hereby relieved of your duties, Minerva. You may return to Aperion until the end of your sentence. Or if you should choose to stay in Anthropa, though I do not recommend it, you will not be given an allowance or any protection from me or my soldiers."

I blink, shocked.

"I trust you will handle this, General Molokai?"

My brother inclines his head.

Groyo nods and flashes himself out of the building, leaving me alone with my brother.

"You can't be serious about this, Kai. You can't strip me of my powers..."

"It is your punishment."

"But—"

"No buts. You broke the rules, you must pay for it."

Opening his palm, he releases a burst of energy that surrounds my entire body. An opaque film settles atop my skin, inhibiting my powers.

"One hundred and five days. At the end of your sentence, the shield will evaporate on its own."

"How am I supposed to fight demons *without* my powers?" I cry out in frustration.

"You are not. You have been relieved of your duties, as I have mentioned," he adds tersely.

"You can't do that! You know how much this mission means to me."

"You should have thought about that before you broke the rules. I would advise you to take your punishment in stride and head home."

"Head home? Absolutely not!"

Does he not realize what will happen once I get home? I've already left when I shouldn't have. The moment they catch me, our parents are going to lock me up until the wedding, and without my powers, I won't have any way to escape.

"That is your prerogative. Should you find yourself in trouble here, however, no one will be able to help you."

He turns his back to me, ready to leave.

"Kai!" I yell. "What does that mean?"

Only his profile is visible as he speaks. "The shield inhibits all your spiritual energy and as such, it will also slow down your healing. It is to your best advantage to leave Anthropa, dangerous as it is now."

"W-what?"

"Go home, sister. You've created enough trouble as it is."

And with that, he disappears.

"Kai! Kai!" I call after him, but it's in vain.

He's gone.

And I'm...powerless.

I rush out of the building and immediately the darkness hits me in the face. I...can't see.

I swallow hard, an array of emotions grabbing me by the throat and threatening to make me ill.

Taking one step forward, I'm hit with an astounding fear.

I can't see.

I don't know what's out there.

I don't know where I am.

I don't have...anything.

"Kai? Please don't leave me here," I whisper. A sob escapes me as I wildly look around but am unable to see anything.

A few more grueling steps and I stop again.

My breathing intensifies and a hole slowly forms in my chest. My pulse is through the roof as fear overtakes me.

So this is what it's like to be powerless. To be...human.

It's to not know where you're going, to not see where your next step might lead you—to know that maybe one wrong turn could prove deadly. And now I could very well die.

Kai said my healing would be slower, too. That means I could get injured. I could get seriously hurt.

And I cannot defend myself.

"Kai? Please," I continue.

A shiver goes down my body, and for the first time in my life, I feel the cold chill of the night.

I am...cold.

I, a goddess of ice, feel cold.

I drop to my knees, struggling for breath.

"I'm sorry," I whisper, rubbing my hands together. "Please, I'm sorry. I won't do it again. Please don't leave me here. Please..."

No one answers back.

Not even my echo.

I'm yet again reminded of the human condition—of those beings that constantly pray to a higher being but never receive an answer in return.

I am that being now.

Here, on my knees, begging. And there is no one out there to hear my plea.

If only I were stronger. If I had my ninth gate open like my brother, he would not have been able to inhibit *all* my powers. Given his rank, his orders have precedence over my wants, regardless of whether we'd have equal spiritual energy or not. But at least I wouldn't have been this helpless...this powerless.

Then the House of Moirai would have found another way to give you a fitting punishment, my inner voice reminds me.

The truth is that no matter how I look at it, I did break the rules. I did something wrong and I *deserve* to be punished. I just never expected I would feel so bereft without my powers.

I squeeze my eyes shut, hoping that when I open them again, everything will be back to normal. That I will be able to see through the darkness again. That I will be able to find my path again.

But it's in vain.

I am utterly powerless.

Moments on end pass, and I'm forced to admit to myself that this is my reality now. For the next one hundred and five days, I am no better than those puny humans.

I am just as helpless as they are.

The chilly wind stings across my cheeks. I cannot remain out here.

I carefully make my way back to the warehouse. Inside, it's not much warmer, but at least I'm no longer shivering so badly that my teeth are clattering in my mouth.

There is a latch at the door, and I pull it to ensure that no one can come inside. With how vulnerable I am...

Think, Minerva. Think.

Admittedly, the only recourse I have is to wait for the sun to rise. Then I can make my way back to my lodgings. But what after?

I have little money left from my last allowance. It might last me until the end of the week but not for another one hundred days. And without money, I will not be able to survive in this world.

Didn't Kai realize that?

Or he did. And he thought I would do the sensible thing and go home.

Go home more of a failure than I left.

No. I cannot do that.

It might be harder to get my footing in this world with no support, but at least I will have my freedom. The moment I go home, I am forfeiting my independence. My parents might even go as far as to rush the wedding to ensure I don't escape.

If my brother truly expected me to give up and go home, then he will be in for a surprise. I will *not* return.

With that thought in mind, I let myself fall asleep.

The next morning, though my body aches from sleeping on the ground of the warehouse, I start out toward my lodgings with renewed optimism.

Yet that quickly fades when I realize how much I have to walk to get home. Several times, I have to ask for directions. Luckily, I know the address of the place, not just the coordinates where to teleport.

Still, I have no money on me to pay for a cab, and that means I must walk for close to six human miles.

By the time I reach my apartment building, I am sweaty, out of breath, and in a foul mood. The only thing that keeps me going is the fact that in just a few steps, I will get to my cozy bed and my stash of cookies. That sounds like the best reward in the world for the effort I had to make.

Disheveled, dirty, and probably looking a fright, I force myself up the stairs of the apartment building.

Why did I have to rent the room on the third floor? Why couldn't I have chosen the ground level one?

Because I was too cocky, that's why. Because now, without my abilities, I realize how many things I've been taking for granted.

One hundred and five days. Or is it one hundred and four days now?

I brighten a little at the thought.

As I reach the second floor, a door opens and the landlady strides out. She looks around, narrowing her eyes when she sees me.

I muster a smile, though even using those muscles hurts.

"Minerva, just the person I needed to see."

"Yes, Mrs. Tinley?"

"There will be an increase in rent by one shilling starting next month."

I stare at her, afraid I haven't heard her right.

"But next month is in three days!"

"Well, yes. But you see, this area is in high demand since everyone is afraid Central London will be struck again. I am only keeping up with the other prices in the area."

I might have been able to pay rent for the next month if I reduced all my spending—including food. But now it's an extra shilling? Where the hell will I get that money from?

"And if I can't pay that?"

She purses her lips.

"You will have to vacate the premises. I already have someone interested to take your place and..."

I tune her out as I trudge my way to the third floor.

"Your answer, Minerva!" she calls out. "Will you stay or leave?"

I close my eyes and take a deep breath.

Of course everything would go from bad to worse in a matter of hours.

"I will take my leave in three days," I reply.

Where I will go remains to be seen. But first I must find a way to make money. And fast.

When I get to my room, I wash up and change my clothes. Then I rummage for the leftover cookies from the other day. But as I open the cupboard, a nasty-looking thing jumps out at me.

A rat!

"Agh!" I cry out, stumbling back.

I teeter on my feet before I land on my back. Tears prick at the back of my eyes.

The rat scurries away but not before I see the crumbs he leaves in his trail.

No. Oh no...

I force myself up and inspect the cupboard, only to find it fully ransacked.

And my cookies?

That nasty creature ate them. What's left is adulterated, and even though I'm salivating at the thought of a sweet cookie, I know I cannot take the chance to eat it. With my healing impaired, who knows what disease I might catch?

Disease. What a thought.

Frustration boils inside of me and I stomp my feet onto the floor. But even the freaking floor strikes back. Now my foot hurts.

I'm hungry, tired, and still cold.

More tears threaten to spill down my cheeks, but I swallow a sob and force myself to think.

One step at a time.

I'll find a solution... I think.

For now, I just need some food so I can go to sleep with a full stomach.

Grabbing a couple of pence, I go out in search of some filling food. Even if it's just bread—that might be the only thing I can afford—that's fine. I just need to fill my stomach with *something*.

The streets are bustling with people—a stark contrast to the silence of the night. Cars crowd the roads, with people sliding between them to get to their destination—sometimes narrowly escaping an accident.

My hair is wet and clinging to my face, making me look quite a fright. Despite the sun shining in the sky, it's only early September, so the temperatures are...temperate. That means my wet hair makes me even colder than before.

The dress I'm wearing is a blend of wool and cotton, but it doesn't seem to help when a chilly breeze makes me shiver from head to toe.

I can't believe I'm even thinking this but... That rat might have been better off than me. At least *he* ate cookies—*my* cookies.

I reach a store and feel for the pence in my pocket. The

smell of freshly baked bread is intoxicating and I am close to salivating. But there is a huge line in front of me that moves slowly.

Happy I will at least get some food, I join the line and wait.

Minutes pass by. The queue slowly dissolves until I'm next in line.

"One loaf of bread, please," I say, presenting my coins.

The seller gives me an odd look.

"Your ration book?"

"What?"

"No ration book, no bread," he adds curtly.

"But I don't have—"

"Next," he calls out, moving his attention from me.

I blink.

Someone from behind shoves me out of the way. I stumble back and barely regain my balance so I don't fall—again.

It takes me a few moments to realize that without my powers, I will need to follow the same rules as humans, and that means getting a ration book in order to buy food.

But how does one even get a ration book?

Where do I go to get one?

Will they even give me one? I don't have any papers, no identification card or anything of the sort. From their perspective, I don't exist in this world.

Then what about food? How will I get something to eat?

A little faint and more than ravenous, I walk around as I think about the best ways to deal with this.

I might be starving for now, but I still won't go home.

Spotting a bench, I head over and take a seat. My feet hurt from walking too much yesterday, and I try to massage my calves.

Out of the corner of my eyes, I spot a pole full of fliers nearby. From afar, they look like job offerings—or perhaps it's my wishful thinking.

Slowly getting up, I take a deep breath as I go to the pole.

I scan the fliers, noting that most of them are either news

about the war or advice for people on what to do in case of another Blitz.

I purse my lips.

There goes my wishful thinking.

My stomach growls in hunger again. What I wouldn't give for at least a slice of bread and some cheese. I won't even be picky and ask for dessert. Just something to fill my stomach *other* than air.

I reach the last flier and stop.

My lashes flutter a few times as I try to make sure I'm seeing right.

Snatching the flier, I bring it closer to my face—yes, even my eyesight is now on par with that of a puny human.

Nurses wanted at RAF Thorpe Abbotts in Norfolk. Will provide accommodation, three daily meals, and a small monthly wage.

I read the flier a few times until I've memorized the lines.

Accommodation—I will have a place to sleep.

Three daily meals—I will go to sleep with a full belly.

A small monthly wage—I can buy cookies.

Giddiness erupts inside of me. I don't know what RAF is, but nursing shouldn't be too hard. I did fix that male the other day, didn't I? I'd say I have the inclination for it—if not the desperation.

This is perfect. The answer to all my prayers. I will survive these one hundred and four days and I will show my brother that not even being on the same level as a puny human will make me return home.

Take that, Kai!

Now there's only one issue. How the hell do I get to Norfolk?

SEVEN

WHAT I LACK IN SKILL, I make up for with charm. Or at least I'd like to think I do. Otherwise, I've just spent all my remaining money on travel to Norfolk for nothing.

Chin up, Minerva. You cannot let something as inconsequential as skill stop you from getting the job.

That's right. I'm a quick learner. I'm not squeamish since I've done my fair share of gutting and maiming. I do rather like the red hue of blood, so that won't be an issue either.

I suppose I just need to learn how to heal instead of kill.

Can't be that hard, now, can it?

The bus stop is a distance away from the location, and I trudge my aching body forward, trying to think about the rewards.

I hope they will provide meals on arrival, or at least upon hiring me. I am far too hungry to be able to wait until tomorrow.

At this point, I am ashamed to say I would take anything. Even stale bread is better than nothing. Last night, as I was twisting and turning in an effort to ignore the pangs of hunger, I even went as far as to consider grilling the little cookie thief in my room. Alas, I found him already dead in the morning—perhaps the landlady took care of him.

The grilling option remains on the table, however. I wouldn't be the first to do so. Of that, I am aware.

People are starving. I am not the only one. But where I once looked at them from a position of privilege my powers and monthly allowance afforded me, now I have a new appreciation for the people who so valiantly fight to live on. It's especially heartbreaking to think of the young mothers whose husbands are on the front and who not only have to find a way to feed themselves but also have to feed their younglings.

From that point of view, I am still a little privileged.

Doing my best to forget about my empty stomach, I march forward. It takes me an hour to get to the location, which I realize is a military base—the headquarters of the Air Force. Well, if that's the case, I suppose they should need a lot of nurses, no? That should be to my advantage.

Or...not.

There is a long line of females stretching all the way outside the military camp. As I get to the end of the queue, I ask if this is the line for the nursing position.

"We are all waiting for registration. There isn't much information yet," a female tells me.

"Thank you," I murmur.

All right. I shouldn't get discouraged about the almost fifty females here for the same position. They should have plenty of spaces to accommodate most of us, no? It's war, after all, and they need all the help they can get. And I need all the food they have available.

I don't do well when I'm hungry. And I don't mean physically. I also mean that I get very, very, *very* angry.

Calm down, Minerva! Everything will work out in the end.

And then my brother will be forced to admit that I am *not* weak—despite having no powers. I can make it and I *will* make it.

I just need to be a little bit resourceful about it. And that involves keeping my ears wide open to the discussions around.

"You went to a three-year program?" someone asks, her voice dripping with awe.

The other female nods.

"I wanted to be a nurse before the war, too."

"I only did the two-year program since it was cheaper and I could help the war effort faster," the girl replies.

I narrow my eyes.

What's this talk of two- and three-year programs?

"Excuse me?" I put on my best smile. "What do you mean by a two-year program?"

The girl in question turns to me, blinking in confusion.

"The nursing program, of course."

"Nursing program?" I repeat slowly.

She looks at me askance.

"You've completed a nursing program, no? That is the minimum requirement for a nursing position."

"Ah, yes, I have. Of course I have. From *way* before the war," I lie.

She nods thoughtfully.

"You're lucky. Those with more experience are likely to get priority in consideration."

Uhm. Right.

I smile at her and end the conversation.

Inside, I am panicking. I am *beyond* panicking. I barely know what nursing is about and these females have completed two- and three-year programs? How am I going to get the job if that's what I have to compete with?

More females arrive and take their place in the line.

I gulp down as I watch my chances of getting this job dwindling by the moment.

It all hits me in the face when one of the females next to me takes out a thick book about nursing from her purse and starts reading.

I angle my body toward her so I can gaze at what's written inside. But I only manage to read a couple paragraphs before she catches me and gives me a glare. She shuffles a few paces away from me and continues to read.

Damn it. These people are treating this as a competition. Not that it's not, since we are all hoping to get one spot. Everyone has their reasons for wanting the job, but I am right here *starving*. That should take precedence. Or at least it does, in my mind.

The line slowly moves forward, and I get the opportunity to see some of the military base. There are one-level buildings and tents erected everywhere, with military trucks running up and down the makeshift streets.

As I poke my head out of the queue, I note that the registration is being held in a similar building. Every female goes in, spends some five minutes inside, after which she comes out with a slip of paper in her hands.

When my turn comes, I'm already bored out of my mind. My stomach is growling incessantly, but I try to put on a smile—though damn, that's hard.

Getting inside the building, I see there are three males behind a desk, shuffling some papers. Two have white coats, indicating they are doctors, while the other one has a military uniform on. The male in military garb is annotating things on a piece of paper, and he barely looks at me as I come in.

One of the doctors invites me to take a seat in front of them.

"Name?" the officer asks.

"M—" I stop myself. My name is not what you would expect of a British female, which might arouse their suspicion. The last thing I need is for them to think I might be a spy or something of the sort. Thinking quickly, I change some letters around to anglicize my name. "Mina Anyan."

"Spell that for me," the officer says.

I do, and he doesn't bat an eye at my last name. I only removed the apostrophe from it because how the hell do I come up with an entirely different name in just a few seconds? Then again, maybe I should have prepared for it in advance.

"Age?"

"Twenty-five."

"Marital status?"

"Unwed."

"Good. Are you engaged?"

"No."

They nod. It seems that was the correct answer.

"Good. Now tell us about your experience."

Uhm...

"I graduated from a three-year nursing program in London."

"Which one?"

I blink. *Think, Minerva, think!*

"The Nightingale one," I quickly say.

"Good program." The doctors nod.

So it is a program. I breathe out a sigh of relief. Was I bluffing? Perhaps, but Nightingale is the most famous human nurse, so I took my chances with her name.

"Any practical experience?"

"I've been working for the past three years at a small clinic just outside of London. We've been caring for the people affected by the Blitz who did not get immediate medical attention," I lie again—an outrageous lie. I hold my breath, waiting for them to call me out on it, but it doesn't happen. They just nod along.

"That is good. We are looking for nurses with practical experience."

I smile.

"Here is your slip with your number. Keep it and wait for it to be called."

"Called? For what?"

"There will be a practical and theoretical exam. It shouldn't be hard for someone with your experience. We just want to ensure we hire the best, given the turnout."

Right, my experience.

"Thank you," I say as I accept the slip of paper.

Gazing down, I note my number is fifty-eight.

There are fifty-seven females before me, and who knows how many after. I'll never get this job, will I?

I dejectedly make my way out of the building and look around for somewhere to sit down while I wait—and devise a new plan.

My muscles are aching, and I'm so tired my eyes are almost closing. Yet I can't afford to let this puny body betray me like this.

No! I will get this job, I will eat, and then I will get a bed to sleep in.

How I will do that? Well, I'll have to think some more.

The line to the registration seems never-ending as more females join in, which makes the competition for those positions more fierce.

If only I had my powers... Alas, if I did, I would not be here, ready to beg for some scraps of food.

And speaking of food...

I close my eyes and inhale deeply as the smell of food wafts toward me. It's coming from one of the buildings.

Before I can even think about it, my feet take me to the origin of the scent. The main room of the building is empty. But judging by the rows of tables and seats, this must be the cantina. That means the kitchens must be around, too.

A few airmen walk around, and I quickly hide so I don't get caught.

Now that the smell has infiltrated my brain, I do not think I can stop.

I round the building a few times until I find a small door. Pulling it half-open, I gaze inside.

It's the kitchen!

Two males wearing aprons are chatting around as they prepare astronomical amounts of food.

There are maybe three or four huge pots on the makeshift stove, their contents simmering and releasing more of that mouthwatering aroma. To the right, there are six, or perhaps eight, trays laid one on top of the other. I strain to make out the contents and my stomach makes a loud noise when I see the meat lined up on the top tray—probably fresh from the oven.

There's bread too. So much bread. Surely they wouldn't miss a little, no? But I doubt they would just give it to me if I asked. I'd more than likely get kicked out for wandering where I'm not supposed to. Perhaps I'd even be punished since they might think I'm trying to do something nefarious like poison the food.

Okay, so asking is out of the question. That leaves...stealing.

Good grief! How low I've fallen. But food is food, so I will deal with my conscience later.

Surreptitiously opening my bag, I take out my carefully wrapped last resort.

"I'm sorry," I whisper. "You're already dead, so you won't suffer."

Opening the door wider, I hurl the dead little rodent in the middle of the kitchen. Then I close the door and I hide behind the building and wait.

The moments trickle by and nothing happens.

Either they're not impressed with my cookie thief, or they didn't see it. But *would* they even react? I'm not sure how males in this world behave, but screaming at rodents is usually a female thing—mostly because they're smelly, sneaky bastards.

Just when I think I wasted my potential meal for nothing, a loud, shrilly sound erupts in the air.

The door to the kitchen bursts open, and the males run out, one after another. I quietly shake my head. If it were me, I would not send those manlings to war.

Alas, now I must be quick.

I dash into the kitchen and straight for the meat trays. Opening my purse wide, I stuff it with as much meat as I can before moving on to the bread and cheese—in between stuffing my face, too. With how hungry I am, I would have carried the entire kitchen out with me. As it stands, I must contend with only what I can carry in my purse.

Male voices resound from outside. I still. Steps thud closer and closer.

The door opens.

Eyes wide, I crouch behind the stove, the only spot hidden from sight.

"A rat? You were screaming about a rat?" The newcomer's voice thunders. He doesn't seem too pleased about that display of cowardice.

I frown. The voice sounds rather...familiar. But I can't quite pinpoint where I've heard it before.

"It's a big one, sir," the other male complains. "So big. Look."

I can almost imagine them pointing to my little deceased friend. And they think *that* is big?

Humph.

They should see the size of rodents in other worlds. That little fellow is *tiny* compared to those.

"And you both ran out of here like screaming girls because you saw a dead rat?"

"A big rat," the cook continues, his voice trembling.

The newcomer releases a loud sigh.

"You're in luck then. I'm saving you from a rat," the male adds drily.

I peek around to see him pick up the rat by its tail and wave it around. The cooks recoil, taking a step back and running out of the kitchen.

Again.

I wait for the other male to leave as well, but he sure takes his time.

He wraps the little rat in some paper and he turns to the door. Before he leaves, however, he stops.

"Next time just ask for food. No one will begrudge you a portion."

My eyes widen in shock.

"Rats are unsanitary, however."

And with that, he leaves. Together with the rat.

He didn't come after me. He didn't tell me off for stealing the food. He just...left.

I wait a few more minutes before I think it's safe enough for me to leave. To my surprise, there's no one around.

Scurrying out of the way, I find an isolated spot and wolf down some more of the food until my stomach is finally full.

My hunger assuaged, I am now brimming with new optimism.

The food was good. This is what will await me if I get the job. Nice, tender meat, fresh bread, and delicious cheese. What more can I ask for?

Well, to be hired.

I mutter a curse under my breath. I might no longer be starving, but I still haven't solved the little issue of *not* knowing a thing about nursing. If only that girl had let me read some of her book...

I have a good memory. If I read something a couple of times, I can memorize it.

But how do I get my hands on a book to read?

As if the fates decided to give me a little grace, I spot the girl carrying the thick book. She crosses the field to go to one of the barracks.

I quickly follow.

She's going to the restroom. Surely she won't go inside with the book, right?

I enter the barrack and note there are two stalls, both in use. The book is lying flat on a counter.

It seems that today is all about perfecting my thieving abilities because I snatch it without a second thought and run out of the barracks, returning to that isolated nook where I plop myself on the ground to read.

I vaguely hear numbers being called, but it's still in the single digits. That means I have some time to get acquainted with the book.

To my surprise, there are pictures as well depicting the art of nursing, and as I read, I slowly gain a new respect for the profession.

Nurses do *everything*. They dress wounds, clean the patients, take their temperature, and observe their bodily functions as well as sometimes administer medication and anesthetics.

I bite my nails as it dawns on me that this is far from the easy job I imagined it to be. In fact, it might be the most grueling of them all. Whereas doctors only diagnose, prescribe treatment, and sometimes do surgeries, nurses do everything else.

It's only one hundred and three days, Minerva. You can do it. Think about food.

Yes, this is my only opportunity. I've already come this far. I might as well push through.

I memorize all the important elements, my confidence growing by the moment.

I'm on my third read-through when I hear voices.

Male voices.

They move closer until they're just a few steps away from me. The only thing hiding me from sight is a big container next to the building.

I make myself smaller and clutch the book to my chest.

"You're disciplining them for running away from rats? Come on, Vitry."

"They're barely eighteen and fresh off the boat. Cut them some slack," another adds.

"Eighteen-year-olds are going to their deaths in this war every day," a male adds.

I frown. It's the same familiar voice from earlier. But where have I heard it before?

"Yes, but—"

"They have it much better than others. They're here, doing their duties away from the front lines. But that might not always be so. If tomorrow they get sent on the Continent, what are they going to do? The first sound of a bomb and they run away screaming? That won't cut it. They'll be shot down the moment they open their mouths."

"But, Major—"

"This is *war*, Lieutenant," Vitry emphasizes.

"And their jobs are in the kitchen. Surely—"

"For now," he states. "The punishment stands. If you have a problem with it, then you two can join them as well."

"Come on, Vitry."

"Is that clear, Lieutenants?" His voice booms, brimming with authority.

There's a pause.

"Is that clear?" he repeats.

"Sir, yes, sir," the two males say in unison.

"You may leave," Vitry tells them.

I hold my breath, listening for the sound of their steps. When the sound recedes, I finally relax and move my stiff body around. I held myself so still for a moment that I think I got a cramp in my lower leg.

I stretch my leg out and massage my calf.

Poor humans. Is this what they have to contend with?

I've been tired before, when my energy levels were low after too much fighting. But it's never been like this—a pulsating ache that's present in my entire body.

"Did you enjoy the food?" the same voice asks. It's that male. Vitry.

I gasp and pull my leg back.

"I already saw you," he adds drily.

"It wasn't me! I didn't steal the meat!" I cry out.

He chuckles.

"And how do you know it was meat if you did not steal it?"

I blink. Is he going to arrest me? Kick me out? Turn me in and publicly humiliate me?

"How do *you* know it was me who stole it?" I counter as I shuffle back and attempt to make myself smaller.

"There aren't too many ladies who wear red shoes," he says,

and I hear his steps as he comes closer. "Especially ones with white polka dots on them."

He stops in front of me.

I'm hiding behind the book—though it's a measly attempt at hiding.

He looms over me, and once more panic takes hold of me.

What is he going to do? He clearly has a high rank if the other lieutenants deferred to him. He might want to make an example out of me in front of everyone—brand me both a thief and a criminal for bringing the little rat inside the kitchen. Then I'll never get the job. I'll never get three daily meals again. And I will likely end up sleeping in an abandoned building, perhaps a barn.

All these scenarios are too unappealing to even think about them.

"Nothing to say in your defense?" he asks.

I bite my lip as I slowly lower the book. Maybe I can find a way to appeal to his sensitive side. Perhaps I can bat my lashes as I've seen human females do to get what they want.

Yes. That is a good strategy.

The moment the book reveals my face, I rapidly flutter my lashes at him. When he doesn't respond to this cue of a damsel in distress, I put in more effort. I bat my lashes at him to the point of aggression.

I can't even see anything but my lashes as they create a dark web in front of my eyes.

Still. He doesn't react.

Is he blind?

I lean in, fluttering them more. Good grief, if he doesn't take a hint soon, my lashes might propel me into flight with how hard they're fluttering.

"Do you have something in your eye?" he finally asks.

What?

Can't he see what I'm doing? That I'm using a trick to appeal to his protective side so he won't turn me in for stealing the airmen's food.

I humph aloud and tilt my head, batting my lashes some more.

I am a female fluttering my lashes at you. You are male. Act like it!

"Are you all right? You don't seem all right," he adds in a low voice.

He comes closer to me.

Yes, this must be working, after all.

"There's something wrong with your eye, isn't it?" he asks.

"No," I say with a groan.

My lids stop moving. I'm staring at him, wide-eyed.

He's in front of me. As in, his face is only a few inches away from mine. Too close. Far too close for comfort.

And to my dismay, I realize why the voice and the name seemed familiar.

It's him. The male from the other night.

The one who made me save the people in the bombing, thereby getting me punished for interfering in humans' fate.

It's *his* fault.

Not only is he the reason why my powers are gone and I am now little more than a puny human for one hundred and three more days, but he is also the reason why I am starving, why I had to steal, and why I was even considering eating my little cookie thief.

It's all *his* fault.

And now? He dares to come so close to me I can feel his breath fanning on my face. It's minty and fresh and ugh! I hate it.

I hate *him*.

"You..." he whispers, his eyes widening in recognition. "Tiny darling." He smiles.

He invades my personal space and now he calls me that derogatory term. I might be tiny, but I don't need to be reminded of it every single time.

My lips curl in a snarl, and before I can stop myself, I draw my fist back and punch him.

Straight in the face.

He whizzes and falls back, blood pouring from his nose.

I scramble to my feet, but powerless and achy as I am, I'm not as swift as I would like to be. He tries to come closer to me, so I use the thick book to swipe his hands away before I smash him over the face with it again.

He staggers back, disbelief written all over his features. Blood drips down his dashing uniform—no, not dashing; it's just a uniform—and he looks at me as if he's seen a ghost.

Before he has the time to recover and apprehend me, probably denounce me publicly for being a thief *and* a violent criminal, I run away as fast as I can.

"There she is!" A girl points her finger at me as I get back to the interview location.

I barely gather my wits about me when I hear her say.

"She stole my book!"

EIGHT

EVERYONE IS STARING AT ME.

"Uhm, I did not steal it," I murmur nervously. "I found it and I was trying to return it," I lie.

The girl narrows her eyes at me. "And where did you find it?"

"In the restroom. It had fallen off the counter."

Once more, she doesn't seem to buy my lie.

"Here," I say and take a step forward to hand her the book. She takes it from my hands, her nose scrunching in disgust when she sees the stains of blood.

"What's *this*?" she shrieks.

"Uhm..." I look around me. Everyone is watching me curiously. "This is how I found it."

The girl glares at me. I can tell she wants to say I'm a liar and that she doesn't believe me. But before she can do so, an army official shows up and tries to placate her.

"There, there. We've solved our little issue," he says with a smile.

Steps follow closely behind me, and as I turn, it's to see the male from before. The front of his uniform is splattered with blood, and he's holding on to the bridge of his nose. He scans the crowd until his eyes land on me.

Damn it!

He's going to denounce me publicly, is he not?

"What are you doing here, Vitry?" the official asks him.

"Checking the progress," he mutters, his gaze on me. "I have a few fellows who require some medical help and I thought you might need some volunteers."

The officer's brows go up and he nods thoughtfully.

"Bring them over. We could use more volunteers for the practical test."

Never once taking his gaze off me, he walks off.

It's not until he's out of sight that I release a sigh of relief. This was such a close call. He could have told on me. For a moment, I was certain he was going to.

The fact that he didn't is...odd. Especially after I assaulted him.

The officer smooths over the conflict over the book and tells us to get ready for our exam. Fortuitously—or not—our numbers are called. Fifty-five to sixty-six are invited to step inside the infirmary for the practical exam.

What is *not* fortunate, however, is that the owner of the book is included in our group, and she is continuously glaring at me, making it clear she does not believe my excuses.

We're ushered inside the infirmary where there are some ten rows of beds on either side of the room. Out of the twenty beds, eight are occupied by patients.

"Each of you, please head to a patient," the doctor tells us.

As I glance around the room, I realize that though there are only eight beds, there are ten of us taking the exam.

A flurry of movement ensues, and all the girls hurry toward one of the beds. It's immediately clear that the first ones choose the easiest cases, while the last ones are left with the hardest.

I am, of course, elbowing my way forward, one step away from shoving the girl with the book to the side. Her name, as I've come to find out, is Lucy.

The most boring name I've ever heard.

I am usually quite competitive, but considering what is at stake here, I find that I must be a little ruthless, too.

I choose the patient who does not display any outward injury. With a little luck, I will only be asked to check his vitals and administer some medication.

But as my luck would have it, Lucy appears to have set her sights on that particular patient, too.

We both reach the bed at the same time, and I sway to the side while simultaneously pushing her toward the other bed. But she won't go down easily. Oh, no. I can tell she holds a grudge for the book incident—which, if I am honest, would not have happened at all if she'd let me read over her shoulder.

She shoots me daggers with her eyes.

I do the same.

"I got here first," I tell her, pushing my chin up.

"No. I did." She glares at me as she takes a step forward.

I inch closer to the bed and grab onto the metal railing.

She won't give up.

She grabs the metal railing on the other side.

"Let. Go," I say through gritted teeth.

"You let go."

"Girls!" the doctor yells from behind.

I pull on the bed to my side and Lucy pulls toward her side. With my powers bound, we are matched in strength, which means that every time I gain a little ground, she pulls on the bed to her side and we're back to where we started.

The bed rattles as we push and pull.

The doctor yells in the background for us to stop.

Slow at first, but becoming louder by the second, the patient in the bed starts moaning in pain.

I blink, startled. Are we hurting him?

But just as I let go of the metal frame, Lucy pulls on it with her entire strength. With no resistance to speak of, the bed slides in her direction, and with it the patient, who's looking quite blue in the face.

"Girls!" the doctor shouts, this time loud enough to shush everyone in the tent.

Lucy's reaction is delayed. But the patient's isn't.

As he tumbles toward where Lucy is pulling on the bed, he half sits, and with a low gurgle, he throws his face forward and empties his stomach on her dress.

Silence ensues.

Bits of food and what I can only surmise must be stomach juice coat Lucy's cleavage and the front of her dress.

Her mouth is half-open in shock.

"Apologies, miss," the patient mumbles. But it's a slurred mumble, and that can only mean one thing.

Don't you worry, strange and ailing man. Minerva is here to save the day!

I move faster than I thought myself capable without my powers as I swipe the bucket from under the bed and throw myself over the bed, aligning it with his mouth just as he starts retching again.

He grasps the bucket with both hands, after which I slowly pull myself off the bed and dust my dress.

Lucy is still in shock, covered in gut contents as she is.

I push my chin up and wait for the applause. After all, that movement was rather impressive, was it not? My aim was faultless. It would have been worthy of a moving picture. Just think—the *super* nurse. With me starring in the main role, of course.

I'm still silently gloating when the doctor rushes to the man's side, pushing Lucy out of the way.

"You. Out," he tells her in an authoritative tone.

She flutters her lashes in confusion.

"But... It's *her* fault," she says as she points at me.

"Me?" I gasp in shock. "But I was just helping him," I add innocently. Turning to the doctor, I start reciting from the medical textbook about the symptoms I'd seen on the patient's face and the fact that he was continuously swallowing as if he had an abundance of saliva in his mouth. I tell him how I took all that to mean he was about to be sick and I wanted to make sure the bucket was close when it happened.

"But he wouldn't have been sick in the first place if she hadn't pulled on the bed," Lucy complains.

I shake my head at her. All right, she may be *partially* right. But this is about survival. I will not go to bed hungry again. I mean, if I don't get this job, I will not have *any* bed to go to.

"Really, Lucy, if you spent as much time studying your book as you do accusing others of stealing it, perhaps you could have identified the signs, too." I smile sweetly at her.

"Miss Anyan is right. This is *not* the type of behavior we welcome here. You are dismissed, Miss Rawlins."

"But please—"

"Please step outside." The doctor's tone leaves no room for argument, so Lucy tucks her metaphorical tail between her butt cheeks—or was it between her legs?—and finally leaves.

But as she opens the door to get out, two other airmen walk in.

I turn, my eyes widening when I spot Vitry.

His gaze quickly finds me and he winks.

He. Winks.

At me.

The gall on this male!

His nose bleeding has stopped, I see. Perhaps he needs a new one. I would gladly offer to help if there weren't so many people around.

"Where do you need us, Doc?" Vitry asks.

The doctor turns to him. "What ails you?"

The male next to Vitry starts complaining about a stomachache, while Vitry rolls up his sleeve to show a wide gash that's leaking blood. From the look of it, it can't be very old. He certainly didn't seem to have any wounds when I saw him moments ago—at least none that weren't inflicted by me.

I narrow my eyes at him.

The doctor tells them to occupy the empty beds at the end of the room.

Happy he'll be away from me, I turn my attention to my patient as I paint a smile on my face. It's best to look as though I know what I'm doing.

"Miss Anyan, you will tend to the major," the doctor suddenly says.

I whip my head up in shock.

"What? But I have a patient already!"

"I've assessed your diagnosis skills. I would like to see how you tend a wound, too."

I gawk at him. What?

"But—"

"Here, Miss Anyan!" Vitry calls out to me, beckoning me toward him with his hand as if I were a dog.

I scowl at him.

"Off you go, Miss Anyan," the doctor says absentmindedly before he turns his back to me and heads to the next bed.

Mumbling a string of curses under my breath, I trudge my way toward Vitry's bed. How can I be so unlucky to have to heal the man I ought to kill—not that I can actually kill him since it's forbidden, though I suppose I might inflict some damage. It's his fault I need a job, food, and a place to sleep.

It's all his damn fault.

And now he wants me to patch his wound?

Oh, just you wait and see, you insufferable male.

"Miss Anyan, huh?" He raises a brow at me as I reach his bedside.

He's sprawled on the bed, his big frame making it seem like a child's bed.

I ignore him and gather some antiseptic, bandage, and some needle and thread. I read about this in the textbook, and luckily for him, I'm not too bad at needlework.

Oh well, just for him, I will be bad at it.

"Nothing to say?" he continues.

I shrug.

"Hmm." He closes his eyes and wrinkles his nose. "I can

smell some beef. I wonder where that's coming from." He smirks.

I glare at him.

His gaze slowly drops to my bag.

The gall of him!

"Let's look at your wound," I say and pull on his sleeve harshly.

The rapid movement startles him, and I note a twitch of pain in his cheek. But the same lazy smile from before quickly replaces it.

"Of course, Nurse Anyan. Anything for you," he murmurs, the last sentence whispered in a very...inappropriate tone.

I swallow and give him another harsh look as I place my fingers on the edge of his gash and press.

He can feel the pain, I am sure. But he's not making a sound.

"Oh my! That's a big gash," I intone.

"Why, thank you for noticing. I tried." Another smirk.

"What do you mean?" I frown.

He just smiles as he pulls himself into a sitting position and makes himself comfortable.

The doctor makes rounds around the room, talking with each nurse to ensure that they know what they are doing. When he stops in front of me, he glances at Vitry's wound and shakes his head.

"That will need stitches," he mentions.

"Of course." I smile. "That is what I am going to do."

I've sewn things before. It can't be that hard. Right?

The doctor nods and leaves.

I mentally rehearse what I have to do. Clean and disinfect the wound, then patch it up and bandage it.

"I am ready when you are," the male drawls.

He's lucky I need this job or I would have cut him up even more than he already is.

I ignore him as I grab some clean cloth and start cleaning the wound.

"Why did you run off the other night?" he asks.

I don't have to look up to know he's staring at me. He's a little too close for comfort. I can feel his breath on the side of my face.

"Please be quiet. I am concentrating," I mutter. *As in, I am concentrating very hard not to take a scalpel and drive it through your heart, you scoundrel!*

"Ah, little thief, I'm surprised you can concentrate at all with the smell coming from your bag."

"One more word and I'll cut your entire arm," I mutter under my breath.

"So bloodthirsty. It's a little too early in the morning for that, although I wouldn't mind it later in the night." He wiggles his brows suggestively.

I press on his wound.

"Be. Quiet."

I get to work on his wound, but in my haste to get this over with, I grab the rubbing alcohol instead of the iodine. The moment the liquid makes contact with his open flesh, he lets out a loud hiss.

It might have been an honest mistake, but I'm not mad about it now. Serves him right.

"You did that on purpose," he grumbles, struggling to breathe through the pain.

I shrug. "I told you to be quiet."

"You wound me, Nurse Anyan. And here I thought this was the beginning of a great friendship."

"Oh, I will wound you all right if you don't stop talking," I grumble.

How is it my luck to get *him* as my patient for this test?

"Please don't," he murmurs in a mocking voice. "I don't think my poor heart can take it."

I glare at him.

He has an innocent expression on, and he releases a loud sigh as he shakes his head.

What is he talking about? Does he suffer from a heart ailment too? Because if he does, I don't know how to treat that.

"I don't know what your heart has to do with this. I am treating your arm, not your chest." I roll my eyes at him.

"But you see, I have a weak heart, and your cruel words are giving me palpitations."

I frown. What is he on about?

"You can ask the doctor for heart medication then."

"There is no medication for this, I'm afraid. It's incurable."

I blink. Suddenly, he takes one of my hands and lays it across his chest.

"See?"

Without my powers, I can just barely make out the beats of his heart. But it does beat faster than any human I've met.

I glance at him.

He's not lying about this, is he? He really has a heart ailment?

"This is concerning. When did it start?"

He sighs. "Three days ago."

"Why? What happened?"

Three days ago... That was the day of the bombing. Did something happen to him then? Did the bomb cause this? He was in its proximity when it happened, so perhaps...

I lean in and press my ear to his chest.

His heart starts beating even faster.

Abnormally fast.

A shudder goes down his entire body, and he releases a muffled groan.

"Are you all right? It's beating even faster now," I ask.

The more I listen, the faster the beats are—so much so that I'm afraid his heart might leap out of his chest at any moment.

"Oh my, this is bad," I mutter. "This is *very* bad."

Without their hearts, humans die. And despite the fact that I hold him responsible for my current predicament, I find that I do not want to cause someone to die. It's not as if he knew who I was or what the consequences of me helping out at the bomb site would be. He was just trying to save people.

I pull back, glancing at him and searching his features. They're tight and drawn up in pain, even more so than when I pressed against his wound.

"Doctor!" I shout, suddenly afraid. "Doctor, there's something wrong with his heart!"

Vitry's eyes widen slightly, and he opens his mouth to speak. But before he can do so, the doctor is at my side, looking him over.

"What's wrong, Miss Anyan?" the doctor asks.

"His heart," I say and point to his chest. "It's beating abnormally fast." I pause as I bite my lip. "He's not going to die, is he? He said he has a heart ailment."

The doctor removes his stethoscope and presses the circular side to Vitry's chest. He listens to his heart for a few moments before he shakes his head.

"This is not a joke, Major." The doctor rolls his eyes. "Stop scaring your nurse if you want to be treated."

A guilty look crosses the male's face.

I look between him and the doctor.

"He won't die?" I ask in a low voice.

"He will not die," the doctor confirms. "He is as healthy as any red-blooded male I've ever seen."

With that, he leaves, going over to another nurse who requires his assistance.

I stare at Vitry.

"Red-blooded male? What does that mean?" I frown. Is that a subspecies of humans? I have not heard about that before.

"Well…" He bites his lip.

"Well?"

"That happens when the heart pumps blood faster and—"

"Is it because of your wound? Because you're bleeding from it?" That seems like the most probable explanation.

He clears his throat. "It's been happening for three days. Before my wound."

"So you've said. But I don't understand. Did something happen to you when the bomb dropped? Is that it?"

He stares at me. I stare back, though more in confusion than anything.

With a sigh, he shakes his head and mutters something under his breath. If I had my powers, I could hear what he was saying. But as it stands, I'm stuck with guessing. Though even that seems to be beyond my capacities at the moment. I am too new at this nursing thing to be able to guess what might plague him, especially since it pertains to his heart. The textbooks didn't say anything about it.

"You should go ahead and treat my wound," he eventually says.

"But what about your heart?"

"We can worry about that later," he croaks.

I nod thoughtfully. Perhaps he's not at death's door as I anticipated.

I set about cleaning his wound once more, but for some reason, I find myself more magnanimous than before and use iodine instead of the stinging rubbing alcohol. I know, very odd.

Maybe I just feel sad for him since he has other ailments, too.

Yes, that must be it.

He's already in pain for an unknown reason. I shouldn't add to that.

After I'm done cleaning the wound, I survey the instruments on the table next to the bed. I need to suture his wound.

Biting my lip, I take the medical needle and thread and set about patching him up.

But as I push the needle through his flesh, I realize this is not as easy as sewing clothes. The skin is thicker and there is more resistance.

The male must sense my hesitation because he places his hand atop mine, holding it steady. I hadn't realized it was trembling.

I give him a forced smile.

"Wash your hands first," he adds.

"Huh?"

He nods to the rubbing alcohol.

"Put that on your hands or you might cause me an infection."

"Oh. Right," I mumble.

I quickly wash my hands with the rubbing alcohol and return to his wound.

"Take a deep breath," he murmurs.

Somehow, I do as he says.

"Now thread the needle through the other side."

His voice is steady, calm. Surprising considering I'm inserting a sharp needle into his skin. Yet his guiding words prove to be very helpful in distracting me from my nerves.

"Good. Now again."

I do as he says. Every time I need to push the needle through his skin, he quietly encourages me, praising me when I'm doing it right.

My lips pull into a smile.

"Good job!" he says. "Now tie the thread at the end and cut the excess."

I can't seem to get the knot right, so he stops me.

"Twist here." He points to the thread. "And loop it through the other thread."

After a couple failed attempts, I manage to tie the thread and cut the remaining bit.

"Perfect. You did so good," he murmurs gently.

I give him a smile. "Thank you."

"Now the bandage."

I grab a roll of bandage and wrap it carefully around his arm, securing it with a knot.

The doctor comes to survey my work and he nods in satisfaction.

"Good job, Miss Anyan."

I preen under the praise, and I'm surprised when Vitry's

hand tightens on top of mine. When did he even grab my hand? Why is he touching it?

I'm about to give him a thorough set down as the doctor leaves, but just as I settle on the perfect words, someone bursts into the infirmary.

"The planes are back! The injured are coming through."

Vitry shoots out of the bed, rushing to the male who'd just delivered the news.

"How many did we lose?" he asks.

The messenger purses his lips.

"Nine."

"Fucking hell!" Vitry curses. "What about Abbots? Is he back? Is he all right?"

I don't get to hear the newcomer's reply as both he and Vitry hurry out of the infirmary.

There's a commotion outside, and the sound of car engines blares in the atmosphere.

"What's happening?" I ask one of the other nurses.

"They must be back from a mission," she answers. "Few make it back usually. It's the curse of the 100th. We'll have our hands full here."

"Curse of the 100th?" I frown. "What's that?"

"The 100th bomb group. There are always so many casualties, some say it's cursed."

"Oh. And the airman I treated?"

"Part of the 100th, too."

I nod, though the information doesn't sit well with me. I don't get to dwell more on it as injured airmen are rushed through the doors of the infirmary. The doctor starts barking orders, asking every nurse available to lend a hand.

Behind him, Vitry rushes an injured male in. He's by his side, holding his hand and telling him to hang on.

Curious, I take a step forward.

The doctor cuts his jacket off, not minding grab the feminine sensibilities around—though I suppose this type of nudity is required for treatment.

My first instinct is to look away, but there's so much blood that you can barely see his chest. There are two deep wounds in his right side and one just above his left lung. They're an angry red, gushing out blood.

"Damn it, Abbots," Vitry curses as he helps the doctor take off his clothes.

"Miss Anyan. Come here!" the doctor calls.

I rush over. Vitry barely spares me a glance, his attention on the bleeding male.

"Press on the wound on the left," the doctor tells me.

I grab some gauze and press against the male's chest. But as I do, I can feel the shallowness of his breath. Every time he inhales, there's a gurgling sound as if he's choking on something.

"His lung must be punctured," I say. "He's choking on blood."

The doctor curses. "Help me turn him on his side."

I grab onto his arms to pull him toward me when suddenly Vitry is there, helping to shoulder the man's weight.

We turn him onto his side, and a few wheezes later, he's breathing a bit better, though still labored.

The doctor works on his two side injuries while I continue to press on his wound.

His pallor, too, doesn't look too good. His eyes open and close as he struggles to stay awake.

Vitry keeps talking to him, small platitudes really, but he doesn't respond.

His breathing slows down.

Long seconds pass before his chest stops moving altogether.

His mouth is ajar, his eyes half-closed.

The doctor draws back, shaking his head.

"He's dead," he declares.

"No, no," Vitry mutters. "He can't be dead."

A bright light emanates from his body as his soul rises, in time for a messenger to come claim it for the other side.

I sigh. I suppose this is the end of his journey.

Another male rushes inside, his face draining when he sees Abbots lying on the table.

"We caught some flak on the right wing, but I didn't think—"

"Save it for the interrogation, Marshall," Vitry's voice thunders.

The male looks stricken. Nodding, he retreats from the infirmary.

"There's nothing else you or anyone else can do, son," the doctor addresses Vitry.

He swallows hard.

"I'll write a letter to his mother," he whispers.

With one last look at the dead man, he turns and leaves.

Hours later and after an entire day's of work, I finally make it to my bunk bed in a room shared with five other girls. At least it's soft and warm, and I even had some more meat to eat for dinner.

But there is something that niggles at my conscience and will not let me sleep.

We saw some twenty men today, all with different degrees of injuries. Of those twenty, five died in the infirmary. And of those five... Only two souls were taken by messengers to P'asala.

Ordinarily, some souls might not agree to follow a messenger to P'asala, and messengers cannot do anything about it. They are not sentient beings to try to convince those souls. But even in that case, I would have seen the souls linger and refuse to leave.

But I didn't.

There was no trace of those souls.

Slowly, a smile pulls at my lips.

Three missing souls. That sounds like a demon, doesn't it?

And the perfect opportunity to appeal to my brother to get my powers back.

I wait until everyone else is asleep, and then I get out of bed.

Sleep can wait.

NINE

IT'S the middle of the night. I would have expected the base to be quiet while everyone gets a restful sleep so they can continue their warring ventures in the morning.

Instead, most of the airmen who returned from their mission are up and partying. A few buildings are lit up, and music blares from inside. I almost bump into a few inebriated males as they stumble around and make crass jokes.

Damn it.

I require a quiet place to concentrate on establishing a connection with my brother. Without my abilities, I don't even know how this is going to work. But it's worth a try.

And if it *doesn't* work, then I'll have to call him the old-fashioned way.

"Why is there nowhere to go fishing around here?" A male groans.

I hide behind a building.

"Lower your voice, Gabe."

"Why should I?" he shouts loudly. "Why? I might as well die tomorrow. Why can't I get laid before?"

"Gabe! Shhh." A pause. "Major Vitry," he suddenly says, his voice taking a serious note.

I peek around the corner and see Vitry facing two males who attempt to maintain a straight posture but fail as they sway from side to side.

"Major," Gabe slurps the word.

"Go to bed," Vitry says with a sigh.

"Why should I?" Gabe counters.

"Because I said so, and I outrank you, Soldier."

"Gabe, please. You'll get in trouble," the other male says, pulling on Gabe's sleeve.

"I don't care. Even better. I'm *done* with this! I'm never going up again. I'm too fucking young to die."

Vitry takes a step toward him.

"You're too young to die?" he asks, his voice low and tense. "And what makes *you* more special than the eighteen-year-old we lost today? What makes *you* more special than any of the other men in here?"

"I didn't sign up for this. I..." he mumbles.

"Let me guess. You signed up for the rewards with none of the sacrifices, am I right?"

Gabe's mouth opens and closes before he eventually shakes his head.

"You wanted to be a hero, but you're not willing to do the heroic thing." Vitry lets out a dry laugh.

"Dying isn't heroic," Gabe whispers.

"Isn't it? Why do you think there are thousands of soldiers dying every day then? Why so many other thousands risk death every day?"

Gabe doesn't reply, so Vitry continues.

"They risk it all because they know it makes a difference. Their sacrifice *saves* lives. Maybe you didn't sign up for this, but do you think those poor people signed up to be butchered by the Germans, too? Do you think they signed up to have their land stolen and their people subjugated by fucking Nazis?"

"But I want to live, too," Gabe whispers.

"Then live." Vitry shrugs. "Go ahead. Run out of here. Go

and live your worthless little life like a coward. It's no skin off my back. "

He takes a step back and waits.

Neither male moves. They stare guiltily at Vitry.

"Well? What's it going to be?"

Gabe swallows.

"I don't want the Nazis to win," he mutters in a low, barely audible voice. "I fucking hate Nazis."

"Me too," the other male whispers.

"Then go back to your barracks, get some sleep, and on your next mission, remember *why* you're flying."

He turns and walks away.

I quickly move back so he doesn't see me as he heads toward the west of the base. As I get further and further away from the military barracks, I can't help but replay that conversation in my mind.

That male's speech was not bad. It certainly did the job of making those soldiers realize the stakes of the war. Though I'm still mad at him for his role in me losing my powers, I have to begrudgingly admit that he is a...decent leader.

Once there are no more people around, I sneak off in search of a more secluded place.

It takes me some ten minutes of walking in circles around the base to find a quiet spot.

Taking a deep breath, I concentrate on Molokai's energy signature. Of course, without my powers, I can barely sense it. But that doesn't deter me from trying to reach out to him.

"Kai? I need you," I say aloud. "If you could put aside your anger with me for a moment and come, I would really appreciate it."

Crickets.

"It's really important. I think I've stumbled onto something here."

I wait.

Once more, the only sound that greets me is the symphony of music and loud voices coming from the base.

I mutter a curse under my breath and try again.

"Uhm, Kai? I think there's a demon here. Maybe a high-ranking one," I say again, doing my best to focus on my voice reaching him.

Of course nothing happens.

Ugh!

Couldn't he have at least left an open channel for communication? He didn't have to shut me out completely.

When he doesn't reply after I call out to him for the tenth time, I realize my only recourse is to physically summon him here.

I let out a sigh. I didn't want to do this since it will physically yank him from wherever he is and bring him here. That means he will *not* be happy with me.

Rummaging through my bag, I take out a knife and press the pointy tip to the inside of my forearm.

Digging the blade inside my flesh, I carve out Kai's personal symbol. That, combined with my blood, will send out the signal and summon him here. This method is usually frowned upon, and only very few people know a god's personal symbol to be able to summon him. But Kai and I are close enough that we know each other's symbol.

I bite my lower lip in pain as I finish carving out the symbol, and as blood pools to the surface of the wound, drops of it dripping to the floor, I mentally prepare myself for his arrival.

Not two seconds later, he's in front of me. He's sporting a scowl that only deepens when he sees the wound on my arm.

"What do you think you're doing, Minerva?" he barks out.

My lips tremble as I force a smile.

"You didn't answer my call. This was the only way to reach you."

He narrows his eyes at me. He's dressed in his battle gear, and there is dried blood all over his clothes.

Oops. I might have summoned him mid-battle.

"This better be important, Minerva."

"It is!" I protest. "Really important."

"Well?" He crosses his arms over his chest.

I clear my throat.

"I think there's a demon here. A high-ranking one. Maybe a Son of Tenebreis," I tell him excitedly.

He tilts his head to the side as he watches me.

"So?"

"So?" I echo. "This is *huge*, Kai!"

"And how would you know that without your powers?"

"Because souls are missing!" I exclaim.

I give him a quick rundown of what happened in the infirmary earlier today and how three souls had vanished.

"Souls don't just vanish! I didn't even see them come out of the bodies of the deceased."

He clicks his tongue against his teeth. "That is unusual."

"Right? There must be something here."

"Except I cannot sense any demon in the surrounding area."

I blink. Without my powers, my senses are not as strong as before. But still, the missing souls alone are an indication that something odd is happening here.

"But there is no other explanation! There has to be something..."

"Minerva." He sighs. "If this is your way of getting me to return your powers to you, then you are making a mistake. It is *not* in my power to do so since your punishment was mandated by the House of Moirai."

"But surely you can see that something's happening here! Think about it. It could be a Son of Tenebreis, Kai. They can also hide their energy signatures."

Kai rolls his eyes.

"The presence of Sons of Tenebreis on Anthropa is a myth, Minerva."

"But Commander Azerius said—"

"He does not have any proof for it. There might be *some* Sons of Tenebreis who were not in Tartareia when it was sealed off. And there might be some that can temporarily leave. But there is no indication they would come to Anthropa."

"There's the war. A lot of souls, isn't that right?" I add weakly.

This isn't going how I envisioned it.

"Anthropa is not the only world ravaged by war."

"But, Kai—"

"You are not getting your powers back until the end of your punishment, Minerva. Do not try to circumvent that. It will not work. Since you decided to stay in Anthropa, you're on your own."

He gives me a harsh look before he flashes himself out of sight.

I blink.

That's...it?

I don't understand. Shouldn't he at least look into this? Missing souls is not a trifling matter. It *never* happens without a reason. So what if he cannot sense a demonic presence nearby? I'm sure there must be something. And I aim to prove it.

So I will show both Kai *and* Commander Azerius that I can operate even under extreme duress, even without my powers. After all, I came first in my theoretical classes. I know plenty of chants and rituals that might aid me. It's just a matter of finding a source of energy to fuel them.

Still annoyed by Kai's lack of faith in me, it takes me a while to realize that my wound isn't healing properly. It's still bleeding, and it hurts.

Damn it all, but it really hurts.

Would I get fired if I snuck into the infirmary to steal some bandages?

Since I've come here, it seems that thieving is all I've been doing. But how else would I survive when this world is not only at war, but I also happen to be an unemployed female with little to no resources?

Well, I am employed *now*, but I might not be in the morning if I get caught. Still, I am not used to such pain and I do not think I can go back to bed with this bleeding injury. Even sleep-deprived as I am, I doubt I would be able to close my eyes.

Muttering another string of curses at my current circumstances, I trudge my way to the infirmary.

In and out. It should be simple.

I wrestle with the door lock for a few moments but finally, I am in.

Going straight to the medicine cabinet, I grab an aspirin—this should be good for pain, no? Then I rummage for some bandages.

The light inside of the infirmary flickers to life.

I freeze.

Who the hell is here at this hour?

Of course my first instinct is to hide somewhere, but as I tiptoe my way around the room, I hear a voice.

"You don't need to hide."

I stop in my tracks.

Slowly, I turn and find myself face-to-face with Vitry.

The last person I wanted to see now.

"What are you doing here?" I burst out.

"I should ask you the same." He raises a brow. "It's the middle of the night. What are you doing here?"

"I... Uhm..."

"Don't tell me you're a Nazi spy, tiny darling."

My eyes widen. That's the last thing I needed—get fired *and* be accused of espionage. I've heard about the abominable treatment of war spies. If I were to be imprisoned and tortured for being a *spy* on top of everything else that's already happened to me already... I shudder just thinking about it.

Then again, wouldn't the House of Moirai have a laugh at my expense if that were to happen?

"Me? A Nazi spy? How could that be..." I mutter nervously.

"Brilliant plan, really. Send a fresh-faced beauty to sabotage our healthcare," he drawls.

"I'm not a spy," I cry out. But then I realize he called me a fresh-faced beauty.

My cheeks flame.

No one's ever called me that before. Or a beauty...

But that's beside the point!

I avert my gaze so he doesn't notice my blush. Heat unfurls inside of me at the compliment. In Aperion, I am hardly a beauty. If I were, I wouldn't have to resign myself to marrying Captain Clown.

But maybe humans have different standards. Or *this* human has faulty eyesight. It's been known to happen.

His amusement fades as he takes in my bleeding arm.

"What in God's name happened to you?" he demands. In a few strides, he's in front of me, grabbing my arm to inspect it.

"Why isn't it healing?"

"W-what?"

"Why isn't the bleeding stopping?" He clears his throat.

"I... Well, I was looking for a bandage," I admit.

"This looks grisly," he mentions with a grimace. "Come."

I don't have time to protest as he seats me on a chair at the back of the room so we're far away from the patient ward. He looks through the cabinets until he finds a roll of bandage and some disinfectant and then he's back at my side.

"How did this happen?" he asks as he pours the disinfectant over my wound.

I purse my lips as I think of what lie to concoct. The wound is clearly in the shape of an odd symbol, so it's not as if I can tell him I accidentally cut myself. It looks on purpose.

"I was playing with a knife and didn't realize how sharp it was," I lie.

Then again, I also did not realize how slow my healing would be now that I'm without my spiritual energy.

"You dummy," he mumbles. "You could have hurt yourself so bad."

"Dummy?" I narrow my eyes at him. "What's that supposed to mean?"

His lips quirk up.

"It's nothing bad, tiny darling." He winks at me.

"Stop calling me that," I grumble.

He smirks.

"What should I call you then? Minerva or... Mina?"

"M-Mina," I say and gulp down uncertainly. "It's Mina."

"Mina?"

"Yes. Do you have a problem with it?"

"Doesn't really suit you," he mentions.

What? It doesn't suit me?

I glare at him.

"Now don't take this the wrong way, tiny darling."

"How am I supposed to take it when you're telling me my name doesn't suit me?"

It's a pretty name. Prettier than Minerva anyway. But now his words are making me doubt it.

He chuckles.

"Mina is much too tight-laced and somber when you're anything but that."

I continue to glare at him as I wait for him to insult me some more. He's done that from the moment we met.

"What am I then?"

"You're a little troublemaker," he says with a smile.

There! I was right. First, he called me an odd duck—I still have not forgotten that, though he tried to explain it's an idiom or whatever—and now he calls me a troublemaker.

"I am not!" I burst out. "I am a perfectly respectable working lady," I say with a humph.

"A perfectly respectable working lady?" He laughs. "One who pranks soldiers with dead rats, steals food, and then lies about being a nurse? Oh, and let us not forget about this incident right here," he says as he pours some more disinfectant over my wound and wipes the blood away.

"W-what?" I stammer.

Certainly, he did see me steal food and use the dead rat as a weapon of distraction. But how would he know that I'm lying about being a nurse? Even the doctor was fooled by my perfect impression of one.

"I *am* a nurse," I feel compelled to add.

"Sure, sure, Minnie darling. You *are* a nurse—one who doesn't know how to bandage a small wound."

"But I do! I patched you up, didn't I?" I protest, nearly jumping out of my seat. He holds me still, not letting me go anywhere.

"Shoddily."

I blink. I do not know what that means, but I am not about to make a fool of myself and ask. I'll just assume it's something bad.

"It was my first day," I mutter.

He merely smiles.

I scowl at him. But then it registers how he called me.

Minnie darling.

"My name is Mina, not Minnie," I tell him squarely. "Just because you don't like it doesn't mean you can change it."

"Minnie suits you better. It's cute, just like you." He winks at me.

My eyes widen.

I swallow.

He thinks I'm...cute?

Heat travels up my neck.

"It's still *not* my name," I argue weakly.

"Sure, Minnie," he replies in an amused tone.

"You! Stop that!"

"No can do, Minnie darling. Besides"—he pauses to clear his throat—"it rhymes better."

"Rhymes better with what?"

He starts whistling as he rolls the bandage over my wound. He doesn't reply to me.

"Rhymes with what, you infuriating male?" I demand again.

"I'll let you figure that out," he tells me.

Oh, no. I barely have a good grasp of this English language as it is. How am I going to figure out what he means? Although, coming from him, it's probably another insult.

"You're awful," I bristle.

"Maybe, but I am taking care of your wound, aren't I?"

"I didn't ask."

"You *never* have to ask," he adds cryptically.

I give him another harsh look, but I'm at a loss for words—shocking, no? But since I don't have a comeback to his odd behavior, I decide to get him back the only way I can—by making fun of his name too.

"I don't know how you can comment on *my* name when people call you Vitry, *Lucien!*" I say pointedly, proud of myself for remembering his name.

"So you remember my name?" he asks with a wicked grin on his face.

My first instinct is to wipe it away with my fist. Alas, I am in a rather awkward position on this chair while he's tending to my arm, so I would just end up hurting myself.

"I have a good memory," I reply and push my chin up.

"Glad you found me worthy to keep in your memory."

"Stop making everything about *you!*"

I've never met someone with a bigger ego and that's saying something since I happen to be engaged to Captain Clown.

"I'm not. You're the one who brought it up first."

"Because you made fun of my name!"

"Fun isn't the right word, Minnie," he states in a somber voice. "I was, in fact, complimenting you."

Aha, as if I'd fall for that. He probably noticed my low level of English and he's trying to take advantage of that.

"Well, then guess what," I say, feeling petty. "I was *not* complimenting you on your name. What type of name is Vitry even? It doesn't sound good."

He shrugs.

"It's my family name and what everyone calls me."

"I'm not everyone. I will not utter such an ugly name."

He quirks his brows at me.

Did I go too far by saying his name is ugly? At least his insults were veiled as compliments, whereas I straight-up told him his name is ugly.

Well, I have already said that. It's not as if I can take it back.

"You can call me something else if you'd like," he mentions with a glint in his eyes. "Something special."

"I'd rather not call you at all," I grumble.

"Such a grumpy little thing you are." He chuckles.

"I am *not* grumpy. I just happen to dislike being insulted."

"And I just told you I was complimenting you," he counters.

"Ugh. Whatever. Are you done?" I ask as I look down at my arm. He's finished bandaging my wound, and though it still hurts a little, the pressure of the bandage makes it more bearable.

Jumping off the chair, I put some distance between us.

"Thank you," I mumble.

I might dislike him, but he did help me, so I can't be too mean to him—though there's nothing I'd like to do more. I'm not sure why he annoys me so much. I'm not one to usually be so rattled—all right, that might be stretching it. I admit I might have a temper, but I usually keep it in check. I am an ice deity, after all. I'm supposed to be cool and collected.

Supposed being the key word.

"You're welcome, Minnie."

I roll my eyes at him.

"Admit it. It's cute," he continues.

"I will admit no such thing," I tell him, though I can't stop myself from smiling. I suppose it is quite a cute name. Not that I'm accepting it. It's just an observation.

"Truce?" he asks and extends his hand toward me. "We'll be seeing each other a lot from now on. It would help to be on friendly terms."

"But not *too* friendly," I note.

He doesn't reply, still holding out his hand for me. I suspect he wants me to grab it in one of those handshakes humans do.

I slide my hand into his much bigger one, and a current of electricity bursts through me. I gulp down at the uncomfortable feeling, but I don't pull my hand away.

"Mine," he suddenly says, tightening his hold over my hand.

I frown.

"You can call me Mine."

I blink.

"Is that your middle name or something?"

He smiles and nods.

"I'm only allowing *you* to use it. Since you're not everyone."

"That's...nice of you," I murmur.

Why is it suddenly so warm in here? Why are my cheeks flaming hot?

"You will, right? Use it, I mean?" he asks, a little flustered.

"Only *I* can use it?" I ask to clarify. I rather like the sound of that.

"Only you." He nods.

"Fine. Then I shall call you Mine."

His lips stretch into a wide smile.

I stare into his green eyes, unable to move.

"Go to sleep, Minnie. I'll see you later."

Too tired to argue with him, I don't bother to correct him anymore about my name. Instead, I just pull my hand back—my palm still tingles.

"Fine, Mine. I'll see you later," I murmur.

As I leave the infirmary, I ponder on our conversation. His middle name is Mine—an odd name for a human, if you ask me. Still, it is much better sounding than Vitry. Or even Lucien.

But something niggles at my mind.

Mine.

Mine...

Mine!

My eyes widen in realization.

Is this why he had an issue with calling me Mina? Because our names are the same save for the last letter?

I nod to myself. That makes more sense.

Maybe he wasn't trying to be rude. Instead, he didn't want us to have the same names—or *too* similar.

Yes, that must be it.

Somehow, that makes me feel better. That and the fact that he promised me I am the only one who can call him by his middle name. I do quite like to be special like that. And as a thank you, I'll even let him use Minnie instead of Mina—just him, though.

I giggle to myself as I slide into bed.

Perhaps he's not *all* that bad.

Mine... His name even rolls easily off my tongue.

TEN

AS I MAKE my way toward the infirmary for a new day at work, I'm surprised to see Mine waiting for me outside.

He's dressed in his uniform, and even I have to admit he looks quite dashing in it. His dark brown hair curls onto his forehead, obscuring part of the scar on his face.

"Minnie," he calls out, his lips curling up into a smile. "Just the person I wanted to see."

I regard him suspiciously. "Why?"

"Here," he says and hands me something wrapped in tissue paper.

I tentatively take it from him and slowly unwrap the tissue paper to reveal a donut. A *glazed* donut.

My gaze snaps to his, new light blooming in my eyes.

"For me?" I whisper.

He nods.

"Eat up."

I lick my lips.

It's been a couple of days since I last had something sweet and I'm already salivating at the prospect.

I was right. Mine isn't so bad. How can anyone who gives me sweets be bad? That in itself is a fallacy.

But as I wait for him to leave so I can eat the donut in peace, I notice he's not moving.

"Thank you," I say, hoping he would get the clue and move out of my way. Since it's a glazed donut, I'll likely get the sugar all over my face, and I don't want an audience for it.

"I'll be flying out today," he mentions.

"Huh?"

"I have a mission. I don't know when I'll be back."

"Oh. All right."

He's still not moving. "Aren't you going to wish me good luck?"

I blink and stare at him. "Do I have to?"

"It would be nice." He shrugs.

"Well... Good luck."

He beams at me. "I'll be back."

He finally leaves.

Odd, odd male. But at least now I'm alone with my donut.

Oh my, it already smells so good. I take a tentative bite out of it, intent on prolonging the experience. But the moment the sugar hits my tongue, I know it's a lost cause. I take big bites of it, all but shoving the last bit into my mouth. Then I take a deep breath and mourn the fact that he only brought me one.

Alas. I may be able to purchase some with my earnings after work.

The prospect of more donuts spurs me and I get to work in a good mood.

Unfortunately, the mood around the infirmary is anything *but* good.

The doctor is in a corner with a few nurses, and as I approach, he comments.

"We lost two more men last night."

"What happened?" I ask.

"The nurses on duty didn't realize it until it was too late." He sighs.

Two men dead. Two more souls missing. It could be that I

wasn't in the vicinity, but after a bit of probing, I found out the men died around the time I was in the infirmary.

Suspicious.

Kai might not believe me, but my instincts are telling me there is something happening here. And I aim to find out exactly what. Then both Kai and Commander Azerius will have no choice but to recognize my outstanding abilities.

I smile to myself.

I quite like the thought of that.

But first.

"Miss Anyan. Please start your rounds."

"Yes, Doctor."

I still need to do my job if I want to buy myself some donuts at the end of the month after I get paid.

Armed with a chart, I start taking notes on each patient.

"They're flying out today. We'll probably have more wounded in by the end of the night," a nurse notes.

"We don't have that many empty beds left. We might have to expand," another answers.

I continue to work, but I cannot help but eavesdrop on their conversation.

When I came here for the job, I did not realize this was an American military base. I had no idea about the bad reputation the 100th Bomb Group had, or the fact that although they have great benefits for hired nurses, a lot of them end up quitting due to the high workload.

Too many injured.

Too many dying.

From what I hear, any other group would have been preferred to the 100th since everyone believes it to be cursed.

I scoff at that.

Of course I don't believe it is cursed. I do not sense any type of witchcraft surrounding the base or its people—well, aside from that ongoing problem with a certain soul snatcher. But with the way people are talking about the 100th, it is clear that it has one of the highest mortality rates—so much so it's not just the nurses who dread working here; the airmen who get assigned to this group think they're doomed, too.

I'm ambivalent on that matter. Work is work. And if nurses quit, then it will be that much easier for me to hold onto my job with my limited skills—I might be clueless about nursing, but I am not afraid of hard work.

Yet as I'm changing the bandage of one of the patients and I note the severity of his injuries, my thoughts stray to Mine.

He said he's a pilot, no? Does that mean he's in the direct line of fire?

I have yet to find out what exactly these airmen do besides fly planes, but I suppose they fight with them, too? I shall have to ask him when I see him again.

If I see him again.

I shake myself. For some reason, I do not want to contemplate the thought of him dying. I suppose it's the donuts. Who else will bring me donuts until I get my first wage if he's gone?

But he's a high-ranking official. He wouldn't be one if he wasn't skilled. In Aperion, you must not only open your ninth energy gate, but you must also be distinguished in the army to advance in rank.

I mutter a string of curses under my breath. Here I am, with only my fifth gate open and no opportunity in sight to advance. If only my parents would see that I make a better warrior than I would a wife.

"Good job, Miss Anyan," the doctor praises me as he takes a look at my chart.

"Thank you."

"You may take your lunch break. Miss Enid will take over for the time being."

Oh, finally!

I look at the clock and realize I've been working nonstop for the last seven hours. My stomach growls in hunger, and if today's course is the same type of succulent meat as yesterday, then I'm in for a treat.

Or...not.

Oh, yes, the high officials get to eat that delicious meat. But I get only a measly potato stew with *no* meat.

On top of that, the nurses are supposed to eat in the same hall as the soldiers, and that means I must grit my teeth and not retaliate against the lewd comments they make about women.

Males. Ugh.

The nurses on break are all sitting at the same table, and I spot an extra seat. Holding on tightly to my tray, I head there. I may not have interacted much with them, but I will try to be friendly—after all, we will be living in close quarters for the next one hundred and one days.

I put on a smile as I greet them. But when I try to go around the table and take a seat, one of the females places her bag on the empty seat.

"We're full here," she tells me.

"But there is a seat there." I point to where her bag is.

"No, there is not," she quips with an even faker smile than the one I'm sporting.

I narrow my eyes.

"Maybe you shouldn't have messed with Eva," another nurse mentions.

"Who's Eva?" I frown.

They all turn to glare at me.

"Lucy Rawlins. It's your fault she didn't get the job."

The name sounds familiar. It takes me a moment to realize they're talking about the girl with the book who got dismissed.

"It's not my fault she did something wrong." I shrug.

"She was our colleague," the same girl adds, giving me a nasty look.

Since I'm not about to sit with people who do not like me, I release a loud humph and turn around, scanning the hall for an empty seat. Unfortunately, all of them are taken either by the nurses or the soldiers and workers.

With no other recourse, I take my tray and head outside. I can eat just fine on the grass somewhere.

I don't want to be anywhere near the cantina so others can

laugh at me, so I walk some fifteen minutes until I find a secluded spot. I take a seat under the shade of a tree and dig into my food. By this point, it's not only meager but also cold. Alas, since I only had a few bites at breakfast and that donut, I am ravenous.

Although I try to pace myself, I end up eating all the stew in just a few minutes. All that's left is a slice of bread, and considering how hungry I still am, I try to make it last.

Breaking it into small pieces, I lay it on my tray and stare at it.

In Aperion, I would have had a banquet with countless delicacies, while here I'm forced to survive on tasteless stew and a few pieces of bread.

I sigh.

At least I'm not eating a rat. I suppose I should look on the bright side.

I take a piece of bread and slowly chew on it.

Out of the corner of my eye, I see people start running in the direction of the runway.

"The planes have arrived," someone calls out.

Grabbing a handful of bread pieces, I shove them into my mouth and get to my feet. Perhaps it's curiosity. But I find myself following those people toward the runway, wanting to see the airmen who came back from their mission.

In the distance, I see the planes heading toward the runway. One after another, they search for a place to land.

A crowd of people has gathered a safe distance away, and a male soldier starts counting the planes as they arrive.

"Five... Six..."

There is excitement, but there is also the underlying fear that some of their friends have not made it.

All the while, as I squint to get a better view of the planes, I wonder which one of them Mine is flying. But they all look the same to me.

"Which one is Major Vitry's plane?" I ask a man in uniform.

He turns to me, his expression tight.

"The Virtuous," he answers with the nickname of his plane. "But it's not here yet."

A few more planes land, and trucks rush to the runway, together with a few ambulances to carry the wounded.

"Is it here now?" I ask after the last plane landed.

He shakes his head.

"We have twelve missing," he says to another soldier. "Must be one of the worst ones so far."

I listen in, hoping for some more information. My understanding of their military is paltry at best, but it's not the first time I've heard of a number of planes going missing.

"What happens when they go missing?"

The soldier shakes his head.

"Shot down by the Luftwaffe, or they crashed from damage from flak."

"Flak?"

I've heard the term before, but I am not sure exactly what it is.

"German anti-aircraft weapons. They shoot at the planes from the ground."

I nod. That sounds bad.

"Are you sure Major Vitry's plane is not here?"

I don't know why I need that assurance. But he's the only person I know here who's been kind to me. He brought me a donut.

The soldier shakes his head.

Worry gnaws at me. Was Mine shot down, too? Did he crash? Somehow, I need to know what happened to him.

Making my way back to the infirmary, I note an ambulance in front being loaded up with nurses. Seeing this as my chance to get to the runway, I hurry in and take a seat in the back of the car.

"They radioed in that three more people are in critical condition. You must focus on the task," the doctor tells us as we ride toward the runway.

"Yes, Doctor," the three nurses present say in unison.

The situation must be dire if they require so many ambulances to head to the runway.

As we reach the planes, I note that most of them have some damage to the wings or the body. There is smoke coming from one of the cockpits and people are rushing to put the fire out inside.

We all get out of the ambulance to intercept the wounded.

From the corner of my eye, I spot five messengers standing in the field by the runway, waiting. If there are five messengers around, there should also be five souls they are waiting to pick up.

I look left and right, but only two souls exit their mortals' bodies, at which point the messengers assigned to them step in to guide them to P'asala. But that leaves three souls unaccounted for.

Damn it! Is the demon around here? Is it feeding on the souls?

I try to see if anyone is acting suspiciously, but there are too many people coming and going, making it confusing. Without my powers, too, I cannot sense the souls, so I can only rely on my sight.

Moments pass as I sift through the many people around in an attempt to identify the missing souls. It's only when one plane is moved that I spot three more. They're standing next to their bodies, their expressions filled with confusion as they watch people fuss around them and cry about their deaths.

The messengers assigned to those souls are now by their side, urging them to follow. Two souls do. The other continues to stare at his body.

He's little more than a teenager, and he's already dead.

I feel sorry for him, but at the same time, he needs to follow the messenger and move on to the afterlife.

The messenger stands there, waiting.

The clock is ticking.

A messenger will not wait forever. If it's clear the soul has no intention of leaving the mortal plane, or if the soul proves to be too difficult, messengers simply depart.

The task of apprehending those unruly souls then falls down on the collectors—vicious creatures that I always avoid at all costs. They're like rabid dogs when they go after rebel souls. Especially since the more time a soul spends outside its body, the more powerful it becomes as it channels onto its emotions—which are usually hatred and regret.

Vengeful souls are the worst, and to deal with them, the collectors have to be equally bad.

I shudder just thinking about those nasty beings.

Unlike messengers, who are not sentient, collectors are deities who've been caught on the wrong side of the law—the ones whose sins were not enough to warrant an execution. They go through rigorous training to become collectors, and unlike in the military, in the collection game, there are *no* rules.

Those bastards play dirty. And they *hate* Aperite warriors, which puts us at odds.

But then there's the other alternative. If the soul doesn't leave with a messenger, it might become food for demons. And if there is a demon nearby...

I don't even know what's worse at the moment—have the soul linger until a collector comes or until a demon senses that juicy energy and wants a bite.

"Nurse Anyan!" the doctor yells at me.

Lost in my thoughts as I was, I didn't even realize when people around me started moving, so I try to keep up.

Yet there, in the distance, the messenger has disappeared.

The soul? It's still around.

I draw in a long sigh.

"Pay attention, Nurse Anyan." One of the girls snickers at me.

A few airmen are carrying out one male who has a nasty wound to the head. Upon closer inspection, I realize that brain matter is dripping out from a hole in the back of his skull. He's still alive, but barely.

The airmen load him into the ambulance and the doctor starts examining him. But soon, another stretcher is brought forward, this time with a male that has an amputated arm. Blood flows out of his limb, and he wails in pain.

I look worriedly around, trying to see if any of the planes is the Virtuous. Most of them have their nicknames etched onto the body of the plane, so I run around, trying to find Mine's plane.

"Have you seen Major Vitry's plane?" I ask one of the pilots as he climbs down from the plane.

His lips are drawn in a tight line.

"He was behind us, but three of his engines were struck. I'm not sure if—"

I tune him out as I gaze up into the sky. There, in the distance, I make out a dark spot against the blue sky.

I bypass one of the planes to get a better view.

There's something there. Something that emits a lot of smoke.

My heart beats fast in my chest as I watch the dark spot grow larger until I can tell it's a plane.

"My God!" someone exclaims. "He's going to crash!"

"Evacuate the runway!" someone else screams.

A commotion ensues as everyone tries to get out of the way, but I stand still, watching the plane wobble in the air.

It goes up and then drops a little, its balance skewed. It leaves a trail of smoke in its wake, and as it gets closer, I see the busted engines on both wings.

"Get out of the way!" a soldier calls out. "Run!"

I can't.

My body cannot physically move. I stand there and watch as the plane becomes bigger and bigger until it fills my entire field of vision.

There, on its right side, I make out some of the letters of *Virtuous.*

It's Mine. He's coming. He's not dead.

I shiver, unable to understand the emotions that information elicits inside of me. There's a warm, tingly feeling in my stomach, and my heart beats so loudly in my chest, it feels as if it's about to poke a hole through it and skip onto the runway.

The plane makes a deafening noise before it plummets down, its nose heading straight for me.

And yet, I still stand there, staring at it.

The lower part of the plane gives way to the wheels, and as the plane makes contact with the runway, a loud, piercing noise erupts in the air.

"Get out of the way!" more people yell at me as the plane moves with increasing speed toward me.

I'm so focused on it, I barely realize how close it is to me until the nose of the plane is maybe a few paces away, at which point it suddenly stops. Shocked, I teeter back and fall backward.

The weary engines make a choking noise as they stop running. A loud pop erupts in the air as the trap door opens on the belly of the plane.

I hold my breath.

"What the hell do you think you're doing, Minnie?" Mine thunders as he slides out of the plane and strides determinedly toward me.

I let my eyes roam over his body, looking for any signs of injury. And when I'm convinced he's all right, I let out a big sigh of relief.

He looms over me, breathing harshly.

"Hi, Mine," I say with a smile.

He stares at me for a few moments before he shakes his head. Extending a hand to me, he helps me off the ground.

"You could have hurt yourself, Minnie," he comments.

"I didn't," I quip. "You could have hurt yourself too."

"I didn't either." Slowly, a smile seeps into his features, and I find myself returning it.

"You were late," I comment.

He chuckles as he glances back at his plane.

"Better late than never, no?"

I nod slowly, still looking at him. It feels nice to see a familiar face.

"I have something for you," he suddenly mentions. He takes off his jacket and reaches inside his uniform to hand me another item wrapped in tissue paper. This time, though, I can immediately see what's nestled within. The sugar has seeped through the paper, soaking it. "It's a little messed up," he explains.

I take the present with both hands. The donut is a little more squashed than the one he gave me this morning, but a donut is a donut.

"Why did you have this with you?" I frown. Not that I mind. In fact, my mood immediately improves as I bite into it and get some sugar in my system. Now this is heaven.

He clears his throat and looks away.

"I wanted to bring you something back."

I frown.

"But you got it from the base, didn't you? You took it with you."

HE NODS. "Yes, but I took it so I could come back with it. It's not as if we have any stops on the way where I could buy some."

His logic is...odd. I do not understand it. But of course, as long as he gives me more donuts—they are more precious than gold in this world—I am satisfied with nonsensical explanations.

"Thank you, Mine. That is very nice of you."

He finally smiles. He places his palm atop my head and ruffles my hair.

"I'm glad you're enjoying it."

I'm about to chastise him for ruining my perfect updo when two cars and an ambulance surround us.

"Glad to see you made it back, Vitry," a male dressed in a military uniform decorated with a myriad of medals exclaims when he sees Mine. "How's the crew?"

At the same time, another male pokes his head out of the plane's trap door.

"Are you done, Vitry? Can I come out? It's getting hot in here!"

"Shut up, Holloway!" Mine shouts.

"Why can't he come out?" the male asks with a frown.

"It's nothing," Mine grumbles.

"Tell me you at least got a kiss," the male peeking from the plane continues.

"Shut the fuck up, Holloway, or I'll kill you with my own hands," Mine retorts, flustered.

I stare at him. I did not realize he had such violent inclinations. Then again, he did kill that male a few days ago—with his bare hands.

My eyes are drawn to his hands.

He has big hands. But that is quite normal. He is a big male too. Big and strong. His muscles are well-defined and quite nice to look at, if I do say so myself. Not that I *want* to notice that, but I couldn't *not* notice it when he took his shirt off the other night. I don't even want to think about his abdominals. I know quite a few deities who would kill to have his body.

But back to his hands.

I've never known hands can be interesting. They're just... hands. But his are. Very, very interesting. A few veins protrude, giving him perfect proportions. There are also old scars and blisters on his palms. He is a male who *uses* his hands.

"Nurse?" the male in uniform asks me.

"Huh?"

"You should check on the wounded."

I blink. "There is someone wounded?"

Mine rolls his eyes.

"It's Holloway," he says with a sigh. "His ears are ringing from when we took one of the hits. I'm sure he's better seen by a doctor, not a nurse."

Now, wait a minute. Is he implying I am not capable of looking after a patient? Of course I've never treated someone for ear ringing, but there is a first for everything.

I turn to glare at him and open my mouth to argue. But before I can say anything, he continues.

"Besides, I have a small injury that needs taking care of myself. The nurse was kind enough to offer to look at it."

I'm confused.

He doesn't seem to be injured anywhere.

He gives me a look as he steps closer to me, all but dragging me to his side.

"You're injured? Why didn't you say so from the beginning?" I ask.

The male from the plane finally slides out, and he wobbles from side to side as he comes toward us. A few other males are behind him, though they seem to be uninjured.

"Damn those fucking Nazis! They nearly blew us off," Holloway mentions in a slight slur.

Mine places his arm around my shoulders and pulls me closer to him. I don't know what he's trying to do. I never allowed him to touch me, or to invade my personal space like that. I may be glad he is still alive and that he is still able to give me donuts, but that is the extent of our acquaintance.

"Take your hand off," I mutter through gritted teeth. My voice is low enough that only he can hear me.

His eyes glint dangerously as he stares ahead. Yet he doesn't acknowledge my words. He merely tightens his hold over my shoulders.

Ah, if only I had my powers... He would have been thrown halfway across the field by now.

As I get a better look at that Holloway male, my entire body tenses.

On his shoulder, perched quite comfortably, is a greed demon. Its reddish gray shadows almost connect to form a humanoid body that has its long arms wrapped all around Holloway's torso, holding on tightly to him. Its eyes are the darkest black as it coils around Holloway, feeding on his energy and controlling its body.

Damn it!

Greed demons are part of a special category of demons that cannot be controlled by the Sons of Tenebreis. They are borne out of mortals' sins and they continue to feed off those sins while keeping their host alive. Whereas a regular demon simply feeds off a soul's energy until there's nothing left, a greed demon can feed off, well, greed, forever, moving from host to host when it suits its needs.

In all my four thousand four hundred and seventy years, I have never seen one of these. They are rare, but they are a handful. There is a special division in the Aperite military that deals with sins demons due to a particular skill set required.

I swallow hard.

Even if I had my powers, I wouldn't know *how* to get rid of a greed demon.

Without my powers?

This entire military base is damned.

ELEVEN

"HOW DID YOU GET INJURED *HERE*?" I ask, scandalized, as I stare at Mine's stomach that is now sporting quite the gash. It's so low down his abdomen that he's had to undo his pants for me to get a good look at it.

"The belt cut into me when we were jolted in the air," he answers casually.

"This looks like a knife injury," I point out.

"And you know that...how?" He smiles, his eyes dropping to my now blemish-free arm. I cover it, but he already saw that my wound has healed. What could I possibly make up to account for that?

On that note, why isn't he *asking* me why my arm is suddenly healed when just last night it was bleeding buckets?

"I'm a nurse," I grumble.

"You're such a good nurse, tiny darling," he drawls. "Good job."

"I hope you're not making fun of me."

"Me? Never! The moment I got hurt, I knew I would be safe in your caring hands."

I narrow my eyes at him.

Why does it seem that everything he says has a double meaning?

He pulls his pants lower, but the moment I see the line of his drawers, I stop him.

"That's enough. I can see it just fine like this."

"As you wish," he says with a twinkle in his eye.

I grab some iodine and dab it all over the surface of his wound. It's not too deep, so it will not require stitching. But I do my best to clean it and then I apply a bandage on top of it.

"Where's the whiskey? I need whiskey!" Holloway shouts from the other side of the infirmary.

I glance back at him, noting that the greed demon is coiled even tighter around him than before.

"More. Need more," the demon whispers in a low, gravelly voice.

"Bring me the whiskey!" Holloway then cries out.

A nurse rushes in, carrying a bottle of whiskey, and hands it to him.

Is that...normal? To just give a patient whiskey?

Holloway grabs the bottle from her and, without a word, brings it to his lips and gulps down greedily. He's drinking at such an alarming speed that both the nurse and the doctor have to wrestle the bottle away from him. I roll my eyes. Why give it to him in the first place?

"More. Get more," the demon whispers. In turn, Holloway cries out for more, wildly moving his limbs around and throwing a tantrum.

As I return my attention to Mine, I note that he's also watching that exchange with interest.

"When did that behavior start?" I ask absentmindedly.

"When we entered the German territory," he mentions, pursing his lips. "He started behaving oddly then. It's why we caught so much flak. He kept giving me the wrong coordinates."

From any other person, I would have taken that as an attempt at an excuse. But Mine doesn't seem like the type to blame someone else for his failures. In fact, his tone is more that of a worried friend than someone looking for an easy way out.

Holloway has now pushed the nurse to the ground while the doctor tries to restrain him.

I gasp and swivel to go help.

Mine grabs my hand and stops me.

"Don't," he mutters. "You'll get hurt."

I shake my head.

"He'll only get stronger," I whisper.

If the greed demon attached itself to him during the mission, then it's only a matter of time before it gains more strength.

As the struggle between Holloway, the doctor, and now a few other nurses continues, the demon slowly shifts on his shoulder, the shadows becoming more opaque until the demon gains a shape. It turns into a small red humanoid reminiscent of a dwarf. Its claws are sunk deep into Holloway's chest, and as it feeds on the chaos, its eyes shimmer and turn a silvery color.

I may not be too familiar with sin demons, but from what I remember from my school days, the more sins they consume, the stronger they become, and just like regular demons, that is reflected in their appearance. After the sin demon has consumed enough sinful energy from the mortal it latched onto, it will be able to control not just *one* human, but multiple at the same time.

If that is the case, then...

I gulp down as a sliver of fear goes down my spine. Not only is Holloway in mortal danger as the demon becomes more greedy, but if it absorbs enough sinful energy, it will most likely be strong enough to tap into the hidden greed of everyone at the base.

No one will be safe from it.

If I let it run amok, it will turn the entire base into a cornucopia of greed.

"Let them deal with Holloway. You're treating me now," Mine says.

"But—"

As both Mine and I watch the fight unfold, the greed demon suddenly turns and glares at me.

"What are you looking at, you ugly female? This is mine. Mine. Mine. Mine," the demon shouts, his tendrils swirling aggressively around Holloway, almost as if it was having a tantrum.

My mouth drops open in shock.

I blink.

Holloway is trying to grab onto the whiskey bottle with the demon encouraging him loudly.

"Nasty demon," I mutter under my breath.

"Ugly female!" the demon retorts. His big eyes narrow at me and he opens his mouth to stick out a black, nasty-looking tongue.

Ew.

"You can't talk like that," Mine adds in a tight voice. I glance at him. Did he hear me cursing the demon? But then he continues, "If you insult Minnie again, I will wash your mouth with soap. At least then it won't emit so many noxious fumes." His nose wrinkles in disgust.

The demon shrieks.

"I will end you! Puny human! You dare to speak to me like that? I will cut you up and feast on your entrails. Both yours and that ugly female of yours. Just you wait. The moment I have enough strength, I will slaughter you both," the demon snarls.

Mine rolls his eyes.

I am too shocked to react.

Did... Did Mine just talk to the demon?

Can he see it? Hear it?

I slowly turn to Mine, my eyes widening with horror.

Because if he did, then there's only one explanation for it.

He's dying.

"Oh, Mine," I murmur in a low, sad voice.

He frowns when he sees my baleful expression.

Without a word, I rip his shirt off. Buttons fly everywhere. His eyes widen, but he doesn't try to stop me, not even when I tear at his white cotton undershirt.

"Where is it?" I ask in a crazed voice.

Time is of the essence.

Maybe I can still save him if I can find the injury. There *must* be an injury.

Humans can only see the spiritual world if they are on the brink of death—or, in some rare cases, if they have unusually high spiritual energy. But I met Mine before I was stripped of my powers, and I did not detect anything out of the ordinary then.

So that only leaves the first option.

He must be mortally wounded.

"What?" Mine asks, his brows furrowed.

"Your wound. Where is it? I must find it, Mine. I must—"

"Minnie, what wound?" he repeats. His hands cover mine and he stops my erratic movements.

"You're hurt. You're dying. I must save you. I must, Mine," I continue on a ragged breath.

My heart is beating loudly in my ears, so much so every other sound dims until the only thing that surrounds me is the deafening sound of my incompetence and the acrid taste of my own fear.

I shouldn't even be attempting to save him when saving humans is what got me in trouble in the first place. If it is his fate to die in the next moments, then I should step back and let fate run its course.

Except I cannot stop myself.

For some strange reason, all sense has fled my body until this ineffable urgency is all that's left behind.

"Minnie, what are you saying?"

"Show me where it hurts. I promise I'll make it better," I add as I swipe my hands all over his naked chest. His skin is smooth and warm, and a slight current of electricity travels from the surface of his skin to the tips of my fingers, making me startle. I swallow, finding it hard to concentrate.

But I must.

I must save him.

There are no injuries to his upper chest. No new ones at

least. There are old scars that I cursorily note but cannot dwell on at this moment. Going lower, I glance again at the wound I've just bandaged, trying to think if I missed anything.

Was it infected? Was there something wrong with it that I did not notice?

It was quite deep, but I cleaned it properly. Even if I'm not the best nurse, I'm certain I did a proper job. Mine was watching me closely, too, and he would have said something if I messed up. Right...?

But if it's not that wound either then...

There must be something else.

He said the seat belt had cut him when the plane had been hit. Maybe he has some injuries on his lower body.

Though I am nervous to do it, I grab onto the sides of his trousers and pull them down his hips.

"Minnie!" Mine calls my name—well, the name *he* decided is now mine. "What are you doing?"

"You're hurt," I whisper. "There must be some other injury I can't see. Does it hurt here?" I ask as I pat his thighs.

I've seen what those cockpits look like and how the seat belts cross over the thighs, too. Maybe he got cut there? There is a rather important human artery in that region, although there is no bleeding that I can see.

My brows are knit together in confusion.

"What about here?" I press right under the wound I just bandaged. Maybe I missed something?

He whizzes and jerks against me. A shudder racks his body, his hips pushing involuntarily against my hand.

"Stop!" he exclaims. His hands are now firmly atop mine, holding me still. "Don't move."

"Are you in pain?" I ask, my worry getting the best of me.

He *looks* in pain.

His features are tightly drawn together, his mouth pressed into a thin line.

He releases a ragged sigh as he leans further into the mattress. His chest rises and falls.

"I am not hurt," he finally replies. "There is no other wound than the one you've tended to," he explains, though he doesn't allow me to move. His grip on my hands is strong. He keeps my palms on top of the exposed skin right under the bandaged wound.

Skin against skin.

Warmth against warmth.

Ever since I've been stripped of my powers, I've found it hard to regulate my body temperature as I did before. In fact, it's rather disconcerting how easily I can get cold and shivery. But his skin is hot to the touch—pleasantly so. It radiates pure heat, and though I am an ice deity, I prefer to roll around in warmth rather than in cold.

And seeing how the weather recently has taken a turn for the worse, I wouldn't mind having some additional heat at night when it is the most chilly. Of course I can't demand him to shed his skin so I can cover myself with it, though the idea does have merit.

Ah, if only he knew I am a goddess, one on a mission to defend his kind, too, he would probably offer me his skin himself, after prostrating himself at my feet and asking for forgiveness for all the instances in which he insulted me.

Mine clears his throat.

"I am not hurt," he repeats. "You can let go."

Although I did not pull his trousers all the way down, I can see the band of his underwear and a line of dark hair that goes down his lower belly until it hides within the confines of his underpants.

I flatten my palm against his skin, surprised to see how soft that hair is.

Males are interesting creatures. I wonder if male deities are built the same. Although... Seeing how the original mortals were created in the image of the Primordials, I assume most are rather similarly built.

As I contemplate the details of the male body, I note something shifting a bit lower. It's a small twitch against the back of my forearm that is pressing against Mine's trousers, but I cannot tell what it is.

I frown as I lean in to take a better look.

"Mine?"

"What, Minnie?" His voice is tense, harsh.

"Are you sure you're not hurt?"

"Quite," he answers in a ragged voice.

"But..." I gulp down as my eyes take in the swollen lump at the front of his trousers. "You're swollen. Did you hit yourself here?" I ask as I move my hand and point to the growing bulge.

Oh my! It's growing so fast. I've never seen an injury swell up so rapidly.

My body tenses.

This must be it! There must be an infection somewhere in his trousers, and if I don't drain the liquid, he might die of septic shock. I've read as much in that damn nursing book.

He's staring at me wide-eyed. His mouth is ajar, and he's at a loss for words.

I'm pretty sure it's the pain.

"Don't worry about it, Mine. I will take care of you," I tell him resolutely. "I will tend to your injury and you'll be as good as new. You're not dying under my watch." I nod to myself, proud of the coherent words that came out of my mouth when everything inside of me is a mass of uncertainty.

Grabbing onto the edge of his underpants, I pull them down to reveal more of that dark hair and the base of the lump.

My hands freeze.

That is...much bigger than I thought.

"Don't worry, Mine," I tell him again, wishing to assure him, though *I* am not in the least assured. "I can fix you."

"Minnie," he groans aloud. His hands are dangling at his sides, almost as if he has no more strength to move.

Poor Mine.

He cut his stomach and now he has a huge lump between his legs.

The base of the lump springs up from a thatch of black hair.

Surprisingly, the skin is not red or yellow as I would have expected. It's the same golden hue as the rest of him.

I purse my lips.

The head must be lower, and to offer him relief from this swollen bump, I must find the head filled with liquid and pop it.

As I pull lower on his underpants, my knuckles brush over the base of the lump. Mine's hips jerk up and he balls his hands into fists.

"Mine? Are you all right?" I ask, fearing I might have hurt him.

"Please... Minnie..." he half groans half moans—from the unbearable pain, I am sure.

"I'll take care of you, Mine. Look how swollen this lump is. If I don't drain it, you'll die," I tell him gently.

"Oh, I'll die all right. But it's not from any lump, tiny darling," he drawls, his eyes closed shut.

"Huh?"

"Stupid female," the demon jibes from behind. His laughter echoes in the room.

I swivel and pin him with my gaze. For a moment, I forgot all about that nasty little demon—although now it's quite a bit bigger. With everyone fighting Holloway and his greed-induced tantrums, the demon is growing stronger by the second.

Taking advantage of my momentary distraction, Mine pushes my hands aside and pulls up his trousers, then buttons them up. He shrugs on what's left of his torn shirt and swings his long legs over the bed.

"No! Don't move! I need to drain your lump!" I call out, following after him.

He strides forward, and in a few steps, he's in front of Holloway—and the demon—who is currently wrestling with the doctor and three nurses.

"Move," Mine commands them. His voice holds so much authority that the doctor and the nurses immediately comply, letting go of Holloway and moving out of Mine's way.

"Say one more thing about her and I will personally send

you back to hell," Mine mutters harshly. Before I can blink, his fist flies, connecting with the ugly demon perched on Holloway's shoulder.

More surprising? His fist *actually* hits the demon, making it sway from side to side as his form becomes distorted. Yet in a few moments, it's back to his initial form. Its mouth opens on a loud, blaring shrill that only Mine and I can hear.

With an annoyed sigh, Mine punches him again, this time in the mouth, shutting the demon up—if only temporarily.

As a young deity, I can't say I've seen *too* much in my lifetime. But not only have I never seen something like this, I've never *heard* of a mortal hitting an amorphous demon. Because though this greed demon might now have somewhat of a shape, he is still in his spiritual form—not strong enough to gain a physical form yet.

Mine's knuckles purposefully skirt by Holloway's face, hitting him in the temple. It's not a harsh blow, but it's enough to knock him out momentarily.

The doctor stares at him in awe.

"Thank you. He was out of control."

Mine nods.

"I need your nurse to tend to me for the night. I trust that will not be an issue?"

"Erm..." The doctor glances at me. Then at Mine. I can tell he wants to say no since he will need a full staff, but for some reason, he cannot refuse Mine. "Not at all," he eventually replies.

"Good. Cuff him to the bed and have a few soldiers guard him through the night," Mine orders before he turns to me, grabs my hand, and pulls me out of the infirmary.

"You're injured, Mine. We can't just leave—" I protest.

He doesn't answer, merely dragging me after him. I don't know where he's going. We walk past the cantina and some of the important military buildings. The sky has darkened and the chilly night air hits me in the face as we walk from one end of the base to the other. Shivers erupt all over the surface of my skin.

Damn it! I hate being this powerless.

Yet even with my rather average abilities, I could easily scream and demand he let go of me. People would hear, and someone would help me, no? But it is even more fascinating the fact that I have no inclination to do so. I am simply curious about him and what he has in mind. Especially now that I am quite certain he will not die—a fact that causes me an unnatural amount of joy.

He gives you donuts, Minnie!

He does, doesn't he? That is a fine quality in a human. He might be insulting sometimes and there might be a gap in our understanding of the English language, but his heart is in the right place.

Why are you thinking of his heart, Minnie?

I shake myself. Although his heart is housed in a rather nice and muscular chest and...

Bad Minnie, bad!

All right, so he might be a good-looking specimen. But he is still human and far below me. This is something I should keep in mind at all times. But that is why curiosity is eating at me regarding Mine and the greed demon.

How had Mine been able to see it? Talk to it? *Hit* it?

Not only is that shocking, but it is quite impressive, too.

After what feels like forever, Mine finally stops in front of a tent-like structure. Stabbing a key into the lock at the door, he opens it and pulls me inside.

The interior is almost bare save for a one-person bed next to a small table. In the back, there is a study desk with a myriad of papers on top of it. Two changes of clothes hang from a railing. Oh, and there's one of those radio contraptions, too, sequestered in a dark corner.

"You want me to treat you here?" I blink in shock. "Through the night?"

I might be curious about him, but this is...unseemly.

We're alone, in a secluded space. It doesn't matter if it's technically both his office and his bedroom. What's important is that I am alone with a male when I am at my most vulnerable.

"There is no need to treat me," he adds with a sigh. "I told you there's nothing wrong with me."

Turning on a couple of lamps, he lets me gaze upon his body.

I study him from head to toe, noting that the bulging lump from before is no longer there.

W-what?

I hurry to his side and fall to my knees to get a better look.

"But how?" I ask, looking up at him. I pat the front of his trousers, amazed to find the lump completely gone!

Mine audibly gulps and averts his gaze.

"I told you it was nothing," he mutters, grabbing onto my shoulders and pulling me up.

"But... How did you see the demon then?" I whisper, more confused than ever. "Only dying people can see them..."

Mine is the opposite of that. He is full of vigor—not at all like someone at death's door. In fact, I should probably *not* be noticing that vigor since it's making me uncomfortably warm and causing my tummy to ache for some reason.

"Does that mean you're dying too?"

"N-no. That's... I mean," I stammer. "I'm different."

"Different how?" he asks as he grabs a suitcase and props it on the bed. He opens it and fishes out a clean shirt, which he puts on.

I let out an unconscious sigh of relief. I'm glad I don't have to stare at his chest anymore. It was quite...distracting.

"You first. How come you could see that demon?" I counter.

I'm not about to reveal all my secrets to someone I don't trust—a human nonetheless. It's forbidden for my kind to get involved in humans' lives and that includes revealing my divine status. Although... I am decidedly *not* divine in this moment. I wonder if the rules still apply to me if I have no powers.

He chuckles.

"Tea?" He motions to a kettle on his desk. The tea is probably long cold.

"Stop prevaricating," I grumble.

He rummages through a few boxes under his desk, thereby ignoring me.

"Mine? I'm talking to you," I tell him, tapping my foot against the floor impatiently. It's late and it's getting increasingly colder. His flimsy tent does little to keep the chill out.

I let out a shudder, which he notices.

"You're cold," he states, straightening his back and letting his gaze roam over my body.

I'm only wearing my nursing uniform and it's made out of a very thin cotton. I suppose these British don't have the funds to make something thicker considering the government can barely feed its own people.

"I'm fine."

"No. You are not," he says.

He goes back to his boxes, and the first thing he takes out is a small wooden container. He places it on the desk and returns to his search. After a few more moments, he takes out a woolen sweater. Getting to his feet, he comes to my side and, without a word, he puts the sweater on me.

I gasp in surprise. But it's too late. He's already pulled it over my head and down my body, going as far as to reach inside and grab my arms so they can go through the sleeves.

Given our size differences, his sweater is like a dress on me. But it's a thick, warm dress, the wool soft and smooth—a high-quality blend.

I let out a sigh of contentment. How can I tell him off when this feels so good? So warm, so comfortable?

"Better?" he asks, his lips quirked up in a smile.

"So much better."

"Good," he purrs.

His voice is deep and calm, and now that I no longer have to mind my trembling limbs, I am back to noticing things about him. Like how his smooth voice travels all the way to my belly in a way that I do not think is biologically possible. Or how his scent envelops me now that I'm wrapped in his sweater.

Ugh! Stop this, Minerva!

"Back to the demons," I state firmly as I force those thoughts out of my mind.

He shrugs. "I've always been able to see them."

He's in front of me now. Although he's put on a shirt, his impressive physique is unmistakable. His arms are thick and bulging with muscles.

"What do you mean?" I croak. Damn him and his perfectly sculpted body. As if it wasn't enough that I had to not only stare at those hard and defined abdominals just moments ago, but I also had to touch them when I was treating his cut and...

I squeeze my eyes shut. This is a serious conversation. I must focus!

"I can't tell you how it happened, when it started, or why, since I do not know it myself," he states casually.

"When you say you've always been able to see them, you mean..."

"Since I was a child," he confirms.

I nod pensively—and if I'm honest with myself, a little relieved. It means he's not on the brink of death. But if that is not the case, then he must have some strong spiritual energy that allows him to see beyond the physical realm.

That is...interesting.

I have heard of such mortals, but since I have not spent much time with his kind, I've never met one before.

"You hit the demon," I add. "You can touch them in their spiritual form?"

"I can touch ghosts, too." He smiles.

"Really?"

Ghosts... I suppose he means mortal souls.

I've never heard of another mortal able to do that. Alas, I don't consider myself to be an encyclopedia of all the abnormalities present in the human world. Perhaps it is possible and he is telling the truth.

On the bright side, this ability of his might come in handy in vanquishing the greed demon.

"I haven't seen a demon like that before, though. One that can attach itself to the body without possessing the host."

"That is a greed demon. They're a different breed and *much* more dangerous. Your friend is in danger," I tell him.

"I gathered that much. The demon attached itself to him while we were over Germany. One moment we were hit by flak, the next I see something swirl around Holloway. I didn't realize what it was until he got off the plane and the demon was clearly visible." He grimaces. "Is Holloway going to die?"

"The demon is growing stronger. If we don't get rid of it, it won't be *just* your friend who will suffer, but the whole base," I explain. "When it's strong enough, it will be able to tap into everyone's greed and feed on it."

He curses under his breath.

"How do you know all of this?"

"Erm…"

"A greed demon. That's very specific information."

"That's because…" I trail off.

I press my lips together as I debate *what* to tell him. On the one hand, I don't want to give away my identity, especially since I haven't known him *that* long to trust him implicitly. But on the other hand, he's the only other person I've met who can see the spiritual world. Without my powers, I will need all the help I can get if I am to vanquish this demon and send it back to the Source.

Yet there's still a seed of doubt inside me. What if I get in more trouble for telling him? Will he even believe me? It's not as if I have a way to prove to him I'm telling the truth considering I am powerless.

"Come, sit here," Mine suddenly says, startling me from my thoughts.

He takes my hand and leads me to the bed, urging me to sit down.

"May I?" he asks.

I frown. He nods to my legs. Unsure of what he means, I just nod.

He undoes my shoes first. Then he gently takes my legs and places them on the bed. He gathers the woolen blanket and covers my lower body, making sure there's not one inch that's exposed to the cold.

I blink.

That is...quite nice of him.

Mine goes back to his desk and picks up the wooden box from before. Returning to my side, he hands it to me.

"What is it?"

"Open it," he urges with a smile.

I pull the wooden top off it and I'm surprised to see a myriad of colorful little balls. They're the size of pearls, so my first thought is that perhaps they're jewels.

"Try it."

"What do you mean? What is it?"

"We call it M&M's," he mentions, taking one of those small balls and slipping it past my lips. I don't even get to act incensed at his much too familiar gesture because the sweet taste of chocolate hits my tongue. Flavor bursts in my mouth and a low moan escapes me.

"Oh my, this is so good!" I exclaim, hurrying to grab more of these magical balls he calls M&M's.

He chuckles.

"You can have the entire box.

My eyes widen. "I can?"

He nods.

I munch on a couple more chocolaty balls as I regard him. His lips are curled up in a smile as he gazes at me, almost as if he can derive the same pleasure just from watching me eat.

And this is certainly even better than donuts. So much sweeter and flavorful. Where did he even get them? Everything is so restricted with the war and the rations... And the fact that he gave them *all* to me.

I gulp down, warmth spreading inside of me. And it's not

from the chocolates, though they make me giddy in a different way. No, it's a different type of warmth, one that starts from the depths of my stomach and travels up, enveloping me entirely. It only gets more potent as I stare into his green eyes. Why, I have no idea. But I've always had good instincts. And this time...my instincts are telling me to trust him.

I'll probably regret my decision in the future. But how can someone so nice be dangerous? How can someone who constantly gives me sweets be a bad person/ Besides, with his ability to see the spiritual world, he can help me vanquish that greed demon. I cannot do it alone.

Yes, I nod, satisfied. Perhaps these are all excuses I create for myself. But at the moment, these excuses are my reality. And perhaps I don't want to look further than that.

"I'm not human," I tell him as I swallow the last bit of chocolate.

His brows rise in question.

"Not...human?"

"I'm an ice deity who hunts demons," I explain, and once I start talking, everything comes out rather easily. I tell him all about who I am and where I come from, as well as what my mission is in Anthropa at this time. He listens intently, never once interrupting me. Of course I have to mention his role in what led to me losing my powers, and I make sure to berate him for that. After I tell him everything—perhaps more than I should have—I press my lips together and stare at him, waiting for his reaction.

For moments on end, he just stares at me.

His eyes bore a hole into me as the silence between us stretches into an uncomfortable eternity.

His lips tremble. I prepare myself for his reply.

But just as he opens his mouth to speak, the only sound that comes out is a dark, rich laughter.

"A goddess." He chuckles. "Sure, tiny darling."

He...doesn't believe me?

TWELVE

I MAY HAVE EXPECTED that Mine wouldn't believe me, but I never realized how annoyed I would be by it. Without my powers, there isn't much I can do to prove it.

Nothing except what I'm about to do now.

It's past one at night. Although the base is fairly quiet, there are still some parties going on in a few tents.

Mine follows by my side as we head to the secluded field a distance away from the military base where I last summoned my brother.

Another summon will *not* make me his favorite person, that is for sure.

"Why are there parties at this time of the night? Shouldn't the soldiers rest?" I ask as we pass by a lit tent teeming with rowdy people.

"Wouldn't you want to have a good time if tomorrow might be your last day alive?" Mine counters.

"I suppose so," I answer tentatively. I've never given that any thought, seeing as how my kind doesn't really die. Given the low chances of that happening, especially in battle with much weaker demons, I've never had to worry about my last moments alive.

Yet now that I think about it... What would I do? If I were to die tomorrow, what would I do on my last day alive?

"What about you, then? Why are you not at those parties?"

Instead, he's out here with me, chasing some supernatural ethos.

He shrugs. The movement makes his arms move, and his hand slides past mine. The smallest touch occurs as his knuckles brush across mine.

I bite my lip to stop a gasp from erupting into the night.

Mine appears unaffected as he continues on.

"I am not led by the same uncertainty they are."

"I don't understand." I frown.

"Their fear of death revolves around the fact that it is the end—that everything they know and cherish will be taken from them."

"That is the definition of death," I agree.

He smiles.

"Sometimes, death is just the beginning, tiny darling." He winks at me.

"No. Not really," I tell him resolutely. "That is not how it works."

He raises a languid brow at me.

"When mortals die, their soul is judged by a Death deity and depending on the merit accrued during a lifetime, they get assigned to different levels of the House of Psyche," I start, not that I mean to lecture him—but I happen to excel at this subject. "Once given a designation, the souls drink from Letharion—the well of oblivion. Only after that they are let to their specific level in the House of Psyche. The virtuous souls who accumulated merit during their lifetimes are sent directly to the House of Moirai to get a new fate. The others have to work for their merit in order to ascend to the level that leads to the House of Moirai.

"Then, of course, you have the most sinful souls. They are sent to the lowest levels of the House of Moirai where they will endure gruesome punishments as payments for their sins. Once their debts are considered paid, they can move up the levels and earn merit toward an eventual reincarnation." I pause to draw in a breath. "But you see, once a soul drinks from the Letharion, they become a blank canvas. While the soul goes on to live again at some point, it will not be as its previous self. From that regard, death *is* the end."

"Is it?" he muses. "Even if they are blank canvasses, they are still the same essence, are they not?"

"They are but—" I frown. "Memories are at the basis of personhood. Without those, the soul becomes malleable to its environment. Take your soul, for example. Let's say you died and went through Letharion and then you got assigned a new fate, but this time it's in a completely different world, one that doesn't remotely resemble Anthropa. You will not be you anymore. You will be a product of your environment."

He regards me skeptically.

"You see, I only half agree with you on that. Yes, the environment likely plays a very big role in shaping someone's personality. But what about inherent inclinations? A soul *must* have certain inclinations."

"That is..." I blink. "I am not quite sure," I admit, to my great chagrin. Not only do I not have an answer to his question, but I realize that I've never questioned the status quo of souls.

"Souls do have an inherent spiritual energy that remains the same regardless of the incarnation," I add slowly.

"Then I don't see why there wouldn't be *other* inherent things, too," Mine points out.

I nod thoughtfully.

"You have given me much to think on," I tell him honestly. "My education, just like that of every other deity, comes from schooling and textbooks. No one but the Psyche deities are allowed to step inside the House of Psyche—and the souls, of course."

"Why is no one allowed inside?" Mine asks.

"There is one thing deities cannot do, and that is to mess with a mortal's soul or fate. The House of Psyche is a fortress in that regard, as is the House of Moirai. We may have a lot of abilities, but even *we* are ruled by fate."

"Abilities? I have yet to see any abilities from you." Mine cracks a smile.

"I told you that I'm being punished for helping *you*!" I roll my eyes. "But I will prove to you I speak the truth."

When we finally reach a more secluded area, I put my hand up to stop him.

Kai should help convince Mine I am telling the truth, but I also have an ulterior motive for resorting to this. If Kai didn't believe me that there was a demon before, he can no longer deny it now. A greed demon, too. Not only will I get an *I told you so* moment, but I will also get the chance to question him regarding greed demons.

Kai is part of the same division as me, so I doubt he would know more about them. But he is much, much older than me, so perhaps he's heard of similar cases in the past. In any case, I will have done my duty to announce the presence of a sin demon and ask for appropriate guidance. Whether Kai decides to let me handle the issue—with information on how to do so, of course—or he notifies the division responsible for hunting sin demons is a moot point.

Considering how rare and dangerous sin demons are, I should be getting *some* recognition for finding one and helping defeat it.

"Go hide behind the barn," I tell Mine as I point to the dilapidated structure a few paces away. He doesn't protest, marching toward it and finding an angle from which he's not visible from my position.

It's better if my brother doesn't see him *with* me. Perhaps he can *accidentally* be in the vicinity, but it's not because I asked him to come—of course not. I would never reveal myself to a human.

I roll my eyes at my own thoughts as I take out a small knife I borrowed from Mine and proceed to cut my brother's summoning symbol in my arm—again.

Ugh.

I am not looking forward to the pain and the slow healing. Alas, it must be done.

When the last line of the symbol is carved in my flesh, a low hum of energy erupts around me. In the next second, my brother appears before me.

I blink, my mouth hanging open in shock.

He's... He's... Naked!

Well, there's only a sheet covering his body, but damn it! I've never wanted to see that much of my brother's naked skin.

"By the Source, Minerva! I am one step away from strangling you," he thunders, clutching the sheet around his waist.

"Kai... I... I'm so sorry. I didn't realize that—"

"That I sleep? That I'm not always at your beck and call? What a novel concept," he adds drily.

"There's no need to get testy with me. I wouldn't have called you if it wasn't urgent."

"Like last time?" He raises his eyebrow.

"It was urgent! It's just that you did not believe me."

Kai shakes his head at me.

"You, Minerva, are hopeless. Do not use my summoning sigil again or you will not like the consequences," he grits out.

"But, Kai, wait until I tell you what happened. You won't believe it—"

Before I can get the words out, he's gone.

Poof.

He just...disappeared.

Again.

"Kaiiiiii!" I yell, though it's in vain. He can't hear me. He probably returned to bed. Because sleep is more precious than my discovery.

I'm so mad, I want to kick something.

"Your brother is so charming," Mine says as he comes up behind me. "Although I don't think I needed to see his bare ass."

I give him a pointed look. Then I frown.

"How did you know—"

"Let me guess. He will not help, will he?"

I release a defeated sigh. "No. He didn't even wait for me to speak. And if I summon him again, I fear he will find another punishment for me."

"Don't you worry, tiny darling. I am at your service," Mine says as he throws his arm over my shoulder. "Together, we will defeat the big bad that's taken over the military base." He furrows his brows as he pulls me closer. "We shall need a ship name."

"A what?" I frown.

"A ship name. You wouldn't know what it is. You're not from here." He winks.

"Explain."

"It's the combination of our names. To signal we're a team. Since we are, are we not?" His voice drops an octave.

"I suppose we are."

"Brilliant. How does *MinnieMine* sound? It's very melodious, isn't it?"

I am confused.

"I suppose?"

"MinnieMine, MinnieMine, MinnieMine," he continues, quite proud of himself. "I like it."

From his pocket, he takes out a bandage. Grabbing my hand, he carefully cleans the blood before he wraps the bandage around my arm.

Surprise washes over me. That is...quite thoughtful of him. I forgot I would need a bandage for the wound until it heals.

But as he focuses on tying the bandage around my arm, he keeps whispering the same *ship* name all over again.

MinnieMine, MinnieMine, MinnieMine.

I don't know why he keeps repeating this *ship* name, or what the purpose of it is. Then again, I have already ascertained that this Mine is an odd duck himself. More often than not, I do not understand him or what he wants to say.

Regardless, right now he is overlooking the most important thing.

"I think you're forgetting something, Mine. We don't know *how* to defeat the big bad," I add in a wry voice.

He sobers. "It shouldn't be too hard, no? You kill demons."

"As I told you before, sin demons are a different category. They cannot be exorcised in the same manner as regular demons. It is why I would have required my brother's assistance considering I am quite powerless at the moment."

"I can assist you," he protests.

I take a deep breath. "You're *human*, Mine. And you have no idea what to do."

He opens his mouth to argue before he closes it. He nods at me.

"You are right. We should first figure out *how* to get rid of this demon."

I narrow my eyes at him.

"You are oddly exuberant about this. Why?"

"Why would I not be? I get to team up with the hottest demon slayer and kick some demon butt. There's hardly anything more exciting than this."

His words echo in my brain, and I'm a bit too slow at dissecting each individual word. He called me hot.

I glance down at my body. I'm still wearing his sweater. Is that a jibe at me being too cold now and requiring his sweater to be warm? I'm well aware I've lost my powers and now I'm susceptible to puny things like cold. He doesn't have to mock me for it.

"You are very odd, Mine," I comment. "I did not anticipate you would take this so well."

"Why wouldn't I? I'm always ready for a fight." He winks at me.

Again.

Why is he always winking at me? Does he have a defective eyelid?

"Minnie Mine. Saving people. Hunting things—"

"I think you're getting ahead of yourself. Just a few hours

ago you had no idea what a greed demon was and now you want to fight one?"

"Well, yes," he says with a nod. "We will do it together." He gives me a smile as he presses me closer to his side.

"Did you not understand anything that I told you? I have no idea how to kill a greed demon. My brother will not even listen to me long enough for me to ask him what to do. Without my abilities, not only can I *not* fight, but I also can't make contact with anyone in Aperion to ask for information on greed demons."

He purses his lips.

"That is, indeed, a quandary."

I let out a tired sigh.

"Tomorrow is another day. I'll try to think of something in the meantime," I grumble. Though, if I'm perfectly honest, I have no idea *what* I could come up with. I could, of course, try again to summon my brother, but that will likely end up in tragedy.

For me.

Kai might have a soft spot for me, but he also has quite the temper and if I push him too much, he might just hand me over to our parents and wash his hands of me—and that is *not* an option.

Ugh. Why can't he ever take me seriously? I had a legitimate reason for calling him. If only he had listened to my concerns instead of dismissing them...

Alas, I must find a way to figure things out by myself. I spare a glance at Mine. He still has that weird smile on his face as he's gazing at me. I suppose I can consider him my partner for now. We are both just as powerless, something that makes me wanna scream in frustration. Hear that. Me, being as powerless as a puny human.

Humph.

It doesn't escape me, however, that if I *do* manage to vanquish this greed demon as powerless as I am right now, that should earn me quite the recognition back home. Commander Azerius would finally recognize my resourcefulness.

I bite my lip as I ponder that. Perhaps this isn't such a bad outcome—as long as I can find a way to kill that demon, of course.

The only positive is that Mine is not only indigent to this world, but he is also a respected member of the autochthonous military, which should help me as I learn to navigate this world. Having him as an ally might be advantageous, after all.

"Good night, Mine. I will talk to you later," I tell him and turn to leave.

"Where are you going?" He frowns, keeping up with me.

"To sleep."

He tilts his head to the side and blinks twice.

"Where?"

"At the dorm." I roll my eyes.

"But—" His words are cut off as he doubles over in pain. Holding on to his midriff, he falls to his knees. Low groans of pain slip past his lips.

I hurry to his side.

"Are you all right?"

He shakes his head. His features are tight with tension.

"I think my wound opened up," he barely lets out.

"Oh, no," I whisper. "We need to head back to the infirmary. Now!" I gulp down. "I should have stitched it," I mutter to myself.

I grab his arm and lay it over my shoulders as I try to help him up.

"No," he grits out. "My...tent. I have everything there."

He must sense that I'm about to protest because he adds, "It's closer."

He has a point.

Nodding, I help him move, though it's quite hard on both of us. Not only is he so much taller than me, but he is also much heavier. Without my powers, I can barely shoulder any of his weight. Good thing that his tent is not *too* far away, and within a few minutes, we make it back inside.

As we enter the tent, he collapses onto the small bed, almost taking me with him. I manage to extract myself from his grasp right as his body hits the mattress.

He groans in pain, turning to his side and clutching his stomach tighter.

"In the...back. White box..." he struggles to say.

Driven by an unusual urgency, I ransack the back of his tent in search of that white box. First, I look in his trunk. It's not there. Then I scan the contents of his suitcase. Only after long, drawn-out minutes do I spot a white box.

I pop it open to make sure it has the right materials.

"Found it," I declare, turning to him.

He removed his shirt and unbuttoned his pants. His bandage is half peeled off, and fresh blood stains his skin.

I press my lips together.

He must have strained too much for the wound to gape wide open like this.

"It will need stitches," I tell him as I place the white box on the table in front of him and take a seat on the bed next to him.

"You can do it, no?"

"Of course." I bristle.

"Good. You should find everything you might need in that box."

I nod, getting to work to wash the blood off his wound.

"This will likely leave a scar," I comment as I see the extent of the injury. How did it get so bad in a matter of hours? I could have sworn it was only a superficial scratch when I first treated it.

"What's one more scar?" He shrugs, pointing to his face.

I glance up, studying the scar tissue on the side of his face. It may be that I've gotten used to him, but I've stopped noticing his scar.

"That's not even the worst," he continues, turning slightly to show me his marred back. "I have scars everywhere."

"Are they from battle?"

He shakes his head.

"I've had them for as long as I can remember."

My grip on the needle and thread falters. His scars denote unspeakable pain if I were to go by the depth and amount of tissue affected. For someone to suffer anything like that...

"Why? What happened?"

He's silent for a few moments.

"I was ill," he murmurs.

"What illness causes this? These scars look as if someone burned the flesh off your body," I ask before I realize that my words might be construed as rude.

He licks his lip and I can sense some hesitation.

"My family is not originally from the United States," he starts.

"You're French, no?" I interrupt. I'd heard some people refer to him as the Frenchman—not that I paid too much attention to what was being said about him.

"You could say so." He chuckles. "Where we're from, there are...divisions in society."

I frown.

"What do you mean by divisions?"

"The government was even more fascist than Hitler's. It wanted to achieve spe—uhm, racial purity. My mother was pureblood, but my father was considered the enemy."

"What does that have to do with your illness?"

He sighs.

"The government devised a disease that would affect only those with my father's blood. By some miracle, he did not catch the illness. But I did." He pauses. "I almost died."

"Is such a thing possible? A disease that targets only a specific group of people?"

He nods grimly.

"What happened?" I ask, barely in control of the tremor in my voice.

"The disease was killing me from the inside out. My parents

tried everything they could to eradicate it from my body. These"
—he points to his facial scars—"are a result of those efforts."

"They...hurt you?" I whisper.

"No. They were trying to save me."

"But... How..." I bite my lip. "Did it work?"

He gives me a sad smile.

"Nothing worked."

"I don't understand. You're still alive, aren't you?"

"Only a part of me is," he answers cryptically. "The only
way for them to keep me alive was to get rid of the part that was
poisoning me."

"Your father's blood?"

He nods.

"Your medicine is that advanced?"

I've never heard of anything like that before.

"Let's say they used an alternative type of medicine," he
mentions with a chuckle. But the flex of his abdominal muscles
causes his wound to contract and he winces from it.

I grab his hand and squeeze it in an attempt to give him
something else to focus on other than the pain from his wound.

His hand is warm, comfortable. His big palm engulfs my
smaller one. Though I was the one with the initiative, he ends
up being the one leading the encounter. Somehow, that makes
my heart skip a beat. Why, I do not know. It's an odd thing,
really. Almost every atom in my being vibrates, jumps around,
and does odd somersaults in the air.

"Is that when you started seeing the spiritual world, too?" I
clear my throat as I slowly pull my hand out of his. I'd like nothing
better than to keep it there, but every time we touch, I seem to lose
my focus. Not only that, but my mind becomes blank. All my
thoughts disintegrate until all I can do is stare at him like a damn
fool. Quite a peculiar thing. I've never heard of such a condition
before, where one is rendered an idiot by a simple touch.

But that means he is dangerous to my well-being and I
should limit these skin-to-skin interactions.

"Yes. Seeing the spiritual world is the only thing I was left with," he adds, once more making me frown in confusion.

He says the most cryptic things, and I have a hard time understanding him. Perhaps it's the fact that though I'm not touching him, I'm still in his vicinity and that may cause a neurological affliction.

I must study this phenomenon more. It's bad enough I lost my powers. I cannot afford to love my brain, too.

"You shouldn't go on any missions for the foreseeable future," I mention as I cut the thread on his last stitch and bandage the wound.

This is it. The end. I will finish this and leave—put some distance between us so I can think straight again.

"It will heal."

Skepticism suffuses me. Just moments ago, he was doubled down in pain and now he's...rather nonchalant.

"It won't if you strain yourself."

"It's fine. You'll be there to put me back together, no?" he asks in a low voice.

I roll my eyes at him.

"Only for the next ninety-nine days. After that, you'll have to find a different nurse."

"What if I want *you*? Only you?"

"Then you're out of luck. I kill demons for a living. I don't heal puny humans," I point out. "I'm only doing this as a last resort until I get my powers back."

"You're a natural at it," he mentions. "And I don't mind being your puny human." He wiggles his brows at me. "I'll let you do anything to me as long as I can feel those pretty hands of yours on my skin."

I glare at him and stab the needle through his skin.

"Ouch," he exclaims in surprise. "Don't be so mean to me, Minnie. I told you I have a weak heart," he murmurs in a low voice. Bringing his hand to his chest, he rubs circles over his heart as if to prove a point.

I follow the movements of his hand with my eyes, and my cheeks flush a deep red as I realize I'm staring at his *naked* chest.

The dim lighting of the tent gives his skin a golden hue. His muscles are hard and well-defined, and for a split second, I picture that it's *me* who's touching his chest. That it's *me* who's rubbing my hands all over those hard planes, feeling his heartbeats and...

"Unless you kiss it better?" He grins. "Maybe then it will heal," he says with a wink.

His words jolt me back to the present. No-no-no, this is out of the question.

"You're one of those shovels, aren't you?" I narrow my eyes at him.

HE BLINKS IN CONFUSION. "What? I'm a...shovel?"

"Y-you think you c-can entice me with your s-sweet words?" I croak, pulling back and giving him a stare down.

His hand stills on his chest, and once more, my eyes betray me as they zone in on his naked flesh. But I quickly recover and bring my gaze back to his face.

"Entice you?" he repeats, a smile pulling at his lips.

"Yes. Shovels do that. But it will not work. I am warning you, Mine. Don't think to try something with me or I will be forced to club you over the head with this box," I say as I grab the white box. It's made out of thick wood, so I think it will do some damage. If he wants another scar to add to his collection, I am more than happy to oblige him.

I expect him to be scared or at least wary. Instead, he just smiles indulgently at me.

"I think you mean rake, not shovel," he adds in an amused voice.

I glare at him again.

"Same thing," I grumble. Who decided to call a defiler of innocents a gardening tool anyway? As if this English language is not confusing enough.

He shakes his head and laughs.

"*I* am a rake? Do you even know what that is?"

"Of course I know!" I burst out, incensed. Getting to my feet, I shoot daggers at him with my eyes. "Rakes are the worst. Flirting with every female and feeding them sweet words to steal their virtue."

He stops laughing. Leaning against the wall, he assumes a relaxed pose as he lets his gaze slowly roam over my body.

"That is where you're wrong, tiny darling. I am not flirting with every female. I am only flirting with *you*."

"Aha!" I point at him accusatorially. "So you admit you're flirting with me."

"Why would I deny it?" He shrugs. "But you see, I cannot possibly be a rake, since yours is the only virtue I am concerned about," he adds in a smooth voice.

"And you think that makes it better?" I cry out, my eyes widening at his easy admission.

He shrugs, a stupid grin plastered on his face.

"My virtue is off-limits, you insufferable oaf!"

"To anyone else, yes." He smiles shamelessly at me.

My nostrils flare in anger as I stare at him.

"Is that why you were feeding me donuts?" I ask, new suspicion entering my mind. "Was that a bribe?"

"Of course not," he answers, and I'm surprised to hear indignation in his voice. "The donuts were to make you smile. I like it when you smile."

I blink.

"You d-do?" I whisper.

He nods and takes a step closer.

"You're the most beautiful thing I've ever seen. And when you smile, you damn near give me a heart attack."

My lips part, but no sound comes out. I just stare at him, unable to find my words. Of all the things he could have said...

My cheeks are flaming hot. A flush spreads down my body until I'm uncomfortably warm and jittery.

"Stop this," I whisper. "Stop talking about my smile, or my virtue, or anything indecent like that."

He smirks. The action folds the skin around his scar, making it seem more prominent. Yet even now, instead of turning me off, his scar only makes him seem more appealing. More...

Bad Minerva! You shouldn't be noticing his smile.

"I fear that's impossible, Minnie darling," he murmurs.

"Not really. Just...don't think about them. Or me. Or—"

"Or?"

Why does he have to still be shirtless at this exact moment? And why is he so close to me—so much so that once more I find my brain turning to mush?

"If your plan was to lure me to your tent and have your w-wicked way with me, it w-will n-not work, Mine," I stammer as I back away. "In fact, if you have *any* nefarious plans with me, this"—I motion between the two of us—"will not work."

"What do you mean?"

"I am canceling our *ship*. I can deal with that greed demon on my own just fine."

I turn to leave.

My heart beats wildly in my chest. I should have realized that all my encounters with Mine were not fortuitous. Males are the same everywhere I go. They only want to use females for their own needs, and Mine is no different. Why else would he have been so kind to me from the start if not to make me lower my guard so he can take advantage of me. And with the way he's messing with my head, it is much better to keep my distance from him.

Alas, he chose the wrong target. I am *not* take-advantageable.

"Minnie, wait!" he calls after me.

Don't look back, Minerva!

Ignoring his thudding steps behind me, I push through the tent entrance.

The chilly night wind immediately hits me in the face, but so does something else. A pungent smell that makes me gag.

THIRTEEN

I SCAN THE AREA, squinting in the dark. Damn it all. How can humans deal with their feeble sight? I can barely see anything.

Taking a few steps, I look around the corner and make out Holloway—mostly because that damn demon glows in the dark—standing next to some three, four males?

The smoke-like tendrils have a shimmery red hue to them as they swirl in the air until they reach the males, attaching themselves to them.

"Minnie, wait for me," Mine continues as he comes from behind. "Please."

I ignore him as I focus on the ensuing scene. Loud shouts erupt in the air and I note more movements.

This time, two of the soldiers who are firmly within the grips of the greed demon are fighting over an object. I cannot make out for sure what it is, but it's a flat piece of paper. A... record? It's hard to tell.

The red tendrils glow stronger as the demon feeds on their greed.

"Give it back," one of the males shouts.

"No. It's *my* record. Let go of it."

Their exchanges center around the same words. One claims it's his, while the other claims it's actually his.

The demon chuckles darkly as it watches the argument. It doesn't matter the outcome. The mere fact that they are focusing on the ownership of the item—on the fact that it belongs to them—feeds the demon.

Holloway stands by the side, dazed and confused. He's no longer in control. The demon is now using him as a puppet to move around until it can gain enough strength to jump to another body.

My lips flatten in consternation. I did not expect this demon to gain strength so quickly. But perhaps it is my mistake to assume it would behave like a normal demon does.

Yet if this continues... We have mere days before the demon takes control of the entire base.

"What are you doing?" another male asks as he joins the altercation. Behind him, a few more males trail behind, their gait suggesting they are intoxicated.

I'm not sure who throws the first punch. But while at first the argument was centered around a record, this time, it's degenerated into two factions. Some of the intoxicated males are defending one of the males while the rest are taking the side of the other one. From a mere conflict about the ownership of an item, it has now turned into a full-on brawl.

Mine is by my side, his mouth agape as he stares at the ongoing conflict. But while brawls are meant to occur in high testosterone environments, this is far from a usual fight.

Holloway is a few steps away from the fight. He's with his back against a building, watching the events with a certain apathy. The demon on his shoulder, however, is getting increasingly excited. Its tendrils slither forward, attaching themselves to the other males, too.

"Why is he feeding on them?" Mine frowns. "He is drawn to greed, no?"

"Violence is another form of greed," I mutter. "The motivations behind the violence must be rooted in some type of greed.

Perhaps it's not the same greed that drove the first two males to fight over the record, but it is a type of greed nonetheless. And it seems our demon is growing stronger by the minute," I add grimly.

The red tendrils glow and shimmer as the noxious emotion travels from the mortals to the demon. It's similar to how an amorphous demon might be feeding on a soul's energy, sucking it dry with every passing moment. But while an amorphous demon requires time to tap into a soul's energy, especially if it's a low-level one, this demon seems to be able to channel the greed energy at an alarming rate.

"The higher-ups will hear," Mine notes. "I should—" He takes a step forward. I extend my arm to stop him.

"No. Don't. The demon already has you in his sights. He knows you can see him, and we don't know what he's capable of at this point."

"But he's only getting stronger."

"Exactly. And before we know *how* to stop him, we cannot be reckless."

He purses his lips, clearly not satisfied with this course of action.

"Break it up!" someone yells. "Everyone, stand down!"

"I guess that's the higher-ups?" I ask.

Mine nods.

I spot a couple of officers coming toward the fighting soldiers. But more surprising is the fact that the boy I'd seen before, the dead teenager, is trailing behind them.

"Do you know him?" I point at the young ghost.

"That's Tommy," he adds in a low voice. "He was a good lad."

"He didn't cross over when he died. Do you know what might be keeping him here?"

"He was only eighteen," Mine adds with a sigh. "He had a sweetheart back home he wanted to go back to."

"And now he won't be able to."

"No, he won't."

With the higher officers now at the scene, the brawl devolves even further. The demon is gleeful as his tendrils swirl in the air in an attempt to connect to the newcomers.

"We must do something," Mine mutters.

I grip his arm tighter to stop him. "No."

I SHOULD BE ENCOURAGING him to break up the fight. Yet all I can think about is the fact that once he's in the demon's proximity, he might become a victim, too.

Tommy, the young ghost, hovers around, staring at the demon. I suppose he doesn't understand what's happening.

Once the officers get involved, everything is a flurry of movement that I have a hard time tracking.

Tommy moves, his arm extended, his mouth open on a loud screech, and I belatedly see what he's pointing at. One of the males has drawn up a weapon—a pistol of sorts. He's waving it around, though with my feeble sight, I can barely make out where he's aiming.

But Tommy can see, and in a loud voice, he calls out a name. *Vitry.*

My eyes widen just as the gun goes off.

I don't know when I move or how I end up covering Mine with my body. I only know that the pain from the bullet is intense.

So. Damn. Intense.

"Minnie?" He blinks. "Minnie, what happened? Are you all right?"

"I will...heal," I croak. He wouldn't.

So what if it hurts a little—*too much*—at least I will be as good as new in a day or so. Mine isn't likely to survive a bullet wound. Based on the fact that the bullet hit me in the shoulder, right above my heart, I assume it was going to hit him low in the stomach.

Without a word, Mine swoops me in his arms and rushes me back to his tent—the brawl from before all but forgotten.

"But the dem—"

"That can wait. It's not as if we can do anything now, can we?" He raises a brow at me.

I reluctantly agree.

My face is screwed up in pain when my body jolts as Mine places me on the bed.

There's blood all over his sweater and my dress, and the wound keeps leaking with no sign of stopping anytime soon.

I'm no stranger to blood. I've decapitated and mangled my fair share of corporeal demons in the past. But I've rarely been on the receiving end of such injuries. In fact, I think I can count on one hand the amount of times I've been wounded to the point of bleeding profusely.

By the Source, how can humans withstand this? How can they go on in life knowing that one little injury and their life can end? How are they not a mass of fear and anxiety?

Even now, as I attempt to regulate my breathing, I can sense a sliver of anxiety coursing through me. It travels up my body, splitting into a million tendrils that take control of every single part of my being.

My breathing grows shallow.

"It's all right, tiny darling. You'll be just fine," Mine assures me.

I blink. For a moment, I'd forgotten he was here.

I grab his arm and squeeze.

"Take the bullet out, please," I beg him.

I can feel that scrap of metal digging into my skin, jolting around with every single movement. It's there—a foreign object in my body. And the mere knowledge that it's there is making me spiral into an unprecedented panic.

His eyes widen.

"Are you...sure?"

"Just do it," I grit out.

"All right."

Leaving me on the bed, he turns to his desk, rummaging

through his drawers. He finally finds what he's looking for—a pair of scissors.

The first aid kit is still on the table in front of me, so when he comes back, I assume he will immediately get to work. The sooner the foreign body is out of my system, the faster my healing will be—well, as fast as the circumstances allow.

He cuts the sweater first. Since the wound is pretty high up on my chest, any movement of my arms would cause me unbearable pain.

But he doesn't stop at that.

He kneels in front of me and grabs the hem of my dress, positioning the scissors and making a deep cut into the skirt.

"What are you doing?" I ask in outrage.

He blinks as he raises his gaze.

"Removing your dress."

"W-what?" I sputter.

HE FROWNS. "How do you think I can remove the bullet from your chest if you're wearing clothes."

"I..." I lick my lips. "Cut around the wound. You don't need to remove my entire dress."

"Minnie..." He sighs. "I can't just cut around the wound."

"Why? I'll do it!" I say and reach for the scissors. But right as I move, a loud groan of pain slips past my lips. Damn it! I can't even move without feeling the most intense pain.

"Sit back and let me tend to you," he commands me. He wrenches the scissors from me again and continues cutting through the skirt of my dress.

"Mine! This is unseemly. You cannot undress me," I protest weakly.

"That's exactly what I am doing, Minnie," he says drily.

"But this is against the rules. No one but my mate can see me without my clothes," I continue, trying to stop him but failing miserably.

"It's nothing I haven't already seen before, Minnie. Stop fidgeting. You're only hurting yourself."

I open my mouth to argue but then promptly close it as I replay his words in my mind. It's nothing he hasn't...seen before?

"What exactly have you *seen* before?" I ask, unable to control the vitriol from my voice. "And *who* have you seen before?"

The thought of Mine seeing another female in a state of undress is...distressing.

He glances at me, then grins.

"Don't worry your pretty head about that." Then he winks.

"Mine!" I grit out.

Alas, with the pain in my chest flaring once more, I suppose I will have to find another time to interrogate him on his past trysts. Although... Why do I care about his past trysts? Why do I care what he does with another female?

Except I do. I very much do. So much so, the rage I feel is giving this damn pain quite the competition.

Humans have loose morals. They engage in all types of unseemly activities—like those people from the party. They touch each other and they eat their mouths and they...

I grit my teeth. Glancing at Mine, I get unusually tense as I picture him doing the same with another female.

"Relax, Minnie," he murmurs. "I'm not going to do anything to you, all right? You have my promise."

I narrow my eyes at him.

"Your promise to what?"

"To not take advantage of you while you're in pain."

He finishes cutting my skirt and is now starting on the bodice. He cuts through my dress until he reaches the top of the neckline, at which point he pulls the two halves of material off my body.

Luckily, I am wearing one of those brassieres females in this world love so much, so my chest is not completely naked. But on my lower body, I am only left in a pair of white shorts that only come up mid-thigh, leaving far too much of my flesh available for his perusal.

The urge to cover myself is overwhelming, but the pain that comes with every small movement is even more so.

"See, wasn't that hard," Mine says as he opens the first aid box.

I grumble unhappily under my breath. It might not be hard for him, but it is for me. Modesty is very important for Aperite high-born ladies. If anyone heard that I might have appeared half-naked in front of a strange male, I would be shamed and ostracized.

"Hurry up then. It hurts."

"I know, sweetie. I'll work as fast as I can," he murmurs sweetly. His eyes meet mine, and he gives me a smile. Somehow, that works to make me less belligerent. I suppose I *am* being rather obtuse. If I want him to remove the bullet, then I have to make this concession.

His gaze dips to my chest—well, above my breasts, to be more precise. I look down too, grimacing when I see the ugly gunshot wound. It's right above my heart.

Redness stretches across a wide radius, all around a deep hole that gurgles out blood.

I may have been injured in battle before. But I've never had to withstand those injuries for more than a few moments before my flesh healed. To see this gnarly wound on myself is rather striking. As blood drips out of me with every movement of my chest—with every breath, really—the pain becomes even worse now that's accompanied by the visual stimulus.

Taking a metal instrument from the box, he leans closer to me—so much so his breath fans over my cheek.

"Uhm, what are you doing?" I whisper.

"Getting the bullet out. This will hurt."

"All right. I'm ready."

He stares me in the eye for a moment before he nods. Redirecting his attention to my wound, he inserts the metal instrument inside my wound.

I gasp. Not only is the metal cold against my feverish skin, but it's also painfully prodding inside my flesh.

"Shh," he murmurs. "I've got you."

"Faster," I say in between short, shallow breaths.

My hands look for something to hold on to—something to keep me grounded as my body feels about to launch itself off the bed in an attempt to escape this pain. With one hand, I grab the blanket underneath me. With the other, I grab the back of Mine's shirt, holding him next to me.

"Easy, easy," he whispers. "Almost there."

"It...hurts," I say groggily.

"There, darling. Almost there," he continues.

The instrument prods deeper inside my wound.

I squeeze my eyes shut.

"Done," Mine proclaims.

Slowly opening my eyes, I see him holding out the bullet fragment. It's smaller than I expected. Though it's coated in my blood, the material is golden and shiny.

"Now let's clean the wound," he continues. Dropping the bullet fragment on the table next to me, he then brings a clean towel that he douses in some disinfectant.

"Ouch," I hiss when the towel makes contact with my open wound.

"How long will it take before you heal?" Mine asks as he dabs the disinfectant all over my injury.

"I think a night? That's how long it took for my arm last time," I mention. Then I frown. "In fact..." I trail off as I peek under the bandage on my arm. "This one's nearly healed."

Mine smiles then.

"Good. I don't like to see you in pain."

Our eyes meet, and a flush envelops my cheeks.

"Uhm... Well—" I swallow uncomfortably. Why does he have to be so nice to me just when I was getting mad at him?

He chuckles and gets to work.

While I think of something to say in return, he cuts up a small piece of gauze, dips it in iodine, and presses it to my wound. Keeping it in place, he takes the bandage and rolls it all around my torso to secure the gauze.

"How's the pain?"

"More manageable now. Thank you."

"Good. Let me get you something to put on."

I rise from the bed, a little more wobbly than I care to admit. Mine grabs a long white shirt from his trunk.

"I'll help," he mentions as he slides the shirt over my head and carefully pulls my arms through the sleeves. The hem of the shirt almost reaches my knees, so I suppose now I'm pretty covered. But I still don't feel too comfortable having this much flesh on display. Perhaps no one will notice when I walk back to my dorm because it's dark out. Hopefully, my roommates will not notice either. Otherwise, that will start rumors.

I let out a deep sigh.

It seems that Aperion and Anthropa have much in common —both are ruled by stringent regulations and social mores. More than anything, both are ruled by gossip and hearsay.

"Can I borrow a coat, too?" I ask as I think better on it. I don't want to risk being the subject of gossip this early into my job. I've heard how the females in this world talk about "easy girls" and I don't want to be branded one.

"A coat?" He frowns. "Why? Are you cold? Do you need another sweater?" He's already rummaging through his trunk for more clothes to give me, which I must admit is rather sweet.

"No, I'm fine. I just need something to cover myself while I walk to my dorm."

He stops what he's doing. Slowly, he turns to me.

"You're not going anywhere," he states in a resolute voice, folding his arms across his chest.

"Yes, I am."

"No. You are not."

"What are you on about, Mine? I can't possibly stay here."

"Why not? You're injured. What if you bleed through the night and someone in the dorm sees? What if someone sees you walking alone across the base when you should have gone to sleep hours ago?"

"Well..." I trail off. He does have a point. "But I can't sleep here," I whisper. "It wouldn't be proper."

"I think we're past propriety, Minnie. Wouldn't you say so?" he asks with a lift of his brow.

"I suppose so." I sigh. "But there's only one bed." I point to the bed behind me. It's small, too. Not that I plan on sharing it with him. That's out of the question.

A shiver goes down my back as I fail to control my imagination and I picture us both on the same bed. He'd be behind me, holding on tightly to me and lending me his body heat throughout the night. His body would be flushed against mine, and with our size differences, he would easily cradle me in his arms. His breath would be in my hair, blowing onto my cheek—warm, sweet...intoxicating.

Eyes growing wide with shock, I shake myself.

"You will take the bed. You are the injured one, after all. I can sleep on the floor."

I glance at the unwelcoming floor. There's some kind of covering put on top of the ground, but it wouldn't be enough to stop the cold from seeping through. And it *is* cold at night. No matter how many blankets he were to put on the floor, he would still catch a chill.

"But it's so cold," I voice out my concern. "You will get sick. And you are human, Mine. A mere breeze can kill you," I point out squarely.

An amused grin pulls at his lips.

"A breeze will kill me? Ah, tiny darling, you really have that little faith in me?"

"Well, yes. You are human."

He blinks.

"That was a rhetorical question. You did not need to answer," he mutters drily.

"But it is the truth. Would you rather I lie to you? You

humans are so fragile. A little cold and you'll catch that dreadful illness. What was it? Consumerism?"

"You mean consumption," he corrects. "Though consumerism isn't a wrong assessment."

"Consumerism, consumption. Same thing. You'll catch that and then you'll be dead and who will help me defeat this greed demon?"

"I didn't know you valued my help so much," he drawls with a smile.

I shrug.

"You are my only ally here. Not only are you human and thus you have a better knowledge of this world, but you are also a part of the military. Given your superior rank, you have more freedoms than the average soldier, so that makes you quite a valuable asset," I tell him objectively.

I might have thrown a *little* tantrum a while ago, but even I must recognize that my chances of defeating the greed demon are much better with Mine by my side.

"Is that everything I'm good for?" he asks in a quiet voice. "If I weren't an asset to you in this fight, would you care whether I die or not?"

I regard him for a moment with narrowed eyes.

"Is this one of those rhetorical questions?"

"No. I would like an answer."

"No," I say with a shrug. "Why would I care whether a mortal lives or dies? It is your fate to die anyway. So what if you're marginally more good-looking than your sad human lot? You're still equally fragile and annoying."

"You think I'm good-looking?" He chuckles.

"Is that all you got from what I said? I also mentioned you are fragile and annoying, which you are, you know. May I remind you that I am now without my powers because you forced me to help you save those mortals?"

"I forced you? Minnie, Minnie. I did not realize you'd have a faulty memory—with you being such a superior immortal being."

I huff aloud at his implication.

"You guilted me into it. Same thing."

"I did not put a gun to your forehead and said, help me or I will kill you."

"You couldn't kill me," I fire back.

"So where is the coercion then? For that narrative to work, I'd need to have something over you. That you helped those mortals is solely because *you* wanted."

"I—" I clear my throat. "Back to the original topic. You cannot sleep on the ground or you will catch your death. Then I will be punished even more for interfering with your mortal fate."

"What do you suggest then? As you've noted, there is only one bed."

"Well..." I glance back at the bed. It's not too big. "I will allow you to sleep on the bed. But"—I put my hand up—"we will sleep on opposite ends."

He tilts his head to the side.

"Is that so?"

"It is the best solution. That way, it cannot be said that we are sharing a bed, since we are merely in each other's proximity. After all, I will remind you I am a respectable unmarried lady," I feel the need to remind him.

Though, perhaps I should be reminding *myself*. Wouldn't it be easier to dash back to my dorm and hide my injuries? The answer is...yes. But I blame my damn imagination for leading me astray. Otherwise, I wouldn't be so curious about semi-sharing a bed with him.

Damn it, Minerva! How low you've fallen if your greatest dream is to share a bed with a mortal.

I bow my head toward my own stupidity, yet I cannot find it in me to go against it.

Just this once, all right?

"As you say, Minnie. As you say," Mine replies.

He moves toward the bed and places one pillow at one end

and one at the other. Then he grabs another blanket so that we don't have to share one. Smart human.

When he's done making the bed, I claim my spot. Getting in bed, I pull the blanket over my body with my right hand, careful not to jolt my left shoulder where my injury is still very much pulsing with pain. Damn it. I'll likely have to sleep on one side only or on my back, which for someone who is quite the fussy sleeper that is going to be a nightmare.

I expect Mine is going to climb into his side of the bed, too, and my heart is in my throat as I wait for my imagination to become reality—well, close to it anyway.

But he doesn't.

Instead, he moves away from the bed and grabs onto the hem of his shirt, pulling it over his head. He doesn't seem to be in pain anymore, even though it's only been a few hours since I stitched him up. But maybe he has a better tolerance for pain. Alas, he must be used to it. His back is a tapestry of scars, some more prominent than others. It makes me wonder what he had to endure to remove that *illness* from his body.

Yet despite his scars, I can't help but appreciate his muscular form. He might be human, but he has such perfect proportions even an Aperite would be jealous.

A gasp slips past my lips when I note his hands going to the band of his pants.

"What are you doing?" I yelp.

He half-turns.

"Changing into my pajamas," he replies nonchalantly.

"B-b-but—"

"If this offends your feminine sensibilities, you're welcome to look away."

My eyes widen.

"You can also watch." He winks.

Cheeks flaming, I promptly turn away. My heartbeat echoes in my ears.

I hear the ruffling of clothes, and the temptation to look back is almost too much. In the end, my common sense prevails and I keep my gaze firmly on the wall. But that doesn't mean I'm not curious.

His footsteps indicate he's getting close. I take a deep breath and prepare myself.

"Does this pass muster?" He points to his outfit. He's wearing a pair of loose pants and a white shirt similar to the one he gave me.

I nod briskly. I'm still terribly flushed and I don't trust myself to speak—not coherently anyway.

He pulls his blanket aside and slides in the bed. Yet it's immediately noticeable that he's purposefully trying *not* to touch me. He keeps his body away from me, and despite his size, he takes the least amount of space.

"Good night, Minnie," he murmurs softly.

"Good night, Mine," I return the words. Though how can I sleep with a gunshot wound to the chest and a handsome male at my feet? What sane person would be able to sleep like that?

Mine, that's who.

In a matter of minutes, his breathing regulates until he's releasing soft, barely audible snores.

Great. Here I am, overthinking this entire situation and his maddening proximity, and he couldn't fall asleep faster.

I grumble some more to myself as my lashes start to feel heavy.

I don't know when exactly I fall asleep, but as sunlight streams inside the tent, I reluctantly open my eyes to see Mine is gone.

FOURTEEN

THE WIND BLOWS through the small opening in the tent, bringing with it a gust of cold air. I let out a shiver. It will never cease to amaze me how uncomfortable the cold can be.

As I blink, a form materializes in front of me.

Tommy. The young soldier.

"You must be Tommy," I greet him, glad I am properly clothed for visitors.

Perhaps Aperion should also fund a school for wandering ghosts so they know what the proper etiquette is—as in *not* to enter a place uninvited, especially when someone is in bed. Alas, he's young and confused. I will forgive him this once.

Keeping the blanket over my legs, I turn to get a better look at him.

He doesn't answer me. Glancing right and left, he appears to be searching for something.

"Tommy?"

At that, he finally looks at me.

"I'm glad you're all right," he mentions.

"Thank you. And thank you for the warning, too."

. . .

HE SHRUGS. "I didn't think you could see me. Not many people do."

"You're a ghost, Tommy. It's normal for people *not* to see you. But why did you not cross over when the messengers came for you?"

"I'm not done," he answers curtly. "Still have things to do." Entering deeper into the tent, he walks around, his attention seemingly far away from me.

"Where is the Major?" he asks.

"Mine?"

"No, mine."

"Yes. Mine."

"No. *Mine*. My Major," he adds, confused.

"That's what I said." I frown. "Mine."

"He's not *your* Major. You're a woman." He glares at me as if I committed the greatest faux pas.

I roll my eyes.

"Mine is his name, silly." I shake my head at him.

"No, it's not," the ghost replies.

"Yes. It is. He told me so himself," I add. "His middle name is Mine. But that's beside the point since I'm the only one allowed to use it," I tell him proudly.

The ghost narrows his eyes at me.

"What are you on about, woman?" He shakes his head at me before he releases a deep sigh. "I will wait for the Major to return."

He moves to the back of the tent and takes a seat at Mine's desk.

"What do you think you're doing?" Getting out of bed, I put on Mine's coat and glare at this daring ghost.

"I need to speak with him."

"Why? How do you even know he can see you?"

"Because he's spoken to me before."

"He...has?"

The boy nods.

"He told me he would help me send a message to my sweet-

heart back home. I've been thinking about what to say and..."
He swallows. "I think I'm ready now." He removes a crumpled
piece of paper from his pocket—surprising that a ghost can do
that. But then again, my specialty lies in demons not ghosts.

"I see..." I mumble awkwardly.

Silence ensues between us as we wait for Mine to return.
It's not on purpose, but what can I talk about with a ghost? The
ghost of a teenage boy at that, too.

Yet as I ruminate on our previous conversation, something
keeps niggling at my mind.

"What did you mean when you said Mine is not his middle
name?"

Tommy raises his gaze to look at me.

"It's not," he answers. "I trained under him. Everyone
knows his full name."

"And that is?"

"Lucian Valerìon de Vitry," he answers in a booming voice,
his tone performative. "The lads used to make fun of his name
all the time." He smiles. "Behind his back, of course."

"Of course," I echo feebly.

"I mean, that's the name of some royalty, is it not? It's not
that hard to think of some duke by the name of Lucian Valerìon
de Vitry." He laughs. "Even his mannerisms confirm that."

"His...mannerisms?" I ask tentatively.

"He never eats with the other soldiers. He never eats from
the cantina either."

I frown.

"Then what does he eat?"

He shrugs. "I don't know. But it's very unusual for someone
of his rank not to eat with his regimen."

"Maybe he doesn't like the food," I suggest. It's hard for me
to imagine that, though, since when I'm hungry, I'll eat just
about anything.

"That's not all. He's known for his insane standards for
flying. No one but him can fly his plane, and his crew must thoroughly wash before each mission. The plane, too, must be spot-

less or he won't take off. He's gotten into a lot of conflicts with the higher-ups over it, but somehow, he was never punished for insubordination when others would have been demoted and thrown in jail. Me and the lads wondered if that's because he has some lofty connections, you know."

I listen attentively, though I have no frame of reference to compare his behavior with. But if Tommy thinks it is so irregular, then maybe there's something to it?

"That's not to say the Major isn't a good guy. He's probably one of the nicest people on the base. He's just...odd," Tommy continues.

"Are you sure he doesn't have another middle name that you're not aware of? He assured me his middle name was Mine."

"If he does, I've never seen it on any official document," the boy answers. "Though gotta say, miss, Mine is an odd name, is it not? I've never heard of such a name before. Except..."

"Except?"

"Maybe he's sweet on you and he wanted you to call him like that...like an endearment, I s'pose."

I BLINK SLOWLY. "AN ENDEARMENT?"

"Yeah, like a claim that he's yours. I call my sweetheart keeper of my heart." His face suddenly drops. "I s'pose now I won't be able to do that anymore."

"I'm sorry, Tommy." I try to comfort the young ghost, though why, I cannot tell. This is the natural order of things. Mortals die and they are reborn. It is the cycle of life. "If you cross over, you might be able to find her again in another life," I suggest.

The odds are slim. Unless they are connected by a thread of fate, their connection will end in this lifetime. But seeing Tommy's ghostly face light up makes me wary of mentioning that one small detail.

"You mean I could be with her again, miss?"

"If you cross over. The more you delay the process, the more you'll mess with the order of things."

HE GRIMACES. "I just wanna give her one last note."

"I'm sure Min—er, Major Vitry will help with that."

"He's a kind man, Major Vitry." Tommy smiles wistfully. "Don't be too harsh on him. I'm sure he didn't mean to deceive you."

"Right," I mutter. The fact that even Tommy thinks he deceived me is telling enough. But is it true? Did M—Vitry deceive me? Did he actually lie about his name? Or could it be that it's something Tommy wouldn't know? I am not sure what to believe. On the one hand, I am very flattered he would share such a secret name with me. But on the other, if he did lie to me to make me call him *mine*, I would be very upset.

I purse my lips. Was Vitry mocking me? Laughing at me behind my back for falling for such a silly thing? I may not be good at this English language, but I would be insulted if he used that against me. And for what end? Is it like Tommy said, an endearment? I must confess I did find it a little odd that his name would be a possessive pronoun, but since I'm not familiar with the rules in this world, I couldn't contest it.

"He must be very taken with you since he's allowing you to sleep in his tent. He never does that."

"Never does what?" I narrow my eyes.

"He never mingles with the chicks. It's a running joke." He sobers up. "Of course not to his face."

"And why is it a joke?"

"Ah, I'm not sure this is fit for the ears of a miss," he adds in a shy voice. If he weren't a ghost, I'm sure he would have blushed.

"Tell me," I command him in a haughty voice.

How dare he pique my curiosity and then not satisfy it?

"Well"—he clears his throat—"we have parties. After every mission, we hit the town—the ones who make it back." His features twist in sadness. He probably realizes he's now one of the ones who did not make it back.

"And?"

"The Major would come with us but would only stay for a drink and then leave when everyone started chasing skirts."

"Chasing skirts?" I ask, not familiar with the term.

"Ladies. Chasing ladies."

"Oh, I see. Continue."

"That's it." He shrugs. "He always left, saying he already had a missus waiting for him."

"Who?" The question is out before I can think about it. Tommy's eyes widen at the vitriol in my voice. Then he smiles.

"He never said. He wouldn't be the first to have a sweetheart back home. But others decide to forget about that. An ocean apart and all that. Not me, though. My sweetheart is the only one for me." His face falls again.

Mi—Vitry has a sweetheart back home? He never mentioned anything of the sort to me. Not that he *should* have—we're only acquaintances, right? But then why do I feel an uncomfortable heat in my chest at the thought of him with another female? And why would he behave so carelessly with me if he had someone else?

He might not have been trying to *chase skirts* before, but the more I think about it, the more I realize he was most definitely trying to chase me.

What was his goal? Make me call him *mine*, invade my personal space, and follow me around until I gave in? Until he invaded my mind and all I could do was think about him, day and night?

My heart stops for a beat.

Oh, no. That's what I have *been* doing. He has scarcely left my mind since that cursed moment when we met. It's become even worse after we saw each other again.

Was this his purpose from the beginning? Make me lose my damn mind? Because I'm almost certain it worked. And if that wasn't enough, he clearly sought to do more. He even convinced me to sleep in the same bed as him! If anyone were to find out about that...

A shudder goes down my back.

He's been lying to me all along. And like a fool, I've been ignoring all my instincts about him. I should have known someone as good-looking and charming as him would be a shovel. To think I slept in the same bed as him... Oh, the horror. My virtue was one step away from being compromised. No, my entire *future* was one step away from being taken away from me.

Thank all the Primordials for giving me this chance to come to my senses and realize what Vitry has been doing. A little more time in his presence and I fear I would have made a terrible, terrible mistake.

"You really mean it?" Tommy asks after a moment "I can meet my missus again in another life?"

"Yes. But that means you must cross over as soon as possible."

He glances at the note in his hands.

"I tried to go back home. But for some reason, I can't go further than a hundred miles or so."

"You're probably tied to the area because it's the place you died," I comment. "And you're a young ghost. That's normal."

He nods slowly.

"How can I cross over then?"

I think for a moment. There's no magic word to call a messenger back. They are soulless, mechanical beings acting on strict orders. If they cannot retrieve a soul, they leave. But...

"When another person dies, you can follow the messenger that comes for that soul," I suggest.

That should work—*I think*. I should *know* this, yet we were never taught about the intricacies of a soul or what happens in irregular scenarios like Tommy's case. We were only taught the basics—mortal dies, soul is taken by a messenger; if not, by a collector later on. No textbook I read ever mentioned what happens if a soul decides to cross over on its own, *before* the collectors come looking for it.

"Thank you, miss. I will do that." He smiles.

I force myself to return the smile.

"You can wait for your Major here. I must leave."

He nods absentmindedly, already focused on his crumpled note as he mouths the words in the letter to himself.

I turn to leave, taking with me both the coat and *his* shirt. After all the lies he's been spouting, the least he can do is make it up to me with physical goods as payment.

The chilly air hits me in the face as I march forward toward my dorm.

My teeth clatter in my mouth, yet I find that it's not the low temperature that's making my body react thusly. It's a deep-seated sense of disappointment.

Despite our arguments, I truly thought Mi—Vitry was a good man, with good intentions. It's disappointing to realize that is not so. All along, he had duplicitous intentions with me.

That damn shovel!

He chose the wrong person to mess with.

My hands ball into fists and slowly, the initial upset gives way to anger.

How dare he?

Not only did he fool me into calling him *mine* just to mock me, but if he already has a sweetheart or whatever waiting for him, then what were his intentions with me? Not that I *wanted* him to have any intentions with me—of course not. Even if he were free and unattached, I would have refused his advances. But it's the mere intent behind his actions. He deceived me from the first, and like a damn fool, I believed everything he told me.

Yet there is one thing that bothers me more than the deceit.

He has a female. Somewhere out there, there is a female he calls his own. While I was calling him *mine*, he was calling another female *mine*.

I stop abruptly. Stomping my feet on the ground, I let out a few expletives.

Stop it, Minerva!

It doesn't matter that he has a female. It only matters that he tried to take advantage of me. That is the only thing I should focus my anger on.

I should have trusted my instincts when they were telling me he was bad news. And to think I took a damn bullet to the shoulder for him.

I should have let the scoundrel die! Or at least bear the brunt of the pain. It wouldn't have been what he deserves, but it would have been a start.

With that thought, I remember my injury. Moving my left arm around, I realize there's no more pain. It seems the wound healed after all.

Ah, the little things. But the lack of pain does little to make me feel better. In fact, all I'd like to do now is find Vitry and give him a taste of pain—show him I'm not the easy target he clearly thinks I am.

"Minnie! Where are you going?"

I swivel and come face-to-face with the object of my annoyance.

There he is, this damned Vitry, in all his handsome glory. Starched uniform, not one speck of dust anywhere on his clothes. His hair is swept to the side in a careful style. There's nothing out of place with him.

I glare at him, but all he does is smile.

Even his eyes smile—those damn green eyes.

"Why did you leave? I got you some donuts."

My stomach rumbles—the traitor.

This time, however, not even sweet, sugary donuts will sway me. I will not become a slave to my cravings.

"I do not want to be around shovels like you," I tell him angrily.

His lashes flutter. They're rather long lashes. For a male, of course. Not that I'm noticing. I'm only focusing on them because I'm secretly wishing some dust would enter his eyes so he would tear at the sight of me.

Yes, oh, yes! Now *that* would be rather marvelous.

Remember who you are, Minerva!

I am a goddess! A demon slayer. I'm not just some nurse he can charm with his smile, green eyes, and sweet donuts...

I'll show him!

"Are we back at that?" He sighs. "I told you I am not a rake."

"Oh, yes. You are. You will not fool me anymore, *Vitry*," I state emphatically as I take a step forward and poke my finger into his chest—hm, a very hard chest.

"VITRY?"

"I know Mine isn't your real name. Don't try to deny it."

He doesn't seem surprised at my accusation. He doesn't even blink an eye.

"I will not."

"So you admit it."

He shrugs.

"You... Did you have fun laughing at my expense?" I grit out.

"It was a lighthearted joke, Minnie."

"Don't call me that. You've lost your Minnie privileges."

"Come on, tiny darling. You know I would never laugh at your expense."

"Do I?" I narrow my eyes at him. "I don't think I do. As a matter of fact, I hardly know anything about you."

"You do—"

"What, that your name is *not* Mine?" I roll my eyes.

"It can be," he answers casually. "For you, it can be."

"What about that sweetheart of yours?"

He tilts his head to the side, frowning.

"Sweetheart?"

"Don't try to lie. I know you have a female. Tommy told me."

His features darken.

"And what did he tell you?" he asks in a low, dangerous voice.

"T-that you told everyone you have a female waiting for you. So don't even try to charm me with your words since I don't believe anything that comes out of your mouth anymore. And from now on"—I pause and straighten my back—"I will actually call you *Notmine*."

His eyes widen.

"Have a bad day, *Notmine*. I hope you"—I try to think of something quick—"trip and land in a pile of trash. At least then you'll be amongst your own."

Okay, not my best comeback, but it will have to do. I add a huff for good measure and stomp away from him.

My heart pounds in my chest as adrenaline clogs my veins.

"Minnie, wait!"

I walk faster.

I may have managed to keep my wits about me the first time, but I'm not sure I will be able to do it the second time.

Vitry doesn't seem to take a hint, though. Where I go, he follows.

Since I can't go to the dorm with him on my trail, I walk around in circles, hoping he'd get tired.

He doesn't.

"Minnie, let's talk, all right?"

I don't answer.

"Minnie, please. Don't be like this. I can explain everything."

Right. As if I'd fall for that.

I keep walking.

After some thirty-forty minutes of walking around in circles, I'm starting to get tired. Vitry has not given up, nor has he stopped calling out my name and all but begging me to give him a chance to explain himself.

Taking a deep breath, I stop.

"Minnie..."

"This won't work," I tell him before he has the opportunity to say anything. "We need to resolve this."

"Resolve this...how?"

"There's too much tension between us."

"Good on you to notice." He smirks.

I shoot him an annoyed look.

"Seeing as how I'm stuck here for two more months, I will have no choice but to keep seeing you."

"Indeed."

"We should do it. Get rid of the tension once and for all," I tell him confidently.

He opens his mouth and closes it. Clearing his throat, he averts his gaze.

"By doing it, you mean…"

"Let out the steam. Get whatever this is"—I wave between the two of us—"out of our systems once and for all."

He swallows hard. His body is tense and he appears uncomfortable.

He's not afraid, is he?

"You want to do it?" he repeats.

"That's what I said." Why is he so slow?

"Here? Now?"

"Of course not here." I groan. Don't tell me this is his first time? "We need a more private setting."

"Private setting," he mumbles, his cheeks slightly redder than before.

He rolls back his shoulders and seemingly infuses more confidence into his stance.

"Are you sure?" he asks, though he does not dare meet my eyes.

Aha! I was right. He *is* afraid.

"Very," I confirm. "Don't tell me you're scared."

He wets his lips and the action draws my attention to his mouth. His lips are rather…nice. I find myself licking my own in response.

"I'm not scared," he replies, though I can detect his fake bravado seeping through. "It's just that…" He mumbles something under his breath. If only I had my normal hearing back, I would have been able to understand what he said. As it stands, I must get closer to him to hear.

"What was that?" I ask.

He gulps down. His Adam's apple—that's what humans call that apparatus, no?—bobs up and down, suggesting his uncertainty. He may maintain that he is not scared as much he wants, but his body language says otherwise.

I knew it! I might be powerless in my current form, but I am still a goddess, while he is a mere mortal. He is right to be afraid. He should be terrified.

Although I do not have my usual powers, I have not forgotten centuries of hand-to-hand combat. I am confident I can take him on—*and* win.

"I've never done it before," he says in a low voice, his gaze still focused someplace else.

"You've never..."

He nods.

That's odd. At his age and level of experience, never mind rank, I would have expected him to be experienced.

"Then I will be your first," I declare. "Don't worry. I'll teach you well." I pat him on the back and wink at him.

He whips his gaze to me. His entire body tenses, and it's almost as if his eyes could see right through me.

"And you've done this before?" There's an edge to his voice that wasn't there before. Gone is the almost stuttering, shy male, now replaced with a dark and foreboding one.

Oh, I see. He realized that letting me see his fear will not aid him in this case, so he's now trying to intimidate me. He probably thinks that as a male he has an advantage over me because he's bigger and stronger.

Well, I'm faster. *And* I have thousands of years of experience under my belt.

"Of course. I've done it many times before."

His eyes flash at me. He probably did not expect me to be so experienced. I may look small and innocent, but I will show him that appearances deceive.

"How many times?"

"Do you think I counted?" I roll my eyes at him.

"How many men?" He takes a step toward me, intruding into my personal space.

"Seriously, Vitry. I don't know. I lost count. I've had thousands of years of practice, all right?"

He stares at me. For moments on end, he stares at me.

"Are you going to back out now? If you're too scared, you just have to say so and—"

"We'll do it," he declares through clenched teeth. "Come," he says and grabs my wrist, dragging me in the direction of his tent.

Realizing his intention, I stop him.

"No, no, no. Your tent won't work."

He frowns at me.

"It's too small. I need somewhere bigger."

"Somewhere bigger?" he repeats, his voice holding a trace of danger.

I nod.

"Otherwise, we'll ruin your stuff. Then you won't have a bed to sleep in or a desk to work at."

"A bed... A desk..." He echoes.

"I'm looking out for you," I assure him. "I know myself and my skills. It will get rowdy."

"Rowdy..." He swallows. His hand is balled into a fist, his veins protruding through his flesh almost as if they're about to pop open. Oh, he's scared, isn't he?

"Let's go to that abandoned barn. No one will bother us there. And I don't want anyone to see us either. It won't be good for my reputation."

He doesn't speak anymore. He lets me lead him to the barn, all the while staring into empty space. It's almost as if he's checked out of the situation, and as we get closer to the barn, I start having second thoughts.

He seems truly terrified.

Did he only agree to do it so he wouldn't lose face? Is it about some manly pride?

Based on his body language, he looks as though he's heading to his execution.

"I won't kill you." I feel the need to assure him. "I cannot kill humans."

His lip twitches.

"So you'll just fuck me to an inch of my life, is that it?" He lets out a dry laugh.

So he knows I am the stronger of the two.

"I'll be as gentle as I can," I tell him. Though considering his deceit, I don't know *how* gentle I can be.

"Lucky me," he mutters under his breath.

We arrive at the barn and manage to sneak inside without anyone seeing us. The place is empty and quite large. It will be the perfect location to finally put this—whatever there is between us—to rest.

The wooden door creaks as it closes behind us and I take a few steps forward, assessing the angles of the barn and committing them to mind.

"All right, now—" I start, ready to set the rules.

But as I turn to face him, my mouth drops open in shock.

His coat is already on the floor and he's now aggressively pulling at his shirt, all but ripping the buttons in his attempt to get it off.

"W-what are you doing?" I ask.

"What do you think I'm doing?" he counters, the same twitch in his jaw as before. His muscles cord and ripple with every movement, his veins more prominent than before. Given his tense state, I can see them on his torso too. Running up his chest and neck and...

"You don't need to take your clothes off for it," I add weakly.

He glares at me.

"Is that how you've done it in the past? Clothed?" He pulls the white shirt off and throws it to the side.

"O-of course," I mutter, taking a step back.

How are the roles reversed now and *I* am the one tense and afraid?

My eyes widen even more when he reaches for his belt. He undoes it, then pulls down the zipper of his pants and...

"Vitry!" I call out, incensed. "What the hell are you doing?"

"What you wanted me to do," he replies through gritted teeth.

Pulling on the belt, he almost rips through the loops. He's so angry, it's like he's an entirely different person.

He pulls his pants down and aggressively pushes them to the side with his feet. He's now bare-chested and wearing only his briefs.

My breathing constricts, and I feel myself getting lightheaded.

"Your turn." He motions to me.

"M-me?"

"Yes, you. Clothes off, Minerva," he commands. It's the first time he's used my full name, and I'm not sure I like it. There's so much aggression rolling off him, it's as if *I* did something wrong, not him.

"I will only take my coat off," I tell him and shrug it off. But unlike him, I place it carefully to the side.

He shrugs. "Suit yourself."

Striding toward me, it takes me a moment to realize that *it* is happening.

We're doing this.

I take a deep breath and count the seconds until he's close enough.

"After this, you will tell me the name of every single male that—"

Before he can finish his sentence, I'm on him. My fist connects with the center of his face, hitting him in the nose.

It...hurts.

"Auch," I cry out, jumping back and cradling my fist to my chest.

"What the fuck, Minnie? What was that for?"

Blood spurts from his nose, dripping down his chin and chest in thick rivulets.

Despite my lack of powers, that was a pretty good punch, wasn't it? But it was so damn painful. I don't know if I can use the same fist to hit him again.

While he's holding on to his nose and muttering a string of curses, I take advantage of his distraction to move to his side.

With my right fist retired, I use my elbow to hit him between his ribs.

Just as I expected, he doesn't see my attack coming, and in no time, he's gasping for breath.

"Come at me, Vitry. I don't want this to be one-sided."

In between wheezing and blinking back tears, he stares at me in confusion.

"What are you talking about?"

"You did deceive me, and it is my right to get revenge, but I am not so cruel as to attack a defenseless man. So come at me," I say and motion with my hand.

I move my right foot forward while keeping the left behind, assuming a fighting stance.

Vitry is still staring at me. He makes no effort to move. He's just standing there, frozen, his blood still pouring down his face.

"Come at me, Vitry! I know it's your first time, but have some courage! I promised I wouldn't kill you. So come, hit me."

"What?"

"I said hit me! Come on!"

He blinks.

Then instead of charging at me, he does something wholly unexpected.

He crashes to the ground, rolling onto his back and releasing a loud, piercing laugh.

Now it's my turn to stare at him in confusion.

He laughs and laughs and laughs until tears are coursing down his cheeks, mixing with the blood from before. He laughs so much, he's barely breathing.

I clench my fists.

I should have been the one making him cry just as I should have been the one to stop his breathing, but not like *this*. Why does it feel as though he's mocking me again?

"Are you laughing at me?" I demand, stomping my foot against the gravelly floor.

He shakes his head, unable to speak due to his persisting fit of laughter.

His amusement only serves to make *me* angrier.

"Vitry!" I shout.

"I'm not laughing at you, tiny darling. Promise," he chokes out. "I'm laughing at myself."

I'm still confused.

"You wanted to do *it*. It being..."

"Fight it out, of course," I answer immediately.

And the laughter ensues again.

FIFTEEN

ANGER DRUMS IN MY VEINS. How dare he laugh at me? It wasn't enough that he fooled me for *days*? Now he has to throw it into my face that not only am I entirely gullible but also a laughingstock?

"Stop. Laughing," I grit out.

He's on his back, rolling around almost naked. And no matter how many times I tell him to cease, he does no such thing.

Perhaps my punch did not do much, despite the blood. No worries. I shall remedy that.

Striding to him, I gather momentum to hit him again. But just as my fist is about to connect with his face, he grabs it with surprising ease. He encases my fist in his palm, and with his other hand, he pulls me toward him. Losing my balance, I topple forward and land on top of him. As if that's not enough of an ignominy, he rolls us over until I am on my back and he is atop me, looming over me.

My breath is knocked out of my lungs, but it is not a result of an external force, rather an internal one. One I am trying my hardest to ignore that it exists.

His features are no longer full of amusement. They're tense. Or, rather, *intense*.

"What do you think—" I don't get a chance to make my outrage known because he shushes me by placing his hand over my mouth.

My words are muffled, and soon I realize it is in vain to even speak since he clearly does not want to listen to me.

Yet the position we currently find ourselves in is not lost on me. His body is nestled snugly between my legs. I am wearing a flimsy shirt for a dress. He's wearing next to nothing. I may not have too much knowledge of carnal matters, but even I can tell this is how everything starts—whether I want it or not.

He is aware of this conundrum, too. A drop of sweat mars his brow as he pulls himself back so he's not touching me so intimately, but he's not completely off me either.

"You will listen to me now, Minnie."

I glare at him. As if I have a choice in the matter.

"I did not deceive you. Mine is the only name I wish to hear from your lips where I'm concerned."

As if I'm ever going to call him that again.

"I do not have a female, as you wrongly assumed. I don't know what you think you heard, but there is no other female in my life aside from you."

I blink. What am I supposed to do with that information?

"I have no interest in any other female. Never had before, and I will never have in the future. Not even when my mortal mind fails to remember the past. Not even then," he continues, an odd cadence to his tone.

Slowly, he removes his hand from my mouth.

"Do you understand what I'm saying?" he asks, his eyes boring into mine.

I stare at him.

"You like males?"

His eyes widen for a moment before he releases a loud sigh.

"Is that all you understood from what I said?" he asks in a hopeless tone.

"You want me to call you Mine, which I will not, of course,

since it is *not* your name. And you're assuring me you have no female and that you are not interested in any female."

He presses his lips together.

"Any *other* female."

"Other than who?"

"You, you silly creature. Other than you."

I frown.

"But that's impossible," I whisper.

"I assure you it is quite possible," he mutters drily.

"You cannot be interested in me. You're mortal! I am *immortal*. Impossible, see?"

"Minnie..."

"All this time... I was right, wasn't I? You're a shovel and you were trying to steal my virtue," I grit out and push against his chest in an attempt to get him off me.

He remains steadfast.

"Get off me!"

"You are once more misunderstanding me," he adds with a sigh, grabbing my flailing arms and restraining me. "I am not trying to steal your virtue, Minnie. I am trying to steal your heart, damn it!"

I STOP MOVING. "YOU...WHAT?"

"Haven't I managed it? Just a little?"

"You aren't serious, are you?" I whisper.

For some reason, his savage expression and the way he's holding me, so close yet too far, makes my heart skip a beat. It's cold outside, but with him on top of me, the cold fades away until there's only a deep sense of comfort as if I'd like nothing more than snuggle in his embrace.

My eyes widen at my train of thought.

I didn't just... I didn't think of him like that, did I?

"Oh, trust me, Minnie. I am *very* serious. You are the only female I've *ever* wanted. No other. Not here, not now, and not for an eternity to come."

"I..." I lick my lips. "I don't know what you want me to say to that."

"The truth would be nice." He smiles, showcasing his perfect teeth.

"The truth is that I am an ice deity and you are a human soldier," I start tentatively. His features tense. "Even if I, hypothetically, returned your regard, it's impossible between us. It's forbidden for my kind to get involved with your kind. It's forbidden for me to even be alone with a male, never mind like this, touching, and—"

"And?"

A shiver goes down my back.

"It's impossible, Lucien."

He seems surprised at my using his first name. It must be the first time I have done so. It feels foreign on my tongue, odd... For some reason, I cannot reconcile that name with the man before me.

"Yet here we are. Theoretically impossible but made possible by our own hands," he murmurs. He brings his hand to my cheek, caressing me lightly. The calluses on his palm are abrasive against my skin, but it's the type of pain that reminds me I'm alive—the type of touch that awakens something within me. Something that should have forever lain dormant.

"And this moment might end up costing me my entire future."

I cover his hand with mine and pull it aside. He stops me.

"I won't let it." He shakes his head.

"What can you do?" I let out a dry laugh.

"More than you can imagine, Minnie." He stares at me, the green in his eyes deepening. "I can love you."

Thud. Thud. Thud.

My heartbeats echo in my ears, as does another sound.

Love. The word *love* is on repeat in my mind, becoming louder and louder until it claims every corner of my consciousness.

Love. What *is* love?

I know *of* it. But I do not know *it*.

I love my brother. I love my parents—to an extent. But love, the type of love that he is implying, is foreign to me.

"What is love?" I ask in a small voice. At his confused expression, I rephrase my question. "How does one...love?"

Slowly, the corners of his mouth tip up until a brilliant smile claims his lips.

"I will teach you."

"I—"

"Give me the remaining time you have left in this world. If by the end of your exile I do not teach you how to love, you may leave and never look back."

"What?"

"Give me until your powers come back. You're here anyway."

"On a mission," I protest. "I must vanquish the greed demon."

"And we will. Together. I would never allow such evil to hurt innocents."

"But—"

"Two months, Minnie. Give me two months. If I cannot teach you how to love, you may leave and forget all about me and your time here."

"But how could I forget if anything happens and I—"

"I will not touch you," he interrupts. "Let me prove to you that I am not after your virtue. Only your heart."

"You're touching me now," I whisper.

"I will not touch you...inappropriately. Unless you ask for it." He winks. "You have my vow."

I bite on my lip as I gaze into his eyes. The mere fact that I am contemplating this is madness. Yet every time I attempt to refuse, to tell him that what he proposes is insanity, my throat clogs up until no sound comes out.

Would it be so bad to admit to myself that I'm...curious?

I am not indifferent to this male. That much I know. Yet do I dare accept his challenge? The risks are enormous. If anyone should catch me, the entire Aperion would shun me—perhaps even sentence me to death. The mere idea of the death of an immortal should make me say a resounding no.

But I don't.

I don't say no. I don't say yes.

I just lie there, at his mercy. My arms have fallen by my sides. His palm still cups my cheek, his body angled toward me.

If he so wished, he could easily have his way with me. If he so wished, he could ruin me. And to my great dismay, I might even...let him.

"Two months. But it better *not* interfere with our mission."

"Of course not, tiny darling."

"But I will *not* call you mine."

"Yet."

He leans forward and lays his lips on my forehead, lingering for two seconds before rolling entirely off me. He lands on his back next to me, and though I expect he must be cold dressed only in his underwear, he doesn't make any attempt to gather his clothes and dress. He lies there, next to me. His hand reaches out tentatively for my own, threading his fingers through mine.

"Don't push your luck," I grumble. I make no attempt to remove my hand from his. It's...comfortable.

"Fine, fine." He sighs.

Now it's my turn to smile.

"You have given me a nickname. Perhaps it's only fair I do the same to you."

He bristles. "What? Luc? Luke?" He rolls his eyes.

I scrunch my nose in distaste. "I don't like that."

"Welcome to the club. I happen to hate my name, too."

"Why?"

He grimaces. "Let's say I have bad memories with the name *Lucien*."

"That is odd," I note. "Is that why you did not want me to call you that way?"

He nods.

"What about Vitry?"

"Vitry is fine, but it's so...impersonal. Everyone calls me Vitry. And you're not everyone." His head turns to the side, and though our hands are linked together, the moment his gaze collides with mine, an unusual warmth washes over me.

"Your *actual* middle name is Valerìon, no?"

He stares at me, wide-eyed. "How did you find that out?"

"The same way I found out your middle name isn't *Mine*."

He nods, though he doesn't seem very pleased about it.

"I am surprised you don't go by that name. It is a very fine name," I add reluctantly.

"Is it?" he asks slowly, carefully.

"One of the greatest Aperite Supremes went by the name of Valerìon. It is a highly regarded name in Aperion."

He grunts.

"I can call you tha—"

"No," he interrupts me. "Only my parents call me by that name."

I frown and await further clarification, but he doesn't seem inclined to explain himself.

"Val?"

He shakes his head.

"Vally?"

"God, no," he grumbles.

"You're impossible."

He lets out a frustrated sigh.

"Can't you see, Minnie? I wanted you to call me something no one's ever called me before." He pauses. "Mine."

A blush stains my cheeks. Perhaps I am too gullible because I did not realize what the name meant from the beginning, but now that I know... I cannot *unknow* it. And that makes me acutely aware of him as...mine.

"It's not proper," I mutter in feigned annoyance. Oh, it is so far removed from proper, I should have seen the red flags from the beginning. Perhaps to a degree I did not *want* to see them. And that is my failing that I will have to reckon with at some point.

"When will it be proper then?"

"Only if you were my mate."

"I will wait then," he utters with such confidence I'm certain my punch must have addled his mind.

"You might wait forever." I roll my eyes at him.

"Forever doesn't seem that long if the prize that awaits me at the end is *you*."

I flush a deeper red. A frisson goes down my back and I cannot prevent my heart from doing a somersault in my chest at hearing his words.

Is it suddenly *too* hot in here?

Because I feel rather warm. And fuzzy. And I'm almost certain there are some winged beings flapping around in my stomach.

Oh my, I think I'm about to be sick...

"What about Rìon?" I ask suddenly in an attempt to change the topic—and hope that I will not get sick and embarrass myself further.

He opens his mouth and I know he's about to rebuke me again, but as the seconds trickle down, no sound comes out.

"That is not a bad nickname," he eventually accedes. "Though it does not feel my own."

"I agree. In High Aperite, Rìon means the loyal one. It remains to be seen if you will live up to it."

The corners of his lips tip up.

"Is that a challenge, Minnie?"

I shrug.

"Is it? I suppose we shall see. You have two months to live up to it."

"If only you knew..." he muses quietly, shaking his head as a wistful smile pulls at his lips.

"If I knew what?"

"It doesn't matter. Two months. I will do my best to teach you *everything* about love."

"Well, not *everything*," I add in a low voice. Wetting my lips, I continue, "Nothing physical must occur between us. I mean it.

You do not realize how strict my world is about chastity. If there is even the smallest doubt that I may have let a male touch me..." I gulp down. "I will not only be shunned, but I may even be imprisoned for it."

"I vowed to you, Minnie. I will only ever touch you if you ask for it."

I nod. His tone appears to be truthful, though what do I know? I've been fooled before. I may be fooled again. Yet if he truly wanted to do something to me, it would be quite easy to do it now. Nothing could stop him if he meant to harm me.

Yet despite the fact that I am now more vulnerable than I have ever been in my life, I do not feel threatened. In fact, the only threat comes from within me, from my impure thoughts.

"There is one thing I am unsure of, though," I start. Turning onto my side to get a better look at him, I place my hands under my head. "Why were you laughing at me?"

His eyes widen. A deep flush goes up his neck until his entire face is red. He averts his gaze, glancing at the ceiling of the barn as he fidgets with his hands.

"Well..." He takes a deep breath. "When you said you wanted to *do it*, that you wanted to *let out the steam*, I thought..."

"You thought?" I frown.

"That is a euphemism in my world for sex."

"Sex..." I repeat numbly. "You thought I wanted to mate with you?" My eyes bulge out in shock.

He tenses, and he shifts around, clearly as uncomfortable as I feel now.

"You mentioned breaking the bed and the desk, and..." He closes his eyes. "Let's just say my imagination got the best of me, all right? It's all my fault for misunderstanding."

He stands up, walks to where he left his clothes, and picks them up.

"No, no. Wait a moment. You can't just say something like that and then walk off. What do you mean by breaking the bed?" I blink. "And if you thought we were going to m-mate, then you also thought that..." My mouth drops open in shock as I replay our conversation. I'd proudly boasted about my experience and the fact that I'd done this many, many times before.

"It doesn't matter now, Minnie," he says in a defeated voice, unwilling to meet my outraged gaze.

"You thought I'd mated with scores of males? That I—"

HE SIGHS. "I am now aware that is not true."

"Of course it's not true! I've never so much as held a male's hand!"

He raises a brow at me.

"Until now," I mutter under my breath. "Nevertheless, how could you misunderstand me like this?"

"Clearly, my head is in the gutter where you're concerned, Minnie." He lets out a derisive chuckle. "To think I was ready to murder every single one of those males you spoke of—"

"Well, you cannot, seeing that I *already* killed them. Really, Mine, you're not doing much to prove me that you are *not* a shovel." The word mine slips out before I can stop myself.

Damn it.

Though I must confess that neither Rìon nor Vitry hold as much appeal as Mine. After all, to me, he *is* Mine...

"Rake," he corrects.

"Whatever." I wave my hand. "How is my virtue supposed to be safe with you when the first thing you thought of was that this was an invitation to mate, not to fight?"

He has the decency to look thoroughly chastised.

"How can I be a rake, Minnie, when yours is the only hand I've ever held, too?" His voice is low, gravelly.

The question takes me by surprise, and I'm reminded of the fact he said he's never done it before, *it* being mating. So he...

"Of course you have not," I huff aloud. "And that is the only reason I am allowing you to court me. If you had so much as looked at another female, I would have never accepted this bargain of yours."

"So I am allowed to court you?" He quirks a brow.

I avoid answering the question directly. Instead, I add, "But be warned that I do expect donuts daily if you want to remain in my good graces."

He smiles.

"Ah, you're such a gem, Minnie. Don't ever change."

"Why would I?" I narrow my eyes at him. "I take it you agree to supply me with donuts?"

"Anything you wish," he says and inclines his head.

I nod. While he's getting dressed, I pick up my coat from the ground and put it on—well, his coat, but I have now claimed it for my own.

But as I head for the exit, Mine stops me. Ugh, I need to stop thinking of him as *Mine*. It's not his name! Yet it's harder said than done... I should at least not utter it aloud. Not when I know how much he would gloat at it.

"Where are you going?" he asks, placing himself in front of me.

"Back to the dorm, of course. I still have a job to do and I must change into my uniform."

He gives me a dazzling smile.

"You will be happy to know that I have spoken to your supervisor and you will not need to return to your station."

"W-what?"

"From today onwards, you are my personal nurse."

"Your...personal nurse?" I repeat, still in shock.

"Indeed. It will be much easier to go about vanquishing that demon if you don't have to report to work daily." Under his breath, he also adds, "And you won't be treating other men, either."

"But, Mine!" I protest. If I could kick myself, I would since this is the second time I'm calling him Mine when I should not. "I need this job!"

"You are still employed. But your only charge from now on is *me*. So you will not be required to room at the dorms, either. In fact, I've spoken with my own supervisor and he's agreed to allow me to move into one of the empty sheds at base. You will, of course, move in with me as my live-in nurse."

I stare at him.

"Your live-in nurse?" I sputter.

"You will still get paid, and you will get all the perks you had as a nurse. You should be happy you now have so much more freedom and—"

Before he can finish his words, I kick him in the leg.

"What is wrong with you? How could you arrange for something so important without my permission?"

"But I thought you would be pleased..." He blinks.

"Pleased? Pleased?" I repeat in outrage. "Why would I be pleased about living with *you*?"

"Because you will have more freedom of movement, and since I know what you are, you won't have to hide and—"

"You are impossible," I cry out. "Males," I muter under my breath. Though I'd like nothing more than to rage at him for not even consulting me, I have to admit that his reasoning is not wrong. I will need more freedom of movement if I am to defeat this demon, and he *is* the only one who knows my true identity and purpose of being here. I suppose for that reason, my new job may have its perks.

But to live *with* him? Did he not understand anything from what I said to him? How can I live with a male? One who's declared his intentions toward me at that, too?

"I promise I will behave, Minnie. There will be separate beds, and I will ensure you have your privacy," he continues as if he doesn't see anything wrong with what he did.

"So I get absolutely no say in this, do I?" I release a defeated sigh after another moment of pondering his words.

Tommy must have been onto something when he said that Mine must have a lot of connections. Who else would have managed to do something like this? I've never heard of a private nurse before just like I've never heard of a Major this influential.

"It's already done," he replies smoothly. "So now that we've put this entire debacle behind us, would you like to come with me to see our new shed?"

Our. He said *our*.

A tiny sliver of excitement goes through me, but I temper it.

"Fine," I mutter. "But remember. The mission comes first. Everything else is second. Is that clear?"

"Of course," he agrees easily. Far too easily. "Who said demon hunting and courting don't go hand in hand?"

SIXTEEN

BY THE TIME the new shed is ready for us to move in—three days later, to be more precise—the greed demon has become stronger. The atmosphere at the base has changed, too. There's a heavy undercurrent, an invisible tension that has formed between people due to the overwhelming effect of *greed*.

Although the manifestations of greed are most evident when it comes to the desire to own physical objects, there is a strong indication that the most sought-after thing on the base is power. And that has caused quite a few conflicts between soldiers and their superiors.

Alas, as I have been observing these changes, I have been unable to come up with a way to defeat the demon. The usual blessed items I've managed to find do not work on it, and every time the demon sees me or Mine, he just...laughs.

I ball my hands into fists.

Have I really become a demon's laughingstock?

Unacceptable.

"Does this not please you?" Mine asks when he sees me frowning.

"It's fine. But you must keep to your side of the shed."

At my request, he'd installed a curtain in the middle of the room to divide it in two. This way, our sleeping arrangements are separate and I don't have to constantly think about whether he will get an extra eyeful of naked flesh.

The shed is not too large. I believe in human size it is about twenty square meters. That means I have ten, and Mine has ten.

Each half has one small bed, a chest of drawers, and a chair. His side has his desk and his many possessions. Since I don't have much, my side is rather...bare.

But the best thing about this shed is that it is warm. I have come to appreciate warmth far too much considering I'm supposed to be made of ice.

Mine smirks.

"I promised I would behave."

"So you should. Otherwise, I will make your life a living hell," I warn.

"Really?"

I nod.

"Humans need sleep. I will not let you sleep until you become crazed with sleep deprivation. I have heard it is a tactic of war and I've decided to borrow it—should you *not* behave, of course," I tell him squarely.

His only response is to laugh.

I frown.

Once more, he shows that he is not scared of me. Even after I broke his nose—though it does appear to have healed quite well—he still won't take me seriously.

"Stop. Laughing," I grit out.

"You are amusing." He shrugs. "I have not laughed much in my life, so think of this as me catching up."

"I am not sure how I feel about being the source of your amusement."

"Good. You should feel good."

I narrow my eyes at him.

"It makes you unique since not much else can make me laugh," he adds.

Well...that changes things. I nod, doing my best not to show my pleasure at his words. He does not need such an ego stroking.

I huff aloud and move to *my* side of the shed, quietly inspecting that everything is in place. I may not have too many items, but I happen to cherish the ones I have. Particularly the pretty dresses I bought with my allowance money—back when I had some. I kept them, though perhaps I could have sold them to buy some food. But I couldn't find it in me to part with them and I did not think that with war raging people would be clamoring to buy pretty clothes.

Two of the dresses, I have still not worn. They are far too fancy for walking around the base. But they will not go to waste. I plan to take them with me when I return to Aperion.

"You arranged everything nicely," I add approvingly as I move around the shed, inspecting every little corner.

I'd offered to do my side, but Mine had insisted that he can do everything. In fact, he'd made me promise not to come inside until he'd had the time to arrange everything. His side, too, is neat and organized, with all his clothes folded to perfection and laid in his chest of drawers. I have never heard of a neat male before, but what do I know? This is my first time sharing such close quarters with a male.

"I am glad you approve." He inclines his head. "The bathroom is in the back. Let me show you."

I frown and follow him. He passes through my side of the shed and opens a door that I didn't realize was functional. The bathroom is small. There is a toilet and something resembling a mix between a bath and a shower, though considering we are on a military base where tens of people share *one* bathroom, I cannot complain. Once more, I'm reminded of Mine's influence.

All the other soldiers shower in a common area while he gets to have a personal bathroom. Not even all the higher-ups get this type of treatment.

Are his parents very rich? Is he, like Tommy said, royalty?

But of course he must be *something* special. Otherwise, I—a goddess—would not have deigned to allow him to court me. It stands to reason that there must be something special about him.

"We should discuss the demon situation now," I tell him as he closes the door to the bathroom.

There is still the small issue that to get to the bathroom he must cross *my* side of the shed, but I suppose we can set the rules about that later. Now, the most important thing is the demon.

Mine smiles.

"Here"—he goes to his desk and removes a small vial from the drawer—"I managed to get this."

I move closer to get a better look.

It is a vial the size of my palm, and it is only half-full.

"What is it?"

"Holy water."

"We've already tried that and it did not work," I remark drily.

"This is *special* holy water. Straight from the Vatican."

"The Vatican?" I frown. I think I might have heard the term before, but I do not know what it means.

"The highest Church authority. It should work better, no?"

I shake my head and sigh.

"There is no such thing as *better* holy water. The blessing chant used on it is the same."

His face falls.

"I spent a fortune on it, though," he mutters under his breath.

"A fortune?"

"Never mind." He chucks the vial back in his drawer. "If holy water blessed by the pope himself won't work, then what will?"

"Who is this pope?"

"The head of the Church," Mine explains. "He resides in the Vatican."

"I have never heard of him. He must not be very good then."

Mine blinks. "What?"

"I would have heard of such a person if he were important enough to the fight against demons. But I was not briefed about any pope or Vatican. That means they are useless."

"Right. Well, if the pope and the Vatican are useless, then what *is* useful?"

"I don't know," I reluctantly agree.

Letting out a loud sigh, I take a seat on the bed and fist the material of my skirt.

"The special division is the only one who'd know how to deal with a greed demon. This type of literature was not in my curriculum."

"Then where can we find that type of literature?"

"Aperion." I take a deep breath. "I wasn't planning on going back anytime soon, but I might have to."

"What do you mean?" He frowns.

"The demon is getting stronger. Every single day, he's one step closer to gaining a physical body. Once he's no longer reliant on Holloway, there's no telling what he might do. The military base is only the beginning."

"But surely there are other ways—"

"No." I shake my head. "I've tried to make contact with my brother again, but he's done something to block me from accessing his sigil. I can't contact anyone else to ask for help because I don't have any spiritual energy left. With how fast the demon is getting stronger, I *must* go back and notify the special division."

There is also the fact that not only will I not get a commendation if I don't do my best to stop the demon, but I might even get punished for not trying hard enough to stop him—or at least aid those who *can* stop him.

It would become negligence on my part, and that is punishable under both the Aperite law and the military one. I would be getting two sentences. And though they might help me avoid a match with that clown, it will also ruin my professional reputation—so much so I might never be allowed to fight demons again.

That is simply unacceptable.

"What happens if you go back without your powers?" Mine asks.

I startle. I hadn't thought about that.

"It would be best if it's not found out," I add slowly as I consider the issue. If my parents find out I'm powerless, they will certainly lock me away someplace until the wedding. The clown himself might decide to pay me a visit and teach me a lesson for the way I publicly embarrassed him last time. And the other warriors...they would laugh at me.

And I hate it when people laugh at me.

Damn it! I'll get in trouble if people find out about my lack of powers, but I'll get in even *more* trouble if I don't do anything and let the demon run amok.

This is quite the conundrum. And I...don't know what to do.

"Can you even *go* to Aperion in your state?"

"I can if I find the portal to go back."

"Find? You don't know where it is?" He stares at me.

I clench my fists.

"There are very few immutable portals. Most are always changing locations. I can detect their energy signature when I have my powers. But without them..."

Mine sighs and joins me on the bed.

"Then how do you propose we get to Aperion?"

"I can—" I stop and turn toward him. "We? *We?*"

"We're a team. Of course I won't let you go alone. Especially since you're vulnerable now."

"W-what?" I sputter. "Vulnerable?"

"Don't take this personally, Minnie. I know you're a force to be reckoned with—when you have your powers. But without them, you're just...human."

I curse under my breath. He has a point.

"Mortals can't just *go* to Aperion," I tell him. "Not only that, but you wouldn't *last* there."

"What do you mean?"

"If a mortal travels to a world that is not his native one, he will get sicker and sicker until he will die in approximately a fortnight. The only way to prevent that is to get a special tincture that would allow you to withstand the atmosphere of other worlds, but I wouldn't have the first clue on how to procure that."

He nods pensively.

"I suppose we'll just have to notify that special division in *less* than a fortnight." He gives me a wide smile.

I roll my eyes at him.

"And you think the special division will take it kindly that a *human* is in Aperion?"

Mine shrugs.

"We won't tell them. I'll accompany you there and wait until you notify them. Then I'll take you back here. You promised me two months, Minnie. I'm not about to waste *any* day."

"You..." I grit out in annoyance.

"Now, now, Minnie. Will you renege on your vow?"

"I don't remember *vowing* anything," I mutter drily.

"You gave me your word."

"You're impossible."

"*Persistent*," he corrects.

"But why?" I suddenly ask. "I don't understand why this sudden interest in me."

"It is far from sudden, trust me." He smiles.

"May I remind you we've only known each other for a few weeks?"

"So? A few weeks might be nothing for your immortal self, but for a puny human like me, it is quite a long time. Long enough to decide you'll do, anyway," he adds happily, scooting closer to me and draping one arm across my shoulders.

I should remind him of the *no touching* rule, but I am momentarily too confused by his words to do so.

"I'll...do? What does that mean?"

"That you are mine," he answers blithely.

I blink. But as I open my mouth to speak, he continues.

"And I am yours, of course. I am all about equality, you see. I am yours and you are mine."

"There is nothing equal between us, human," I grit out. I decide to ignore the rest of his statement because I find it rather charming and it makes me feel better about still calling him Mine. Though it's not because he *is* mine, of course. It's only because...well, he *feels* mine. My temples throb. This is more complicated than I expected. I cannot believe that I am having such difficulty with one paltry pronoun.

"You're right," he adds with a nod. "You are far superior."

An unwitting smile pulls at my lips. At least he knows that.

"As a mere mortal, it is my duty to worship you. From that perspective, you are right. We are not equal."

My lashes flutter in surprise.

"Worship...me?" I whisper.

He smirks.

"Don't tell me you've never thought about it. You're a goddess, after all. Wouldn't you want to have a male at your feet"—and to prove his point, he slides off the bed and onto his knees in front of me—"worshipping and adoring you?"

"What are you—" My words are cut off abruptly as he places his head in my lap, nuzzling his face against me.

"I can do that and so much more, Minnie," he rasps. His breath travels through the material of my dress until it reaches my skin. It makes its way inside of me, warming me in a way that makes me shudder with pleasure.

"This isn't appropriate," I croak. "We should—"

"But it wouldn't be *just* your body that I would worship," he continues. "I would worship your soul, too."

My eyes widen.

"I would pleasure you day and night, until your body is a bastion of pleasure, until your soul—"

"Stop." I place my fingers against his lips. "Please don't say any more."

He grabs my hand and kisses the inside of my palm before turning it and kissing the back of my hand.

"As you wish, my goddess," he murmurs.

He gets up, dusts his suit, and walks around the room as if nothing happened. As if he didn't just make my heart stop in my chest with his nearness and his honeyed words. Low tremors that I'm having a hard time controlling rack my body.

"Back to the issue of the demon," Mine says. His voice and demeanor are both steady and calm—as if he's completely unaffected by what just happened while I'm barely hanging on by a thread.

"Yes," I croak. "The demon..." I take a deep breath and try to settle my nerves. "In order to get to Aperion, we must find the portal first."

At my mention of the word *we*, he gives me a dazzling smile. My breath hitches.

"You need spiritual energy for that, no?"

I nod. "My own energy flow is blocked. But that doesn't mean I cannot siphon some. The only issue is that there isn't much I can siphon energy from in your world."

"The demon?" He offers.

I shake my head.

"With how strong he is now, I will never get close enough."

He makes a tsk sound.

"What about souls? You said they're the purest form of energy. Would absorbing a soul work?"

"Absolutely no," I burst out and jump to my feet. "It is forbidden." At his confused expression, I continue. "If I consume a soul, I will become the same as a Son of Tenebreis. My energy signature will change forever and I will be branded both a traitor and the enemy. And there is only one fate for that..." I squeeze my eyes shut as I remember the first execution I ever witnessed. "Death."

"Death? Even for an immortal?"

I nod.

"I might be immortal as far as time goes, and I might even withstand most injuries. I might even die and be reborn if my energy is depleted to the point that my body fails me. But the type of death that awaits anyone who breaks the law is the permanent type. There is a sword in Aperion that has the power to exterminate a god's essence. And the owner of that sword happens to be ruthless when it comes to meting out justice."

"Who?"

"He is called Azerius, and he is my commander. But he is also...as scary as he is fascinating and strong."

Mine's features tighten.

"Fascinating? Strong?" he repeats.

"He is thought to be the strongest deity alive. Everyone looks up to him just as everyone is afraid of him."

"Let me guess. You look up to him, too," Mine adds drily.

"Of course. He might be ruthless, but he is just. And I've never seen someone with a more admirable work ethic than him."

His nostrils flare.

"You seem to hold him in *very* high esteem."

I nod excitedly.

"And if this mission goes well, I'll get a commendation from him. You have no idea how valuable that is in my world. And then I won't have to mar—" I promptly stop myself when I realize I've said too much.

Mine narrows his eyes at me. In two thudding steps, he's in front of me, towering over me with his impressive height.

"You won't have to do what?" There is something different about him. It's not just the chilling quality of his voice, but there's also something else. Something that makes the hairs on my body stand up.

"Go ahead, Minnie. Finish what you were about to say."

"Nothing."

"It wasn't nothing." His eyes glint dangerously. "Go on. Tell me."

"Mine..."

"Tell. Me."

"I won't have to get married," I whisper.

"And when were you planning on telling me about that

marriage of yours?" he asks in a low voice as he moves closer to me.

My breathing intensifies from his nearness, drowned only by the incessant drum of my pulse.

"W-why should I have told you?" I muster in a shaky tone. "It does not concern you. We're nothing to each other. I'm a goddess and y-you're a puny human."

"We are *nothing* to each other?" he sneers. "So it does not concern me that I am courting you while you're promised to another?"

"I didn't mean that. I just..." I take a deep breath. "It's an arranged marriage, Mine," I hurry to say. "I was not consulted about it."

"I will ask you again, Minnie. Do you think it does not concern me that I am courting an engaged woman?"

He takes a step toward me. I take one back. Our bodies are in motion, but our gazes are stagnant.

My eyes are on his, trapped by an ineffable intensity.

I back away, and he charges forward.

Until my back hits the wall. He's in front of me, crowding me with his body. Placing his hand above my head, he leans in, his eyes narrowing at me.

He doesn't speak again, though.

He just waits.

"I..." I close my mouth. He's right. Maybe before this would not have concerned him. But I did agree to give him two months to court me—a lapse in judgment on my part now that I think better of it. A human courting a goddess. It would be laughable if I wasn't in such a dire position. The position being the fact that I am *not* unaffected by said human.

Even now, my heart beats so wildly in my chest, it might just leap out of it. Yet it is not fear.

Here I am, trapped by the massive body of a male who's seen war, who can not just best me but also subdue me, and I don't feel the slightest bit afraid.

There is something else, though. A tremor low in my

stomach—one that worms its way through my entire body until every single cell hums with awareness.

"I'm sorry," I whisper. "I should have told you. But you have to understand that though I may be engaged to him in name only, I do not see myself as such. In fact, I've been doing everything in my power to evade the match. It's just that in my world—"

He presses a finger against my lips and shushes me.

"I know your virtue is intact," he starts, and I'm shocked at the cadence of his voice. It's rough and barely subdued, with a hint of malice. "But I must know what else happened between you and that fiancé of yours."

"What?" My brows shoot up. "What do you mean? Nothing happened, of course."

He isn't mollified by my words.

"Did he kiss you?"

"Of course not!"

"Hm." He clicks his tongue. "How could he resist the temptation?"

"Temptation?" I snort. "Trust me, there is *no* temptation on his part," I mutter, annoyed at the mere thought of that clown.

"More the fool he is then," Mine scoffs.

"Right..."

"What else, Minnie?"

"I don't know what you mean—"

"Did he touch you in *any* way?"

"He doesn't see me that way, all right? He hates me as much as I do him. I bet he's only going through with the marriage because his mother told him to."

"Did he touch you in *any* way?" he repeats.

I frown at him. What does he want me to answer?

"You're being ridiculous, Mine. He probably only grabbed my hand once."

"Your hand..." He nods to himself. "Which one?"

I blink. What?

"Do you think I remember?"

"Which. One?"

"Left?"

He nods.

Grabbing my left hand, he brings it to his lips. He blows hot air on my knuckles before he asks, "Which fingers did he touch?"

"Now you're just making fun of me," I add under my breath as I attempt to pull my hand back. But his grip is too strong. And considering my position between him and the wall, my movements are rather limited.

"Doesn't matter," he mentions right before he places his lips on my big finger. He kisses the entire length of it, slow, languid kisses that make me break out in goose bumps. When he's done with that finger, he moves on to the next. He does this until he's kissed every single inch of my hand.

"W-what's gotten into you? Why are you behaving like this?"

He stares at me for what seems like forever before he releases a long, tired sigh.

"I am courting you, therefore you are *mine*, Minnie."

"But—"

"No buts. This is the way of my world and you are now in my world. If I am courting you, it means I am laying claim on you. You will not look at other males. You will not touch other males. Hell, you will not even *think* of other males."

I blink in shock.

"Did you just say I cannot *think* of other males?" I repeat in outrage.

"Damn right. And your nursing duties will be reserved only for me. You will not attempt to treat any male who is not me. Is that clear?"

I am waiting for him to laugh and say it's a joke. Because how can it be anything *but* a joke?

But as the seconds pass, his gaze only intensifies, his breathing even more so. His nostrils flare—in and out—almost as if he's doing his hardest to control himself. But control himself for *what*?

I don't understand this, or him, or the customs of this world. I agree that I should have told him about my clown of a fiancé, though I don't even claim him as such, but other than that, I'm stumped as to what he'd have me do or how to behave.

"Surely you realize how absurd this is, no?" I ask when he doesn't show any hints of amusement.

He merely shrugs.

"There is nothing absurd about this, Minnie."

"You're telling me I cannot even *think* of another male? Do you realize how absurd that is? You cannot control my thoughts—"

"Oh, but I can," he cuts me off.

I stare at him. "What?"

Slowly, his lips tip up. But it's not the usual carefree smile I've come to expect from him. No, it's something more menacing, something almost sinister.

"I can occupy every second of your day so that you have absolutely no time to even think of another male."

"Are you...serious?"

"Why would I not be serious?"

"Because I've never heard of anything as outrageous as this before."

He shrugs again.

"It's because you are not familiar with my world. But rest assured, Minnie, that I am here to teach you everything about it. Including the fact that once a male claims a female, there can never be anyone else for him."

"Oh. Really?"

He gives me an assured nod.

"In Aperion, there are so-called blood bondings or true matings that happen between two people whose threads of fate are irrevocably linked. This type of territorial behavior happens between true mates, though those pairings are exceedingly rare. I did not realize that humans engaged in it, too," I add pensively.

Though extremely rare, true matings are incredibly romantic. The fates are the ones who assign true mates, and some sources state that every single being in this universe has an assigned true mate—or a linked thread of fate, as others refer to it. But to find one's true mate, one must exchange blood to trigger the bond. Otherwise, both beings continue to go through life oblivious to their one true mate—which is why the phenomenon is so rare.

Yet once two beings have been blood bonded, they are completely in tune with one another. Accounts differ on how the bonding manifests, with some claiming that each bonding is unique. But the mates are extremely territorial of each other and they can never desire or lie with anyone but each other.

Ah... Blood bondings are as romantic as they are taboo in Aperion, though. Aperites are prohibited from sharing blood with *anyone*. It is an offense punishable by death if found out. It's almost as bad as consuming a soul and it's reported that it has a similar effect in tainting one's spiritual energy. Perhaps it's because both things are characteristic of the Sons of Tenebreis—soul sucking blood drinkers.

My own theory is that the Houses prohibited blood sharing because they were afraid people would be finding their true mates left and right. If they did, there would be no more advantageous marriages, no more selective breeding or political alliances. Everything would be left to...fate. And as much as the House of Moirai likes to believe it's in charge of everything, so do the other Houses like to prove that is not the case.

"But wait," I suddenly say. "What about those humans at the party? Or those soldiers bragging about the many women they slept with? How can they do that if they are territorial?"

My question throws him off as he scowls.

"I did not say that everyone is like that," he mumbles.

"But you implied it."

"I did no such thing," he counters. "I just informed you of a custom I happen to engage in. And since I am *in* this world, then this custom is automatically characteristic of this world."

I go over his words, growing more confused the more I replay them in my mind.

"What type of logic is that? I did not understand a word of what you said."

He smiles at me.

"And that is all right, Minnie." He pats me lightly on the shoulder. "I will guide you. Just remember the main rule—I am the only male you can ever think of, look at, touch, or desire. Ever."

"That's more than *one* rule," I grumble.

"It's a combined rule."

Once more, I find myself very confused. How did we get here? We were talking about the demon, weren't we?"

"What happens if I don't?" I ask innocently.

His expression darkens.

"That is the issue, Minnie. I am doing this for your own good." He presses his lips together, looking at me with sudden concern in his eyes.

"What?"

"If you don't follow the rules, then I will be forced to kill any males involved. And you cannot kill humans, can you?" he murmurs sweetly as if he's reciting poetry, not telling me about his murderous intentions.

"But I wouldn't..."

"They would die *because* of you, Minnie. It's just as if *you* killed them. And we cannot have that, can we?"

"N-no."

"Good girl." He winks at me and ruffles my hair. "Now back to that demon..."

And just like that, he's back to his previous laid-back self.

Me? I'm more confused than ever.

SEVENTEEN

THE MORNING LIGHT streams into the shed. I stretch in my bed and let out a yawn. But I stop mid-stretch when I realize something is wrong.

The light should *not* be streaming into my side of the shed. There's a curtain for that.

I dare pry my eyes open, and at first, the light is blinding.

But moments after, I note the lack of curtains. But that's nothing compared to the fact that there's currently a bed attached to my own.

Mine's eyes are wide open. He's on his side, his arm tucked under his head as he watches me.

"Morning," he whispers.

I blink. Once. Twice. On the third blink, I let out a loud screech and scoot back, seeking distance from him. Unfortunately, these beds are far from luxurious or big. And in less than a second, my body makes contact with the hard ground. A loud groan escapes my lips as pain ricochets through my bones.

"Minnie?" Mine asks in a worried voice. "Are you all right?"

He shuffles closer and peers down at me over the edge of the bed.

"What are you doing there?" I ask in outrage, momentarily forgetting the pain.

"What do you mean?" He frowns.

"We agreed on something. You'd stick to *your* side of the room, and I would have mine. Why is your bed suddenly next to mine?"

"Ah, that." He sighs. "I did not mean to break our agreement. But you see..."

"What?" I narrow my eyes at him.

"There was something odd when I got back last night."

I wait for him to continue. After an unsuccessful conversation on the subject of the demon, he'd left to do *work*. By the time I went to bed, he hadn't returned. And that was around midnight. It's on the tip of my tongue to ask him where he was—and with whom—and what he did. But it's more important to ascertain the reason behind this blatant violation of rules.

"I was returning from the cantina and I felt that someone was following me. Even when I entered the room, I kept having this feeling that I was being watched." He lets out a shudder. "I tried to fall asleep but couldn't."

"I still don't see why you got rid of the curtain and put your bed next to mine?"

"Because you're the strong one," he states suddenly. "Where else would I have felt safe if not close to you?"

I stare at him for a moment.

"You..."

"I was afraid it was a demon or something watching me from the shadows. But they wouldn't have dared to do anything with you close to me. Right, Minnie?"

"Right."

"Because you're a strong demon slayer."

"Right."

"And I'm just a puny human."

"Right, right," I mutter.

"So you see, it wasn't a breach of rules, per se. Isn't your role as the badass goddess in this relationship to protect your weak human?" He looks at me sweetly.

I open my mouth to agree but then stop.

"Relationship?"

"Partnership," he corrects. "Really, Minnie. Here I am going against my manly pride to tell you how much stronger than me you are and you're misconstruing my words."

"But you said relationship—"

"You misheard. Partnership," he emphasizes.

"But—"

"So the situation is now settled, no?" He interrupts me.

Swinging his legs over the edge of the bed, he grabs my hand and pulls me to my feet.

"I suppose so," I mutter, still a little unsure.

"Excellent. Now we can discuss what I have learned."

My ears prick at that.

"What did you learn?"

He smiles at me.

"I was out late last night because I was conducting some research of my own. You said you can channel spiritual energy from an object."

I nod.

"Would a magical object work?"

"Magical?" I frown.

"Used by a witch," he clarifies.

"But where would we find a witch?" I ask as I get to my feet and dust my nightgown. Mine is dressed in a white shirt and a pair of loose pants, nothing scandalous, nothing interesting. So why are my eyes straying to his side? Why can't I help the way my gaze rakes over his body, noting each hard muscle and the way it pushes against the material of the shirt.

I swallow hard—audibly so.

Good thing he is too focused on bringing me a tray of food to notice. Though I could always blame my reaction on the food.

"I don't know about finding a witch. But we might be able to find objects *used* by a witch. They should work, no?"

"If they're imbued with magic," I reply absentmindedly.

He pulls a chair for me to sit at the table—we've already

converted his desk to a table—and lays in front of me an assortment of breakfast items.

My mouth salivates at the sight and smell of them.

There is my daily donut, of course, but a variety of scones with butter and jam on the side accompany it. That is just the sweet part of the meal. Next is the savory, which is comprised of bread, ham, and three types of cheeses.

I have to wonder where he could have procured this from. Army food might be a tad better than civilian food, but it's still nothing fancy.

Nothing like *this*.

It's an entire feast—and it's just breakfast.

I should probably question him about it, but later. Now it's eating time.

Before he takes a seat next to me, he brings over an electric kettle and pours hot water into two cups, each containing a tea bag.

"What qualifies as *imbued* with magic?" he asks as he finally joins me at the table.

He grabs a scone, cuts it in two, and adds jam on one side and butter on the other. I emulate his movements.

"If it's been used in a ritual," I say as I take a bite of the scone.

This is wonderful. Oh, my!

I quickly eye the number of scones on the table. Six more left. Then my gaze flies to Mine. He's a big male, so it stands to reason he would need plenty of food. Does that mean he will eat most of the scones?

As the thought enters my mind, I quickly shove the rest of the scone in my mouth and grab another, repeating the process —though this time I only add the jam since the butter takes away from the sweetness.

"I asked around," he says as he slowly and methodically butters his second scone, "and there is a place that might house such items."

"House? As in they're just...there?"

"It's a museum. Some forty-fifty minutes away from here by car. It houses a lot of artifacts from the witch trials in the seventeenth century."

"But..." I chew slowly as I think about what he said. "How do we know they were *actual* witches? I've heard about the so-called witch trials you humans had. Most of the women accused of witchcraft were innocent."

"Maybe." He shrugs. "But it's worth a try."

"All right. We can try it. But I have questions."

He smiles. "Of course you have. Go on."

"How will we get there? We have no car."

"I'll get us a car."

Of course he'd have access to a car. I think that proves my suspicion that he's incredibly wealthy for this world.

"What about your duties? You're an airman. Won't you get in trouble if you leave the base?"

"Already talked to my CO. I've been granted leave for a week due to my last injuries."

"But they weren't that bad," I mumble.

"Trust me, Minnie. They *were*," he replies in a tight voice.

"Fine. So you can leave the base and we have a car. But how can we access that museum? Aren't all centers closed because of the war?"

Another shrug.

"Maybe. But we will get in somehow."

He seems so sure of himself, so...

I put down my scone and narrow my eyes at him.

"Just how rich are you?"

His brows go up in surprise. Then he chuckles.

"How rich?"

"Yes. Tommy said you come from a wealthy background. But it must be *very* wealthy for you to afford all of this." I wave to the food in front of us. That in itself is a luxury. Never mind the fact that he can get a car, leave the military base as he pleases *and* get into a closed museum.

"You could say so," he murmurs in a low voice. His cheeks are slightly flushed.

"You could say so? What does that mean?"

"My family is very wealthy. We moved to America when I was younger and we invested in the right ventures. With time, our wealth and influence accumulated."

"WHY ARE YOU HERE THEN?" I ask suddenly. "I mean. If you're so wealthy, why would you risk your life in war? I'm sure with your influence you wouldn't have had to join, no?"

"You are correct. I did not have to join the Air Force."

"Why did you then?"

"Because you're here," he answers smoothly.

"Hey!" I slap his arm playfully. "I'm serious."

"So am I. You don't believe me?" He feigns an offended tone.

"I can't believe you're being so shameless this early in the morning," I grumble and roll my eyes.

"Why else would a man risk death if not for the love of a beautiful woman?" He wiggles his brows at me.

"You're impossible." I shake my head. It's clear I'm not going to get an answer out of him, though the curiosity remains. If he is so wealthy, why court death in the Air Force? It's...baffling.

"Might be." He chuckles. "But my brand of impossible is getting you a way to siphon spiritual energy. You should thank me." He leans back, pushing his chin up and smirking at me.

I glare at him.

"Right. I'll thank you after I've successfully siphoned the energy, since we don't know if it will actually work."

"I'll be waiting." He winks.

I let out a frustrated groan and kick him in the shin under the table.

"Ouch."

"Serves you right," I say as I grab the rest of the scones—and the donut—and bring them to my side of the table. He can have the savory stuff. I'll keep the sweet.

He has a perpetual smile on his face as he looks at me. Even when he should be annoyed, he's not. Is this part of his courting ritual? I suppose the food is, but what about the rest? The fact that he's both teasing me *and* letting me get away with being mean to him.

And to my shame, I *am* mean to him. I'm not yet sure why exactly, but whenever I see him being too nice to me, I want to kick him.

Then I want to hug him.

I shake my head to dispel those dangerous thoughts.

Perhaps this is his plan. Drive me to be mean to him so I can be apologetic afterward and allow him to get away with things I wouldn't normally do. Like the bed situation.

Ugh! I don't like this. I don't like feeling out of my element, and I certainly don't like the fact that I'm not very versed in this courtship thing.

In battle, at least you know what to expect. In courtship? I fear it will hit me harder than in any battle I've taken part in.

"Finish your meal and change. I'll get the car ready."

"THIS IS NOT A MILITARY CAR," I add with a frown.

"It's my personal car." Mine smiles as he opens the door for me.

I get into the front passenger seat and make myself comfortable. Leather seats and a luxurious interior. I am once more reminded of how wealthy he is.

I glance back. "What's that?"

"Oh, that? I packed some food to have on the road. You'll get hungry."

"That is thoughtful of you," I murmur.

It doesn't escape me that he said I will get hungry, not he or we. He did this with me in mind. Warmth spreads through me. I've never had anyone be so nice to me before.

He might be trying to impress me now that he's made his intentions clear about courting me, but even before that, he's been nothing but kind. I might have been a little harsh on him in the past, but that was because my sudden misfortune colored my perception. And though I searched for anyone else but me to blame, the truth is that no one forced me to break the rules.

I did it because I wanted to.

And if I were to go back to the past—though messing with time is forbidden too—I would make the same choices.

I'm startled from my thoughts when Mine starts the car. We barely leave the base when something catches my eye in the mirror on the car.

I swivel, my eyes wide with shock.

"Tommy! What are you doing here?"

He gulps down guiltily.

"I don't want to stay behind with that demon!" he bursts out.

"HE'S A GREED DEMON. He won't eat your soul."

"No, but he's awful to me! He makes fun of me every day when he sees me. I hate him," he cries out.

Based on my own experience with that greed demon, I'd have to agree. He is very obnoxious and if he realizes you can see him, he derives pleasure from making you squirm. Perhaps he's found a way to channel greed in that, too?

While Tommy prattles away about his experiences with the greed demon, Mine smiles indulgently behind the wheel. Somehow, I would have expected him to be annoyed that a ghost has come into his car uninvited. But it doesn't seem to be the case.

"Have you sent the letter to my Delilah, Major?" Tommy asks.

"Of course. I am sure she will be happy to read your last words."

Tommy's face falls.

"If only I didn't die..."

"It's the order of things, Tommy. We die and we get born. All over again," Mine says in a stern yet oddly wise tone.

"And if you move on, you still have a chance to be with her," I chime in. It might not be my duty to escort souls to the afterlife, but given the abundance of demons on Anthropa, I don't want to take any chances that one might prey on Tommy before he's able to leave.

"I know." He nods solemnly. "But I need to find one of those messengers you spoke of."

"Nothing yet?"

Tommy shakes his head.

"All the recent deaths occurred off base," Mine adds. "The planes were shot down over Germany."

"Damn it," I mutter a curse under my breath.

"Is there no other way, Miss Minnie?"

"I'm afraid not."

He sighs. "Do you think I can join you? Or will I be whisked back to the base?"

I spare a glance at Mine. He doesn't say no, so I don't either.

"We'll see how far you can go."

He smiles brightly at me. "You're so kind, Miss Minnie. Thank you!"

"Don't mention it," I mumble.

"He's right, Minnie. You're so kind," Mine drawls in an odd voice. He looks at me from the corner of his eyes, his hands wound tightly around the steering wheel. What is wrong with him now?

I decide to ignore him and find out more about Tommy.

"Why did you join the military? You're so young." I bite my tongue when I realize I spoke in present tense instead of past. He doesn't realize it, though.

"All the eligible men in my town had to."

It's Mine who speaks next. "Men were only allowed to refuse if they had a robust reason. Depending on the state, some faced prison time while others were required to pay fines."

"I had no money for fines," Tommy adds. "And I was deemed too healthy to be exempt."

"What about you, then?" I ask Mine. "Wouldn't these"—I point to his scars—"help you escape mandatory conscription."

He shrugs. "Perhaps. But I never tried to evade it."

"Why? And don't give me that flimsy excuse that it's because of me." I roll my eyes.

He smirks. "This war? Of course it was for you." He winks at me.

"Come on." I punch him lightly in the shoulder.

Tommy also joins me in asking the question. "Tell us, Major."

Mine doesn't appear too comfortable with this line of questioning, and my smile slowly dies on my face. Is it a sore subject for him? From what I've gathered from my time on Anthropa, the military is a dignified profession. It is as respectable as it is in Aperion, though much more dangerous. Of course, not in terms of *actual* danger, but because humans are such fragile beings that they can instantly die.

It takes a lot more to kill an Aperite. And since our military's sole purpose has been to hunt demons across the universe after the war with Tartareia ended, fewer and fewer Aperites have died in battle.

Mine clears his throat.

"My best friend was in the military. He was a few years older than me and I always looked up to him. So I started training to join him."

"Your best friend?"

He's never mentioned a friend before. If anything, Tommy has been saying just how much of a recluse he is. I've never seen him on overly friendly terms with anyone at the base.

"Where is he?" I ask.

Mine grits his teeth and I instantly regret asking the question.

"He died of the same sickness I had," he answers after a moment.

I blink. When he mentioned that sickness, I assumed it was some type of childhood illness—humans seem to be particularly susceptible to those. I did not realize it would have been so late in life.

"Oh, no!" Tommy exclaims. "Was it influenza? My mam's sisters died of it, too."

"Something like that," Mine adds in a low voice.

I look at him intently as if waiting for him to add more. But he doesn't. He's staring up ahead, almost as if he's lost in his mind, or I should say, his grief.

But what I'm most surprised at is my reaction to it. I want to apologize for bringing up bad memories. If my best friend died—though I suppose I don't have one unless you count... Mine—I would be sad too. Devastated, really.

My brows bunch together as a cold shiver racks my body.

The thought of Mine dying doesn't sit well with me. In fact, it threatens to make me physically ill. I shake my head. This isn't the time to think about death—despite the fact that we have a ghost in the back of the car. Though as I glance back, I note that Tommy has momentarily disappeared. Perhaps he's been dragged back to the base? Somehow, I'm thankful for the reprieve, for being able to be alone with Mine when I can sense the turmoil underneath his calm facade.

His features contort with pain, and a restless desire grows within me to comfort him and alleviate his pain. I reach out for his hand—a move as antithetical to me as acknowledging that he might be my best friend. He startles, and his sad eyes slowly find mine.

"I'm sorry," I whisper.

The corners of his mouth tremble as he gives me a small smile. He grabs my hand and squeezes it before bringing it to his lips for a light kiss. Yet it's a kiss that I feel in my bones. The warmth from his mouth spreads up my body, enveloping me and causing my skin to erupt in goose bumps.

"You're sweet," he murmurs. "But such pain can never go away."

"Was the sickness...painful?"

He nods. "In his last days, the pain was crippling."

"And you felt it too? That pain?"

Another nod, a bitter one.

"And you said there was no cure for this sickness?"

"None that his parents would have been able to enact in time. He was already dead when I exhibited the first symptoms. And with the knowledge of what was to come, my father decided to take matters into his own hands and do something extreme."

"I'm happy," I tell him.

His eyes widen in surprise—I surprise myself, too.

"I'm happy he found a way to save you." I pause and wet my lips. "Otherwise, I would have never met you."

He stares at me for what feels like moments on end. He's not paying attention to the road, though the car never veers off course. He's only looking at me. A hard, pressing stare that befuddles me just as much as it fills me with an odd certainty.

Holding my hand tightly, he brings it once more to his lips. His eyes are on mine as he whispers against my knuckles, "I survived so I could meet you."

EIGHTEEN

THE IMPOSING castle looms in the distance, dominating the landscape with its massive stone walls and turrets. Jagged stones and darkened windows dot the exterior, adding to its menacing appearance. As we approach, I find myself appreciating the architecture and ancient craftsmanship. Mine had mentioned that the castle was built a millennium ago. That in itself is astonishing considering humankind has been slow to develop until very recently.

The sky is a dark blue, a foreboding aura, though there is nary a cloud in sight. The town is quiet, too, though that is to be expected with the threat of attack looming over villagers' heads. They've all heard of the Blitz, and they're afraid they might be next. After all, fear and uncertainty are the two most prevalent feelings in times of war.

The car drives up the hill toward the entrance of the castle.

Although it's closed to the public due to the war, Mine said he has a way to get us inside. One glance at him, and I have to calm my rabid heart rate. It's getting out of control and I do not know what I can do to stop it. One look at his harsh and domineering profile and I find myself fidgeting in my seat. I suppose it's because he's handsome.

I hum to myself. Yes, very, very handsome.

I am a little surprised they make humans *this* handsome. I have yet to see one that comes anywhere close to Mine, and that is with his scars. If he did not have his scars... Oh, my! He would be far too dazzling. I'd have to fight every single female who laid eyes on him.

I stop for a moment, my thoughts startling me.

Why would *I* fight for him? He's the one courting me, not the other way around. He should be the one to fight for me. Not that I condone senseless violence, but I rather like the fact that he's willing to kill other males for trying to get my attention. Whoever taught him this particular courting technique did well.

But then I scowl even more as I start thinking that someone might have taught him that technique—as in, a female.

"Mine," I start, shooting him a warning glance. His next few words will save or end him.

"Yes?" He gives me one of those dazzling smiles and I have to force myself to focus on the task at hand.

"Have you wanted to kill other males for another female before?"

His lips tremble with mirth.

"What is that question, Minnie?"

"Answer me! Have you felt the urge to kill other males for even looking at another female?" My voice drops a notch just as my eyes narrow at him so he knows how much hinges on his answer.

"Are you asking me if I've been jealous before, little darling?" He smirks at me.

"That is exactly what I am asking. Have you, or have you not?" I lean closer to him, doing my best to intimidate him— which, of course, fails abysmally, seeing as how he's only regarding me with amusement.

"I have."

My hand finds his arm and my fingers dig into his flesh. Seconds pass as he doesn't elaborate, seconds in which I'm pretty sure I draw blood.

He doesn't mind the pain. He barely registers it as he suddenly stops the car.

His gaze is on mine. He doesn't break eye contact even for a moment.

"Only for you, little darling." His eyes twinkle with mischief. "If I could, I would hide you away from the world so that no one else can see you. No other male, nor female. No one but me."

I wet my lips.

"Only you?" I whisper. The idea doesn't seem as unappealing as I would have thought. In fact... I find myself imagining it quite easily. Me and him, far from the world, away from the world...in spite of the world.

"But I know that is not possible. I cannot hide you from everyone because you shine far too bright, Minnie. Alas, I will settle for killing everyone who looks at you the wrong way."

Butterflies dance in my stomach.

"And what is the wrong way?"

His lips slowly curve into a smile.

"Like they forget you are mine and you will *always* be mine."

The conversation comes to a sudden halt when someone knocks on the window of our car.

Mine lowers the window.

"How may I help you?" the elderly man asks. He's dressed in a dark uniform that signals him as the guard to the entrance of the museum.

"We're looking for the entrance to the castle," Mine answers with an affable smile.

The man frowns.

"The castle is closed to the public. I am sorry, but you will have to go back."

Mine's smile doesn't falter.

Rummaging through the inside of his coat, Mine removes a couple of crisp banknotes and extends them toward the man.

His eyes widen and he stares at the money a few seconds too long before he shakes his head.

"I cannot let you in. I'm sorry," he adds with a nervous gulp.

That's a lot of money. Anyone would say yes to that type of money considering the scarcities of the war.

"Perhaps you can reconsider," Mine continues, getting another stack of banknotes and adding them to the bunch.

The man's Adam's apple bobs up and down as he eyes the money warily. He wants to accept the bribe. I mentally will him to do so.

But in the end, he shakes his head again.

"I'm sorry. You'll have to leave."

The man doesn't linger. As soon as the words are out of his mouth, he turns to leave.

Mine grinds his teeth in annoyance.

"Was that your *secret* way of getting in?"

He mumbles something inaudible under his breath and puts the car in reverse to turn back. Yet we don't go back down the hill. Instead, he finds a clear path through the forest and drives between the trees. The branches hit the sides of the car, the path too narrow for the width of the vehicle.

"What are we doing?" I startle when a thick branch slaps against my window.

"Plan B," he says.

The path becomes too narrow for the car to advance and he is forced to stop.

"Uh, Mine?"

He swivels to look at me.

"I don't think your plan B is a plan at all," I mutter, pointing at my side of the door. Tree branches block the visibility out the window, and a thick trunk rests against the door, putting pressure on it. Some goods might be expensive in this world, but that doesn't mean they're worth it. Case in point, this fancy car. A little pressure from the tree and the metal is already bending inward.

Mine curses aloud. I assume he's going to put the car in

reverse once more to try to remove us from this situation. Instead, he leans over to me, places his hands under my arms, and plucks me off my seat.

I squeal in surprise.

"Shh," he murmurs. "I need to focus."

"What are you—"

My words are cut off when I fall on top of him. The wheel digs in my back, forcing me to press myself into him.

Big. Mistake. He immediately realizes it, too.

I can feel him everywhere.

His hard chest. His rippling muscles. The tension in his body.

His scent envelops me, leather and darkness made more potent by the heat of his body.

I slowly raise my eyes to his. They're such a vivid green, like freshly grown grass at the height of spring. I've always been in awe of his eyes but also rather mesmerized by them. It's as if they don't quite fit on his face, yet at the same time, the depths mirrored in them encompass his entire essence.

Crisp. Clear. Orderly.

His eyes *are* him. And now they're watching me just as intently, that vivid shade of green swirling a darker hue. At first, I wonder if it's his pupils that are growing in size, but as I lean forward to get a better look, I realize it's the color of his irises. There are myriads of minuscule patterns that swirl in concert, creating a changing canvas, one that tells a story, but that I fear I have yet to learn the language needed to decipher it.

Stark green. Dark green. And a hint of rust.

My tongue peeks out to wet my lips.

His eyes follow that movement.

"Stop moving," he whispers in a low, almost pained voice.

I blink. "What?"

"I need you to stop moving, Minnie," he repeats. His voice is much softer now, a caress to my ears that results in a whole-body shiver.

I shift around until I hit something. I frown.

"What's this?" I ask as I half turn.

Mine's hands are on my shoulders, keeping me in place.

"There's something there, Mine. I think I hit your stick," I add, panicking.

"My...stick?" he croaks.

"Yes, the car stick."

I push his hands away and rotate so I can get a better look. But then I spot the *actual* car stick, a distance away, not at all so close to me I would feel it poking me in the back.

I slowly turn to Mine.

His cheeks are scarlet as he mumbles, "It's my stick all right."

"What?"

He clears his throat, but the silence stretches as he refuses to answer my question.

"Mine! What's wrong?"

"You...know," he adds in a low, bashful voice.

Frowning, I shake my head.

"I don't."

He lowers his hands to my waist and moves me a bit further as he adjusts himself in the seat. Still frowning, I'm trying to grasp what's happening when I happen to glance down at his pants.

Mine follows my gaze and he curses under his breath.

"Uhm..."

Before I can scramble for the proper words, he kicks the door open and deposits me outside the car. He doesn't join me out immediately, though, and when he does, the rather large outline in his pants from before is gone.

I want to ask more questions, but for some reason, my cheeks redden to a shade to match his own. Our gazes collide and we both swiftly look away.

"So..." He's the first to start. "We should leave the car here since we won't be able to drive through the forest."

He grabs my hand and steers me toward the forest. The

trees are so tall, they create a dome above our heads, barely allowing any light to come through.

I hate to admit it, but the fact that he's holding on to me makes me feel better. More...protected. Which is ludicrous since *I* am the one who should be protecting him. I suppose it's still nice to have someone next to me, lending me his strength. And despite being human, Mine has quite the strength.

I eye him up and down surreptitiously. Oh, yes. His body is hard with muscle. I blush as I remember feeling that hardness under the tips of my fingers. Seeing that he's officially courting me, perhaps he'll let me touch his muscles again. And *maybe* I will show him my own too—after all, I did not spend so much time training in the army not to feel proud of my toned muscles.

"So what's the plan?" I ask in an attempt to steer myself away from those thoughts. I need to think about killing demons, not feeling hard, hot muscles...

"We're going around the forest to find the entrance to the castle ourselves." He pauses and clicks his tongue against his teeth. "I don't understand how anyone would refuse that type of money. Especially during wartime," he grumbles under his breath.

"Some people have principles," I tell him with a shrug.

"It's a *lot* of money," he emphasizes.

"So? There are some things I would never do for all the money in the universe."

He narrows his eyes at me, but I swear I spot a smile creeping up his face.

"Is that so?"

I nod.

"No amount of money would make me marry that clown-faced Theron, which is why I need this to work. If I'm successful and earn myself a commendation from Commander Azerius, my parents will not be able to force me to marry him."

"Or you could run away," Mine suggests with a wicked glint in his eyes.

"You think I never thought of that?" I roll my eyes at him. "I would, of course, get away. But then I would be branded a traitor. Anyone willing to betray their family is ruled a traitor in my world. I'd be a pariah in the *entire* universe."

"Wouldn't that be better than marrying someone you don't like?"

"Of course it would. But you're missing the point. I wouldn't *just* be a pariah. I'd also be hunted wherever I go. Aperion has very strict rules, and anyone breaking those rules must be made an example of. What do you think me running away from an unwanted marriage would signal to the rest of the noble families?"

"That you're a brave and independent female?"

My lips quirk into a smile.

"That too." I chuckle. "But it would set a precedent that it is permissible for a female to say *no* to a match decided by her family. The entirety of Aperion derives its strength from strategic marriages that have the potential to yield the next Supreme."

"I'm not sure you explained what a Supreme is," he mentions slowly.

"I haven't?" I blink. "Oh, my bad. The Supremes are the most powerful deities. Each one of the fifteen Houses of Aperion has a Supreme that oversees everything to do with the Houses and the order of the universe. You could say they are the original gods of your mythology, except there is never one fixed god. You have the mythological god of water, Pose something, but in reality, there is only the House of Hydros that controls all matters related to water and its Supreme is the ultimate authority," I explain.

"So these Supremes are changeable?"

"Yes. Deities might be immortal, but they are not invincible. Thousands of years ago, when Aperion was at war with Tartareia, the life expectancy for a Supreme was only a few hundred years while holding the position. As the most powerful entities, they were usually at the front lines, leading the war. But since we live in times of relative peace, the Supremes have been faring much better, so there haven't been many changes in the last few thousand years."

"I see." He nods pensively. "So how does one become a Supreme? Could *you* become one?"

Laughter bubbles inside of me.

"Me? A Supreme?" I throw my head back and laugh at the absurd notion.

"Why not?" He challenges.

"When a Supreme dies, there is a selection for the next one within that specific House. The ruling monarchs of the House will nominate a few candidates who will compete for the title. But it's a much more complicated process. To qualify, I'd need to have opened my ninth gate. That is a minimum. I've only opened my fifth one." I pause, gritting my teeth at that thought. It's not for the lack of trying, though, just for lack of opportunity. "I'd also need to have a series of accomplishments in the service of Aperion that would recommend me."

"Well, considering what we are about to do, I would say you are doing something in the service of Aperion, no? And you can always train to open your ninth gate. It's not impossible."

I blink.

Now that he puts it like that, he's not wrong. It wouldn't be *entirely* impossible.

"But even if I passed all the necessary tests and reached the top, I'd still need the approval of the other Supremes. It's a very difficult process that can last hundreds of years."

"But *not* impossible," he counters.

"Yes." I smile. "Not impossible."

Although seeing how Commander Azerius has been a contender for the title of Supreme for the last few hundred years with no avail, I fear it would be pretty impossible for someone like me to become one. He's the most powerful deity I've ever met, and yet, the other Supremes will not appoint him for whatever reason.

"I have full confidence that you can achieve whatever you

set out to do," he murmurs, pulling me closer. "If anyone *can* do the impossible, it's you."

My lashes flutter in surprise and my face heats.

"Thank you. That's nice of you to say," I whisper. I don't quite know how to respond to that, especially as he regards me with such intensity. Perhaps this is just part of the courtship and he doesn't mean it. But the truth remains that no one's ever spoken to me like this—no one's ever had *full confidence* in me. If anything, my entire life, the opposite has been true. People have been doubting me at every turn.

I gaze up at him. He's smiling at me, a full-bodied smile that makes the corners of his eyes crinkle.

A *genuine* smile.

How is it that someone who's known me for mere weeks can believe in me more than my own family ever has?

"It's the truth. You're capable of so much more than you realize."

I snort.

"You don't believe me?" He appears wounded.

"You don't need to sing me so many praises, you know. I've already allowed you to court me," I add drily.

"You think I'm singing you praises?" His eyes widen in shock.

"It's nice that you think so highly of me, but you hardly know me or what I'm capable of. Yes, I might be a goddess, but I happen to be a rather mediocre one."

He extends his arm in front of me to stop me from walking further. Planting himself in front of me, he stares at me with an odd expression on his face.

"You're anything but mediocre, Minnie," he states in a serious tone. "Perhaps no one's told you this before, but you are *extraordinary*."

My lashes flutter in confusion at the vehemence behind his tone.

"You've never had anyone tell you this before?" he asks softly.

I lower my chin in a barely perceptible nod.

He smiles.

"Then I will tell you this every day until you believe it. You are extraordinary."

Once more, I'm rendered speechless. This courtship of his is working because my heart is beating like crazy in my chest.

He takes a step forward until his chest bumps into mine—his *very* hard chest.

A shiver goes down my back.

The word *extraordinary* echoes in my mind while I stare at his plump lips and gulp down nervously.

Oh, something is certainly working, and I'm not sure if it's his honeyed words or the fact that his body is like an ancient sculpture come to life. Or maybe both.

I'm suddenly dizzy and warm and as he slowly leans toward me, I grow even hotter.

Is he... Is that... Is he going to do that kissing thing with me? That eating of mouths I saw other people do? Is he going to put his lips on mine? Before, I would have said absolutely no—disgusting.

Now, I'm...curious.

Instinctively, my eyes squeeze shut as I hold myself still and...wait.

I wait and wait, convincing myself I'll tell him off *after* the fact.

But nothing happens.

I blink my eyes open.

Mine is a few steps away from me now, shooting daggers with his eyes to poor Tommy, who is looking back and forth between the two of us.

"Did I interrupt something?" he asks, confused.

"No," I say at the same time that Mine says, "Yes."

His nostrils flare as he glares at the ghostly lad. Oh, he was definitely going to do that kissing thing with me. My cheeks heat at the mere mental image of it. Yet Tommy's arrival proved fortuitous as I am still not sure I can go that far.

I might have allowed him to court me, though I am still not sure to what end. All I know is that I like being around him. He makes me feel like I matter. That doesn't erase the fact that an entanglement with a mortal is forbidden. But as long as no one knows...

"How did you manage to come here? It's quite a distance away from the base. I thought you'd have been dragged back by now," I ask.

"I can go a bit further, too," Tommy mentions with a proud smile.

"Why did you leave so suddenly then?" I frown.

"Because I was a third wheel!" he exclaims. "You were having a moment and it was uncomfortable to watch."

"A moment? What do you mean? We were not having any moment."

"Oh, we certainly were," Mine agrees, his stance now more relaxed.

"What?"

Mine comes around and takes my hand.

"And we were having a moment before you interrupted just now, too."

Tommy's eyes widen. "I-I-I... I'm so sorry, Major!" he cries out in horror.

Mine still has a sour expression on his face as he regards the stressed ghost. He must have *really* wanted to do that kissing thing with me. I wet my lips and look at him from beneath my lashes. I think I rather wanted it too... So what if it's not technically allowed since I am unwed and he is mortal? The more I think about it, the more sure I am that he is the only person I'd like to try kissing with.

He catches me staring at him and raises a brow at me.

"We'll have other moments," I tell him with a smile. "Stop berating the poor boy."

He stares at me for a second, his touch insistent and hot.

"Other moments, huh?"

I slowly nod.

"Plural?"

I nod again, caught in his mesmerizing gaze.

"I'll hold you onto that," he murmurs softly before he turns back to Tommy. With a heavy sigh, he decides to let the poor ghost off the hook. "You're fine, lad. Just as well, you can help us find the entrance to the castle."

Tommy readily agrees and promises he will make himself helpful.

We resume our journey, this time with Tommy a few steps ahead as he surveys the area. Mine still holding on tightly to my hand. Some might say *too* tightly.

But I rather like it. And him. Especially him and his warm presence. It's comfortable and it feels like home—or what I imagine an *inviting* home would feel like. I wouldn't mind it if he decided to *never* let go. In fact, I lean closer to him and twine my arm around his while holding his hand so I can also have a good grip on him and never let *him* go.

I smile blithely until I realize what I just admitted to myself.

I...like him?

Mine?

I like Mine.

I like *like* him.

Oh my, this is bad!

NINETEEN

"THERE'S AN OPEN DOOR OVER THERE," Tommy
signals us as he walks out of the castle wall.

"Thanks, lad," Mine mentions as he goes to the door. The
rusty hinges rattle and it takes him a few tries to open it.

I follow after him, taking in the dusty surroundings. There
are cobwebs everywhere, and goose bumps cover my skin as I
see a few insects scurry out of our path. Tommy wrinkles his
nose in disgust too, even though the insects cannot crawl on his
ghostly body. He hurries ahead, disappearing from sight.

"I don't think anyone's been in this side of the castle in a
long time," I mutter.

"At least since the war started," Mine agrees. "With a castle
this size, I doubt they had the staff to maintain it after the
museum closed."

"You said you read about it. So you know where we're
going?"

"The Early Modern wing. The artifacts should be there."

I nod. "I hope this works. Otherwise—"

"It will work," Mine corrects. "You trust me, no?"

My brows knit together.

"No?"

He blinks. "What? You don't trust me?"

"Why would I trust you? I barely know you," I add drily.

"Because I'm courting you? Because you're alone with me without your powers? Because…"

"I get it." I put my hand up and roll my eyes. "I suppose, from that point of view, I trust you. Although"—I narrow my eyes at him—"we've already ascertained that I would beat you in a physical fight, so that is moot."

"Of course. You are so much stronger than me, Minnie. It is me who should be worried about being alone with you. God knows, you might even take advantage of me and steal my virtue," he adds dramatically.

I lower my head to avoid a cobweb and turn to stare at him in confusion.

"What do you mean?"

"It was a joke." He shakes his head as he walks ahead.

"No, really, what do you mean by stealing your virtue? That's impossible."

He half-turns to raise a brow at me.

"Minnie darling, you wound me. You wouldn't want to steal my virtue?" He crosses his hands over his chest.

I purse my lips. "I never thought about it like that."

"Like what?"

"That I could be a virtue thief, too. But that seems fair. Why should males get to have all the fun? I can be the one to steal your virtue too," I add pensively.

"You can be my virtue thief all you want," he murmurs as he comes closer to me.

I do my best to fight a smile, though my lips have a mind of their own as they curl up in pleasure. I slap his shoulder playfully, then lean in to whisper in his ear, "You're lucky you're still in possession of said virtue. Otherwise, I would have had blood on my hands."

"My blood?" he asks slowly.

I smirk. "First, that of the person who would have taken your virtue." I pause. "Then yours."

"Ah, Minnie, you're so bloodthirsty," he murmurs appreciatively. "Don't stop. I like it."

"You're morbid." I chuckle.

"Morbidly yours." He winks.

I gulp down and look away, afraid that if he gazes at me like this much longer, I will forget all about who I am, my duty, and the reason why we're here in the first place.

"But I thought you can't kill humans?"

"I never said I'd kill you. But I would have my pound of flesh."

"Your pound of flesh, huh? That means that I am yours, too?" He licks his lips as he takes one more step toward me. He's now so close I can smell his fresh soap—a relief considering the musty, old smell of this room.

"You are, Mine. You are." Patting him on the chest, I try to ignore the way my heart beats in my chest or the fact that my cheeks are likely scarlet red. I move past him and walk further into the castle.

Mine's chuckle echoes behind me. That scoundrel! He's probably gloating that he's able to tease me like this.

The grand hall stretches out before us, its soaring ceilings accentuated by clear glass that gives a glimpse of the sky. The walls are adorned with ornate tapestries, and sparkling chandeliers hang from above, casting a warm glow over the space.

"And Tommy—" My words are cut off when I spot him from the corner of my eye.

He's coming back into the grand hall from another entrance, and he's not alone.

"That is..."

"Major, Miss Minnie!" he calls out to us. "I met someone," he adds effusively as he gestures us to the ghost of a young lady. Seemingly in her late teens, she's dressed in a long linen gown that is tattered around the hem. The color is washed out, with spots of a vivid green and others of a pale green. Her black hair is braided down her back, with a few strands curling down her face.

"This is Annie. She's been here a long time."

"Oh, I bet," I mutter under my breath.

Mine shakes his head and releases a long sigh.

"Some four hundred years?" He ventures a guess.

Tommy's eyes widen. "How did you know?"

"She's dressed in a seventeenth century dress," he notes drily.

Tommy stares in wonder at him, probably idolizing him even more now. The girl, Annie, however, regards us both with suspicion.

I put on my best smile. It's never wise to upset an old ghost. After a hundred years or so, they start gaining enough power to blast a human. And the last thing I want is the ghost of a young girl blasting me.

"How did you come to be here? Did you live in the castle?"

She's still staring at me intently. But she doesn't answer.

"Uh, Annie? Can you answer Miss Minnie? She's a nice lady, I promise," Tommy interjects.

Her hand shoots out and she grabs Tommy's arm, the hold bruising, but in a ghostly way. I frown. His energy signature flickers in and out under her touch.

"Minnie, stay back," Mine whispers as he pulls me close to him.

"Something's not right."

He nods.

"Tommy, can you come here?"

"Why? Annie's nice. Right, Annie?" He turns to look at her. Her lips curl up in a sinister smile.

"Of course," she murmurs in a sultry voice.

Tommy's eyes glaze over with a type of adoration bordering on obsession.

Oh no. This is not good.

His ghostly signature continues to flicker in and out, and within seconds, his ghost is gone.

"Demon," I grit out.

Some demons are known to take the form of an innocent ghost to lure people to their deaths and thus consume even more souls. It's a strategy that works in a lot of worlds. If only I had my powers...then I would have been able to sense his demonic energy.

And now poor Tommy's fallen prey to this blasted demon.

"We can still save his soul," I tell Mine. "But it will prove difficult."

The girl's features contort and morph until the true form of the demon is revealed.

"This stink will never get old," Mine mumbles under his breath.

"They're made up of decaying energy. Of course they're going to smell not so pleasant."

The demon roars, opening its mouth to reveal two rows of sharp, canine-like teeth.

"Is there no demon dentist? Or at least demonic toothpaste. I rather think that would be an easy business venture, what with all these demons and their nasty cavities..."

"I don't think it's the right time to talk about demon cavities, Mine. Especially not when we are about to become this demon's next meal."

He scrunches his nose in distaste.

"Does he need to bite me to take my soul? Because why else would he need all those sharp teeth if he can just absorb the energy?"

"He can only absorb the energy when your soul is out of your body," I explain with a roll of my eyes. "Until then, he will use his sharp teeth to make sure the soul gets out of your body."

"Ew. He's not putting that stinky mouth anywhere near me, Minnie. You won't let him, right?" He flutters his lashes at me. I can't tell if he's genuinely afraid or if he's mocking me. Sometimes I don't know if Mine is joking around or is being serious, and that is rather annoying.

"I will protect you," I assure him.

But as I face the demon head-on, I realize I have no idea how to fight him without my powers.

As if reading my mind, Mine dashes to the side and brings his elbow down upon a glass case, then takes something out of it.

"Here," Mine mentions as he brings me one long bone. He's holding on to another identical one as he assumes a fighting stance, looking quite proud of his quick thinking.

I look at his great find and release a long sigh. If this demon doesn't eat us today, I'll never live down this shame. Hear that. Fighting with a bone.

"Are you serious?"

"I'm not touching that demon with my bare hands," he says with a look of disgust.

Rolling my eyes, I take a step in front of him, shielding him with my body as I wait for the demon to strike. Be it what may, but I can still heal—albeit much, much slower. Mine cannot. I suppose I can deal with a little pain as long as this demon is destroyed.

As I grasp onto the bone, however, my palms start sizzling and I feel the latent energy inside it. Eyes wide, I focus on that energy, drawing it out until it envelops my entire body, making it glow a deep blue.

"Minnie..." Mine whispers in awe.

"Energy. The bone has energy," I whisper.

He gives me the other bone, too, and I hold on tightly to it, siphoning all the remaining energy until I feel a strong burst of power.

The demon lets out another wail that's followed by a pungent smell of putrefaction.

"Ew!" Mine shields his nose.

"I have this handled. Stand back."

Mindful of using the little energy I have carefully, I don't summon my ice sword. Instead, I use the long bone and only freeze the end of it, making a sharp, spear-like head.

Just as the demon rushes forward, mouth wide open and ready to chew us out, I stab the bone in between his upper and lower jaw, digging the spear-like head into the roof of its mouth. It wobbles back, letting out a loud wail of pain. Before it can recover and charge again at us, I call back my makeshift weapon. As my fingers wrap around the middle of the weapon, the ice from the spear-like head flows down, enveloping the entire body of the bone and turning it into the perfect cold and deadly weapon.

I grab it tightly, letting out a sigh of satisfaction at the familiar icy feel. It's so cold, the air itself is pebbled with ice crystals all around me. Yet for the first time in months, the cold is welcoming. It's a part of me, no longer the enemy.

My body hums with pleasure at this little burst of power, and perhaps it's rather cliché of me to say this, but I don't think I've ever appreciated my spiritual energy as much as I do now, knowing how it is to live without it.

I don't get to dwell much on the nostalgia of it, though, as the demon quickly recovers in the process, growing even more spikes around its body and emitting more foul gases.

"Gross," Mine mutters.

A glance back reveals him sitting quite relaxed a distance away, arms across his chest, back against the wall. I blink. That is rather...odd of him. This is an *ascended* demon, not just a regular one. I doubt Mine would have seen one in his lifetime and, well, remain alive. They are that vicious with living beings as well. But based on his countenance and the way he's cheering me on, you'd think he's just a spectator watching a show.

"Go, Minnie! Show him you're the *bestest* goddess in the whole universe."

My lips fight against a smile.

"I'm the *only* goddess you've met." I roll my eyes.

"So? That just makes you the standard and I shall judge all other gods and goddesses compared to you."

The demon roars. I turn back my attention to him. His body is straining as more foul energy oozes out from within.

"I don't think he likes not being the center of attention," Mine says.

"He's trying to ascend again," I mutter.

Mine sobers up. "If he does... Tommy will be gone, no?"

I nod tightly.

"I'll get you more magical objects," he suddenly says and rushes toward one of the wings of the castle, leaving me alone with the demon.

I sigh. He could have just said he was afraid. I wouldn't have judged him. He's just a human, after all. Alas, there's no time to think about Mine's display of bravery—or lack of.

The demon's back splits open and spike-like tentacles come out from his skin. There are three of them, all coming toward me. Still concerned about conserving energy, I use my body to dodge them, leaning backward when one aims for my head and sideways when the other two try to hit my body.

Pressing hard on the ball of my left foot, I propel myself in the air and jump behind him, using my makeshift icicle to sever one of the tentacles. The demon cries out in pain, but my victory is short-lived when two more tentacles appear from the same spot.

Damn it!

He's ascending fast. He's probably consuming the leftover souls at an alarming rate so he can reach the next level.

A demon of this level wouldn't be a problem when I'm at my normal capacity. But like this...

With each use of my icicle, each movement of my body, I can feel the borrowed energy seep out of me. I have only a few movements left before I'll be out, so I need to think about this strategically. There's also the added worry that I might not act in time to save Tommy's soul.

As the tentacles reach for me once more, I jump up and imbue the rest of my energy into the tip of the icicle. Getting in front of the demon, I rotate my body around to evade the tentacles while I mentally attempt to identify the demon's core where his energy is stored. If I manage to land a powerful blow to its core, I can end him quickly. But I only have one chance before I'll be depleted of energy.

But just as the tip of my icicle hits him in the chest, it disintegrates.

My eyes widen.

The demon laughs at me, and in a moment of inattention, his tentacles hit me straight in the chest, flinging me to the back of the room. I hit the wall and crumble to the floor, pain erupting in my entire body.

Blood pours from two incision sites where the sharp spikes of the tentacles hit me.

It's hard to move without groaning in pain, but I push myself to get up.

More blood stains my clothes and drips to the floor.

I close my eyes and take a deep breath. All my years of training come back to me in a split of a second. This is likely a level two demon trying to ascend to level three. Dangerous, but not unmanageable. With a level one, I could have had an easier time finding its energy core and destroying it, but this demon seems to have built an armor around his chest. Somehow, I need to penetrate that armor.

Yet my wounds are not closing, so I am completely out of energy.

"Minnie, here!" Mine's voice echoes in the hall. I turn to look at him, surprised to see the multitude of items he's holding in his arms. Items that might have spiritual energy in them.

My optimism resurfaces.

But before he can reach me, he has to evade the demon's tentacles. To my surprise, he does.

Quite easily.

I blink.

He's nimble on his feet, moving almost as if he's floating while dodging every attack. I suppose his physical prowess might be attributed to his training in the military, but it is my first time seeing him like this.

He's...magnificent.

And he's not even doing anything.

He's just evading every blow with such grace, it's like

watching a dancer on the great stages of Aperion mimicking an ancient battle where the protagonist easily subdues the demonic forces.

I don't even *like* Aperite dance performances. Yet I find myself mesmerized by Mine's performance.

He's entirely unscathed as he reaches my side and gives me a handful of different objects—a mirror, an ancient comb, a small silver box, and a brooch.

The moment I touch them, pure energy washes over me. My wounds knit together until I'm completely healed. This time, there's so much energy, I get lightheaded.

His shrewd eyes look me over, noting the blood stains.

"You're all right?"

"Now I am." I smile.

"Good. Go kill that demon."

I give him a nod, though for a short moment, I'm unable to take my eyes off him. Danger swirls around us, and the demon is one second from attacking again, yet the look in Mine's eyes as he watches me makes something within me vibrate.

It's strange. Unfamiliar. But it makes me giddy in a way that only killing demons did before—which is itself odd since I'm hesitating to kill the demon just to get another glimpse of him. He might be *just* a human, but he is a magnificent one. A brave one, despite my previous misgivings.

A tentacle strikes in our direction. I push Mine out of the way and summon a shield of ice around him. If he moves, it moves with him, making sure he's protected at all times.

He doesn't protest. In fact, he seems rather pleased with it.

Good.

At least he's not like those males who do not like a female doing things for them. He's taking his role as a human companion to a goddess quite seriously, even going out of his way to help me. I suppose that earns him some extra points in this courtship of his.

The magical items yielded enough energy that I'm able to fight close to my regular standard. I summon my ice blades, rotating them around just as the demon sends his tentacles flying toward us again. When he notices he cannot hurt Mine, he strikes at me.

I deflect the blow and cut through the tentacle, but this time, I infuse the sharp edge of my swords with a dash of cryos—the secret ability my clan is known for. Instead of regenerating or even duplicating, the tentacle flesh is cauterized with a layer of ice that consumes it from within until the entire thing falls off.

I do the same to a second tentacle, all the while flashing myself closer to the demon. He's much uglier the closer I get, and the smell of putrefaction is rather noxious. I can't blame Mine for wanting to be as far away from him. But as it happens, I'm used to this. I've even had worse. The higher a demon ascends, the more they reek of putrefaction since the energy becomes more and more polluted. It's only when they're at the eighth level that they are able to control everything perfectly and mask the stench.

As I flash myself right in front of him, he roars loudly, sending a gust of putrid wind toward me. I dodge it and lower myself to the ground. Time is of the essence here. Otherwise, Tommy might not make it.

I scan his chest carefully, looking for any weak spot. The skin is a hard shell, similar to that of a reptile. No wonder it barely budged when I tried to penetrate it the first time. Yet on a closer look, I notice a darker spot close to the center of his chest.

It's small. Barely visible. My aim must be incredibly precise to hit it, and with the thickness of the shell, I will need momentum too.

Pursing my lips, I jump back. My eyes are still focused on that small dot. I take a deep breath and let the remaining energy flow through me. Combining my two blades together, I turn them into a translucent spear. The sharp end is a deep blue as I infuse cryos into the tip.

The remaining tentacles move wildly around in an attempt to pin me down.

I move faster.

And when I've gained enough momentum, I sprint toward the demon, spear aimed toward the tiny black dot.

He attempts to protect himself with his tentacles, but I cut through them before pushing the sharp tip of the spear into his chest.

He shrieks in pain. His hands reach for me. I'm holding on to the spear that's still lodged into his chest as he frantically moves around, pulling at me and trying to get me off him.

I hold on.

His wails of pain intensify as my cryos spreads within his energy core. When the outside of the armor starts turning a light blue, I finally let go and propel myself back.

Breathing hard, I wait for the result.

The cryos acts from within, and in a matter of seconds, his entire body becomes a light blue before it explodes.

To my surprise, Mine pulls me inside the shield, placing his body in front of me as pieces of the demon fly everywhere.

"It's done," I whisper when there's nothing left behind.

The shield flickers in and out before disappearing too now that I am running low on energy.

Mine slowly turns.

"And Tommy?"

"Look." I nod to the middle of the hall, where a shimmery light becomes stronger and stronger.

From a small, golden energy ball, tens of flickering lights burst out. Some are weaker than others, but they are still intact.

"There he is." I point to one of the shimmery dots. It may not have Tommy's previous form, but I can recognize the energy signature.

The air crackles with a new type of energy, and my eyes widen in surprise.

"We need to go. The collectors will come to take the souls. Take me where you found those items."

He nods and grabbing my hand, he leads me down a windy path

out of the main hall and into a smaller wing of the castle. As we enter one room, there are glass cases on every wall and some in the middle. A couple of them are broken—the ones Mine took the items from.

"You did a good job. How did you know which ones had energy in them?"

He shrugs. "I didn't. I just hoped." He flashes me a confident smile.

"You were lucky then."

"Perhaps. But *you* were spectacular. Is that how you usually kill demons?"

I surreptitiously preen at his praise. Good on him to recognize it. He is a fine observer.

"A demon of that level? No. With my powers, I can dispatch him much quicker."

"That's impressive. *You* are impressive," he praises as he gets closer to me. His shoulders brush against my own and I stifle a shudder. The image of him running with the items toward me as he evaded the demon's tentacles is still fresh in my mind. It makes my heart beat rather wildly in my chest. My stomach, too, is a little unsettled, though that might also be from the demon stench.

"Let's get more items," I announce, stepping forward and putting some distance between us.

I walk straight to the broken cases and read the description of the artifacts. They are, as he first mentioned, believed to have belonged to witches. So he was right that they would be imbued with energy. Nodding to myself, I browse the intact cases, cross-referencing the descriptions to make sure the items also belong to witches.

When I find one that is similar enough, I prepare to break the case, but Mine stops me.

"Allow me," he murmurs, trying to push me aside.

I narrow my eyes at him.

"You've already done plenty. I can do it myself," I say as I shove him back.

Does he think I can't break a damn case? I just killed a demon *and* kept him safe within my shield.

He opens his mouth to protest, but I'm quicker as I bring my elbow down on the case with the remaining bit of energy I have left.

The glass shatters and I reach inside. The item is a slight, golden hairpin with a leaf design at the top. Pretty. I might even keep it after we're done. I quite like the color gold. And humans do make pretty jewelry.

I hum to myself in satisfaction, but Mine is mumbling on about doing it himself.

"Minnie, you'll hurt yourself." His hand is inside the case, too, as he tries to grab the item before me.

"No. I can handle myself," I fire back, reaching for the pin.

Our hands bump one against the other and I pinch him. He releases a small yelp of pain, and that distraction is enough for me to get hold of the pin.

Holding it tightly in my hand, I focus on the energy within.

My mouth parts in shock as I feel the enormous amount of spiritual energy it contains, but for some reason, I am unable to siphon it.

I try again, focusing harder.

Nothing.

On the third try, I give up and open my eyes.

"It's not working," I whisper dejectedly.

There *is* energy inside. I can feel it. But I cannot get hold of it.

"Can I see it?" Mine asks.

I extend my arm to give him the pin when a voice resounds from behind us.

"That belongs to me."

We both turn around at the same time.

I freeze in shock, and the pin drops to the ground with a thud. Mine doesn't seem to realize the danger we're in, so he stoops down to grab it.

"Another ghost? Demon?" he asks in a laid-back voice.

"Worse," I whisper.

"You have taken what is mine," the voice continues. "I will now require something in exchange."

"What do you mean worse?" He frowns.

I purse my lips.

"That...is a faery. And a bargain with a faery is a bad, *bad* idea."

TWENTY

"LEAVE THE PIN. We'll find another object," Mine whispers in my ear.

"Unfortunately, it doesn't work like that. I've already touched it."

"So?"

"So she will not let us go until we agree to a bargain."

"The goddess is correct," the voice says as it finally materializes before us.

She has long white hair that's framing a heart-shaped pale face. Her pointy ears peek through her hair, adorned by golden jewelry. She's wearing a long emerald green silk dress. A thick gold necklace is wrapped around her neck, and a thin chain falls from it, turning into a golden mesh corset that emphasizes her small waist. Her arms, too, are fully adorned with golden bracelets.

She's stunning like her wretched kind usually is. But as the thought crosses my mind, I immediately look at Mine. He better not think that.

To his credit, he's regarding her with narrowed eyes accompanied by wariness and distrust.

Good male.

He is a decent judge of character. Of course he must be if

he's chosen to court me and I took pity on him and allowed to do so.

The faery's glance moves toward Mine, and I note a glimmer of interest.

"He will do," she states, taking a step forward.

Immediately, I put myself in front of him.

"He is off-limits."

She smirks and regards me curiously.

"It is him that I want for this bargain to be fulfilled."

"And I am telling you that you can't have it." Glancing back at Mine, I elbow him in the ribs and mutter, "Say something."

"I am not available," he adds in an amused voice.

I glare at him.

He doesn't realize the danger we're in, does he? The mere fact that I tried to siphon energy from an object belonging to a faery entitles her to payment, and from what I have heard, faeries drive hard bargains. They see what one prizes the most and they demand that in return.

I don't dwell on the fact that Mine might be my prized possession. That sort of mental gymnastics is better left for another day when we're not facing a powerful faery while I am currently powerless.

Even if you were not powerless, you would still have to play by her rules, my inner voice notes drily.

The faery race was created by the Flora Primordial and it's almost as old as Aperion itself. The faeries were her prized offspring and she was always particular to them, going as far as to make them guardians of all plants. Before the Primordials disappeared, Flora wanted to ensure that her children would not be taken advantage of, so she bestowed on them a gift—nothing would be taken from them without something returned. But it was up to the faery enforcing the bargain to approve the item returned.

Just like the vows to the Source are unbreakable, so are the bargains between a faery and any other race—Aperites included. That is one of the reasons why Aperites hate faeries, since they can wield a power over them no one else can. It is also why we are taught from childhood to sense if something belongs to a faery and avoid it altogether.

Damn it. Yet another thing that could have been avoided if only I had my spiritual energy.

"I require a groom for my granddaughter. He is a fine male." She points straight at Mine, her eyes moving up and down his body, assessing him as one would cattle.

Never mind that she doesn't look old enough to be a grandmother—though I've heard her race ages quite gracefully over a number of hundreds of years—but to set her sights on my male?

Unacceptable.

"Yes, he is a very fine male. But he is mine. You can't have him," I tell her, barely in control of myself.

"You've heard the lady. I am spoken for," Mine drawls as he throws his arm over my shoulder. "I do like it when you're jealous," he whispers in my ear. "Don't stop."

I take a deep breath and seek to calm myself so I don't clobber him over the head—mine or not mine.

"This is a delicate situation. Shut up."

He feigns a gasp.

"I am at my lady's mercy," he adds with a smile.

Can't he take a hint? This isn't a game.

"See, I could never be parted from her. I am a rather weak human who is in need of his protector. My darling Minnie has deigned to take me under her wing and I have sworn her my loyalty," he informs the faery, and I can't for the life of me tell if he's joking or not.

But then his tone suddenly changes, as does the atmosphere around us. "Forever," he adds, punctuating each syllable in a dark voice.

The faery takes a step back, her eyes slightly widening. She quickly averts her gaze from Mine, almost as if she didn't dare look him straight in the eye.

Good male. I pat him on the shoulder. At least he knows

who he belongs to. But that still doesn't solve our current quandary.

"What else would you accept?" I ask.

"As I have mentioned. I require a groom for my granddaughter," she says. "I will bargain for that or nothing else."

Mine moves closer to me. The heat from his body permeates my own as he aligns himself right behind me. His chin comes to rest on my shoulder as he regards the faery with a laid-back expression.

"What does she mean by nothing else?" he whispers. "Does that mean we can be on our way now?"

I shake my head.

"It means she will not let us leave until we agree on a bargain. And trust me, she has time," I add drily. "Time that we do not have with how fast things were evolving on the base."

"All right. Got it. So we must close the bargain then."

My muscles tense. I slowly turn my head around, my nose almost bumping into his.

"You are not going to her," I tell him. "You are courting me, or have you forgotten that little detail?"

Even if he were not courting me, I would not have relinquished him. I found him first. He belongs to me.

"Me? I would never." He feigns a horrified expression. "Don't you worry, tiny darling, you're not getting rid of me that easily."

"Then what do you propose we do?" I narrow my eyes at him.

The faery is watching the exchange with great interest.

"I will accept your first male born," she interjects.

"No."

"Never."

Both Mine and I burst out at the same time, and the faery lets out a soft chuckle.

Mine leans back and straightens his shoulders.

"What are your requirements for a groom for your granddaughter?"

The faery's lips curl up.

"Handsome, of course," she says as she continues to stare appreciatively at Mine. In turn, I glare at her. How dare she look like that at my male. Yes, he is handsome, but that is only for me to note.

"He must be strong and be able to protect her." Her eyes linger on his muscles. I grab his arm and pull him closer, splaying my palm over his muscles so she can see they're taken. They're my muscles. Well, not mine, but I am the only female who can touch them.

The faery notes the possessiveness in my grip and she chuckles. Mine, on the other hand, like the good male he is, places his hand over mine and gives me a comforting pat. His eyes, too, are on me, even when the faery is speaking.

Good. Otherwise, we would have had words later on.

"He must also be faithful and loyal. He must not step out on my granddaughter."

"There you have it, then. It cannot possibly be me," Mine interjects. "I only have eyes for one female, and it's this tiny one over here."

I shoot him daggers with my eyes, though I am quite pleased with his statement.

"Hmm." She clicks her tongue against her teeth. "Then we find ourselves in a bind, do we not?"

"I wouldn't say so," Mine continues. "I happen to have the perfect solution that would satisfy all your demands."

"You do?" I blink in surprise.

He winks at me.

"I happen to know a male who is not only strong and handsome, but he is also currently unattached."

"Who?"

"Your brother, of course."

My mouth parts in shock.

"Molokai?"

He nods.

"But he would never agree to this," I whisper. I don't deny

that he is a good choice. He also happens to have wronged me as of recently, so I wouldn't mind handing him over to this faery's granddaughter. That would serve him right. Especially since he has quite the distaste for faeries.

Well, Kai happens to have a distaste for all non-Aperite beings, but faeries are at the top of the list because when he was just a fledgling, he accidentally went to the faery realm and got lost. He doesn't speak much of what happened there, but he's always been vocal about his hate of their kind.

"He doesn't have to agree."

"I don't follow." I frown.

"The sigil. Whoever has his sigil can call on him, no?"

"Yes, but—"

"Would you accept that? A sigil that can call on a powerful god at any time?"

The faery tilts her head to the side as she considers this.

"And who is this god you are talking about."

"Mine. I'm not sure—" I pull on his sleeve, but it's in vain as he continues.

"His name is Molokai from the House of Cryos. He is a general in the Aperite army and he is unattached. No one outside his family knows the sigil that can call on him at any time."

"Molokai from the House of Cryos you say?" The faery's eyes sparkle with mischief. "I accept."

"Mine!" I pinch him. "Kai will kill me."

"Will he?"

"Well, he won't exactly kill me. But he will be so angry with me."

"And you think he doesn't deserve it after everything he's done? I should think someone as straitlaced as him would benefit from some fun."

"How do you know he's straitlaced?" I frown.

"Isn't he?"

"Well, yes, but—"

"It's settled. Think of it as a little revenge."

I bite my lip. He's right. Kai behaved abysmally with me. He will likely be enraged when he finds out, but oh well. He deserves it.

"Fine. You can have my brother's sigil. In return, I want your verbal confirmation that I may avail myself of the energy inside this pin."

"You may avail yourself of the energy inside the pin in exchange for your brother's sigil," the faery confirms.

"I need a pen and paper—"

The faery materializes both and hands them to me.

I scribble down the sigil.

"This will only go in effect if it is drawn with blood, on the flesh of the summoner."

The faery inspects the drawing close.

"And how will I know it is genuine?"

"I vow to the Source that this is my brother's sigil."

She nods. "You have a bargain."

After grabbing the paper, the faery disappears from sight.

I release a loud sigh. That was a close call.

"What about your sigil?" Mine asks. "What is it?"

"I won't tell you."

"Why? I'm your male." He pouts.

"Perhaps. But I have not agreed to be your female. Until then, you will not get my sigil."

"Minnie!" he complains.

"Let us go now. We have a portal to find," I say and head to the exit.

All things considered, we have resolved quite a few issues. I killed a demon, made sure Tommy's soul went to P'asala, and now I have an item that's overflowing with powerful energy.

"Now wait a minute," Mine calls out from behind as I get out of the castle. I'm about to tap into the energy of the pin when he snatches it from me.

"What are you doing?" I thunder at him.

"I am not going anywhere like this." He points to his clothes that are stained with some of my blood and demon grime. "You are not going anywhere like that either."

I glance down at my dress and purse my lips. Whereas he only has a few light stains, I am covered from head to toe in disgusting demon bodily fluids. Alas, that comes with the job.

"It's just blood and demon grime." I roll my eyes at him.

"Minnie! It's not just blood and demon grime. It's disgusting! It smells bad too."

"So?"

"What do you mean, so? We're dirty."

"I've had worse." I shrug.

"I'm well aware," he adds drily, with a roll of his eyes. "And while you might be fine smelling so foul, I am not. We need to wash and change."

"No."

"Yes."

"No. Time is of the essence."

"I'm not going anywhere carrying this stench with me."

"Good thing I do not need you to come with me." I humph and turn to go. To think that just a few moments ago I was praising him for being a good male. More like a fussy male. Who's bothered by a bit of demon grime? Certainly not me. As I told him, I've had worse.

"Then I guess you don't need this too." He smirks and pockets the pin.

"Mine!" I tackle him to try to get the pin back, but he's fast, dodging me at every turn.

He hops back a few steps and chuckles at me.

"Wash and you get your pin."

"Mine! It's not the time to joke around! The greed demon must have grown stronger already. If we return to base and he senses the energy from the pin, he might realize what we plan and he could try to stop us."

"We're not returning to the base."

I cross my arms over my chest.

"And how do you propose we wash?"

"There's a river down the hill. We'll wash there."

My eyes widen with outrage.

"A r-river? Have you gone mad? It's cold!"

"You're a goddess of ice," he shoots back.

"Whose powers are currently on a leave of absence. I do not like the cold."

He shrugs. "That makes two of us. But I dislike being dirty more than the cold."

Pressing my lips together, I debate the matter in my head.

"You can wash and I'll wait," I offer. No matter how much I'd like to snatch the pin from him, it's clear he's not going to give it to me without a fight—and I'm currently too worn out to engage in one.

"No. You will wash, too."

"But—"

"I'd like to be able to stand next to the female I'm courting without holding my breath, Minnie," he adds with a sigh.

I nibble on my lip. He does have a point. Although... I could certainly use this to keep him at arm's length. Though logical, I find that the idea doesn't appeal.

"But we don't have a change of clothes—"

"We do. I made sure to pack some since I assumed something like this would happen."

I gawk at him. He's ready for everything, isn't he? Though I'd like nothing more than to be mad at him since he clearly went through my clothes, I decide to let it slide—this time.

"Fine," I acquiesce.

He beams at me. We go back to the car to get the change of clothes, after which he leads the way to the lake. All the while, I'm trying to brace myself for the cold I'll encounter.

The lake is not as close as he'd made it out to be. It takes us more than thirty minutes to reach it. It's on the other side of the hill! How did he even know it was there is beside me.

Luckily, it's surrounded by trees, meaning that no one will be able to see us.

"You take that side, I will take this side," I say as I dig my foot into the dirt and draw a line to delineate each half of the lake.

"Minnie!" He groans.

"And you will go in first and stand with your back to me," I add.

"You'd better not try to leave and steal the pin," he warns.

Well, I did not think about that, though now that he mentions it...

"Vow it. Vow that you will not steal the pin and leave. And vow that you will wash."

I roll my eyes at him. Smart male.

"Fine, fine. I vow to wash and not steal the pin and leave."

"Good."

Without further ado, he unbuttons his jacket and throws it to the ground. He's wearing a white shirt underneath that he quickly chucks, too. He's now only in a tank top and I blink nervously at his muscles.

Is it suddenly warm?

I should turn away like I told him to do. I shouldn't be watching him undress, especially since with every piece of clothing he removes, something vibrates in my lower belly.

He doesn't tell me to turn, though. He's smirking at me as he removes his tank top.

Now he's bare-chested and my heart thuds horrifically loud in my chest. Goodness, it's definitely getting warm.

Then his hands are on his belt, unbuckling it and throwing it to the side. The sound of the zipper going down finally punches some sense into me and I quickly turn just as he lowers his trousers down his legs.

I'm mortified but also too damn curious. It's a battle with myself not to turn and watch him in his naked glory, something I've been thinking about quite a bit as of late.

Who am I kidding? I've been thinking about it every single night while we've been sleeping in the same cabin.

Only when I hear the sound of water splashing around do I finally turn.

"Don't peek, all right?" I call out to him.

"I am a gentleman, Minnie. Of course I will not peek."

I make quick work of removing my dress and shift. I don't take off my brassiere and underwear, though. That would be too scandalous.

As if everything I've been doing so far hasn't been the definition of scandalous.

With a sigh, I step toward my half of the lake.

Mine is still in his half with his back turned to me. He's washing his face and hair, going underwater before resurfacing.

A shudder goes down my back.

This is going to be so cold. I can already feel it.

Bracing myself, I squeeze my eyes shut as I dip one foot in the lake.

"Oh," I whisper in surprise. The water is lukewarm and not at all unpleasant. It's colder outside than inside. Without giving too much thought to how this difference in temperature could happen, I get inside until the water reaches my collarbone.

I splash it over my face. Perhaps this wasn't such a bad idea. It does feel nice to be clean.

Stepping a bit further into the lake, I emulate Mine and submerge myself to wash my hair. The bottom of the lake is slippery, and as I try to find my footing to resurface, I trip and fall further into the lake.

The water here is much deeper, now well over my head.

And there is one aspect that I did not consider.

I cannot swim.

I move my arms around in an attempt to bring myself to the surface, but just as I get a mouthful of air, I find myself being drawn under the water.

In my panic, I forget to close my mouth and water rushes in, making me splutter.

That lasts only a moment. In the next, two strong arms haul me back to the surface.

I wheeze and spit the water in my mouth, my lungs on fire

both from nearly drowning and from the panic that I might drown.

"There, I've got you," Mine whispers. He's holding me close to his body.

His naked body.

As my panic recedes, I realize he's crossed into my half of the lake. And now his naked body is next to my own and...

"Go back to your half of the lake," I attempt to protest.

He gives me a lopsided smile. "A thank you should be in order."

"Thank you. Now go."

He needs to leave. Now. This is not only improper, but it is also too much for my feeble senses. It's already bad enough that I can feel the strong muscles of his arms, and that if I leaned forward, my chest would brush against his chest and...

I redden instantly.

"My, my. You're blushing."

"M-me? Blushing. Of course not," I stammer.

"Yes. You are." He chuckles. "You're so cute."

"You need to let go. This is unseemly. Improper. Please," I croak.

"What is improper about me saving you?" he asks as he angles one brow.

"What? Everything! This." I attempt to push him off, but then I realize we're still standing in the middle of the lake where the water is too deep.

"Stop fidgeting, Minnie."

"Help me get over there." I motion to the edge. "Then let go."

"No one will see us." He tsks.

"So? I am an unmarried lady. A respectable unmarried lady. I cannot be this close to a naked man. Especially a shovel like you."

He tightens his hold over me and draws me closer. So close that my hard nipples bush against his warm chest. Oh my, I'm going to faint. Right here.

"Why are you still going on with that? How many times do I have to tell you I am not a rake?" His voice is different now, tighter. No longer playful like before, he's staring at me with a dangerous intensity.

The sun shines against his tanned pallor, intensifying the green hue of his eyes. If before I'd thought he was beautiful, like this, with droplets of water clinging to his lashes and some dripping down his skin, he is...mesmerizing.

I cannot take my eyes off him, though I'm painfully aware I must.

"I—" The shift in his countenance swallows my words.

"How can I be a rake when you're the only female I've ever looked at in all of my existence? Past, present, future. How?" The wind carries the last question, echoing in the valley and in my mind.

"I... That is to say... You may not be a rake, but that doesn't mean females don't desire you. I saw how the faery looked at you. There's also the women at the base and..."

"And? It is out of my control if other females look at me. But what is in my control is to never acknowledge them, never look at them."

I blink at the vehemence in his voice.

"Would you like me to be more disfigured than I already am? Say the word and I'll do it." He grabs my hand and brings it to his face, placing my fingers on his scar. "I can add another scar. And another. Until I'm so badly deformed no one will ever look at me. Would you like that?"

"W-what are you talking about?"

"I will do it. For you, I will do it. Just so you never think of another woman looking at me or desiring me."

"Are you mad?" I whisper.

"Yes, Minnie, I am raving mad," he grits out in a low voice. "If my words cannot assure you, then my actions should." He pauses, a sardonic smile pulling at his lips. "But then the question is... would you still look at me?"

"Of course," I blurt out without thinking what I'm admitting. "You'd be handsome to me anyway, just because you're you."

His lips curl up in a smile. "So you think I'm handsome?"

Damn it! I fell into his trap.

"Uhm, that is to say..."

"Your blush is confirmation enough," he says playfully. "That pleases me."

He leans forward and my mind blanks on me.

Is he going to...is he...

"Let go!" I shout, sliding out of his grip.

But seeing as how I'm still in deep waters, I immediately sink to the bottom.

He dives after me, grabs me—tighter this time—and he finally takes me to the shore.

Bad, bad idea.

At least the water was covering us before. Now?

My eyes widen as I look him up and down. Water drips down his muscled body, emphasizing every curvature. He looks like one of those marble statues, all hard angles and chiseled flesh. But the man before me is full of life, not an immobile statue. And as my eyes dip lower, I feel my heart thudding louder and louder.

I'm curious when I shouldn't be.

Luckily—or not—he's still wearing his underwear. But they're white. And soaking wet. That means I can see the contour of something.

Why am I suddenly this feverish? Why am I both hot and shivery at the same time?

There's something there. Something that arouses my interest. But before I can investigate further, he leans over to me.

"Minnie, Minnie." He tsks at me. "What am I going to do with you?"

"What do you mean?" I ask slowly, confused.

He smiles.

"I wonder...will I get a kiss in this lifetime?"

"A k-kiss? You want a k-kiss?" I stammer.

My pulse echoes in my ears, both at his suggestion and his nearness.

"Not just a kiss. I want *all* your kisses."

I gasp.

"All?" I repeat weakly.

"All."

I bite my lip as I stare into his eyes.

"I've never done this kissing thing before," I whisper.

"Me neither."

Giddiness erupts in my chest.

"Never?" I ask in a low voice.

His lips are pulled up in a smile as he shakes his head.

"I've been waiting for the only lips I'll ever kiss."

Then he leans in, and I close my eyes.

TWENTY-ONE

HIS HOT BREATH is on my lips, his clean scent invading my nostrils. I tilt my head back, giving him unspoken consent to continue with this kissing business. Forbidden or not, I'm far too curious about it. And seeing how many rules I've already broken, what's one more? A small one at that.

It's only one kiss.

To assuage my curiosity.

Yet just as I feel the mere brush of his lips against mine, a loud noise cuts through the air. We both fall apart. My heart is racing as I look wildly around.

"You're trespassing!" an old man shouts at us from within the woods. He stomps onto the ground, fast approaching us, carrying with him a hunting rifle.

Mine's eyes widen, but he doesn't lose his composure. He gives me half a smile and whispers, "Oops," after which he gathers our clothes, using my dress as a makeshift bag to hold them all. Before I can gather my wits about me, he pulls me up and swoops me in his arms. Well, perhaps swooping me in his arms might sound a tad too romantic.

He mostly swings me around his shoulders like a sack of potatoes and runs in the opposite direction.

The old man continues to shout at us. He even fires a warning shot.

But by the time the echo of the gun meets my ears, we're already a distance away, nestled within the thick forest.

He's fast, Mine. Very fast.

And strong. He carries me and our clothes with such ease, no wonder he has such impressive muscles.

"You can put me down now. I don't think he's behind us anymore."

He finds a fallen log and places me down to sit on it.

Thoughtful too, I muse.

He dumps the bundle of clothes on the ground before he takes a deep breath.

His eyes meet mine and as we stare at each other, laughter bubbles inside of me. I release the sound into the wild, and his own laughter joins in. We're both laughing. At the situation. At each other. At the fact that I was seconds away from having that kiss but instead a man with a shotgun chased us around.

The situation is amusing.

Yet soon the laughter gives way to mortification as I realize I'm still in a state of deshabille, as is he.

I lean forward to shield some of my nakedness. I could get my clothes and dress and put them back on, but that would call on him to do the same and ruin the moment. Besides, I find that my curiosity is not yet satisfied. I want to see more of him, know more of him.

He's standing proudly in front of me, hands on his hips, and I let my eyes roam over his body.

His abdominals are hard and pronounced. On his lower belly there is a light trail of dark hair that the band of his briefs swallows.

I've seen this part of him before when I treated him. Yet the scar from his wound is all but gone. There's nothing but healthy, virile male flesh.

Heat travels up my neck at the thought. Yet worry for him as

I notice his briefs start to tent and become more constraining accompanies that excitement. I nibble at my lip as I instinctively lean forward to investigate more.

"Done staring?" he asks, amusement in his voice.

"I'm not staring. I am observing. I am a nurse after all," I add shakily.

"And what are you observing?"

"The lump is back." I point to his white briefs. "Are you certain you're not hurt?"

He blinks and stares at me quietly for a few moments.

"The...lump?"

I nod. "You had it when you got injured, too. But it seemed to go away on its own. Now it's back."

His gaze dips down to where I'm pointing. The material of his briefs is now tightly wrapped around his flesh. Still damp, the white cotton molds to the outline of his swollen intimate parts. But I am still confused as to how his flesh could change size so suddenly if he's not ill. That is the only logical explanation.

"Minnie," he groans my name as he tilts his head back and scrubs a hand over his face.

"Are you in pain?" I whip my gaze up.

His eyes are closed and he's breathing hard. That makes the swollen lump become bigger, pushing against the material as if it had a life of its own.

Releasing a long sigh, he takes a step toward me. Getting to his knees in front of me, he rests his hands on my thighs as he looks into my eyes.

"Minnie, do you know how sex, uhm, mating works?"

I blink in shock.

"O-o-of c-course," I stammer.

"How?"

"W-what? That's improper. I can't answer that."

"We're far past improper. Indulge me," he murmurs.

"But—"

"Please?"

I clear my throat against the sudden discomfort. It's not just the fact that we're discussing such a forbidden topic but also the way he's holding on to me, so close...

"I'm not entirely sure of the mechanics of it, but I do know that it happens when a mated couple is intimate with each other and the male spills his seed inside the female."

"And how does he, erm, spill his seed?"

My face flames.

"I... uhm..."

"You don't know?" He raises a teasing brow.

"Mine! Of course I..." I squeeze my eyes shut. "I grew up sheltered, all right? I was not allowed to read any material regarding mating, and in the army, no one would speak about such improper subjects in my presence. I only know what I've gathered from the movies I saw in Anthropa. But they were not too informative."

"How so?" he asks. This time, he's not mocking me. It's a genuine question.

"Well, the people in movies were in a bed, naked under the sheets." I shrug. "But I've also seen humans kiss and touch around the base."

"So when you thought I wanted to steal your virtue, what did you think was going to happen?"

"Can we change the subject? This is mortifying," I add under my breath.

"Tell me, Minnie."

"What I saw in movies. Naked bodies tangled together, I suppose," I finally admit, averting my gaze. I can barely stand to look him in the eye after this mortifying conversation. It's not just the impropriety of it all, though I suppose the subject was bound to be tackled seeing as how I've allowed him to court me. No, it's also because I'm embarrassed about my own lack of knowledge. I am over four thousand years old, for goodness' sake. I should know more than some incomplete observations.

Yet the sad reality is that I am not the only Aperite deity this ignorant about what goes on between mated couples. Every respectable unmarried lady is forbidden from exploring such matters. Even for someone as myself, who's had more freedom than others by being allowed to join the military, my knowledge is still painfully lacking. And that's because it's not just the parents who try to shield females from this information but also the other people in the military.

They don't talk about it, and we don't ask. That is the policy. Just mentioning something related to the act of mating would not only be highly scandalous, but it would also ruin one's reputation.

Fear perpetuates fear and in the end until the entire society is shaped by that which we strive to avoid.

"Look at me," he suddenly says, pushing my chin up. "It's all right not to know."

"Is it? Aren't you silently laughing at me?"

"I would *never* laugh at you, Minnie."

"In my defense, highborn ladies marry soon after their three thousandth birthday. I am a bit of an exception because I went into the military. That's the only reason why I don't have as much knowledge as other ladies my age."

He smiles at me.

"That swollen part of me, erm... it's swollen because it's full of seed."

I stare at him. This time it's *him* who's red from head to toe.

"Oh," I whisper. "So it..."

He nods. "It goes inside of you. And after it's, erm, emptied, it goes back to its normal state."

It's not hard to imagine *where* it would go inside of me, and instead of getting more embarrassed, I find myself growing hot. Right in that region. But then I suddenly frown.

"What about that time, though? It went back to its normal state and you didn't... Or did you..."

"Of course not," he hurries to assure me. "I can take care of it on my own. It can also go away on its own after a time if I force my thoughts away from you."

"And you forced your thoughts away from me?"

"I did my best." He flashes me a guilty smile.

"How often does this happen to you?"

He's taken aback by my question.

"Often enough," he says in a tight voice.

"Because you want to... mate with me?"

"It's not a conscious thing, Minnie. You just have to be near me and I..." He gulps down uncomfortably. "My body just reacts to you, all right? *Only* you."

Warmth spreads through me at his words. I don't like that he has to suffer from this condition, of course, but I do like that his body reacts *only* to me. And to think that he's been such a gentleman while suffering... It's giving me a new appreciation for him.

"But don't think that I'm pressuring you in any way," he hurries to add. "It's just a biological response. It doesn't mean anything."

I stare at him.

"I'll *never* pressure you about this. So what if you give me a hard-on every time you look at me with those beautiful eyes of yours, or if you give me blue balls every time you brush your hand against mine? I'll just have to find novel ways to get rid of it." His shoulders angle in a lazy shrug.

Blue balls? That sounds rather...painful.

"Novel ways..." I watch him through narrowed eyes. "That means thinking about something else?"

"Something gross." He nods.

"I don't like that," I suddenly announce. "I don't like you not thinking of me. You're courting *me*. You're supposed to *always* think of me."

His eyes widen.

"That's... erm..." He looks away.

"What's the other way? How do you take care of it?"

"Minnie..."

"How?" I insist.

"With my hand," he awkwardly admits. "While thinking it's you."

I gulp down.

"Do you... need to take care of it now?"

"I'll be fine. Just give me a few moments."

He gets up and walks away, turning his back to me. His chest rises and falls as he takes deep breaths. But he doesn't attempt to touch himself.

"Do you need help?"

A groan slips past his lips.

"Please be quiet, Minnie. This isn't helping."

"Why?"

"I'm trying to picture that gross demon from before."

I frown.

"But you said you'd think of me."

"Minnie..." Another groan.

"You said you'd take care of it. With your hand."

"If I do, I would have to..." he trails off. "I don't think you'd consider it very proper." He lets out a dry laugh.

I lick my lips. None of this is proper, yet here I am.

"I think..." I pause and wet my lips. "As long as I'm a distance away, my virtue is not in danger."

He glances back at me, his eyes boring into me.

"I can watch. And you can... think of me." I take a deep breath. "I *want* you to think of me."

"Are you sure?" He still hesitates.

He wants my approval.

The mere fact that he's asking whether I am certain about it warms my heart. It certainly proves to me I made a good choice in allowing him to court me.

He is a worthy male.

"Show me," I whisper, doing my best to temper the excitement that brews inside of me.

He slowly turns. His fingers go to the band of his briefs and he pushes them down his legs.

My hand flies to my mouth as a gasp slips past my lips.

"That..." My eyes widen in shock. I suppose nothing could have prepared me for the sight of his swollen flesh.

Swollen for me.

Oh my, that is much larger than I thought it would be.

His member juts forward, long and thick. Angry veins protrude on each side. There is a black drop of moisture at the tip that he swipes with his finger as he gives his length a quick stroke.

That movement alone awakens something within me, and I find myself squeezing my thighs together to alleviate the discomfort growing between my legs.

Almost instinctively, my body yearns for him. It is a foreign sensation. One I've never experienced before.

But as I continue staring at his naked body, all I can think of is how it would feel to touch him—have him on top of me, inside of me.

I turn a hundred shades of red as I realize the direction of my thoughts. We've yet to have a proper kiss and now all I can imagine is how it would be to mate with him—*fully* mate with him.

His length grows even thicker under my eyes, and he grabs onto the base of it, giving it a light squeeze. His flesh is big and strong like him, and to my surprise, I find that it's just as beautiful.

A soft moan escapes me.

"I can put my briefs back on if you want." His eyes are on my face, looking for any trace of uncertainty.

"No. Continue." I don't know how the words came out without a stammer—not when I can barely think of anything else but the image in front of me.

Thick, towering evergreen trees envelop us in a lush, fragrant embrace. The grass beneath our feet is a patchwork of earthy browns and vibrant greens, swaying gently in the breeze. And there he stands, completely exposed to the elements, his tanned skin gleaming in the sunlight. The rawness of his nudity is striking against the backdrop of nature's own nakedness.

I can't help but sigh dreamily as I take in his form. Every inch of him is captivating, from the defined muscles rippling beneath his skin to the faint scars that add character to his body. They tell a story of battles fought and challenges overcome, making him even more alluring in my eyes.

He might be human, but no god could measure up to him.

His right hand is on his length, slowly moving up and down. It's a tentative movement as if he's still wary about doing this in front of me.

"Show me," I whisper. "Show me everything."

My voice bolsters his confidence, and his movements gain speed.

He encases his length in his fist as he pulls roughly on it.

His head falls back, his mouth ajar. But his eyes never close. He's looking at me. They might be hooded and droopy, but I can feel his intense gaze. It never once leaves my face.

But then something shifts within me, and in a moment of madness, I lean back, baring my semi-naked body to him.

He hisses, his movements becoming brisker.

"Fuck, Minnie," he rasps. The combination of his deep, husky voice and his ecstasy-filled expression makes me erupt in goose bumps. "So beautiful. So fucking beautiful."

As his hand moves faster and faster along his shaft, beads of sweat gather on his brow and drip down the side of his face. His muscles tense and flex with each thrust, and as he jerks once more, a low moan escapes from his lips.

I can see the arousal in his eyes as he shouts my name, his release finally coming to a climax. A torrent of liquid shoots out, some splattering onto the ground while a few droplets coat his hand and stomach.

His seed.

He's spilling it for me. His body is wracked with pleasure and desire, and I watch in fascination as he lets go completely, giving himself over to this primal act.

Despite being four thousand years old, I have never felt such a rush of emotions. It's overwhelming, this raw display of carnality.

As the tremors subside, he continues to gaze at me intently, studying my every reaction. As a satisfied smile tugs at his lips, I realize he must be pleased by what he sees.

Standing up, I reach for the dirty shirt in our makeshift bag and make my way over to him. He looks surprised but doesn't move as I approach.

"Scandalized yet?" he drawls.

My cheeks are flaming hot, yet I find that rather than being scandalized, I am...left wanting.

"Not yet," I whisper, dabbing the material of his shirt over his abdominals to clean the remaining residue.

"You're not...disgusted?" he asks uncertainly.

"Why should I be? This is a normal bodily response. Perhaps it is something new to me, but I found it rather...exciting," I admit.

Yet in spite of my bravado, I don't dare look down. His flesh is still hard and so close to me... I gulp down.

"I'm glad to hear that," he murmurs.

The thick, dark substance coats his knuckles, giving them a menacing appearance. As I reach out to clean his hand, he suddenly grabs my wrist and throws the dirty shirt to the ground.

I raise my gaze to his, my confusion evident in my furrowed brows. But before I can ask him anything, his hand is on my face. His thumb traces my lips before sliding inside and pushing his finger past the barrier of my teeth.

I still, unsure of how to react. Part of me wants to pull away, but his intense stare keeps me rooted in place. Slowly, I allow my tongue to touch his finger, tasting the surprisingly sweet seed that he pushed into my mouth. It's even sweeter than the glazed donuts he brings me every day.

Feeling bolder, I grasp his wrist and turn his hand so I can run my tongue over every inch of his knuckles. I feel him gulp hard as I clean the remaining seed from his skin.

But then he abruptly pulls away from me, leaving me startled and unsure if I did something wrong.

Instead of answering my unspoken question, he takes hold of my cheeks in his strong palms and leans down toward me.

"My brave, brave girl," he whispers, his warm breath caressing my face. He presses gentle kisses first to my forehead, then my nose before hovering over my parted lips.

"One kiss. Just one kiss and I can die a happy man."

I wet my lips, still tasting the sweetness of his seed.

"How can you be satisfied with just one kiss when I promised you *all* my kisses?"

That's all the encouragement he needs, and on my next breath, we're breathing together.

His lips are soft yet firm as they mold perfectly to mine. At first, he lays light, almost chaste kisses on my mouth before he nibbles at my lower lip. A gasp escapes me, but he swallows it as he seeks entrance in my mouth.

His lips meet mine in a delicate, almost hesitant touch. But as I mimic his movements, he releases any restraint and pulls me closer to him, his mouth devouring mine. Our tongues dance together in a passionate yet chaotic battle for dominance.

He lunges, I counter. He withdraws, I chase after him.

It's a never-ending cycle of give and take, push and pull. We're both equal adversaries in this intoxicating game of desire.

Despite the forbidden nature of our encounter, I can't find it within me to care about the potential consequences.

His touch is worth every risk.

With my fingers digging into his muscular shoulders, I stand on my tiptoes to get even closer to him. The heat between us is palpable, igniting a fire within that threatens to consume us both.

"Sweet Minnie," he murmurs in between kisses. "You have no idea how long I've been waiting for you."

He's breathing hard. *I* am breathing hard. But as I look into his eyes, I note a light sheen of unspilled tears. My lashes flutter in confusion.

But as he covers my mouth again with his own, I don't get to dwell on his odd words and even odder expression.

I simply give myself over to the kiss.

It might be my first, but it might also be my last.

I must make the best of it.

TWENTY-TWO

FRESHLY BATHED and dressed in clean clothes, we're standing at the precipice of what could be the most dangerous part of our mission. I hold tightly onto the small pin, drawing just enough energy from it to lead us to the portal. With a nod to Mine, we start our journey.

I can't help but feel a slight twinge of apprehension as we move forward. Mine must sense my unease, for he gently grabs my hand and pulls me closer to him.

"You're awfully quiet. Do you regret what happened?" he asks softly.

I bite my lip, averting my gaze.

"I don't regret it, but..." I trail off.

His expression softens as he tilts his head down to look at me.

"I'm embarrassed," I whisper, my cheeks flushing with heat.

"Why would you be embarrassed?" he questions, his voice laced with concern.

"How can I not be? I...I...I behaved like a feline in heat," I admit, a flush of embarrassment flooding through me again.

A small smile tugs at the corners of his lips and his eyes sparkle with amusement.

"A feline in heat?" he repeats, raising a brow.

"Don't you dare make fun of me!" I playfully jab my elbow into his side.

"Ouch! Fine, fine. I won't make fun of you," he concedes with a chuckle. "But really, there's no need to be embarrassed. What happened between us is completely natural—"

"But—" I try to interject.

He cuts me off with a finger pressed lightly against my lips.

"Answer this. Do you want me to kiss you again?" he asks quietly, his eyes searching mine.

Without hesitation, I nod. How could I not want more of his intoxicating kisses?

With a mischievous glint in his eye, he leans down and presses a quick peck against my lips.

"Then there you have it," he says with a grin. "You should never be embarrassed with me, my tiny darling. Never."

"All right." I smile shyly. "But remember. You promised your courtship would not interfere with the mission," I remind him sternly, my brows furrowed as I search for the right word. "As such, I would ask of you to temper your..."

"My...?" he prompts, a teasing glint in his eye.

"Your appeal," I say firmly, trying to quell the fluttering in my stomach his charm and playful banter caused. "Please tone it down so I can focus on the matter at hand."

"Right. I must not distract you with my handsomeness and my skillful kisses." He grins, leaning closer to me.

I elbow him playfully, trying to hide my own smile.

"Eyes on the road," I scold, though my lips curl up in amusement.

"Minnie, would it cost you too much to admit that I'm handsome?" he asks with an exaggerated pout. "Or that you all but melted in my arms?"

"I will neither admit nor deny," I reply coyly. "The matter is adjourned."

"Cruel, cruel female." He sighs dramatically, pressing a hand against his heart. "See, my heart ailment has now returned."

I roll my eyes at his theatrics. Though I may still be learning about human customs and emotions, I am not as gullible as I once was.

"If your heart ailment is truly so serious, perhaps I should leave you behind," I suggest slyly, stealing a quick glance at him. "I wouldn't want you to get any sicker. Traveling through a portal can be quite strenuous, especially for someone with a delicate human constitution."

He blinks in surprise before recovering with a grin. It seems he didn't expect such a response from me.

He suddenly stops, his eyes closed and arms outstretched, taking deep, measured breaths. The sun casts a warm glow on his face as he basks in the open air.

"What are you doing?" I frown, checking my watch. "We're on a tight schedule."

"It's gone." He sighs in relief, a smile spreading across his face. "I am now cured. Let us continue."

"Just like that?" I raise an eyebrow skeptically.

"I think it's the fresh air. But also your presence," he says, turning to me with a soft look in his eyes. "It's like a healing balm to my heart, Minnie. And I have a feeling another kiss from you would ensure my ailment won't come back for some time."

"The mission?" I tap my foot impatiently.

"Just one more kiss. Think of it as charity," he pleads, practically batting his eyelashes at me—*I* used that technique first!

Smirking, I stop in front of him and rise up on my tiptoes. He closes his eyes expectantly, but instead of kissing him on the lips, I place a gentle kiss over his heart and hold it there for a moment.

"There. My charitable duty is done. Now let's get going."

He gives me a puppy look—he does that quite often, though I'm not sure why. It does make him endearing in an odd way, but he needs to learn that such blatant cuteness doesn't easily sway me—well, maybe just a little.

After his heart is miraculously cured, we get back into the

car and start driving toward the location of the portal. Mine unfurls a map in front of us and asks me to point out where the portal is located.

I focus on the energy of the pin, being careful not to use too much as I must conserve some for any unforeseen circumstances that may arise in Aperion. Since Mine is coming with me, and he is only human, it is my responsibility to protect him.

"Over there." I point to a spot on the map.

"A field. Figures," Mine mutters under his breath. "Luckily, it's not too far from here. We should be able to reach it before nightfall."

The sun begins to dip lower in the sky, casting a golden hue over the green fields and scattered trees. The roads are empty save for a couple of cars here and there. And as we make to exit the county, we come across a military checkpoint.

Mine flashes his credentials and we are quickly let through.

"We're getting closer," I tell him. The portal's energy signature is becoming stronger.

Mine glances at the map and traces the location with his finger.

"We'll need to stop the car here and continue on foot." He points to where the main road meets the field.

As we get there, he parks the car by the side of the road and we start toward the field.

When the energy signature of the portal is at its strongest, I borrow some power from the pin and sprinkle it around us to reveal a dark blue swirl of light.

"And this will take us to Aperion?" Mine questions pensively.

"It can take you anywhere. But you're lucky you're with me since I can direct it to take us to our destination."

"We just go inside?"

I nod.

"But before..." I trail off as I borrow a tiny bit of energy from the pin and tap his forehead. "This should help you understand the language of Aperion for a short period of time."

He nods thoughtfully.

"Come." I grab his hand and step into the portal.

He opens his mouth to say something, but I'm already pulling him inside. The blue light surrounds us and in a matter of seconds, we're expelled on the other side of the portal.

I stumble around to find my footing, but Mine catches me in his arms.

"Huh," I whisper. I've heard that mortals have a hard time when going through a portal for the first time, usually involving dizziness and nausea. But he seems perfectly fine.

His gaze is sharp as he looks around, taking in his surroundings.

"Where are we?" His voice is laced with disbelief as he surveys our surroundings.

I gently extricate myself from his embrace and take a moment to look around. He keeps a firm grip on my arm as if afraid to let go.

A bustling crowd of people surrounds us, all engaged in their daily activities. The air is filled with the sounds of chatter and laughter, creating a lively atmosphere. In front of us, a line has formed outside of a shop, with people eagerly waiting for it to open.

"This is... Aperion?" He raises an eyebrow skeptically. I can tell he's not impressed with the seemingly mundane surroundings.

The buildings here are much shorter than the ones in London, only three stories high at most. But they are made from a unique grey brick that gives them mystical properties. Only those invited inside can enter, making each business feel exclusive and secretive. Well, that, and it also serves to keep conflict to a minimum, though there is one exception. The military can come and go from *any* building in Aperion.

"We're in a small town at the edge of the Capital of Polemos. I suppose it's not too glamorous," I add pensively.

"These people are gods?" He points to the bustling streets. The sound of laughter and conversation fills the air, mixed with the clanging of pots and pans and the calls of street vendors. In the distance, we can hear the faint sound of music coming from a nearby street performance.

I shake my head. "Only about ten percent of the population of Aperion is descended from deities. The remaining ninety percent are called s'Aperiotes and while they have *some* spiritual energy, it's minimal and does not translate into any abilities. There is, of course, the rare case in which a s'Aperiote has an unusual spiritual energy," I explain.

"I suppose I was expecting something different."

"Aperion has a very strict hierarchy. At the bottom are the s'Aperites, often treated as second-class citizens due to their lack of abilities. Power is everything and the hierarchy is determined by who holds the most of it. Sitting atop this pyramid are the Supremes, followed by the monarchs of each Royal House, then the nobility, military leaders, and minor deities. These upper classes all possess abilities and our laws prohibit those with abilities from mating with s'Aperites, although accidents do happen, and that is how you get the rare s'Aperite with abilities. But that is only possible among the minor deities since conception only occurs if both parents' levels of spiritual energy are similar," I continue.

"The only advantage s'Aperites have is that they are not really bound by our strict mores. They can mate among themselves without outside interference, though they do require the permission of the Higher Office of their Commune before they are allowed to marry. Although they have more freedom, they still have to answer to Aperite laws. That means that they have a certain...dislike for deities. So let's not advertise who I am to anyone around, all right?"

Mine is staring at me.

"Your world is strange."

I shrug. "Your world is strange to me, too."

"Where to now, then?"

"We must make our way to the Capital on foot," I declare, my voice echoing off the surrounding buildings.

His eyebrows shoot up in disbelief. "On foot? How far is that?"

I nod firmly. "Yes, it's just over there," I respond, pointing west and gesturing toward a cluster of tall structures piercing the sky in the distance.

His mouth falls open in shock. "There?" he repeats incredulously.

I give a curt nod. "Yes, it shouldn't take us more than a day," I state matter-of-factly.

He stammers, struggling to process the information. "A day? Did you just say a day? On foot?"

I raise an eyebrow at his reaction. "You're a military man, Mine. Act like it," I scold before striding forward.

"Wait a minute. Surely you have some sort of transportation? A car or something?" he protests, scrambling to keep up with my pace.

I sigh and shake my head. "We do have access to vehicles, but using one would risk drawing attention to ourselves as only elites are allowed to ride in them. Horses would cost us money we don't have. So walking is our only option."

"Minnie! This is ridiculous," he complains loudly.

My patience wears thin and I turn sharply toward him, hands on hips and giving him a stern look. "If you're going to continue whining, perhaps I should have left you behind after all."

He lets out a string of curse words under his breath.

I narrow my eyes at him. "And if you think walking on foot will be too difficult for you, I'll find you another portal and you can head back to Anthropa."

Suddenly, he grabs my hand and starts marching forward with determination. "Don't you worry, Minnie. Walking is one of my specialties," he declares confidently.

Humans, I shake my head in annoyance.

As we stroll through the bustling streets, I can sense the eyes of the locals following us with curious glances. It takes me a moment to realize it's because of our attire. My simple cotton gown, dyed a deep emerald green and adorned with delicate embroidery on the bodice, instantly gives away that I am not from here. Mine, too, clad in high-waisted trousers and a perfectly tailored shirt, also stands out as someone not from this region.

If we are to continue our journey through Aperite towns and villages, we'll surely attract unwanted attention with our distinct clothing. Instinctively, I reach into my pocket and grasp the pin. I was hesitant to use it again until we reached the Capital, but it seems like we may need new disguises sooner than expected.

As I turn to Mine, I suggest we stop by a nearby clothing shop. But his gaze is distant, concerned, and my words die on my lips as a loud commotion erupts just a short distance away from us.

A crowd of people has gathered in front of a shop, their voices rising in panic and distress. Some are screaming for help.

My heart races with fear as I whisper to Mine, urging him to keep moving. "We can't afford to get involved."

But his jaw tightens, his expression determined. He pulls me forward but stops abruptly as we pass through the thickening crowd. More voices echo from within the circle of people, some wailing in pain.

"Mine, we need to go," I plead urgently.

"Someone is injured," he mentions, his sharp gaze scanning the tumultuous scene before us.

"We can't risk getting noticed," I protest.

But he shakes off my grip and pushes through the throng of people. My heart sinks as I follow reluctantly behind him, praying we won't be caught up in whatever chaos has unfolded before us.

As I race after him, my heart pounds in my chest and my breath comes out in ragged gasps. He elbows his way through the throng of people with a sense of urgency that makes me quicken my pace.

"Mine, wait!" I call out to him, desperate to catch up, but

just as I reach his side, he pulls me close. His grip is strong and his eyes are wild with fear and anger.

"What the hell is that?" he asks in a rough voice, gesturing toward the center of the conflict.

I turn my attention to the chaos ahead. Three people lie on the ground, their cries of pain piercing through the air. Blood has stained the pavement, creating a gruesome mosaic of red and brown.

One victim clutches at a large slice around his arm, blood gushing out between his fingers. Another male writhes in agony from a stab wound in his abdomen. And then there's the woman, her face bloody and bruised, her once-beautiful dress now marred with red spots.

But what catches my eye is the figure swaying back and forth next to them. It's a fourth man, seemingly unharmed but with a crazed look in his features. And as my eyes scan down to see the light blue powder stains on the inside of his elbow, I realize what the problem is.

He's on *zantrax*. And he's on a drug-fueled rampage.

My heart races as I grab Mine's arm and beg him to leave. "We need to leave. Now," I add, my voice tight with urgency. But he doesn't budge, his eyes still fixed on the woman cowering from the mad man.

She begs for help from the bystanders, but they all back away in fear. Someone mentions calling the militia, but no one dares to intervene and stop the wild-eyed man. He takes a wobbly step toward the bleeding woman, and suddenly a burst of energy explodes from him.

"He's a deity?"

I shake my head. "He's on a black market drug made from the energy of a god," I explain. "It gives the user temporary powers, but it's highly addictive and dangerous. And now that it's wearing off, he'll be searching for more."

"Zantrax? That's still a thing?" Mine asks incredulously.

I nod grimly. "The military has been trying to crack down on it, but every time they think they've found the source, more sellers appear. And there have been reports of minor deities disappearing, all linked to the production of this drug."

Before we can continue our conversation, another blood-curdling scream pierces the air. The crowd begins to back away as the man unleashes another burst of uncontrollable energy. He lets out a loud bellow and an invisible force pushes us back.

Mine quickly shields me with his body."

We need to leave now," I say urgently. "The militia will come soon and we can't be caught here."

Too late for that, though, as the thudding steps of the soldiers part the sea of people to get to the assailant.

There are only three soldiers, and by the look of their uniform, beige with black stripes, they are from a lower division comprised of minor deities. But that also means they have low to no abilities, which might prove difficult in handling a *zantrax* case.

The man turns his attention to the three soldiers, and as he opens his mouth, a burst of energy flies toward them, injuring one and momentarily confusing the other two. With that distraction in place, the man looks for a way out. People are running right and left, seeking shelter, and the commotion jostles us around.

As the man scans the crowd for an exit, his eyes register our presence.

Oh, no!

One by-product of zantrax is that its users are highly sensitive to spiritual energy since it's the only thing they seek once the addiction has sunk its claws into them.

He takes a step forward, and my fears suddenly materialize.

He must sense the energy of the pin, or he might even be able to sense the shadow of energy I still emit.

"Run!" I shout to Mine.

But it's too late.

Without hesitation, the man locks his crazed gaze on us. He charges forward, heedless of the militia still lingering in the background or the innocent bystanders caught in his path. His sole focus is on me, his next source of energy. His eyes are wide and wild, dilated and unfocused as they search for their target. Blood, tainted with zantrax, oozes from his nose in a dark purple stream. Just as he prepares to pounce, Mine quickly shoves me aside, taking the brunt of the man's attack himself. A blur of motion and chaos ensues as they collide in a desperate struggle for power.

"No!" I scream.

He's human. He can get injured. And here we won't be able to find medical help if that happens.

The man attempts to release another energy burst, but Mine is quicker. He realizes that he uses his mouth to release the energy so he covers it with his hand while he brings his knee up and hits him in the stomach. Gripping his nape, he yanks his head backward, releasing his hold on the mouth at the same time the man unleashes the blow of energy. It flies into the sky, not injuring anyone.

The soldiers moan in pain, but they attempt to regroup and grab the man. Yet instead of falling, the man once more turns to stare at me.

He takes a step forward, but Mine grabs him again, this time putting pressure on his neck in an attempt to immobilize him.

It works—for a second. Another wave of energy rolls off him, the force once more pushing everyone in his vicinity back.

I fall backward and onto my back.

He can't control it, I realize. He can fire blows with his mouth, but he cannot control the pure energy that's dripping from him. Goodness, but how much zantrax did he consume to get to this level?

Mine stumbles back, but he manages to keep upright. His eyes widen as he sees the man advance toward me, now only a couple of steps away.

I push my hand in my pocket, searching for the pin in an attempt to fight him off. But Mine is quicker. He glances back at the soldiers and, rushing toward the one closest to him, he snatches the sword from his scabbard, and with an unusual speed, he charges at the addict.

The sword swishes in the air. One cut in the middle of his body. There's such precision in the blow, such force, that the man is cut into two. The upper part tumbles onto the ground, his blood a mix of blue, red and purple from the amount of zantrax in his system.

I stare at Mine in disbelief.

Did he just... cut him in half?

He rushes to my side, his hand reaching out to help me up. I am a little disoriented by the chaos around us, and it takes a moment for me to realize that most of the crowd has scattered at the sight of the militia. Their arrival has sparked fear and panic among the people.

"We need to make a run for it. Now," I tell him as I note the soldiers set their sights on us.

We take off running, the sound of our footsteps echoing loudly in my ears. The soldiers are close behind, their weapons drawn and ready to fire. My heart races as we weave through the chaotic streets, trying to evade capture.

Damn it! Mine may have acted heroically by eliminating a zantrax addict who posed a threat to the public, but to the militia, he is just another criminal who dared to kill a civilian and steal a soldier's sword.

As we near the end of the boulevard, two more soldiers appear in front of us, cutting off our escape route. Three more approach from behind.

"Damn it!" I curse under my breath. "This is all your fault," I grumble at Mine, giving him a harsh stare.

"Me? What did I do?" he asks innocently, a mischievous smile pulling at his lips. "I saved you, didn't I? I think I deserve a kiss for my chivalrous behavior and—"

Before he can finish his sentence, I kick him in the shin.

"And now we're caught," I say exasperatedly. "Exactly what we needed to avoid."

The soldiers surround us, their weapons aimed at us in case we try to resist arrest.

"So what's going to happen?" Mine asks curiously, not seeming too concerned about our dire situation.

"They'll take us to jail," I reply through gritted teeth. "And when they uncover my true identity, I'll be in deep trouble."

"Jail. And where is that?" Mine asks with a sly grin.

"Capital, of course," I say, rolling my eyes.

He smiles in satisfaction and takes a step forward, willingly offering his hands to the soldiers to be cuffed. Another soldier does the same with me.

"What's wrong with you?" I ask in disbelief as we're loaded into a militia vehicle, a large container operated by *yovas*—magical beings with wings. "How can you smile in this situation when I specifically told you how important it was for us to keep our identities hidden?"

Mine simply shrugs, still wearing a slight smile on his face.

The soldiers get in their capsules and urge the *yovas* to take flight.

"Think of the bright side. Now we won't have to walk to the Capital," he says in a lazy voice as he leans back and makes himself comfortable.

TWENTY-THREE

THE AIR IS thick with the stench of sweat, urine, and blood. The smell of mold and mildew permeates the air, making it hard to breathe. The rusty bars of the cell are thick and aligned closely together, letting very little light come inside.

But the ground is the worst. Semi-moist, cold, and uncomfortable.

As soon as we arrived at the jail, we were dumped here quite unceremoniously and told a superintendent would see us at some point.

The jail is littered with small cells on each side of a small hallway. The moans of the other prisoners echo in the air, some filled with pain, some barely audible as they're close to death.

I've heard about these provincial jails. The militia is tough on the s'Aperites who commit crimes, and often, the punishment for a transgression is death. There is little nuance in the Aperite society, both at the top and the bottom. Either you're guilty or innocent, and if you qualify as the former, you must be punished accordingly.

My fear of being recognized takes a back seat as I now have to think of a way to make it out of this jail alive. Or, rather, to ensure that Mine makes it out alive, though I'm still put out with him for what he did.

Mine and I were put in a small cell, and luckily, we're the only ones inside, though I can vaguely make out the shape of another dying prisoner in the cell across from ours.

We're sitting on opposite sides of the small, dingy cell, though Mine keeps trying to inch closer to me and I continually shift away. The putrid scent of urine and decomposition hangs heavy in the air, making my stomach churn.

"What's this atrocious smell?" Mine asks, crinkling his nose in disgust.

I give him a hard stare, incredulous at his complaint.

"You're complaining about the smell? Now? You did this!" I snap at him.

"I did not expect this to be so...dirty," he mutters, running a hand through his disheveled hair.

"It's a jail! What did you expect? Royal treatment?" I roll my eyes at him, unable to hide my annoyance.

"Well..." He smiles sheepishly, his charm momentarily faltering.

"This is ridiculous," I huff aloud. "I should have left you behind in Anthropa."

"Now, now, darling Minnie, do not be cross with me." He drags himself closer to me for what feels like the hundredth time, though this time he doesn't stop until our bodies are pressed against each other.

I make to move—again. But he's faster as he grabs me by the shoulder and all but pulls me onto his lap.

"Don't be mad, pretty please?" he whispers in my ear, his hot breath fanning over my face and sending shivers down my spine.

I let out a shudder, torn between punching him and kissing him.

"I am very mad at you," I tell him sternly, though with his proximity and seductive words, I have trouble keeping the same cold tone as before.

"I acquired us free transportation. Surely that deserves some credit," he says, wrapping his strong arms around my waist and pulling me close to him. My initial reaction is to head butt him and distance myself from his touch. But the warmth radiating from his body is surprisingly comforting. I am cold, after all.

He leans into me, nuzzling his nose against my neck and taking in a deep breath. My instincts tell me to squirm away, but his hold is firm.

"What are you doing?" I ask, trying to wiggle out of his grasp.

"Stay still," he demands, inhaling me once more. "You smell divine."

"Thanks...I think. Now let go."

"No." His grip tightens around me. "Your scent helps me forget about the unbearable stench of this cell."

I roll my eyes, mentally blaming him for our current predicament.

As I continue to shift my weight, attempting to break free, he responds by holding on to me even tighter.

"Stop moving," he growls in a low, primal voice.

My movements freeze and I gulp nervously.

"You...you..." I stammer as the hardness of him presses against my backside. A blush creeps up my neck as a shiver runs through my body. "H-how can you..." I squeeze my eyes shut. "How can you be aroused in this situation?"

"I have no control over it," he whispers in my ear.

A shiver runs down my spine, but this time it's not from the biting cold. The intense heat emanating from his hardness seeps through the thin material of my dress, making me acutely aware of every inch of him as a person and as a male.

Strong. Virile. Hard.

It awakens something deep within me, a primal desire that I had long buried and thought did not exist.

Despite his laid-back personality and constant joking and teasing, there is an undeniable masculinity about him that calls to my hidden femininity and makes me crave to submit to him.

It's outrageous. It's terrifying.

But somehow, all the walls I've built around myself seem to crumble in his presence.

"You need to control yourself," I croak out, though my stomach is filled with jittery knots and I can barely speak without stuttering.

He simply smiles against my skin, sending a rush of warmth through my body.

"How can I when you're near?" he responds playfully.

"Mine!" I squeal when he presses even closer, his body molding perfectly against mine. "Can't your...your...male part understand that we're in a filthy jail cell?"

"It doesn't matter." He chuckles. "You're here."

"Well, tell it to behave. I can't focus with...with it pressing into my back."

"It won't listen to me," he says with a mischievous glint in his eye. "It's completely enthralled by you."

The thought is both thrilling and unnerving. But now is not the time for such thoughts.

I wiggle more and he lets out a muffled groan.

"Stop moving."

"Why?" I ask innocently.

"You're torturing me."

"You're torturing yourself with impure thoughts while we're in this situation—that you caused, too."

"Minnie, have some mercy on me. I'm hanging on by a thread here."

"That's your problem. Not mine." I huff aloud. "Deal with it so we can plan how we're going to get out of this situation."

He doesn't reply, merely releasing more guttural sounds into my neck. I continue to move in his lap, hoping it will drive him crazy enough that he'll let me go. No matter how much I like the fact that he reacts to me, this is not the time for any reaction save for self-preservation.

"Stop." His breathing is harsh and barely controlled. And when I don't stop, instead releasing me from his grasp, I find myself on my back on the floor with him looming over me.

The cell is dark save for the few rays of sun making it through the bars. But as I gaze upon his face, the shade of swirling green of his eyes takes me aback.

The hunger in his gaze startles me. As he lodges himself with his hips between my legs, I feel that hard part of him right at my core.

I whimper. He smiles, his white teeth gleaming dangerously. Then he wiggles, and the breath is knocked out of my lungs at the onslaught of sensations traveling all over my body.

But I am not one to be ruled by my baser needs. And if he plays dirty, then I shall too.

Licking my lips, I lean forward until my mouth is close to his.

His brows go up in surprise, his breathing becoming more accentuated. His eyes droop and focus on my lips.

"Mine," I whisper, getting closer to him.

"Minnie," he rasps.

But just as he thinks I'm going to kiss him, I headbutt him. He reels back and lets out a groan of pain. It's enough for me to slide from under him and resume my position at the other end of the cell, all the while glaring at him.

"Don't you dare get more dirty thoughts," I warn. "We have enough trouble as it is."

I watch him closely, thinking he's going to be mad at me. But to my surprise, he simply slumps back against the wall, his head thrown back as he lets out a laugh.

"You win, Minnie. You win."

"Of course," I huff. "Now—" I stop myself from continuing as I hear footsteps down the hallway. Mine is on alert, too. This time, when he comes to my side, I don't tell him off. We both wait, and soon two guards appear into view.

Mine's body tenses, and he grabs my hand, giving me a soft, comforting nod.

They stop in front of our cell, and just as I think they're going to open the grilled door and get us out to meet the superintendent, they turn and unlock the cell opposite ours.

The guards barge inside and drag out a nearly dead man. His clothes are tattered and even in the poor lighting I can tell he's badly bruised all over his body. The only sign that he's still alive is the wheezing sound he makes as he breathes.

After they take him out of his cell, they dump him to the ground and one of the guards stomps angrily on his chest.

Once. Twice.

They both stomp on him until the wheezing sound stops. Until he no longer breathes.

Mine suddenly stands up and walks to the door.

"Hey!" he calls out to the soldiers.

"Mine," I grit out. "Stop!"

He doesn't mind me, continuing to address the soldiers.

"Cowardly of you to kick a defenseless man," he jibes.

One of the guards turns to him, his eyes narrowed.

"Bet you've never tried to hit someone who can hit back," he continues.

"I will deal with this," the guard tells the other.

He strides to our cell. Reaching between the bars, he grabs Mine by his shirt and pulls him close.

"Next time, it will be you," the guard sneers, releasing a burst of energy that sends Mine flying against the wall of the cell.

I gasp.

The guards laugh as they see him cough blood as he tries to get his bearings together.

I scramble over to where Mine is, glaring at the guards.

"Or perhaps we will do her next," they say mockingly.

Mine's muscles tense, but I beg him not to mind them.

"Focus on me," I whisper. "Only on me."

He brings his eyes to me, his gaze thunderous and ready to kill.

I caress his face softly, wiping away the blood from his mouth.

"Only focus on me," I repeat.

When the guards realize they won't get another rise out of

him, they grab the dead prisoner and drag him away. As they pass by the other cells, more sounds erupt as the other prisoners hurl insults and curses at the soldiers.

The steps recede.

"Are you all right? What was in your mind?" I ask as I scan his body. He must have taken quite a hit if he's spitting out blood.

"I'm fine." He smiles, his teeth bloody.

"What was that?" I grit out at him. "You could have gotten yourself killed."

He shrugs.

"I didn't. But I did get this." He opens his palm to show me a key.

My eyes widen.

"You..."

"I got us here. I'm getting us out."

"You idiot!" I hiss. "Why didn't you ask me before you did something like that?"

Another shrug.

"This won't help. We might get out of the cell, but we can't get out of the prison." I take a deep breath as I try to calm myself. How could he take such a risk without even consulting me?

"What do you mean?"

"There are wards all over the prison. Jailbreak is impossible. Only the soldiers have runes etched into their bodies to allow them to freely walk in and out of the prison."

"You can use energy from the pin and bypass the wards," he says.

"You think I wouldn't have offered if that was an option? I don't know what wards they're using and as such I wouldn't be able to replicate the exit runes."

His lips tighten as he mulls on that.

"What about the dead guy? How are they taking his body out? Are they etching a rune on his body?"

I shake my head.

"The dead are taken to the morgue and placed in a special wooden coffin that has the runes etched inside. And if we don't find another way to leave, that's going to be our fate, too."

"Not necessarily," he comments.

I raise a brow.

"I have an idea." He smiles sheepishly. "And this"—he holds up the key—"will help us."

"Let me guess. Another stupid idea that will put your life in danger. No, thank you."

He tilts his head to the side as he regards me.

"My life? Only mine? You don't have powers, remember?"

"I still likely won't die. But you can. And I'm not about to stand by and watch you die."

His lips curl up, his features lighting up.

"So you do care for me. At least a little."

"You're impossible," I mumble and look away.

Suddenly, though, his expression changes.

"There are worse things than death, Minnie. They might not kill you, but they can certainly do other things."

"By other things you mean..."

He grabs my chin and turns me to him.

"Rape. Yes. You saw how he looked at you. I wanted to gouge his eyes out for the mere fact that he dared to look at you."

"They can't. Rape isn't allowed," I protest. "We have very stringent rules and the higher-ups would never condone that."

He lets out a dry laugh.

"Is that what you think? Ah, Minnie, you're much more naive than I thought."

"I'm not naive."

"Idealistic then. You think your rules mean anything when there's no one watching?"

"But—"

"I wager if they can kill a defenseless man, they can very well rape a woman, too."

"No, that's... It can't be."

"Men will be men, no matter what world they're in."

I nibble on my lip. He does have a point. And though I still don't believe any militia or military personnel would engage in that, I don't want to risk it.

"So what's your great idea then?"

"Simple. We get out of here and head to the morgue. We find an empty coffin and that's our way out of here."

"Are you...serious?"

"Very."

"You think they won't check the coffins before they take them out?" I roll my eyes at him.

"Oh, I'm sure they will. But you will use your magical pin and make it so they don't see us. You can do that, no?"

"I can but—"

"It's settled. Now we just have to find the perfect time to leave the cell."

A little more back and forth, and it seems his plan is the only viable one, so we wait until everyone is asleep before we use the key to get out of the cell. I borrow some energy from the pin and cloak our presence as we walk down the hallway.

The conditions of the prisoners in the cells are appalling to see. All of them are beaten and starved, moaning in pain and barely able to move. They are one step away from dying, and I assume that's what the guards are waiting for. And if they don't die by the time they're supposed to, they'll apply the same treatment they did to the other prisoner.

Disgust rolls in my stomach. If I hadn't seen this firsthand, I would have never believed the militia to be capable like this. And this begs the question: who allows them to do so?

I am sure Commander Azerius would be against it. Not for any moral reason, but because it goes against the law.

Yet the only reason why the laws are not as enforced here is because these people are s'Aperiotes, not Aperites with divine origin. They are just a stepping stone for those in power.

I'd known the system to be broken—my forced betrothal to that clown being a prime example for it—but I never thought the situation would be so dire.

We are not allowed to interfere with mortals' fates, but what about s'Aperiotes? Aren't they mortal, too? Aren't these soldiers who kill them descendants of the Primordials, too, even if far removed? It is a conundrum, and once I get back my powers and resume my position, I aim to get to the bottom of this.

Mine holds on to my hand as we carefully walk the long, windy hallway that's littered with darkened cells. It's like a never-ending maze as we turn right and left, only to find more cells, more dying people.

He doesn't seem too happy about it, either. His face is screwed up in disgust, his nostrils flaring every time a shout of help resounds through the hallways, followed by the incessant moans of pain.

By chance, we stumble onto the door that leads to the exit. But now it's a matter of finding the morgue where they prepare the bodies to take them outside of the jail.

"This way," Mine suggests. With no idea where to go, I follow him. Turns out his luck is still going strong today because he leads us straight to the morgue.

The moment we enter the room, the smell of rotting flesh assaults us.

"Good Lord, I hate the smell of putrefied flesh," he mutters as he covers his mouth and nose.

I purse my lips. The smell is indeed a bad one, but this is not the time to mind his sensibilities. I've noticed he's not very good with strong scents, and it makes me wonder how he managed to last so long in the military—after all, no matter the world, soldiers end up doing the dirty jobs, more often than not in dirty conditions too.

"Stop complaining," I mutter in annoyance.

"If you give me a kiss, I'll be able to keep my mind off it," he mentions shamelessly with a wiggle of his brows.

I give him a deadly glare.

"This is not the time for jokes, Mine. We need to get out of here. Now."

"Fine, fine." He lets out a disappointed sigh. "It was just an idea."

"Get an idea about how we're going to fit in one of those." I point to the rows of wooden caskets.

They aren't very big and Mine is a very tall male, taller than most s'Aperiotes, in fact.

He scrunches his nose in disgust.

"Are they all going to be taken outside?"

"All the ones with bodies inside."

"Wait, wait, wait," he blurts out as he pinches the bridge of his nose with two fingers. "You don't mean we'll have to share a space with a dead body."

"What did you think I meant?" I raise a brow at him.

"It's a dead body, Minnie! It smells, and it probably already has maggots running through it." He makes a disgusted face.

I shake my head and purse my lips.

What am I going to do with him? I knew I should have left him behind. He has the sensibilities of a pampered female.

"You want to get out? That's the only way."

"But—"

"No buts. In fact, move your butt into a casket."

"You'll join me, though?"

I roll my eyes.

"Of course. I have the powers, remember? Don't you worry, Mine, you will be safe with me." I pat him on the back and look around the caskets.

I find the largest one and move the lid to the side to reveal a portly man inside—in a quite advanced stage of putrefaction.

Ew. Alas, it must be done.

Drawing energy from the pin, I levitate the dead body out of the casket and I dump him into an empty, smaller one. It's a tight fit, and it takes a few tries for me to finally dump him inside.

Mine chokes as the belly of the man pops, liquid flowing out of him into the casket.

Double ew.

I put the lid on the other casket and motion for Mine to join me into the newly empty one.

"Can you... do something about the smell?"

"You're impossible," I mutter under my breath. But alas, he is right that we do need at least a semi-decent casket since we don't know how long we'll be in there.

I use my powers to clean it and step inside, fitting my body close to the edge to make room for him. There is still a slight musty smell coming from the wood, but considering this must have been used to carry out hundreds if not thousands of bodies, I suppose it's normal for the smell to be ingrained into the material.

"Are you coming?" I ask in annoyance.

He lets out a defeated sigh before slowly stepping closer to the dark wooden box. His gaze is pensive and his forehead creased with a frown, his lips pressed tightly together.

"Ahh, the things I do for you, Minnie," he murmurs, almost to himself. With a shake of his head, he climbs into the casket, taking a moment to look around before settling down inside.

"It's going to be a tight fit," he remarks slyly, giving me a mischievous look as he lies on his side against the wall of the casket. Our bodies are pressed flush against each other in the confined space.

Everywhere we touch, sparks fly between us.

His breath is hot against my face, his chest rising and falling with each breath just inches from mine.

I swallow nervously.

"I guess we're having a Dracula moment," he whispers with a playful glint in his eye.

"A what?" I furrow my brow in confusion.

"Never mind." He shakes his head. "I suppose I was wrong. This is actually quite comfortable. Especially..." He shifts slightly and his hips press against mine, letting me know he is once again excited by our close proximity.

My cheeks heat up with embarrassment.

"We need to focus." I clear my throat, trying to ignore the fluttering in my stomach his closeness causes.

He smirks at me knowingly.

"I am focusing on you," he retorts smoothly.

"Enough. This is serious—"

But before I can finish my sentence, he presses a finger to my lips and his expression turns serious. He tilts his head to listen carefully.

"Someone is coming."

My eyes widen in alarm.

Palming the pin, I use some energy to move the lid of the casket off the ground and place it on top of us.

Darkness engulfs us.

The door to the morgue opens and steps thud onto the floor as soldiers march in. They're deep in conversation, making ribald jokes and poking fun at each other. I would have rolled my eyes at the situation had I not been backed into a corner like this—literally.

Although it's dark inside the casket, Mine's breath fan over my face, the air getting warmer and warmer. The old, musty smell of the wood is all but forgotten as his scent invades my nostrils.

We've been in close quarters before. Yet somehow this seems more intimate, more...important. Despite the fact that neither of us speaks and that the only noises around us are the raised voices of the soldiers, the silence is heavy. Perhaps it's *because* we're both silent that I am so acutely aware of him next to me, of his warm body warming my own when cold is all I've ever known.

I squeeze my eyes shut against the barrage of feelings that threatens to consume me. From the start, I set out to focus on the mission and get my powers back. But just as well, from the start Mine set out to thwart me at every turn. Even when I feel most confident about what I'm supposed to do, he still makes me waver.

Now, as I feel his presence, steeped in all the senses *but* sight, I start to realize that no matter how strong my resolve is, his might be stronger.

He never once balked in the face of a challenge, even after knowing my true identity and my goals; or after all our misunderstandings.

He's been steadfast where I have been wavering. And that realization makes me pause. Not only because a relationship with him as a human goes against everything I am, everything I was taught, but also because for the first time, I am someone's *goal*.

Have I ever had someone put me first before? I find the courage to ask myself. And the answer is evident: no.

I was born for a purpose, I was raised for a purpose, and I was always treated *as* a purpose. Even during my time in the military, an avenue I sought out to establish my *own* purpose, I was just another soldier in a sea of equally or better qualified ones. I did my job, but I was never indispensable, as evidenced by the way the military so easily washed its hands of me. To my family, aside from the advantages my union with Theron would bring, I am rather...dispensable.

Never in my life have I felt that I was the sole focus of someone; the sole ambition.

"I'm here," Mine whispers. "I'll keep you safe." He takes my hand in his and squeezes it tightly, that gesture alone imbuing me with more strength than any magical object ever could

I blink my eyes open, though I still cannot see him.

"W-what?" I whisper back, the word spoken through trembling teeth.

His hand slides up my arm: up and down. That's when I realize *why* he is trying to comfort me. My entire body is trembling.

Shudders consume my body and I am unable to stop them. Fear, frustration, and desolation compete for supremacy within me. It's an overload of emotions, and it's all because of him.

Because he goes against everything I should want. Because

he made me his purpose when all I've ever been was an accessory to a purpose, never one in itself.

"Shh," he continues, holding me as best he can in this tight space.

Such a precarious situation we're in, and my emotions decided to suddenly surface just now.

"I'm here, with you. Always with you. Nothing will happen, all right?" He continues to whisper, to comfort, as if he had the power to change everything even when I know he doesn't.

Strangely enough, I find myself believing him.

"Follow my breaths. In and out," he continues.

I attempt to emulate his breathing, the adrenaline within me crashing down until there's only a dark hole in my chest, a feeling of relief but also one of loss.

Another realization hits me.

There is only one thing that can fill the void within me—the one thing that might damn me for all eternity.

As I continue to struggle for breath, more sounds erupt in the morgue. The soldiers carry out a few caskets and debate which ones to take out next to fill their quota.

My eyes widen in fear. I should have realized when I saw so many bodies that they don't carry them out as they die, rather when it's comfortable for them. And if they don't choose ours...

Their steps become closer until they stop next to ours.

I quickly summon energy from the pin to create an illusion over Mine and me so that if they open the lid, all they'll see is a dead body.

"This one doesn't smell as bad. I think we can stop for today," one of the soldiers says, stopping just as he's about to peek inside.

I borrow more energy and unleash the strongest, most foul smell I am able to—which is tricky sins itself. I cannot create things out of thin air, but I can borrow already existent ones. And to pull this off, I borrow some of the stench from the overweight man from before and imbue it around us.

Mine squeezes my hand.

"It doesn't smell? Is your nose all right? This one stinks the worst!" another soldier intones.

They don't even bother to open up the lid, immediately sliding it closed and sealing it with a couple of nails—most likely they don't want to smell that again.

They struggle to carry our casket to the back of a vehicle, after which they just carelessly dump it on top of others.

Some more chatter, and the vehicle is moving.

Since they will likely not check on us again, I clean up the air and replace it with fresh one.

Mine lets out a long breath.

"I didn't know you could do that," he mentions in a low voice.

"I can do a lot of things," I huff. "I will have you know that what I may lack in spiritual energy I make up in creativity. There are some tricks that use less energy than others and that get the job done just as well," I tell him, almost as if I feel compelled to explain myself.

I might not be the strongest, but I am still a level five. That is more than halfway to nine, which means I am well above average. If only I were higher, though... I wouldn't have been put in this situation in the first place—the marriage conundrum, not the Anthropa debacle. I now see that what happened in Anthropa was my fault alone, and how can I regret it when I've gotten to meet Mine, who's proven to be quite the loyal follower. Yes, that part I do not regret.

"Minnie?"

"Huh?"

"I asked you a question. Where do they take the dead bodies?"

I mull over the question for a moment.

"I don't know," I answer honestly. "I am not too familiar with how militias work, and every region does it differently."

"We'll just have to wait and see then. I just hope they won't bury us. It will be hard enough to get out of this casket with the lid nailed shut."

"Bury us?" I snort in disbelief, my voice muffled by the walls of the casket. "Too much effort for them. Did you see how lazy those soldiers are?"

"Then I certainly hope they won't incinerate us," he continues with a nervous edge to his tone.

I roll my eyes at his pessimism. "Why do you have to be so grim? I'm certain they'll just—"

Before I can finish, the vehicle comes to an abrupt halt, causing our bodies to jostle within the confines of our coffin-like prison.

"What's happening?" Mine asks as we hear shuffling all around us.

The sound of heavy footsteps and gruff voices grows louder and closer. A loud thud echoes through the air, followed by another one.

Our casket suddenly starts moving, swaying back and forth as if being transported by a group of clumsy pallbearers. I cling onto Mine as we prepare to be discarded with the casket. But instead, the nails on the lid start rattling as the soldiers take them out one by one. Suddenly, it slides open, blinding light penetrating the darkness inside.

I quickly grab onto the pin and use its energy to once more camouflage our appearances and scents.

As the soldiers take off the lid of the casket, they move around it and tip it forward with a grunt.

"Faster. It stinks!" one of them yells, clearly not pleased with their task.

Mine and I hold on to each other tightly as we suddenly come face-to-face with a steep cliff. Without warning, the soldiers give us a rough shove and we tumble out of the casket, falling over the edge of the cliff.

TWENTY-FOUR

"FUCK!" Mine curses as he shifts mid-fall, grabbing me in a tight embrace. I barely have time to realize what's happening or to help cushion our fall before we hit the ground.

Something soft breaks our fall, and we roll together down a steep slope. His arms are around me, never once letting go even though he stands to get hurt worse than me.

"Mine," I call out as we come to a halt. "Are you all right?" I ask hastily as I visually check his body for any sign of injury.

He lets out a harsh groan and I immediately panic.

"Are you hurt anywhere?" I pat down his body.

"What is this smell?" He curses in disgust as he brings up his hand and pinches his nose with two fingers.

So worried I was about him that I didn't register my surroundings, or the fact that Mine is indeed right. The stench is overwhelming.

Yet it's not surprising as I look around us.

"What the—" My words get swallowed up by shock.

Mine opens his eyes and raises himself on his elbows, his expression mirroring mine as we realize where we are.

"Jesus fucking Christ, what the fuck is this, Minnie?"

"Stop swearing so much," I grumble, though I feel like spewing some expletives of my own.

"Well, no shit. If this isn't swear-worthy, then I don't know what is."

He gazes down at his body, his face turning a tad green. He's covered in...bodily fluids. Of the decomposition type.

The entire ditch is filled with corpses. One on top of the other, they litter the entire landfill in a grotesque display.

At the top of the slope, the corpses are fresher, perhaps only a few days old. At the bottom, it's mostly skeletons and scraps of clothing that survived the harsh heat of the blazing suns.

Yet it's exactly that heat that turns this environment into a noxious one, the smell from decomposition making it hard to breathe.

Even if a prisoner wasn't dead when he was dumped in this ditch, he certainly would be shortly. I have no doubt disease lingers around too.

"We need to find a way out," Mine says in between muffled breaths. "Fast."

I nod in agreement, though I can't help but glance around at the mistreated corpses and think that they were someone's family once upon a time. And instead of releasing the bodies in the care of their loved ones for a proper funeral, they were thrown in here, disposed of as if they were worthless.

No matter the crime, no person deserves such an abhorrent treatment.

How is this allowed? Somehow I doubt that the central command would allow for such egregious behavior. Then again, there is so much bureaucracy between the regional militias and the central command that I doubt this would ever reach the ear of someone important—someone with enough say to demand change.

"Fucking hell!" Mine continues to grumble as he gets to his feet and notices the stains on his clothes. "I've dealt with plenty of bodily fluids in my time but never without protective gear. Never mind that this is gross, but can you imagine the diseases?" He lets out a shudder. "What if I catch something? What if it's something native to Aperion and it ends up killing me for good? We must find a way to get clean, Minnie. As soon as possible."

"I'll get us out," I assure him as I reach into my pocket for the pin.

Mine might have a propensity for drama, but in this instance, I can't say I blame him. He survived a terrible illness in his childhood, which is why he's probably always so concerned about cleanliness and disease.

Even to my battle-hardened senses, this corpse landfill is not only unhygienic but also disrespectful and profane. Though all souls who die in Aperion head directly to the House of Psyche, I can't shake the feeling that there's a lot of bad energy tied to this place. The sooner we're out of here, the better.

My brows furrow in concern when I can't find the pin.

"Uhm... Mine?" I start nervously.

"Here." He extends his hand toward me and gives me the pin. "You dropped it," he adds nonchalantly.

I blink. Then I release a sigh of relief.

"That was very sharp of you," I murmur. Just thinking of losing the pin among hundreds if not thousands of corpses was already making me spiral.

"I have my moments." He shrugs, though I can see he warms at the compliment.

Drawing energy from the pin, I transport us up on the cliff and I remove most of the stench clinging to our clothes. The stains, however, are out of my control.

"We can head into the Capital, get some fresh clothes, and grab a shower at an inn," I offer.

"I hope it's not far," he grumbles as he starts walking.

I keep up with his aggressive stride. "You were bragging about getting us free transportation just a while ago. Seems like we still need to walk."

I expect a smart comeback from him, but he surprises me when he pulls me by the shoulders to his side.

"At least I have great company along the way."

"You...you think I'm great company?" I ask, taken aback.

That's yet another thing no one's ever said to me. If anything, it's usually the opposite because I never live up to people's expectations.

"Of course," he replies instantly. "There's no one else in the entire universe I'd rather walk with for miles on end." He winks at me.

The two Aperite suns are blazing from both east and west, making the heat unbearable. Still, the flush climbing up my neck has nothing to do with the sweltering heat.

"Thank you..." I whisper shyly. "You too."

He gives me a dazzling smile. He doesn't let go of me as we march forward, keeping me close as he tells me all about Dracula and Bram Stoker, a classic tale in his world. I listen attentively, surprised by the way vampires are portrayed in this story. The ones I have heard of, some of which happen to make their home in Anthropa, cannot turn into bats, nor do they sleep in coffins. Although the latter I haven't personally verified and cannot say for sure. Still, it makes for an interesting story to pass the time.

It's almost the end of the day when we reach the outer district of the Capital.

There are very few shops still open, but we manage to secure clean clothes and a room at a nondescript inn for the night. Although I insisted on getting separate rooms, Mine managed to convince me that it would be a bad idea since I'm the only protection he has, therefore I must be with him at all times.

I agreed.

It might not be the most proper arrangement, but I think it's a little late to worry about propriety at this point.

The room consists of a small bedroom and an even smaller wet area. Due to the fact that this is a rather poor part of the Capital, the amenities aren't that great and we are warned that warm water would only run for fifteen minutes.

All wet areas in Aperion are operated by magical runes, for which people who lack abilities must pay a premium to use.

As soon as we walk through the door, Mine dashes toward the shower and locks himself inside.

"Don't use up all the water," I call out as I head to the window and pull the curtains aside to inspect the street. Although I don't think anyone's recognized me so far, I don't want to take any chances, especially in the Capital since it's not the same as a small village in the middle of nowhere. Fellow soldiers and courtiers could be walking around, and if they see me...

I shake my head. It's better not to think of the worst outcome just yet.

The door to the bathroom slams open and Mine appears in the room, wearing only his pants, which rest dangerously low on his hips.

I blink and gulp down. I'm too tired for this type of temptation.

"Don't tell me you already washed," I say jokingly in an attempt to mask the low tremor of my voice.

He rolls his eyes at me.

"We only have fifteen minutes of warm water. Might as well make the best of it."

"What do you mean?"

"Take off your clothes and come to the bathroom."

My mouth hangs open in stock.

"W-what?"

"Come on, Minnie."

"We might be sharing a room, but I throw the line at sharing a shower," I sputter.

He raises a lazy brow at me and then shrugs.

"I might take too long in the shower," he adds suggestively. "A full fifteen minutes perhaps."

"Mine!" I stomp my foot. His only reaction is to laugh.

"Come?"

When I don't move, he turns back to the wet area and turns the water on.

The minutes trickle by and as I realize he has no intention

of stepping out of the shower. I quickly take off my dirty clothes and run toward the washing room.

Yet the sight in front of me stops me dead in my tracks.

The water courses in rivulets down his body, and my eyes are drawn to his firm buttocks and toned back. Scars riddle his body, most of them concentrated on his back. Thick jagged lines start from his neck going down to his buttocks, with a few continuing down his left leg. His left side is the most visibly scarred, and the marks continue on the front of his body, with the thickest one being on his upper chest.

His skin might not be flawless, but it's those imperfections that give him character and make him so appealing in my eyes. They make him seem real, flesh and blood, pure...masculinity.

"Done staring?" he drawls. "Only five minutes left."

I shake myself from my reverie. My only two choices are to hang onto my modesty and go to sleep dirty or...

I let out an annoyed sigh and take off the rest of my clothes before I join him under the warm jet of the water. Although this is the first time I'm fully naked in front of someone, I try not to dwell on it. I can feel his eyes on me, examining every little inch of my flesh. Yet he doesn't say or do anything.

I expected to fight him for some peace to wash myself, seeing as how he used such an underhanded method to get me to join him, naked, in the bathroom. But he shocks me when he lathers a good amount of soap onto my hair and massages my scalp while I go about removing the dirt from my body.

His touch is gentle yet firm as he carefully rinses the soap out before applying another layer and cleaning my hair properly.

With his help, I manage to get clean just in time for the water to run out.

He's the first to get out. He takes a towel and pats down his body before he wraps it around his waist. I do my best not to notice the fact that he's aroused, although it's kind of hard with his male part tenting the material of the towel.

Even so, he was a perfect gentleman. Never once did he

come too close to me or made me feel uncomfortable about my nakedness and the vulnerable position I was in.

Taking the other towels, he hands one to me as I step out of the shower and uses the other one to dry my hair. I quickly cover my nakedness, though he must have gotten more than an eyeful by now.

"We could have just split the time," I grumble as he works on separating my strands of hair. After all, if he didn't have any designs on me, why did he insist on sharing the washing space?

"I don't trust your washing skills enough," he answers, amused.

"What?"

"You have long hair," he clarifies. "It takes longer."

"So you wanted to shower with me just to make sure I washed properly?"

"Yep," he hums as he continues to squeeze the moisture out of my hair. "You're welcome."

"You're weird," I say with a chuckle.

"Maybe, but now you'll get a restful sleep."

"Speaking of sleep..."

"Yes, Minnie, we are sharing the bed, too," he adds indulgently.

Somehow I am too tired to argue with him on this, so I simply grab a cotton shirt from the clothes we'd bought earlier and shrug it on before getting in bed.

His eyes never leave me as he continues his ablutions, and once he's done, he joins me under the blanket.

We're both on our sides, looking at the each other.

Despite the horrendous detour we've taken and the horrors we saw both in prison and outside, Mine is surprisingly relaxed. He has a small smile on his face, his eyes twinkling with mischief.

"What are you thinking about?" I ask, curious.

"You, me, one bed."

I frown at his wording.

"Never mind. Sweet dreams, my dear Minnie," he murmurs

and he lays a kiss on my forehead. He closes his eyes and goes to sleep.

Despite how tired I am, I can't seem to do the same. My thoughts are in disarray as I find myself more confused than ever about my situation and my purpose. The time is dwindling and the thought that I'll have to leave Mine behind leaves me... cold.

Yet how can I allow myself to stay when a relationship with a human is not only forbidden but would make me an outlaw for all of Aperion. We might be together, but we'd always be hunted because I don't for a moment believe the Aperite Supremes would allow a deity to get away with such an egregious rule break without making an example out of us.

If only I had been born a human, too...

"THIS IS how males dress in your world?" Mine asks as he fastens a dark blue linen tunic around his waist before donning a thick leather belt around his midriff.

"The common folk. The nobility wear much finer cloth. Although for females, the dresses are also a bit more extravagant," I say as I go about putting on my own ensemble.

The dress is made from the same ordinary linen as Mine's, but this one is a lighter cream color. It has an empire waist and a high neckline, not leaving too much exposed flesh. After I tie back the dress, I add a thin brown leather belt under the bodice.

"The shoes are comfortable, though," he comments after he's put on the leather boots.

"Yours maybe. Not mine." I crinkle my nose as I wiggle my toes around in the narrow toe box. Female clothing, whether poor or rich, is not made for comfort. These shoes are no different. They have pointy toes and a small, rounded heel at the back. As opposed to the male shoes, these ones are not made out of leather, rather of some satin imitation.

Once dressed, we leave the inn and head to the military headquarters that is in charge of sin demons.

The Capital is huge, so to get there faster—and without the chance of running into someone recognizing me—I buy us tickets on the *Prohodos*, a tram-like vehicle that services all the districts of the Capital.

It's mostly used by s'Aperiotes since they make the bulk of the commuters from the outer districts to the central ones.

"Try not to speak too loudly," I whisper to Mine. "We don't want anyone taking notice of us."

He nods.

"I'm surprised how similar Aperion is to Anthropa," he comments in a hushed voice.

"In many ways, yes. After all, most other worlds *are* modeled after Anthropa. It's just that those lacking a magic-based system had to resort to other alternatives."

"Technology," he mentions thoughtfully.

"Exactly. Although there are other worlds that have magic as their main infrastructure, Aperion is unique in that it is the source of *all* magic in the universe."

"What do you mean?"

"I told you about the Supremes. There is one designated for each House of Aperion, and they are in charge of their element for the *entire* universe. Take someone from Anthropa for example, who is born with above average spiritual energy."

"A witch?"

"Yes, a witch." I nod. "Usually, they invoke higher beings to grant them power to perform magic. That increased spiritual energy allows them to create a direct link to the Supremes, which in turn allows them to perform spells. Say a witch desires to control nature. She will either invoke the Gaia Supreme or the Flora Supreme."

He clicks his tongue against his teeth.

"That's assuming the magic they practice is good, no?"

"Not necessarily."

"What?" He chuckles.

"There is *always* an exchange. The goal does not matter as much as what the performer of the spell is ready to relinquish." I shrug.

"And you say demons are bad?" He raises a brow.

"Of course. Demons feed on souls. They *destroy* creation. Our Supremes would never do that."

"Huh…" he murmurs, seemingly unconvinced.

"Nothing is free in the universe, Mine. All types of magical beings that are not of divine origin will have to exchange something for their powers. Like that faerie for example. Her kind might be powerful, but they cannot *ever* give or receive something without striking a bargain. They are *compelled* to do so. Those vampires you spoke of. Their kind traces its origins to the House of Skia, and they exchanged immortality for an unquenchable thirst for blood."

"Then where do you draw the line? If the goal doesn't matter, then why do you crucify demons so much when your Supremes are equally capable of doing damage."

"I told you the difference." I roll my eyes at him. "The Supremes will never destroy a person's soul."

"But what *if* a mortal offers up their soul to a demon, of their own volition? What if they want wealth and fame and whatnot and are willing to forfeit their soul for it?"

"That is their prerogative." I shrug. "But the only ones who are able to strike those deals are the Sons of Tenebreis. Since they technically have divine origin, they are able to fulfill wishes. But since the soul has unimaginable power, the bargain will always be in their favor."

"But why is it so bad if it's people's prerogative whether to sell their soul or not? As long as no one is forcing them…"

"Ah, but that is exactly what regular demons do for the Sons of Tenebreis. They tempt people, corrupt their souls until they either enter such a bargain, or until they become demons themselves after death," I correct.

"So they don't consume them? They let the souls become new demons? So magnanimous of them," Mine comments drily.

"They do consume them in most cases, at least until the demons are able to take on a physical form and get to a higher level. That's when they prefer pure souls, so they simply kill people."

"Fine, I'll grant you that demons can be destructive. But what about witches and other beings who borrow powers from the Supremes and end up doing bad things with them. I'm sure that happens."

"It does," I reply nonchalantly. "That's why there's a special place in hell for them." I smile. "As much as the House of Moirai controls certain points in people's lives and their fates, there is always a certain degree of free will. And that free will verges on whether people do the good thing or the bad."

"So your Supremes purposefully allow the bad?" he asks, his lips curling up. "Making abstraction of the demons and their role in corrupting souls. Doesn't that free will mean they *allow* evil to exist?"

"That's... The world is made up of balance. For good to exist, bad must exist too."

"That doesn't answer my question," he probes deeper.

The *Prohodos* comes to a stop.

"It's our stop. Let's go," I say as I pull on his sleeve.

He has a droll smile on his face.

"You don't have an answer, do you?"

I scowl at him.

"I just told you my answer. Just like the first primordials were made up of good, neutral and bad, so is the world. Everything is a copy of the first creation."

"That's not an answer," he presses on.

"Yes. It is."

"Fine. We can agree to disagree." He shrugs, his expression akin to gloating. My competitiveness rises to the surface.

"I don't have time to continue this now, but don't think for a moment that you've won."

"Fine, fine." Another smile.

The military headquarters are only a short distance from the

Prohodos stop. It's a rather nondescript building that blends in with the background. Only those who've been inside any military compound would know most of the conference rooms and training spaces are underground.

"We're here. Wait for me, all right?"

His smile drops.

"How long will you be there for?"

"I don't know. It shouldn't be too long. I will just inform the General of the situation and I'll be back."

He half turns and motions across the street to the statue of a woman holding an hourglass.

"You have until the hourglass has run its course."

I frown.

"Until what?"

"Until I come for you."

TWENTY-FIVE

A RUNE SYSTEM that scans one's energy print against the database locks the entrance to the military complex. I borrow some energy from the pin and run it through my body to recycle it and make sure the runes won't detect any foreign energy. When I'm done, my energy signature swirls around my hand and I press it against the doorframe.

A loud click resounds, and the doors open.

Stepping inside, I note that this complex is different than the one I operate in.

The walls are a stark white, bare of any adornment. At the front, two soldiers are standing in front of two large doors, who immediately look me up and down suspiciously.

"Minerva An'yan here to see the General Leotar," I state confidently as I march up to them.

"The general is busy and not open to the public."

"I am a soldier under General Molokai An'yan, and I've been working in Anthropa for the past few months. I have information about demon activity in Anthropa that will interest the general."

One of the soldiers gives me a bored look, but the other takes a step back and closes his eyes.

"The general will see you," he replies. He must have gotten approval via a mental link.

With a nod, I wait for them to open the doors and stride inside.

A long staircase leads to a lower level. On my way, I encounter more soldiers who ask me for my identity before letting me pass through another set of doors, and then I go down another staircase.

After I repeat the process three times, I finally arrive to the level where the general's quarters are.

A soldier greets me.

"This way. The general will allow you ten minutes of his precious time. Make sure to state your purpose clearly," he advises.

I bite back a rude remark since it does not bode well for me to get into conflict with his soldiers before seeing the general. Still, the stringent rules are yet another reminder that this branch of the military does things differently.

The soldier scans his energy signature against another set of doors. As they open, he doesn't follow me inside, merely inclining his head for me to go in.

There is a large pool in the middle of the room, the water a deep red. The walls in this room are a dark gray, and evenly spaced around the room are statues of the fourteen Primordials.

As I pass by the pool, there are two velvet sofas and a table, and to my surprise, I notice a female lying on one of them, only a red satin sheet covering her naked body. She doesn't seem surprised to see me as she pops a bite of food in her mouth. She gives me a smile, undulating her body as if she were unashamed of her nakedness.

I gulp down.

That is...something. A bad something.

Although I am aware there are males in Aperion who engage in affairs with courtesans and other lowly females, I've never seen someone be so forward about it—particularly a general who should be setting an example.

In the second half of the room, the walls are covered in bookshelves, and in the middle, there is a study with golden carvings of historical Aperite events. Behind the desk, there is another set of locked doors.

Yet the most surprising thing is that the general is not here.

I half turn to question the female when the doors open and the general strides forward. I only get a brief peek inside the other chamber and spot a large bed, which would suggest those are the general's private rooms.

None of the generals in my branch of the army have personal rooms within the military base. As far as I know, not even Commander Azerius, but that's most likely because everyone would be too uncomfortable to be around him at all times.

The general stops when he sees me, his eyes narrowed to two slits.

He's wearing a black satin pair of trousers and a half buttoned shirt.

"Miss An'yan, was it?" he asks in a bored voice.

"Yes, General."

"I heard you had something to say to me?"

"Yes, I—"

He makes a motion to stop me. He walks around the study, grabs a glass, and pours himself a drink. He asks me if I would like one, too, and since it's not polite to decline, I nod.

He hands me a glass, then waits.

I stare down at the blue liquid and the smell of alcohol drifts up my nostrils: Aperite *tringos*, a strong but expensive Aperite alcoholic beverage. I've had it before, but I can't say I liked it. Now, with his eyes focused on me, I force a sip.

"You were saying?" he continues, a sly smile spreading on his face.

"We've been conducting a mission in Anthropa and—"

He stops me again.

"Last I heard, you were about to be married? To Theron of House of Pyros?"

"Yes, but—"

"An engaged female is not supposed to be gallivanting around, and she is especially *not* supposed to be around other males. What does your betrothed say about this?"

"We are not married yet, and I am a soldier. My duty is foremost to Aperion."

"Huh." He clicks his tongue against his teeth. "Was your duty foremost to Aperion when you interfered with the Moirai?"

I blink. "What?"

He lets out a dry chuckle. "The rumors have been going around, Miss An'yan. You've certainly been doing everything in your power to brand yourself unmarriagable."

"No, that's..." I mean yes, technically, he is right. But the way he's saying it doesn't sit right with me.

"Is that why you're here?" he asks as he takes a step closer.

"No. I have a legitimate concern. I came across a greed demon in Anthropa and—"

"You think I would not know if there was a greed demon in Anthropa?" He raises a brow. "Now tell me why you're really here."

I frown.

"Blissa, leave us," he commands.

The female scrambles off the sofa, tying the sheet around her body before scurrying out of the room.

My eyes widen.

"What is going on? I only came here to let you know about the greed demon and ask you act swiftly. I don't like any of your implications."

"Miss An'yan... Minerva." He smiles, a seedy smile that makes my insides recoil. "Let us do away with the pretense. Everyone in Aperion knows you're not keen on marrying Theron, especially after you humiliated him publicly."

I take a step back as he advances toward me.

"I think I was mistaken in coming here," I murmur as I slowly retreat.

"Stop!" he bellows. His energy seeps out and I find my body unable to move. He comes closer, his smile widening. "I also happen to know what your punishment was for messing with fate. You're powerless, aren't you?"

"General Leotar, please release me and I will be on my way," I say through clenched teeth. I *hate* the way I'm so powerless against him now, even more so as I see how happy he is to see me so helpless.

"I have a proposition for you. Why don't you become my female?"

"W-what?"

"Of course I am not any more thrilled about your disobedience than Theron would be, and I find that you're not exactly" —he pauses as he rakes his gaze over my body—"my type. But I suppose you will do. An alliance with your family will serve me just fine."

"Uhm, no, thank you," I say, staring at him in shock.

He tilts his head to the side. "You don't have to agree. If I take your maidenhead, you will *have* to marry me."

A sliver of fear goes through me at his pronouncement. By the Source, how did I end up in this situation when I just wanted to do the right thing? And how is such a debauched person a general? The mere fact that he's threatening to violate me goes against the rule of conduct, and I will gladly inform Commander Azerius of the fact.

After I get away from Leotar first.

I force my limbs to move, at least so I can grab onto the pin and syphon some energy. But he's far too strong.

"I said no," I grind out. "Release me, now, or next it will be *your* head that falls for even insinuating that."

He looks me in the eye for a moment before he throws his head back and laughs.

"And who's going to believe you, Minerva? You who's already broken rule after rule? You who's run away from her betrothed?"

Pure rage flows through me at his words, but not only at

him, at myself too. Because he *is* right. I did break the rules. Yet I know that Commander Azerius is a fair man. If I tell him...

I squeeze my eyes shut—the only part of my body I can move. To tell him, I'll have to make it out of here first. *With* my virtue intact.

"You're wrong," I tell him in an even voice. Despite the fact that I am seething, I need to keep my wits about me.

"Am I now?" He smirks.

"Oh, yes. So very wrong."

He stops in front of me, his hand reaching out to touch me. My first instinct is to flinch, but I'm frozen to the spot as he touches my cheek.

"You won't be able to take my maidenhead," I say as I look him straight in the eye. "It's already gone."

Shock briefly flitters across his features before he schools them.

"You're a poor liar."

"Not lying," I counter. "If you know so much, then you should also know I've been living on Anthropa for the past few months, among humans." He stares at me intently, so I add, "Human males."

"You *lie*," he accuses.

"Do I? You might want to marry me for some political gain, but you would likely have to accept that you will never know if your firstborn is yours."

"You whore," he thunders, his mouth drawn up in a sneer. "I think I will find out for myself if you're lying or not," he adds in a cruel voice. Before I can react, he grabs my belt and rips it from my body.

"Stop!" I yell, panic unlike any other coursing through me. "I said stop!"

A sneer paints his face as he grabs onto the top of my bodice. The material tears, a loud noise that permeates the air, though it barely registers through the gaze of fear that's taken over me.

I'm so helpless I cannot do anything but watch as he pulls at my dress until the top of my breasts is laid bare. The cold of the air hits my skin, making me both shiver and internally recoil from his touch.

Seconds trickle by as I realize the enormity of what is about to happen. He's going to taint me with his touch and I can only stand by and witness my own defilement.

One more pull of the material and my entire chest will be completely naked.

He reaches for me, and I summon all the strength I can muster to fight against his power.

A series of loud bangs reverberate outside the main room. Shortly, the doors open as soldiers yell, "Demon!"

Leotar stops right before he's about to touch me, his expression one of disbelief.

"What?" he barks out.

"He's... he's..." the soldier stammers.

Yet before he can enunciate clearly what he wanted to say, a shrilly wail of pain echoes through the room.

A heavy, almost intoxicating presence fills the space.

"Impossible," Leotar mutters.

I cannot see behind me, yet as Leotar shoves me to the side and out of the way, his control over my body ceases.

I stumble to the ground, breathing hard from the excess adrenaline running through my veins. Lifting my gaze up, I watch, almost dazedly, as a dark figure shrouded in a dark gray smoke enters the room. Only the shape of his body is visible, tall, lean, and muscular. Black tendrils flicker around his body.

"You... it cannot be," Leotar gasps. "The Sons of Tenebreis are locked in Tartareia!"

The dark figure makes a clicking sound that resembles a chuckle before one dark tendril shoots out, wrapping itself around Leotar's midriff.

I watch in shock as the general tries to gather his power and strike the dark figure, but instead of being hit, he merely absorbs each blow.

Laughter echoes in the hall, followed by a semi-distorted voice, "Die."

The tendril tightens around the general's body until it snaps it into two.

W-what?

I wait for the general to regenerate or come back to life. This should be a trifling wound for someone of his caliber.

Nothing happens.

He is...lifeless.

In all my life, I've never seen something like this. Such raw power that he is able to kill an Aperite general without expending any effort.

I shrink back, reaching for my pin but knowing that if a level nine general stood no chance, then I stand even less so.

The shadowy male stops in front of the severed parts of the general's body. Waving his hand over the body, he pulls forth a shimmery mist that sways in the air before forming a sphere.

He palms the ball and advances in the room, and I prepare myself for the attack. At least death is more welcome than being defiled. The seconds trickle down as he moves lithely toward me, and all I can think of is the fact that I don't want to die. I've barely lived, despite my advanced age, and if I'm honest with myself, the most I've truly lived has been in the last few months, with Mine.

Mine... how is he going to return home without me? He will be in danger if he's discovered in Aperion. But if he does make it back... An image flashes in my mind, of him, in the future, long after I'm gone, with some faceless female.

No!

I tighten my fists, ready to fight. I'm not about to allow Mine to live on without me. He decided to court me. He is mine, and he can only be mine.

Fear morphs into anger as I struggle to my feet, assuming a fighting stance. I borrow all the energy I can from the pin and summon my armor.

"You have my thanks for killing that bastard, but I'm not dying today," I grind out as I wait for his tendrils to strike.

He stops a few feet away from me, the dark shadows of his body swirling in darker hues.

"Come on!" I shout, materializing my ice sword.

With a small movement of his hand, he makes my sword disappear.

I blink in shock.

He comes closer.

So close, he's almost touching me, the blurred edges of his shadows caressing my body.

The same semi-distorted voice then speaks, "Yours, for when you will need it the most."

I frown at his cryptic words, but I don't get to question him before he pushes the ball of energy in my chest.

I wheeze and cough as the potent energy burns my insides, spreading around before seemingly disappearing. One moment, my body brims with power, the next it's all gone.

"What did you do?" I ask in a low whisper.

"You will know. When the time is right, you will need it."

I wait for him to say more or finally strike at me.

But just as he utters the last word, the shadows coil onto themselves before slowly evaporating from sight.

Alone in the room, I stare at the space he just vacated, slowly getting myself under control.

The general is dead. The other soldiers must be dead, too, or they would have come rushing in. Everyone at the base must be dead.

By the Source, that demon or whatever he was killed an entire military base with barely any effort. I've *never* seen anything like this before. Yet the mere fact that I'm here, still alive, is bound to raise eyebrows.

A ragged breath slips past my lips. Another one follows until my lungs work properly again and until my limbs stop trembling.

I must get out of here. I must...

Looking around me, my gaze connects with the walls full of books. I came here searching for help. If no one is going to help me, then at least I should help myself. Knowing time is of the essence, I grab the cloth covering off the sofa and lay it on the ground. There's only a little energy left in the pin, and I must ration it wisely to ensure we can still get back to Anthropa.

With a twist of my wrist, I pull forward all the books that have anything to do with greed demons in them and lay them in the middle of the cloth. There are, however, too many, so I limit myself to ten.

After carefully tying the corners of the cloth together, I swing the makeshift bag over my back and teleport myself out of the building and back to Mine.

"We must leave, right now," I tell him the moment I spot him. I don't give him time to ask what happened as I simply grab his hand and teleport us away from the scene of the crime.

Since I'm running low on energy, I need to choose a nearby location, so I settle for one of my family's properties on the outskirts of Polemos. It's a small cabin that my grandmother used to retreat to when she wanted to be away from the perils and anxiety of politics.

The area is protected by wards, and only someone with An'yan blood can enter the grounds. That should at least offer some protection in case anyone might come looking.

We land in the middle of the drawing room.

Letting go of Mine's hand, I place the makeshift bag on the floor and stoop down to sift through the titles.

A frown creases my forehead as I realize something is amiss. Mine, usually chatty and animated, has not uttered a single word since we arrived here. My unease grows when a loud thud echoes through the room, causing me to jump to my feet.

"Mine!" My heart races as I see him lying on the floor, his skin unnaturally pale and his body unmoving. Panic rises in my chest as I kneel down beside him, cradling his head in my lap and gently touching his flushed cheeks.

"You're burning up! What's wrong with you?" I ask frantically, searching for any sign of injury or illness.

He groans in discomfort, his face contorting in pain. His lips part to speak, but the words that come out are slurred and garbled, full of distress and confusion.

"Will...be...fine."

My heart thuds in my chest. "No, you won't. We're in Aperion, Mine. There is no human doctor around."

"Need to...rest. Will be...fine." He takes a deep breath, trying to steady himself.

"What's wrong with you? Did that demon do something to you? Did he hurt you?" I ask frantically.

"What...demon?" He frowns, looking confused.

I shake my head. "Never mind. Just tell me how to help."

He forces a feeble smile, but I can see the pain etched onto his features.

"You cannot," he says through gritted teeth, his breaths becoming more shallow. "I must have...overtaxed myself."

"But this isn't normal!" I protest, my entire body trembling at the thought that something might happen to him.

His hand covers mine, trying to reassure me. "Remember my childhood illness," he starts slowly. I nod. "I was never cured. When I am weak...the symptoms reappear."

My panic grows as I realize the gravity of the situation. That illness almost killed him, didn't it?

"But..." I start to argue before he cuts me off with a sudden turn to the side. His body heaves as a dark substance spills out of his mouth, staining his lips and clothes.

He continues to retch and vomit more blood. I pat him lightly on the back, my heart lodged in my throat as I watch helplessly as he suffers.

It feels as though an eternity passes before he stops.

The floor is covered in the dark red of his blood, his clothes equally stained.

There is. So. Much. Blood.

"Mine?" I whisper, needing to make sure he's still conscious.

"I'm...fine..." He lets out a dry cough.

"Tell me how I can help. Please," I beg.

With a loud, labored breath, he strains to sit up, the muscles in his arms quivering from the exertion. Slowly, he turns toward me and attempts to muster a weak smile.

My hand flies to my mouth, a gasp of shock escaping my lips at the sight before me.

"Mine...you..." I choke out.

He blinks, and in that moment, I can see his eyes widening in realization. His hand trembles as it reaches up to touch his right cheek.

An angry gash runs across his cheekbone, trailing down to his chin and disappearing under the collar of his tunic. It looks as if his skin has been violently torn apart, with thick, dark blood seeping out from the wound.

The hand touching his face, too, begins to lacerate until blood drips from the injury. More blood rushes to the surface down his body, staining and sticking to the material of his tunic.

His entire right side has been split open and is violently bleeding.

What in the Source is going on?

TWENTY-SIX

HIS EYES ROLL in the back of his head and he drops to the ground, out cold.

"Mine!" I call out, cradling his face in my hands. His blood is everywhere, staining my hands and making me hyperventilate.

I've never been one to shrink at the sight of blood, but it's never been the blood of someone I care about.

His entire body is a mess of cuts and slashes that bleed profusely.

My heart in my throat, I try to ground myself and find a way to help him.

Even my brief training as a nurse fails me as I realize I have nothing around that could help him. There are no human medicines around, nothing that could help fight an infection if he happens to get one due to his open wounds. But perhaps I can use my powers to get some... I'm not sure if I still have enough energy to move things from one world to another, but I must try.

Knowing time is of the essence, I hold tightly onto him and teleport him to the inner bath house.

The bath house is cold and bare. The pool in the middle is dusty and devoid of any water.

Briefly leaving him on the floor, I hurry to start the heating system and clean the pool before activating the runes that control the water supply.

Steam soon wafts around the room, the wood crackling as it gets warmer and warmer.

While the pool fills with hot water, I get back to Mine and start undressing him. He's unconscious, but every touch of my hands seems to pain him as he lets out low groans of pain.

Pursing my lips, I manifest a blade and cut through his tunic and underclothes, revealing more of the deep gashes that run along the right side of his body.

Before, the scars had been mostly focused on his left side. Now, new ones will mar the other side of his body.

My heart weeps for him and the pain he must be going through. But more than anything, I am terrified that I won't be able to help him—that whatever's happening to him might be fatal. He said not to worry, but seeing this much blood, this much mangled flesh, how can I not worry?

I remove the scraps of material from his body and gently lead him to the steaming pool.

"Minnie..." he groans in pain as his skin makes contact with the hot water.

Discarding my own tattered clothing, I join him inside, modesty be damned.

Manifesting a soft sponge and some iodine from Anthropa, I start slowly cleaning his wounds.

"It will be all right. I'll take care of you," I whisper, pressing the sponge against his ravaged cheek.

He squeezes his eyes shut as he pushes against the pain.

I wish my words would turn into reality, but the more blood I wipe from his skin, more pools to the surface. His wounds are angry and nothing seems to appease them.

Leaning forward, I wrap my arms around his neck and drag my tongue against his cheek, hoping that my saliva would help. His blood flows into my mouth, harsh and metallic but surprisingly addictive.

A shudder goes down his body, and slowly, but certainly, his arms come to rest against my midriff, holding me close.

That gives me hope that his strength is slowly returning. Yet as I pull back to regard him, I note that nothing has improved.

My lips flatten into a tight line. Perhaps it's because my energy is so low that my saliva is not working as before. But there is one thing that is more potent and that is...

I still at my train of thought.

As an Aperite, blood exchanges are strictly forbidden for us —it's one of the things that sets us apart from the dangerously reckless demons. But even though I am low on energy, my body still possesses remarkable healing abilities far beyond those of humans. Perhaps I can use this to help ease his suffering.

Swallowing hard, I know that what I am about to do could potentially lead to my downfall if anyone were to find out...but the sight of his pain-ridden face pushes all hesitation aside.

His eyes slowly flutter open, filled with so much agony that my own heart constricts in sympathy. His mouth curves up slightly in a futile attempt to comfort me, despite being the one in excruciating agony. And in that moment, I make up my mind.

The chance to alleviate Mine's suffering is worth any potential consequences that may come my way.

"Mine," I whisper, my voice barely audible. "Look at me."

With great effort, he focuses on me through his hazy pain-induced daze.

Gently retrieving my blade, I press its sharp tip against my sternum.

His eyes widen in shock.

"Minnie—"

Without hesitation, I slice into my skin and allow the blood to flow freely.

Guiding his head forward, I thread my fingers through his hair and I urge him to drink from the wound.

He hesitates for a split second, his nostrils flaring as he takes in my scent.

"Drink," I command softly, determination evident in my tone.

"You know what this means," he rasps out hoarsely.

"None of that matters," I counter firmly, "as long as you get better. Drink."

This time, he needs no further persuasion as his lips eagerly latch onto the wound, his tongue lapping up the droplets of blood. My body arches instinctively and I encourage him to take as much as he needs, willing to give everything to ease his suffering.

His hot breath against my skin causes me to break out in goose bumps. The feel of his tongue as he laps up my blood makes my body hum with unreleased tension. I recognize how wrong it is for me to feel like this when he's suffering, but I never realized that sharing blood would be so erotic, so fulfilling.

My breath catches in my throat. He lets out a low moan before he wrenches himself away from me. His lips are red and smeared with blood. His eyes swirl a deep green as he stares at me intently.

The gashes on his body slowly stop bleeding, but they don't heal. They close up, still red and angry, turning into harsh scars.

My eyes widen. That's... That shouldn't happen. My blood should *heal* him completely, not merely make the wounds turn to scars.

"Mine... Your wounds."

"They don't hurt anymore," he adds in a low voice. "Thank you, Minnie."

"But they haven't healed. They're..."

They look like injuries that have been healing for a few weeks, but the scar tissue still remains.

He lifts a hand to his cheek, tracing the new bumpy scar tissue.

He closes his eyes and sighs in resignation.

"That does not matter. If you hadn't..." He takes a deep breath. "If you hadn't given me your blood, I would have likely suffered for days on end. Thank you."

"Don't thank me." I shake my head. "I would do anything to take away your pain," I say as I cover his hand with mine.

"Ah, Minnie mine, you're too sweet." There is a sad lilt to his voice as he regards me. "I must look like a fright. As if I weren't already scarred enough," he adds bitterly under his breath.

"It doesn't matter to me. It only matters that you're alive."

His face lights up.

"Are you uncomfortable in any way? Is there anything else I can do to help?" I ask.

He shakes his head, a small smile still on his lips.

"I will be weak for a while, but I should be fine now. Thank you," he repeats.

"Oh, Mine, you scared me so much," I confess. I cup his face between my hands and get closer to him, then press my lips against the bumpy scar tissue and lay feather-like kisses against his flesh.

"I've never seen anything like this before. Your entire body..." I trail off as I let my hands roam lower, down his neck and chest. The scar tissue is pronounced there, too, but at least it's not bleeding anymore.

What type of illness could have caused something like this? Something so painful and insidious? Something with no cure in sight?

"I know. The scars will fade a little over time, but this happened before, too." He scrubs a hand over his left side. "The first time it affected only my left side. But as you can see, with time, it's not so bad," he adds, almost self-consciously.

"I don't care about your scars. I never did. I just want to make sure you won't get ill again. Are you sure there is no cure? Nothing I can do? Perhaps get some information from Aperion?"

"No," he states. "You cannot meddle with fate, can you?"

"But—"

"Curing my disease is akin to meddling with my fate, Minnie," he advises darkly.

"The punishment would be worth it. So what if I get another few months without my powers?" I grumble.

"You forget something. That was your first infraction. I doubt they would be lenient the second time."

"I don't care. If I can help, I will."

"No." His tone is firm. "I don't want you to put yourself in danger for me. Ever."

"But, Mine. If I can do something—"

"No," he repeats. "This is enough for me." He wraps his hands around my midriff and pulls me flush against his body. "Just being with you like this is more than enough."

I gulp down.

Since he's no longer unconscious, I suddenly become aware of our proximity and the fact that we are...naked. It didn't seem to matter before when the main purpose was tending to him. But now...

The hot water surrounds us, but there is no mistaking the heat coming off his body and transferring onto my own.

His eyes too, blaze with desire, and it's getting harder and harder to ignore his growing male part poking against my belly.

"Perhaps we should get out. You need rest," I stammer as I avert my gaze.

"Not yet," he whispers. "Let me hold you a few moments longer."

"I'm sure you can surmise this isn't exactly proper and—"

"Fuck propriety."

I raise my eyes to look at him.

"I'm not going to ravage you, Minnie. No matter how much I'd like to, I am too worn out to do anything but hold you. So please..."

Something in his voice makes me waver.

"All right. I suppose we can stay like this a bit longer," I acquiesce.

My reward is a beaming smile and a tight hug as he presses a kiss on my forehead.

"You have no idea how long I've waited for this," he whispers. "To have you in my arms, to breathe you in and hold you..."

"A few months?" I offer jokingly.

"A lifetime," he answers. I expect him to laugh it off, but as I tilt my head to look at him, I realize he's serious about it.

"A lifetime?" I echo.

He takes my hands in his, threading our fingers together and staring at the tight link.

"It was all worth it," he continues, disregarding my previous question. "Everything was worth it," he mumbles, more to himself.

"What do you mean?" I frown.

He gives me a tight smile.

"I knew you'd come along, my very own Minnie." He tightens his hold on me. "I knew I'd find you and that you'd be mine and mine alone."

"That's...very nice of you?"

"You will understand. At some point, you will understand. But for now just know that you were the one I was waiting for all along, the one for whom I was glad to go through hell and suffering as long as I knew I'd one day have your lovely hands take the pain away."

I bite my lip, unable to ignore the giddiness building inside of me. My stomach is in knots, and though this feeling coursing through me is similar to fear, it is not fear. It's something new, something that makes me want to take a step forward instead of backward.

I may not understand very well what he's talking about— these are the ramblings of an ill man after all—but I do know something. His words are sincere.

"I'm glad you waited for me," I say shyly. "I love knowing I'm the only one for you just like you're the only one for me. It's...special."

He nuzzles his face against my hair before placing his chin on my shoulder.

"Then you must take responsibility for me," he whispers mischievously in my ear.

"W-what?"

"You must take responsibility for making me wait this long, Minnie. Why couldn't you come earlier to Anthropa?" he muses, almost to himself.

"You wouldn't have been born," I stammer.

His dark chuckle echoes in the steam-filled room.

"Maybe for you, I would have."

"What are you talking about? You're not making any sense," I say, struggling to get out of his embrace and take a look at his features. Is he getting more ill? Is that it? Because his words confuse me to no end.

He hugs me tighter. For someone who was on the brink of collapse just moments ago, his strength is rather remarkable.

"You have to thank my mother for this. I got my patience from her," he adds.

"What do you mean?" I ask, frowning. He's never mentioned his parents much before.

"I probably inherited my love sickness from her too," he continues, once more not making any sense. "She is the type to love with all her heart and to only love once. One male. Her entire life, she's only loved one male, even though it brought her far too much heartache." He slides his lips across my shoulders in the lightest kiss.

"Your father?"

He nods.

"I wouldn't be here if my mother didn't have endless patience and too much forgiveness in her heart for everything my father put her through."

"You sound as if you don't like him," I add warily.

For some reason, I'm curious about his family. No matter how many deep talks we've had, whenever the subject of family came up, he was always tight-lipped. Perhaps I'm taking advantage of the situation by probing, but I can't help myself. I want to know everything about Mine.

Everything.

"I like him well enough." He laughs. "I just don't agree with some of the things he's done and the choices he's made in the past. If it were me... I would never allow anything or anyone to stand between me and my beloved," he rasps. He emphasizes the word beloved in such a way that I *know* he's talking about me.

He trails up my neck until he reaches my ear. He parts his lips over my flesh and uses his teeth to nibble at the most sensitive part.

A shiver travels down my back, and I instinctively lean into his touch, seeking more of it.

"What happened?" I ask in a strangled voice.

Yes, please talk. If you continue this, I don't think I'll meet the next day with my virtue intact. And he won't even have to ask for it. I'll likely offer it on a platter as long as he can touch me more like this, elicit more of these foreign sensations from my body.

"My mother was very sheltered growing up. She was sent to an all-girls boarding school, but her education was mostly on how to be a good wife for her future husband. Her parents had a match for her already and they were waiting for her to reach her majority so they could announce it to the public.

"I think it happened some time before her graduation. My father ended up in the vicinity and they met. He was older, wiser, and I think that appealed to her at the time. She started sneaking around to meet him every time she could."

"How old are we talking about?" I interrupt, not liking where this is going if she was still a schoolgirl.

"Old enough." He lets out a dry laugh. "He might not look it, but he's lived more than anyone I know."

"Oh, all right."

"It's actually not what you're thinking about. It was my mother who kept seeking him out, wanting to spend more time with him. From what she tells me, he was quite reluctant in the beginning. But he eventually fell in love with her too."

"And that's when you came to be?"

"No. Not yet. You're quite the impatient little minx, aren't you?" He chuckles.

"Fine, fine, go on."

"He knew she was engaged, but he still slept with her. She soon got pregnant, but before she could tell him, he was gone."

"What?" I burst out in shock.

"I know. That was my reaction too," he adds wryly. "In his defense, he did not think he could father biological children, so he didn't think that was a risk."

"But it happened. What next?"

"My mother had the child while she was still at the boarding school. By the time everyone realized she was with child, she was already in labor."

I wait for him to continue.

"The baby was taken away from her," he adds quietly.

I gasp loudly.

"What? They took the baby from her? How? Why?"

He nuzzles his face against the crook of my neck. "Her parents still wanted her to go on with the match. They couldn't have rumors going around about her pregnancy, so they made the baby disappear.

"And no, that was not me. It was my older brother."

My mouth falls open in shock. This is the first time he's mentioned an older brother.

"Where is he now?" I dare ask.

He stills. "No one knows. They couldn't find him," he adds, his tone sad.

"Your mother married the other male?"

"Yes and no. She kept hoping my father would come back for her—she was sure of it. She waited until her wedding day, and she waited even as she was forced to marry the male her parents decreed. But she would never betray her beloved and..."

"And?" I repeat, trying to temper my excitement at the story.

"She took matters into her own hands and almost killed her husband on the wedding night."

"She what?"

"She was lucky she didn't kill him, otherwise she would have been executed for it. But she did injure him enough that he repudiated her. She was shunned by her entire family and exiled to live far away from them, with no money, nothing."

"Mine, that's horrible."

"And yet she kept hoping my father would come back. Year after year, she didn't lose hope. Year after year he didn't return. She doesn't speak much about that time she spent on her own, barely surviving, but I think it was hard on her. Everyone knew her as a fallen woman, and she had to fight to protect herself."

His voice is full of respect as he talks about his mother and it's evident how much he loves her. Now I'm even more curious about her. Maybe at some point I can meet her?

"Eventually, my father did return. He searched for her until he found her living in a small cottage, subsiding on an even smaller vegetable garden because the soil was so barren in that area."

"Please tell me she didn't take him back immediately."

He smiles.

"In her heart, I do believe she did. But she also made him work for it, and she told him that she would only take him back once he managed to make the ground fertile again."

"Oh my." I laugh. "That sounds rather hard."

"It was," he agrees. "It took him a long time to do it, but he never stopped trying. I think my mother needed to see that he was committed to her and that he wouldn't leave again. On the day of the first harvest, she took him back. And that's when I appeared."

"Did your father find out about your older brother."

"He did, and he couldn't find him either, which can only mean one thing..." he trails off.

"I'm so sorry," I whisper.

"It's fine. I never knew him. But I don't think my mother ever moved on from it."

"And she never blamed your father for that?"

"Strangely, no. But I think he blames himself for it. If only he'd come sooner. If only he'd taken her with him. So many ifs..."

I ponder over his words for a moment.

"I get now why you don't want to be like your father. He let your mother down when she needed him the most."

"I would never let you down, Minnie. I hope you know that. No matter where you are or what separates us, I will always find you."

"Ah, Mine, that's so sweet of you to say." I don't add that it's likely impossible for him to stay true to his promise due to the fact that he's human and I'm...not.

"It's not just a platitude. I mean it. There might be a time when you are alone and afraid. When that time comes, please remember my words. I will find you. I will be there for you. Be like my mother and never lose hope."

I lean into him, soaking in his words.

Yet as I blink, the world starts spinning, the image in front of me flashing in and out. Instead of the bright light of the bath house, darkness glides over my eyes.

There's something there. Something that isn't quite right.

A sharp pain erupts in my head.

"Go back, Minerva. Show me what happened next," a dark, unfeeling voice commands me. The compulsion is so strong I can only obey.

TWENTY-SEVEN

I OPEN my eyes and find myself alone on the large bed in the main bedroom. Slowly, the events of the day before flash through my mind.

After Mine had significantly recovered, he'd washed all the blood from his body before doing the same with me. He has a strange fascination with washing me but since he seems to enjoy it and I'm rather partial to it, too, I let him do it. When we were both clean, he took me out of the pool and dried me before carrying me to the main bedroom of the house.

He was all purpose and determination as he laid me on the bed and went to look through the various chests of drawers. He found some dresses, some male clothing, and even a silky night-gown, which he'd promptly shrugged over my head.

I'd looked at him perplexed. Not a few hours before he'd been barely able to move and now he was taking charge as if he owned the house...and me.

He'd put on a cotton tunic, too, and he came to bed, though retrospectively I realize he must have done it so I didn't look at the extensive damage his bout of illness had wrecked on his body.

"Let's sleep," he'd whispered as he pulled the blankets aside, nestled both of us within, and hugged me to his chest.

Too weary from everything that had happened, I could only let my body relax knowing he was fine. He was alive and next to me. The tight hold of his arms was all I needed to feel safe and at peace, so I'd drifted off to sleep almost immediately.

But as I take in the empty other half of the bed, my anxiety returns in full force.

Where is he? Is he fine? Is he suffering in silence?

Panic burrows in my breast until I can barely breathe. The thought that he could so easily be taken away from me awakens a fear in me I previously thought myself impervious to.

Jumping out of bed, I look dazedly around the room and when I don't find him, I go to all the rooms of the cabin, one by one.

A sigh of relief escapes my lips when I see him on the floor of the drawing room, surrounded by open books. The color has returned to his face, though the new scars are still red and angry.

"You should have woken me up," I tell him as I take a seat next to him on the floor. I breathe in and out to calm myself, though my heart is still giving me palpitations.

"You were tired from yesterday. You should have slept more," he replies with a soft smile as if I had been the one at death's door just hours prior. A flush goes up my face and a sliver of guilt spears its head as I think I might not have done enough for him.

Here he is, worrying I didn't get enough rest when his entire body had been split open and bleeding from this mysterious illness.

Although I appreciate his concern, I wish he took better care of himself too. I'm the immortal one here, and he's the human with a debilitating illness.

"I slept enough," I grumble. "Did you find anything in these books?" I switch the topic, still not very used to these new feelings he awakens inside of me.

Before him, I'd had concerns. But true fear? I'd never encountered that. And I'm still not sure if it's a good or a bad thing that I now have.

"Not on greed demons in particular. Yet." He closes the book in his hands and places it next to him. He's barely looking at me. "How come the general let you borrow all these books?" he suddenly asks.

"He didn't. I took them."

He half turns and raises a brow, the scar tissue puckering around his eyebrow.

"Just what happened in there?"

I purse my lips. I don't know how much I should tell him because I don't want him to worry too much. After all, the general might have tried to harm me, but he was killed before anything happened. By a demon of all things. Truth to be told, I am still trying to wrap my head around what happened at the base because I've never seen a demon so powerful to be able to take out a general with the least amount of effort.

"Let's just say that my visit there wasn't welcome. But the general and the soldiers had other things to worry about"—like being killed, though I don't say that—"so while they were busy, I made away with the books."

His lips tremble.

"Minnie, Minnie. Breaking more rules?"

I shrug.

"If they did not want to listen to me, then I might as well take it upon myself to solve the issue."

"That's a good initiative. Then you should be rewarded even more, no?"

"I suppose so," I mutter, though the desire to be praised and rewarded seems like a faraway one. Especially after what happened at the military compound. Commander Azerius will no doubt hear of it soon and he will launch an investigation into what happened. He will want to interrogate me, too, and I'll need to come up with a narrative that will least impact me or Mine. Alas, good thing he waited for me outside. Because the commander will likely employ the truth diviners to see what occurred and if he saw a human with me...

"Then we better start working," Mine says. He's still

avoiding facing me directly, and I frown. Grabbing a book, I shuffle in front of him so I can have a clear view of him. I do like his eyes on me, and perhaps while he's reading and not paying attention, I can also steal some glances at him.

He seems startled by my move, but he doesn't say anything. He merely continues reading.

I force my attention on my book, but every time he turns a page, the sound captures my attention and I find myself glancing up.

He has a slight frown as he concentrates on the words at hand. I wonder how my little spell worked in aiding him to understand the language and if he has any difficulty deciphering the written form.

I should be putting in the same effort to research this demon —it is my reputation and maybe even life at stake here. Yet time and time again, my eyes slide up, ending on his face.

Is he still in pain? Did my blood help with that too, or it just closed the wounds? The questions are so many, yet I find myself tongue-tied when it comes to voicing them aloud.

Suddenly, his gaze collides with mine.

I immediately straighten my back and avert my eyes, but I've already been caught.

"Do my new scars bother you?" His voice, laced with a combination of wariness and resignation, surprises me.

I blink in shock, this time looking directly at him.

"No. Why would they?"

He lets out a tired sigh as he threads one hand through his thick locks.

"You don't have to lie to me. I looked in the mirror this morning. I saw..." he trails off.

"What did you see?"

"I look like a monster," he replies quietly.

"What?" I stare at him. "You what?"

His hand comes down from his hair as he traces his new scar.

"I'm sorry if this offends you. It should get better with time." He pauses, frowning. "I hope," he adds under his breath.

"You think it offends me?" I repeat in outrage. That was the last thing I would have ever thought about. "Have you gone daft, Mine? Did this illness also addle your brain?" I shoot back.

His eyes widen in surprise.

"You don't look like a monster, and they don't bother me in the least." I roll my eyes. "Here I was admiring you, in a rather positive way, I might add, and you think I'm offended by your scars?" I huff aloud. "The only thing I am offended about is that you would even think tha—"

I squeak in surprise as he grabs me by the waist and moves me to his lap as if I weighed nothing.

Our faces are inches apart, the green of his eyes making me gulp uneasily as my stomach makes a sudden somersault.

"You maddening, beautiful, brave female," he whispers.

Slowly, I lift my hands and frame his jaw within my palms, tracing the scars with my thumbs.

"Does it still hurt?" I ask in a whisper. Up close, I can see that though closed, the wounds are still red and puckered.

"No, not anymore. Because of your blood," he says as he takes my left hand and presses a kiss to the inside of my palm. "I'm fine now, though a little worse on the eyes." He lets out a dry laugh.

I pull my hand away.

"Stop this," I tell him firmly. "I don't care if you had a million scars. I only care about this," I say as I stab one finger into his chest. Then I move it up to his head. "And this." I press against his temple. "I'm not shallot," I declare.

He blinks and stares at me. Then he suddenly bursts into laughter.

"Shallow," he corrects.

"Whatever. I'm not that, all right?"

"All right," he replies softly.

"Good," I huff.

He chuckles and leans in to place a kiss on my nose. Then he slowly hovers over my lips. But before he can kiss me, I press my finger against his lips and push him back, narrowing my eyes at him.

"No, no, no. We still have to talk about this."

"Got it, you're not shallow," he adds with amusement.

"That too. But I need to know more about this illness of yours. You said it's recurring. Will it happen again?"

His lips flatten, his mood changing immediately.

"It is likely," he answers slowly, reluctantly. But I'm not about to drop the subject, so I push on.

"What does that mean?"

"I don't know when it will happen again. Sometimes I'm fine, and sometimes an over exertion can cause it. Despite my father's efforts, the illness remains dormant within me."

I stare at him.

"Will you...die from it?"

He lets out a nervous laugh. "I'm mortal. We all die at some point."

I swat his shoulder. "Stop joking about this. Will you die from it?" I repeat, this time more forceful.

Seconds pass by as he takes a deep breath, his brilliantly green eyes eclipsed by a wariness I haven't seen before.

"If it gets bad enough, yes, it can be deadly," he admits.

"You..." My lips tremble. "You lied to me. You told me you're fine and you're clearly not. If this can kill you. If..." I ball my hands into fists and bang lightly against his chest. My eyes are moist, achy, and no matter how much I blink, I cannot get rid of this irritation.

He catches my fists and holds on to them.

"Don't panic," he whispers. "It's not my time to die yet, Minnie."

"But you will die."

"Eventually, I will."

How can he say this out loud so carelessly?

"No, no." I shake my head.

"I'm mortal, Minnie. My fate has been decided a long time ago."

"No, I won't let you," I tell him vehemently.

He gives me a tender look.

"If I were to die, soon, at some point...will you stay with me until the end?"

"I'll find a cure. Whatever illness you're suffering from, I'll do everything in my power to cure you."

He gives me a sad smile.

"You'd be messing with fate again," he notes wryly.

"So be it." I shrug. "I can take whatever punishment they dole out for me. But at least you'd live."

"My tiny darling," he whispers as he pulls me to his chest, pressing one of my hands against his beating heart.

I raise my gaze to his, and with our gazes locked together, I lean in and press a light kiss against the scar on his chin. Slowly, I make my way up, kissing each and every one of his scars.

"You'll live," I tell him. "I don't care how many scars you get. You will live. For me."

"Ah, Minnie, have I told you how much I love you?" he whispers as he turns his face so that our lips are mere inches apart.

I blink and stare into his eyes.

"You...do?"

"I love you," he states quietly. "More today and even more tomorrow. Every day, I'll love you more."

I pull back, my heart racing in my chest. He's talked about love before, but this is the first time he's said the words so clearly, so directly.

"I..."

Do I love him, too? I don't know, but I think I do. If these feelings growing every day in my chest are any indication, then I'd say I'm well on my way to loving him too, if I already don't. But because there is so much standing between us, so much that is outside of my control, I find it hard to say the words aloud and give him my confirmation.

"I…"

He waits expectantly as I stammer and stutter in an attempt to find my words.

"I think you're not too bad," I end up saying, though I mentally beat myself over it.

I wait for the disappointment to appear on his face and try to think of ways to explain myself, that there is something there, but I'm having a hard time to define it because I've never experienced this before.

But as I open my mouth to speak, he suddenly laughs. His eyes crinkle with warmth and amusement.

I frown. What…?

"Oh, Minnie, Minnie. You really do know how to stroke a man's ego."

"Are you…mad at me?"

He shakes his head, a smile still on his lips.

"I could never be mad at you. In fact, I probably deserved that." He chuckles. "Funny how history repeats itself," he mutters, more to himself.

"I don't understand."

"You don't need to understand, Minnie." He caresses my cheek. "My love for you is unconditional, and it always will be."

"That's…" I clear my throat. "That is very nice of you."

He pulls me close and presses his lips against mine in a swift yet maddening kiss.

"We have work to do."

I nod, though that doesn't mean I'll have an easier time focusing on my work while he's still here, especially after he said those words to me.

We spend half a day going through the books, though we don't find much information about greed demons. As we put aside book after book, I wonder if I made a mistake when I chose the titles. I didn't have much time for an in-depth search, but it would be disappointing to know everything I did was in vain.

Mine releases a tired sigh and my eyes are suddenly on him,

looking for any sign of illness. He seems fine, though a little tired.

And that's when it hits me.

When did he last eat?

I'm built differently and I can withstand hunger better. But he's human. He needs daily nourishment.

Suddenly, I get to my feet.

"I'll make some food," I declare.

His brows go up.

"Can I watch?"

"Of course," I tell him. "Perhaps that will make you love me even more." I wink at him playfully.

"Of that I have no doubt."

We head to the kitchen and I open a couple of cupboards and get some items from inside. The cabin is designed to be self-sufficient, and each cupboard door is engraved with runes that ensure the food inside is always replenished when the door opens.

Mine takes a seat at the table, a book still with him as he watches me.

I smile to myself. Cooking is something I'm quite good at, if I do say so myself. Spending so much time on the battlefield meant I had to make do, so I've learned quite a lot from the many worlds I visited.

While I prepare the food, I take care to only select ingredients that wouldn't be incompatible with Mine's biology. I end up making a hot spicy stew with vegetables to be eaten aside something similar to the rice in his world.

I plate the food and bring it to the table, but this time, instead of watching me, his brows are furrowed in concentration as he reads from the book.

"Greed demons are descendant of the first Greed Primordial. While they are rare, they are insidious and can make a community rot to its core."

"You found something?" I take a seat next to him.

"It recounts how greed demons act and how they spoil a

person's character by influencing them to give in to their inner greed. But then it says 'There is only one way that has been shown to have some success in stopping a greed demon. Since they get stronger on greed, the only way to weaken them is to give them the opposite.'"

"The opposite?" I frown.

"Charity," he states.

"What does that mean?"

He purses his lips.

"The instructions are not too clear, but if I understand this correctly, it means that instead of letting the demon get to our heads, we should treat him with kindness instead. Charity. Perhaps offer him things?"

I nod and think on it.

"That easy? Impossible."

"That's all it says. But it might not be impossible. Think of the other sin demon references we found. For a lust demon, the weapon to defeat them is chastity. For a wrath demon, it's peace and calm. It seems that what they lack is their weakness."

"That makes sense. But how do we even give charity to a demon?" I snort. The entire idea seems preposterous.

"I'll check the rest of the books too, but I think this is a starting point," Mine says as he closes the book and grabs his bowl of food.

I wait for him to taste it, and once he lets out a moan of approval and he starts eating faster as if he can't get enough, I can finally focus on my own food.

"Charity. Easier said than done," I add thoughtfully. "What can one even *give* to a demon?" My words are filled with venom, and Mine's head suddenly snaps up, staring at me with an inscrutable expression.

"Demons are beings, too, Minnie. They have wants, just like you do."

I snort and roll my eyes. "*Insidious* wants."

His lips press together as he stares at me for a few seconds. Then, with a sigh, he turns his attention back to his food.

<h1 style="text-align:center">TWENTY-EIGHT</h1>

WE RETURN to Anthropa the following day, though the entire time we spent walking to the portal, I worried the army would come after me. A general murdered in his own military base is not a small thing, and soon the news will break all over Aperion. I just hope I'll be able to destroy the greed demon before someone catches up to me to interrogate me.

Though we've only been in Aperion a couple days, the different time flow means it's been weeks already in Anthropa, far more than I'd expected.

Back at the military base, Mine leaves me at our quarters so he can go speak with his supervisors and explain the reason for his absence so they don't take it as desertion. It's when he comes back that he has bad news for me.

Although his CO had seen his new scars and had understood it had been a health issue, he'd called over the doctor to give him a checkup.

He was deemed healthy.

"I have to fly out tomorrow," he states. "Will you be fine by yourself?"

"Of course," I answer immediately, almost annoyed he'd imply otherwise.

"Try not to get yourself in trouble, all right? Don't go too close to the demon until I come back."

"I'll study that book more," I tell him with a smile, although I also plan to put into action what I'm studying. "You should take care of yourself. Those missions are dangerous."

He shrugs. "I'll be fine. I told you, it's not yet my time to die."

As if he can know when his time to die will be. But I refrain from adding that. He brought me some donuts, including a chocolate-covered one, and I aim to enjoy them in peace.

As we get back to our routine, it makes me better appreciate this type of life, away from the prying eyes of the Aperite aristocracy and its burning rules. Perhaps it's not such a bad idea to leave it all behind. I'll at least have Mine and...

I sneak a look at him as he buttons up his nightshirt. Freshly showered, his wet locks hung over his forehead and a few drops of moisture drip from his lashes and onto his cheeks.

I lick my lips instinctively.

"You promise me you won't try anything while I'm away?" he asks again.

"Uhm, I told you I would."

He tilts his head to the side and stares at me.

"Is that so..." he trails off.

"You should sleep. You need to be rested for tomorrow so you can kill as many of those horrible Nazis as possible," I suddenly say, getting up from my bed and going to his side. I tuck him in and lay a kiss on his forehead. "And remember. You come back to me."

"Yes, yes, Minnie." He chuckles.

As I head to my own bed, I continue to steal glances at his form even as he goes to sleep. I'm worried about his missions. No matter how skilled he is, the danger is always there. For a moment, while we'd embarked on our adventure, I let myself forget this aspect of his life—of our lives, since mine isn't any less dangerous.

The next day, the anxiety doesn't dwindle. If anything, as I wave him off on the runway, my heart aches in my chest when he becomes a smaller and smaller dot on the horizon.

He said he loves me.

"Don't you dare leave me until I can tell you I love you, too," I whisper to the wind.

Since my primary patient is gone, the other nurses ask me to help them with some chores around the base. I happily agree as it gives me more freedom of movement to observe how the greed demon has evolved in the time we've been away.

The first thing I notice when I head to the infirmary is that all the beds are full.

"There you are, Miss An'yan," the doctor greets me when he sees me. "Thank you for joining us. We're completely in over our heads. We have no more beds and the staff cannot cope with it anymore." He takes a deep breath. "Any extra help is appreciated."

"What happened? All these men have been injured in battle?"

He shakes his head bitterly. "If only. More than half the injuries have been sustained on the base."

"What happened?" I ask as I follow him inside the full infirmary. All the other nurses are inside, rushing from one bed to another to take care of the patients.

"Beats me," the doctor replies with a weary sigh. "It started shortly after Major Vitry went on his medical leave. Soldiers would fight over the smallest thing like food or drink. At first it wasn't very alarming, but then they started targeting the women on the base."

"What?"

He nods grimly. "Most of the soldiers currently in the infirmary got their injuries by fighting over the women and who would claim them. It got so bad, the women barricaded themselves in the cantina and stayed there for days until the fighting died down."

I glance at the injured soldiers and note most of them are

sporting bruises on their faces from punches. The worst of the injuries are gunshot and stab wounds.

"By that point, most of the men had been too injured to fight over them. By God, I barely convinced them to treat them. They were terrified, and with good reason."

"Any casualties?"

He grimaces and nods. "Five men. The higher-ups have been notified and we're expecting an investigative crew to come here any moment."

"And what's going to happen to the men who survived?"

"They will be tried in the military tribunal. Those who survive, that is. We have nine who are in critical condition, and the smallest infection might kill them. It's why I need all the help I can get."

He looks gaunt and haggard, his eyes bloodshot and tired.

"Of course I'll help," I add. "May I also inquire about Holloway? He's a good friend of Major Vitry and he's been asking about him."

He purses his lips.

"He is...perhaps one of the worst cases. He's been placed in isolation and I fear something might have broken in his mind. He's not himself anymore."

"Isolation? When was that?"

"A short while after the altercation. He was uttering some insane things and telling people they should fight to the death."

"And that altercation was...?"

"Five days ago," he answers.

"And has anything more happened after?"

"More?" He raises a brow.

"Any other acts of violence or unusual behaviors."

"Not that I know of," he answers, scratching the back of his head.

If Holloway was put in isolation, perhaps that explains the overall air of normalcy around the base—sans the injured men. That also means the greed demon has not devoured enough sinful energy to become corporeal or jump hosts.

A smile pulls at my lips.

This could prove easier than I thought.

"Who has been in charge of Holloway, Doctor?"

"We have nurses on rotation going to him. No one wants to, though, as they all complain about his language and behavior."

"I can do it."

"I was thinking you'd help in the infirmary..."

"I can take care of Holloway so other nurses won't have to. That way they can focus on the infirmary."

"I suppose that helps as well. But are you sure? He is not a pleasant fellow."

"Of course. Leave it up to me."

"All right. Let me give you a short summary of the medicines he's supposed to take and I'll show you to his cabin. He's tied to the bed, so he cannot hurt you. A soldier will be outside should he need to relieve himself, so you will not have to deal with him without his constraints."

The doctor gives me the list of medicines and tells me they should be administered three times a day, after which he leads me to where Holloway—and his demon—have been sequestered.

"Shout if you need anything, miss," the soldier on guard tells me.

I nod.

He opens the door for me and I step inside with my tray of medicine.

The entire cabin has been emptied of any belongings. There is only a small lamp close to the door that barely illuminates the room.

The bed is in the middle, and Holloway is strapped to the metal hinges by his hands, feed and midriff.

His eyes are blank, almost as if there is a white film covering them.

I step closer, but he doesn't seem to take notice of my presence.

The demon, however, now almost as tall as the ceiling,

stands next to him, fuming in anger. A part of him is still attached to Holloway, so he cannot move unless his host does.

The moment the demon detects me, he forces Holloway to spout obscenities at me. When that doesn't scare me or make me react, the demon gets increasingly mad.

"Hello, Mr. demon," I say as I address him directly.

His eyes widen in shock. "You!" He points his finger at me—the previous mass of mangled energy has now become more anthropomorphic. I doubt he has much longer before he can become corporeal and separate himself from Holloway. And that truly makes me question what I'm about to do next. Alas, trial and error, no?

"You ugly wench." He throws the insult at me, but I just shrug, keeping the smile on my face.

He's almost normal-looking, if not for that scowl dripping with malice as he realizes who I am.

"And you're so very handsome. You've been eating well, haven't you?" I ask as I pat his semi-translucent belly.

If he could, I have no doubt he'd have steam coming out of his nose and ears like those cartoon people do at the movies. Alas, his only weapon for now is to glare at me.

"I brought you a little something," I say.

He starts cursing me out before abruptly stopping. "You brought something...for me?" he asks in disbelief.

"Two somethings, in fact."

His eyes slowly widen and I could swear I detect a hint of anticipation in his features—but he masks that quickly.

"What could you, an ugly wench, have to give me?"

"How about a donut?" I ask as I burrow my hand in my pocket and remove a paper-wrapped donut.

While studying the book this morning, I noticed a passage that spoke about sweetening a greed demon. It didn't specify how or if it was a figure of speech. So I decided to try my hand at the literal meaning first. Considering I'm wasting a precious donut on him, this better work.

A whiff of the powdery sugar reaches my nose and I have to

force myself not to think of it being devoured by a beast. Not when Mine got it for me right before he left this morning.

With more difficulty than I anticipated, I push the donut in front of him.

"It's for you. I want you to have this sweet treat and enjoy it."

He opens his mouth to speak, but no words come out. For moments on end, he stares at my donut and I wonder if perhaps I read the text wrong.

"For me?" he asks again, unsure.

"Specifically for you. It is freely given," I add as I push it even further into his face.

Moments trickle by. He doesn't move. He's just staring at the donut with an odd expression. But just when I think this plan was all in vain, he snatches the donut from me and pops it into his mouth, paper wrap and all.

Loud, disgusting munching noises echo in the room.

By the Source, I didn't even know non-corporeal demons could eat solid things.

In a few bites, the donut is gone, after which the demon releases the most vile and disgusting burping sound. It's so strong, it blows my hair into my eyes.

Ew.

I tuck the stray strands behind my ear and as I get a good look at him, I realize something is off.

I scan him from head to toe and then back to the head again. Suddenly, it dawns on me that he's no longer as tall as the ceiling.

What? Did this trick actually work? Don't tell me all we had to do until now was to offer him sweet things and we would have defeated him? Although I am slightly smarting from the fact that he would have that in common with me.

Happy with my new discovery, I quickly administer the medicine to Holloway and leave.

My next goal? Find as many sweet things as possible. In

fact, double that. After all, I do require my own commission for it.

And since I still have a little bit of energy left in my pin, I use it to infiltrate the kitchens. But after an hour of surreptitiously rummaging through all the cupboards, I realize there's nothing here.

I frown. Where would Mine have gotten them from then?

My lips tighten in annoyance. If I can't find them anywhere on base... I suppose I could manifest them, but the energy from the pin is quickly dwindling. I'll likely only have a few more uses for it if I get the donuts.

After a little mental back and forth, I decide to risk it.

Manifesting a dozen donuts, I head back to the cabin where Holloway is sequestered. I'd placed the donuts on a try and covered it so it doesn't raise suspicions.

"Back so soon, miss?" the guard asks.

"I forgot to give him one medicine. I'll be in and out." I give him a smile and he opens the door for me.

When he sees me, the demon starts shrieking.

"You ugly wench! What did you do to me?"

"Me? Nothing. I just wanted to give you more donuts. You like them, don't you?"

His eyes flicker.

I step closer and reveal the twelve donuts.

He stares at them, licking his lips.

"They're yours," I add.

He grabs the first donut and shoves it into his mouth—again, I have no idea how he can even eat since he's not corporeal. One after another, he's eaten about eight as I watch closely for any changes in his shape.

To my shock, nothing happens.

What? But it worked before. He shrank after the first donut. So why is he not changing at all after eight?

I quickly pull back the tray and glare at him.

"Give me!" he shouts.

By the Source, if anything, his body has returned to the previous size.

I stare at him in shock and befuddlement. How could this be?

Clearly, it's not the donuts that can make him shrink. And to think I used my precious energy to get these...

Angry, I take a step back.

"Enough!" I tell him sternly.

My gaze dips at the remaining four donuts, and my mouth waters. Annoyance continues to bubble within me and out of spite, I grab one of the donuts and shove it into my mouth. *Take that, you ugly demon. Now you have to watch me eat these delicious treats.*

He continues to shout at me, calling me all sorts of names as he pulls onto the right side of his body that's still tied to Holloway. Oh, I don't doubt he'd like nothing better than to get his hands on me.

I grab another donut, but this time it's less about the spite and more about the fact that the addictive sugar is already laying claim to my decision-making processes.

The third one is soon gone, too.

The demon stares at me in disbelief, and just as I bring the last donut to my mouth, he starts shouting as loud as he can, the sound slowly turning into a shriek.

I'm about to bite into the donut when he utters the one word I never expected him to.

"Please."

It's low, barely audible, but it makes me stop before eating the donut.

Hope flickers in his eyes as he sees me stop, and I take a moment to analyze the situation.

Something doesn't add up here.

The smell of sugar continues to taunt my nostrils, and I'd like nothing better than to bite into the donut and be done with it—at least then I'd have gotten something out of it since I've already used the energy.

But there's something in the way the demon is writhing and salivating at the sight of the donut that makes me pause.

His previous angry words are now replaced with anguished ones.

It's the greed talking. It wants something and it's not getting it.

What happens then if he wants it and gets it?

This might backfire if it makes him grow even more, but I reluctantly part with the donut and hand it to him.

He snatches it from my hands, and to my surprise, he seems to almost...cherish it?

He takes a small bite. Then another. But it's no longer the same frenzied feeding as before. This time, he's savoring it.

And by the time he's done, he's shrunk back again.

I blink. That's... How? How did this happen?

Before he can realize that he's once more changed size, I leave the cabin, thank the soldier, and head back to the infirmary to help.

All the while, I keep trying to make sense of what happened. What was the difference between the first donut and the next eight? And then how did the last donut change the situation?

Was it because he craved it so much he dared to beg me for it? Is it because I didn't want to give it to him? Do things that are not given to him matter more?

Or...is it because I also wanted it?

The first donut, I felt sad parting with. The following eight were just part of the plan. But the last one? I was salivating for it as much as he did. Does that change things? If the item being given is something precious to the giver?

It must.

Otherwise, anyone could be defeating greed demons by simply showering them with gifts.

It has to be meaningful gifts.

Charity... My eyes widen in realization. It's not about giving someone useless things, it's about doing a selfless act, going against one's desires.

My heart beats faster with excitement. It's not a foolproof theory, but it's better than what I had before. Now it's just a matter of trying it out to prove if it's right.

The sirens go off on the base. Soldiers run from their posts and rush toward the runway. The doctors and a few of the nurses go to the ambulance and board it. I follow after them, excited for Mine's return.

I might have gone against his warning not to engage with the demon, but I can't wait to share my findings with him.

We huddle together in the back of the ambulance as the car starts heading toward the runway.

The sounds of planes fill the air. The anxiety is high as everyone tries to see if their friends made it back safely.

For some reason, I am not worried that Mine will not return. Not only did he promise me he would, but I also have full confidence in his abilities. He's a good fighter, and that is a high praise for a human. But he is *my* human. Of course he must be a good fighter. Otherwise, I would have never entertained his courtship.

Once we reach the runway, I scan the planes around looking for Mine's. When I see that he's landed, a bright smile spreads across my face. The doctors and nurses hurry to get the injured, but my first priority is making sure Mine is all right. After all, I am his personal nurse, no?

I barely get out of the car when I see him jumping out of the plane. He takes less than a second to spot me, after which he's running at full speed toward me.

I blink, and in the next moment, I find myself in his arms as he twirls me around.

"I missed you," he whispers against my ear.

"Mine! People will see!"

"So? I don't care. Let everyone see that you're mine."

Heat travels up my cheeks, but I don't make any effort to push him away, simply melting in his embrace.

"You're all right? No injuries?"

"None."

"And your crew?"

"Perfectly fine as well."

"Good. That is good."

"It was a good mission. Not too many fallen, and it seems everyone made it back in one piece," he mentions as he looks around. It dawns on me he's speaking about the souls of the dead. There aren't any around.

"Come, I need to speak to you," he says urgently as he all but drags me away from the commotion on the runway.

We get to the cabin and he locks the door behind him. Hands on my hips, I tilt my head and frown as I wait for him to speak.

"I need you," he rasps as he wrenches the uniform from his body, shedding his clothing until he remains bare-chested.

TWENTY-NINE

MY EYES GROW to the size of two saucers as I gawk at him.

"What are you doing?" I squeak and jump back.

Once his chest is bare, I note that his scars are an angry red, far worse than before.

"Minnie," he says my name in a harsh voice.

"What do you need?"

"Blood," he states simply. "Your blood."

I don't need to ask why he needs it because I can see it in the way his scars threaten to split open. They're raised and jagged, almost like a dress whose seams cannot hold it together any longer.

I grab a knife from the table and press the blade to my forearm. The pain is swift and sharp. I extend my arm to him and he's in front of me in two strides, fitting his lips to the bleeding wound.

He sucks it in greedily, his throat bobbing up and down.

Warmth spreads through me as I push myself into him, urging him to take more until he's sated.

With a low, guttural sound, he wrenches himself away from me. He's breathing hard, but the scars on his body are no longer as threatening as before. The redness has now dulled to a light pink.

He lets out a sigh as if a massive weight's been lifted off his chest. He takes a few second to compose himself before he moves to his dresser and takes a small box from the top shelf. He quietly wraps a bandage around my arm before laying a kiss to my inner wrist.

"What happened?" I ask

"We were hit hard," he replies.

"But you said it was a good mission." I frown.

He shrugs.

"The end result was good. We didn't have a lot of planes go down. But for that we had to make certain maneuvers."

"We or you?" I raise a brow.

Another shrug.

"I did what I had to do for my men."

"Mine!" I grit out. "You promised you'd be careful."

"I'm here, aren't I? And a lot of good men will live to see their families. My mission isn't only to bomb German factories but also to take care of the men under my command."

"So you exerted yourself too much, didn't you?"

"Come, Minnie, don't be mad, all right?" He lifts his lips in a smile as he gathers me in his arms. "I missed you," he whispers against my hair. "It feels good to have someone to come back to, something to fight for."

My heart skips a beat, and I blush furiously at his words. He certainly knows how to make his case. And the fact he's such an honorable soldier makes me even more proud of him. I might be mad that he's putting himself in danger, but that doesn't mean I don't respect his choices.

Good male.

"Now I just need a bath to wash off the sweat. Help me?"

"W-what?" I stammer. "I'm certain you can b-bathe yourself."

"Usually, yes. But I find myself quite tired. And I won't be able to wash my back properly. Will you do it for me?"

When he puts it like that...

"All right," I accede.

"And my hair, you can wash my hair too."

"Fine." I roll my eyes.

"And—"

"That's enough. Don't push your luck," I warn.

He chuckles.

On the way to the bathroom, he sheds the rest of his clothing before turning on the water and getting inside the tub.

It's a small one, not really meant for lying inside, especially for a big male like him. But he makes do, sitting with his knees to his chest, which makes it much easier for me to ignore that growing part between his legs.

Turning in the faucet, I take a small bucket and fill it to the brim. First, I pour it over his head and back before I lather some shampoo in his hair. I work my fingers through his locks, massaging his scalp.

He lets out a long sigh of contentment as he leans into my touch.

"I hate the war," he admits quietly. "I hate that so many innocent people have to die."

"And I hate that you're always in danger. Do you think it will end anytime soon?"

"It will. But by that point too many will have died."

"I know your intentions are noble, Mine. But you can't save them all."

"That's what guts me." His voice is low and broken and something shatters inside of me. We've never talked much about the emotional side of the war and the toll it takes on him, but I can only imagine.

I might have only known him a few months, but it was evident from the start that he was an honorable male.

Our first encounter briefly flashes through my mind and how he'd heroically run toward the site of the bomb, intent on helping anyone he could.

I lean in and press a kiss against his jagged temple.

"Tell me something good. What do you plan to do when the

war ends?" I change the subject so he can take his mind off the bloodshed for a moment.

"You mean we," he corrects.

I roll my eyes, though a pang of sadness reverberates through my chest. I will like not to be here when that happens. But I will not ruin this moment by reminding him of that.

"Fine. We."

He smiles.

"I'll take you out on a real date, to the fanciest restaurant, and I'll feed you delicious cakes."

My brows go up.

"Delicious cakes, you say?"

"I bet you've never had an eclair."

"I have no idea what that is, but if it's sweet and delicious, I'm all in."

He leans back to look at me.

"And I want to take you somewhere."

"Where?" I frown.

"It's a place I used to call my own in the past, waiting for time to go by."

"That doesn't tell me too much about it," I add drily.

"It will have to be a surprise then. A little haven for the two of us."

I bite my lip so hard I draw blood, anything to stop myself from imagining what that haven would look like when I know our future is precarious. We might not even have a future.

Yet is it so bad if I let myself dream about it?

"I can't wait," I tell him softly.

I continue to wash his hair, pouring more water over his head to rinse the shampoo out.

Silence descends between us, the only sound that of the water splashing. He doesn't move, merely letting out small sighs of contentment when I massage his skin.

There's something oddly satisfying about this and the way he trusts me so implicitly, lowering his guard in my presence.

I've been around too many military men to know that this is a rare thing.

"I will need to head out for a debrief with my CO after. It shouldn't take too long. But after I get back, we can plan how to tackle the greed demon."

"I...might have done some investigating of my own," I admit sheepishly.

He sharply turns to me.

He still has shampoo clinging to his hair, and the bubbly foam slowly dripping down his face makes his scowl amusing rather than intimidating.

"Really, Minnie?" He raises a brow at me. "What did I tell you?"

"Did you really expect me to follow your orders?" I huff aloud. "I am not foolish, Mine. I know the dangers and I was careful."

He shakes his head.

"You're right. I didn't expect you to do as you're told, but a man can at least hope, no?"

I glare at him.

He stares back, his expression the definition of stoicism.

Seconds pass as we engage in a rather odd staring contest before we both concede at the same time with a rather well-timed bout of laughter.

"Good on you that you know," I add with a giggle.

One corner of his mouth tugs up and he regards me with amusement. He's so handsome when he smiles. Especially when he smiles at me. There's something magical about the way his green eyes light up.

My gaze glides over his features, and a shiver goes down my spine.

He is too handsome for his own good. And despite what he might think, the scars only enhance his allure. Although his slanted eyes are big and clear, with long dark lashes that I can only characterize as beautiful, the rest of him is sharp and rugged, all angles and muscles, all male. He is an odd combination of beauty and strength, and not for the first time, I feel proud to call him mine.

He notices the change in my demeanor and a smolder enters his eyes. His nostrils flare, and a twitch appears in his cheek.

Before I can utter another word, his arms are around my waist as he effortlessly picks me up and deposits me in the tub with him, in his lap.

I straddle him, my dress getting wet as I press my palms against his naked chest.

One breath. One independent breath and then we're breathing together.

His lips press against mine hard, his tongue pressing past the seam of my lips. His attack is merciless, frenzied. But as I dig my nails into his shoulder, holding him close, I welcome the aggression rolling off him, rolling onto me.

He tugs and bites my lips, consuming me, devouring me. The taste of him is as maddening as I remember, and I wonder why, since our first kiss, our lips haven't been glued together. Yet as he continues to stroke his tongue against mine, to make me shiver from a mix of want and anticipation, and then even more want, I realize how dangerous this is, how addictive it could become.

It might be too late, though.

Desire unfurls inside of me as I press myself closer to him. That hard part of him is nestled between our bodies, growing even harder by the second.

His hand glides over my back before settling on the nape of my neck, his big palm encircling the entire surface before pressing lightly.

Our mouths are fused together, moving wildly, in a maddening chaos. There's only instinct as I swipe my tongue over his lips and cheeks before returning to his mouth, tugging on his tongue with my teeth and biting hard on it, drawing blood. He does the same with me, plunging in my mouth deeper and deeper until the chaos becomes a coordinated mess.

His blood flows into my mouth, filling me. The eroticism of it makes my heart stop in my chest.

Am I still breathing? I don't know. My body might have forgotten how to. The only drive I have right now is to be as close as possible to this male, to feel his big hands on my naked body, to do things to me I should have never thought about.

There's an ache inside of me that's becoming more and more painful with each passing moment and the touch of his lips against mine only further stokes the fire.

His other hand moves to my chest, cupping my breast through my soaked dress. He finds the hardened bud in the middle and pinches it between his fingers. A shot of electricity travels through me, and I let out a moan against his mouth.

He swallows the sound. Reaching for my neckline, he rips the buttons at the bodice, pulling the material aside until he has access to my almost naked breast, now covered only by a flimsy brassiere.

"Mine," I whisper.

"Just a little. Please." The words are wrenched from his mouth, low and tremulous.

My reply is to kiss him again, peppering his jaw with small kisses while he reaches inside my brassiere and finds my flesh.

My back arches instinctively as I lean into his touch.

He strums my nipple between his fingers. I've never imagined my body could achieve such sensations, but every time he caresses my breast, a flash of light travels through me. Everything converges in the spot between my legs and the ache intensifies.

"Fuck, Minnie. You drive me crazy," he rasps against my lips. "So. Fucking. Crazy."

He draws back until our lips are barely touching, our breaths mingling together. I stare at him. He stares at me.

"Fuck!" He groans. His eyes shut close and small tremors rack his body. His hold on me tightens, both at my nape and over my breast.

His hips push into me. Once. Twice. The third time, he lets out a moan and he smashes his lips against mine again.

His hips push into me. Once. Twice. The third time, he lets out a moan and he smashes his lips against mine again. He moves lower, down my chin and neck, and when he reaches the top of my breast, he bites onto my naked flesh.

"M-Mine," I whimper, digging my nails into his shoulders. He bites harder, a mix of pain and pleasure crashing onto me.

"Harder," I tell him in a voice I barely recognize. "Take my blood."

He follows my instructions, his teeth surprisingly sharp as he bites again, this time breaking the skin. The blood flows to the surface and into his waiting mouth, and a wave of euphoria envelops me. Everything tingles. Everything is overstimulated.

He continues to thrust his hips against me, that hard male part of him brushing against my soaked dress. There might still be a barrier between us, but I can feel the heat radiating from him as if we were body to body.

His breathing becomes harsher. His hand is still on my breast, massaging my nipple while his mouth feasts on the blood pouring from me.

For the first time, I understand why this is forbidden—why demons do it despite being prohibited. Although it borders on eroticism, it's so much more than that. It's the exchange of life, of one's own essence. I don't think there's anything more intimate than this.

With a last lick, he gathers all the remaining blood and kisses his way back to my lips again.

Resting his forehead on mine, his eyes swirl a dark green as he's trying to catch his breath.

"You..." I trail off as I note the dark stains on his stomach. His seed. "But how? You said you needed your hands."

He lets out a small chuckle.

"I don't need anything when you're so close to me," he murmurs. "When you're such an erotic vision come to life."

My eyes widen and a flush envelops my cheeks. I never realized males could spill their seed so easily, but I am flattered he finds me so attractive that he doesn't even need to touch himself.

"I suppose I wouldn't mind helping you like this again in the future."

He's taken aback by my words, but as his lips tug up into a smile, he leans forward and gives me a sweet kiss.

"This is all I needed to feel refreshed," he tells me, nuzzling his cheek against mine.

"More than a bath?" I ask cheekily.

"Darling, as long as I have your kisses, I can spend an eternity without washing, though I very much doubt you'd want to kiss me then," he adds, amused.

I pull back and pretend to be scandalized for a moment. But then I give him another quick peck and whisper, "I think I might be persuaded to kiss you even then."

His laughter echoes in the small bathroom.

Truth to be told, if he could be mine for an eternity, I wouldn't mind anything else.

MINE GOES to his debriefing session while I wash his clothes and hang them to dry alongside my dress. When he comes back, he brings me a couple of donuts, some M&M's, and a chocolate croissant. Ah, this male certainly knows how to treat his lady right.

While I eat, I explain what occurred with the greed demon and what my suspicion is about the charity rule from the book.

"So you're saying not everything counts as charity?"

I nod, popping another M&M in my mouth.

"You can give him plenty of things, but it seems his power only decreases when he receives something that means something to the owner. All the other times, nothing happens. In fact, he even recovered some of his strength when I gave him something I didn't care for."

"That's...interesting. It would make sense, though, since true charity is giving something you yourself need or covet."

"We should make a list of things we care about that we might offer to the demon," I say, though right as the words come out of my mouth, I realize there aren't too many things I'm personally attached to.

Mine, though, surprises me when he takes a piece of paper and starts writing. Curious, I scoot over and peer at his paper.

The first thing is, of course, soap. I roll my eyes. He could have written Minnie—not that I want him to give me to the demon. But why shouldn't I be at the top of the hierarchy anyway?

I surreptitiously watch him fill out his list with pretty mundane stuff, still waiting to see my name written in that pretty script of his. He does have nice handwriting. But I suppose it is to be expected of someone as perfect as him.

When he still doesn't write my name, I decide to probe a little and give him a slight nudge.

"What did you write? Let's compare lists."

His brows go up. I am so close to him I can see everything, and he knows it. But he decides to indulge me as he reads off his list. When it's my turn, I start with the obvious, "Lucien de Vitry," I say pointedly.

His eyes widen.

"Me? You'd give me to the demon?" He blinks.

"It's the list of the most important things to me. You are first," I say with a huff.

"I appreciate that, but I hope that doesn't mean you're ready to relinquish me to that nasty demon."

I roll my eyes at him. "Of course not, Mine. But you are first on the list nonetheless."

"So you don't plan to sacrifice me?" He wiggles his brows.

"No. I would never give you up, not even to destroy a demon."

"My, my, but that's high praise indeed," he adds in a satisfied voice. "Am I to understand I am more important to you than defeating the big bad?"

"Of course." I don't see how that's not evident. "There are

countless other people who can defeat the demon, but there is only one of you." I pause to look at him. He has a dreamy look on his face, his chin propped on his hand as he stares at me with a languid smile.

"Would you make the same decision if people's lives were at risk?" he asks quietly.

I shrug. "It doesn't matter."

He purrs his approval. He actually purrs.

"So now you know my position. Why am I not first on your list?" I ask directly since he can't seem to take a hint. "Am I not the most important for you?" I narrow my eyes at him.

He's taken aback by my outburst.

"Ah, Minnie." He chuckles. "You are far too important." Getting out of his seat, he comes before me, drops to his knees, and takes my hands in his. "I don't need to make a list for that. And the reason your name is not first is because I would *never* entertain giving you up for any reason at all."

"Not even to save innocent lives?"

"No. You see, there are millions of innocent people out there and only one of you. I will *always* choose you."

"You...would?"

"Without a second thought."

"Good male." I pat him on the head. He gives me a brilliant smile before he stands up and starts poring over his sheet of paper again.

After most of the camp has gone to sleep, we sneak out of our cabin and head to where Holloway is being held. Mine has a few of his precious items with him, including his favorite soap, a shirt his mother gifted him before he went to war, and a letter from his parents. Since I have very few belongings in this world, I decided to opt for the fancy items of clothing I bought with my allowance, though I am a little sad to see them gone. But I suppose that is the entire purpose of this so-called charity.

Like before, a soldier guards Holloway, but with one word from Mine, he allows us inside.

Holloway is in between states of consciousness due to the

medication the doctor prescribed. And this seems to make the demon even angrier. When he spots us, he starts shouting at us —though that is not anything new either. He tends to be a rather loud and belligerent creature.

"We've come bearing gifts," I tell him as we stop in front of Holloway's bed.

Despite his anger, the demon's interest is piqued when he hears about gifts, his greed reflected in the way his beady eyes sparkle with want.

Ew.

I wonder how previous Aperite warriors discovered that a greed demon's weakness is charity. To have noticed that, someone must have given one a gift, no? And not just *any* gift, but something that mattered to them. Who could have been inclined to do that to a demon, the enemy?

Alas, their knowledge is useful to us.

Mine takes out his soap first and hands it to the demon.

"Now I'll have to go to town to grab another bar. This is custom, you know?"

"Why would you need a custom soap?"

"I have sensitive skin, all right? And I also have a very sensitive nose. I am very particular about the fragrances used in soaps."

"Right," I mutter drily. He's certainly a fussy male. But he's been a good boy, so I suppose I can gift him one of those soaps when I get my next pay.

The demon grabs the soap with urgency. With donuts, I expected him to eat them, though it was rather strange considering he is only semi-corporeal. But I am curious what he's going to do with the soap. Mine is, too, watching him intently.

The demon throws the soap into his big mouth and munches on it. I cringe internally, but he seems quite gleeful about it as he smacks his lips together in pleasure.

"More," he demands at the same time as his energy signature flickers in and out, and he dwindles in size.

"You were right," Mine whispers in awe. "This is spectacular."

I preen at his praise.

"I am a good soldier," I simply state.

"You are a hell of a soldier, Minnie. You did this in one day. That's commendable."

I was already blushing, but now I'm blushing some more. It's quite nice to have my achievements recognized, especially by someone whose opinion matters to me.

"Let's see with the next one."

Mine takes out his shirt and gives it to the demon, who like before, stuffs it into his mouth. As he munches on it, he releases moans of pleasure as if it were the tastiest morsel of food. Odd demon.

He dwindles again.

When it comes to the letter, Mine is a bit apprehensive to hand it over, but it is that reluctance that makes the demon shrink sizes twice as much as before.

"Damn," Mine whistles after the demon's finished eating the letter.

He's now a little bigger than a garden gnome.

Since it's my turn, I hand him one gown at a time, anxiously waiting for him to become smaller and smaller. And while that happens, by the time I'm out of items, he's still there. Small, but still present.

"Do you have anything else?" I ask Mine.

We're both in a rather peculiar situation since we are both away from home and possess very few items that truly matter to us.

He shakes his head. "You?"

I purse my lips, thinking. "Maybe we can give him another donut?"

"I doubt that's going to make him disappear."

At hearing our conversation, the demon starts to shout again, though this time his voice is high-pitched and sharp, almost that of a toddler.

"There is something else..." I trail off, unsure. Digging into my pocket, I take out the pin. It only has a bit of energy left, but it could make the difference between a life-and-death scenario.

"Minnie, no," Mine immediately interjects. "It has spiritual energy within it. It might *feed* him and make him stronger."

"I know." I sigh. "But compared to the dresses, this is far more important to me."

"We can't take any chances that he might regain his strength. We have nothing left to give him."

I think on it for a moment. "Charity is also about trust."

"Huh?"

"Think about it. You're giving a person something that matters to you and you hope they will prize it just as much. There are beggars in Aperion as I presume there are here as well. A lot have become addicted to Zantrax, and they've lost everything while trying to fund their addiction. Most people don't want to give them money because they fear they will just buy more Zantrax."

"In this world that is true as well," he mentions thoughtfully.

"So when you're giving the charity, you're doing so on a basis of trust. Trust that they will use the money, or the items, in a beneficial way, but at the same time, you leave it up to them to make their own decisions."

"He's a demon, not a regular beggar, Minnie."

"Aren't demons a form of beggars, too? They are so empty on the inside, they can only thrive by draining others."

"That might be so, but—"

Before he can voice out another objection, I hand the pin to the demon. "It is freely given," I say.

"Minnie..." Mine groans.

He grabs my hand and pulls me back as we watch the demon stare at the golden pin for a moment before popping it into his mouth, glee written all over his features.

"Foolish female!" He laughs as he absorbs the pin and its

energy. But his words turn into a screech as his energy starts flickering at the speed of light , followed by a blinding light.

Mine pulls me to his chest and covers me with his body.

Once the light is out, we both slowly turn to look at the demon.

"I'll be damned," Mine mutters. "You were right. You did it, Minnie."

The demon is gone, no trace of him left behind.

"I...was?" I ask in disbelief.

Perhaps now I will get my much-desired commendation *and* my powers back. But with that realization also comes the sad reality that when that happens, I will have to leave Mine behind.

"I guess I did it," I whisper softly, sadly.

THIRTY

I STARE at the calendar while Mine takes a shower and prepares himself for his next mission. The last few days have been something out of a fairy tale, just the two of us without the threat of the demon hanging over our heads. The base, too, is back to normal, and much more lively and healthier.

Five more days. Only five days until I'll get my powers back. What once would have been something I desired with all my heart, now it's something I dread with my entire being.

What will happen to me once I get my powers back? What will happen to Mine?

I squeeze my eyes shut to prevent the tears from falling.

"You seem down this morning," he mentions as he puts on his uniform.

"I'm always down when you must go on a mission. It's dangerous."

"While I appreciate your concern, my tiny darling, I'll have you know I'm a damn good pilot. Nothing will happen to me in the air."

"I know but—"

"Give me a kiss," he murmurs as he plants himself in front of me, his hair still a little damp.

I raise myself on my tiptoes and brush my lips against his.

"Come back to me."

"Always," he promises with a wink.

We walk together to his plane, and after a quick kiss, he's off to the skies.

The other planes depart too, and slowly, the remaining people leave the runway and head back to their tasks.

I'm still standing in the same spot, staring at the now clear sky, a sense of doom unfurling inside of me. Then again, every time he leaves for a mission, I worry for him. He might be the most competent male I know, but he is still mortal and prone to injury and...death.

For the thousandth time, flashes erupt in my mind of him being hurt, of him dying and leaving me alone. If that were to happen, what would I do? What would become of me?

The more time I spent with him, the more irreplaceable he has become in my life.

I know my concerns are illogical since he's bound to die at some point. All mortals are. And yet, the thought of that occurring fills me not only with an unspeakable sense of grief, but also with anger and a desire for retribution.

By the Source, if anything were to happen to him, I fear I would once more break the rules and rain hell on anyone who did him harm.

I take a deep breath and attempt to ground myself. These are all unfounded seeds taking root in my brain. Mine is alive. And he is mine.

I slowly turn to head back to our cabin when I bump into someone I didn't expect to—at least for a few more days.

He's dressed in his non-combat attire, a dark blue pair of pants and a matching tunic held together by a thick belt, with the family's insignia engraved on the middle and encrusted with dark blue sapphires.

My sense of doom intensifies.

"Molokai, this is a surprise," I say in a cold tone, pretending to be unaffected by his presence, days earlier. This can only mean something bad's happened.

"Minerva. I see you've done well for yourself," he mentions with a bored swipe of his gaze over my nurse uniform.

"I had to. You left me powerless in a foreign world."

A twitch appears in his cheek, the only sign of emotion. Since he was a child, Molokai has always been quiet and withdrawn, rarely exhibiting emotion. He can be kind. I know it since I've been the recipient of that kindness on more than one occasion. But he can also be scathing in his indifference when someone disappoints him, and I seem to have done just that.

I've gotten used to his frosty personality over the years. It's odd that out of all the offspring of the King of Cryos, Molokai is the only one who embodies the icy designation of our House. Our older brother is a pleasure seeker, which is acceptable for him being a male and the heir. I am bound by my gender and the expectations placed upon me, though I've always had a rebellious streak.

Not Molokai.

From birth, he displayed an unusual amount of spiritual energy despite not being the first born. In fact, it's well known he is far more powerful than our brother. And with that power came the expectation for him to enroll in the military and gain recognition, paving the way for him to one day become the Cryos Supreme. He's still young, at only six thousand years of age.

Most Supremes are elected into their position when they are well over ten thousand years old—though there is an exception to that, too. Lispera, the Ananke Supreme that sacrificed herself to seal off Tartareia seven thousand years ago, had been the youngest Supreme ever recorded, gaining her position at only five thousand six hundred years old. But Lispera is a legend. No one expects anyone to measure up to her, now or in the future.

But as the years pass, the expectations placed upon Molokai grow. Although the current Cryos Supreme is still strong, with the slow but steady stream of demons appearing everywhere and the possibility that the seal of Tartareia might break at any point, everyone is waiting for a war to break out.

The Supremes will be the first line of action then, the only ones able to go against the elite of the Son of Tenebreis. And if by any chance the Cryos Supreme is defeated, a new one has to be ready to fill that role. Immediately.

One brother is going to be king. The other is going to be a Supreme. To say I'm jealous would be an understatement since my only role will be that of a wife and broodmare.

Unacceptable!

"The possibility to return to Aperion was presented to you. You refused," he points out.

I shrug.

"And what does that tell you? If I'd rather be powerless in a strange world than go home?"

He doesn't answer.

I move past him. He follows.

With him on my trail, I cannot return to the cabin and risk him seeing I've been sharing a living space with another male. Instead, I head to the abandoned field a distance away where no one can spot us. The last thing I need is for someone to see Kai and think him the enemy in his strange attire.

Once we are far enough and with no possibility of anyone spotting us, I face him.

"What is the purpose of your visit?" I ask, still maintaining an otherwise calm appearance. Inside, however, I'm panicking.

Is he here about what happened in Aperion? About the death of the general? Have the truth diviners been called?

The death of a general, especially one in charge of a special unit, would be immediately noticed. Commander Azerius would be informed and asked to investigate.

Do they know I was there?

Molokai's expression is clouded and inscrutable. I cannot tell what he's thinking, but him coming to see me before my punishment is over can only be a bad thing.

Not only did I witness a demon—or whatever that creature

was since it's unlikely a Son of Tenebreis would not only escape Tartareia but would enter Aperion—I didn't report it. The first thing I should have done was to ring the alarm and inform my superiors. Instead, I ran away from the scene. With a mortal in tow.

Molokai doesn't speak for a moment, and my mind runs wild trying to count all my transgressions. If they know the full extent of everything I've done... Actually, the punishment for that would be nothing compared to what would happen to me if they even suspect I shared blood with someone, a mortal.

That has a definite punishment. Death.

A shudder goes down my back.

Truth diviners aren't called as such for nothing. Part of the House of Psyche, their abilities allow them to reconstruct a scene or an event from any trace evidence.

I scanned my energy signature when I entered the military compound.

I squeeze my eyes shut and berate myself for having forgotten that little detail. If anything, the fact that it took this long for Molokai to come for me is a wonder.

I should have been arrested and sentenced immediately.

"I have heard what happened at the base," he finally speaks.

I hold my breath.

"You're here to arrest me, aren't you?"

He narrows his eyes at me.

"On the contrary. Commander Azerius has decided to award you for your accomplishments."

"My...accomplishments?" I ask with a frown.

He takes a deep breath. "Perhaps I shouldn't have dismissed you so easily when you called on me. But you handled the greed demon spectacularly. Without powers, too."

"The greed demon?" I repeat. "How do you know about that?"

"You mean to tell me you did not submit the anonymous tip yourself?" he asks with narrowed eyes.

"Anonymous tip? I have no idea what you're talking about," I tell him, confused.

He continues to regard me with suspicion.

"Commander Azerius received a tip that you've successfully defeated a greed demon—something no one outside the special squad has done. You say you had nothing to do with that tip?"

I blink. Who would submit such a tip? Who would even know about the greed demon in the first place?

"I really have no idea about any tip. I vow it."

He nods thoughtfully, his body relaxing slightly.

Is that why he was so frosty? He thought I'd sent an anonymous tip in about myself? I scoff at the thought but only because I didn't think about it first and someone beat me to it.

Who?

"The tip was rather detailed about how you worked day and night to find a way to vanquish the demon and protect the mortals. You did this without the full scope of your abilities, too, and as such, Commander Azerius wishes to reward you."

"He does?"

"He has spoken to the House of Moirai on your behalf." He takes a few steps until he's in front of me. Touching two of his fingers to my forehead, he neutralizes the shield he'd placed before. My energy returns with a vengeance, flowing through me from head to toe.

"Your powers have been returned."

"That's very kind of Commander Azerius," I choke out, feeling overwhelmed from the raw power flowing through my veins.

"He requests your presence in Aperion. I am here to deliver you to him."

"Me? He wants to see me?" I ask incredulously.

"Yes. We should depart." He turns to leave, expecting me to follow behind him.

"Wait a moment! I can't go right now!"

Kai half turns and narrows his eyes.

"You cannot go right now?" he repeats, his voice dangerously low.

Given my so-called accomplishment, you'd think Kai would have forgotten my small indiscretion. But seeing how cold he is with me still, it seems he has neither forgotten nor forgiven me for it.

Is it because it put a blemish on our family name?

"I have to say goodbye to people. Can't it wait until tomorrow?"

Mine will be home in the afternoon. I can't just leave without saying goodbye, no matter how much harder that will be on me. Even now, my heart is heavy in my chest as I imagine the look of disappointment on his face when he finds out my time has come to an end.

I dread telling him that. But at the same time, I cannot possibly leave without letting him know. I must say goodbye to him and assure him this is not the end. That I'll come visit him as often as I can.

"Minerva, no one makes Commander Azerius wait."

"But—"

"No buts. He expects to see you shortly. Let us depart."

Panic flutters inside of me.

"Wait! Can I at least grab my things? I won't be long."

He stares at me.

"You have five minutes. Not more. Be back here when you're done."

Knowing he will count the seconds down, I teleport myself to the cabin. There are very few things to take with me, but I needed this excuse so I can at least write a note to Mine.

I rummage through his desk for some pen and paper and then force myself to come up with the right words so he won't be mad at me for leaving without saying goodbye.

He won't be upset with me, right...?

"Damn it!"

He will be. I'm sure of it. He will be disappointed in me too, and the thought of seeing his expression change from one of love to one of disappointment cuts through me.

I never told him I loved him, too.

I stare at the paper. This isn't the moment to say it, though. It needs to be uttered face-to-face.

Think, Minnie, think!

Words will be meaningless when he sees I am gone. But there is something I can offer him that might lessen the impact.

Grabbing the pen tighter, I scribble a short message, followed by a drawing.

> *My brother came to get me back. I am returning to Aperion. If you need me, call and I will come.*

Leaving my sigil out here in the open is dangerous. Giving my sigil to a human is even more so. But I need Mine to know that he matters to me and that I did not abandon him.

I tuck the folded paper under his pillow and take a moment to gaze at the cabin one last time. Mine's shirt catches my gaze in the laundry basket and before I can think it through, I grab it and hide it among my own clothes. At least I'll have his scent to keep me going until I see him again.

My time is running out, so with one last glance, I teleport myself back to Kai's side.

He takes one look at me and my meager bag of belongings and nods to follow him. He leads me to a portal nearby that takes us to Aperion. When we arrive, we teleport to the military base in Cryos where Commander Azerius is apparently waiting for me.

We walk down a long corridor before entering the War Room.

Commander Azerius is with his back to us, staring out his window. On standby near him are his two generals, Aethon and Cerenios.

"Commander Azerius," Molokai and I greet him.

He turns, his face expressionless.

"Minerva and Molokai. Welcome."

"I was told you wanted to see me, Commander?"

"Congratulations are in order for your deeds in Anthropa. I have heard of your bravery even when your powers were bound."

"T-thank you," I mumble.

"However, it is odd that the Sin Squad did not act when the greed demon started to get stronger, is it not?"

"I tried to communicate, but—"

"The Sin Squad does not need any communication to sense if a sin demon makes its appearance anywhere in the universe. It is why they deal exclusively with sin demons."

"Perhaps they were busy," I add with a tight smile.

He doesn't return the smile, merely staring at me with those dark eyes of his as if he could see through my very soul and unravel all my secrets.

"They were not busy. They were attacked."

"W-what?" I whisper, feigning surprise.

"The Sin Squad was attacked?" Molokai inquires, his reaction genuine.

"Another odd situation of which we were only apprised days after it happened."

"When you say attacked, you mean?"

"General Leotar is dead, as is his entire military base."

"General Leotar? But he is a level nine. Who could have killed him?" Molokai asks, his jaw tense.

"That is what we are currently investigating," Aethon replies. "Only another level nine or above could have done this. But there is something else amiss with this murder." He pauses, glancing at Commander Azerius for confirmation. "His soul is gone."

"His soul?" My eyes widen.

"Indeed," Commander Azerius drawls dangerously, his eyes

never leaving my face. "The souls of everyone present at the base are gone."

"Only a demon could have done that," Molokai states.

"A demon, yes. A regular demon? No. The soldiers present at the base were all levels six through eight, and the general level nine. A level twelve demon would have had a hard time defeating *one* level six soldier, let alone a score of them and a general."

"What do you suspect, then?" Molokai asks.

I'm still silent, doing my best not to betray any knowledge of the murders, though I can't help but feel Commander Azerius' hard and probing gaze on me.

"A Son of Tenebreis," Commander Azerius replies curtly. "An *elite* Son of Tenebreis."

"Impossible."

"So we said about their presence in Anthropa, and while we have not officially confirmed it, there are a number of clues that point to that being the case."

"But they cannot get out of Tartareia," Molokai adds.

"They should not be able to, no. But this can only mean one thing. The seal is weakening. And if these murders are any indication, whoever managed to escape Tartareia is incredibly powerful."

"Have you called on the truth diviners?"

Commander Azerius' lips tip up dangerously.

I hold my breath. If he has called on them, then he knows. And this meeting was only a pretext so he could apprehend me. If he has yet to do it, then he will know soon and I will be equally doomed.

"That is another odd thing. For some unknown reason, the truth diviners cannot get a read on the base. They could not detect any energy signature, not even the one of the deceased soldiers."

"That's impossible..."

"As impossible as me receiving a tip that a powerless goddess vanquished a greed demon outside of her area of expertise?" he asks pointedly as he raises a brow.

"I hope you are not implying that my sister would have been involved in this." Molokai surprises me when he jumps to my defense. "As you said, someone powerful must have killed the general and his soldiers. Minerva is only a level five."

"Is that so?" Commander Azerius flashes himself in front of me in the blink of an eye. "Then why is it that I feel more energy coming off her than a level five should possess?"

He looms over me, his height and proximity terrifying.

"I…" I take a deep breath. I cannot show him how afraid I am of him. "I could have tested for a higher level, but I was never allowed to."

He tilts his head to the side, studying me. His obsidian eyes are two bottomless pits of apathy and despair, and I *know* that one wrong word and he will have my head.

"Azerius, she's not a threat," Molokai intervenes, pushing me back and placing himself between me and Commander Azerius. "What she says is true. Our parents forbade her from testing further because they arranged a betrothal for her. She's always been a good soldier."

That… That is high praise coming from my stiff brother.

Commander Azerius doesn't move, his eyes on me still. He barely registers my brother's presence.

"Perhaps I should test it out myself," he muses, purple energy swirling around his palm and up his arm.

Sweat beads on my forehead as I realize I'm staring death in the face.

His arm moves. I await the blow.

"Molokai is right," Cerenios finally speaks, flashing himself next to Azerius and placing his hand on his upper arm, stopping him. "Lady Minerva is unlikely to have had anything to do with this."

Azerius momentarily backs down, though why he would stop at Cerenios' request, his subordinate, is a mystery. But the suspicion doesn't leave his eyes.

"Why don't you tell us how you managed to vanquish the greed demon, Minerva?" Cerenios turns his attention to me.

His amber, cat-like eyes slide over me with indifference. He is of similar height and build to Commander Azerius, but whereas half of Azerius' face is covered in ancient runes, Cerenios' face is devoid of any mark.

Although Commander Azerius is terrifying, Cerenios is not far behind. They could pass for twins, and not only in appearance but also demeanor. The only difference is that Cerenios has emotions, albeit muted by intention. He has a family I've heard he adores, so he has a soft spot within him that does not exist with Azerius, although the commander would call that a weakness instead.

Azerius is all alone. All powerful, but all alone.

"It was by chance actually," I start, telling them how without my powers and my allowance I had to resort to becoming a nurse in the military. "The greed demon had attached himself to one of the soldiers and he'd started influencing everyone on the base. I realized that the more greed he consumed, the more powerful he became. But the reverse was also true. If someone was kind to the demon, his power decreased."

"Interesting," Cerenios mentions with a nod. "So you killed the demon by being kind to him?"

"Yes."

"And without her powers, too," he says, this time addressing Azerius. "I believe that deserves a reward."

The commander doesn't speak. Suspicion is written all over his face. He *knows* something. He just doesn't have the evidence to back it up. Otherwise, I would already be dead.

"Cerenios is right. Minerva should be rewarded for her achievement," my brother agrees. With how curt and icy he's been with me, it comes as a surprise that he would so readily take my side.

"I am nothing if not fair," Azerius relents. "What do you wish for, Minerva?"

I blink. That was even more unexpected. My first thought is to ask for Mine, but that is impossible. So I ask for the only thing that can bring me closer to him.

"May I continue my work in Anthropa? I believe there is more to be done there. The war is escalating and with it the number of casualties."

"That is all you desire?" He raises a brow.

I nod.

"Your parents reached out when you disappeared. They would like you back."

My heart stops in my chest.

"I promised them I would return you, and I do not break my word. But I would also not disregard your wish." He pauses.

A tremor goes down my back.

"You will go home to your family and you will grace them with your presence until the end of the Skya. After that, you may continue your duties in Anthropa should you wish to do so."

"Until the end of Skya? But that is months if not years in Anthropa time," I whisper. Skya is the eleventh month of the Aperite calendar. A tendril of telepathic energy slithers out and I find out today is the tenth day of the month of Ananke. That means I will be stuck here for almost three Aperite months. I'm not entirely sure what the conversion rate is to Anthropa time, but it should be close to a year if not more.

"Indeed. But according to my sources within the House of Moirai, the war in Anthropa will not end for at least another two years. In fact, the bloodiest of the battles are yet to come. You will not lack for work." His commanding voice leaves no room for negotiation.

That is so much time, though... What will Mine think? He will assume I abandoned him.

I open my mouth to argue, but one look at Azerius' unyielding expression and I know it would be in vain. His word is law, and if I want to be smart at this so I can eventually see Mine again, I cannot argue with Azerius.

"Thank you, Commander. I will do as you say."

He nods and turns with his back to us, thereby dismissing us.

"Come. I will take you home," Molokai says as he grabs my arm.

"Molokai," Commander Azerius' voice rings out. "I have need of you. Minerva can find her way back by herself."

"Yes, Commander," he immediately agrees.

With a nod, Molokai leads me to the door.

"Mother is furious with you. Take care." With those words, he leaves me to the wolves.

Although the last thing I want to do is go home, if this is the price I have to pay to return to Mine, then so be it.

I teleport myself to my room in the palace.

My energy signature will have triggered the defense mechanisms of the palace, thus alerting my parents of my presence.

I quickly shower and put on a new dress befitting of my status before heading out to greet them—and I brace myself for the battle ahead.

Servants hurry up and down the hallway, barely sparing me a glance. The opulence around is almost blinding after months of living with the bare minimum, and I find that I would rather be destitute and barely surviving than endure a lifetime of pain and regret.

Oh, Mine. You've probably seen my note already. Are you mad at me? Disappointed? Will you call on me?

If he uses my sigil, I will be bound to go to him in an instant. I will not need a portal or even conscious teleportation. I will simply be carried away to where he calls.

I hope he won't hold a grudge for too long and he will call on me. If I see him even for a few brief minutes, I will be able to withstand anything that comes my way.

Lost in my thoughts, it takes me a moment to recognize a foreign energy signature in my proximity. I stop and look around.

"Theron," I spit out the name of the last person I wanted to see right now.

THIRTY-ONE

"MINERVA. FANCY SEEING YOU HERE," he grinds out, his distaste for me evident in the way his nostrils flare.

"Why are you here?"

He sneers at me. "I am a guest of your parents, of course. Commander Azerius informed them you would be coming home and they wanted me to be present."

I narrow my eyes at him.

"As you can see, I am home. Now get lost." I move past him, heading toward the throne room.

"Your parents are not at home currently."

That makes me falter. I half turn.

"What are you talking about."

He shrugs. "The Duke of Hirsham is having a banquet. They should be back shortly."

I sigh in relief. I'll have a little more time to get ready to face my mother's wrath.

"Then I bid you good night. I shall retire to my room."

"Not so fast," he snaps, grabbing my arm. "I believe you and I have unfinished business."

"Do. Not. Touch. Me," I grit out. Energy rolls over me, enveloping me from head to toe as I blast him to the other end of the corridor.

His face betrays his surprise as he barely lands on his feet. Soon, his expression turns to one of pure anger as he glares at me, unleashing his own energy and sending a blast toward me.

I lean backward, dodging the attack.

Ah, but it feels good to have my powers back.

Rumors say Theron is a level eight, soon to take his level nine exam. Yet I don't care that there are multiple levels of energy separating us. The mere fact that he dared to show up here, that he dared to put his slimy hand on me, awakens something primal inside of me.

Turning to face him fully, I manifest a sword in each hand. His eyes widen.

"Scared?" I tilt my head and smile at him.

"You fucking bitch," he curses before he manifests his own sword and charges at me.

Hie energy is a muted red as it swirls in waves around him. A descendant of the House of Pyros, his main specialization is fire. Not ideal considering mine is ice. But it appears it's finally time to put to the test which element is stronger.

Before he can reach me, I teleport behind him. His reaction time is a couple seconds delayed as he breathes harshly and sends a blast of fire toward me.

Jumping up, I evade the first blow, but he sends a second and a third in quick succession. Rotating in the air, I avoid all the blasts while moving closer to him. As my foot touches the floor when I'm a few paces away, ice forms on the surface of the ground beneath his feet.

His sword comes up to block my blows, infusing his blade with his fire energy, which melts through my icy blades. But as I give him a slight push, he slides backward, slipping. He startles when he notices the icy floor and I take advantage of this to kick his leg until he drops to his knees.

"My, my, Theron. Is this the great soldier I've heard about?" I laugh in his face.

His pride seems to take a steeper fall than his body. Red

blotches appear on his face, going down his neck. His eyes blaze a deep red as he releases a loud cry and presses his hands to the floor, melting the ice.

He strikes at me with his sword and while I parry his blows, he uses his left hand to form a ball of fire that he launches at me.

I move to the side, but it's too late to avoid it.

A ragged groan of pain escapes my lips as the fire burns through my dress and the skin of my stomach. I clutch onto the injured area, glaring at him with murderous rage.

"Pain looks good on you, Minerva." He chuckles.

My nostrils flare, and with a loud cry, I launch myself at him, letting all my energy loose.

I strike and he parries. Aiming for his face, he brings his sword up to stop the attack, imbuing it with scorching heat in an attempt to melt my ice swords.

A smile curves at my lips.

Fire might melt ice, but he forgot about a certain trick my family is known for.

There is regular ice, and there is also unbreakable ice.

The heat does nothing to damage my blade, and with a strong push, I cut through the metal of his sword.

His eyes widen when the upper part of his sword clinks against the ground, but I don't allow him any time to recover. Brandishing my sword against his cheek, I cut from his forehead to his neck. Blood oozes to the surface as a gaping hole appears on his face.

He lets out a whiny shriek before he catapults himself away from me. He raises his hand to his left cheek, feeling for the damage. More blood pools around his fingers, dripping down his arm. It's a nasty sight.

The perfect Theron is not so perfect anymore.

"Blood looks even better on you, Theron," I shoot back.

My injury is already healed.

Undoubtedly, he's waiting for his own wound to do the same.

But as the seconds trickle by, the blood continues to ooze, showing no inclination to stop.

I put my swords away and regard him with overt satisfaction.

The seconds now turn to minutes. His flesh attempts to knit itself together but is unable to. Just as it heals a little, the wound breaks anew, more blood coming out.

"What did you do?" he demands in a rough voice laced with fear.

"I did something?" I ask with a shrug. "I don't know. I just defended myself against an assailant."

"Cut the crap, Minerva. Why is my wound not healing?"

My smile turns to pure contempt as my lips flatten into a tight line.

"Because I don't want it to," I tell him. "I'm rather enjoying the sight of you like this. Defeated and in pain."

"You bitch! What did you do?" he demands louder.

"You didn't know who you wanted to marry, Theron? An oversight on your part." I laugh at him. "The royal House of Cryos has a technique called eternal ice, or cryos. Not only does it not melt like regular ice, but it can also infiltrate tissue and become a parasite attacking from within."

"What the fuck are you talking about?"

I walk casually to his side.

"Ah, you didn't do your homework, I see. Well, consider yourself enlightened now. This is what awaits you on our wedding night, except..." I let my eyes trail lower. "In other areas of your body."

"You fucking bitch! How do I get rid of this?"

"Not my problem." I shrug and continue walking past him and toward my quarters.

"Minerva!" he cries out. "Minerva!" His shouts echo through the hall.

I note the various servants hiding in corners, not daring to make a sound.

When I hear a very low, "Please." I stop.

I'm not this heartless to leave him with a perpetual gaping wound in his cheek. Shaking my head at the pathetic figure he makes as he clutches onto his injury, I go back to him.

"Give me your hand," I demand, grabbing the blood-stained hand clutching onto his cheek.

His eyes regard me warily. He's scared. His body is trembling both from the pain and the fear he might be permanently disfigured. Alas, my kindness extends only so far.

Manifesting my blade again, I point it over his inner forearm. He tries to pull his arm away, but I hold it still.

With the tip of the blade, I carve a small rune into his arm meant to neutralize the parasitic remainders of the eternal ice.

The rune melts into his skin and disappears.

His wound finally stops bleeding, but as the flesh surrounding it starts to knit together, it does so in a mangled fashion.

The wound may be closed, but it is far from gone.

"Just because you said please." I smile sweetly at him. "But next time you try to touch me again, I will not stop even if you beg. I am not someone you want to mess with, Theron."

With that, I leave him behind. In a short while, he will find out that he's been permanently scarred in ways in which deities rarely are. Still, I can't find it in myself to feel sorry for him.

Nasty clown that he is.

Hear that, a level eight and he was bested by a mere level five.

A satisfied smile pulls at my lips.

I wonder if he'll try to get out of the betrothal now that he knows what I am capable of.

Perhaps I should have done this before, scared him so badly he would have jilted me from the beginning.

"THEIR MAJESTIES ARE WAITING FOR YOU." A servant knocks to let me know.

I take another look in the mirror to ensure my appearance is spotless—one less thing my mother can complain about. Noticing a stray strand in the back of my updo, I quickly pin it back.

The walk to my parents' quarters is short, but with trepidation building inside of me, it feels far longer. A few maids walk behind me, and when we reach their apartments, they go ahead to announce me.

It's surprising they would call on me in their quarters rather than the throne room, but this only tells me I should be more prepared for an attack. Their quarters are more private in case they need to tell off their daughter.

The doors close behind me and as I walk deeper into the anteroom, I notice my parents sitting on a sofa in the drawing room, their expressions solemn.

A deep breath and I announce my presence, "Hello, Mother, Father."

My mother doesn't turn to look at me.

"Minerva. Welcome back," my father says as he gets up to give me a hug. "Please, take a seat."

Mother glances at me from the corner of her eye and scoffs.

"Before you say anything," I start. "I know you are not pleased that I disappeared without word. But I was not doing anything bad. I just wanted to participate in one last mission before giving up my career."

Another scoff from my mother, this time with an added roll of her eyes.

"Please understand that I *love* my job. I love fighting demons. It's part of my identity and I don't understand why I have to give it up."

"Because your husband does not want you to work," my mother snaps.

"He is not my husband yet."

"But he will be. And his family has made it clear that they

want you to give up the military. No noble family would like an unladylike daughter-in-law."

I bite back a retort because what I'd like to say would *certainly* be unladylike.

"Your mother is correct. Theron's family has some expectations that you must meet."

Before I can answer, my mother continues, "We heard about your altercation with Theron yesterday."

Of course they would.

"Really, Minerva. We've raised you better than this. Where are your manners?" My mother gives me a sharp look. "We know you're proud of your time in the military, but surely you have more sense than to try to attack someone who is far above your level."

I raise a brow. She's heard about the fight but has not heard about Theron being the losing party? Interesting.

"And how could you even think of attacking your fiancé? You must, of course, apologize to him."

"You're not even going to ask me why I attacked him in the first place?"

"Because you had something to prove," she states confidently.

"No. It's because he touched me when he should not have."

She rolls her eyes at me. "Minerva, no more excuses. Your behavior has been abysmal as of late. Do you even know what people are saying? They know you ran away and they're now questioning not only your upbringing but also our security wards."

"Yes, Mother, because everything has to be about you."

"Minerva!" She gasps.

"*Mother?*" I tilt my head and glare at her.

"Now, now, there is no need to argue," Father adds in a low voice.

"Of course there is," my mother interjects. "Look at her! First, she disappears without a trace, then she initiates a fight with her betrothed? Savage behavior! No child of mine should behave like this."

"Then are you sure I am your child, Mother? Perhaps I was switched at birth," I add drily.

She wheezes. Her mouth drops open in shock and she stares at me.

"If I am such a disappointment to you, why don't we just go ahead and cancel the engagement? I will return to the military and live on my own away from the family. That way I will no longer bring shame to our House."

"Minerva! You're being impertinent."

I sigh. "Why do we even need a connection to the House of Pyros? Maledo is the heir and he will become king one day. Molokai is well on his way to become the next Cryos Supreme. Why do you need me?"

"No child of mine will be a failure!" she shrieks.

"How would I be a failure if I continue with my career?"

"Dear, I think failure is a bit harsh. Minerva has earned a commendation from Commander Azerius himself. That is quite a feat," my father adds, sending a small smile my way.

That he would take my side is...surprising.

"You know I have never been a fan of females in the military. That is something better left to the males," my mother grumbles.

"Regardless, Minerva achieved something worth of praise. Not only that, but she brought honor to our House. Everyone was talking about it at His Grace's banquet last night."

Mother huffs in disapproval.

"While I am proud of your deeds, you must also listen to your mother, Minerva. She is right that people will keep talking if you behave in an unladylike fashion, regardless of whether you're good at your job or not."

"Thank you, Papa," I tell him sincerely. It might be the first time he's said he was proud of me, and that in itself warms my heart.

My mother glares at me and opens her mouth to speak, but

one look from my father and she swallows her words. Instead, she straightens her back and adds in a monotone voice, "We will be meeting Theron and his family in a week's time. Make sure you will behave."

"Of course, Mother. If that is all, may I go now?"

"You may," Father says.

Taking advantage of his decree before my mother decides to find more fault to me, I scurry out of their quarters and head back to my room.

To my surprise, the meeting went far better than expected. Of course my mother's words were scathing, but I am used to that. The fact that my father defended me, even in that quiet manner of his, was a pleasant surprise.

He said he was *proud* of me. Me! Not Molokai or Maledo. Me, Minerva!

I giggle to myself as I throw myself on the bed and burry my head in my pillow.

Finally, I have done something praise-worthy! It doesn't even matter that Mother thinks I am unladylike and a disappointment.

Even more surprising, they did not lock me in my room, nor did they say anything about restricting my access to the outside. Perhaps, as long as I behave well, I might be able to delay this betrothal indefinitely and earn some more commendations while I'm out in Anthropa. Perhaps by then, my father will tell my mother that I don't need to get married.

Ah... I smile to myself. Suddenly, life isn't so bad.

If only Mine were here too...

I still, a thought suddenly crossing my mind.

My powers are back. I am not grounded. I should be able to sneak into Anthropa for a couple of hours and meet Mine, and then I'll come back. No one has to know. At least I'll be able to tell him face-to-face what happened and that I did not abandon him. It would break my heart if he assumed the worst.

I wait until everyone's gone to sleep before I fashion a copy of myself from ice. It looks the same from a distance, and you would only realize it's made of ice if you touched it.

Moving it to the bed, I slide the blanket over the body so it appears I'm sleeping. This copy should last for a full day before it starts melting, but I will be back by then.

Once more, instead of teleporting directly, I sneak out of the palace to evade the sensitive wards. After my first escape, my parents put even more in place as well as hired some additional guards to stand at every point of exit. What they don't realize is that I know of a secret exit through the garden that is still a blind spot.

Outside the palace wards, I use my powers to locate the nearest portal and teleport myself there.

My heart is thudding in my chest with excitement. It's only been a day, but I already miss Mine so much, I can't wait to have his arms around me and his lips on mine.

Ahh! I redden from head to toe as I remember our bathroom interlude and the way he'd touched me. Perhaps we can do more of that. Or just more of anything as long as it involves his body against mine.

The portal is located a short distance from the palace inside a dense forest. There isn't anyone around, so crossing to Anthropa shouldn't be a problem.

The bluish tint of the portal shines bright as I approach it. I set the time and place in my mind and take a step forward.

"You are supposed to remain in Aperion until the end of Skya," a voice calls out.

Eyes wide, I swivel. I didn't sense any other energy signature around. But as the figure steps out of the shadows, I realize why. With his power, he can perfectly mask his energy signature.

"General Cerenios," I mutter, half in annoyance and half in fear.

His amber eyes are trained in me, his expression blank.

"Where are you going, Minerva?"

"Erm..."

He takes a step closer. He's dressed in his military uniform, a dark burgundy tunic fashioned with a brass plate on top of it that has his House insignia. His sword is sheathed at his side, the top of the handle encrusted with a large ruby.

"Were you following me?" I ask.

He shrugs.

"Did Commander Azerius put you up to it?"

Another shrug. I don't believe any answer is forthcoming from him.

"I was just taking a stroll around the woods. It's been a while since I've been here," I lie.

"Is that so?" he asks casually as he plants himself in front of me.

I have to crane my neck back to look up at him due to our height differences. Yet the moment my eyes make contact with him, a sliver of fear goes down my back.

"I will be getting back now..." I add nervously and make to move past him.

With lightning speed, he blocks my way with the sheath of his sword.

"There is something about you," he says, his eyes narrowed. "You haven't been completely truthful, have you?"

"I don't know what you're talking about—"

He leans toward me until his nose is inches away from my neck. I keep myself still.

"I smell a male on you."

"Uhm... probably my betrothed? He was at the palace yesterday," I stammer.

"No." One word, full of conviction. "This scent..." he trails off, closing his eyes and breathing me in again. "There is a faint trace of ancient power that clings to it. Something I have never scented before."

"I'm sure you're mistaken. What other male could it have been?" I force a laugh. He doesn't share my amusement.

Cerenios straightens his back.

"Go home, Minerva. Now."

I don't wait for him to change his mind and I immediately teleport myself near the palace gates before making my way back inside.

My pulse is through the roof, my breathing erratic as I collapse onto my bed.

I was wrong to think everything was fine. For Cerenios to be at the portal, it can only mean one thing.

Commander Azerius is suspicious of me.

THIRTY-TWO

IT'S BEEN MORE than a week. Months in Anthropa. Mine hasn't used my sigil yet.

Although my parents decided to keep me busy by going to seamstress fittings and getting a new wardrobe for the meeting with Theron's family, not even the prospect of new, pretty gowns has managed to improve my mood.

It's the night before the meeting, and as I restlessly toss and turn, thinking about Mine, an idea forms into my mind.

The House of Cryos has an armory full of magical objects passed down through generations. I haven't been there in hundreds of years, but I seem to remember a certain item that might help me.

Getting out of bed, I surreptitiously go to the armory, successfully passing the security wards. There is a myriad of objects inside, ranging from deadly weapons to more mundane items like enchanted jewelry and magical mirrors.

There is a certain mirror I'm looking for that allows you to spy on what a person's doing at a certain moment in time.

It takes me a few hours of going through the different mirrors before I finally find it.

It's the size of a table mirror, it's frame a secret combination of gilded runes that give it its power.

I hide it underneath my nightgown and head back to my room.

Once I'm alone, I prop it on a table and, slicing my finger open, I let a few drops slide in between the carvings of the runes to activate it.

A bright light shines from inside the mirror, and I take my bloodied finger and write Mine's name on the surface of the mirror.

Lucien de Vitry.

With bated breath, I wait for the image to form on the surface of the mirror.

Moments pass, and nothing happens.

I frown. Did I do something wrong?

To test that the mirror works, I wipe his name and replace it with my own.

Immediately, an image forms of me. It's as if someone held a camera to my back and filmed me, the image showing me staring into the mirror with a frown between my brows.

All right. So it works. Then why doesn't it work for him?

A faraway memory drifts into my mind of Tommy mentioning Mine's full name is Lucian Valerion de Vitry.

I prick my finger again and write that name.

Nothing.

What in the Source?

I wipe the mirror again and this time, I write only Valerìon de Vitry.

The mirror shines brightly and this time, an image forms on its surface.

I blink in confusion. Is Lucian not his name? Otherwise, why would the mirror only work when I write Valerìon de Vitry?

The question slides to the back of my mind as I focus on what I'm seeing.

He is in a foreign room, leaning against a counter and sipping on a cup of dark liquid that I assume to be that human coffee he enjoys. He's not dressed in his military uniform but rather in a casual white shirt that molds to his muscular body and a pair of dark slacks. My eyes are drawn to his big and strong arms and a sigh escapes me as I remember being held in his embrace only a week ago.

He seems well. He certainly doesn't look upset or distraught at my absence. His scars too, have healed much better since I last saw him, another sign of the passage of time in Anthropa.

He's smiling and nodding at someone.

I narrow my eyes. Who is he talking to?

As I study his surroundings more, I note it's some sort of a kitchen, but not the type I'd seen at the base. This is smaller, more personal. Something that would be found in an apartment in the city.

His lips move. He *is* speaking to someone. But I can't see yet who is around him.

Biting on my lips, I clench my fist in annoyance. Why doesn't the mirror have audio too?

His mouth moves too quickly and I can't make out too much of what he's saying except for the words *fine* and *tomorrow*.

A flash of navy blue material catches my eye in the periphery of the image. The person whom it belongs steps closer, and a gasp flies past my lips.

She's a woman in her twenties, her hair primly tied at her nape in a clean bun. A few strands of hair flow down her fore-head in a thin fringe. She half turns and I get a better view of her face. Small heart-shaped face, china-like complexion with a smudge of blush on her cheeks, she has big blue eyes framed by dark long lashes. Her nose is small and upturned, her lips full and pink.

I gulp down uneasily.

She is absolutely gorgeous. I don't think I've seen a more beautiful female. Most of the goddesses I know cannot compare to her either. *I* cannot compare.

She walks closer to Mine and as he places his cup on the counter, he opens his arms for her to hug him.

I grip tightly onto the desk until the wood cracks so I don't break the mirror instead.

She's shorter than him, her head reaching his chin. He leans forward and lays a tender kiss on her forehead and I see red.

I. See. Red.

The temperature drops abruptly in my room and errant energy seeps off my pores in dangerous waves, freezing everything in its path. My eyes become glazed with jealousy as I stare at Mine, *my* Mine, hugging and putting his lips on another female.

How. Dare. He?

Who is she? Who in the Source is this beautiful female and what is she to him?

My energy is so uncontrollable, it reaches the mirror, enveloping it in a film of ice. I'm close to my tipping point. I can feel it. I am *so* close to forgetting about all the rules and going back to Anthropa to *kill* her. And him. If he dared to cheat on me, then he is next too. Because *how dare he?*

I've only been gone a short period of time and he's found someone else already? What about all those promises and sweet words he told me? Is he telling her the same thing? Is he telling her she's his only one, that he's never looked at another before?

You are so dead, Valerion de Vitry. When I catch you, I'm going to make you suffer in ways you've never in your life imagined for making a fool out of me.

Before my rage can morph into devastating heartbreak, another figure appears in the room. The angle of the mirror shifts, pulling back to reveal the entire kitchen rather than just the angle where Mine is.

The male is around Mine's age. I can only see his profile as he approaches Mine and the female. He has a straight nose and a tanned complexion, his hair the darkest of black. He's dressed casually in a pair of gray pants and a black sweater.

The female turns to him, her lips spreading into a dazzling smile. She leaves Mine's arms and launches herself at the other male, who takes her in his arms, his hands moving possessively down her back. Then he pulls her in for a kiss.

A full-on, mouth to mouth kiss.

I blink in confusion. What is happening?

Mine rolls his eyes and says something to them. They break apart a few seconds later and more words are exchanged, after which Mine looks up, directly at the angle of the mirror.

His eyes are narrowed to two slits, but as the other male continues talking, his face erupts in a bright smile.

The couple are now holding hands, with the male throwing one arm around her to keep her close. His face is tilted toward her, his lips curved up in a perpetual smile. I cannot see his features clearly or the color of his eyes, but his bone structure reminds me of Mine in a way.

As that thought enters my mind, my eyes widen in comprehension.

He must be related to Mine! A cousin or something. Which means the female is family too.

I let out a sigh of relief. It seems I will not be murdering anyone tonight. Though when I see Mine again, I must let him know that regardless of whether he's related to those people, unless that's his mother, he cannot put his lips anywhere near her.

Nodding to myself in satisfaction, I watch them for a few more minutes as they busy themselves around the kitchen to prepare food. Well, it's mostly the female and the other male. Mine just stands there, looking into empty space with a rather stupid grin on his face—stupid because it's not for me, of course.

Suddenly, the image from the mirror dies, and no matter how much I try to reactivate it, it's in vain. I suppose these aren't meant for constant surveillance. Since I don't know how to power it up again, I toss it in a drawer and go to bed, satisfied I won't have to kill my beloved for wronging me.

Ah, it's always the little things that make me the happiest.

But that happiness is short-lived when the following day my maids fuss over me to make me *beautiful* for Theron and his family. A constant frown is etched on my forehead as I have to withstand being poked and prodded.

The most work goes into my hair as the maids add jewels and embellishments. The entire ensemble is heavy and uncomfortable. My mother comes by a short while later, nods her approval, and asks the maids to add a few more pieces of jewelry to my neck and hands.

In the end, I no longer feel like myself, just a pretty display piece. But that is exactly what mother intended.

The meeting takes place in the blue room of the palace of Cryos—a dining room reserved for special guests whose walls are painted with the rarest shade of blue in Aperion.

My parents and I are the first to arrive. Both Maledo and Molokai had begged out due to previous engagements.

When Theron and his parents arrive, a succession of greetings ensues as well as false platitudes that I have a hard time *not* rolling my eyes at.

"Theron, dear, what happened to your face?" my mother asks when she gets a better look at him.

I raise a brow at him. Though the wound is not as bad as before, there is a rather ugly scar running down his face.

"He got it in his last mission. It was a hard one. Commander Azerius has praised him for it, of course," his mother interjects.

Theron glares at me, a warning in his gaze not to say anything about the real cause of his scar.

I smile to myself. So he had to lie... I'm sure his pride would have been shattered if anyone found out a female scarred his *perfect* face.

Clown.

"I'm so sorry to hear that, Theron. It must have been a very difficult mission. Was it a level twelve demon?"

His nostrils flare. "Yes," he answers in a clipped voice.

"Oh my, I've never even seen a level twelve demon. Are they very scary?"

He looks ready to explode. "Yes."

"Yes what?"

"They are scary."

"You're so brave," I praise him in a high-pitched voice.

Everyone seems convinced by my act, thinking I've just been impressed by Theron's military prowess. But Theron realizes I'm secretly laughing at him, and this only makes everything so much funnier.

We take a seat at the table and wait for the courses to be served. Our parents make small talk while Theron continues to glare at me, occasionally touching his scar and remembering my promise from before.

As the conversation turns to our upcoming nuptials, our parents are discussing the best time for a wedding when Theron suddenly interjects.

"I am going to be involved in a long mission at Commander Azerius' request. I believe it would be best to postpone the nuptials."

Both our parents gasp in shock.

"You want to postpone the wedding?" my mother asks in a tremulous voice.

"I believe it would be best to take advantage of this opportunity," he states.

"I think Theron is right," I speak out. "Of course I am eagerly awaiting the wedding, but this is a rare opportunity for him to establish his career. We would not want him to miss out on it, no?"

"I suppose you are right," my mother comments reluctantly.

"It is an important mission," Theron continues.

Olivia, his mother, looks from her son to my parents, suddenly at a loss for words. I see they did not discuss this in advance and it makes me wonder what made Theron speak out. It's well known he's not an independent thinker and always relies on his mother to make decisions for him.

Perhaps I *did* scare him. I stifle a smile at the thought. Ah, but if I had known, I would have done this from the beginning so we wouldn't have gotten engaged in the first place.

Alas, the past is the past. There's no need to dwell on it.

"If Theron thinks that would be better, then I agree as well. Do you have a date in mind, my dear?"

"Since it is such an important mission, I cannot say how long it would take."

Both parents are quiet.

"I suppose we can reconvene once Theron is done with his mission," my mother says. She's not pleased with the outcome, but she cannot object to it, not when Theron's accomplishments would reflect good on our match too. Mother is nothing if not a strategist, and no matter how much she'd like to see me married tomorrow, she knows she must tread carefully.

"It is settled then. The wedding will be postponed indefinitely until Theron finishes his mission," my father finally speaks after quietly observing the exchanges.

The conversation becomes stilted and awkward and Olivia declares that they should leave.

I give Theron one last threatening look as I watch him go. It seems he's not entirely stupid. He still has some self-preservation since he realizes he will never get a tame and biddable wife in me.

"Minerva," my mother calls out. "What did you do?" Her eyes are shooting daggers at me as she strides to my side and grabs my arm roughly. "You think I was fooled by that demon excuse?"

"I don't know what you're talking about." I smile sweetly.

My father sighs and shakes his head.

He grabs my mother's hand off my arm and pulls her to his side.

"You're taking *her* side?"

"I am not taking anyone's side," my father says in a weary voice.

"Yes. You are." She glares at him. Stomping her foot against the floor, she leaves the dining room with a huff.

Alone with my father, he turns his attention to me.

"He's terrified of you," he adds quietly.

"Who?"

"Who do you think?" He laughs. "Theron."

"But I didn't do anything."

"You don't need to lie to me, Minerva. Others may not see it, but I would recognize the effects of the *eternal ice* anywhere."

Oops.

"He started it."

"And you finished it."

"Of course. I defended myself."

He nods silently at me.

"You are stronger than I thought."

"Have you *ever* given any thought to me at all?"

"I don't understand what you're asking of me."

"It's simple. You've never concerned yourself with me. You've allowed Mother to make all the decisions. I still cannot believe you allowed her to betroth me to Theron."

He scratches his chin. "I suppose he might not have been the best choice."

"He is supposed to be a level eight, Father."

"And you defeated him."

"Quite badly."

"I see."

"What do you see? That not only is he weak but he's also a liar? That's *not* an honorable male."

He purses his lips. "You are correct."

"So? Are you going to do anything about it?"

"What can I do? The betrothal has been approved by the House of Moirai."

"It can be petitioned to be broken."

"No. It cannot."

"There has to be a morality clause in there, isn't it? We can just unmask Theron as a liar."

"We would make the House of Pyros our enemy and that is not the goal," he replies drily.

"There has to be a way. Surely you see how badly matched we are. Think of your future grandchildren. I should at least be matched with someone stronger than me."

He hums in approval.

"I will see if there is anything to be done."

My eyes widen. Hope shines in them, perhaps for the first time ever.

"That's... That's very kind of you."

"It is not kindness, Minerva. I happen to be as concerned about this match as you are, though my reasons might be a little different."

"What do you mean?" I frown.

"I have said too much. Do not concern yourself with that."

"But—"

"You may retire to your room."

He moves past me to leave. Suddenly, though, he stops. He half turns and stares at me for a moment.

"The birthday of the Duchess of Sigmore of the House of Arche is in a fortnight."

"So?"

He takes a few moments to answer.

"Your presence is required."

"What? Why?"

I've never been *required* to go to the celebration of a monarch's birthday before. Certainly, I've never had the inclination before since I hate those parties. My parents are always the only ones who go, sometimes with Maledo, but he is the heir.

"I do not know. The duchess stated she would like you to be present."

"How does she even know who I am?" I've never met the Duchess of Arche before. I don't think I've ever even *been* to Arche.

"That I cannot answer. But since she specifically asked for your presence, she must know of you. I wonder..."

"What?" I stride to his side.

"She has a son. You may have met him. Perhaps she has heard of your achievements in the military and she might be interested in a match, though it would be irregular for that to happen since it is widely known you are engaged to Theron."

He pauses, deep in thought. "Though if someone could break your betrothal contract, it would be the Duchess of Arche. She not only has influence with the Supremes but also with Commander Azerius."

"Who is her son?"

"He's Commander Azerius' right hand. Cerenios."

My body freezes as a sliver of fear washes down my back.

"If that is a viable option, and the duchess is indeed seeking a mate for him, then I would be amenable to break the betrothal with Theron."

"That is..." I whisper, unable to find the words.

"Alas, I will have to discuss with the duchess first. Good day, daughter."

He leaves.

I cannot will my limbs to move as his words replay in my mind.

The Duchess of Sigmore, Cerenios' mother, specifically asked for my presence at her birthday celebration. My father may think it has to do with a potential match between us, but I know better.

Cerenios knows something—suspects something.

He just needs the evidence to get me convicted.

A birthday celebration is the best place for him to interrogate me without anyone raising a brow.

By the Source! I am in so much trouble.

THIRTY-THREE

A FORTNIGHT LATER, I find myself once more at a crossroads. My anxiety is at an all-time high as we step inside Sigmore Palace for Duchess Rhea's birthday.

Maledo is by my side, holding on to my arm and leading me inside the ballroom as our names are announced. He is the spitting image of our father, with his light blue eyes and dark hair. He is a handsome male and he is well aware of his appeal, his eyes immediately drawn toward the females present, who bat their lashes suggestively at him.

Our parents are a pace behind us, the voice announcing them reverberating loudly in the ballroom.

Molokai once more excused himself due to a previous engagement. It's not irregular for him to miss out on social events. After all, it wasn't him who was personally invited by Duchess Rhea to the party.

The ballroom is the size of an entire training field. It is almost double the size of the ballroom in our palace, which in itself is quite a feat. Rumor has it that Sigmore Palace might be the most extravagant in Aperion, not only because the Sigmore family is one of the wealthiest but also because over time, the family has supplied the largest number of Supremes from any one lineage.

Their connections are legendary, too. It is said that the great Lispera herself was a close friend of the Duchess of Sigmore and a frequent guest at the palace.

For a moment, I let myself absorb the history of my surroundings and imagine what it might have been like seven thousand years ago when Lispera had been alive. As the youngest person ever to become Supreme, she's the role model for a lot of fledgling deities. But it's not only because of her impressive career. She represents the struggles of females against the archaic practices of Aperion.

No one thought a female could achieve what she did, and rumors say her power was so great it couldn't even be measured with the normal level system. She not only became a Supreme, but she also sacrificed herself to seal Tartareia so the Sons of Tenebreis could not leave their realm, thereby ensuring a relative peace in the universe.

If she were still alive... I wonder if Commander Azerius would have such a monopoly on power in Aperion.

I force a smile on my lips as I turn to the crowds forming in the middle of the ballroom.

There are several hundred people if my estimates are correct. I am not particular to such crowds, but perhaps they will provide a shield for me as I get lost between the countless faces.

The entire room is surrounded by runes that inhibit the use of spiritual energy. All large gatherings implement this rule so deadly conflicts are avoided. Aperion might seem united as a whole against demons, but inside there are numerous factions always fighting for supremacy. Without these safety runes in place, this would turn into a bloodbath, especially since most of the rulers of the Houses are present—the best time for an attack, from the outside or from within.

Some faces I recognize from other official functions in the past. But I am not familiar with most of the nobility. My eyes scan the crowd in search for Cerenios, knowing he will be watching me, but so far I don't spot him anywhere.

A small reprieve.

The duchess and the duke are at the end of the ballroom, greeting their guests one by one.

My parents, Maledo, and I head to where they are to pay our respects.

"Happiest of birthdays, Duchess Rhea," my mother intones as she drops into a small curtsy as a sign of respect, though she technically outranks her. I do the same, avoiding looking her directly into her eyes.

"Welcome, welcome. Thank you for your presence."

"We brought you a special gift," my father says, manifesting a platinum necklace with a light blue stone accent. "It is made from our specialty, the eternal ice."

"Oh, how wonderful. Thank you," the Duchess murmurs, accepting the gift.

"This is our son and heir, Maledo," Father introduces my brother. "And this is our daughter, Minerva."

At the introduction, I glance up. The duchess is startlingly beautiful. Her bright red hair is coiffed up in a bun atop her head, with multiple jewels adorning the updo. Her skin is a warm caramel shade, her eyes a deep green. She looks nothing like Cerenios.

I glance at the duke. He, too, does not resemble Cerenios in the least with his dark hair and black, slanted eyes.

Even more surprising, both the duke and the duchess are warm, pleasant people, whereas Cerenios is downright terrifying. If before I would have given Commander Azerius the title of the scariest person in Aperion, I think I'm slowly learning to reconsider the hierarchy.

According to the research I'd done into the Duke and Duchess of Sigmore, they aren't the most gifted deities, although their line is a rather famous one, who's yielded a number of legendary Supremes. Yet the most interesting thing is that two rather average individuals could have produced such a powerful offspring. It's not just because the Sigmore family is influential in Aperion that Commander Azerius took Cerenios under his wing. It's due to the male's abilities, which he displayed from a very early age.

"Pleased to meet you," I murmur.

"I hope you will enjoy the festivities," the duchess mentions. "I have to go around to greet the other guests, but we shall have to find the time to converse," she mentions to my parents.

Once the introductions are over, my parents find some of their acquaintances and they strike up a conversation. Maledo has surreptitiously disappeared from our side, and as I scan the crowd, I see him a distance away, talking to a couple of young ladies.

I roll my eyes.

A servant carrying punch glasses stops by my side and I take one glass, planning to nurse it for the rest of the evening.

As my parents continue to get lost in their conversation, I slowly move to the side, hiding behind a pillar to avoid detection in case Cerenios is looking for me.

Tapping my foot against the floor as I wait for the time to pass so we can finally head home, I find my mind drifting to Mine once more. It's been days since I've last been able to survey him. The mirror simply stopped working one day. It was already only working a few minutes per day, but now that it's completely out of power, I'm left not only speculating the worst but also bored out of my mind.

Spying on Mine gave me something to look forward to every day, even though it enraged me to no end to see him go about his days without sparing me a thought. He never once even glanced at the sheet of paper I left him with my seal.

My absence barely seemed to affect him. It's almost like he completely erased me from his mind.

The only positive aspect is the fact that he never met with another female—as far as I've been watching. He spent some more time with that couple, but since that pretty female is mated and seemingly happily so, I've decided she is of no threat to me.

At least he's been a good male in that regard.

I've also gotten a front seat to some of his missions and I've been watching his with pure astonishment and bated breath as he operated his airplane, skillfully evading any incoming flak or fire.

He truly is an amazing male. So competent.

I may be mad at him for not calling on me yet, but I must admit I have greatly enjoyed secretly watching him. Of course no one needs to tell me how great he is, but it is quite nice to see him in action, kicking Nazi butt.

If he were an Aperite soldier, I have no doubt he would have easily made general in no time.

I sigh dreamily as I remember his lips on my own, the taste of his blood on my lips... I've found myself craving it more and more. Perhaps this is why it's so forbidden. Not only is the sharing of blood the height of eroticism, but it's also the closest one can be to another being—bar mating, though I cannot speak of that. Yet.

I squeeze my eyes shut. When did my regard for rules crumble that I am now contemplating mating with that male at some point? But the truth is that I know it will happen once I see him again.

I want him. That much is clear.

But do I want him so much that I would forsake all the rules that have been drilled into my head since I was naught but a fledgling?

Yes!

My skin suddenly pricks with awareness as my entire body grows cold with fear. It's immediate as if my body recognizes the danger before my mind can process it. Shaking myself from my thoughts, I look right and left, scanning my surroundings.

There he is.

Cerenios.

He's staring at me from across the ballroom. Dressed in a white suit with his family's insignia embroidered in golden thread across his chest, he is both handsome and terrifying as he holds himself completely still. His eyes are on me, and when he sees me take notice of him, his lips curve up in derision. He holds up a gobbet with punch and mockingly inclines it toward me.

My face falls.

He seemingly derives pleasure from my discomfort, his smile becoming wider. But it never reaches his eyes.

Looking for an opening, I seek to escape his unflinching gaze. But just as I move, he moves, too.

The room is surrounded by runes. He cannot do anything here, can he?

But it is his home. He may have hidden advantages I know nothing about. I cannot risk the encounter, though I knew it was going to happen the moment the duchess insisted on my presence tonight.

I wade my way through the crowd, keeping an eye on him as the distance between us dwindles. He's on my heel, about to catch up with me at any point.

And I have nowhere to run to.

Unless...

I suddenly stop.

Just as he is about to get close to me, I turn in his direction, and as I walk toward him, I purposefully bump into him and spill my drink on him.

His eyes widen in shock.

The people around us stop what they're doing to try to help him and engage him in conversation, at which point I take advantage of the limited time he's not paying attention to me to slide away.

The moment the party started, the ballroom was sealed so no one can wonder the palace grounds without permission. But as I take a detour to the lady's room, I find a small staircase that leads to an alcove above the ballroom.

It's so narrow, only someone with my slight frame could fit up the staircase. And as I get to the top, I note the small ceiling of the alcove that requires me to pull up my gown and shimmy inside on my knees.

It's darker here than in the ballroom, the lighting source shining away from this hidden spot—the perfect nook to hide into.

But just as I reach the railing to gaze down onto the ballroom, I note I'm not alone.

"Argh," a small voice whimpers as I bump into a warm body.

"Who's there?" I whisper.

"I should be asking you the same," she huffs, though her tone is more bordering on amusement than annoyance. "This is my spot."

"Mind if I borrow it for a while?" I ask as I get a closer look at her when a beam of light shines over her face. She's young. Much younger than me. Her hair is black and lustrous, falling down her shoulders in rippling waves. Her eyes are a deep green with specks of gold in them.

She eyes me up and down. "You're small enough to fit in here. I suppose I can make an exception," she adds, her eyes sparkling with mischief.

"Minnie," I introduce myself.

"Wyn," she replies with a smile. "I gather you are not too fond of these parties."

"Is it so obvious?" I chuckle.

"Why, though? It's so magical and wonderful," she adds with a wistful sigh.

"Then why aren't you there on the dance floor?"

She pouts. "I'm not allowed. I haven't reached my majority yet." She sighs.

"You're not missing much," I tell her honestly.

"Oh, I am missing far too much," she replies as she directs her attention to a cluster of people at the ball. She has a dreamy expression on her face as she gazes at one of the males deep in talk with a couple other people.

"I wish I could be there. Then I could dance with him and —" She stops herself as she realizes she's said too much. "Sorry, you didn't come to hear me blubber about my love interest."

"Aethon?" I raise a brow, recognizing the object of her rapt attention.

Her eyes widen as she drags in a sudden breath.

"You know him?"

"I know of him. He's a general in Commander Azerius' army."

She narrows her eyes at me.

"And what do you think of him?" she inquires, though I recognize the underlying jealousy behind her question.

"I have no opinion on him." I shrug. "I've heard he is a good soldier. Nothing else."

A smile curves at her lips, making her seem dazzlingly beautiful. "Good, that is good," she murmurs, more to herself.

She pauses for a heartbeat before she blurts out, "He is so wonderful, though." She gushes. "He's the most handsome male in the entire of Aperion. The sweetest too, though he would hate to be described as such."

"How would you know that if you haven't reached your majority yet?"

It's common knowledge that unless a female has reached her majority and has had her come out, she is not allowed to meet any unattached males.

"He's a friend of my brother's. I've known him my entire life."

"Isn't he ancient?" I frown. From what I remember, he must be around fifteen thousand years if not more. He's the star of the House of Pyros, the last surviving blue dragon. And although he's said to possess great power, he's never had great ambitions for himself, preferring to be a mere general when he could have been king or even a Supreme.

"Bah." Wyn snorts and waves her hand. "Love has no age."

"Does he know that too?" I giggle.

"Not yet, but he will. He's going to come at my come out ball, and I already have in mind a gorgeous gown that will surely dazzle him. He's going to look at me and see me as a female for the first time and then—" She stops midway through her passionate speech. "You must think me rather silly. We've just met and here I am rambling like a fool."

I smile.

"On the contrary. I hope it all works out for you. I have my own person that I cannot wait to see."

Excitement shines in her eyes and she suddenly grabs my hands. "Marlowe, right?"

I blink. "What?"

"His name is Marlowe. He is a very dangerous male, but he loves you very much."

"I... I'm not sure what you're talking about. I don't know any Marlowe."

Her brows knit together in confusion.

"I apologize. Sometimes I blurt things out without thinking."

"No, it's fine, but I don't know any Marlowe."

The green of her eyes flickers to a pale opal color.

"You will. Not now, but you will. He has faced death three times to be with you. And he has sacrificed much, much more. But his sacrifice is not in vain."

"What are you talking about?" I frown.

"Your male. He is ill." Her face falls. "It is an incurable illness, at least for now."

"How... how did you know?"

Her eyes are glazed over as she continues.

"This will be his second death. But to rid himself of the core of the poison, he must die."

"No, no, he cannot die."

"He must. But he will come back to you, Minerva," she adds in an ominous voice, and I realize I never told her my full name.

"W-who are you?" I ask in a whisper as a shiver goes down my back.

"When the time comes, you must make two visits. One to the House of Moirai and one to the House of Psyche."

"Why?"

"That thread must be cut before a new one can replace it. If you do not cut it now, you will perish with him."

"I don't under—"

"Blood will tell," she mentions before her gaze moves past me, her head tilting to the side.

"You should not be here," she states suddenly, but she's not talking to me. I turn, but no one is there. "It is not nice of you to come here uninvited."

The air thickens and a wave of pure electricity sweeps around us.

Suddenly, her eyes are back to normal and she jumps back, startled.

"I apologize again if I said something wrong," she murmurs, her countenance withdrawn.

"What did you mean by that?"

She shakes her head. "I don't know either. Sometimes I just... see things." She gulps down. "There is someone after you, Minnie. Someone very, very powerful. You should fortify your mental shields."

"Who—"

I don't get to finish my question because she vanishes. One moment she's there, the next she's gone.

What... this room is supposed to be full of inhibiting runes. How did she do this?

Was she even real?

As I stare at the empty space, I wonder if perhaps I didn't make her up.

But the things she said... How could she know Mine is sick?

Yet what she said about the House of Moirai continues to ring in my mind long after she's gone. I've never given much thought to the fact that I might have a fated mate, someone other than Mine.

Fury grips me in a tight vise. No, that cannot be. There cannot be anyone but Mine for me.

Would doing what she said, cutting my thread of fate, allow me to be with Mine without worry?

More doubts spring to my mind. I don't know whether I should pay attention to anything she said. But it wouldn't hurt to investigate, no?

After all, I would do anything to be with Mine. Even cutting all the fated ties to my world.

The same pricking sensation washes over me, and as I gaze down the railing, I see Cerenios in the middle of the ballroom, dressed in a new suit, his eyes on me.

I gasp and fall backward. Scrambling out of the crammed space, I almost fall down the stairs in my attempt to flee. But as I reach the bottom, I come face-to-face with him.

"What were you doing with her?" he rasps out in a harsh voice.

I stare up at him bewildered.

"Who?"

"Arwyn. Why were you with her?"

The girl... She was real then.

"I—"

"Come." He grabs my hand and pulls me away from the crowd toward a hidden door. As soon as he steps in front of it, the door opens and we're out of the ballroom.

The absence of the inhibiting runes is immediately noticeable as a whisper of power tingles in my fingertips. But if I have my powers back, then so does he.

By the Source, he can and *might* kill me.

THIRTY-FOUR

HE DRAGS me into a small room at the end of the hall and closes the door behind him.

"I will ask one more time. What were you doing with Arwyn?"

"You mean Wyn? I just met her."

"You will not go near her again, Minerva."

"Or what?" I raise a defiant brow.

His lip twitches and he takes a step toward me.

"I know you are hiding something," he starts in a low voice. "Something that would get you punished."

My eyes flare open. "Why? Because I talked for five minutes with Wyn?" I ask, confused at his sudden outburst. The Cerenios I know is usually more composed than this.

"Five minutes too long. She cannot be near those of your ilk."

"My ilk? What's that supposed to mean?"

"Someone who has no regard for rules," he states tensely.

"What is she to you?"

"It does not matter what she is to me. All that matters is that you keep your distance. Or the next time we will see each other will be on the execution block."

"Is that a threat?"

"I do not make threats, Minerva. I act."

I bite my lip as I eye the door, but to get to it I must get past him.

"I am not hiding anything. You know all there is to me and what happened with that sin demon."

He moves closer, once more leaning in to sniff me. "Tainted blood. You smell of tainted blood."

A shiver goes down my back. I don't know what that's supposed to mean, but it cannot be good.

"You are mistaken. I am a princess of the House of Cryos. You'd best respect me," I say in a forced voice.

He smirks, though his eyes remain cold and unfeeling. "I do not give a damn about your rank or your family, Minerva. Respect is earned in my world."

"You..." I take a step back. He follows.

"Azerius tasked me with finding out what you are hiding about the demon attack." He pauses. "One word, and you will be executed."

"You would fabricate something on me?"

He shrugs. "There is no need to fabricate anything. I just need to find out what you are hiding."

"Well, good luck with that. Now I will be taking my leave."

I move to the side to avoid him as I head toward the door.

"Stop!" he commands, his voice infused with pure energy that makes me freeze in my tracks. W-what?

My body refuses to obey me as I attempt to move.

"You will answer some questions for me now," he states casually as he circles around me, his hands behind his back.

Against my will, I find myself saying, "Yes."

What the...

Panic takes hold of me.

I've never heard of Cerenios having the ability to control someone. But this... I can't move, can barely think as he plops himself in front of me and pins me with his gaze.

"How did you destroy the greed demon?"

"With charity," I reply automatically.

He narrows his eyes at me.

"And how did you know about charity?"

"From the books on sin demons."

"Those books are only found in very particular collections in Aperion. Where did you procure a copy?"

I clamp my mouth shut, biting hard on my lip until I taste blood. Still, as if under a spell, I am compelled to answer.

"From General Leotar's library."

"Ah. There it is," he murmurs in satisfaction.

My eyes widen in fear. Anything I say is going to damn me at this point. Somehow, I must break free of his control.

Since my body is immobile, I focus my energy on the surroundings, dropping the temperature until his breath comes out as a fog.

He appears surprised by this, but he barely chuckles to himself.

I add a little more strength to the cold weather until the floor becomes glazed with ice. My limbs, too, start getting frosty, and instead of combating the cold as I would have usually done, I let it envelop me, sending my body into an overdrive of sensation.

The first crack appears.

I move my arm, the pain of frostbite jolting me out of whatever mind control he's using.

"Commander Azerius was right. You are not a mere level five, are you?" he asks curiously.

Gritting my teeth against the pain spreading through my body, I force my other limbs to move.

By the time I am relatively free of his control, though, it's too late.

He grabs me by the throat and lifts me in the air.

"Nice try." He tsks. "But I am not done with you yet."

"Damn you, you sanctimonious pig."

"Now, now, Minerva." He clicks his tongue against his teeth in derision. "Who taught you such unseemly words?"

"Leave. Me. Alone! This is against the law!" I cry out. "If

you want to investigate me, do it formally, you coward," I spit at him. "But wait, then you wouldn't be able to use your mind control on me. Because it's forbidden."

He smiles at my threat, tightening his hold.

"Ah, but who would believe your word over mine?" He chuckles.

"You dare tell me off about breaking the rules when you're doing the same thing?"

"It is different. I am doing my job, and Azerius knows that sometimes different techniques have to be employed. The end result is all that matters."

I glare at him. What did I expect from Commander Azerius' lap dog? The rumors have always implied that Azerius was relentless in his pursuit of his justice, but I never realized how far he would go.

Worse? Azerius is the highest authority in Aperion. Even if I wanted to seek help from someone else, not even the Supremes could do anything to stop him since he has free rein over the military. The mere suggestion that I might be a traitor and he'll be allowed to torture all the answers out of me.

My fingertips tingle with energy as I ready myself to attack. But before I can do so, the door swings open and a female walks in, her eyes wide with shock.

"What is the meaning of this?" she shrieks.

"Thea, out," Cerenios replies without even looking at her.

"What are you doing?"

"Out!"

She doesn't obey his command. Shutting the door behind her, she strides determinedly toward Cerenios. She's taller than me, but he still dwarfs her with his height.

"I turn my back for a moment and you are out here assaulting someone?" She shakes her head at him. Her nails morph into claws and she digs them into his neck, then rakes them down his flesh and draws blood.

Cerenios is unmoved.

He regards her with a bored expression on his face, barely moving a muscle.

She launches herself at him again until he finally throws me aside and slowly faces her.

Stumbling back, I massage my neck absentmindedly as I watch them with confusion.

"Thea, I told you to leave."

"No. I must defend her against your tyrannical ways." She points to me as she glares at him.

He rolls his eyes.

"Should you not first ask *why* I was doing it?"

"Of course not. Whatever it is, you're likely at fault. Though I must say, Cer, I've never known you to be this aggressive toward a female. Have you finally lost it?"

"Thea..." He sighs.

"It's evil Ze's influence, isn't it? He's turning you into a monster, Cer! How can you work for him?"

"Work. That is exactly what I am doing. So please leave and let me continue my *work*."

"I knew it." She stomps her foot. "Never mind that you're taking orders from that evil male, but now you're doing this here? Unacceptable."

She turns to me. "Don't you worry. While you are here, you are under my protection."

I nod numbly. I think I like her. Though she's a bit odd. Going by her dark green empire waist gown, she's likely a guest at the party. Her red hair is pinned atop her head in a basic updo, but the simplicity of it does nothing to detract from her beauty.

"How did you know I was here?" A glint of suspicion appears in his eyes.

"Wyn told me. She also said you were up to no good."

"Wyn?" Surprise flickers across his face.

"She told me to stop you, so that is what I am doing," she adds, nodding to herself.

Belatedly, I note that the wounds on his neck are not healing. If anything, they continue bleeding.

"Do not make me repeat myself, Thea. Leave. Now," he adds with a sigh as he scrubs a hand over his face. Moving lower, he realizes his wound is still bleeding, but instead of panicking, he merely rolls his eyes. He brings his hand to his lips and licks the blood off his fingers.

"I am taking her with me," she declares as she grabs my hand and heads for the door. But as she tries to open it, the door doesn't budge.

"Cer?" Thea taps her foot against the floor impatiently.

"I am afraid I cannot let you take her. As I told you, I am working."

"I don't care. You are not allowed to work here. If you have anything to resolve with this female, you can do so officially, at the interrogation office, not at a party. Unless you have something to hide?" She watches him with narrowed eyes.

His jaw tenses and they engage in a battle of wills as they stare at one another.

"Is there something more untoward happening here?" Thea asks.

"Untoward?" I blink, finally finding my voice. "No, no, he—"

"I am talking to him." She shuts me down with a harsh stare. Maybe I don't like her that much after all. I don't know who she is and what her relationship to Cerenios is, but it is clear they have some history. If I could, I would leave and let them solve their issues alone. But as it stands, now I'm trapped between two belligerent deities and seeing how Cerenios' wound is still not healing, this Thea might be a strong opponent too.

By the Source. I could barely face Cerenios alone as it was before. Now I have to contend with another one?

"You brought a female to a closed room. Do you realize the optics of that?"

"Thea, please cease your histrionics. Nothing untoward was

happening. I do not have a taste for..." he trails off as his eyes find me and his nose wrinkles in distaste. "This type of female."

"This type?" I blink. "What's that supposed to mean?" I ask, not knowing whether I should feel offended or not at his words.

"Yes, Cer, what type? And how dare you call me hysterical?"

His jaw is locked tight. "The lying type," he states tersely.

My face falls. "That's not true—"

"What?" Thea blurts out.

"I do not care for liars and for rule breakers. Minerva is both. And she must be punished."

A series of emotions crosses Thea's face before she schools her features. A tremor runs through her body.

"So you are not only consorting with a *lying* female, but you're also trying to punish her?" she asks suspiciously. "At a house party?"

"Yes, that is exactly what I am doing."

"Is this some kinky thing I didn't know about?" she suddenly asks. "Are you..." Her voice goes down a notch. "Is that why you were choking her?"

"Thea." He takes a deep breath. "You have an overactive imagination. Where would you have even heard the word *kinky*?" he demands sharply.

"It's what humans use for this sort of thing," she replies flippantly.

"This sort of thing?"

"You know, choking and stuff. You *were* choking her."

"And when did you see humans choke each other?"

"We are talking about *you* here, Cer. Not me."

"You will answer me, Thea. Where did you witness humans engaging in *kinky* behavior?"

"I'm well traveled, you know." She huffs and raises her chin.

"Who, when, and where?"

"I am not the one doing it! You are."

"And I have told you, nothing untoward is happening here. You are jumping to conclusions."

"If it is nothing, let us leave."

"No. I must continue my work." He pauses, glancing at me as if just remembering I am still present. "You are making a fuss about nothing, Thea."

"Nothing?" She raises her voice. "If anyone else were to have seen you go into a closed room with her, you would have a scandal on your hands."

"My reputation is spotless. No one would doubt I was conducting an investigation. *Work*, Thea."

"You will not *work* here. Now I will take her back to the party and you better not do this again."

"Thea," he adds with a low growl.

"Open the door, Cer."

"No."

"Open the door this instant, Cerenios. Do not make me repeat myself."

He swallows. Is he...afraid of her?

"Thea, you are—"

"Thea this, Thea that." She rolls her eyes as she cuts him off. "You are in so much trouble, Cer. Let us not forget about the fact that you called me hysterical. I assure you I will not be forgetting about that soon. Now open the door."

"No."

I stare between the two of them in confusion.

Thea lets go of my hand and strides to his side.

"You are being outrageous. If you don't let us go—"

"What? If I don't let you go, then what?"

"I will... I will..." She presses her lips together. "I will be forced to hurt you again." She raises her hand to his face, her nails elongating into claws.

His lips quirk up and he tsks at her.

Grabbing her hand, he pulls her close, his mouth moving up her inner arm.

"What are you doing?" she stammers.

"Making sure you *cannot* hurt me," he murmurs before he

parts his lips. His canines elongate and he lodges them in her flesh, biting her.

He's...

My eyes widen in shock.

Thea's body goes still as he feeds from her.

He. Feeds. From. Her.

Red flecks stain his irises, making him appear even more dangerous.

To my surprise, Thea doesn't seem too concerned with the fact that he's *feeding* from her—something that is forbidden in itself. And he dared criticize me?

Moments go by and she finally wrenches her hand away from his mouth. He's smirking at her as he wipes the residue blood from his lips. It's then that I realize his wound has closed.

"What is wrong with you?" Thea grinds out.

Cerenios shrugs. He leans in to whisper something in her ear that I can't quite make out even with my advanced hearing. After that, his eyes connect to mine.

I take a step back and hit the door just as he flashes himself in front of me. This time, Thea does not interfere, merely standing back and massaging her arm long after the bite mark healed.

"See something familiar, Minerva?" he asks in a derisive voice.

"W-what are you talking about?" I stammer.

He leans in and inhales deeply. "Tainted blood. I can smell it on you. And there is only one way that could be the case."

I blink. Why does he keep repeating this *tainted blood* issue? What even is that?

Can he tell I shared my blood with Mine? But no, that's impossible.

Unless... Awareness slowly seeps in. I did not *just* give Mine my blood. I also tasted his, though nothing like Cerenios did with Thea. It was a few drops at most. And why would his blood be tainted? He's human!

Is it because of his illness? Is that what he means?

I'm more confused than ever as I stare at his self-assured expression.

"You know exactly what I am talking about. Let us dispense with the theatrics."

"You're wrong," I whisper.

"Am I?" He raises a brow. "Perhaps others are not able to detect the stench, but I can. Commander Azerius can. It is just a matter of finding out the cause."

"Your nose is faulty," I counter. "I've never even heard of tainted blood or whatever it is you're talking about."

"Thea? Mind telling Minerva here what tainted blood means?"

I glance at Thea and she bites her lip, averting her gaze.

"Blood sharing with a different species," she adds in a low voice.

My heart stops in my chest.

"You're one to talk?" I burst out. "You just drank her blood." I point accusingly to him and Thea. "So what if you're the same species. Blood sharing is forbidden altogether."

His lips slowly curl into a dangerous smile.

"You're trying to prove a point, but you're breaking the rules too," I continue.

"Is that so?" He chuckles. "Except I am not. Blood sharing is allowed between first degree relatives in extreme situations. My injury not healing qualifies as an extreme situation."

"You mean..." I look between him and the other female.

"Thea is my sister," he confirms.

"B-but..." The loud beat of my heart drowns every noise around me.

"I know what you have done, make no mistake of that. I only require enough proof for a conviction."

"No, no. I didn't do anything."

"Really?" He raises a brow. "Let me break it down for you since it seems your small brain cannot comprehend the situation you are in. You somehow acquired books from General Leotar's personal library. The same general who was murdered in cold blood by a demonic entity, likely a Son of Tenebreis. A murder that occurred in Aperion, at a military base that is supposed to have the highest degree of security." He pauses as he sees my face fall. "A murder that even the most eminent truth diviners cannot see."

I shake my head.

"You're insinuating that I—"

"That you worked together with a demon. Yes."

"I would never!" I protest, this time fully confident in my answer. "I would *never* collude with a demon."

He seems taken aback by my outburst.

"Then how do you explain all the above?"

"I can't explain it. That is true. But I vow to the Source that I would *never* willingly engage with a demon or aid one in any way. I am a soldier, Cerenios. I've dedicated my entire life to fighting them. I would *never* betray our cause."

He doesn't reply, merely staring at me. A vow to the Source is unbreakable. Even he knows that.

"That's it, Cer. You got your answer. She vowed she is not involved with a demon," Thea intervenes.

Cerenios' nostrils flare. He doesn't seem impressed by my vow, but even he cannot refute that if I lied in my vow, I would be writhing in pain now.

Thea strides to the door and places her hand on the knob. "Open the door."

He still doesn't react.

"I am not done with you, Minerva. There is something off about you. I know it. And I will not stop until I find out what that is," Cerenios states ominously as the door clicks open.

I don't bother replying. The moment Thea opens the door, I dash out, not looking back.

When I get back to the ballroom, I find my parents and stick by their side until the event is over and we get back home. I don't see Cerenios anymore, nor his sister, but I know he will *not* give up.

I am in more danger than ever, and it's not even for something I've done! I was a bystander at the demon attack. But admitting that will only get me in more trouble. They will likely not believe me, even if I vowed it. And then they will ask *why* I did not come forward with information after it happened.

Every situation ends with me endangering Mine since he was with me in Aperion at that time, and I cannot allow that to happen.

Back in my room, I pace around like a madwoman as I try to make sense of what my next steps should be.

As we returned home, my father made some comments about Cerenios that still bother me.

"He is the most eligible mate in all of Aperion. It's not a coincidence that Commander Azerius took him under his wing. He is relentless in furthering Aperion's interests and wiping all traces of corruption from our institutions of power. You would be lucky if the duchess considers you," he'd mentioned.

All I could hear was *relentless*.

He is several thousand years older than me, which means there must be some records about him in the library, especially if his deeds are celebrated. Although I hold disdain for the male, I am smart enough to realize I must know my enemy.

Late that night, I barricade myself in the royal library and scour any mentions of Cerenios.

Yet what I find only exacerbates the dread forming inside of me.

Cerenios finds. Azerius kills.

Azerius might have the reputation of a God Killer because he is the executioner of deities, but Cerenios is just as dangerous. He is the one who does all the dirty work so that Azerius has the necessary proof to execute someone.

The deadly duo, some chronicles call them.

Cerenios exhibited extraordinary abilities since his first years. The Duke and Duchess of Sigmore beseeched Azerius, then still a general, to take young Cerenios under his tutelage and train him. Cerenios went to live with Azerius when he was only a few hundred years old, spending over two thousand years in close proximity to the God Killer. It is not surprising that he would be as deadly and precise as his mentor.

This information is not scary at all.

Closing the book and putting it back in its place, I massage my temples.

Anxiety runs through my veins, and my hands have a slight tremor to them that I cannot stop.

I don't see any way out of this. He *will* find something on me. And I will be arrested, then executed.

No! There has to be something I can do.

Wyn's words from before echo in my mind. What had she said?

I must make a visit to the House of Moirai and cut my thread of fate.

But can I trust her? She sent Thea to help me, and if she had not come at the right time, I would have been forced to divulge everything to Cerenios. Perhaps she *does* have good intentions.

"Senea," I call out to the library wraith.

"Yes?" A ghostly being materializes.

"Show me all the books on the House of Moirai that mention the threads of fate."

A few books light up at the end of the library.

"Do you require anything else, Your Highness?"

"No. That is all."

I take out the books the wraith highlighted and spread them out on the table.

Although everyone knows the power the House of Moirai wields, not only in Aperion but in the entire universe, there is very little information available on the specifics of their work. Both the House of Moirai and the House of Psyche are the most elusive parts of Aperion, and the only ones closed to anyone outside of their jurisdiction.

I remember learning the basics about them in school, but beside their hierarchies and the fact that one deals with the eternal cycle of souls while the other weaves the parameters of each soul's fate, there was little else we were taught about them.

As I peruse the books, I realize there isn't much more here either.

One chronicle mentions there are nine threads of fate, pertaining to the self, family, friends, love, potential, fortune, misfortune, life, and death. The *self* thread is imbued with the innate characteristics of a person, good and bad. The *family* thread decides within which family the soul will be born into. The *friends* thread connects to other souls and makes a tapestry of connections; it's all about the other people a person might meet in a lifetime. The threads for *fortune* and *misfortune* as well as *life* and *death* are rather self-explanatory. They relate to when a person will be born, their trials and tribulations during their life and ultimately death. The *potential* thread is more mysterious and the only one the chroniclers can't decide on a definition.

Yet as I read on, I realize that while these threads provide some parameters, they are not precise. There is still a certain degree of free will. But once more, the chroniclers cannot agree on the weight of free will versus the threads spun by the Moirai.

Nine threads of fate. Wyn said I must cut *a* fate thread.

But she forgot to tell me which one...

THIRTY-FIVE

I CANNOT BELIEVE I'm taking such high risks based on a few words from a stranger. Yet here I am, at the gates of Moirai, about to either manage to get inside or get arrested for even trying.

Taking a deep breath, I square my shoulders and head to where the armored soldiers guard the portal that leads to the inside of the House of Moirai.

Although it is technically located in Aperion, the only way to get inside is to be approved by the door watcher, who then inputs some coordinates in the portal that take you to the heart of House of Moirai. This system ensures that even if the armed guards guarding the portal were to be defeated, no one would be able to step inside without the proper coordinates.

As I step forward, the guards look me up and down with suspicion before the door watcher materializes.

"Name and purpose of the visit," he demands.

"Minerva An'yan of the House of Cryos here to see Groyo of the House of Moirai."

"Is he expecting you?"

"No, but I am here to relay my gratitude for his influence on my development," I say, adding some flowery language for good measure.

The door watcher does not seem convinced.

"What is it you are carrying?" He points at the basket in my hands.

"This is a gift for Lord Groyo. It is a dish I made specifically for him," I add sweetly.

"If you do not have an appointment, you cannot go in."

"I'm sure an exception can be made. Lord Groyo will be happy to see me and listen to all the lessons I have learned after our interaction."

"No exceptions," he states firmly.

"Not even for a princess of the House of Cryos?" I smile. "You should ask Lord Groyo first before turning me away."

He ponders my words for a few moments before he disappears. In a matter of seconds, he is back.

"Lord Groyo will receive you," he declares.

I let out a small sigh of relief as I follow the door watcher to the portal. He inputs the coordinates and as a light blue color swirls around me, my surroundings change.

A lush, green valley extends in the horizon. The sky is clear and perfectly blue—a stark contrast to Aperion's usual semi-orange sky, whose hue is given by its two blazing suns. The entire landscape is picturesque and the main color palette is a pastel version of the vibrant Aperion colors. A sudden calm settles over me. I'm not sure if this is due to the tranquility of the environment, or if there is something in the air in the House of Moirai that takes away all my worries.

"Balabas will lead you to Lord Groyo," the door watcher mentions as a wraith materializes in front of me.

"Thank you!"

The wraith's ghostly eyes meet mine. "Follow me, Lady Minerva," it says in a monotone voice.

We walk down a small, paved road that seemingly stretches for miles.

I try to interact with Balabas, asking some questions about the threads of fate housed within House of Moirai, but I'm greeted with a very generic, "I am not programmed to answer such questions."

Wraiths are soulless beings with no mind of their own. Their only purpose is to serve the commands of the person who created them. Although they are not sentient, all wraiths derive their knowledge from the Source, which means they are a wealth of information if one can get them to talk. Sometimes, there are loopholes in how wraiths are programmed, and one can get some tidbits of information. But as I continue to rephrase my questions, it seems Balabas is not one of them.

As expected of a wraith from the House of Moirai, I think drily to myself.

We walk for minutes on end until a massive construction appears on the horizon.

As we get closer to it, my eyes widen in astonishment at the sheer size of it.

It's a circular tower with the radius of an entire Aperite city. Though that's impressive on its own, it's the fact that it's so tall, it brushes against the sky, with no visible roof in sight.

That's hundreds if not thousands of floors.

"This is..." I whisper, more to myself.

Balabas promptly replies, "This is the seat of the House of Moirai, Lady Minerva. Lord Groyo's lodgings are on the one thousand and third floor."

"One thousand..." I trail off. "How many are in total?"

"An infinite number, just as there are infinite worlds out there and worlds not yet formed," Balabas surprises me when it answers my question.

"Is that where the fates of souls are located?"

"Yes. They are arranged according to their place of origin."

"By origin you mean..." I probe carefully.

"The world they are born into for that particular lifetime. There are an infinite number of wraiths that work to sort out any changes in placement as a soul enters and then departs the House of Psyche."

Finally, I'm getting some relevant information.

"Who decides what world a soul will be born into? The House of Psyche or the House of Moirai?"

"The House of Moirai, of course," Balabas answers in the same monotone voice. "While the wraiths move souls from one level to the other, the clerks working for the Moirai Council delegate the tasks so order is maintained in the universe."

"The Moirai Council? What is that?"

"It is a fourteen-member council handpicked by the Moirai Supreme, who dedicate their lives to spinning the threads of fate."

"Fourteen members? And they spin all the threads of the universe? How is that possible?"

"I cannot answer that as it is beyond my knowledge."

"What about the Supreme? What does the Supreme do?"

"The Supreme is in charge of spinning the threads of fate of the most influential people of each generation. Those souls are picked based on their potential to influence millions of other souls."

There it is, that word again: potential.

"What is potential exactly?"

"I cannot answer that, Lady Minerva."

I sigh. It seems the only information the wraith is willing to impart is the general kind. But considering I did not find any such information in the books from our library, this is quite novel for me.

"Where would I find my own thread of fate?"

"I cannot answer that."

I roll my eyes.

"Where would the threads of fate of Aperion be?"

"You will have to be more specific, Lady Minerva."

"What do you mean more specific?"

"The souls of deities are different from the souls of s'Aperiotes and they are given a different type of consideration."

"You mean they get special treatment?"

"I cannot answer that."

"Where would the souls of deities be then?" I rephrase my question, though I brace myself to get the same non answer.

"Each council member is assigned one House of Aperion."

"Which council member is assigned House of Cryos?"

"Lord Groyo, of course."

Ah, perhaps luck is on my side after all.

"And how are these council members fair to their own fate? Can't they cheat and assign themselves good fates?" I ask since this has been on my mind for a long time.

"Cheating does not exist in the House of Moirai," the wraiths promptly replies.

"How so?" I frown.

"A requisite of any living soul working in the House of Moirai is to relinquish their emotions. Without emotions, there is no incentive to cheat."

Wait, what?

"You mean the Moirai Supreme and the council members are emotionless?"

"Together with any living clerk who works here, yes."

That is interesting, and something to keep in mind when interacting with Groyo. He will not be easily swayed by my awkward charm, and perhaps not even by the delicious food I cooked for him.

Damn it!

"If they are emotionless, do they mate?" I ask suddenly.

"No, every worker for the House of Moirai is required to live a life of celibacy."

"Then how do they reproduce?" I frown.

"They do not."

"I don't understand. They don't have any offspring? How do they appoint successors? Do they even have successors or is it the same people all the time?"

"Each council member has a term of ten thousand years after which they are relieved of their duties. Each Moirai Supreme has a term of fifty thousand years after which they are relieved of their duties and a new Supreme is chosen. Each clerk has a term of five thousand years before they are relieved of their duties. All House of Moirai deities are from the other Houses in Aperion and after they finish their term, they are allowed to return to their respective Houses."

"What?" I squeak.

"It is public knowledge," Balabas adds. Of course everything Balabas is telling me is likely public knowledge, but that does not mean widely available. Certainly, I have never been heard most of the things the wraith told me so far. In my defense, I've never been interested in the affairs of the House of Moirai before.

Balabas continues, "Fledgling deities are recruited within their first thousand year of life if they display certain abilities that might be a good fit for the House of Moirai. They are then trained and molded into their role."

That sounds vaguely familiar, and I think I remember some rumors about these recruitments during my school years. But I never paid them any mind.

We are getting closer to the tower. Since my time to ask questions is limited, I bring up another thing that's bothered me since my parents decided to betroth me to that clown. But it seems that the wraith cannot answer any question related to the threads of fate, so I carefully choose my next words.

"How does the House of Moirai decide which matches to approve for deities?"

"A hypothetical model is built to test the potential of the offspring between two deities. Should the potential offspring have equal or better potential than at least one of its parents, the match is approved. Should the potential offspring have less potential, the match is denied."

"What about true matings?"

Balabas stops and turns to me, the first time he's done so.

"True matings are forbidden in Aperion. They disrupt the order of things."

That much I knew as well, since true matings are triggered by blood-sharing and sexual intercourse. The first is forbidden by Aperite law, while the second is frowned upon *before* marriage.

"How do they disrupt the order of things?" I inquire.

"I cannot answer that."

"When did true matings become forbidden?" Balabas should be able to answer that since wraiths have an encyclopedia-type knowledge.

"When the Primordials left."

I frown.

"What do you mean by that?"

"I cannot answer that," Balabas replies.

I purse my lips in annoyance and rephrase my question, "What is so bad about true matings that made them forbidden?"

"Bad is subjective," the wraith responds. "True matings were not conductive to the purpose of Aperion. They were deemed to be against the interest of the realm."

I blink. "Why?"

"True mates only care about each other at the expense of anything and anyone else. It stands to reason that if they only care about each other, they will not do their duties to Aperion and the rest of the universe."

"Does that mean that Moirai only approves matings that have no chance of being true matings?"

"I cannot answer that."

Yet the answer is evident. Moirai's process of approval hinges on two important criteria: the potential power of the offspring and the impossibility that the parents would be true mates.

Slowly, it dawns on me that Moirai has been actively working against us. So what if true mates only care about each other? By denying people the chance of finding their one true love, they are denying them true happiness.

I'd long suspected that the rarity of true matings had to do with the political game of advantageous marriages in Aperion, but I never realized it would be so insidious. Retrospectively, it makes sense why in my over four thousand years of life, I've only read a handful of accounts of true mating—all references from obscure, unofficial sources.

Despite the fact that true matings are considered taboo and they are not talked about, those accounts stayed with me because they gave me a sliver of hope—that perhaps I, too, would be able to find my one true love at some point in time. But with the House of Moirai working to ensure that *never* happens, it dawns on me that it's never been possible in the first place.

All this time, I've been holding out some romantic notions about true mates, thinking that although they are rare, they still happen. I would look at a couple seemingly in love and hope that, perhaps, they'd found their true love.

By the time I can think of another question to ask Balabas, the wraith stops.

"We have arrived."

The door to the first level of the tower opens in front of us and Balabas leads me inside. To my surprise, there is nothing of note inside, only a slew of other doors. Balabas chooses one, seemingly at random, and opens it for me. The wraith doesn't follow me, merely nodding for me to go in.

Once I step through the second door, I find myself in the middle of a corridor. The walls are a stark white, devoid of any decor or artifice.

Not knowing what I'm supposed to do now, I take a tentative step forward.

"Lady Minerva. What brings you here?" Groyo's voice rings out and he flashes himself in front of me. He's wearing the same pearlescent gown as before, his face full of runes that have been etched in his face in two rows on each cheek. His eyes are a very odd, light yellow color.

"Lord Groyo." I clear my throat. "This is a nice room you have here," I add nervously.

He stares at me, his face devoid of any emotion.

"What brings you here?" he repeats.

"I have come to pay my respects and thank you."

"Thank me?" he echoes.

"Your interference in my life has helped me see that I was on a wrong path and I have since mended my ways."

"You are welcome," he replies tersely. "You may leave now."

"Eh?" I blink. He's already turning to leave, so I shout, "Stop."

He half turns, a question knit between his brows.

"This is for you. My gratitude," I muster with a tremulous smile as I extend the tray with the pie I baked for him. It's a recipe I learned in Anthropa, so I have no doubt he will be impressed with it. He's probably never had anything of the sort before.

He glances down at the tray with curiosity, but he does not take it.

"I do not...require such things."

"But it is a gift," I insist.

He brings his gaze to mine, apparently not really comprehending the idea of a gift.

I don't know how old he is or how long he's been in his role, but if he's been taken from his family when he was a mere thousand years old and had his emotions suppressed, it makes sense that he would not know.

But emotion or not, he should still abide by polite etiquette. And that means he cannot refuse my gift.

"I see. Thank you," he mentions after a moment's thought. He doesn't reach forward to grab it from me, merely using his telekinesis to move it to his side.

"You may go now."

"Wait!" I call out again as he makes to leave.

By the Source, but this male cannot wait to get rid of me. And I cannot allow for that to happen if I need to fulfill my mission.

"You must tell me how you like it."

Once more, he frowns, not comprehending my words.

"You are not from the House of Cryos, right?" I wager a

guess. If he is in charge of our House, then with all the House of Moirai checks and balances, chances are he is not.

"I am not. I am from the House of Anemo," he answers slowly, methodically.

"That explains it. In Cryos, it is extremely frowned upon to receive food and not sample it."

He tilts his head to the side, glancing from me to the tray floating by his side. He ponders my words.

"I do not...eat this type of food."

"This type?"

"Cooked food," he mentions in a low voice, though his eyes are on the pie.

"What do you eat?"

"Nutrient powders to keep my energy levels at optimal levels."

"Is it forbidden for you to eat it?"

"No. It is not." He's still looking at the pie, almost longingly —though if he has no emotion, I doubt he is capable of experiencing longing.

"Then you could try it? It's the polite thing to do since I made it specifically for you."

He still hesitates.

"You can have just a bite and if you do not like it, I will not take offense," I add. "Though I am a rather good cook, so it should be delicious." I wink playfully at him.

He barely pays me any attention, his eyes on the pie.

His throat bobs up and down. He *wants* to try it.

"I suppose I could take a bite," he murmurs. Using his telekinesis—which on second thought might be him manipulating air since he's from the House of Anemo—he slices a piece of the pie and without even touching it, he brings it to his mouth and takes a bite.

I watch him with bated breath, waiting to see his reaction.

"This is good. Thank you, Lady Minerva," he mentions as he takes another bite, then another until the slice is finished.

He doesn't reach for another one, but I'll have to hope that the amount he ate will be enough.

Seconds trickle by and as I'm starting to lose hope, his eyes roll back in his head and he wobbles backward.

He opens his mouth to speak, but he cannot do so—not until he is prompted anyway.

I've been breaking rules right and left recently, so if I'm going to sneak into the House of Moirai, I might as well bring my full arsenal with me. Which is why I may have decided to use a forbidden rune I found while rummaging through the Cryos armory. It's an unusual one that has not been used in eons, but it holds extreme power, granting its user complete control over a person for exactly thirty minutes. Of course the catch is twofold: the rune's magic has to be ingested, hence the pie, and it can only be used once by a person.

But now that Groyo is under the influence, I quickly pose my questions.

"Where are my threads of fate located?"

He flinches but cannot stop himself from replying, "The seventh door on the right."

"There are no doors," I mention with narrowed eyes. "Show me!"

He presses his hand against the white right wall and a shimmery light erupts from within before a row of infinite doors materializes in front of me.

"How do I recognize which are mine once I go inside?"

"They will shine the brightest for your eyes only."

I nod. That's quite easy.

"Thank you, Lord Groyo. Now wait here until I return and do not move!"

He obeys me, his body becoming slack.

I count the doors until I reach the seventh and go inside. Using my energy, I manifest a timer to tell me when the thirty minutes are about to elapse.

My mouth opens in shock as I enter the room. There are millions of spider-like threads of an opalescent color. They are all linked and interwoven with each other in a complex tapestry that my brain cannot even begin to comprehend.

They all pulse with light, some stronger than others. And as I walk among them, careful not to touch any that are not my own, I realize that this room also stretches to infinity.

Time is of the essence, and fear grips me that I will not be able to find what I'm looking for before the rune's power runs out.

Taking a deep breath, I stop in the midst of the layers of threads and focus on my surroundings. Summoning my energy to the tips of my finger, I weave a small ice eye on which I carve a transfer rune so I can borrow its sight.

Adding more energy to the eye, I send it flying forward to explore the unknown.

Closing my own eyes, I let the wandering eye see everything for me.

It travels miles per second, taking in the multitude of linked threads with their beautiful colors. But while most of them shimmer with a combination of other colors, none yet shine the brightest.

More distance traveled. More webs explored.

I've never given thought to the infinity of life, of creation, of fate. Yet seeing it all for myself now, I find myself in awe at the sheer magnitude and complexity.

I'm just one small part of it all, an insignificant part in the large scheme of things.

Yet it's that small part that I wish to have control over, that I wish to shape and mold as I want and not let some ancient deities decide for me.

I've already lived four thousand years according to the fate assigned to me, never stepping out of that predetermined mold.

And if I hadn't met Mine, I probably would have never done it either.

I would have rebelled against my betrothal to Theron, of course, but I don't think I would have had either the courage or the determination to run away, to risk becoming a pariah in the only world I've ever known.

That is no longer the case.

I can shun away everything and everyone as long as I have Mine by my side, my best friend, my beloved. And for that, I will willingly exile myself from Aperion so long as I can be free to love him as I long to.

The eye stops. A web of tangled threads shines so brightly, it's almost blinding. Registering the surroundings, I flash myself there, absorbing the energy of the eye within my palms.

Here it is. My fate.

Nine blinding threads of fate, and one of which I must cut.

Wyn might not have said it explicitly, but after some deliberation it is clear she meant my love thread. Since Mine is mortal and our energies signatures differ so much, it is impossible that he might ever be my fated love.

A bitter taste assails me as I think of another male who might have a claim on me. Yet it's also the opposite that worries me. If at some point I stumble upon that male fated for me and the true mating corrupts my feelings to the point that I forget Mine.

Unacceptable.

That can never happen.

There can never be anyone else for me. Now or ever.

I turn my attention to the bright threads and study them intently. Some of them have different colored hues, ranging from pure white to light blue, green, red, pink, orange, purple, yellow, and black. The pure white and black ones I assume to be the life and death ones respectively.

But the others... Which one is the love thread?

THIRTY-SIX

THINK, *Minnie, think.* What else had Wyn said?

Blood will tell.

Does that mean red? Red like blood?

I glance at the reddish thread, but then there's also the pink one and depending on the angle the light hits, the first one becomes more pink and the second one more red.

Fantastic. How in the Source can I tell them apart—if red is even the one I should be cutting.

I should go back and ask Lord Groyo to tell me which one to cut. But as I glance at my timer, I realize I'm rapidly running out of time, and I need to spare at least a minute to make sure Groyo forgets all about our interaction today.

With no other choice but to gamble, I take a deep breath and materialize my ice dagger. The blade hovers between the pink and red threads, which shift from one color to the other almost in a hypnotizing manner.

I conjure up Mine's face and the warmth of his body against mine, and as I glance again at the threads, I see a stronger flicker of red.

I cut.

The snap is soundless. At first, the thread breaks in two. But within moments, those half-threads twist and turn in the air before heading straight to me. I stumble back, accidentally hitting some other threads, but I'm not too quick to react as the shimmery half-threads hit me in the chest simultaneously in the same place, just above my heart.

My breath is knocked out of my body and I fall to my knees, wheezing as I struggle for air.

The pain is sharp and lingering.

I press my palm against my chest and a tingling sensation starts spreading all over my body.

Images flash before my eyes, swift and relentless, but I can't make sense of any of them. There's only a sense of dread developing deep inside my chest. Panic rises within me until I'm a chaotic mess of fear and anxiety.

A deep breath, and it's gone.

I exhale slowly, still reeling from the attack. The thread I'd cut is gone, and so are the other tiny connections tying it to the other threads.

I struggle to get to my feet, but I sway from side to side, barely able to get my bearings together.

Something else shimmers behind me, a foreign thread that I'd bumped into and that now coils around my arm in a suffocating vise.

I look around, but I cannot detect its origin. It's not like the others, clustered together and intertwined with each other.

This one is solitary. A deep blue seeps into my skin as it continues to vine over my shoulder and around my neck.

Suddenly, it tightens, cutting my air flow.

I grip it with both hands in an attempt to wrench it away from me, but it only grows tighter and tighter.

I cough and wheeze as my breath slowly leaves me. With all the energy I can muster, I focus it around the thread, freezing it.

With a small pull, it shatters all around me, falling to the ground in a myriad of icicles that dissolve into dust.

I'm lightheaded. My throat aches from the pressure. But as I note the ticking clock by my side, the sobering realization that I have mere minutes before the rune runs its course springs me into action.

I flash myself back to the hallway.

Lord Groyo is still on the ground, unmoving.

His eyes widen when he sees me.

"You will forget that I went through that door and interfered with the fates. You will only remember that I came to bring you food as gratitude. You ate the food and enjoyed it and then I was on my way. You will not remember that I did anything forbidden."

"Yes," he answers, his eyes blanking.

As the time elapses, he regains mobility of his body and he stands up. He blinks as he looks at me.

"Thank you for the food, Lady Minerva. I enjoyed it."

"I am happy to hear that, Lord Groyo," I add with a smile. "I will be on my way now. Good day."

"Good day to you too."

I turn my back and leave, doing my best to stay calm even though my heart is racing in my chest.

Only once I am safely out of the House of Moirai can I let my guard down and let out a sigh of relief.

I did it.

I cut the thread.

I...

The enormity of what I did hits me with a staggering intensity. Doubts crawl inside my mind as I ask myself if I did the right thing.

I took the words of a stranger as gospel and in my desperation to rid myself of this unwanted fate, I did the unthinkable, the forbidden.

If word gets out about this, I will not only be imprisoned but most definitely sentenced to death.

Did I just gamble away my future? Or did I free myself of the past?

Yet even as these thoughts plague me, the reality is that what is done is done. I cannot undo it.

If I'll be punished for it...then so be it. As long as I can be with Mine for the rest of his days—and beyond—this is a risk I am willing to take.

A while ago, I agonized over a small rule break. Now look at me, disregarding all rules. And though I'm afraid of the consequences, I cannot bring myself to regret my decisions.

Ultimately, they all led me closer to him.

Mentally and physically exhausted, I return to my room at the palace, surprised to see my brother waiting for me.

He's with his back to me, staring out the window, his hands at his back.

"What do you want, Kai? I'm not in the mood to argue."

"I did not come to argue," he states.

"Why did you come then?"

He turns, his eyes meeting mine.

"Are you...all right?"

My brows go up in shock.

"What...do you mean?"

"I've spoken with Father and he seems to favor a union with Cerenios. He thinks you've caught his eyes."

"No," I immediately reply. "That is to say he is mistaken."

"Is he? He seemed quite sure. The Duchess of Sigmore even invited you personally to her banquet."

"I think it's a misunderstanding. What could Cerenios see in me?" I attempt a laugh.

He doesn't share my amusement. His eyes are icy cold as he regards me intently.

"You would do well to stay away from Cerenios, Minerva. Theron is a good enough match for you."

I blink in shock.

"Good enough? What is that supposed to mean?" I blurt out.

"You are misunderstanding me, Minerva." He sighs.

"There is no misunderstanding. What, you think Cerenios is too good for me?" I step closer to him, folding my arms across my chest. "That the only male I'm worthy of is that pompous Theron?"

His lips flatten.

"Theron is safe," he adds cryptically.

"What's that supposed to mean?"

"You should stay away from Cerenios, Minerva," he starts but suddenly stops. "Knowing your nature, telling you to stay away from him will make it even more likely that you'll do the opposite."

"Damn right."

His lips curl in a slight smile.

"Let us leave the rebellion for a moment and not antagonize every word I say. Think you can do that?"

"Depends on what you say."

He curses under his breath.

"Cerenios is dangerous. The way he and Commander Azerius showed interest in you does not sit right with me. If he seeks you out, please try to avoid him, or only see him in a populated area so he cannot do anything."

"By doing anything you mean..."

"I do not know yet. But something is strange and I do not like this sudden interest he has in you."

I happen to know all too well what Cerenios wants, but to see my brother worried about me tells me the matter must be even more dire than I imagined.

"I see. I will take care. I happen to dislike him immensely."

"Good. He is...not all bad but not good either. Despite working under Commander Azerius for so long, I still do not know much about Cerenios. The only other person he interacts with other than the commander is Aethon."

"He was the other general in the room when I spoke with them, no?"

He nods.

"You don't have to worry about Aethon. He is an honorary general who lends his skills in battle when there is need. But he does not like to get involved in politics or conflicts. He keeps to himself."

"Thank you for the warning, Kai," I add softly as I reach his side and press my hand against his arm. "You're a good brother."

His features tighten.

"Not as good as I would like to," he whispers, his voice conflicted.

I open my mouth to assure him that I know he struggles drawing a line between duty and family, but I cannot utter a word because I feel a tight pressure in my heart.

My skin prickles with awareness, and a whoosh of air wafts past my ears.

I blink.

The moment my eyes open again, I am no longer in my room, nor is Kai next to me anymore.

It is dark. It's never this dark in Aperion.

The ground is laden with heavy snow, the temperature in the air in the negatives—far too cold for humans to be out and about, especially in flimsy clothes. Yet that is exactly the case of tens of human males who work on clearing a path of snow, their clothes tattered, their boots almost soleless and full of holes.

I look around. There are barracks on each side of the ground, and in the distance there are security towers littered all around the area.

Light shines from the towers, the only glimmer of light in the otherwise dreary environment.

What is this? Where am I?

Barbed wire surrounds the barracks, a sign this is an entrapment of some kind.

I don't even know what date it is in Anthropa or how long I've been gone. But by the looks of it, the war is far from over.

I pivot, cloaking my presence to the normal eye.

If I was teleported here without notice, there can only be one explanation.

He used my sigil.

"Mine?" I call out. Since he can see the spiritual world, my voice should be for his ears only.

More males move around the courtyard, some taking up shovels to clean the snow while others return to the warmth of the barracks.

"Mine?" I shout again, looking all around me.

So many people. All males. Even more inside the barracks. And they all look the same—haggard, tired, and cold.

Fear that Mine would be experiencing a similar fate grows in my breast, and I run around the area, my only purpose to find him.

As I go around one of the barracks, I finally come face-to-face with him. Or rather, with his blood dripping onto the white snow.

He's wearing only a shirt, one of sleeves folded up his arm to reveal a bleeding wound—my sigil carved in his flesh.

My eyes instantly move up his body, scanning him for other injuries. He's dirtier than I've ever seen him, smudges of coal all over his once white shirt, his collar, and face.

Yet, as he takes me in, his features suddenly light up.

I don't waste a moment as I run toward him. He doesn't waste a moment to open his arms.

And there I am, held tightly in his embrace, feeling him against my body.

He's alive. That's all that matters.

"Ouch," he groans in a low voice. "Easy with my ribs."

"You're hurt?"

"Bruised. It will heal. Now that you're here, nothing else matters." He gives me his signature dashing smile that would usually have me melt on the spot. At this moment, however, I find myself rather put off with him.

"Why wouldn't you call me earlier? What is this? Where are we?"

"Prisoner camp. My plane got shot down," he adds casually.

"What? When?"

"A few months ago."

"A few months ago?" I repeat in disbelief. "What did they do to you? Show me!"

"It wasn't as bad as you'd think. A few beatings here and there," he adds sheepishly.

"A few beatings here and there?" I echo. "Who? Show me who dared to lay a hand on you and I will make them regret it, Mine."

"Easy, easy, Minnie. They're human, remember? You can't hurt humans."

"I'll make an exception," I mumble.

I scan him from head to toe several times over to ensure that he is as I left him. Hear that! Someone dared touch my human? Hurt him?

Unacceptable.

"Why did you not call me until now?" I ask in outrage.

"I didn't want to disturb you."

"You..." I shake my head at him. "How could you even think that?"

"There, there. You're here now, no?" he asks sweetly. "And just in time for the worst of it."

"What do you mean?" I frown.

"There are rumors that the Soviets are heading toward us. They're going to evacuate the camp soon."

"Evacuate where?"

He shrugs.

"I don't plan to be here for that."

"You should have planned to not be here at all. Seriously, Mine, did the plane crash addle your brain?"

"Not the plane crash," he murmurs, burying his nose in my hair. "Your absence. I've become an idiot since you left me, Minnie."

"I can tell," I mumble drily.

His chuckle vibrates against my ear.

"But I'm *your* idiot, no?" he adds in a suave voice, thinking that will diminish my anger.

"Of course you're *my* idiot. Who else would have you?"

"You're so magnanimous, tiny darling. Only you could deign to overlook my glaring faults."

"At least you recognize your good luck," I mumble.

He holds me even tighter in his arms, and I use my powers to shield him from the cold, covering him in a cocoon of warmth.

He sighs happily.

"I gather your powers are back?"

"Obviously," I huff out. "And I am here to cure you of that idiocy. And save you, of course."

"Of course. What would I do without my powerful goddess?"

"Good that you know it. Now we should leave. Come, I'll teleport us to the base."

I pull on his hand, but he remains frozen to the spot.

"We cannot. What will people think when they see me suddenly appear there?"

"That you were smart enough to escape?" I roll my eyes.

"Smart enough?" He raises a brow, the corners of his mouth curling up. "Until a few seconds ago, I was an idiot."

"You're both smart *and* an idiot, all right? And that's all because you seem to lack any type of self-preservation. Which is why I am here."

"I missed you, Minnie," he whispers, his eyes locked on mine.

"You could have missed me less if you called me earlier," I retort.

"I wanted you to have enough time to put your affairs in order. I hope you kicked that fiancé of yours to the curb." Though still playful, his voice has a tense edge to it.

"It isn't in my power to do so," I start, and his body immediately tenses. "But consider him not only kicked to the curb but also thoroughly kicked in his curb," I add proudly.

He blinks.

"Kicked in...his curb?" he repeats.

"Yes! You should have seen his face." I let out an evil laugh.

"Do you mean you kicked his ass?"

"Same thing." I wave my hand. "The ass is curbed."

"It's curved, Minnie, not curbed."

I frown.

"Whatever. I kicked his curved ass. And it felt good."

"I'm happy for you, tiny darling, but I'm not sure how I feel about you saying he has a curved ass. That would imply you looked at it and—"

"What? Never!" I blurt out.

His lips tremble with mirth.

"Right, right."

"Enough conversation about curbs and curves and whatnot. We need to leave."

"Not back to the base, Minnie. I can't afford to suddenly show up there. They will think I may have betrayed them and gotten help to get back. They will ask me exactly what route I took and how I got back and I will not be able to answer."

"Then what do you propose we do?" I narrow my eyes at him.

"We wait until the evacuation—" Right at that moment, a loud alarm blares in the air. "Well, that was rather fortuitous."

German soldiers demand that every prisoner come to the courtyard. The instructions are simple: they will march west and abandon the camp.

"They will call my name since I am a ranked officer. But when the march begins and we find ourselves close to the woods, I will give a signal and we can stealthily move out of the line."

"Why can't we just do it the simple way? That's so complicated, Mine," I cry out.

"I have a reputation to maintain, Minnie. Surely you of all people should understand that."

I grind my teeth in frustration. He does have a point.

"So how will we return back to the base, then?"

"We won't. We will make our way to France where my parents are and I will report to the U.S. officials there."

"Damn it, Mine. You know I can only teleport to places I have been to before."

Unless someone uses my sigil like he did, I can only go to places I have visited before.

"Once we get rid of the Germans, we'll be on our own. Think of it as a road trip."

I purse my lips as I consider his words. I don't know how I feel about this so-called *road trip*.

"It will be just the two of us. No one will know our identities. We can be anyone we want." He pauses, his eyes glinting dangerously. "We can be a married couple, husband and wife. No one will question your reputation."

My eyes widen at his outrageous suggestion.

"What? Your wife? When did you even ask me? You are getting ahead of yourself, Mine. And don't think this will give you liberties with my person," I tell him sternly.

"I would never think of that, Minnie. God forbid I take advantage of you."

"Good on you to know," I say and cross my arms over my chest.

He drops to his knees in front of me on the cold ground, his eyes on mine.

"Will you have me, Minnie? Will you have this idiotic, feeble human who gives you so much trouble?"

My lashes flutter in surprise.

"Wha—"

"Will you have me as your male? I vow to always love and cherish you, to always put you first, above anyone and everyone else."

"Mine, that is—"

"Those two months elapsed, Minnie. Did I not win your heart? Even a little?"

I look away, a blush going up my cheeks.

"You did," I whisper.

"Then be my female. And let me be your male."

I gulp down. Slowly, I sink to my knees and join him on the ground.

Placing my hands against his cold cheeks, I cradle his face in my palms.

"You silly, silly male. I've been yours from the moment you called me Minnie," I murmur, for that had also been the moment I started calling him Mine.

Leaning in, our breaths mingle for a split second before his lips are on mine in a kiss that makes my heart weep: of joy but also of sorrow because my love for him might be infinite, but our time together is not.

Yet even knowing the heartache that is to come, the punishment I'll likely face, I cannot bring myself to part with him again.

Never again.

THIRTY-SEVEN

MINE'S NAME is called and he grabs my hand to go with him.

Sensing a shift in the air, I tell him, "Go ahead. I will be with you after I check something out."

He glances at me but doesn't ask what. Instead, he only says, "Vow you will come back to me."

"I vow it."

With a slow nod, he heads to the crowd forming in the courtyard. I watch his retreating figure just as a mass of energy materializes next to me.

"What in the Source do you think you are doing, Minerva?" Molokai demands in an angry voice.

I should have expected he would follow me since I disappeared from his side. But I was too concerned with Mine's well-being to worry about that.

"I have something to take care of here," I answer.

"With a human? I saw you."

I slowly raise my eyes to meet his. "And what did you see?"

"You were embracing," he spits out in disgust.

I shrug. "Are you going to tell on me?"

He presses his lips together, and there is my answer.

"Someone else will find out."

Knowing how strong Kai's sense of justice is, his reply surprises me in a way I hadn't dared hope before.

"Not if I'm careful. At least not for a period of time."

"You are playing a dangerous game, Minerva. How long has this been going on?"

"Long enough to know his intentions are genuine. As are mine."

He snorts as if he could never fathom such a thing. But I wouldn't expect my brother to understand things of a sentimental nature. He's too frigid for that. Yet the mere fact that he's not forcefully taking me away gives me a modicum of hope.

"You have no idea what will happen to you—"

"On the contrary," I interrupt him. "I do, and I am willing to face the consequences."

He tilts his head to the side, studying me.

"I do not understand you."

"It is not for you to understand, Kai. But I would appreciate it if you did not tell anyone."

His lips are pursed, but he gives me a tight nod that must have cost him a lot given his strict adherence to the rules.

"Do you sense something odd about this place?" I ask and change the subject.

Another thing I'd noticed the moment I got here but couldn't analyze further because my entire focus was on Mine.

Kai frowns. Looking around, his nostrils flare as his eyes shine a dark blue. Suddenly, he flashes himself to the barbed wire fence and traces his hand over its surface.

Then he's back.

"Runes," he states quietly. "Not Aperite."

I nod slowly. I'd suspected as much.

Pressing my palm against the wall of the barrack, I reveal even more such runes.

"This is a prisoner camp, but there are also rumors of extermination camps. Do you think—"

"That these Nazis are using demon magic to harvest the souls?" He completes my thoughts.

I nod.

"It is possible." He sighs. "I will report this back and go around the other camps to investigate. If demons are working together with humans to harvest souls, then—"

"This war and wars in other worlds could be a result of demon interference."

"It would not be regular demons either. Elite Sons of Tenebreis, since only they have the power to make such bargains. But the question remains if they've made their way to Anthropa or if they communicate with humans through other means."

"High-level demons. It's possible."

"Or those high-level demons could be in positions of power to dictate the terms of the war. We've been so focused on opportunistic demons who might come across the carnage and feed on the souls that we did not even look at the people ordering that carnage. That would change everything."

He has a grim expression on his face as all the implications become clear.

"These demons... they might be far more powerful than we gave them credit for."

"Perhaps you should head back and let the commander know," I tell him, hopeful he would get the hint and leave.

"I'm not done discussing this madness you're engaging in."

"And what do you think is left to discuss? I've already made up my mind."

"That is—"

He stops. His entire body freezes as his eyes glaze over. Shimmery particles appear around him, almost like a cloak.

In the blink of an eye, he's gone.

I stare at the place he just vacated in shock, knowing fully well what his sudden departure means. His sigil was used.

And if it's the faerie who did it...oh my, Molokai will be so angry with me!

Why did it have to happen just now when he promised he would keep my secret?

Muttering a string of curses under my breath, I go in search for Mine.

The prisoners are all forming a long line to the gates, ready to depart.

Mine is in the middle, and as I squeeze next to his side and grab his hand, a slow smile curves up his lips.

"You came," he whispers.

"I promised I would."

He squeezes my hand tightly and keeps me flush against his body so I don't touch any of the other prisoners.

We walk slowly until we reach the woods he mentioned, at which point I shield him with my powers and we make our way surreptitiously out of line and away from the marching soldiers.

I tug him toward the cover of the trees, but he keeps glancing back toward the men marching forward.

"Do you want me to help them?" I ask, noting the worry lines etched on his face.

He shakes his head.

"You cannot mess with that many fates."

"For you, I will. If you want me to..."

"No." His answer is clipped. "History must go forward. I've already done too much."

"What do you mean?"

"It doesn't matter," he murmurs, finally following me deeper into the forest. "I suppose I feel bad for those men. With nothing else to do in all these months, we got to know each other and...they're good men."

"I can—"

"No," he states again. "Some will survive. Others won't. It's life."

I accept his reasoning, but I can't help but feel the sadness seeping out of him.

It makes me wonder what truly happened in that camp while I wasn't there for him. But I can do something now. I can ease his suffering...somehow.

We walk for a few hours in a perpendicular direction so we don't meet any other soldiers.

"We'll need to find a place to sleep for the night. It's late and you must be tired," I tell him when I note he's gone too quiet.

He takes a deep breath and looks around.

"We won't find anywhere warm or anywhere that they won't try to kill us on sight."

I snort at him.

"You happen to be traveling with a goddess, in case you haven't noticed. Come."

I look around for a spot that's both hidden by the trees and has even ground. When I find a good one, I nod to myself and kneel down, pressing my open palms against the frozen ground.

Particles of ice meld together and rise forth, slowly knitting themselves into a solid structure in the shape of a small cabin. I fortify the roof and floor with two thick layers and add a second one for the walls so they can conserve heat.

When I'm done, I blow the hair out of my face and turn to Mine.

He's staring at me in shock, or rather, admiration?

"This is..."

"Eternal ice. It will not melt if we make a fire inside. It is also impenetrable in case of an attack. I think this should be a nice place to sleep for the night, no?"

"Nice? Minnie, you're a queen," he says as he swoops me in his arms and lays a loud kiss on my lips.

"Princess," I correct.

"Maybe princess by birth but a damn queen in your own right. This is spectacular."

Pink spots dot my cheeks. Well, if he says so...

Giddiness erupts inside of me as I pull him inside the small ice cabin so I can show him what more I can do. If he thinks this is amazing, he should wait and see my other tricks.

After we go inside, I move one block of the eternal ice over the entrance. It seamlessly blends together with the other walls, giving the impression that the entire cabin is just one big block of ice.

The inside is not too big—I did not have the best space to play with. But this should be enough for us to sleep and move around comfortably.

It's also tall enough for Mine to stand up without slumping his shoulders, and he notices my attention to detail as he walks casually around.

I preen under his silent praise.

"Let's get you warm," I mention and manifest coal from the camp and wood from the forest. They appear laid out in the middle of the cabin and I move them around until they're in the best position. With a snap of my fingers, a fire comes to life, both lighting and heating up the enclosure.

Mine gives me a wide grin before he shrugs off his dirty shirt, which I promptly manifest away. Then he crosses his legs and sits in front of the fire.

Ah, but this is just the beginning! I must show him I can do more.

Focusing on the objects in our hut at the base, I first manifest some clothes for him and my nice dress. But as I think on what else to get him, I realize there's only one thing that would make him truly happy.

To be clean.

Manifesting the tub across such a distance is no small feat, but for him I do it.

The tub fits quite well at the end of the cabin, and while Mine stares in shock at the items that keep appearing in our little space, I transport some ice from outside, dump it in the tub, and melt it.

Since heat is directly opposite to my ice abilities, it takes me almost three times the amount of energy to get the ice melted and turned into nice warm water.

"Minnie," he breathes out in wonder.

Oh, the effort is well worth it as his previous morose expression turns joyful.

He wastes no time in shedding the rest of his clothes and getting inside the tub, releasing a loud sigh of satisfaction as the hot water touches his skin.

I will the rest of his dirty clothes away and remember to grab some soap from the military base. The back and forth of teleporting items is also quite draining, but to see that smile on his face, I'd do it all over again.

Even his nakedness no longer bothers me, though I only got a short glimpse before he dunked himself in the tub.

"I fucking love you, Minnie," he suddenly says. "This is the best gift I've ever gotten."

I smile happily. "Of course. Who knows you better than me?"

He chuckles.

"You'll have new clothes to change into, and—" I pause as I locate one mattress and a thick blanket and teleport it inside the ice cabin, then place it flush against the other end.

"See, now I've thought of everything."

"That you have. You're so strong, tiny darling."

"See? I told you! You're probably falling even more for me now, no?" I bat my lashes at him, for the first time succeeding in doing this odd gesture. "My supernatural charms must be overwhelming your feeble human mind."

"How did you know?" he asks. "I do find myself rather speechless. I didn't know it was your supernatural charms..." His lips curve up.

It takes me a moment to realize he's making fun of me.

"Mine!"

"I'm more in love with you today than ever before. Is that better?" he asks with a wiggle of his brows.

I huff aloud, though the words please me immensely. And to show him how magnanimous I am, I roll my sleeves up my arms and go behind him to wash his hair.

He leans into my touch, sighing as my fingers massage his scalp.

His eyes are closed, and he hums a low melody.

I smile as I lean forward and press a kiss to his forehead.

His eyes snap open, his irises a light green that sparkles with intensity. He suddenly grabs one of my hands and holds me in place.

"How long will you stay in Anthropa this time?" His voice is no longer playful.

"I don't know," I answer truthfully. "I will do my best to stay as long as possible."

He's quiet. Wrenching himself from me, he turns around in the small tub so he's facing me.

"Will you stay with me until my last days?" he asks quietly.

My brows furrow in confusion.

"What do you mean your last days?"

A sad smile touches his lips. "I am still ill, Minnie. Though your blood can heal the immediate manifestations of the disease, it cannot cure me. Now more than ever it is slowly festering inside of me."

"W-what?" I mutter in shock.

"It is the truth. I don't know how much longer I have left."

"Don't say that!" I cry out. "Don't even think it, Mine. I'm warning you."

"It is not up to you, or me, though I am thankful I lasted this long so I could meet you."

"You're not dying! I am not going to allow you to die, Mine. You hear me?"

"I hear you, Minnie," he replies softly. "But if it happens... Will you stay with me for the time I have left?"

"I would never leave you willingly."

"Good." He nods, then resumes his bath as if nothing happened, as if he didn't just stab a dagger through my heart with his words.

He finishes washing and dries himself before putting on the clean clothes.

Though still troubled by the notion of him dying—no, he will *not* die. But the fact that he believes he will... It makes me wonder if he told me everything about his illness. If he omitted some information.

As I ponder how to approach the situation and learn more about his condition—it is the only way I can find a way to help him—I realize this is not the best time to open the discussion again.

He's tired and in pain. Who knows what type of torture he experienced at the hands of those nasty Nazis? In Aperion, enemies are pushed to the brink of death if they are captured. I can only assume humans do the same in times of war.

Closing my eyes, I mentally search some of the venues I've been to in Anthropa and find a high-end hotel with good food. This is technically stealing, but what's one more rule broken?

Mine audibly gasps when he notices an array of fine foods appear in front of him.

"I told you I can do a lot of things," I tell him.

"I can see," he notes drily. "Half of this is dessert."

"Well, you can have the meat, and I'll have the cakes. But first, the appetizer."

He raises a brow at me as I extend my arm and materialize my dagger, making a small incision over my wrist.

"You need to heal."

He doesn't need to be told twice as he pulls my wrist to his mouth and wraps his lips around my flesh. He sucks on the blood until the skin starts to mend, after which he slowly laps at the dwindling incision.

"More?"

He shakes his head. "You're going to turn me into an addict, Minnie."

"So? I don't think I would mind it if you were addicted to me," I add pensively. "You'd never stray."

He blinks. "I'd never stray?" he repeats in shock.

"Yes. You'd be so thoroughly addicted to me you wouldn't be able to function otherwise." As the words are out of my mouth, I realize I would rather like that.

"Minnie, are you blind?"

"What?"

"Are you blind? It's the only explanation as to why you would not see that not only would I *never* stray—truthfully, the implication that I would is offensive—but if you looked well enough at me you'd realize I am already *that* addicted to you and I cannot function without you."

I purse my lips. "You functioned well enough while I was away," I counter. "You think I don't know you were out carousing with your friends while I was gone?"

"W-what? Carousing with my friends?" he sputters.

"Yes. Don't think I don't know that." I place my arms across my chest and glare at him. "You were supposed to be missing me, not having fun with other people."

"And how would you know that?" He raises a brow.

"I spied on you, of course."

"Of course," he repeats drily. "As if that is normal."

"It is *very* normal. You are mine. Of course I have the right to spy on you at any moment. Since you are mine, your time is mine too, as is whatever you do in that time."

"Is that so...?"

"Yes," I state firmly. "You could have missed me more, by the way. I did not see any tears," I accuse, remembering the way he'd smiled with those friends of his while I was suffering because I was away from him.

"You did not see any tears..."

"Why do you keep repeating my words?" I narrow my eyes at him. "Don't think of changing the topic. I want to know how much you missed me."

His lips tremble, and I wonder if he's angry at me.

"What exactly did you see me doing while you were spying on me?"

"Well, for one you were spending time with a male and a female. And don't think I did not see you hug that female and put your hands on her." I point threateningly at him. "The only reason you're still intact is because the other male was clearly her lover."

"By intact you mean..."

"You know what I mean," I add with a harsh stare.

"I don't think I do."

My eyes slowly dip down to his pants.

"That thing. I may not be able to kill humans, but I can certainly maim them."

His brows shoot up. "You would have..." He points to his crotch.

I nod gravely. "I would have," I confirm.

"Damn, Minnie. You're more bloodthirsty than I thought."

"You have no idea what I am capable of, Mine, which is why you've been warned."

"I don't think I needed that warning, but it's duly noted."

"Good."

"And you don't have to worry about those people. They happen to be related to me."

"I assumed so. The male looked rather like you."

"That's because he's my father."

Now it's my turn to gawk at him in shock. "Your father?"

"And the female was my mother."

My lips part open in shock.

"Your...mother...?"

"Indeed. So you see, I was not carousing with them. I was just spending time with my family."

"But they're so young..."

"They had me young." He shrugs.

"But..." I swallow. This changes things. If those were his parents, then he was not doing anything bad, and I can hardly reproach him for hugging his mother. Although with how young and pretty she looked...

It's his mother, Minerva!

"That still does not erase the fact that you did not seem to miss me overly much," I add with a huff.

"I should have shed some tears, no?"

"Correct." I nod.

"And because there were no tears you think I did not miss you enough."

"Correct again."

"Ah, Minnie. Did you not see my heart weep?"

"No, I did not. And don't you Minnie me with that poetry language stuff or whatever."

"Poetry stuff?" He chuckles.

"Hearts do not weep. At least not while they're still inside the body. Now if I were to cut you open and squeeze the blood out of it, maybe then—" I don't get to finish my words before he pulls me into his arms.

His hot breath is on my lips as he stares intently into my eyes.

"Bloodthirsty again," he whispers, dragging his nose over my cheek. "Is that what you want, Minnie? To cut my chest open and see if my heart weeps for you?"

"It's a figure of speech," I point out wryly.

"Perhaps. But what if it wasn't?"

"What are you talking about?"

"You seem to be having some doubts where I am concerned. First you imply that I could ever stray and that I can function just fine in your absence—both of which are false, by the way. Then you say I did not miss you enough because you did not see any tears. Now I am not a male who is prone to emotional displays. I keep my feelings close to my chest. But for you"—he licks the lobe of my ear—"for you I'd make an exception and show you *inside* my chest."

"Mine... I think this talk has gone a little too far and—"

He pushes me from him, and before I can say anything more, he takes off his shirt and places it to the side. He's bare-chested now and I gulp down as my eyes slide over his hard, rippling muscles.

Why does he have to be such a beautiful specimen of a male? It's not fair.

"Your sword. Give it to me," he commands. And though I

could very well deny him, I find I am unable to do so. I am the power, but I am *not* in power.

Almost mechanically, I manifest my blade and place it in his waiting hand.

"If this is what it takes for you to stop doubting me..." He brings the blade to the center of his chest.

"Mine, stop," I finally snap out of my trance. "You're wrong. I don't doubt you."

"Oh, but you do, tiny darling. If you hadn't, you wouldn't have spied on me. You would have simply *known* that I would never stray. But you doubted me. Is that not so?"

I bite my lip and give him a small, barely perceptible nod.

"You doubted me and you *still* doubt me."

"I—"

"No lies."

I take a deep breath.

"I suppose I am used to betrayal. Or perhaps I am far too used to people disappointing me."

"And you thought I would, too."

Another nod.

"Minnie, Minnie," he chides in a low voice. The tip of the blade sinks into his skin.

"Stop! You don't have to prove anything. This will only hurt you."

"Maybe. But you can heal me, can't you?"

"I can, but—"

"No buts." The blade cuts deeper in his skin. He drags it down his sternum until he reaches his belly button. His hand is steady, the cut straight. There is no trace of hesitation. No trace of pain.

"Mine, this is insane," I say and call back the blade to me, manifesting it away.

Blood pools down his stomach. He's already tired and weary. This wound would only make everything worse.

"You need *more* of my blood to heal," I start, but he ignores me.

With his bare hands, he grabs onto the cut he made upon his sternum and pries the flesh apart. He pulls on each side with such force and determination that his muscles and rib cage become visible.

"Mine, this is too much. Please stop."

"No. Not yet. Not until you see my heart *weep*."

THIRTY-EIGHT

THE SHOCK at seeing him cut himself with my blade is slow to fade. I'm staring at him wide-eyed, not knowing what he's going to do next.

I have the power to stop him—to coerce him to stop hurting himself. But even knowing that, I cannot seem to move.

Shame eats at me as I realize that deep down, I want to see his heart weep for me. I want him to show me how deep his love for me runs, no matter how crazy that demonstration might be.

He meets my gaze with his determined one. His fingers plunge deeper inside the incision he made, pulling harder at the skin. It slips off the ribcage with ease, but even more surprising is the way he looks at me unflinchingly.

The pain must be unbearable, especially for a human. Yet he does not back down.

Digging his fingers inside his own chest, he presses hard against the bones until they snap, the sound a loud echo in the small enclosure.

He just...broke his own bones, his own rib cage? For what? To prove what?

Yet more importantly I ask myself: why am I not stopping him?

He bangs against his sternum, each time harder than before until that bone breaks into a myriad pieces that fall onto his lap.

"You..." I whisper. Surely this is too far. Surely I should stop him now.

His breathing is harsh but even. He doesn't look down at the bloody residue of bone falling from his chest or the rivulets of scarlet liquid dripping onto his lap.

He's only looking at me.

His fingers dig deeper and deeper until his entire rib cage has been broken. I may not be an expert in human anatomy, but if it's anything like a god's, then it would take enormous strength to break those bones.

But he did it with such ease. Without flinching. Without a grimace of pain.

He slowly peels away flaps of skin and bone until he reveals the top part of his heart. It thuds against what's left of his ribcage, the sound almost deafening.

"Do you see it, Minnie?" he murmurs as he brings one bloody hand to my cheek. "Do you see how this poor heart of mine beats only for you?"

"What have you done?" I whisper in awe. "How could you even think to do this?" My eyes move from his earnest expression to the painful image of his wide-open chest. It's a complete dichotomy; one I cannot even begin to understand, not as a deity and certainly not from the perspective of a human.

Mortals, defined by their finite lifespans, are driven by a certain self-preservation even more so than deities are. They avoid pain and hurt and any type of injury that might pose a danger to their lives.

So as I look into Mine's eyes, I cannot understand how he is able to do this, go against his very nature to prove something to me.

The more I think about it, the more I realize that not even a deity would have ever willingly done something like that. Though immortal, some injuries can prove fatal even for the strongest of us. No one would risk the danger such a weakened state would pose since an enemy could attack at any moment.

He isn't just enduring immense pain to show me his love and loyalty. He is also leaving himself completely vulnerable and at my mercy. I could strike him down, but he knows I would never. I could refuse to heal him, but he knows I would never.

By trying to assuage my mistrust, he showed me how fully he trusts me. And that realization floors me more than anything in my life.

Tears prick at my eyes as a wave of emotion builds inside of me, threatening to spill over. I've never been the demonstrative type, always keeping my emotions in check because outbursts were frowned upon.

But if Mine can go against his biology and self-preservation to prove something to me, then I can only repay him by shedding my inhibitions and showing him the real me, too.

The tears fall, this time unbidden.

The blade materializes in my hand and bringing it against my throat, I cut a straight line down my chest. The material of my dress falls to the sides to reveal my naked breasts. I dig the blade deeper, emulating Mine's cuts.

He stops me. Pushing my hand away, he leans in and licks the blood trickling down my skin. He makes his way from my navel to the valley of my breasts and up my neck, not letting even one drop go to waste. He cups my breasts as he continues to suck on my flesh even as my wounds heal.

I let out a ragged breath. From the corner of my eye, I see his chest is healing, too. His bones are regenerating while his skin is slowly mending together until the only trace of his madness are the smudges of blood painting his skin red.

Grabbing my blade, he cuts through the remaining material of my dress before roughly pulling it with his hands and throwing it to the side.

I'm almost bare except for a scrap of material covering my privates.

Leaning forward with deliberate slowness, he presses a

torturous kiss to one breast before lavishing the same attention on its twin. His lips trail a path of electric sensation down the valley between my breasts until they reach the curve of my stomach. With delicate care, he places a tender kiss just below my belly button before pressing his cheek against my stomach.

The heat radiating from his body warms me from within as he wraps his hands around my hips and holds me close.

"You have no idea how long I've been dreaming about this," he whispers in a low voice, his breath hot against my skin.

"How long?" I ask, unable to hide the excitement in my voice.

He smiles against me, his lips grazing over my flesh.

"An eternity? Maybe more?"

A shiver runs down my spine at his words, sending sparks of anticipation through my body.

"I want to see more." He raises his head slightly so he can look into my eyes. "Can I?" His fingers trace over the side of my hip, hooking onto the material of my underwear.

My mind is reeling, but I manage to nod in consent.

All the reasons why he shouldn't do this flash in my mind, but with each passing moment, they seem less important than the desire coursing through my veins.

"I suppose it's only fair since I've seen all of you too," I murmur, trying to sound nonchalant despite the fluttering in my stomach.

"And you're all about equality, aren't you?" He raises a playful brow.

I nod again, feeling a surge of confidence and vulnerability all at once.

"Uh-huh."

"Good girl," he praises in a husky voice that makes me blush from head to toe.

With a swift motion, he slices the sides of my underwear with a sharp blade. I gasp in surprise and irritation. "That was the only pair I had," I protest, trying to cover myself.

He clicks his tongue disapprovingly. "I'll buy you as many pairs as you'd like when we get to Paris," he offers nonchalantly.

My fingers thread through his unruly hair as I try to process his words. "Paris? Is that where we're going?" I ask, intrigued.

He nods, a proud smile on his face. "My parents live in France, and I have a beautiful house just outside of Paris. Remember when I said I would take you to my sanctuary someday?"

A feeling of anticipation builds in my chest. "Is that where your sanctuary is?" I inquire, unable to hide my curiosity.

He grins mischievously. "Yes, and I can't wait to see your reaction when we arrive."

"Why? What's so special about it?" I press.

"Let's just say that I built it with my future wife in mind," he explains, his gaze lingering on me.

I raise an eyebrow in response. "Future wife? You're getting ahead of yourself."

He chuckles and gazes at me with affection. "I have no doubt that you will become my wife, my female, my everything..."

"I might be persuaded..." I tease, though a smile tugs at the corners of my lips.

"Then let me start persuading you," he says with determination.

With a swift, fluid motion, he tosses aside the flimsy scraps of fabric, exposing every inch of my bare skin to his intense gaze.

It suddenly hits me like a wave crashing against the shore.

I am completely and utterly naked.

In front of a man.

But instead of feeling vulnerable or embarrassed, I find myself unable to look away as he hungrily takes in my body.

My arms fall back behind me as I lean on my elbows, my legs parted slightly to give him an unobstructed view. He looms over me, his touch no longer present but his eyes blazing with desire.

His piercing blue gaze meets mine for a moment before

slowly trailing down my neck and over my breasts. My stomach tightens at the raw intensity in his gaze. Slowly, it travels lower, skimming over my curves until it reaches the apex of my thighs.

A low hum builds inside of me, and I fight the urge to squirm under his unwavering stare. But I remain still, unable to tear my eyes away from him.

He swallows audibly, his Adam's apple bobbing up and down as his focus becomes fixated on that intimate place between my legs. A surge of moisture floods through me, pooling between my thighs and trickling down my inner leg.

I gasp in shock at the sudden sensation.

"Mine, I..." I start, about to find an excuse for it.

"Shh," he murmurs, pressing a finger to my lips. I hold my breath as his hand hovers over my most intimate area. "May I?"

I give a sharp nod, my eyes on his.

His touch is both hesitant and reverent as he traces the seam of my sex with one finger. A shudder runs through my entire body, reacting to the contrasting sensations of heat and cold.

"So beautiful. Your pussy is just like the rest of you. Perfection."

"P-pussy?" I repeat, the word unfamiliar.

"This pretty little thing that's mine and only mine—that will ever be mine," he rasps.

"Yes," I agree, my voice throatier than ever before. "Only yours."

He's raptly staring between my legs, intently studying that secret place that's now weeping for him.

"Have you ever touched yourself here?" he asks, his voice low and husky.

I shake my head, feeling embarrassed at the question. "Only when I...wash myself," I admit in a whisper.

He smiles knowingly, a mischievous glint in his eyes. "I bet even then you aren't as wet," he says as he coats his finger with my moisture.

My cheeks flush with heat as he continues to explore, his movements firm yet gentle. "You're so damn wet," he remarks, his voice filled with both surprise and satisfaction. "Soaking my entire hand."

But just when I think things couldn't get any more scandalous, he shocks me further by lifting his finger to his lips and sucking it into his mouth. My jaw drops open in disbelief. Did he just...

His eyes snap closed as he releases a low moan, savoring every drop of moisture from his finger with such indulgence that his chest vibrates with pleasure.

My breath catches in my throat, completely scandalized by his bold actions. "W-what?" I stammer, my words barely audible.

But instead of answering, he gives me a devilish grin and leans in closer, his eyes sparkling with mischief. My heart pounds in my chest as his hand slides between my thighs, teasingly tracing the outline of my folds.

"I knew you'd be delicious, tiny darling," he murmurs, his hot breath tickling my ear. "But I never realized it would be this good." He swipes his finger between my folds again, bringing that wetness to his mouth. "Fuck..." His voice is low and husky as he smacks his lips together, savoring the taste of me.

A flush rises to my cheeks as I watch him with a mix of shock and desire. The memory of his own taste, sweet and intoxicating, reminds me that this is not entirely out of the ordinary. Perhaps it's because we love each other and find each other irresistibly attractive that naturally we are drawn to one another's flavors. It's just biology, right?

But as he continues to touch me, his fingers dancing lightly over my skin, I find myself squirming and yearning for more. His touch ignites a fire within me, a burning need that intensifies with each passing second.

"Stay still," he commands suddenly, and before I know it, my body obeys him without question. "I'll give you everything you want, tiny darling. And everything you never knew you needed."

My heart races at the promise in his words, and an urgent

electricity courses through me. Despite staying perfectly still on the outside, my insides are pulsing with anticipation for what he has in store for me.

"You've never had an orgasm, have you?" His tone is both teasing and knowing.

"An orgasm?" I echo, my frown deepening. "What do you mean?"

"Pleasure," he murmurs, his finger tapping against a small spot between my legs. I gasp in surprise, unsure of how to react.

He continues, his voice low and seductive, "If I touch you here, do you feel pleasure?"

My body betrays me, instinctively arching toward his touch. "I...I don't know," I admit, biting my lip.

"That's because you've never experienced it before." His lips curl into a wicked grin. "But don't worry, this is just the beginning."

Without warning, his hand is between my legs again and he resumes his ministrations. Every touch feels like fire on my skin, driving me mad with desire. He circles around that sensitive spot for what feels like an eternity before moving lower and coating his fingers in my wetness.

I can barely think straight anymore as he expertly manipulates me, sending jolts of pleasure through my body. But just as I feel myself getting lost in the sensations, a fleeting thought crosses my mind—one that reminds me that this is all new to me and begs the question: what exactly am I getting myself into?

"H-how do you know that?" I blurt out. "How do you know where to touch me?" The venom in my voice is evident. Perhaps I should just shut up and let him continue to do his thing since he already does it so well. But I cannot stop my brain from wondering how he knows this and where he learned it.

He tilts his head to the side, his gaze heavy with desire as he watches me. His expression is languid, but there's a fiery intensity in his eyes that sends shivers down my spine.

"I prepared. For you," he says in a deep, seductive tone.

My heart races at his words, anticipation building within me.

"And how exactly did you prepare?" I ask, breathless.

"I read a lot," he murmurs, sliding his hands under my naked buttocks and lifting my hips closer to his face. My skin tingles at his touch, and I can feel myself growing wet with need.

He presses his face against my sex, inhaling my scent deeply. "I read all the ways I could pleasure you. With my fingers, with my tongue..." And to prove his words, he leans forward and swipes his tongue over my sensitive flesh.

The sensation is so unexpected, so overwhelming that I let out a loud cry of pleasure.

He chuckles, the warm breath from his mouth causing me to shiver with delight.

"But that was just the theoretical side. Let's see how I do in practice."

With that, he wraps his lips around my pleasure bud, sucking it into his mouth. The combination of pressure and suction sends waves of pleasure through me, rendering me completely lost in the moment. My mind goes blank as I give in to the intense sensations brought on by his touch.

"Exquisite," he purrs against me. "You taste so damn good, I could spend an eternity feasting on you."

I gasp and dig my heels into the ground as I grab onto his hair, pulling hard. Yes, an eternity sounds rather good so long as he keeps doing that to me.

He doesn't seem to mind when I tug too hard onto his hair. In fact, my reaction only spurs him further as he swirls his tongue around my bud before sucking on it again, this time putting more pressure on it.

His fingers dig in the flesh of my buttocks as he holds on to me tightly.

Using his teeth, he nibbles on my bud, scraping it lightly at first before biting so hard on it I jump up and release a high-pitched scream.

His chuckle reverberates against me as he slowly licks me again to make up for that brief moment of pain. Yet as much as it surprised me when it happened, the bite of pain only served to intensify the pleasure as he teases me with his tongue.

But just as some type of pressure builds inside of me, he stops. He gazes up at me, a mischievous smile on his face.

"How am I doing so far?" He has the gall to ask me when I'm so close to the precipice I can almost feel it. I may not logically recognize this feeling I'm seeking, but on a primal level my body seems to know.

And it wants more.

"Don't you dare stop!" I cry out and tighten my hold on his hair.

He rewards me with a small bite against my inner thigh before slowly—far too slow for my liking—going back up between my legs.

"May I take your blood?" he murmurs, his mouth so close to where I want him.

"Yes, yes. Just..." Do something!

He waits a second before he swipes the flat of his tongue all over my sex, from the bottom up. As he reaches my pubic bone, he stops. His teeth scrape the sensitive skin at the top of my sex before moving slightly lower right atop my bud.

Sharp teeth penetrate my flesh. The sensation is unlike any other. Both pain and pleasure shoot through me in competing waves, and as blood drips out of the puncture wounds and into his waiting mouth, a strange euphoria claims my limbs.

I'm barely aware as my arms become slack by my side, my chest rising and falling as I labor to breathe.

He drinks deeply, and as the wounds heal, his attention returns to my bud, now drenched in a mix of blood, moisture, and his saliva.

Oddly enough, the thought of it makes me even wetter, but I suppose I'll have time to question that later.

Still holding on to me, he moves one hand to my hip. His other hand joins his mouth between my legs as he trails his fingers through my wetness while his tongue continues to lap at me.

Then suddenly, one finger is there. At my entrance. He circles it around the small hole before pushing it slightly inside.

It's a tight fit as he barely squeezes it halfway in. But the feel of him inside me sends a wave of shock through me.

I let out a small moan, followed by some incoherent sounds that might have been something along the lines of, "harder."

"You're so tight, tiny darling. So damn tight..." he groans. "I can't wait to fuck you properly, to feel you strangle my cock."

Any other time, his words would have scandalized me. Now they just whet my desire even more.

At first, he slowly thrusts his finger inside and withdraws it, and it dawns on me that he's simulating the act of mating.

The faster he moves, the easier it is for his finger to slip in and out of me.

The friction is delicious, and combined with that wicked mouth of his...

By the Source! Now I know why females aren't allowed to be alone with males. If they knew about this, there would not be a chaste deity in Aperion!

If just one finger of his can drive me so crazy, I cannot imagine how it will be when he uses his other thing on me, that much, much bigger thing.

Oh my! He will truly break me. But the prospect of it only makes me giddier and strangely...wetter.

"Fuck, Minnie. You're doing so well, tiny darling."

"Something is happening," I say in between moans. "There is something. I don't..." I grab onto his hair again and press his face closer to me, needing more pressure.

"Use me. Use my mouth to get what you need."

Hooking my legs over his shoulders, I undulate my hips up and down, then side to side, creating a rhythm to the way his mouth touches that pleasure spot.

He flicks his tongue in and out, keeping up with my speed.

And as the pressure builds and builds, I can only go faster, cling to him harder.

My back suddenly arches and my muscles become stiff as a loud sound slips past my lips.

My eyes are wide open, my head thrown back. Everything is so much clearer around me. I can feel and hear every little pulsation in the environment.

But that spot. Right where he's now kissing me. It's pulsing with heat and something else, something that...

I writhe again as another wave crashes into me, this time ten times stronger, so much so that an icy wind sweeps through the small enclosure, freezing everything around us.

I cannot move or control my abilities as I watch ice covering every single thing around.

My body is hot, but all around me it's icy cold.

Seconds after, or perhaps an eternity, I finally manage to regulate my breathing.

So that was what he meant by pleasure. And here I thought kissing was the best thing ever, followed closely by chocolate donuts. But this? No donut can trump this.

Perhaps instead of daily donuts, I should ask him to give me one of these orgasms. Yes, that sounds perfect.

I sigh happily as I stretch my arms, feeling more invigorated than ever.

My energy points are all wide open, allowing all my spiritual energy to flow with more ease than ever before. Raw power travels through my veins, and for the first time in my life, I feel rather...invincible.

"That was..." I can't even express into words what that did to me, both as a female and as a goddess. It's almost as if I've been asleep all my life until now, and that pleasure he gave me opened a secret door inside of me, letting out some type of mystical power.

"I think you passed your practical exam with floating colors, Mine. I only have one question. When can we do this again?"

Please say now, I think to myself.

I don't even know if it's possible to experience that again so soon, but I'm willing to try. The build-up to the explosion itself was quite yummy too, and since he also finds me yummy, well, isn't that a win-win?

I frown. Why is he not answering me?

I gaze down at him.

Damn it! I can only see a thick sheet of ice.

"Mine?" I cry out, pulling him from between my legs.

Oh no! He's frozen, too.

THIRTY-NINE

I FEEL the surge of energy coursing through my fingertips as I press them to his frozen face. The chill of his skin slowly gives way to a warm, rosy hue as life returns to his features.

He blinks and drops of moisture fall from his lashes, remnants of the ice that had once encased him.

"Are you all right?" I ask, my voice shaking with anxiety.

He tries to speak, but the chattering of his teeth muffles his words.

"Oh, what have I done," I whisper, my heart racing in panic.

Forcing myself into action, I help him to his feet and guide him to the tub at the end of the ice chamber. A quick glance behind me reveals that even the fire has been extinguished, so I hurry to rekindle it while carefully lowering him into the tub.

Summoning every ounce of my strength, I focus on the ice around him, willing it to melt. The temperature of the water rises with a powerful surge of energy.

"My powers haven't been this uncontrollable since I was just learning to use them," I admit through gritted teeth as sweat beads form on my forehead.

Slowly, his body begins to regain its healthy glow as he lowers himself into the tub. The hot water envelops him, warming every inch of his once-frozen skin.

"Don't blame yourself, Minnie," he says with a reassuring smile. "It was rather...hot."

"No, it was freezing. I froze you!" I exclaim, more guilt washing over me.

He resurfaces from under the water, droplets cascading off his slick hair. Leaning forward with a mischievous glint in his eyes, he rests his arms on the edge of the tub. Despite nearly succumbing to hypothermia just moments ago, he appears lively and playful.

"I must say, though," he teases, "before I became a human popsicle, I got to see you climax and that alone is worth everything." His smirk widens.

"Did you like it?" he asks knowingly.

"Of course I did," I reply breathlessly. "But I almost killed you!"

He shrugs nonchalantly. "Nah. I'm stronger than you think."

With a flick of his hand, droplets of water land on my chest. Steam rises in the air as the hot water makes contact with my icy skin. A disappointed sigh escapes me as I realize just how close I was to seriously harming him.

"No, no." I shake my head. "We can't risk this again. I did not realize that my powers would be out of control if I...if I..." I blush.

"If you orgasm?" He raises a brow.

I nod and avert my gaze.

"And here I was going to ask you to give me one daily," I grumble under my breath. "I guess I'll settle for donuts instead."

His fingers, now much warmer, are on my chin, turning it so he can see my eyes.

"Am I to understand you liked it better than donuts?"

"Are you kidding me? It's ten thousand times better. I've never felt so alive, so powerful, so..." I trail off as I realize my words are too enthusiastic when I should be the opposite now that I know the consequences of this.

"So what? Tell me," he insists, still keeping his hold on my jaw.

"Invincible," I whisper.

He stares at me, his expression inscrutable.

"I made you feel invincible," he murmurs proudly.

I nod.

He smiles and shakes his head. Scrubbing his hand over his face, he suddenly lets out a laugh.

"Thank God! I was so worried you wouldn't like it, that I wouldn't do a good job at it..."

"If you had done a better job, you would be dead, Mine," I point out matter-of-factly.

He chuckles.

"Dead but in heaven."

"It's not the time to joke about this. It's serious! I could have killed you."

He surprises me by grabbing me by my waist and pulling me into the tub on top of him.

"Maybe, maybe not. But it was just your first time. I have no doubt you will learn to control your powers if we practice more."

The mere notion that we might do it again has me squeezing my thighs together as moisture seeps out of me.

By the Source, he's ruined me! I will never be able to think of anything sexual again without remembering what he did to me with his mouth and how that made me feel. Am I bound to get wet every time he smiles at me for the rest of my life? With no relief in sight?

"We will not," I feel compelled to add, though my voice lacks conviction.

"Is that so?" he asks playfully as he sneaks his hand between my legs and finds out just how soaked I am.

"Uh-huh," I croak as his fingers part my folds and he teases that bud again.

"You don't seem too sure."

"You have a death wish," I counter, pushing my hips toward his palm.

"I can't think of a better way to die than between your thighs."

Heat travels up my cheeks.

"Stop it," I whisper.

He trails his lips over my own as he continues to languidly touch me.

"Let me prove you wrong," he murmurs before he kisses me.

But this kiss is unlike any other. His tongue plunges deep in my mouth just as he thrusts his finger inside me.

I gasp and he swallows all my sounds, sucking my tongue in his mouth as he continues to pump his finger in and out of me.

The flat of his palm is against that pleasure bud, and the delicious friction is starting to make me tingle again.

This time it's faster than before. Almost as soon as he increases his speed, the pressure inside me mounts.

For a moment, I try to contain my power since I know that release is coming. But as he claims my mouth again, all thoughts fly away from me.

He holds my nape with one hand, kissing me deeply, and he ravages my sex with the other.

Without warning, that wave of pleasure crashes over me. My energy points snap open again, and a flood of raw power travels through my veins.

I gasp into his mouth.

My eyes snap open and I remember in time to push him away from me.

I'm frozen in place, my back against the icy wall of the house as the tremors wrack my body. Pleasure and power both pulse through me, and a wave of ice bursts out of my body.

By the time I can breathe again, I blink and realize Mine is fine.

This time, he's not frozen, though everything around us is. The fire I'd started is gone. Everything is covered in another layer of ice.

Everything but Mine and the water we're in.

Mine's gaze is heavy and hooded as he looks at me. He palms himself through his pants, squeezing the outline of that big, big thing.

"Do you..." I clear my throat. "Do you need help?"

He smiles sheepishly at me.

"Too late. You came so hard, Minnie, I came in my pants just from watching you."

"Oh," I whisper.

I remember him mentioning that males can do that if they find a female attractive.

"That is very nice of you," I add. How could I have ever found a better male? His touch not only brings me pleasure, but it also makes me stronger. And he's so attracted to me he can spill his seed without any stimulation.

"Nice..." He chuckles. "Only you would call it nice."

"How else would I call it?" I frown.

"Never mind. Let's get cleaned up and start up that fire again." He yawns. "We need to get some rest before we start our journey."

I nod.

After a quick, refreshing wash, we slip into clean clothes. I then replace the ruined mattress and pillows with fresh ones.

But as I start to conjure a new fire, I am hit with the realization that something has changed within me. It usually takes great effort for me to manipulate heat or create any kind of fire—actions that are completely opposite to my natural abilities. With my normal energy reserves, I would only be able to do so a few times before feeling completely drained.

Yet as the flames dance to life, burning hotter than ever before, I feel only a small dip in my energy levels. It is almost as though my powers have strengthened, evolved even. The fire crackles and flickers, casting a warm glow over our surroundings. And for the first time in a long while, I feel a novel sense of control and strength coursing through me.

That's... interesting. I must investigate this more. Do deities experience some type of energy charge when they engage in sexual activities? Is it only females or do males experience this too? Is this something that happens across the board regardless of the level of the deity or only for those who have attained a certain level?

"Come here." Mine beckons, pulling back the warm blanket to make room for me. I slip in beside him, his warmth radiating against my body.

"Since a little ice won't kill me, I'll gladly do my duty and worship my little goddess every single day," he murmurs, his voice low and intimate.

My heart flutters at his words, hope and excitement bubbling up inside of me. "You will?"

"And I'll even treat you to some donuts," he adds with a playful smile.

"Both?" I ask in disbelief.

"Both," he confirms with a nod, delight shining in his eyes.

"You spoil me too much," I tease, though I'm secretly reveling in his attention.

"What about you? Don't you want..." I trail off, hinting that he might want me to reciprocate. I'd gladly do it, but we might need to take it slower. While he's had plenty of material to read, the only knowledge I have is, well...what I know from him and what occurred between us.

Mine shakes his head without hesitation. "All I want is you," he declares, his tone suddenly becoming serious and intense. "Marry me, Minnie. Say you will marry me."

"That again." I sigh. "What do you mean by it? I know what marriage means in my world, but what does it mean in yours?"

"A vow. A promise. A celebration." He pauses. "We don't have many traditions, but I would love to vow my love to you in front of my parents and get their blessing for our union."

I turn sharply.

"Your parents?" I ask, half panicked. "But what if they don't like me? What if they don't give their blessings? What if—"

"Shhh," he says as he presses a finger against my lips. "They already adore you."

I blink. "But—"

"They know all about you and how much you mean to me and they can't wait to meet you."

Biting my lip, I nod along, though I can't help but be nervous about meeting his parents.

He gathers me in his arms, kissing my temple and murmuring how much he loves me.

And that's how we fall asleep.

But it's not how we wake up.

"W-what?" I groggily open my eyes, my mind still foggy from sleep. But Mine is already on his feet, his expression tight and focused.

"We're under attack," he says gravely.

That's when I hear it. The unmistakable sound of gunfire hitting the outside wall in rapid succession. My heart races as I realize the gravity of our situation.

"The ice won't break. It's indestructible."

"Might be, but that will only pique their interest. They won't leave us alone until they find out what this is," Mine replies, his tone resolute but tinged with worry.

"Damn it," I curse under my breath. "And I can't hurt humans."

"You can't. But I can."

Mine's words hang heavy in the air. It takes me a few moments to shake away the sleepiness and understand what he wants to do.

"What?" I jump to my feet. "Are you insane?" I demand, panic rising in my chest.

But then, a loud boom shakes the ice structure, startling me even further.

"They have guns. And bombs," Mine's voice remains calm but urgent.

"You have nothing!"

"So get me something," he counters matter-of-factly.

My lashes flutter in surprise. In fact, not only is he too calm about this entire situation, but it's almost as if he's...excited about it.

"Teleport some weapons from the base and I'll use those."

"But—"

"Trust me, Minnie. I can take care of them."

More shots echo outside, accompanied by loud explosions. The hostilities are getting worse by the second.

Taking a deep breath, I close my eyes and mentally go back to the base, looking around for any weapons. Inside out little shed, I find a couple of pistols and a larger weapon. I teleport all of them back to us.

"This is perfect," Mine says with a nod as he inspects the guns. "Can you tell me how many people are outside?"

I press my lips together. How much can I help him before I am considered directly responsible for what befalls those humans?

Alas, before I can contemplate the intricacies of Aperite laws, I flash myself outside. As I wander around, invisible to all but those with a strong spiritual energy, I take note of the surrounding situation.

Ten soldiers stand next to the towering ice structure, their weapons at the ready. In the distance, a tank and five more soldiers can be seen, while three tanks and five cars line the main road.

Returning to the ice room where Mine awaits, I relay what I observed. He nods solemnly, his expression grim.

"They're most likely here as part of the evacuation," he explains.

My brow furrows in confusion.

"Shouldn't they move on then?" I inquire.

"Not if they suspect this may be of interest to their leader," Mine replies darkly. "Hitler is known to have a fascination with the occult."

"Occult?"

"Things outside of the realm of possibility. And what would be more impossible than a house of ice that is impenetrable?"

"That makes sense. So you don't think they will leave us alone."

"No. They will not."

I let out a heavy sigh. "It's a lot of people. And they have tanks."

He shrugs. "I can handle them."

"You're one person."

"Still don't have enough faith in me?"

"I do, but I'm also a realist and—"

He shuts me up with a kiss.

"I'll be fine. Wait for me here, all right?"

"No dying. Promise me."

"Promise." He gives me a lopsided smile.

"And if you need help, I'll teleport you back to safety here."

"All right." He winks at me, his tone dripping with confidence.

"We can still just teleport back to the base and—"

"Trust me," he repeats.

"Fine. Go kick some Nazi butt."

"It will be my pleasure."

He swiftly reaches for his weapons, the gleam of metal reflecting in his intense gaze as he gives me one final kiss. "Teleport me out," he commands, urgency lacing his voice. "And wait for me inside."

I comply with the first request, but the second... I may not be able to physically intervene, but that doesn't mean I won't keep a watchful eye on my male.

As soon as Mine leaves, I transport myself to the top of the ice structure and sculpt a comfortable chair out of ice.

Settling into my icy throne, I also pilfer some more dessert from that fancy restaurant. Unfortunately, today they don't have any donuts, so I have to make do with some oddly shaped pastries drizzled with a bit of chocolate. Sighing in disappointment, I take a bite and savor its sweetness nonetheless.

Good enough, I suppose.

I settle back and watch the ensuing action, ready to intervene and save Mine should he need it. I might not be able to harm those nasty humans, but I can save my human.

The moment the soldiers notice Mine striding toward them, they direct their weapons toward him. A barrage of bullets ensues.

I tense as I wait to see what Mine does.

He easily moves through the curtain of bullets, his fluidity and speed baffling the soldiers.

It baffles me too.

It's not the first time I've witnessed his fighting skills, and for a human, he is certainly impressive.

But is that enough in this instance?

He spots the nearest man and heads toward him, all the while moving around the bullets with unnatural speed and precision.

I take a bite of the pastry. The chocolate is nice, but something is lacking.

As I chew, I note he's shot the man in the face, right between his eyes.

A kill shot.

I smack my lips together, enjoying the sweetness of the pastry. For someone whose job is to pilot a plane, he's certainly got a good aim. And good fighting skills.

He reaches the dead man and grabs the body before it hits the ground, positioning it in front of him and using it as a shield.

And good strategy!

Ah, but how can someone be so perfect?

I sigh dreamily as I take another bite of my pastry.

More bullets rain down on him, but they hit the dead man instead. Mine moves to the side—surprisingly at the same speed, considering he's dragging another body with him. He goes for another soldier and repeats the process.

Shielding himself, he lets the corpse take the bulk of the

bullets while he positions his gun through the crook of the man's shoulder and takes aim.

Another soldier falls.

With impressive swiftness, he drops the first body and grabs the second.

I can see his plan now, and to be perfectly honest, I'm surprised it works.

Those soldiers must be idiots because they can't get one proper shot at him. Not that I want them to, but it would make the fight a little bit more exciting.

As it stands, I'm watching a one-man show.

Why did I have qualms about him before? I should have never worried. Mine is far, far superior to all those men combined.

In fact, by the way he dances around the snow, switching one body for another, I'd say he's having fun with this.

His new clothes are covered in blood, and there are splatters of red all across his face as well.

He's dirty, but he's smiling. That's enough for me to know he's enjoying this far too much. Otherwise, he wouldn't have drawn this out. He would have killed them and demanded another shower and a change of clothes.

I smile fondly and shake my head. Oh, he will certainly demand a shower after he's done. And like the supportive lover that I am, I will get him one.

Minutes pass by and more soldiers drop to the ground.

I'm almost finished with my pastry when one crucial thought flashes inside my mind.

Where. Are. The. Souls?

I should have seen them exit the dead bodies, yet as I scan the ground littered with corpses, there is nothing.

Nothing.

Mine shoots the last of the ten men before dropping the body shield to the ground and turning to look at me. He has a bright smile on his face as he waves excitedly at me.

But I'm not looking at him. My eyes are focused on the man he just executed.

He's lying in a pool of blood, a hole between his eyes. I focus on his body and listen to the sound of his heart.

Nothing.

He is dead. But his soul is nowhere in sight.

And that can only mean one thing...

Demon.

I flash myself by Mine's side.

"The others are coming. They must have heard the shots," he says, his voice edged with anticipation.

"We must leave. Now. There's a demon somewhere here."

His brows go up.

"Demon?"

I nod. "The souls are gone. He must be a high level too if he consumed them so easily."

"But—"

Marching footsteps echo in my ear. They are getting close. It seems that the woods are not hospitable enough for them to bring their tanks or other vehicles. But that doesn't help our situation.

If there is a high-level demon there... I will have to fight him. And though I am confident in my abilities, such a confrontation would draw the attention of any nearby deity and that is the last thing I need right now.

"Let's go. I can carry you," I tell him and turn with my back to him so he can mount me.

Even without teleportation, my speed should help us get far enough away from them and avoid a direct confrontation.

"You want me to..." he croaks.

"Yes. Hurry!"

He blinks, his lips trembling. Is he cold? It is quite cold and he is only wearing a shirt. Even more reason why we must leave now.

With a wave of my hand, the eternal ice dissolves. Nothing

remains of the ice hut except for the tub, which I promptly send back to our shed at the base.

"Hurry!" I repeat, pointing to my back.

He shakes his head, his mouth curved in a smile.

Why is he smiling? Can't he see the danger?

I roll my eyes at him but just as I'm about to berate him, he moves.

He places his arms around my neck and hauls himself on my back, his legs on either side of my waist. I grab onto the back of his knees to support him.

"Hold on. This is about to get fast."

"Sure thing, tiny darling. Show me what you can do," he purrs in a low, velvety voice.

I huff at him. He might not realize it, but with my enhanced strength, I could carry him with one arm only, too.

"Right," I mutter drily. "Don't say I didn't warn you."

The soldiers are behind us, only a small distance away.

Holding on tightly to him, I start running.

I hope he's not concerned about his male pride and sensibilities. It is his fault, after all, for falling for a goddess much stronger than him. And it is he who wants to marry me and make it official. Not that I'm not a willing participant. I am rather enthusiastic about it too.

Though he seems to find this situation amusing, it is good he is at least cooperating.

"Oh wow," he breathes out when he realizes how fast I can run.

I breeze through the trees, logging in a mile per minute at first before getting to my maximum of ten times that.

"This is amazing," he adds in awe. "You are amazing."

He tightens his hold on me and leans back, closing his eyes and enjoying the way the breeze brushes against his face. I use some energy to wrap him in a warm cocoon so he won't get cold in this weather.

"You weren't kidding when you said you were fast."

To my surprise, there isn't anything remotely insidious

about his statement and it makes me gain a new appreciation for him. I don't think any other male would have so willingly jumped on a female's back and allowed her to save him.

In Aperion, a male would rather face death than suffer such ignominy.

I glance at Mine's carefree expression and exuberant smile, and I find myself sharing his sentiments, too.

This is amazing. He is more amazing than I ever dared to imagine my mate would be.

Because that's what he is, whether the fates will it or not.

My mate.

"Oh, fuck," he mutters when we come to a halt. He jumps off me, grimacing as he looks around.

It's dark out, the air frigid and cold for the mere mortals walking the streets at this hour. A church looms ahead, its dome tall and proud as it scrapes the skies. All around it, there are other majestic buildings displaying stunning architectural opulence.

A long bridge extends over the river, dots of light making it seem almost ethereal in the way it connects one part of the city to another.

I may not have intentionally decided on this location, but now that we're here, I am not mad.

Mine does not seem to share the sentiment.

"What's wrong?" I frown.

"We went too far and in the wrong direction."

"I don't understand."

He points to the imposing church in front of us. "That's the Frauenkirche. And that"—he nods to the building next to it—"is the Semper Opera House."

I still don't understand why he is so concerned about that.

Turning to me, he presses his lips in a tight line. "We're in Dresden."

"And that's bad because?" I raise a brow. "We can just take the train to France as you said."

This city is comparable to London in its beauty—well,

before the bombing. But it's clearly a cultural center, so I am sure it is also a hub of transport. If anything, we probably ended up in the *right* place.

"Not so easy, I'm afraid." He takes a deep breath just as the wail of sirens rip through the air. The piercing sound shatters my optimism since I know fully well what it means. I have experienced it before.

"This city is about to be bombed."

FORTY

THE LOUD SOUND of a plane flying close overhead resounds in the air.

"Hop back on. We have to leave," I tell him.

I've experienced enough bombing in London to know how dire the situation will get. This area will be teeming with lost souls, demons who seek to prey on them, and messengers trying to get them to cross over.

And where there are demons, there will also be Aperite warriors hunting them down. The last thing I need is for someone to recognize me and later comment on my whereabouts.

"Mine?" I repeat, but he's not listening to me. He's not even looking at me. His gaze is focused on the skies as more planes abound. The air becomes a cacophony of engine noise and loud booms rippling all around.

The city is not about to be bombed; it is currently being bombed. And we need to leave as soon as possible.

"Mine!" I call out to him again. "We must leave before—" A bomb dropping over the church, mere feet away from us, cuts me off.

I grab him by his sleeve and pull him behind me while I summon a shield around us.

A loud explosion lights up the sky as the walls of that beautiful construction crumble to the ground. Dust and debris flies toward us. The ground, too, is shaking underneath our feet.

This is not the only building being leveled to the ground. Right and left, more bombs drop from the sky, some hitting the targets while others simply fall on the street, making huge holes in the asphalt.

I hold on tightly to Mine as tremors similar to an earthquake make the entire foundation of the city shake.

Screams erupt in the air. So many pained, wailing voices, I wish I could close off my ears to them.

Just as the physical world reels from shock as building after building collapses or catches on fire, so does the spiritual world.

Messengers line the street all around, herding confused souls toward the afterlife.

"This isn't right," Mine whispers.

"It's war."

"Perhaps, but this...this is never warranted."

Right as the words are out of his mouth, the scream of a child pierces the air. We both turn toward the source and witness a little boy on fire run out of a building. His clothes are burning badly, the flames seeking to engulf his skin.

Mine gives me a look.

"No," I say immediately.

He purses his lips and sighs.

"I cannot..." I add in a low voice.

Yet what I see in his eyes shocks me, the disappointment, the dead expectations.

Shaking his head at me, he runs out of the cover of our shield, going straight for the child. He takes off his coat and swats it at the areas where the child's skin is on fire.

Seconds stretch into an eternity as I stare at them, alone in my little bubble. Regret slowly eats at me even as I tell myself all the reasons why I should not get involved.

It's not right.

People will die. Humans are fated to die. If not today, then tomorrow. And if I save someone, then someone else will die in their stead.

Death comes to all.

Yet even knowing that, an uncomfortable feeling settles in my breast.

I watch as Mine continues to care for the child. More bombs go off around him. More fires spark to life. He doesn't budge. He is steady in his conviction as he continues to help.

The child looks up at him and after thanking him in German, he tells him his sister is still inside the building.

My eyes widen.

"Mine, no!" I call out.

He half turns, his profile shrouded in darkness and the shadows of the dancing flames. His resolve is resolute.

Telling the child to come to me, he dashes toward the burning building.

"Fräulein," the child mutters uncertainly as he steps closer.

My instinct is to ignore him and shield myself from human eyes. But the look in his eyes, so hopeless, so pained, makes me extend my hand toward him.

And when he grabs it, I take away some of his pain.

This should be fine—at least this. If he is meant to die, he can do it painlessly.

Moments later, Mine exits the building holding a little girl in his arms. Surprisingly, she doesn't seem to be harmed.

The boy calls out her name and rushes out to her.

"Go to the river," Mine tells them. "You should be safer there."

The children run in the direction of the lake, as many others do, too. The streets are crowded with people running right and left, some seeking cover, others seeking their missing loved ones. Then there are those who are so injured they've lost all sense of space or time, wandering aimlessly around until they fall to the ground, never to rise again.

So many of those are children.

"You're right. This is not right." I take a deep breath. "But what can I do?" I ask as I glance up at him, tears building in my eyes.

"You're already doing it, Minnie. You care, and that's the first step."

"But—"

"I know you can't interfere. But I can. And maybe...if I am the one you're helping, it wouldn't be a direct interference?"

"But you'd be putting yourself in danger. And I would be interfering with your fate then..."

"I told you. It is not my time to die. But this... I can't turn a blind eye to it, Minnie."

"I know." I sigh. "What do you want me to do?"

"Shield me. I'll do the best I can, focus on the women and children."

"Even if they're the enemy?"

He raises a brow at me. "Women and children are never the enemy. But they're always the victims."

"You can't save them all."

"I can try." He shrugs.

I glance at him. What an odd male. He's on the other side of the war and yet his first instinct is to help the enemy. I've seen the way his side regards the Germans. They want to see them all destroyed.

Anyone else in his position would have turned a blind eye and derived joy from the fact that the Allies are bombing such a big city.

Not him, though.

Warmth spreads through me as I add one more item to the endless list of things that make him the perfect male.

Perfect for me, of course, and no one else.

"I'll help you try then."

His brows shoot up in surprise.

"You're a gem," he murmurs as he gives me a quick kiss.

Heading to the crowd of people, he instructs them to head to the river in perfect German. I did not realize he would be fluent in the language, but it makes sense since they're the enemy. One should know his enemy.

I keep a shield over him so nothing can touch him. By extension, that applies to anyone who comes in contact with him.

Despite justifying it to myself that I'm not doing anything technically against the rules, I know that even this small intervention is having an impact on people's lives. The mere fact that a fearless male rides into the raging fires to save and help people, the fact that he's interacting with them and telling them where to go, all of those are interferences.

I cannot say how many people will be saved, or if others will die as a result of our actions. But I also cannot stand by and do nothing. Half of the reason is because I do hate seeing helpless people suffer thusly. The other half, however, is much more selfish, much more self-serving.

I want to do it because he wants to do it, because if I didn't, he might never look at me the same. The mere glimpse of disappointment in his gaze when I suggested we should leave was enough for me to realize how much this means to him.

Good, good male, as much as I am a bad female.

Perhaps it's my age and the countless deaths I've seen; countless bloodsheds; countless wars. Perhaps it's the fact that I know that death is not the end. Perhaps all of these have jaded me.

But he makes me care again. He makes me want to do better, want to be better.

If I break more rules in the process...

I take a deep breath.

So be it.

The area teems with lost souls and messengers. My senses become high on alert to the presence of demons, too. Closer and closer, a handful of warrior deities make their appearance.

Without giving my presence away, I scan the energy signatures around, noting they are all mostly novice deities, with the highest level I sense being a four. That means I should be able to shield myself from them.

As messengers disappear with their charges, demons start appearing in greater numbers to prey on the remaining souls.

I take a deep breath and spread my energy around. Rough estimates would put the casualties at around eight thousand. Maybe a little more. Considering that nearly ten percent of souls refuse to move on, though in the case of violent demises that number rises considerably, I am looking at almost a thousand lost souls.

I sense three deities. Two level threes and a level four. More worryingly, I sense at least five mid-level demons, with one that is certainly a high level; perhaps even a level eleven or twelve.

"Damn it," I mutter under my breath. Those novice deities won't be able to handle high-level demons. Even I have a hard time with them.

"You save the living. I'll save the dead," I shout over to Mine.

He stops and turns to me.

"Demons?"

I nod.

"Be careful," he adds before getting back to his task.

From the corner of my eye, I keep an eye on him as he continues his rescue mission, but my attention is otherwise engaged to the demons approaching.

Extending my arms to my sides, I manifest my ice swords. A swirling fog envelops me as eternal ice builds all over my body in the shape of an armor.

A demon flashes herself in the middle of the square. There are some twenty souls roaming around. The period immediately after death is the worst because all souls are disoriented, with some being incredibly angry and confused.

The demon, whose current physical body is that of a woman in her mid-twenties, notices me right away. The souls move around her mechanically, not registering the danger they're in.

She barely minds the souls, her attention solely on me.

Her eyes glow a deep red as shadows arise from her body like tendrils. In the blink of an eye, they reach for me.

Level eleven.

Damn it! Of course I'd have the luck of encountering a blasted level eleven exactly when I'm trying to keep a low profile. Why couldn't I have met her before, when I was trying to rack up accomplishments and impress Commander Azerius?

The most I've fought has been a level eight, which is considered upper mid level. Eleven, though? These bastards are strong and vicious.

I may have not fought one myself, but I've seen my brother do it. Though their energy is not organic like that of a deity or a Son of Tenebreis, once they get past level ten, their abilities are on par with both.

Their power comes from the amount of souls they've consumed, but compared to born deities or Sons of Tenebreis, that energy is not naturally replenishing. Even if they reach a high level, they must constantly consume souls to maintain their power.

Of course those bastards Sons of Tenebreis would also rather consume souls to speed up the replenishment process. Rumor has it that they don't even require food if they feed on souls.

Sniveling bastards, all of them.

The attack pushes me backward.

I put my blades together in the shape of an X to stop the tendrils, and just as they retreat, I flash myself at the half point and slice through them.

Sure enough, in the next instant, they regenerate.

I nod to myself, filing every bit of information away. Regular weapons are unlikely to help.

"Bitch," she spits at me before she launches another attack. This time, instead of two tendrils, four more that extend from her back join in.

"Says the bottom feeder," I retort, quickly flashing myself between her tendrils and snapping them, this time closer to the base. "You might be used to eluding deities to get to this level, but you can blame today's misfortune on the fates." I smirk at her.

"Who said I've been eluding them?" She laughs. With a snap of her fingers, she opens her blouse to reveal her neck. Hanging low down her chest is a necklace comprised of small crystals that seem to shimmer in the darkness of the night.

For a moment, I cannot comprehend what she's showing me. But as the energy inside the crystals swirls in a familiar pattern, I realize *how* she managed to get to a level eleven.

She killed deities. Many of them, by the looks of it. Perhaps some were novices, and thus easy prey, but to have defeated that many deities is nothing short of impressive. What is infuriating, however, is the way she'd trapped their energy in those orbs to keep them as spoils of war—after consuming their souls.

Her lips tug up. "One more and I will fully ascend," she drawls.

And that's when I realize she's not here for those poor human souls.

She's here for me.

An ascended demon's power is similar to that of a Son of Tenebreis. Though I've never personally faced one since most if not all of them are trapped in Tartareia, the rumors say that only a Supreme could previously defeat a Son of Tenebreis.

My lips flatten and my nostrils flare as I regard her. She has a smug expression on her face, likely thinking she's already won this battle. Well, she'll have a mighty surprise on her hands. It's not just my reputation on the line here—and I'm quite partial to it—but Mine's safety also depends on me.

"I'll have a little fun with you before I eat you," she murmurs, smacking her lips together.

"You're welcome to try." I roll my eyes.

Her tentacles spring from her back, coming toward me with a speed ten times the one from before.

My eyes widen, and I react right on time to manifest a shield and place it in front of me. As the tentacles hit the surface of the shield, I use my sword to cut through them, infusing particles of enteral ice at the tip of the blade.

As they touch the black tentacles, the particles quickly move forward, freezing the length of the spare appendages and making their way toward her body.

She startles when she realizes what my eternal ice is capable for, but she's smart enough to know it will kill her should the particles reach her main body. Her claws extend and she slices all the tentacles at the root before the eternal ice can reach her. They fall to the ground and a dark mist envelops them as the matter starts to slowly dissipate.

Her mouth twitches in annoyance.

Her tentacles regenerate, but she doesn't direct them toward me again. They float above her head, twirling in the air as if they had a mind of their own.

Hovering one palm over the other, she moves them in a circular motion to create a blast of energy.

Before she can send that flying my way, I flash myself behind her and strike. She, too, swivels, and her right hand turns into a lance, blocking my attack. The energy blast she'd been trying to create dissipates.

She swings her lance at me, aiming for one of the few spots that are not covered by my armor: my upper neck and my face.

I move from side to side, narrowly evading nicks of her blade: who knows what poison might reside inside it. She advances on me, and suddenly we're back in the same familiar dance: she attacks and I defend. Yet to win this fight, I'll have to switch the dynamics.

The demon steps closer to me, her lance making contact with my sword. She uses her entire strength to push me, but I stand my ground. When she moves close enough, I lean in and blow cold air toward her, which immediately turns into frost when it meets her skin.

She lets out a loud shriek that the ice enveloping her face soon mutes.

I flash myself away from her and take a deep breath. My

body is starting to feel the effects of exhaustion after everything I've done. I must end this soon, otherwise my abilities will start to weaken.

All around us, the mayhem continues as merciless fires consume the buildings. Screams permeate the air, and people with all types of degrees of burns run around in search for shelter.

My gaze immediately seeks out Mine, needing to ensure he's fine. He's a distance away, trying to help two kids get out from under a mass of rubble.

My attention must have lingered too much on him because as I glance back at the demon, the ice has already melted and her line of sight is set on...him. A smile curls up her lips and with blinding speed, she sets out for him.

Alarmed, I chase after her, pushing myself way past my limits to ensure I make it to his side before she does. Mine seems to notice it too because he shields the children with his body and looks back toward us.

She's almost there when I flash myself in front of him.

Her tentacles swing out, and before I can protect myself, one of them penetrates the exposed skin at the top of my neck.

A croaked sound escapes me as I choke on my own blood. Pain erupts everywhere as the tentacle continues to dig inside of me, pushing forward and moving from side to side to create as much damage and decapitate me.

"Minnie!" Mine's voice rings out.

He pushes the children behind him as he reaches out for me, his fingers brushing lightly against my own.

My eyes turn a vivid blue as a burst of energy explodes through me. Focusing on my neck, I build up particles of eternal ice that explode from within me, from every cell in my body. The ice claims the tip of the tentacle, but this time, I change my strategy.

Having learned from the last time this happened, I quickly swing my sword at her in an attempt to distract her so she doesn't realize what the eternal ice is doing.

Cutting just over the part where the eternal ice is slowly eating into her tissue, I wrench myself free of her tentacle. With my free hand, I grab the broken piece and pull it out of my throat, then fling it to the side.

More blood spills down my armor and onto the ground, but without the tentacle, my wound is swiftly healing.

The demon's nostrils flare.

"Master did not mention you would be so hard to kill," she mutters under her breath as she takes a step back.

"Master? What are you talking about?"

She lets out a dry laugh. "Wouldn't you want to know?" She snickers. "The end is near. The gods will die. And in the end, we will reign over everyone."

I narrow my eyes at her. "Who is *we*?"

She doesn't answer. Her lips spread into a sinister smile as she presses her hands together again to build an energy blast. Luckily for me, while she's gathering her energy to put into that blow, she doesn't realize the eternal ice particles slowly make their way toward her body.

Just a little more.

Rather than using the ice to obliterate *all* of her tissue, I imbued it with more energy than usual in an attempt to control the trajectory of the damage and focus only on the core of the tissue. By making it die from within while still maintaining an outer healthy appearance, the demon might not notice it immediately like before and sever the tentacle again.

This is not something I've tried before, and it might not fully work.

But as she continues to work on her energy blast, not minding the poison heading her way, I'd say the odds are in my favor.

I smack my own palms together, rubbing them to create a wave of energy—I should at least create the illusion that I'm still fighting and not that I am waiting for something to happen.

Just as she thrusts forward a small ball of gray energy, I also send a wave of my own ice energy.

They meet in the middle, and as they clash, they start fighting for dominance. It all happens in the span of a few seconds. The demon's energy releases a dark mist that at first covers my energy, seeking to put it out.

I don't think she's fought other ice deities in the past, or at least none with my lineage because she would have known that technique is futile.

Just as the two energies seemingly become one—the gray one—an explosion erupts in the air. It's so powerful, it sends all of us flying.

Eyes wide with worry, I create a shield to protect Mine and those children, using a big part of my energy to move them to safety—telekinesis always takes a toll on me. Mine urges the children to run toward the river before turning his attention to me, giving me a sharp nod of acknowledgment.

The demon uses her powers to stabilize herself some yards away, turning her arms into lances once more and pressing them into the ground to stop being shoved backward by the blast.

She's breathing harshly. Half her face is bloody from being in the direct path of the blast.

"You will pay for this," she cries out. She propels herself in the air, her entire body contorting and becoming a gray mass of demonic matter.

My smile slowly grows wider.

"Not today, demon. Not today," I say gleefully. The eternal ice has not only reached her main body, but by shifting into her true demonic form, she's allowing the ice to penetrate to the depths of her physical embodiment.

Mid-air, her shriek resounds for all to hear. It starts from within. Slivers of ice breach the surface of her body, freezing everything in their path.

It lasts a few seconds. Her body freezes before it explodes into tiny particles that lose themselves in the wind.

I exhale deeply as I plant my feet onto the ground. I sway from side to side from exhaustion. My armor vanishes, leaving me naked. Strong arms wrap around my midriff, pulling me to his side as he covers my nakedness with his coat.

"You did good, tiny darling. So, so good," he whispers in my ear.

He smells of smoke and leather. He smells of home.

I only need to inhale his scent to know I am safe.

"Sleep now," he murmurs.

Despite my exhaustion, I wouldn't have said I was close to passing out. But his words trigger something within me. My body goes slack against his, and my eyes flutter closed.

Without meaning to, I'm lost to the world.

FORTY-ONE

THE RATTLING of tires against a hard ground startles me awake.

"Mine!" I shout as I open my eyes.

"Here, Minnie darling. I'm right here."

I glance to my side. He's in the driver's seat of a car, confidently steering the wheel down a raggedy path. I blink, then look down at myself.

I'm wearing a long cotton gown that's surprisingly soft to the touch. Over the dress, his jacket rests over my shoulders, providing extra heat even though he knows I don't need it—he is the one who can get cold, not me.

"Where are we?" I ask groggily.

"Close to the border with France. In fact, we should be there in less than ten minutes."

"Close to the border?" I furrow my brows. "How long have I been out?"

"Some three days," he answers casually.

I gawk at him.

"Three days? Did you just say three days?" I take a deep breath as I try to make sense of the situation. But as I open my mouth to speak again, it's to panic once more. "What do you mean it's been three days? How is it possible I was out that long?"

"You must have exhausted your energy and needed time to replenish it—"

"No. I've been low on energy before and it's true that I usually need sleep and food to replenish it, but I've never been asleep for three days straight. That is outrageous."

"You did defeat a high-level demon. Cut yourself some slack. You needed the rest."

I grumble under my breath, annoyed that he's right. The fight with that demon took a toll on me, but even so, I clearly remember being tired but not exhausted. I still had plenty of energy to function at normal levels. That I just passed out... It's odd.

Alas, now I am invigorated and my energy is brimming.

"So what happened in those three days?" I ask, curious.

"Hmm, let's see. We evacuated Dresden, and I pretended to be a German soldier saving my dear wife. I do happen to have a flawless accent, so everyone believed it. After we left the city, I bought us a car, some clothes for you, and some food for the road. Then I started driving."

I stare at him. "You bought things? With what money? You had none."

He shrugs. "I am resourceful."

I narrow my eyes at him, thinking what he might have done for that money.

"Well, the dress is nice. You have good taste," I add reluctantly.

He gasps aloud. "Good Lord, Minnie! Was that a praise? Did you just praise me?"

"Easy now, don't let it go to your head. You have a big enough ego as it is."

"It's certainly bigger now," he counters with a wink.

"Are you... I hope you're not using one of those inundations on me."

He frowns. "Inun—what?"

"Don't think I didn't see your pants." I point out in outrage. "You're always thinking dirty thoughts, Mine. Why else would your...your...thing be up and an about?" I continue. "I was asleep until moments ago, so don't tell me you were scheming something with me like this?"

"Up and about?" He blinks in confusion. "He's not going anywhere, Minnie."

"Don't you Minnie me. I was asleep until moments ago, so what were you thinking of me that your thing would get up?"

His chest vibrates with mirth.

"Tell me, Mine. What sort of nefarious designs did you have on my person while I was asleep?"

He's still chuckling. "Minnie darling, I thought you liked that particular type of nefariousness."

Images of our night in the ice chamber flood my mind and I blush.

"W-well, y-yes," I stammer. "When I'm awake and present. I will not have you cheat me out of one of those organisms, Mine."

"Orgasms," he corrects. "And innuendos, not inundation."

"Orgasms, organisms, whatever. You will not cheat me out of them."

"So let me get this straight," he starts, turning to me with a serious expression on his face. "You are not actually upset that I might have nefarious designs on you, just that you might miss on an orgasm while asleep?"

"Of course. You promised to give them to me daily. It's been three days that I was unconscious. So either you gave them to me while I was asleep, which I will take issue with because I did not feel anything and thus they do not count. Or..."

"Or?" He wiggles his brows.

"Or you owe me three days' worth of orgasms."

"Then I suppose I am indebted to you," he adds playfully.

I huff. "Good that you know," I mutter as I materialize a notebook and a pencil.

He frowns and leans forward to see what I'm scribbling. I

give him a deadly glare. He watches intently as I write down the heading.

Debts

Underneath, I write the days he owes me.

"I am holding you accountable," I tell him as I close the notebook and materialize it away.

"You're so thorough, tiny darling. You should add some interest, too."

"Interest?" I frown. "What do you mean?"

"Every day I'm late for paying my debt, you add more to it."

"More?"

He nods with a smile.

"Good idea. More is always good."

"I've turned you into a pleasure fiend!" he exclaims in feigned outrage, his lips curled up in satisfaction.

"I'm glad you recognize your part in this because you must take responsibility."

Another bout of laughter.

"I said I'd marry you, didn't I?"

"Yes, you did. But since that is not a ceremony officiated by a high priestess who solidifies the union between two people, how will this marriage you speak of be official?"

"Simple. My father will officiate it. He can make it very official."

"What does that mean?"

"He can make it so that it's not contested in any world, or in any life. We'd be bound, forever."

"Impossible."

"I can assure you, he knows his stuff." He winks at me.

"No, it is impossible to be bound forever. For that, we'd have to be true mates and we, though it pains me to admit, are not."

He glances at me, his hands tightening on the steering wheel.

"And how would you know if we were?"

"According to rumors I've heard, true mates get initially bound together after they exchange blood. Their union is then cemented after they consummate the bond. We've shared blood before, and nothing happened."

"So you're saying we are not fated to be?" He raises a brow, his voice tense.

I shrug. "I don't care whether we are or not. I chose you, didn't I?"

Would it have been ideal if we were fated? Yes. But I would be satisfied with living a full loving life alongside him

"Maybe. But what if your true mate came along at some point?"

"Nothing would happen since I'm not about to share blood with anyone else. Ever," I answer truthfully.

"But it must go beyond blood sharing. You must have an affinity with that person from the moment you meet."

"No, that will not happen."

"How can you be so sure?"

"Because I cut my thread of fate, all right? That means I don't have any mate in this universe. Not now, not ever."

He's silent for a moment.

"When?" he asks softly.

"When I was away. I found out it might be the only way to be with you and—"

"You risked everything, didn't you?" he murmurs in a low, pained voice.

"Maybe I did. But I'm here, am I not?" I give him a tremulous smile. "I'm here and your father will officiate our wedding and we'll live happily ever after."

"Oh, Minnie," he adds in a ragged voice. "What have you done?"

"It's fine," I mutter.

"No. It's not fine. It will never be fine, no matter how much this needed to happen." He takes a deep breath. "I wish things were simpler. That we could be together without the entire universe being against us."

"Well, what is done is done," I say, a little weirded out by his ominous words. "But on the bright side, it's not the entire universe that's against us since no one knows about us."

He bites his lip, lost in thought. "For now."

"For as long as we can keep it that way."

He sighs.

"I love how optimistic you are when you, better than anyone, know just how much this, being here, with me, is going to cost you."

I shrug, though his words root themselves in my mind.

"I knew the risk when I did it."

"And you did it anyway..." he trails off. "Minnie, Minnie..." There's something odd about him. I frown as I try to decipher the expression on his face. It's a mix of sadness and resignation, but I don't understand exactly why he would feel that.

"I hate how much you have to sacrifice for me. But I'm also so damn selfish that I wouldn't have it any other way. As long as you're mine..." He presses his lips together as he stares at the road ahead.

Slowly, he glances at me and gives me a sweet, sad smile.

"That probably makes me a horrible person."

"It makes you human."

He shakes his head. "If you only knew..." His voice drops an octave.

"What? What should I know?"

"Never mind."

"What?" I repeat. "You can't just say that and not continue."

He's silent for a moment, so I badger him some more.

"In a perfect world, I would have shouldered all your burdens. I would have loved you, protected you, and kept you in a tight cocoon close to my heart where no one could hurt you."

"Might I remind you I am the powerful goddess here?" I ask drily. He doesn't mind me as he continues.

"But it's not a perfect world. And one thing I've realized in the time I've lived without you, waiting for you, is that some things just...must happen. If not, we would not become who we are meant to become."

"Mine, what are you on about? You're not making any sense. Did you perchance hit your head? Do you need blood?"

He chuckles. "You don't need to understand me now."

"But I want to." I cross my arms over my chest. "Tell me."

He smiles indulgently at me.

"There are some events in our lives that define us—that make us who we are and prepare us for who we are meant to be. I may hate the fact that you interfered with your fate. But that in itself is perhaps part of your fate."

"Isn't that circular logic?"

"Ah, my Minnie is so smart," he coos as he pats my head affectionately.

I push his hand aside and punch him lightly—he's human, after all—in the shoulder.

"Don't change the subject."

"How about I pause it then? We're at the border." He nods to the militia cars waiting up ahead.

"Will we have any issues? We don't have any papers."

"Don't worry about it."

He drives to the barrier and stops. A couple Frenchmen dressed in military uniform come toward us, and one of them knocks on the window.

Mine lowers it and smiles affably at the soldiers.

"*Bonjour,*" he drawls in perfect French. Just how many languages does he speak? His German was perfect, too.

I pay close attention to his words, managing to understand some of what he's saying.

He claims we got robbed and we lost our papers, but he has proof of his identity. When the soldiers ask about the proof, Mine only says to call his superior, who then should call his superior until he reaches the Army General and say Lucien de Vitry is asking for safe passage into France.

Skeptical, one of the soldiers walks back to his outpost to make the call. The other soldier waits by our car, surveying us suspiciously.

"And she? Who is she?" He points at me.

"My wife."

I preen at the words.

"*Oui, je suis sa pousse*," I say in a haughty voice in French. I might not be fluent in it, but I am quite good at it since I happen to love French cinema too.

Mine turns to look at me, blinking repeatedly.

The soldier stares at me, too.

I frown. "What?" I mouth to Mine.

"*Elle est anglaise*," Mine adds apologetically as he turns to the soldier. He starts laughing and nods at him.

"No, I am not," I blurt out.

The soldier stops laughing, his eyes widening. His hands are suddenly on his rifle and he gets into position.

"*Non, non. Vous n'avez pas besoin de dégainer votre arme. Elle est juste très mauvaise en français et n'a pas compris*," Mine quickly says. "Right, Minnie? You only speak English."

Mine glares at me and I slowly nod. "Yes," I say in my best English accent. "I only speak English. I apologize if I said something wrong."

The soldier does not seem convinced.

"*Sortez de la voiture*," he barks out. "*Mettez les mains où je peux les voir*." He takes a step back and points his rifle at us.

"What's going on?"

The soldier lets out a loud whistle and more men in uniform come out of their outposts, all of them with their weapons raised.

"Minnie," Mine starts in a tense voice. "Can you get the car to fly over the barricade?"

"Yes, of course." Though that will require quite a bit of energy.

"Good. And a shield. We'll need a shield."

"I can do that," I say and create a shield around the car.

His lips are a thin line of tension.

"When I give the signal, we fly."

I nod and gather my energy, letting it surround the car.

The soldier who'd left before comes back, confused to see everyone pointing their weapons at us.

"*Repos*," he calls out, his voice thundering. The he follows with, "*Il est le fils de Ciel de Vitry*."

The soldiers look at one another for a few more tense seconds before they holster their rifles.

"Apologies, Mr. de Vitry. You may go," the man says with a salute.

"Thank you," Mine replies.

The barricade is raised, and our car continues on.

A mile or so after we've crossed into French territory, I turn to him.

"Explain! What just happened?"

Mine shakes his head, his lips curled up in amusement. "You said *pousse* instead of *épouse*."

"So?"

"It means sprout. You said you were my sprout."

"Oh," I whisper.

He laughs.

"At least now I know your vocabulary mishaps extend to languages other than English."

I glare at him. "I hope you're not laughing at me."

"I am not. You are just too adorable. Even when you're about to get us shot at, you're adorable."

He might have said something else in that sentence of his, but all I can hear is adorable.

Mine thinks I'm adorable.

I smile to myself. He's a smart one, all right.

In fact, I'm so happy at his praise that I forget everything I wanted to ask him about—like who Ciel de Vitry is.

It takes us another three hours to get to the mysterious location he calls his safe haven.

All the while, he's extremely tight-lipped about what I'm going to find there, making me more and more curious.

We reach two sprawling metal gates with intricate designs consisting of skulls and scenes of eternal torture. Almost at will, they open and Mine drives on, following a serpentine driveway toward one of the most stunning mentions I've seen in Anthropa.

From afar, I note the sheer magnificence of the four-story building. The facade is reminiscent of those gothic cathedrals I loved to visit back in England, but the overall shape is square and angular. Where those cathedrals had high domes and ribbed vaults, his home has none.

Yet there's something almost magical about it.

"This is it," Mine declares as we get out of the car. His voice is reserved, bordering on bashful.

"You're nervous," I note immediately. "Why?"

He's taken aback by my question and he gives me a reserved shrug.

"I built this," he mutters, low and barely audible.

"You..." I look from him to the mansion then back at him. "You?"

He nods. "It was a personal project."

"Then you did these, too?" I ask as I point to the art on the main facade of the building.

Another nod.

I walk closer until I can reach out and touch the bass-relief carvings in the stone with my own hands.

My breath almost leaves my body as I trace the characters of the odyssey. It all starts at the bottom, with scenes of friendship, of war, and of longing for love.

"Minnie..."

"Shush," I say, not looking at him.

Using my energy, I float up so I can see the second part of the story.

More battles, some ending in victory, some in defeat. There is companionship, family, but also a sense of loneliness.

It's at the third level that another motif appears.

Pain, illness, and loss.

The scenes depict a plague sweeping through the land and killing the hero's friend. He, too, succumbs to the illness, but he eventually survives.

And there is only one reason why he kept on going.

Love. He was waiting for that one person he could call his. Even when his illness was too painful and the will to live nonexistent, he still prayed that his beloved would come.

Then I reach the end.

I'm almost scared of what I'm going to see. So far, I recognize the many chapters of Mine's life and how important they were. He's spoken about waiting for someone special too, so this is nothing new.

But in the last scene of the carving, there is a meeting.

She gives him her heart. He gives her his soul.

"Who?" My voice is carried by the wind until he can hear me. "Who is this?"

As I lower myself to the ground, I come face-to-face with him.

"The woman I was waiting for. The only one who could save me from damnation." He pauses. "You."

"But how did you know—"

"I did and didn't," he interrupts me. "I trusted that fate would bring you to me, and she did."

"You're such a charmer," I grumble, though I am beyond pleased.

Of course I wouldn't have expected anything else from him. Only a male worthy of me would have worshipped me before we even met.

"Show me the rest of the house. You said there are more surprises?" I ask, my eyes glistening with excitement.

Perhaps he will have a personal chef who can cook me all the pastries in the world. Now that would be the best surprise. I'm already hungry. How long has it been since I last ate? Four days? More? Outrageous!

The doors open and we step inside.

The first thing that strikes me is the sheer minimalist decor that's somehow paradoxically shrouded in opulence. Sprawling staircase, black and gray marble columns, as well as four human-sized sculptures that look like antiques.

Everything is gleaming and spotlessly clean. The floors are so polished, I almost feel bad stepping inside.

"Come," Mine says as he grabs my hand and takes me up the stairs. I let him lead me, though my attention is on every detail of his house, trying to make sense of what that says about him.

So far, one thing matches. Cleanliness. His obsession with cleanliness matches his house, too. There is not one corner that is not sparkling clean, in a way that I doubt even most Aperite houses are—and those deities can snap their fingers and clean everything.

"Where to next?"

"The first level houses the master suite."

The first floor has a long hallway filled with all types of antiques. I'm not that versed in Anthropan art or history, so I don't know if they are genuine or not. But they look old.

At the end of the hallway, there is only one door. Mine leaves me alone for a moment while he takes exactly five steps to the right and six backward, his steps thudding hard against the hardwood floor. The rhythm appears to be a code of some sort because as he stops, I hear a low ping in the wall. He reaches toward one painting, and pulling it aside, he reveals a secret compartment that houses a row of keys.

"I take my privacy very seriously," he adds when he sees my questioning expression.

Unlocking the door, he holds it open for me to step inside.

I expected to see his bedroom. Instead, it seems to be yet another foyer that leads into a waiting room. This one is much more intimate. Though the ground floor seemed rather cold and bare, this part of the house is fully furnished and exudes a sense of warmth.

"The layout of your house is confusing," I say when I, once more, don't see his bedroom.

"It's not. Think of this as an apartment within the house. This is the waiting room. Through that door there is the study and the library." He points to the nearest door to my right. "Those two doors right there are the bedrooms, with a large bathroom in the middle. There's also—"

"Bedrooms?" I interrupt him. "More than one?"

"Technically, though the second one does not really qualify as a second bedroom since there is no bed. Come." He grabs my hand and drags be toward the room he claims to be the master bedroom.

"This is huge," I whisper when he opens the door.

A large double bed is in the middle. Actually, I think it might be double-double, not just double. So double I could swim in it. Before he can say anything else, I forget myself and let my instincts run the show as I dash at full speed toward the bed and throw myself on it.

A giggle escapes me when I sink into the plush mattress, only to resurface as I spring back in the air. My, that's a strong mattress. I bounce around the bed. Mindful of his love of cleanliness, I shed my shoes and then get to my feet and jump up and down.

"Oh my, Mine! This is such a good mattress."

His mouth is ajar as he stares at me.

"Minnie, I'm not sure—"

"Come! This is so much fun!"

He shakes his head and for a moment he hesitates. But my lips tug into a wide smile when I see him carefully take off his shoes. Then he shrugs his dusty coat off. Then he also takes his socks off—I probably should have done that too. Finally, he comes over.

Yet it's almost as if he's reluctant to get on the bed.

Grabbing his hands, I tug him forward until he loses his balance and has no choice but to fall on the bed. He seems stunned at first, but he quickly recovers and charges at me.

I jump back, aided by the strong springs of the mattress. I bounce on the bed and make him bounce up and down in return too.

"See? This is fun!"

He mumbles something under his breath that is along the lines of 'typical Minnie.' But then he gives me a bright smile and he pulls me into his arms. Together, we crash into the mattress and we bounce up and down a couple more times before we stop.

"You like the mattress, I gather?" he asks in a low voice that sends shivers down my spine.

"It's so bouncy. I love it!"

"Good, because you'll be sleeping here."

"H-here?" I turn in his embrace and shyly look up at him. "Together?"

"Of course. There's no other bed."

"Well, I suppose it will be easier for you to pay your daily tribute if we sleep next to each other," I murmur, batting my lashes suggestively at him—I think I've finally mastered this art!

"Damn right. I also have quite the accumulated interest to pay." He nuzzles his face in the crook of my neck, slowly trailing his lips over my flesh.

"Yes," I whisper. "Three days and counting."

"I think we should not count in days."

"What?"

"Hours. Let's do hours. Three days is seventy-two hours. I have seventy-two hours of overdue payment. That's quite a lot, isn't it?"

"Oh my, that is indeed a lot. Do you plan to pay for all those seventy-two hours?"

"Let's not forget the other hours in between that will keep adding up while we sleep and eat."

"So every hour I don't get an orgasm is an orgasm owed?" I ask huskily, liking the idea of this. Before, I would have called him a pervert. Now I declare him a genius.

"Yes, and I get my treat, too, between those pretty legs of yours, right where I belong."

"I guess you'd better start paying your debt."

I grab onto him, holding tight as I push my body against him. But just as I think I'll finally get one of those delicious orgasms that gives me extra strength, something else happens.

My stomach growls in hunger.

Mine pulls back, a worried expression on his face.

"I haven't eaten in four days," I confess.

"Fuck!" He lets out a string of curses as he hauls me off the bed. "I need to feed you. The kitchen is downstairs."

He doesn't let me have a say as he takes me in his arms and carries me back downstairs.

The kitchen is right by the staircase, and to my surprise, this area is also spotless.

That's when I finally think to ask.

"Is there anyone else around?" I say with a frown. I cannot hear anyone in the house or on the grounds.

"Who would be here?"

"Staff? Workers?"

"No. There's only me. I don't like foreign people in my space."

"That doesn't surprise me," I mutter drily. "But who takes care of the grounds? And the house? This is so big it must require at least ten to twenty workers maintaining it on a regular basis." The kitchen, too, is industrial in size—almost as big as the one at the military base. To my disappointment, there is no private chef waiting to cook me a special meal.

"No. It's just me and occasionally my family comes over," he says.

I'm still confused. "You've been away for months, Mine. How is this so...clean?" I point to the gleaming tiles and the spotless steel appliances that reflect my appearance—which is rather disheveled and should be fixed sometime soon.

"Oh, that..." he trails off nervously. "My mother must have done it. She comes in every week on Saturdays to clean and oversee the estate. She's the only person I'd trust to clean my place."

"I see." Though I don't really.

I jump out of his arms and go to the fridge, then open it to find it fully stocked with food.

Odd.

The meat and produce are both fresh. The cheese, too.

Another growl from my famished stomach. Ah, but that cheese looks good. I take it out of the fridge and take a bite out of it before I can help myself.

"Do you want me to cut some for you?" Mine asks.

"No, don't worry. I can eat it like this." I grab another bite. Hmm, I wonder what type of cheese this is. I can taste some nuts in it, and it's quite creamy, not at all like that hard English cheddar.

"Are you sure? I can cut you a few slices and give you some bread."

I shake my head. Why bother when I can just bite into it like this?

I'm halfway done with the block of cheese when I suddenly stop mid-chewing.

The sound of another set of footsteps reverberates through the house.

It's close, far too close. And I was so damn focused on this cheese I barely realized another person had made it onto the grounds.

Sloppy, Minnie! What if it is an enemy? Surely cheese isn't more important...

Yes, it is.

"You said there's no one here." I tilt my head to the side, listening to the sound as it approaches.

"It's not..." he trails off as he hears the sound too.

"Mine, what day is today?" I think to ask right as I pocket the rest of the cheese.

A guilty look flashes on his face. He hadn't thought of it, had he?

"What day is it?" I repeat, this time with rising panic.

"Saturday."

By the Source, can the earth split open and swallow me now?

The last thing I needed is to meet his mother. I'm not only disheveled after three days of traveling in a car, I'm probably also a little—a lot—smelly and in need of a good scrub.

What will she think of me? That I'm some homeless beggar her son picked up on the streets?

I squeeze my eyes shut in defeat just as the kitchen door opens and someone steps inside.

"Mother."

FORTY-TWO

MY BACK HITS the plush mattress before I can even think it through. Panic takes over and instead of facing Mine's mother as I should have, I'm hiding in his room.

But I have a good reason for doing so!

How could I meet his mother for the first time while looking and smelling like a sewer rat?

It's his mother. I need to make a good impression on her. Based on how he's been speaking about her, it's clear Mine loves her dearly and as such, he would also be partial to her opinions.

Not that I think she would convince him to leave me. Mine would *never*.

But she could try.

She could think I'm some homeless bum who's trying to get with him for his status. He is a rather decorated airman, and a recent POW, too. Add to that the fact that his family is wealthy —only someone very influential would be able to ensure our border crossing so smoothly. His father's name was the only thing necessary for us to be allowed to cross even when we looked rather...suspicious.

He's rich. They are rich. She'll think I'm trying to get his money. It's not like he can tell her about my real identity and the fact that I am a princess in my own right—his money does not faze me. Though certainly, money seems to make life easier here in Anthropa and since we will be living here from now on, I suppose I am quite lucky that he is rich.

That is *not* to say I'm with him for his money. Him first, money second.

Now how do I make a good impression, though? First, I have to get clean, of course.

Remembering which door Mine had said was the bathroom, I go inside. Of course it would be enormous, with the biggest tub I've ever seen in the middle of the room.

Shedding my clothes, I throw them into a basket that I assume is for dirty laundry before I go straight for the bathtub. I don't even care for the water temperature. It can be freezing cold for all I care as long as it washes the grime off my body so I can look semi-decent for that meeting.

Yet as I start furiously scrubbing my skin, I can't help but tune in my hearing to what's going on downstairs.

"What a surprise to find you here, dear!" His mother's voice is soft and melodic. There is some shuffling as she walks closer to him and what I assume to be a hug.

I force myself to disregard the fact that another female is touching him.

She's his mother, Minerva. Stop being so outrageous.

"I did not realize today was Saturday," Mine mumbles awkwardly.

"That's right. Last I heard, you were in that awful camp. How was it, by the way?"

"Awful as you can expect. Though the males there were all valiant and resilient."

"And you had enough food?"

"Of course. You know those camps. There's always food."

"Good, good. I know why this had to happen, but I hate it for you nonetheless."

"We just got here, actually," Mine cuts her off.

"We?"

"Yes. Minnie is with me. Though I don't know where she's off to at the moment."

"I'm going to meet her? Finally? That is such good news, dear. I am so excited about it. I should let your father know too so he can come. Maybe organize a feast. There should be food in the fridge, but perhaps she'd like something else. I can—"

"Mom," Mine says affectionately. "Why don't you meet her first before bringing Father along? I think she's rather...anxious about meeting you."

"Anxious? Why would she be? You've told her not to worry, no? I've heard so much about her so far that I think I already know her. You have no idea how excited I am that she's finally here."

"Just... This once, all right? Next time she can meet Father too."

A pause.

"I suppose. I should at least prepare something to eat?"

Immediately, I take a liking to her.

Yes, please! Make something yummy for me to eat because I'm starving!

"Maybe later. I should check on Minnie first—"

"No!" I yelp out, jumping out of the bathtub. How dare he postpone my food?

"What was that, dear?" his mother asks.

"Nothing. I think some food would be nice."

"Is Minnie partial to anything?"

"She loves sweet things. And she only eats beef."

"I can make a steak and some rice to go along. Do you think she'd like that?"

And some dessert? Maybe, hopefully?

"I'm sure she would. I think we have some cherry jam. Do you mind making some donuts too?"

"Of course not."

I sigh in relief. Food is coming. Oh my, but his mother is so nice. I already love her. Well, *almost*-love her. I'll reserve judgment until I see how good her donuts are.

But until then I should make sure I'm presentable.

I lather myself in soap two more times so I'm particularly clean. The last thing I need is for his mother to have a similar obsession with cleanliness and judge me for being dirty.

Perhaps I do go a little overboard with scrubbing my skin until it's red and tender, but that quickly heals and I'm as good as new.

Using some energy, I dry my hair and comb it perfectly in place. To my surprise, the bathroom has everything I might need, including some feminine products I've never heard of.

That perfect male. He thought of everything, didn't he?

Smiling to myself, I grab my dress and proceed to try to wash it. Although I get out most of the smell, it still has some oil stains from the car that will simply not come out.

Sighing, I put it on and mentally prepare myself to go downstairs.

But just as I'm about to leave the bathroom, I notice there's another door on the other end. Though pressed for time, curiosity gets the best of me and I open it.

This must be the second room Mine mentioned, I think to myself as I step inside. My eyes widen in shock as I take in the sheer size of it. It's perhaps twice as big as the bedroom, and it's filled with things—feminine things. Are these his mother's by any chance? Yet the more I look around, the more I doubt that.

There are tens if not hundreds of gowns hung tidily in an open closet, with a couple of spectacular pieces worn by mannequins. On the other side, there are rows and rows of shoes, each pair more beautiful than the other. And then at the end of the room there is a wall covered in jewelry cases.

I'm...speechless.

Tentatively stepping inside, I stop in front of the first mannequin. It's wearing a long burgundy dress. The bodice has a square neckline and a tight corset while the skirt flows out, aided by the countless layers of lace and material underneath.

Yet what strikes me immediately is the fact that it appears to be my size. And to confirm, I gauge my waist with my palm length and then do the same with the dress.

It fits.

Confused, I check the other dresses. All are in my size, some of them almost as if they were custom made so that the waist is small while the upper bodice is more generous for my chest.

I gulp down, a wave of emotions rolling over me.

Did he...did he do this for me?

These are some of the most exquisite clothes I've ever seen.

Turning to the shoe wall, I grab a couple random pairs and slip them on. If they all fit, then these are for me.

I try pair after pair, and not surprisingly, they all fit.

My heart beats loudly in my chest and my eyes fill with tears. He did this for me.

I don't know when he did it, or why, or even how. How did he even know my sizes so well? But a deep sense of awe and appreciation fills me.

For someone who's not very concerned about clothes or shoes, or even jewelry—although I do like pretty things like any other female—the sight of this room fills me with more joy than I've ever felt in my life. But it's not for the material things. It's for the meaning behind them.

He thought of me. Even when I doubted he did, he thought of me.

He never stopped thinking of me.

The door behind me opens again and he steps into the room. So lost in my thoughts I was that I let my guard down and he snuck up on me. I didn't hear him. Not when the loudest sound in this room was my thudding heart.

"I planned to show you this a little later," he mentions.

I slowly turn and wipe the moisture from my lashes.

"When did you do this?"

He shrugs. "Here and there, while I was waiting for you."

My brows go up. "You bought so much in so little time?"

Another shrug. "I've been waiting for what feels like an eternity."

I gulp down. "Thank you."

"My mother is making food. Why don't you choose one of these dresses and come down with me to meet her?"

I nod slowly. He doesn't ask me why I bolted when I did, as if he already knew my deepest thoughts and worries.

"How about this one?" he asks as he picks a blue day dress.

"I want the red," I say as I point to the same dress but in red.

"Blue is my favorite. Wear it for me?" His voice is soft, warm. How can I refuse him?

I take it and shed my dress so I can put it on. Mine comes around to zip me up at the back.

"And these shoes?" He holds up a pair of black slippers.

"Thank you," I murmur.

He leads me out of the room and down the main stairs toward the ground floor. My anxiety is all but gone as I stare up at his handsome profile. There's a fluttering in my lower stomach that I would have confused for hunger in the past, but now I know better. It's him; my reaction to him; everything he makes me feel.

It's *only* him. And a little bit of hunger, but that's almost forgotten at this point.

We head toward the dining room, and I'm surprised to see the table has already been set up. There is a basket of bread on the table, a tray full of juicy steak that's having me salivate on the spot and another tray filled with roast potatoes. Although I'm starving, it's not the food that has my full attention.

It's the platter of donuts at the end of the table. Just as promised, his mother made donuts from scratch. Though I know they are filled with cherry jam, I'm surprised to see the chocolate drizzled on top of them.

Of course I can't be a heathen and start with dessert. I must show her my best side, and that means highlighting how good I am for her son, how proper and polite.

Nodding to myself, I straighten my back and try to momentarily forget about the donuts.

"Mother," Mine says as his mother enters the dining room, carrying a platter with a variety of cheeses.

I slowly turn, plastering a polite smile on my face as I curtsy —perhaps that's a little overkill, but if it wins me points...?

I might have seen her before in the divining mirror, but seeing her in the flesh is completely different. She's slightly taller than me and very slender. Dressed in a dark green dress that reaches her ankles, she has a thick belt wrapped around her waist, emphasizing how slight she is.

Her hair is a dark brown like Mine's, her face small and dainty with huge blue eyes and pouty lips. Yet even more surprising is how young she looks. One would think she's his sister, not his mother.

"You must be Minnie," she says with an affable smile on her face. "I am Rità. I am so happy to finally meet you."

"Hello, Rità," I greet softly. "It's good to meet you too. Your son has told me so much about you." How do I even call him? Lucien? Valerion? I can't very well call him *Mine* in front of his mother, no?

"He has? That's news to me." Her brows go up as she sneaks a glance at Mine.

"Just that I take after you, Mom." He winks.

"Thank you so much for the food. You didn't have to bother," I add a small platitude.

"It was no bother! Valerion told me you helped him escape that wretched place. For that alone I must thank you."

"It was nothing." I wave my hand. "He would have handled it without me too. Your son is a great warrior," I say, a genuine praise. Glancing at Mine, I note a slight blush on his cheeks.

"That he is. I've always been proud of his achievements, though I don't like how often he puts himself in danger. Especially with his health..."

"I'm fine, Mom. I told you there's nothing to worry about," he adds in a pointed tone as if there's something more to the conversation I'm not aware of.

"He's told me about his illness and so far he hasn't had another episode."

"He...has?" His mother blinks in surprise. "You have?" she asks, this time addressing him directly.

He shrugs nonchalantly. "I figured this time she should know."

I frown. "This time? What does that mean?"

Mine gives me a smile. "Nothing of consequence."

"Why don't we sit down and eat?" his mother interjects.

Still a little confused, I follow suit and sit at the table. Mine, ever the perfect gentleman, grabs my plate and fills it with beef and potatoes. He cuts each item into small pieces so it can cool off, forgetting I don't need any help on that front. Still, his gesture is duly noted and I graze my fingers against his when I accept the plate back.

The urge to dig in is overwhelming, but I temper myself. This isn't about showing what a starving animal I am. On the contrary, this is about making a good impressing on his mother and showing her what a polite lady I am.

"Valerion tells me you worked as a nurse in the war?"

"Yes, that is correct." I grab one small bite of meat and place it in my mouth, then chew slowly, properly...demurely.

"Awful thing, this war. I'm so happy it's about to end."

"It is?" That is news to me.

His mother glances quickly at Mine before she clears her throat.

"The Allies have invaded much of Germany. It is only a matter of time before it surrenders."

"I suppose so. Though there is something odd about this war..." I muse aloud.

"Odd?" Rità frowns.

"You may speak freely, Minnie. My mother knows about my particular abilities."

"She does? And she believes you?" I lean in to whisper. From what I have gleaned from my time in Anthropa, very few humans are accepting of the supernatural. Most of them pretend it's only a fanciful notion or that the people who believe in it must be mad.

He nods. "She's actually an academic on the topic of the occult."

"She...is? You never mentioned."

That's odd. Shouldn't he have said something about it at some point? We've been dealing with facets of the occult since we met, and there were numerous times when we would have needed more information. Someone with her background could have helped us.

He shrugs and gives me a silent smile. "It must have slipped my mind."

I blink and furrow my brows. That's not something to slip one's mind, is it?

"Then there are people who study the supernatural in your world?" I ask.

"Something like that." He chuckles.

"That's how you knew about the museum, then?"

"Yes."

"Does she know about Aperion, too?"

"She can hear you, you know. You can ask her yourself."

I sneak a glance at his mother and she's regarding me with a pleasant smile.

"Did you tell her about me?"

"Of course not," he quickly adds in the same low voice. "I would never do that without your approval."

"Good. You're a good male." I pat him on the back affectionately.

"You may tell her however much you want, but I can assure you she is trustworthy."

"She's your mother. Of course I would never think to doubt her."

That makes him smile. He grabs my hand and lays a kiss on my knuckles.

"If I may ask," his mother begins, "what is it about this war that you think is odd?"

"I am not sure yet, but when we were at that prisoner camp, I detected some strong runes. Demonic in origin."

His mother stops eating, slowly laying her cutlery down.

"Demonic, you say?"

I nod. "I did not recognize them, and I have not yet had the chance to look further into what that could mean. But I think it might have to do with the rumors that those Germans are running extermination camps. I am not sure how much you know about demons, but most of them feed on souls and—"

Rità stops me. "I am aware. There are a few covens of witches that have declared themselves demon hunters, though without much success over the years."

I nod. "Depending on the type of demon, they can be very hard to kill. Especially if they are a Son of Tenebreis, natural-born demons," I mutter, disdain dripping from my words.

His mother strains a smile. "And why do you think demons might be involved?"

"I am not sure. But demons have always been drawn to conflict due to the large number of deaths. The Sons of Tenebreis are said to use those made demons to get stronger so they can finally escape their prison realm. It wouldn't be far-fetched to believe the SoT are trying to create more conflicts so they can consume more souls."

"The only issue I would have with that is the fact that people were not killed in cold blood at my camp. Sure, there were those who tried to escape, but otherwise, we were left alone."

"Perhaps your camp, but I have heard rumors of medical experiments."

"What type of experiments?"

Rità straightens her back and leans forward.

"Underground laboratories where disgraced doctors perform all types of tests. Some of them are merely biological, testing the limits of the human body. But others..." She glances at Mine. "I have heard from some sources that they are trying to see what happens after death."

"How would they do that?"

"By killing someone and then reviving them."

"How is that possible?" I blink in confusion.

"There are some ways to momentarily stop the heart," Mine explains. "Freezing temperatures can do that to the human body. If submerged in freezing water, the heart eventually stops. If the body is then immediately taken out and electric impulses are sent to the heart, the person can, technically, revive from the dead."

"What?" I whisper, shocked. "I have never heard of anything like that."

"There are cases in which this type of death occurs naturally, which is why we have accounts of people's experiences of the afterlife," his mother explains.

That only makes me more confused. Life and death are black and white. There are no shades of gray in the middle. No dying and coming back—under any circumstances. Well...technically, there is no coming back if we're talking about mortals. There are other ways to come back, one being as a made-demon, or as one of those rare vampires created by the House of Skia.

"But..." My brows knit together. "If they are to go to the afterlife, that would mean they would follow a messenger to P'asala. They cannot return once they do that."

"They can and they do," Rità mentions. "I've seen it in my research. In fact, I've interviewed a great number of people who've experienced these near-death episodes and they all described similar things. They recall being led down a long, barren road toward an unknown destination and seeing some type of apparitions before being yanked back into their bodies."

"That..."

"I can only conclude that it must not be their time to die yet and thus they are allowed to return to their bodies while their mortal biology still allows it."

I mull on her words for a moment. Although it seems impossible to believe, there is a logical explanation to it. Mistakes happen, as evidenced by my interference with fate. And the

House of Moirai is always striving to fix those mistakes. If the mortal in question can still survive in their original body, then it stands to reason that the House of Moirai would send them back. Given that the messengers are not sentient beings, they cannot stop a soul from being sent back by a higher power.

What strikes me the most is the fact that I was never taught any of this. If Rità interviewed multiple people who experienced this, then it's not a one-off phenomenon. Why was I never told this could happen?

I also assume that since the soul exits in P'asala and returns to its original realm, it once more becomes vulnerable to demon attacks. For this reason alone, we should have been taught about it.

"You think they are experimenting with killing people and reviving them?" I ask carefully. If that is true, it could change everything

"Yes, though I am still trying to understand what the aim is," she notes with a sigh.

My hand tightens around the fork before it falls onto the plate, a thud echoing in the room.

"Minnie?"

"I think I'm going to be sick," I mutter, suddenly getting up. A wave of dizziness assails me as I stumble forward. Strong arms catch me, pulling me into his embrace.

"What's wrong?" he asks, his voice worried.

His mother jumps out of her seat, coming toward me and regarding me with concern.

"You know what they're trying to do," she mentions quietly.

I nod.

Mine strokes his hand down my back in soothing motions while I regain the ability to speak.

"A low-level demon usually possesses a mortal while slowly consuming their soul," I start. "But what if..." I gulp down uneasily. "What if they didn't consume the soul and merely suppressed it. What if they cohabited with it in the same body?"

"Then if the body dies, they both..." Mine trails off.

"If, and without proper proof, this is merely a theory, but if the demon finds a way to bind to the soul while it's being led toward P'asala, then it has a direct path to Aperion."

"But wouldn't other deities hunt down the demon?"

"They would need to know it could travel to P'asala in the first place. They would never even think to look there because no living demon has ever breached the realm."

"But that's only a low-level demon." He frowns. "Surely they wouldn't be able to do that much damage."

"You don't understand. No pure-blooded Son of Tenebreis can enter Aperion. Every portal has runes to ensure that. But if someone were to remove those runes or override them..."

"The Sons of Tenebreis could invade Aperion."

"Exactly."

"But they're still trapped in their realm. How could they—"

He suddenly stops and slowly looks over my head toward his mother. "This shouldn't have happened," he whispers in shock. "This wasn't supposed to happen."

"What are you talking about?" I take a step back and study him. He's gone utterly still. His mother, too, looks perturbed.

"I've messed everything up," Mine adds with an anguished groan.

FORTY-THREE

"WHAT ARE YOU TALKING ABOUT?" I ask as I look between the two of them.

He ignores my question, instead asking one of his own. "Are you sure the Sons of Tenebreis are still trapped in Tartareia?"

I tilt my head to the side, my brows knitting together in confusion. His tone is curt and decisive, not at all that of someone who barely knows anything about the SoT.

Against my better judgment, I respond. "Yes, but there are rumors of some being able to temporarily leave Tartareia."

"Where did the rumors originate from?"

"Commander Azerius heard it from a source. I assumed he had reason to be concerned, which is why he told us to be vigilant, but we still have not had any confirmation of that."

Mine paces around the room. His mother has a tight expression on her face too, one I cannot read, nor understand.

Why would it concern them if the SoT have left Tartareia?

"How can they temporarily leave Tartareia?" he asks in a low, ominous voice.

I'm more confused. Why would he be interested in this? He's never been much concerned about the Sons of Tenebreis before. Although I am wary of revealing classified information, since this is Mine, I end up replying.

"Commander Azerius believes elites of the Sons of Tenebreis are using the Chalice to temporarily travel out of Tartareia while they are searching for a more permanent solution."

"The Chalice?" He frowns.

"Every House of Aperion has an artifact left behind by the fourteen Primordials. They have immense powers and are heavily guarded. The Chalice was the artifact held by the House of Bronte. Some time ago, the King of Bronte and his high priestess colluded together and stole the Chalice before leaving Aperion," I explain.

"I have read about these artifacts you speak of," his mother suddenly says.

I turn to her, eyes wide in shock. "You have? How?"

"A book I stumbled upon," she replies vaguely. "It described artifacts similar to those you are talking about and their power."

"Is that so?" I quirk a brow. "And what did that book say?"

"Any liquid drank from the Chalice gives the user the ability to physically withstand any injury for a short period of time. But I do not see how that would allow them to exit their realm."

Once more, I find myself suspicious of her knowledge. How would a book describing ancient Aperite artifacts be in Anthropa? Who wrote it? When? For what purpose?

Nothing makes sense the more I think of it.

They're hiding something from me and I don't know what.

I don't detect any spiritual energy from her just like I did not detect any from Mine. But that doesn't mean anything considering anyone with great spiritual energy can hide theirs.

"Because the barrier Lispera created corrodes all matter that crosses on either side of it. In theory, by using the Chalice, a Son of Tenebreis is able to pass through the barrier without damage to his physical body," I explain. "Commander Azerius theorized that after the effects of the Chalice wore off, the barrier would still affect the body unless he returned back to Tartareia."

"This Commander Azerius seems to know a great deal," Rità notes.

I nod begrudgingly. "He is in charge of protecting Aperion and by and large the entire universe. He should know everything."

We might be enemies now, but that doesn't take away the fact that Azerius is the best at his job.

"Let's postulate that this is true and the Sons of Tenebreis are using the Chalice to travel outside of Tartareia. Why would they be doing these experiments to get to Aperion?"

"They might be trying to find a way to permanently free themselves," his mother adds. "That's always been the goal."

"Yes and no. We believe they are, of course, trying to free themselves. But there is something else that we're suspecting."

Both Mine and Rità look at me expectantly.

"Together, all fourteen artifacts might be able to free the Seven from Tartarstasis."

They both blink and share a concerned look.

"Might?"

"The chances are very high."

Rità squeezes her eyes shut.

"And if that happens, that greed demon we met? There are going to be legions of those and other sin demons, unleashed in every single realm."

"Oh dear, that sounds rather bad," Rità murmurs.

"Say that again, Mom," Mine adds in a dry voice. "None of this happened before," he mutters in a low, barely audible voice.

"You keep saying that. What do you mean it didn't happen before?"

"The Seven have been in Tartarstasis for a long time, no?"

I nod.

"So we don't know how the universe would look like if they were set free. That's what I meant."

"Oh. Yes, it would be very bad."

"Perhaps we should leave this grim topic for another time and finish eating?" his mother interjects. "I must leave shortly."

"Of course," Mine says with a smile.

He leads me back to the table and all of a sudden, the

conversation switches to mundane topics like politics and the latest news about the war. I half-listen and mumble some replies, but deep down I am still unsettled by the previous conversation.

I quietly finish my steak and move on to dessert. But even the delicious sweetness of the donuts cannot calm my racing mind.

Something is off. A heaviness develops in the pit of my stomach that weighs me down, making it hard to breathe.

Soon, the dinner is over and Rità gets up to leave.

"It was lovely to meet you, Minnie. I will see you again soon."

Rità gives me a warm hug before she leaves, promising to arrange a dinner with her husband present as well. She seems in a hurry to leave, which once more makes me suspicious of the entire exchange.

"Thank you for the food. It was excellent," I tell her, mustering a small smile.

"See you soon, Mom." Mine waves her off.

After the door closes behind her, Mine and I find ourselves alone again.

Silence descends between us, heavy and palpable.

We're sitting a distance away from one another, both looking at the now closed door, both not daring to look at the other.

Something is wrong. I can feel it, not only in the way Mine and his mother behaved, but also in his body language.

A strange tension rolls off him as he stares into empty space.

"What are you hiding from me?" I ask him directly.

He swallows hard. "I don't know what you're talking about." Yet he averts his gaze.

"This, everything. Something doesn't add up and I need you to tell me what it is immediately."

"Minnie—"

"Don't you Minnie me. I might be a little naive, but I'm not stupid. Perhaps I should have questioned this more when I first learned you could see the spiritual world, but though rare, that can happen. I should have questioned it every time you had the right solution to my problems."

I move and plant myself in front of him. Hands on my hips, I stare at him, scanning his face for any reaction.

"But I was far too enamored with you to see any signs. Whenever I thought something was off, I convinced myself it's just a coincidence, or that I'm overthinking it."

Retrospectively, more things start to become suspicious. It wasn't just his so-called ability to see and touch ghosts and demons but also his unusual athleticism and speed. The time he'd cut that male in two in Aperion comes to mind.

Back then, I thought he was only a good soldier. Now it makes me wonder.

Just days ago, he took out multiple soldiers in the blink of an eye and with barely any effort.

Are there humans out there who are skilled fighters? Sure. But I've never seen someone of his caliber.

Then there's the greed demon. How many times did I read through those books and found nothing, yet he easily found exactly what we were searching for? Almost as if he knew...

Still, I didn't think much of it.

Until now. Until I find out that both him and his mother know far too much about my world—more than it is humanly possible.

"Don't even think to deny it. You promised you wouldn't lie to me."

"I won't."

His lips flatten in a tight line. He glances at me with a combination of pain and longing.

"Then tell me. How come your mother didn't blink at the mention of SoT? She didn't even ask who I was as if she already knew..."

"I did not tell her."

"And yet she knew."

"She...did."

"How?" I demand.

"Minnie..." he groans aloud. "I wish I could tell you."

"Then tell me. What's stopping you?"

"I can't. Not yet. Can you just...trust me?"

"Trust you about what? Because I did trust you, but it seems that was misplaced since you've been deceiving me from the start."

"That's not true," he quickly protests. "I may not have told you everything. But I never once told you a lie."

"What about omissions?" I raise a brow at him. "What about vague statements that may not have been lies but were not entirely truthful anyway?"

He takes a deep breath. Placing his hands on my shoulders, he looks me straight in the eye, his gaze conflicted and anguished.

"I vow to you that everything I did was for your well-being. I would never hurt you. You know that."

"Do I?" I whisper. "I know I'm not the sharpest when it comes to language and word play, and now I can't help but feel that you took advantage of that."

"Minnie..."

"Your mother looks to be around twenty-something in human years. Even if she had you extremely young, it's impossible she would look this young."

He doesn't speak.

"How old is she?"

He doesn't reply.

"How old is she, Valerion?"

At the mention of his given name, he snaps out of it.

"If I answered that, I would have to lie," he whispers.

"She isn't human."

Silence.

"You aren't human either."

More silence.

"What are you?"

"I can't tell you yet, Minnie. Please." He pulls me into his arms, holding me tightly. "Give me some time. I will tell you everything when I can. I promise," he murmurs in my ear. "Everything I've ever done has been for you, Minnie. Everything."

He takes a deep breath.

"Time and time again, I tried and tried, and yet it's never good enough. It always ends the same... So please..."

I push him off me.

"What are you talking about? What ends the same?"

"I can't say more. Not yet." He shakes his head.

"I see." Though I don't. If anything, I'm more confused than ever.

If he's not human, what is he? And if he is something else, how come I never sensed it?

Taking a step back, then another, I find my back slamming against the front door. Tense, Mine is frozen on the spot as he follows my every movement.

"I need space. I can't think when you're this close to me," I mutter, seeking the doorknob at my back.

"Minnie, please." He takes a step forward.

I give him a sad smile and shake my head. Opening the door, I run at full speed away from the house.

His voice echoes in my ear as I continue on, never once looking back. I keep thinking he might follow, that he might somehow reveal some unexpected abilities.

But he never does.

Only his voice follows, his anguished scream. Though perhaps that's just my mind playing it on a loop as I feel more and more guilty about my departure.

Yet how could I stay?

How could I remain there and listen to his non answers, knowing that the more he talks the more I'll overlook everything and go along with his nonsensical explanation.

Just being in his presence clouds my mind, and I need to be able to think clearly to make sense of everything.

Moments later, drawn by the bustling noise of the city, I reach Paris.

I stop in the middle of a busy road and barely avoid a moving car. Jumping to the side, I roll over on the pavement.

The sharp rocks dig into my elbows and knees, and I let out an annoyed groan of pain.

Someone asks me if I'm all right. Pulling my dress over my injuries to hide the healing flesh, I tell them I'm fine and thank them for their concern.

Nodding, they move along.

I remain behind, rooted to the spot.

More people move by me, talking animatedly about their day, about their hopes for the future. The war is ending, they say. The Nazis are defeated, they say.

The world is changing.

And I have a feeling my world is changing, too. I just wonder if it's for the better or for the worse.

My feet eventually move, and I start walking slowly, mechanically.

The smell of fresh pastries wafts through the air, but instead of whetting my appetite, it only turns my stomach inside out.

What could Mine be hiding from me that he cannot possibly tell me? And how are his parents involved? It's clear that his mother is not human, and by extension he is not human, either.

But what could he be?

Descendant of a deity? Other species?

There are so many supernatural species that live hundreds to thousands of years, and I'm not an expert on most of them. They could be anything for all I know. But he must know that wouldn't change how I feel about him. So why all the secrecy?

Why can he not tell me now?

The more I think about his vague words and musings since I met him, the more confused I become.

If he's not human, doesn't he realize that's perfect for us? Not only would his life span be much longer, thereby giving us more time to be together, but we might also be biologically compatible. We could, in theory, become mated.

I might be mad at his lies by omission, but that doesn't mean I am mad at the end result. So I cannot understand why he would hide it.

Unless...

I stop in my tracks.

He wouldn't hide it unless he thought he should hide it.

Demon.

The possibility is like a punch to the gut.

But that cannot be. I've trained my entire life to be able to detect demonic spiritual energy. There is nothing about him that signals demon. By the Source, I drank his blood and I never sensed anything unusual about him!

I shake my head and mentally berate myself for even thinking something like that.

He cannot be a demon for the simple reason that he is good. He's kind and heroic and the best male I've ever known. And he is mine.

So what if he technically lied and hid things from me? So what if he's not ready to tell me what he is? He asked me to trust him, and that is what I should have done from the start.

I should have never left his home in the first place. Instead, we should have talked more until I understood more of his reasoning—even if he could not reveal everything.

He accused me of not trusting him before, and I fear I may have proven it to him this time that I, in fact, do not trust him. Even if that can't be further from the truth.

I do trust him. If I didn't, he'd probably be missing a limb or two right now.

I suppose I am a little miffed about not seeing the signs earlier. They were right in front of me, but unfortunately, I'm on the slower side when it comes to catching on. He was aware of this too, because he revealed just enough not to make me question him.

So I can see it from his perspective too. He did, in fact, not lie.

It's getting dark. Winter in Anthropa means their days are much shorter while the nights are longer. Used my entire life to the ever-present light of Aperion, I find that I quite like the night.

Street lamps light up. The area is bustling with people coming and going from the many stores littered on each side of the road.

Once more, the smell of something sweet assails me. Should I get something to eat?

Though we just had dinner, my mood throughout the meal prevented me from enjoying the food even though it was delicious.

Materializing some coins—it seems thieving is much easier after you've done it a few times—I buy a chocolate croissant from one of the pastry shops.

The flavor is delightful and I slowly savor it as I look around the other shops.

Most of them seem to be clothing stores, and looking at the mannequins in the window wearing the latest fashions seems to take my mind off my dilemma for the moment.

Nibbling at the chocolate core, I stop in front of a different type of shop. My gaze is arrested to the white dress in the window. It has a tight bodice with thousands of shiny beads and a silk skirt.

It's a wedding shop.

I'm staring at a wedding dress.

Since the topic of marriage has become so ubiquitous between us, I've learned a thing or two about traditions in this part of Anthropa. A white wedding dress is the standard, as is the sharing of rings on the wedding day to symbolize eternal love—or something like that.

In Aperion, there is no set color for a wedding dress. Instead, the bride and groom wear their family's colors and insignia.

The House of Cryos has a combination of light blue and white in two concentric circles. On top of the color scheme is a black dagger with one skull on the top right side and another on the lower left side.

If I were to marry Mine in an Aperite fashion, my wedding gown would feature a dress with that color combination as well as the crown that's been in my family for eons—a crown made up of a succession of small skull daggers.

When I was a fledgling, I was fascinated by that crown, and I have, on occasion snuck into the artifact room to try it on. Back then it was too big for my head, but I still loved the regal aura it lent me.

Alas, I will never wear that now.

Still staring at that wedding dress, I pop the last bit of the croissant into my mouth, lick my fingers, and decide to stride inside.

"May I help you?" someone immediately asks.

"That dress. I want to try it on." I point to the mannequin.

"Excellent choice! It's the new style. It just came in on Friday."

The sales lady takes me to the fitting room and brings me the dress in my size.

"Let me know if you need anything," she adds as she closes the door, leaving me alone with the dress.

It's even more stunning in person. The beads are arranged with such care and craftsmanship that I'm almost wary to touch it.

After shedding my dress, I slowly put it on, using my powers to pull up the zipper at the back and button myself up.

The dress is a little long, though given my short stature, most ready-to-wear dresses in this world are on the longer side.

I close my eyes and think back to Mine's secret closet. Choosing one of the heeled sandals, I manifest them in the cabin with me and put them on.

Patting the skirt down, I'm impressed by how soft the silk is and how well it fits my body.

I take a step back and regard myself in the mirror.

Can I picture myself wearing this while getting married to him?

The answer is an immediate yes. And it's not just the dress. It's also because it's him.

Perhaps I am an idiot, but there isn't much that would turn me off him. He could be anything; even an ogre for all I care—though I hear those live in a different world.

With this dress on, the intention materializes deeper and deeper in my breast.

I will trust him no matter what. And I will marry him no matter what, too.

"I'll take it," I tell the sales lady after I've changed into my own clothes. Of course I'm once more paying with stolen money, but the joy of having a wedding dress of my own is too strong for me to care.

I'm a thief, so what? To be with Mine, there isn't anything I wouldn't become. Rule breaker? Check. An outcast? Already done. Inter-realm criminal? Already done that too. Killer? Well, I was one long before him if we're talking about demons. Mortals, though? For him, I would do that too.

Smiling to myself, I grab the bag with the dress from the cashier and leave.

I think I've been gone long enough now. I should go back so he doesn't worry too much. I should also apologize for my reaction and assure him I will trust him, whatever it is that he is hiding from me.

With that in mind, I hide my presence from mortals and prepare to teleport.

But that never happens.

The hair on the back of my neck stands up. A current of energy travels through me, shocking me into submission.

I cannot move. A familiar sensation.

Within seconds, my hunch is confirmed when Cerenios appears in front of me.

"Hello, Minerva. It's been a while."

He smiles slowly at me, a predatory smile that does not reach his eyes.

If I could, I'd spit him right between those cold eyes of his. Then I'd knee him between the legs—not sure if that would hurt him as much as it does mortals, but wishful thinking.

Of course I can do none of that, seeing that he's once more holding me captive with whatever mind control he's got going.

Bastard!

"I have been looking for you since your energy signature disappeared from Aperion, but I have been unable to detect it until now. Interesting, is it not?"

That is indeed quite odd. I didn't shield my energy signature properly, mostly because I didn't think anyone would be looking for me so soon.

"More interesting is the fact that General Molokai is missing. You wouldn't happen to know where your brother is, would you?"

With a flick of his wrist, he allows me to speak.

"I don't know," I answer drily. "Probably screwing some faerie."

"Language, Minerva." He tsks at me. "You should not be allowed to speak like that."

"Is that so?" I grit out.

"Of course, if it were up to me, you would not be allowed to exist. But all things at their time."

I am not sure why he hates me so much, but this pretty much confirmed he's looking to have me executed. Given his clear distaste of me, he'll probably find any reason to put me on that execution block.

"And what will Commander Azerius say about your targeted attacks? I'll make sure everyone knows how you threatened to fabricate lies about me."

He shrugs.

"Good for me that I will not have to fabricate anything. You created your own circumstances without any interference from my part." He smirks. "I will say, though. Whatever shield you used to mask your energy worked very well until now. It took me longer than I would have thought to find you."

"Ah, such a high praise from one such as yourself," I spit out mockingly.

"I can both recognize you are a pest to be exterminated and admit your abilities are...decent."

If only I could move... I'd wipe out that stupid self-assured grin off his face.

"Then why are you so bent on destroying me and my reputation? I'm a good soldier. I've only ever been a good soldier and I've made solid contributions in the fight against demons!" I cry out in frustration.

"Perhaps." He tilts his head to the side and studies me. "But you are also everything that is wrong with our society."

"What are you talking about?"

"You have a rebellious streak that is prone to breaking the rules. Aperion is Aperion because of its rules. Therefore, you are incompatible with Aperion," he states matter-of-factly.

"You're insane," I whisper.

"Maybe. But you are lucky I've decided to be magnanimous."

I regard him with a mix of fear and disdain. Nothing he has in mind can be good for me.

"I have decided to spare you from execution."

"Very magnanimous," I mutter and roll my eyes. Let's see, for what price?

"In exchange, I will kill you myself. You will then get the opportunity to be reincarnated and your mind can be reprogrammed. It is, after all, a pity to waste someone with your potential."

"What—"

"Of course I would never attempt to kill a defenseless person. There is no honor in that."

In the blink of an eye, the scenery around us changes to an empty field.

His mind control wears off and I can move my limbs. I take a step back, stretching my muscles.

He appears in front of me, fully armored, his hand on his sword.

"You may defend yourself and fight me. I would encourage you to do so since I would rather like the exercise." He pauses. "But know you will not leave this field alive."

Then he strikes.

FORTY-FOUR

ICE SPREADS OVER MY BODY, creating a protective armor just as the first blast of energy hits me. I'm thrown back with a force that slams me against a tree. My lungs constrict as the air is knocked out of me, but I am shielded from any direct injuries by the icy shell.

With great effort, I push myself off the ground and watch as Cerenios approaches with casual ease.

"I hope you will provide some entertainment before your inevitable death," he taunts. "Though it pains me to end the life of such a pathetic weakling."

"You're a despicable being," I manage to say through labored breaths, trying to regain my composure.

He simply shrugs. "Perhaps. But an efficient one."

In an instant, another wave of energy is hurtling toward me. This time it takes on a deep burgundy hue, swirling and pulsing with increasing intensity as it closes in on me.

Just barely avoiding its deadly trajectory, I drop to the ground and watch in horror as it slices through trees, leaving a trail of destruction in its wake. The severed trunks thud against the forest floor with a sickening weight, followed by more trees toppling over in the aftershocks of the attack.

My heart races as I gulp down nervously, my palms slick

with sweat. His muscular frame towers over me, his presence alone enough to strike fear into my bones. If that had hit me, I would be dead.

"You say you must kill me. Why? Who gave the order?" My voice trembles as I attempt to reason with him.

"In cases such as yours, no order is necessary. I am allowed to act as I see fit," he states coldly, his expression betraying no hint of remorse.

"This will cause a scandal. You forget I am part of the royal House of Cryos." I try to use my status to appeal to his sense of duty and honor.

"And you think anyone will miss you?" His lips slowly tug up in a mocking smile. "I did my research on you, Minerva. Your family will be rather pleased to see you gone." His words hit me like a physical blow, but I refuse to let him see my weakness.

He's right. The only one who cares about me is Mine—the only one who will feel my absence. A sudden wave of guilt washes over me as I think of my beloved and how he always stood by my side.

My eyes widen in sudden realization. What will Mine think when I never return to him? The thought brings tears to my eyes, but I quickly blink them away, refusing to give this cruel man the satisfaction of seeing me cry.

I may put up a fight here, but I know I am no match for Cerenios. He will kill me.

Mine will never know what happened to me. He might think I abandoned him. That I decided to go back to my world and forget about him.

Tears stab at my eyes. I don't care about my own death as much as I care about Mine's opinion of me. I never want him to think I don't love him or that I could turn my back on him.

Determination within me surges with fierce intensity, propelling me forward. Failure is not an option. No matter the odds stacked against me, I must find a way to return to Mine.

Cerenios advances toward me, his sword still sheathed at his side. But his true weapon is the raw, pure energy emanating from his body. In this battle of strength and power, I am clearly outmatched.

Each time he unleashes a barrage of energy blast at me, a surge of panic courses through my veins. My armor may be impenetrable, but I know all too well that it has its weak points. Should one of his blasts find its mark, even the most minor injury could prove fatal. The thought alone is enough to send shivers down my spine.

But I cannot give up. Death may be looming over me, but I refuse to surrender. There must be a way to turn this fight in my favor.

With a flick of my wrists, two swords made of solid ice materialize in my hands. Against Cerenios' energy attacks, close combat may be my only chance at survival.

I charge toward him, swinging my swords with calculated precision aimed for his neck. He raises his sword in defense, effortlessly blocking my strike without ever unsheathing his weapon.

My speed proves advantageous as I quickly teleport behind him and thrust my blades toward his unprotected back. But just before they make contact with his flesh, he vanishes into thin air and reappears behind me.

"Nice try," he whispers in my ear just as he pushes the handle of his sword into my back. The blow is imbued with energy, and what would have been a light injury becomes a ravaging one as I'm thrown farther into the field, flying past the cut-down trees until I finally hit the trunk of a still standing one.

I struggle to control my harsh, ragged breathing as intense pain radiates from the spot where I was struck. My hand probes around my back, searching for the source of the injury, and my eyes widen in shock when I feel the unmistakable cracks in my armor. The damage is concentrated on my lower back, a large crack followed by hairline fractures that spiderweb across the surface. But it's not just my back that's affected. As I glance down at my torso, I see the fine lines etched into the once impenetrable ice armor, tracing their way around my stomach and chest. A shiver runs down my spine at the realization.

It can't be possible...

This armor is crafted from the strongest ice in the universe. Yet here I am, already injured from a single strike that didn't even use the sharp end of Cerenios' sword. How could this be?

Cerenios materializes in front of me, his sword securely sheathed at his waist. His expression is one of boredom as he gazes at me with cold detachment.

With a disappointed shake of his head, he asks, "That is all?"

I grit my teeth and stand up, ignoring the sharp pain that courses through my body. Every movement seems to exacerbate the fractures in my back, causing me to hold back any cries of agony.

But then I feel it—a loud snap that echoes through the air. My hand flies to my back and I realize with horror that the crack has turned into a gaping hole, one that threatens to spread even further.

Fueled by determination and desperation, I grab my swords and let out a fierce battle cry before launching into attack mode.

I can't go down without a fight. I won't.

My strikes are wild and untargeted, driven solely by instinct and adrenaline. But as I continue to attack, I start to notice something—my speed is slightly faster than my opponent's. It may only be by a nanosecond at first, but with each strike, it stretches into multiple ones while I keep his other senses distracted.

Finally, it all culminates in one powerful strike, using my swords to create an illusion of attack while simultaneously conjuring a dagger of eternal ice from my wrist and shielding it under one of the swords.

As I swing my swords toward him, he gracefully deflects them with a flick of his wrist. But in that moment of distraction, I seize the opportunity to send a shard of ice flying toward his chest. The sharp edge pierces through his skin just as he opens his palm to unleash a powerful wave of energy toward me.

The impact is deafening and my armor can barely withstand it. A loud snap echoes through the air and my protective gear shatters into pieces, falling to the ground in a heap. The spot where the energy blast hit me turns red and throbs with intense pain, causing me to double over and spit out a mouthful of blood.

But despite the agony coursing through my body, I can't help but feel a sense of satisfaction. My eternal ice has made contact with his skin, sending thousands of particles throughout his body, ready to wreak havoc on his cells.

In response to the foreign substance invading his bloodstream, his armor quickly envelops his body, trying to contain and counteract the effects of the icy particles spreading inside him.

I focus on conjuring all my energy, pushing past the searing pain that radiates from my wounds. With every ounce of strength I possess, I will tiny particles of eternal ice to form within Cerenios' heart, commanding them to freeze and create a barrier to stop the blood flow. His brows furrow in shock as his body stiffens, his black armor pulsing and dissipating in the areas where the eternal ice takes hold.

His expression morphs to one of anger as he turns his gaze toward me.

"Not so smug now, are you?" I smirk at him, my own pain temporarily forgotten.

"This...eternal ice." He grunts, small patches of frost forming on his chest. If my pain is a nine out of ten, then his must be unimaginable. Eternal ice is known as one of the most excruciating substances in existence, coveted by many for its power. It's no wonder Theron's family sought an alliance with mine.

"Neat trick," Cerenios mutters.

"Neat trick?" I raise an eyebrow. "I don't think you'll say the same when your heart freezes and bursts in your chest. Any moment now."

He stares at me.

"Any moment?" He raises a brow skeptically. "Do let me know when that moment comes."

I frown. Moments pass. Nothing happens. The ice at the surface of his skin recedes.

Summoning more of my energy, I attempt to make contact with the ice particles inside of him.

But no matter how hard I try, I cannot sense them.

They're gone. They're not inside his body, or anywhere else for that matter. It's like they never existed.

"H-how?" I ask in a broken whisper.

All my hopes were pinned on that one trick. It had never failed me before, regardless of my adversary's strength or abilities. Though I may not boast a high level like others, my inherited powers were enough to see me through any challenge.

But this...this is something new entirely.

Eternal ice—the name itself hints at its indestructible nature. This substance cannot be melted, vanquished, or even destroyed. It is one of the strongest and most resilient materials in existence, with no being in the world able to survive it. And when fine particles of it enter the body, clogging arteries and stopping vital organs, there is no chance for survival. Not only does it cause harm, but it also prevents any form of healing.

No matter how strong one's spiritual energy may be, if they can't heal, they are doomed to die.

But Cerenios isn't dying. Far from it. He stands before me with an amused look on his face as if he were indulging a small child with a simple party trick.

"I have heard, of course, of your eternal ice," he starts, walking casually toward me.

I take slow steps backward, each one sending a jolt of agony through my abdomen. My heart races in terror as I see the nonchalant expression on his face, a stark contrast to the pain and fear consuming me.

My body feels like it's being weighed down by chains, my energy levels drained from the intense battle. But despite my weakened state, I refuse to back down.

"You think you know enough about eternal ice? You can barely control it," he taunts.

My eyes widen in confusion. "What are you talking about?"

He smirks. "Eternal ice may be invincible in theory, but in practice, it is only as strong as its wielder."

"That's not true!" I argue desperately.

"Isn't it? Then how do you explain the fact that I am still standing?" he challenges.

I stumble backward and fall to the ground, the impact causing more pain to erupt from my already injured stomach. My movements are sluggish and weak, and I feel like I'm drowning in my own blood.

He looms over me now, just a few paces away. "If your energy level was even close to mine, perhaps your attack would have been effective. But as it stands..." His voice trails off with a mocking chuckle. "I suppose it just tickled."

"It...tickled?" I gape at him in disbelief.

He shrugs casually. "A cold tickle," he clarifies with a smirk.

I don't know whether I should laugh or cry at his statement.

I end up doing both.

The tears are from the pain while the laughter is from the hopelessness.

I was quite arrogant to think someone like me could defeat the great Cerenios, wasn't I?

I can still fight. I still have energy left. But as my stomach injury heals, I realize that it is moot.

Everything is moot.

With one motion, he lifts me in the air, staring at me.

"You might have lived still, if you did not cross paths with Wyn," he tells me. "I take her safety very seriously, and your mere presence jeopardizes it."

"I only talked to her for a moment," I protest. "And we didn't speak of anything scandalous!"

"Perhaps you did, perhaps you did not. I do not take risks with her safety. Therefore, you will have to be exterminated."

"You're crazy."

He shrugs. "I am crazy good at my job." And with that, he opens his palm and gathers a ball of dark energy that he presses into my stomach.

A guttural cry bursts from my throat, my body thrashing wildly as I struggle to break free from his telekinetic hold. But his grip on me is unyielding, his powers acting like a searing laser that slices through layers of skin and muscle to reach deep into my organs.

Blood gushes up my throat, forcing me to choke and gasp for air. The pain intensifies with each passing second, the hole in my stomach expanding at an alarming rate under the relentless assault of his energy.

Desperately, I try to use what little control I have left over my own abilities to heal the damage he's inflicting. Every slight pause in his attacks is met with a burst of healing energy, but it's only a temporary reprieve. I know that no matter how hard I fight, my death is inevitable.

Still, some stubborn part of me refuses to give up. Through the agonizing pain, I focus on the simple mantra: Bear. Heal. Bear. Heal. Over and over again, I bear the excruciating agony before mustering all my strength to heal myself. Each time, it's only a small amount, but it's enough to shield my heart from his destructive onslaught.

More blood comes out of my mouth, and in an act of defiance, I spit it right in his face.

His nostrils flare in disgust and he thrusts me away from him. Despite the pain coursing through my body, I take advantage of the distance to heal my wounds. My energy is rapidly draining, but I can't help but wonder if I've found a weakness in him.

He brings his sleeve to his face to wipe off my blood, repulsed by its touch. He's so disgusted that he doesn't even realize when I flash behind him and tackle him to the ground.

Without enough strength to summon my swords, I resort to using my fists. Straddling him on the ground, I rain down punch after punch on his face until my skin is scraped raw and my knuckles are bleeding.

But as my own blood threatens to mingle with his, something flashes in his eyes and he delivers a powerful blow that sends me flying across the field. I dig my feet into the ground, skidding backward until finally coming to a stop. Every breath is ragged and painful, my throat still raw from our earlier encounter.

I see him get to his feet, his expression a mixture of panic and annoyance. He wipes at his face, cleaning himself until there's no more trace of me left.

It's odd. Yet that oddity might be my winning ticket. So far, he hasn't touched me. Every time, he used his telekinesis or his energy blasts to strike me.

Using my nails, I prick my skin at the back of my elbow on each arm, letting a small rivulet of blood flow down my wrist. Once my skin is stained red, I flash myself to his side.

His eyes are on my bloody arms and even bloodier clothes, so much so he doesn't notice the blast of energy behind him.

It hits him in the back of the head, making him reel. He stumbles forward, and pressing his hand to his nape, he finds it sticky with blood. My brows knit into a frown when I note that the color of his blood is such a dark red, it's bordering on black.

What...

His expression suddenly changes into cold, murderous intent. If before he'd been mostly amused by little old me trying to fight in the big leagues, now he's killing me with his gaze alone.

Coldness seeps into my bones as I step back.

He swipes his fingers over his bloody nape and brings them in front of him, staring at that oddly colored liquid with an odd glint in his eyes.

"Game over, Minerva." He slowly lifts his eyes. It's almost

as if a film covers his irises. They're no longer a golden hue, but a dark burgundy one that flashes dangerously at me.

His next strike, I don't even see.

I'm still rooted to the spot, terrified of what's to come, when the first stab of pain brings me to my knees.

I look down to see his hand. His gloved hand shoved deep into my chest cavity.

I let out a loud gasp, followed by a wheezing sound as his fingers dig around the inside of my chest until they find their target.

He grips my heart and pulls, ripping it out of my chest.

One last breath leaves my lips, enough to see that vital organ drop to the ground next to me, enough to realize that this is the end.

"Mine," I whisper or attempt to. He needs to know; he needs to...

Coldness surrounds me and my gaze becomes blurry.

A dark cloud descends into the forest, or is it a tornado? I cannot tell for sure, just as I cannot tell any longer what is real and what is not.

This swirl of dark matter lands on the ground next to me and starts gaining the shape of a person, a male.

His features are shrouded in mystery, but there is something familiar about him.

Something...

A loud, shrilly sound erupts from that swirl of dark mist as it witnesses my death. The dark matter fills the entire area like a thick fog, making it impossible to see what's happening.

That I'm still conscious—if this is real—is a miracle in itself. But the real miracle happens when I feel something touching me.

I cannot move. I cannot blink. I can only think, and even that is from a faraway place that doesn't seem like me.

Something warm and wet is placed within my open chest. Probing hands look for the perfect placement, and once the piece fits in the puzzle, a burst of energy explodes within me.

Healing energy travels to my newly returned heart, repairing my arteries and all connective tissue.

Slowly, so very slowly, my body recognizes this is not the end. I am still alive.

But I am not sure my mind does, too.

The mist is everywhere. I want to open my mouth and warn it about Cerenios, but I cannot speak, not yet.

I lie still on the grass, my body slowly healing but still bleeding.

In the distance, I hear a tight exchange, words I cannot understand. Explosions, crashes, and loud thuds reverberate through the air. There is a war going on somewhere, but the mist makes it impossible for me to see.

Moments pass. Silence ensues. Though still alive, I do not have enough energy to keep my mental functions active. Slowly, I drift into a deep, healing sleep.

FORTY-FIVE

MY LUNGS FILL with air and I let out a loud, piercing scream.

"Minnie?" Mine calls my name, his voice filled with worry as he rushes to my side.

I open my eyes and take in my surroundings. We're at his house, in his bedroom. But...how? When did this happen? The last thing I remember is having my heart ripped out of my chest and seeing it gurgle blood next to me on the ground.

I was so certain I was dead. After all, who can escape Cerenios? And he'd definitely been there. Or...had he?

Glancing down, I note I'm wearing the same dress from before, except it's not tattered or stained with blood.

"What happened?"

"You had a bad dream. I was downstairs cleaning up when I heard you scream."

I frown. "No, no. I left. I wasn't here..."

"You did, but you returned a few hours ago. You don't remember?"

"I...returned?"

He nods. "I was so worried you wouldn't come back, that you would leave me." He takes a deep breath. "I meant what I said before. I will tell you everything when the time is right—when I'm sure it won't cause any harm."

"What harm could it cause?"

"More harm than you can imagine," he murmurs, a resigned expression on his face. "I fear I've already done that."

I do a quick scan of my body, and to my great surprise, I find my energy levels intact. There is nothing in need of healing, nothing that might point out to a previous injury. Not only that, but my outer appearance is spotless too. Nothing to suggest an altercation. No blood when I remember clearly I shed enough to be painted in red from head to toe.

"You're sure I came back by myself?"

He tilts his head to the side as he regards me, a question in his eyes. "What do you mean by yourself?"

"I came here with my own two legs?"

He chuckles. "That is a strange way of putting it. But no, you did not. You were simply here. I assume you teleported back?"

"I did...?"

"Minnie, are you all right? What happened while you were away?"

I bite my lip. "I followed the sound of the city until I reached Paris. I visited a couple of shops and then—"

"Then?"

"I don't know. I could have sworn I encountered someone from Aperion and got into a fight. But there is no evidence of it on my body."

"That is...odd."

"Tell me about it." I laugh nervously. "It must have been a dream, but I've never in my life had such a vivid dream."

"Was that why you woke up screaming?"

I nod. "It was...disconcerting. Perhaps it's just stress."

"And I added to that stress," he whispers apologetically. "I am sorry. I did not think my mother would come here today of all days."

"We would have had to meet eventually."

"Yes, but she would have been prepared."

"To what? Lie better?"

He presses his lips together in a thin line. "You will understand what I mean soon enough, Minnie. But for now, I want you to know how thankful I am you returned to me."

He slides off the bed and to his knees. Pressing his head on my lap, he wraps his arms around my midriff and holds me tight.

"You have no idea how it felt to watch you leave. To see the disappointment in your eyes. I've made a mess of things, haven't I?"

"Yes...and no." I thread my fingers through his thick locks. "I just wish I could understand why you're doing this. I've already run through every scenario, and I am quite confident you are not human. Nor is your mother. But I cannot sense anything out of the ordinary with you two."

He raises his gaze to look at me. "Whatever I am... I can give you something." He gulps down hard. "I vow to the Source that my intention is only to protect you, to love you, to be with you. Everything I have done, past, present, future, has been for that goal."

I stare at him, stunned into silence.

Did he just... Was that a clue?

More confusion swirls in my brain as different theories take root. But at the core of all of them is a deep calm that washes over me.

Leaning forward, I press my lips against his forehead.

"I trust you," I whisper, knowing the words to be true the moment they leave my lips. "I will always trust you."

"Minnie..." he rasps. Unshed tears gather along his lower lash line, his eyes glistening with ineffable emotion.

"In my dream." I take a deep breath as I squeeze my eyes shut. Perhaps it was a dream, but it affected me all the same. The feeling of dying...of having my heart ripped out of my body... I've never felt such pain and terror before. It wasn't so much physical as it was mental. I stood at the precipice and I saw what my death would bring and I was terrified.

"I realized there is only one person in the entire universe who would miss me should I die. You. No one else. My family couldn't care less about me as long as I don't sully their name. My brother may tolerate me, but even he would wash his hands of me if I become an outcast. But you..."

I press my palm against his cheek, feeling the pebbled skin under my touch.

"You've not only accepted me for who I am, for what I am, but you've also taught me to not be ashamed of it and embrace myself. You gave me courage, Mine. When everything fell apart around me, you helped me believe in myself again. Perhaps you made me believe in myself for the first time ever."

"Ah, my sweet Minnie," he murmurs lovingly. He raises himself on his arms, his mouth a razor's edge away from mine. His breath fans my lips as he closes the distance and skims his mouth over mine.

"You're the only one I would ever die for, Mine, just as you are the only one I would ever live for. You *are* mine, just as I am yours. And tonight, I want to be fully yours," I whisper.

His eyes snap open, so vividly green, so beautiful.

"You mean..."

I nod. "I've been yours in spirit all along. Tonight I want to be yours in body, too."

"Ah, Minnie mine. My sweet treasure," he groans against my lips. Pressing his palms into the mattress, he takes a deep, tired breath as he lays his forehead on my shoulder. "You're dangling in front of me such a dangerous temptation..."

"So take it. It's yours."

He shakes his head, his forehead sliding over my half-naked shoulder. "Not yet. Not like this."

"But—"

"You promised you would marry me," he interrupts me. "So let's do it. Tomorrow. My father will officiate it."

"Tomorrow?" I gasp.

"You bought the dress. I peeked in your bag and saw it," he admits in a low voice.

The memory of the dress comes back to me. In my dream,

I'd dropped it in the middle of the street before Cerenios had teleported us to that forest. But if it's here...

It must have been a dream after all—a frightful one but only a dream.

Thank the Source.

Perhaps it's because I am so fresh after that wretched nightmare, but now more than ever I realize that though immortal, my existence is precarious. All it takes is the right adversary for my life to end. That terror continues to plague me as I hold on to Mine and revel in his closeness. How could I ever hold a grudge against him when he's all I have?

"Tomorrow then. I'll be your wife."

He pulls back slightly and gazes at me, his lips tugged up into a big smile.

"My wife," he mutters, almost to himself. "And I shall be your husband."

I chuckle at the way he repeats the words all over again as if he cannot get enough of them.

"Then I will claim you. The proper way," he tells me with a smile.

"I don't think there's any improper way with you." I giggle.

"Is that so?" He raises a brow. "Just a while ago you thought a mere hand touch was improper."

"Well, you helped me see the error of my ways."

"Always at your service, my fair lady," he murmurs with amusement.

"Always?" I bat my lashes.

"Always," he confirms.

"Good. Then take off your clothes," I command.

He blinks as he looks at me stupefied.

"T-take off my clothes? Me?"

"You, who else?" I roll my eyes.

"But—"

"Don't tell me you're the prude now and I'm the one with nefarious intentions?"

"But tomorrow," he protests, though it's a weak attempt as his eyes are already roving over my body suggestively.

"Tomorrow is the main dish. Tonight can be the appetizer."

His brow quirks up. "Why is everything about food for you?"

I shrug. "Food is yummy, and so are those orgasms, and you're still in debt."

"Right, right. I am a puny debtor who needs to pay up."

"I'm waiting," I say and lean back on my elbows to watch the show.

"Shouldn't you be the one to undress? So I can pay my debt properly," he adds as he trails his finger down my leg until he reaches my uncovered ankles. He rolls down my stockings, one at a time, all the while keeping his eyes on me.

Heat builds up inside of me, making my breathing heavier, more punctured. He grabs one of my feet and presses a kiss on top of it before trailing his tongue to my toes.

"Mine..." I let out a startled gasp when he sucks my toe into his mouth.

This wicked man... he's staring at me while he flicks his tongue all over my toes. I never imagined something like this could be so...erotic. But the tight knots forming inside my stomach tell me otherwise. Goose bumps appear all over my skin as I squirm against the mattress.

"C-clothes off," I reiterate, though slightly more flushed than before. "You, naked, is part of the debt."

"Is it? Then of course I must pay up," he answers dutifully as he takes a step back and reaches for the buttons on his shirt.

"At least you're a well-behaved debtor. But I will have you know the interest rate has gone up."

"How much are we talking about?" He carefully unbuttons his shirt before he throws it to the side, revealing his muscled chest.

"Pants, too."

"Ah, so demanding," he drawls as he unbuckles his belt. But

once that's off, his fingers hover over the zipper of his trousers, teasing me.

"Too much talking and too little undressing. I am the injured party here and thus I require my recompense."

"Of course, my fair lady."

I don't know where he came up with that nickname, but I don't dislike it.

He pulls down his trousers, taking his drawers together with them. Just like that, he's stark naked in front of me.

My breath catches in my throat. I might have been the one to initiate this, but now I fear I might be in a little too over my head.

His body is pure perfection. His scars, too, are part of that allure, making him seem both sexy and dangerous at the same time. But as I peruse his body, I notice new scars. Some are starting from his navel and going down his legs. They're reddish still, suggesting they're recent. The worst one is right above his hardened male part, a mosaic of scar tissue that spreads to his back and buttocks.

"Mine," I start, but he's quick to press a finger against my lips and shush me.

"Not now," he whispers.

I gulp down. Concern blooms in my chest.

"When did this happen?" I demand. When did he strain himself too much? Was it while I was out those three days? Was he suffering while I was sleeping, oblivious to everything he was going through? Pain laces through me as I stare into his anguished green eyes. The same pain is there too, but his is hidden, shrouded in the thousand secrets he keeps from me.

"Not now," he repeats, his warm breath tickling my neck as his skilled hands begin to unbutton my gown. Each button comes undone with ease, revealing the smooth, creamy skin underneath. I feel a deep flush of embarrassment as he slowly removes the gown, leaving me standing naked in front of him.

But his focus is not on my nudity. He presses soft kisses against my exposed skin, murmuring words of adoration and love as he trails down my neck and over my shoulders. His hands roam freely over my body, caressing and exploring every curve and dip.

"My beautiful wife-to-be," he rasps.

Feeling a sudden rush of desire, he flips me onto my stomach on the bed and pulls my hair to one side. His lips leave a trail of fire as they move down my spine, stopping to suck and mark every inch of skin along the way. I moan and writhe beneath his touch, eagerly giving myself over to his control.

"Yes, take me...take everything," I whisper, arching my back as his hands grip my buttocks firmly. Heat builds between us, the desire pulsing through both our bodies.

He moves lower and lower until he reaches the swell of my buttocks.

"What are you doing?" I gasp out.

"Paying off my debts," he replies with a low chuckle, his hot breath sending shivers down my spine. "Making up for all that accrued interest."

"Oh. And how do you plan to do that?"

"You will see," he replies as he chuckles against my back.

His hands move over my buttocks, kneading the flesh between his fingers before biting me. My back arches in surprise. His teeth nip and scrape the skin, at first softly, playfully. But then his sharp teeth penetrate my flesh until he draws blood. He licks every drop, lapping at my blood while I fist the sheets and thrust my body toward him.

I gasp and shiver, the pain only making me want the pleasure that much more. Moisture gathers between my legs, pooling down the inside of my thighs.

He drags his mouth lower until he finally finds my sex with his tongue.

"M-Mine," I whimper. He laps the moisture from between my legs, his chest vibrating his pleasure.

"So wet for me," he whispers. "My little wife-to-be is a naughty, naughty girl."

"Please..."

He buries his face between my legs, flicking his tongue over my pleasure bud before sucking it in his mouth.

Fisting the sheets, I wildly thrash around. Pleasure shoots through me. At first, it's tiny needles of pleasure that spread to the tips of my toes. But as he continues to torture me with his skilled mouth, my entire body begins to tremble in preparation for the climax.

Then he stops.

"Mine!" I cry out. "Don't you dare!"

"But I do dare." He chuckles. "Perhaps you should add more interest."

"Oh, I'm adding ten times the interest for every second you don't touch me and—" My words are cut off as a scream rushes past my lips.

He pushes a finger inside of me, curling it inside of me and hitting a hidden spot.

W-what? I nearly jump off the bed at the first sign of intrusion. But as he adds another finger and thrusts them in and out of me.

"That's it. Show me how much you love being fucked by my fingers."

My eyes widen at his sudden use of profanities, but my body seems to respond to it. I clench around his fingers as contractions start in my lower body.

They're small at first, but with each masterful thrust of his fingers and flick of his tongue, they build up. More and more until my mouth opens on a loud, earth-shattering scream.

I bury my head in the sheets as I hold on for dear life while that delicious orgasm rolls through me. And to my surprise, the room isn't completely frozen. Just a tad bit colder than before.

"Not done yet," Mine says. He trails his tongue once more over my drenched sex before he gets up. Then something else is between my buttocks. Something warm, big, and hard.

He slides his length between my cheeks, coating it with my wetness. Just as I think he might have changed his mind, that he will take me now, he surprises me once more when he flips me on my back.

Grabbing me by my ankles, he pulls me toward him until my ass is on the edge of the bed.

"Fuck, Minnie," he mutters under his breath as he presses his erection against my center.

He slides it up and down, but he doesn't push it inside me.

"Do it," I tell him—I *dare* him.

Sweat beads on his forehead, his expression a mix of anguish and frustration. He shakes his head at me. "Not. Yet."

"Please." Does he want me to beg? Because I will do it.

Another shake of his head, though this time, the head of his erection bumps along my entrance. He circles around it before sliding upward and settling over my mound.

His hands are tightly holding on to my thighs as he thrusts against me.

Once. Twice. The third time, he throws his head back and lets out a low, guttural groan. His shaft pulses and twitches as he climaxes. Spurts of his dark seed coat my stomach, some landing between my breasts and on my chin.

He's still grinding against me as his orgasm subsides, and in a moment of madness, I turn the tables on him. Using my powers, I switch our positions so he's the one sitting on his back on the bed. I climb on the bed between his legs and wrap my hand around his still hard shaft.

It's surprisingly soft and warm to the touch and much bigger than I thought just by looking at it. He lets out another groan as he watches me with hooded eyes.

"You don't have to..." He trails off when I lean in and take the tip of his maleness into my mouth. His head falls back onto the mattress.

"Fuck," he curses, his hands finding their way in my hair.

"It's sweet and creamy," I mention as I lick the beads of moisture. "Tastes almost like chocolate."

His lips quirk up.

"There you go again with the food comparisons."

I smile against his shaft. "You should be pleased about it since I happen to love sweet things. It means I will love this too," I continue, giving it another swipe of my tongue.

"Oh fuck. Fuckkkkk," he growls. "I'm too sensitive. I'm going to..."

I don't let him finish as I open my mouth wide and take as much of him as I am able to, using my tongue to caress him as he's done to me. Going by the way his body is turning and twisting, his fingers gripping my hair tightly, I think I'm doing a good job.

Pulling back, I suck on the tip, gathering every bit of that delicious seed. Who knew lovemaking would be so yummy? First, he introduced me to orgasms, which are on par with dessert, and now he's *giving* me dessert?

A more perfect male doesn't exist.

I notice that whenever I lick the underside of the head, his body erupts in shivers, so I assume that's a sensitive area. I focus my efforts on it, and more guttural sounds escape his lips. I don't know what he's saying. It's almost as if he's speaking another language I've never heard of—and I've heard plenty. But I don't stop to wonder about that. I continue my ministrations until his release erupts in my mouth, filling me up with the most delicious flavor.

I don't swallow immediately. I twirl my tongue around it to get more of the flavor.

He stares at me in shock.

"Minnie, you..."

His hand is on my cheek, caressing me lightly before his thumb pries my lips open. My mouth is full of his seed and I swirl it for him to see.

"Fucking hell. You're the hottest thing I've ever seen, you know that?"

I close my mouth and gulp down but then notice some errant drops still leaking from the tip. Leaning in, I lick him clean, all the while he continues to caress my cheek.

His gaze is one of wonder as he stares at me.

"So damn worth it," he whispers.

"Huh?" I raise my brows in question as I wipe my mouth.

"Everything was so damn worth it."

"Oh, come on! I didn't make you wait *that* long," I fire back.

"Longer than you think." He chuckles. "But you also surprised the fuck out of me. That was..." He whistles. "I've imagined your mouth on my cock plenty of times, but I never thought I'd blow up as I did."

"That's good, no?" I bat my lashes at him.

"Good? It's beyond anything I would have imagined. You're a natural, aren't you?" he murmurs low in his throat. Pulling me by my nape, he smashes his lips against mine in an aggressive kiss. "My wife-to-be is a natural at sucking cock."

My lashes flutter in embarrassment at his words.

"T-that's because you taste good," I admit bashfully.

He chuckles.

"Do all males taste like this?"

He suddenly stops. His expression becomes feral as his gaze darkens. His hold, too, tightens.

"Erase the thought of *other* males from your mind, Minnie. You will *never* taste anyone else."

"I didn't mean it like that. I was just curi—"

"Don't."

"All right. I'm sorry," I whisper, afraid I ruined the moment.

His gaze immediately softens.

"Don't look at me like that." He gathers me in his arms and hugs me to his chest. "I didn't mean to snap at you. But I'm a goddamn jealous asshole. The thought of *any* male in your vicinity threatens to drive me crazy."

"No, you're right. I am the same. I wouldn't want you to ask that about a female either."

"Ah, my tiny darling, you're so precious."

"It seems we're both jealous assholes." I giggle nervously.

"Nope. Can never refer to you as an asshole. You can be my jealous goddess."

"You don't mind it then? If I'm jealous, too?"

He smiles at me.

"Tiny darling. You can be as jealous as you want. If you didn't have that weird rule about not harming humans, I would be encouraging murder day and night. You are quite hot when you get all riled up and jealous over your male." He gives me a quick kiss on the mouth. "Alas, I will have to be content with *just* maiming. Such a bad lot in life I have," he adds with a sigh.

I raise a brow at him. "What?"

"Of course I will do the murder after you've done the maiming. I think that's only fair. *And* I will do both the maiming and the murder when *I* get jealous. See, I'm all about equal opportunity."

I blink. "You're an odd duck, Mine."

His lips tremble with mirth, remembering our first exchange.

"See, I finally got to duck you."

"Finger-duck me," I correct.

He throws back his head and laughs. "Finger-duck. Yes, yes. That I did."

"And soon you will duck me properly."

He tilts his head and regards me with a sad smile.

"Soon," he repeats, an edge to his words. "For now, let's get you cleaned up."

"You too. I got some on you too." I point to where our chests meet and where his seed now stains both of our bodies.

"Race you to the bathroom," he suddenly says as he deposits me to the side and jumps off the bed.

"Oh, you want to lose, you puny human?" I call out and teleport myself to the bathroom.

By the time he opens the door, I'm already in the tub, laughing at him.

"You're not playing fair," he accuses me as he stands by the tub, his hands on his hips. His male part is on eye level with me and already starting to harden.

"You may take it up with the GR."

"GR?" He frowns.

"Gods resources."

It takes him a second to get the pun, but once he does, he howlers with laughter.

We spend a rather un*godly* amount of time in the tub, washing then playing with the bubbles from the soap. Like the good husband-to-be he is, when we're done, he dries me and puts on my nightgown before doing the same to himself. After such a long interlude, sleep comes surprisingly easy.

Sometime in the night, my eyes snap open as a feeling of dread courses down my spine. I stand up, breathing hard. Was it another dream? I cannot remember.

Something moves in front of the bed, and as I glance up, I note it's Mine.

Confused, I raise my voice to ask, "What are you doing?"

But he doesn't answer. Instead, his gaze falls upon me with the saddest expression I've ever seen.

As my eyes adjust to the darkness, I slowly realize that the bed is not empty. There is a figure lying next to me...

With a gulp, I force myself to look and a gasp escapes my lips when I see his body lying there. He's here, but he's also there? How can this be?

The truth hits me as I reach out to shake him awake. His flesh is no longer warm and alive. It's icy cold and growing colder by the second.

My heart pounds in my chest as I place two fingers on his throat, searching for a pulse. But deep down, I already know the answer.

No... Please, no...

I turn to face the form standing at the foot of the bed.

"You...you're dead," I whisper hoarsely.

He closes his eyes and gives a small nod.

A chill runs down my spine as I sense another presence in the room.

The messenger. He has come to take him from me.

"No! You can't leave," I plead desperately as I leap out of bed.

He takes a step back, moving away from me and toward the ethereal being that seeks to steal him from my grasp.

"Mine? No...please don't go," I beg through tears, my voice breaking with emotion.

The messenger materializes in the corner of the room, his intent clear.

Still gazing at me, Mine silently mouths something just as the messenger reaches out for him.

"Come find me."

And then he's gone.

FORTY-SIX

THE SHEETS ARE WARM, but his body is cold. I reach for him as I always do, waiting for him to reach back in return. In that moment, I delude myself into thinking that I didn't just see his soul being taken away. That was just a bad dream. He isn't dead. He's just sleeping.

But he never reaches for me. His body is still, unresponsive.

"Don't you dare," I mutter under my breath. "Wake up, Mine. This isn't funny." My voice trembles as I speak, my body tense with fear. I push at his shoulder. No answer.

No, no, no. This is just another nightmare. He's not dead. He cannot be dead.

With growing panic, I shove him again, my voice becoming frantic. "Wake up," I demand, my voice cracking. "Wake up!"

His head tilts slightly at my touch, his once vibrant face now slack and lifeless. My heart pounds in my chest as I refuse to accept this reality.

No. This can't be happening. It's not real.

I grasp at him, cupping his cheeks, willing for any sign of life. But there is none. "This isn't funny! Please, stop it!" Tears stream down my face. "Wake up, please wake up—" I shout, all over again, a command meant both for him and for me. If this is a dream, then I will just wake up and everything will be fine.

Mine will be there to hug me, kiss me, love me. He will be there for me.

But my cries go unanswered. He remains frozen in place. I remain present and awake.

My hands move down his body, feeling the chill of death under my fingertips. Madness overtakes me as I lay my cheek against his heart, trying to transfer some warmth, some vitality back into his still form.

Wake up. Wake up. Wake up.

My own powerlessness stares back at me. I might be a goddess, but even I do not have power over death.

How did this happen? How can this be real? He was alive just last night, his warm body next to mine.

Now there's only coldness.

I am made from cold, to love the cold. But I've never in my life hated it as I do now.

A guttural scream tears from deep within me, clawing its way out and echoing through the empty room. It's a sound of anguish and denial, raw and primal, like that of a wounded animal.

I dig my nails into his chest, hoping to elicit a flinch or a sigh, anything to prove that he is still here with me.

But there is nothing.

More cold descends in the room, the walls slowly becoming covered in frost—a physical manifestation of my grief. My powers become uncontrollable as I give the ice that's building inside of me free rein to consume the outside. Yet it never touches him. It engulfs everything but never him.

Because he's already been consumed by the cold...

I continue to plead, my fingers now tangled in his hair as I shake him in desperation. "Don't you dare leave me!" I cry out, half commanding him, half begging him.

I press my lips to his, some delusional part of me thinking that my kiss will revive him. But he remains unresponsive, his mouth slack against mine.

Slowly, I pull away, my tears falling onto his expressionless face.

True terror grips me as reality crashes onto me.

He's gone. His soul is gone. Now there's only this lifeless body that means nothing to me without its spark.

Numbness engulfs me as I slide to the floor next to the bed. I stare into empty space as I breathe in and out and try to clear my head. I won't resolve anything by devolving into a hysterical mess. Time is of the essence here. He might be gone, for now, but his soul is still alive.

He is not completely lost to me.

He is probably in P'asala right now, making his way toward the Letharion—the well of oblivion. And as soon as he drinks from that well, he will forget everything.

He will forget *me*.

Come find me.

The words echo in the frozen room.

Come find me.

How? Where?

There is no way for me to go to P'asala and get his soul before he reaches Letharion. I would be killed on the spot if I tried to trespass—that much I know.

Once he's drunk from Lethe's well, he will be assigned a level in the House of Psyche while he awaits his next incarnation.

The logical thing would be to wait for him to be reborn. But there is another thing to consider.

He's a soldier, a killer. He's killed countless people, both in the name of this senseless war and to protect me. That alone would likely relegate him to Katras, the lowest level of the House of Psyche, where he might be tortured for an eternity.

That I cannot countenance.

Not only must I prevent him from being tortured, for I have heard stories of how harsh the punishment is for damned souls, but I cannot let him rot in there for an eternity.

While damned souls can create enough merit for themselves

to move up the levels of the House of Psyche before eventually getting their turn at reincarnation, there is also the possibility that they will never make it that far.

He might be sent to Katras, or he might be sent to a slightly higher level. As long as he is at the bottom of the House of Psyche, he *will* suffer, and that is unacceptable.

My hands ball into fists as I imagine the horrors he's about to endure.

You're a goddess, Minnie! You have power.

I do, don't I? I might not have the power to bring him back to life in his original form, but I can get his soul back. It might be hard. It might be close to impossible. But I've already done the impossible when I went to the House of Moirai and cut my own thread of fate. Breaking into the House of Psyche should be easy compared to that.

Wyn's ominous words ring in my mind.

When the time comes, you must make two visits. One to the House of Moirai and one to the House of Psyche.

She knew this would happen. Somehow, she knew everything.

I trusted her once and went to the House of Moirai. Now I will trust her again and go to the House of Psyche.

Hopefully stealing a soul is not too hard.

But how do I enter the House of Psyche? Can I just barge inside and wander through the levels? There is very little I know about the workings of the House of Psyche aside from the standard information we're taught in our schooling. The House of Psyche is not open to visitors, just like the House of Moirai, so I could be turned away.

Alas, if all things fail, I suppose my last resort is killing myself and going to the House of Psyche as a spirit, though I don't know how I would avoid the Letharion so I don't lose my memories and thus lose sight of my goal.

I groan. Why is this so hard? Not only that, but why am I so damn ignorant of the workings of my own world? I don't even know what I'll do once I find him. What does a soul look like after it arrives in the House of Psyche? Is it the same as before? Does it change? Can I carry it in my pocket? Do I need a special soul-carrying bottle or vial?

I let out a heavy sigh.

But there is another question that lingers in my mind.

Did Mine know he would die?

Closing my eyes, I massage my temples and think back to the night before.

He hadn't seemed any different than usual. I've already witnessed how his illness behaved and last night he seemed healthy. Except...

His new scars. There were fresh marks on his flesh. While they weren't bleeding, they were red-pinkish in color, suggesting he'd gotten them fairly recently. But how? When? Why did he not tell me about it?

And to think I might have added more stress to his already weak constitution when I argued with him and left him...

A pang of hurt reverberates in my body.

Oh, Mine. Why didn't you tell me if something was wrong? Or was this part of your secretive plan, too? Something you couldn't yet divulge?

Luckily for me, all souls are treated equally in the House of Psyche regardless of their species. It's only when they move from the House of Psyche to the House of Moirai and they get assigned a new fate that their species is determined.

Getting to my feet, I'm wobbly at first, devoid of any will to live on as I once more see his lifeless form.

But this pain is ephemeral. It will all be fine once I get his soul back. We'll be together again and all will be well.

I chant that to myself until I'm fully convinced of it.

Staring at him, I'm both wary to leave him alone like this and restless to erase the image of him dead from my mind. But I will only achieve the latter once I get him back. Until then...

What is going to happen to his body? I can't very well leave it here to decompose. His mother will come back next Saturday. By that time, he will already start to rot.

It might only be an empty carcass now, but his face is still the face of the man I love.

I should find a way to let his family know so they can treat his remains with the respect they deserve.

As I ponder how to get in touch with his family, a succession of noises draws my attention.

There is a continuous rattling of a door handle somewhere downstairs, followed by a voice that calls out, "Valerion!"

His mother. She's...here? Now?

What are the odds? I think wryly to myself. But I cannot waste time wondering about that when I can go about my mission.

With a heavy heart, I lay a kiss on his cold lips and murmur a binding vow.

"I vow to the Source that I will get you back, or I will die trying."

———————

BACK IN APERION, I note that only a day has passed since I've been gone. The palace is quiet as I make my way toward the library to consult some books on how to gain access to the House of Psyche. Since it seems to be midday here, I don't expect to run into any one of importance. My father has meetings at this time and my mother usually has her beauty afternoon sleep.

I barely reach the door to the library when my senses become high on alert.

"You!" my mother shrieks at me when she sees me.

I turn and frown.

"What have you done, stupid girl?"

I blink in confusion. "What?"

She charges toward me, her energy shimmering around her. Instinctively, my shields go up to protect myself from an incoming attack.

"How could you do this? How?" she shouts, and the ground under my feet trembles from her anger.

"I have no idea what you're talking about."

"No idea? You have no idea? You've ruined us! All of us!"

"Wait a moment. What happened?"

She's still a distance away, but I keep my shields up in case she decides to unleash her energy toward me. Her once beautiful face is mottled with anger, her cheeks red, her eyes almost bulging out of her face. I don't think I've ever seen her like this before, and a sliver of fear envelops me. What could have happened to cause her to react like this? I was only gone a day. Not much would have changed in that time, no? But perhaps she's heard about Cerenios' true intentions toward me; that he isn't interested in a potential marriage, but rather he's investigating me at Commander Azerius' orders.

"What do you mean what happened? Soldiers should be here any moment to arrest you," she continues in the same shrilly voice.

"Arrest me?" I ask, dumbfounded.

"How could you do this, Minerva? How could you lay with a human?"

"W-what?" I stammer. "I didn't—"

"There's no point in denying it. Theron has not only publicly repudiated you, but he's also shared evidence of your behavior. By the Source, how can you be my child? How could you do something like this..." she continues. "The entirety of Aperion knows what you've done. How you've shamed all of us. But with a human, Minerva." She shakes her head. "I never had much hope for you, but I never believed you would do something like this."

I stare at her. Theron repudiated me? For lying with a human? But... How would he know?

"What evidence did he show?" I ask slowly.

"He used a divining mirror to show everyone how you lay like a whore with that scar-riddled human."

"Don't call him that," I snap.

Her nostrils flare at me, the corner of her lips tugging down in disdain.

"You know what the punishment is for this. Death. And neither your father nor I will do anything to help you. In fact." She pauses. In the distance, I register thudding footsteps. She hears them, too. "I disown you. You are no daughter of mine."

Perhaps that type of statement deserves a comeback, but it seems she was not joking when she mentioned soldiers are coming to arrest me. They're in the palace, on their way toward me. I give her one last look of disappointment before I flash myself in the library. After gathering as many books on the House of Psyche as possible, I teleport out of the palace just as the library doors burst open to reveal the incoming soldiers.

To make them lose my trail, I teleport all over Aperion, leaving small prints of energy behind before shielding myself altogether. Then I go to the only place I know no one will think to look for —the cabin in Polemos. They will eventually come here, too. But it should buy me some time to study the books and figure out a plan of action.

But as I arrive at the cabin, I realize I didn't count on the memories of Mine hitting me with such a fierce force. I see him in the middle of the living room, poring over books. I see him smiling at me and kissing my forehead. I see him hugging me from behind as we go to sleep.

The tears fall unbidden as I stand in the middle of the room, staring into empty space. The books fall from my grasp, thudding against the hardwood floor.

"How did I mess everything so badly?" I whisper to myself.

I was careless, so damn careless. I should have seen the signs of Mine's deteriorating health just as I should have been more careful about my presence in Anthropa. From the moment I got there, I used my powers liberally with no thought to shield my energy signature. Theron could have easily followed me around. And given the way I humiliated him, he would have wanted revenge.

He got it. Oh, he got it in spades.

Not only is he free of me now, but my biggest fear has finally materialized. I am officially a fugitive sentenced to death. Ironically, it's not even for the worst of my offenses—messing with the threads of fate. A dry laugh escapes me. I suppose they haven't found out about that. Yet.

Well, considering my next little heist, the offenses will keep on piling up. It's not like they can kill me three times. Not that it's of any consolation.

Taking a deep breath, I get to reading.

Although the House of Psyche is closed to anyone born outside its boundaries, there is one way of getting inside. Every hundred of years, a deity is allowed to lodge a complaint with the House of Psyche if they feel that a soul has not been judged properly. The complaint can be either in favor of the soul, arguing that the punishment has been too harsh, or to the disadvantage of the soul, arguing that it should be sent to a lower level and thus delay its reincarnation.

If I seek entrance to lodge a complaint... Won't they know who I am and that there is a pending arrest warrant for me?

With no other choice, I suppose I will have to try my luck.

To ensure I will be at my optimal strength, I quickly eat something and ransack the cabin for any leftover items that might hold some spiritual energy. At the moment, my energy is nearly full, but there is no telling what I might encounter in the future, so I will need some backup. When I get to the study, I find a pen that my grandmother used in the past and note it's overflowing with energy. I place it in my pocket.

Careful to shield my energy signature, I teleport to the entrance of the House of Psyche. Similar to the House of Moirai, there are two guards in front of a portal. I introduce myself and tell them I am here to lodge an official complaint about an errant soul. After I'm done speaking, I wait with bated breath to see if they recognize my name.

"You may proceed," one of the guards says.

The portal blinks twice and I go inside. At the other end, a deity garbed in a blue gown awaits me. "I am Fina and I will be your guide today."

"Thank you," I murmur.

"Please follow me to the Office of Complaints."

She starts walking. I follow after her, glancing around and studying my surroundings.

The entire background is a light blue. There is no earth or sky, nor a beginning or an end. There isn't anything but a big void, and we are walking on a marbled bridge that materializes in front of us as we step forward. The entire area is like a board of chess, waiting for us to make the next move before it makes its own.

I lean over to the edge as I try to see what's underneath this bridge, but Fina suddenly stops me. She pulls me back and shakes her head.

"You would do well not to look down."

"Huh? Why?"

She gives me a smile that does not reach her eyes.

"Anything below this bridge is the domain of Ishaktar and she does not like to be gazed upon without permission. Anyone who dares to look at her without permission is pulled down into the deepest pit in Psyche."

Ishaktar... The books mentioned her. She is the former Psyche Supreme. No one knows why she retired from the position when normally, a deity has to die to relinquish the Supreme position. Some rumors say she's gone mad because she's lived far too long, seen too much. She's so ancient, the books referred to her as an entity rather than a being; ever-present, ever-knowing. No one knows her age, or what she looks like. She just...exists.

But the books never mentioned that she still controls areas of Psyche.

"The deepest pit? By that you mean..." I feign a shudder and paint an expression of terror on my face.

"You may know it as Katras."

My destination.

"That horrible place?"

She smiles again, as fake as my attempts at bodily tremors.

"It is only horrible for those who have something to fear," she replies cryptically.

Turning, she continues to walk, beckoning me to follow. The bridge extends in front of us with every step, almost as if the entire construction was sentient.

"You are from the House of Psyche, Fina?"

"Yes. Of course."

"Where do your people live if this is what Psyche looks like?"

She stops and glances at me from the corner of her eyes.

"Your questions are intrusive."

So it's a secret. All right.

What surprises me the most—besides the self-building bridge—is the fact that we're the only ones here. Shouldn't Psyche be bustling around with beings? At the very least, there should be other people around.

That's when it slowly dawns on me that the realm itself is alive and showing us only what we need to know or see.

Ishaktar. She *is* the realm, isn't she? Directing the ongoing traffic in a way that keeps most of the workings of Psyche hidden.

And if she is so anger-prone she sends anyone who glances down to Katras, perhaps that is my ticket there.

What if Mine isn't there?

If he's not there, I'll claw my way out to the next level and then the next. I've vowed not to rest until I find him unless I die and that's what I'm going to do.

Squashing aside all my doubts, I take a deep breath and channel my energy. When Fina realizes I'm not following her, she stops and comes to my side.

"What is the matter?" she asks.

"Nothing, just..." I grab her hand and infuse icy energy into her, her limbs becoming swallowed up by a layer of ice that later consumes her entire body.

She's frozen to the spot, unable to move. Since I don't know what her skills are and how quickly she's able to break free, I quickly move to the edge of the bridge.

And since Ishaktar might not notice me staring at her immediately, I take it one step further and simply jump.

The fall is steep. So steep, in fact, that I fear it's never-ending.

Without warning and after what feels like an eternity, I crash onto a hard, scorching ground. My body twists and contorts, with broken bones protruding from my flesh and half my face caved in.

Well... Damn.

Pain erupts everywhere in my body, so much so I can barely roll from side to side to take some pressure off my injured side. Once I'm on my back, I feel for the broken bones and push them back into place. My shoulder goes in easy enough. My cheekbone, too. My jaw proves a little harder as I find the right angle to pop it back on. It's my hip and shin bones that are the worst, mostly because the bone has broken off, leaving a sharp, ragged edge.

I'm not sure why, but there is something off about this place. My movements are slower than before, and I have to make a conscious effort to carry out even the easiest of tasks.

I tear some material from the bottom of my dress and wrap it around my hand in a thick layer. Using my clenched fist, I knock on the bone with the layered part of my hand until it moves back into place. It takes me minutes on end to successfully put all my bones back inside my body. But even with nothing else poking out, I find that my healing is not as sharp as it should be considering I'm at full power. The skin mends, but there is a noticeable delay, which means there is a noticeable delay in my pain subsiding too.

Goddamn it, as Mine would say. Considering the pain I'm enduring right now for him, I will add a one hundred times interest to his debt. He will owe me orgasms for not only his next life, but the next one and the next-next one too.

Muttering a strong of curses under my breath—another

thing I've learned from him—I wobble to my feet. But it's when I try to stand up that it hits me that this is not a normal place at all.

A suffocating heat envelops me, making it hard to breathe. My lungs work at double capacity to make up for it. But it's not just my breathing that's affected. This scorching heat makes me want to strip off every layer of clothing, even shed my skin. My mouth is dry and I'm suddenly struck by an unquenchable thirst.

I take a step forward, but it feels as if I'm taking a step back instead.

My vision blurs and I'm unable to make out anything around me. The air is thick and oppressive, bearing down on me mercilessly, making me unable to carry my own weight.

I crash to my knees, unable to stand up anymore.

My breathing is shallow and ragged, and I start gasping for air.

But just as I think I might suffocate, fresh air fills my lungs until I can finally breathe properly.

What?

"Better?" a voice asks.

I look up to see a female. Her slim figure is garbed in a flowing red dress. Her hair is pulled back tightly into a neat bun at the back of her head. Green, vibrant eyes overlined with a black kohl stare down at me.

"Who are you?"

She smiles slowly at me, revealing sharp, predatory teeth. She crouches down in front of me.

"You may call me Anami."

I frown. "Are you here to escort me out? Because I'm not leaving. Not yet."

"On the contrary. I am here to help. But first..."

She raises her gaze, looking at something over my head.

"He's here, watching. Shield your mind, Minerva," she commands. "Now!"

FORTY-SEVEN
APERION, PRESENT DAY

HIS FINGERS RETREAT from my eye sockets. Blood spurts forward, flowing down my cheeks in rivulets. I choke and sputter as more blood and bile rise up my throat from the onslaught of pain.

My throat is raw and sensitive as I heave and attempt to spit out all the buildup. But the position I'm in, frozen upright, my neck paralyzed, does not allow me to do anything but swallow up the foul liquid.

With no more constant pressure, my eyeballs start to heal. It's a slow process. I'm so depleted of energy it takes every ounce of strength to force my body to heal and stop it from shutting down.

My sight, too, slowly returns, only to see him wipe his bloody fingers with a disgusted expression on his face.

I draw a sharp breath in and grind my teeth against the pain.

But he doesn't care. For him, I'm just a means to an end—a task he needs to perfunctorily perform.

My eyes slowly accommodate to the blinding ceiling lights as I register my surroundings. The room is bare of any furniture. Translucent runes are etched into dark gray walls, blinking a stark white every now and then—a sign they are active. Some, I recognize. Others not so much. But they collectively keep me hostage here, pinned to the spot, unable to move a muscle.

These runes are used for high-level interrogations, with some of them activated only by an astounding amount of spiritual energy—I suppose Azerius has that in spades.

As my body begins to heal, so does my mind, and confusion sets in.

I blink and frown as things I knew to be true suddenly are not so true anymore. Memories are slipping away from me by the second, replaced by foreign images that are somehow extremely familiar.

My first kiss. I could have sworn it was with Marlowe. But now... All I can see is Mine.

Wait. Mine? I called Lucien Mine?

But as the question echoes through my mind, it becomes a certainty. He was Mine. I could never call him Lucien. That wasn't him. Valerion either.

To me, he was only Mine.

Yet more things become confusing. Like our first meeting and the fact that I got punished by the House of Moirai for intervening in human fate. Didn't I meet him at the movie theater? There's a vague recollection of that happening, but the more I try to visualize it, the farther it gets from me until it disappears.

No, I met him at the site of the bombing and I helped him save those people. Why I would ever do that when I knew the consequences... I have no idea. But I did.

Our relationship, too. Wasn't he too ill to do anything? As we moved from friendship to love, his illness became considerably worse.

Yet as I remember the past now, though he was still ill, he was far more capable than he should have been, stronger, more... virile.

We engaged in forbidden physical relations, and to my surprise, not only was I accepting of that, but often I was the one initiating them.

If it weren't for the dire conditions I find myself in, I would have blushed at the new pieces of information flooding my mind.

I allowed him intimacies I never thought I would, at least not before. I asked him to claim me with no promise for the future—a mistake on my part, or at least it should have been.

It was him who wanted to wait, him who wanted to make it special. How? Why?

Then there's his death. He was supposed to have died of a human illness. Tuberculosis, I believe. But my memories of his illness are changed. He never named the cause of it, only that it was engineered by people in his country to destroy minorities. Even now, after having absorbed so much information about the new, technologically advanced Anthropa, I have doubts that it's even possible.

But he was ill. And his symptoms were unlike any I've ever seen before.

My brows furrow in confusion as some information disappears altogether. Tuberculosis? No, he never had that.

A sliver of terror grips me. What is going on? Why am I misremembering things? Why am I forgetting things?

I...

What's wrong with me?

What did Azerius do to me?

All the other big events in my life remain unchanged, except for the order. Or is that something I'm getting confused about right now?

The logical thing would have been to go to the House of Psyche after he died and then to the House of Moirai. Then why do I remember heeding some unknown female's advice and going to the House of Moirai first? And how did she know Marlowe's name when even I did not know it?

In fact, why am I suddenly remembering direct confrontations with Cerenios when before I would have sworn we barely ever crossed paths?

Everything is confusing.

Even my interactions with Theron seem different, though they all ended in the same outcome—he repudiated me.

This time, however, he had proof that he presented to the authorities. And this time, it's because of that proof I was imprisoned and cursed to have all mortals look upon me with adoration so I could never know their true intentions.

Except it never worked on Marlowe. Because he's not mortal. He never was...

My eyes widen in shock at the biggest change. Mine could see the spiritual world—he couldn't before. Whereas before he was my solace of normality, now my memories are shifting, pointing him out to be my partner in crime rather than my silent comfort.

My head feels as if it's about to burst open, though I have no doubt Azerius would like that far too much. Every time I try to remember a specific event, a sharp pain spears through my skull. There is an echo of what *should* have happened in that memory. But when I recall it, it's completely different.

What the...

All the changes seem to only revolve around him. Mine. Everything else feels the same, though at this point I don't know how I can trust myself anymore.

Everything is changing in the blink of an eye, and I can't keep track of what's real or what's not—what's perhaps made up by my mind to survive this torture. Or...what he might have done to me.

Azerius, the God Killer.

He's been trying to get information on Marlowe by digging into my brain—literally.

I don't even know how long I've been here, or how long he's been torturing me. I only remember the beginning. Being secured in place with magical runes and Azerius digging my eyes out so he can directly connect with my brain.

After that, everything is fuzzy, though the one constant is pain; my body being ravaged and trying to heal before being ravaged again.

Perhaps that's why everything is different. Because Azerius has been messing so much with my mind, he might have caused permanent damage.

"W-what d-did you do t-o me?" I croak, my throat raw from pain.

He doesn't answer me, merely going on about cleaning his fingers so there isn't one drop of my blood on them.

"A-answer me!" I shout.

Moments trickle by. More memories resurface. They seem new and old at the same time, making me think I'm going crazy.

"Y-ou did something to m-my memories," I shout. That makes him stop and glance up at me.

"I did no such thing," he replies in a bored voice. Straightening his back, he walks toward me. "Though I find it odd that you would think so."

"You d-did! Everything is wrong. Everything!" I cry out. Yet as I open my mouth to tell him what is wrong, I can't remember. The new memories are now the only memories. I stare at him, mouth agape, unable to form a coherent sentence.

What did I want to tell him in the first place? I know something is wrong, but I cannot verbalize it. What in the Source is going on?

"Interesting," he notes in the same robotic voice as before. "Though this session has been nothing short of enlightening."

I blink. "Why?" I ask, almost afraid.

"There was something there, someone..." He presses his lips together. "They knew I was watching and did not want me to see something. Now that makes me even more curious. But it seems I will not be able to do it while you are alive, so I will just dissect your brain for any new information after your execution."

His words are spoken casually as if he engages in such activities daily.

"Dissect my brain?" I repeat bleakly.

"I am still unsure what shields you used to keep me out, but I will find out," he continues, more to himself.

"I don't know what you're talking about," I say. My voice is finally healed enough that my throat isn't on fire every time I say a word.

"Of course you would not." He rolls his eyes at me. "You are not a very bright individual, Minerva."

There he goes again. Even when he locked me up in this room, all he could talk about was how dumb I am.

And to think I idolized this male... He's nothing but a bully. A robotic bully.

"Your insults are useless," I fire back. It's not as if I don't already know I've made mistakes, that perhaps I was far more naive than I realized.

"It is not an insult. Merely the truth. I saw the same things you did, and yet you never questioned what was right in front of your eyes."

I frown. He continues, "Perhaps you did not want to see it, but that does not make a difference."

"What are you talking about?"

He stares me right in the eye.

His eyes are two bottomless pits. His lack of emotion has never been more clear to me than now.

He looks at me, but he doesn't see me as a being. There is no empathy behind that cold gaze of his, only the mechanical impetus to do his duty. Unfortunately for me, his duty consists of punishing me.

"I initially theorized that your impetuous meddling in the House of Psyche caused a human to be reincarnated as a demon —something that is in itself an abomination. But based on the information I gleaned from your memories, the opposite is true."

"You're talking about Marlowe?"

"Valerion," he corrects. "Your meddling likely shifted his reincarnation timeline forward, but I doubt it did anything of consequence. I would, in fact, theorize that you did more damage to yourself than him when you interfered with your thread of fate." He pauses then and shakes his head. "You could not even get that right, Minerva, could you?"

"W-what?"

"Of course you would not. Only someone with your... decreased intellect would confuse the *potential* thread for the *love* thread. But perhaps you are as visually challenged as you are mentally."

"Can you stop commenting on my intellect?" I grit my teeth.

"Why? It is rather challenged."

"So you've said." I roll my eyes. "But back to my mistake. Did you just say I cut the wrong thread?"

"Indeed. *Because* of your challenged intellect, and vision, perhaps both at the same time, you cut your *potential* thread instead of the *love* thread. I must confess that was quite amusing to witness. It's not every day that I see such idiocy."

I decide to ignore his continuous jibes and instead focus on the core of the issue.

"And what does that mean?"

He shrugs.

"It has not been done before, therefore there is no frame of reference for it. But you do not need to concern yourself with it since you will die soon enough and it will be of no consequence then."

"But did my cutting the wrong thread have anything to do with Marlowe and what happened to him?" I press on.

Azerius sighs in frustration.

"Valerion. And you do not follow, do you?"

"I...don't?"

"Of course you do not. Valerion *was* a Son of Tenebreis. The Son of Tenebreis that breached Aperion and murdered General Leotar. You lived with him for so long and you never suspected he might be the enemy?"

What? No, that cannot be. Yet as I attempt to deny it, the clues start to assemble in front of me, forming a rather alarming picture.

"Impossible..."

"Very much possible," he interjects. "And given the illness

he had, I would put his age at a minimum of seven thousand years old," he adds pensively. "Most likely far older than that since he must have left Tartareia before it was sealed."

My eyes widen in shock.

"What?" I blurt out. "What are you talking about?"

Mine, over seven thousand years old? No, I refuse to believe that would be the case. And yet...

"I have heard rumors of that illness, though it is now considered extinct. It ran rampant through Tartareia some seven-eight thousand years ago, targeting anyone with predominant Aperite blood. The disease died out once Tartareia was sealed off, but I have never heard of anyone surviving it or living with it." He pauses. "There is no cure for it, so I would be curious how he managed to live with it for so long."

Mine's words echo in my head as he explained how the disease was made to target a certain bloodline. He mentioned his father's bloodline specifically. Could Azerius be right?

"If this illness affects those with predominant Aperite blood, doesn't that mean he's one of ours? He's not the enemy!"

"Perhaps in your skewed perception. However, Aperite law does not recognize half-bloods."

"How could he be a half-blood? Aperites and Tartareians were once the same race..."

"Ah, but that is where you are wrong, Minerva. There might be similarities between Aperite deities and Tartareian Sons of Tenebreis, but they are not the same race. That is a common misconception. If that were the case, the disease could not *only* target Aperite blood. It would inadvertently also affect Tartareian."

"But—"

"Why do you think Sons of Tenebreis consume souls?"

"Because they are evil?" I snort at the obvious answer. "Because they always want more power?"

"Perhaps in the case of demons, yes. Their core is so corrupt, their only goal is to gain more power. But it is not the case for the Sons of Tenebreis."

I frown. "What are you talking about? This is what we've always been taught. That the Sons of Tenebreis are born evil."

"And of course you would never question the logic of it, would you?" he mutters under his breath.

Hands behind his back, he walks around the room, deep in thought. "Aperite deities were created by the combined efforts of the Seven of Light and Seven of Nether Primordials. The core of your souls, is as such, in harmony. There is a balance that is not present in the Sons of Tenebreis, whose creators were the Seven of Darkness. The Sons of Tenebreis consume souls in search of that harmony."

"You may think of their soul as a mass of chaos that is one step away from imploding. The energy of a soul stabilizes that chaos, for a period. But soon that wears out and they need yet another soul, then another, in a never-ending cycle."

"So it is their nature, not out of inherent evil but because their biology requires it. Why are they so reviled then?"

He claps at me. "Bravo, Minerva. It seems your intellect is only half-challenged."

"Just get to the point," I mumble.

"It is the way of nature. The Sons of Tenebreis are part of that nature. And all predators become prey eventually. It just so happens that Aperite deities and the Sons of Tenebreis are in a perpetual predator-prey relationship that swings like a pendulum."

"Then by that logic it shouldn't be possible for Aperite deities to consume souls, no? Yet we're always reminded how forbidden that is. Why would we need the warning if that is not part of our biology?"

His lips tug up.

"Another brain cell has awoken, I see."

I roll my eyes.

"You are correct in that assessment. Aperite deities' souls are originally in harmony. If you were to consume a soul, your energy signature would change because your own soul would become pure chaos. You would be tainted. And to keep yourself from going mad—which, by the way, is what happens to the Sons of Tenebreis who do not consume souls regularly—you would have to continue consuming souls. You would, essentially, become the same as a Son of Tenebreis." He pauses. "Well, in your case, a Daughter of Tenebreis."

"Wait a moment!" I cry out. "What do you mean they go mad if they do not consume souls?"

"The chaos inside them eats at them until they go mad. When that happens, they usually self-destruct."

"W-what..." I gulp down. "You mean *all* Sons of Tenebreis consume souls? Even now when they're trapped in Tartareia?"

"Why do you think they have demon thralls, Minerva? They are using them as proxies to get them souls when they are unable to."

"But that means... Mine..."

He rolls his eyes in exasperation.

"You were the one who noticed the missing souls at the military base. How you did not think of it before is beside me."

"But the greed demon..."

"You know as well as I do that this happened before the greed demon appeared."

"But—"

"You may continue in denial for as long as you would like. Frankly, I do not give a damn about you. Valerion, on the other hand... I am interested in him."

"Why? It can't be *just* because he's a Son of Tenebreis outside of Tartareia."

"That is not for you to know. Alas, I have spent far too long in here. It appears duty calls."

He turns to leave.

"Wait! You're leaving me here? Like this?"

He stops just in front of the exit.

"Well, no. Tomorrow you will be taken to the public square for your execution. I did mention it will be a public execution, no?"

My lashes flutter in surprise—though at this point, why is any of this surprising?

"Public execution?" I stammer.

"Aperion must know we do not abide any rule break. Your death will serve as a good example for it," he says. "I look forward to killing you. Until tomorrow."

With that, he leaves the room.

SLEEP DOESN'T COME EASY. Though I know I should be resting after the continuous torture I endured, the thought of what's going to happen tomorrow keeps me awake and perpetually petrified. Yet it's not dying that scares me. That should be fairly quick—after Azerius has paraded me around the main square so everyone is aware of my sins.

No, death does not scare me, which is surprising in itself considering how much I've agonized over the act of dying. It's the thought that *he* might die again that terrifies me.

Because if Azerius is so interested in Marlowe, he will most likely use this opportunity to draw him here, using me as bait.

Marlowe might be a Son of Tenebreis, but he is undoubtedly no match for Azerius.

No one is.

Perhaps I should spend my last waking minutes contemplating my life so far and how blind I've been to what was there in front of me from the beginning.

Perhaps.

But I find that I don't have the energy to care that Marlowe is or isn't a demon. The missing souls in his basement make sense now, as do the missing souls from the military base. But he needed them. Azerius himself said that it's not always malicious. Sons of Tenebreis need those souls to survive. How can I condemn him for doing what I, too, have been trying to do all this time? Surviving...

I am disappointed he never trusted me enough to tell me.

Not in this life when he did not remember, but in the past when he knew fully well what he was, what I was. He knew everything and yet he kept it from me. Perhaps he knew far more than I ever did, at his advanced age and such.

That gives me pause. He's over seven thousand years old? Though still hard to believe, retrospectively, I can see the instances in which his maturity and experience shone through.

Wait a moment, though!

He knew so much, was capable of so much, and yet he still made me do all the work. Was he silently laughing at me all those times he portrayed himself as a puny human in need of help?

When I catch you, Marlowe... You're going to regret making a fool out of me.

If anything, I'll find a way to defy death just so I can get revenge for all the times you made me a fool.

He made me carry him on my back... The gall on this male. Back then I was impressed he would go along with it without taking a hit to his male ego. Now I know better—he was laughing at me all along.

I grind my teeth in annoyance—the only movements I am able to do with my body held still by those runes.

Every little interaction I had with him where he hid behind me, asking me to protect him because he's just a puny little human flashes before my eyes. I was so proud then, that he would trust me to keep him safe. Now all I feel is a growing rage.

Marlowe, Marlowe. You will pay. It doesn't matter what I have to do to get back to you, but you will pay. How dare you use my weaknesses against me? Ply me with sweets and praises while silently laughing at me?

The door suddenly opens. There are no windows inside the room to notice the passage. Though I did not get the opportunity to rest, with my mind so busy working up scenarios to torture that blasted male, I do feel much better than the day before. My body is as healed as could be considering my low levels of energy.

Yet my mood immediately plummets when I note it's not Azerius who comes inside.

It's Cerenios. His gaze meets mine and a slow, sadistic smile pulls at his lips.

"We meet again, Minerva."

FORTY-EIGHT

AROUND THE SAME TIME, AKKAYA

Marlowe

AN UNKNOWN FIGURE suddenly shadows the light streaming through the window. He's with his back to me, dressed in all black, his long hair flowing down to his shoulders.

"You are awake, I see," he comments as he stares out the window. His voice is strange, both familiar and foreign.

"W-what happened?" I croak and pull myself in a seating position.

I remember bits and pieces since being blasted by Minnie through that portal. My eyes widen as I quickly feel my abdomen for that gaping hole Azerius caused, then sigh in relief when I realize it's not there anymore.

But how? What happened?

More importantly, where is Minnie? What happened to her?

The man turns. His eyes are a piercing gray as he stares at me with a hint of sadness.

"You are healed, if that is what you are wondering."

"Who are you? Where am I?"

"You are in my home, in a realm called Akkaya."

I barely register what he says when it dawns on me the gravity of the situation. I'm in a foreign realm, away from her. The image of her, being held down by those two men flashes in my head, making my blood boil anew. She couldn't fight them. She's so strong, my beautiful Minnie, and she couldn't fight them. They held her down, touched her. They...

The pain in my chest surpasses my physical pain.

They'll kill her. They will execute her and I will lose her forever.

"Fuck!" I curse aloud, my heart thudding sickeningly fast in my chest. "Fuck, fuck, fuck! I need to leave. I need to get to Minnie," I mutter and attempt to get to my feet. I barely manage to move an inch before my body explodes in pain.

The man comes closer, his lips flattened into a tight line.

"You should probably not move much. Not yet anyway."

"What's...wrong with me?" I ask, tension knotting in my muscles.

"Your body is still adapting to your new circumstances. The pain should fade soon."

"What circumstances? What the hell is going on? And who the fuck are you?"

He doesn't answer.

"You know what? Fuck you and fuck this. I'm leaving."

"You are welcome to try."

I give him a hard glare as I swing my legs over the bed and plant them firmly on the ground. But as I stand up, I wobble forward, crashing to the floor.

The fall knocks the air out of my lungs and I let out a harsh curse.

He walks around me, giving me a pitiful stare.

"I need to get to Minnie," I grit out. "He's going to kill her. He's going to..." I squeeze my eyes shut.

"You cannot do anything right now. Not in this condition."

"I need..." I ball my hands into fists and drag myself forward. I only manage to move a few feet before my body betrays me. Out of breath and ravaged by pain, I let out a loud wail.

He crouches in front of me, his expression marred by a great sadness.

"You must be strong enough if you want to get to your female," he tells me. The fact that he calls her 'female' tells me he's likely not human.

"Who are you?"

"You will remember soon enough," he says. Reaching out, he stops himself just as he's about to touch me. "You have no idea how lucky you are to even be here," he murmurs cryptically.

"What are you talking about?"

He smiles sadly. "You must be the only one of your kind to not only have survived that illness for so long but also make it to the other side of it."

My brows knit in confusion. What the hell is he talking about?

"My kind?"

"A hybrid that neither Tartareia nor Aperion will ever recognize...or accept."

My eyes widen. "What?"

"Is it not hypocritical that Aperites preach fairness and balance, but they behave just as immorally as Tartareians?" he asks, almost to himself. "If it had not been for your female personally getting you out of the depths of Psyche, you would have languished there for an eternity."

"I don't understand what you're saying—"

"Of course you do not." He sighs. "You will, soon. But you must remember how lucky you are, whereas anyone else with the blood of Tartareian elites can *never* escape Psyche, never reincarnate." He pauses. "There is a special place in that hell reserved only for us."

Us. He said us. More confusion swirls in my mind.

"You're...a Son of Tenebreis?" I croak.

He nods. "Though it has been a long time since I identified

with my kind. Nonetheless, the blood in my veins and my stained soul brand me as one of their own."

There's something so familiar about him, that a strange thought suddenly crosses my mind.

"Are we related?" I ask carefully.

His lips quirk up. "If you are asking whether I am your father or not, the answer is no," he adds with a chuckle.

I gulp down. He knew exactly what I was going to ask. Can he read my mind?

"Your thoughts are very loud," he says, confirming my suspicions. "But that, too, shall pass once you learn how to shield your mind again."

"How do you know all that?"

"Your powers are back. Your essence is once more whole."

His head tilts to the side as if he's listening to something. "This is my cue to leave." With a snap of his fingers, I'm once more back in bed. He lingers for one more moment as he says, "I am happy you are back. Truly. Sol'Ren would have been, too. All he ever wanted..." He pauses and closes his eyes. "All he ever wanted was for you to be happy."

I stare at him in confusion as he heads for the door. Just as he opens it, another man comes inside. "Thanks for looking out for him, Nyk."

The man, Nyk, inclines his head. "Always, old friend."

The door closes and I'm left alone with the newcomer.

He's around my age, if not younger. He's dressed in a pair of loose beige pants and a white shirt, with a red cardigan on top. That is some...questionable fashion choices right there.

"And you are?" I quirk a brow at him. I've decided to save my strength for later since every small movement causes me intense pain. Even though I need to leave here and get to Minnie as soon as possible, until I get better, I'm stuck here.

Unless these people who clearly know so much about me can help me.

Alas, there is *one* good thing about this entire ordeal. It appears I am not quite human. That might be a cause of concern at one point—I did freak out initially when my blood turned black—but not anymore.

I'm not human. I have powers. That means I can save Minnie!

And if I'm just as immortal as she is, then I can be with her *forever*. No more dying and no more worrying that she might find someone else. That's never going to happen now.

She's stuck with me for eternity. How cool is that?

The newcomer doesn't answer. He's staring at me, almost in awe.

"It really is you, Valerìon," he murmurs.

"Valerìon? Who's that?"

He snaps his fingers and a mirror materializes in front of me. "You."

I blink slowly, then move my hand to my face, feeling for my features. The person in the mirror does the same, emulating each movement. Because it *is* me. Yet it's not.

It's familiar but foreign at the same time.

I look like myself but different. My hair is pitch black now, whereas before it was a dark brown. My irises, though still green, are more vivid, my eyes more elongated. My jaw seems more angular and pronounced.

"What the hell?" I burst out and punch the mirror. Of course the one hurting is me while the mirror disappears in thin air.

The man stops in front of my bed and regards me with a sigh.

"You are still in pain, are you not?"

"Who the hell are you and what's happening to me? I need answers. Now!"

"Perhaps this will help allay some of your worries," he says, and just as he finishes talking, his form changes to a familiar one.

"Giles?"

"Good to see you again, Mr. Spencer-Astor," he replies, the accent and cadence the exact same as Giles.

"What the fuck? You're not Giles. You can't be—"

"On the contrary." He smiles. "I have been this Giles character for many years."

I gawk at him. His voice is now different but coming from Giles' mouth. Fuck. This is creepy as fuck. Maybe I'm hallucinating? Yes, that might be. I've never done crack, but I guess this is what it feels like.

For fuck's sake...

"Giles is not human? Was never human?" I repeat in disbelief.

He smiles and nods. "Well, technically he *was* human until he died. Then I simply replaced him."

"Does my mother know?" I hurry to ask. But then I realize what this would mean. "Fucking hell! Did you seduce my mother as Giles, you fucking weirdo?"

He does not seem to take offense to my language. He continues smiling at me.

"No, no... Don't tell me—"

The door opens, and another person walks in. She's slender and petite, with big blue eyes and dark hair. She appears to be in her early twenties, but if she's one of them, then fuck knows how old she is.

"Oh," she murmurs when she sees Giles by my side. "Are we doing that?"

"That?" I ask, at the same time as Giles-not-Giles says, "He's in pain."

"He's in pain? Still?" she asks, alarmed. She hurries to my bedside and looks me over. "Where are you hurting, dear?" She extends her hand to touch me.

"Don't you 'dear' me!" I blurt out and pull myself away even though the movement itself hurts.

"I'm taken," I tell her. And him, just in case they might be into some kinky shit. "My fiancée is a goddess. A *very* powerful goddess. And she's very jealous, so don't even think to put your hands on me. She will turn you into ice."

She glances back at Giles-not-Giles, her lips trembling with mirth.

"You should probably tell him already, dear," Giles-not-Giles says.

The woman gives me a worried glance before she shifts her appearance right under my eyes.

You have got to be fucking kidding me.

"Mom?"

"My sweet Marlowe," she coos as she wraps her arms around my neck. "I was so worried about you."

"Get off me. Now!" I push her off me.

"That is not how you speak to your mother!" Giles-not-Giles says sternly.

"You two." I point to them. "You'd better explain every-thing. And fast. Every second counts and I need to get to Minnie."

"I'll handle that," Giles-not-Giles tells my mom-not-mom or whoever she is. He reaches for me and I instinctively back away. But as he presses his fingers against my forehead, a blast of energy travels through me. Millions of images flash in my mind, so many, I'm having a hard time distinguishing between what's real and what's not.

Soon, I'm gasping for air as the pressure inside my head increases.

"Easy," my father tells me as he pats my back. "Let it all come back to you."

My eyes roll in the back of my head as more currents of energy go through me.

Then, suddenly, everything clears.

"Better now?" he asks.

"He should be fine, no? He was fine before."

"Of course, dear. He should start healing from the inside out now."

"Why is he not saying anything then?"

"You're worrying too much, Rità. You know it takes some

time. We're talking about thousands of years' worth of memories, across multiple timelines. He's probably overwhelmed."

"My poor baby," she murmurs.

"I can hear you, you know," I add drily as I open my eyes, this time seeing them with lifetimes of history between us.

"See, he's fine," my father points out.

"You are?" Mother asks tentatively, moving closer to me. "Can I hug you then?"

"Come here," I say and open my arms for her.

She lets out an excited squeak and rushes to hug me—a little too tight.

"That's enough, Rità, he's still recovering."

"I missed my baby," Mother murmurs as she kisses my cheek.

"Missed you too, Mom." I chuckle. As she finally draws away, I grab my father's arm and pull him into a hug. "Missed you too, Dad."

"It's good to have you back, Valerìon."

My father is not one for overly overt displays of affection—unless you happen to be my mother—so he quickly resumes his place next to my bed.

"How did we do this time?" I ask them, ready to focus on the most important issue at hand.

My mother glances at my father sheepishly. "We think we're on the right track this time."

"She's still captured," I point out the obvious.

"Yes, but it took much longer for that to happen. In fact, I had a great idea—"

Father stifles a laugh.

"What great idea?" I raise a brow. Mother somehow always has *ideas*.

"Well, as you know, the order already changed when Minnie went to the House of Moirai first and *then* to the House of Psyche. That, and she cut the proper thread this time."

"Okay, and?"

"I've been thinking that since last time your soul triggered the defense mechanisms of Psyche due to your Tartareian essence, perhaps I could remove it before you died and then it would be easier for her to steal your soul."

"That sounds logical." I nod.

"But your mother failed to think about the fact that you would eventually *need* that essence back to be whole, so we had to come up with a different plan."

"Just for the record, *both* of us came up with this plan, all right?"

"What?"

"Well, your body. It was the perfect vessel for the remaining energy. And it stayed safe and hidden until—"

"Until I asked Giles, *you*, to track down Lucien's body." I groan at the memory.

"A little unorthodox, but we both know you far too well and assumed you would want to destroy it."

"So when I destroyed it..."

"You released the remaining energy, which is why you are at full strength now," Mom adds.

"Soon to be at full strength," Father corrects. "His body needs to get used to the full extent of his energy again."

"All right. As much as it is a little odd, I can get behind it. What else?" I ask.

They share another look, but this time it's a grave one.

"You messing repeatedly with the timeline has had...consequences," my mother says.

"What consequences?" I ask as I comb through the new memories. "The Sons of Tenebreis?"

"Not only are they able to temporarily leave Tartareia, but the seal is weakening," she adds grimly.

"It will not hold for much longer, son. A few decades, perhaps less."

"Damn it," I mutter.

As my energy slowly fills every cell in my body, the pain becomes only an echo. When I find myself fit enough, I get out of bed, pacing around as I try to think of my next steps.

"I must go to Aperion," I tell my parents. "Get Minnie back before the execution."

Enough things have changed that I bought myself some more time to save her before her execution. But time is still of the essence.

"I prepared fresh clothes for you and some fresh food. It's been so long since you've fed, you must be already feeling the effects of it." She materializes some clothes as well as a vial with a shimmery substance inside. The moment I snap it open, the energy of a soul flows through me, helping me ground myself even more.

"Thank you, Mom." I kiss her on the cheek.

"There is something else, son," Father starts.

I glance at him and raise my brows in question.

"After you get Minnie back, could you two go to the House of Psyche and check something?"

"For you?"

He shakes his head. "Nykander."

"Oh. Sol'Ren."

"Nyk thinks his soul is at the bottom of Psyche, below Katras. I've tried to look into it, but I can't sense anything remotely."

"Of course I will. Ren was my best friend—still is..." I gulp down, swallowing the wave of sadness that grips me. "How has Nyk been?"

They both shake their heads at me.

"That bad?"

"He's made it his mission to destroy the people who engineered that illness. But he needs to find a way to Tartareia first. I told him to wait, that the seal is weakening, but he doesn't believe that will happen soon enough."

"Nyk has always been hot-headed," Mother adds.

"I would be too if my wife and son were killed by that damn illness." I purse my lips. "I still expect to break out in blisters every time I use my powers," I add, almost to myself as I clench and unclench my fist and feel the surge of energy washing through me.

"Val—"

I drop to my knees, a sharp, barbed vise wrapping around my heart and causing it to bleed in my chest.

"What's wrong?" both my parents quickly ask.

I slowly raise my gaze, tears streaming down my cheeks.

"I can't feel her anymore. She's...dead." I choke on my words. "She's dead. Again."

"My sweet boy," Mother coos as she wraps her arms around me, though nothing can console me at this point. Nothing.

"Why? How?" I ask, barely able to breathe. One would think that after experiencing this hundreds of times, it would get easier. But it always gets worse because I always expect things to change and they never do.

"I don't know. We need to review everything and—"

"I should have told her the truth when she asked. I should have told her everything."

"She couldn't have known then, Val. She needed time to come to terms with what we are," she mentions softly.

"No. I asked her to trust me and she did. I must trust her too that she will not react badly. I must..." I pause and take a deep breath, steely determination flowing through my veins.

"I'm going back to where everything went wrong."

TO BE CONTINUED

**For more stories in the same world, check out:
Barbi and the Villain**

BONUS CONTENT

**Scan the code below for FREE bonus content!
Or visit www.veronicalancet.com/bonus-content**

9 781959 854197